Praise for *1*
"Author, Frank Rocca, in story through Jackie's eye uncompromising stance a ride!

[...] The artwork utilizes daring colors that I feel fit the story. I like how the word *MORE* stands out. The model holding the gun will immediately capture the writer's intended audience, which I believe to be predominately men looking for a no-holds-barred story that will immerse them in another time and place [...]

First person can be tricky, but the author does a fine job with this point of view. This is a man many readers, especially those living in a day-to-day world, will enjoy living vicariously through. The raw language is not for everyone, but does add to the character's personality. Indeed, this book in many ways is a character study, something many readers will appreciate.

All in all, a book sure to be enjoyed by readers looking for an exciting read." **Judge, *Writer's Digest* 21st Annual Self-Published Book Awards**

"When I began this book I knew it would not be an easy read for me. That is because I have experienced nothing of the life into which Jack had been thrust by the sheer accident of birth. The visceral reactions I felt as I was coaxed to walk through Jack's maelstrom of addiction and chaos – even from my vicarious vantage point of miles and decades away – gnawed a hole into my sense of existential security. It is a powerful depiction of raw life, which is never easy to digest. Though I did not think I could be drawn into the reality of Jack's existence, there I was...

Ultimately, I wanted to see Jack as a tragic figure. His existential nihilism and abject confusion about what would constitute a better future –or a better Jack – seemed to drive his addiction as much as his addiction drove his attitude. Even his drug-addicted friends said he was out of control – just as some could also see the good in him, when for a long time he could not..." **William Hale, Ph.D., LICDC, Psychologist and CD Clinical Supervisor**

"I've just read this book "*Jack*" for the second time. It is a gritty, hard hitting story about difficult people living in difficult circumstances. I'd never heard of Collinwood prior to reading this novel. Now, I have associated it with other stories and movies set against a similar backdrop as "Jack."

The book is set in a time and place where a specific American sub-culture is at its peak or arguably in its decline. The author has re-created characters that are definitely products of their environment, violent, funny and tragic..." **Anaru Marshall, New Zealand, Corporate Executive**

I'M JACK & I'M BACK:
THE BASEMENT PIT

FRANK ROCCA

#28 12·25·2013

TO MARSHALL

THANKS

[signature]

2013

Copyright © 2013 Rocca Enterprises
Collinwood International
All Rights Reserved
ISBN: 0941223000
ISBN-13: 978-0-941223-00-3
LCCN: 2013919141

"We live together, we act on, and react to, one another; but always and in all circumstances we are by ourselves." ~ *Aldous Huxley*

For: Indigo Pierson,

my grandson

TABLE OF CONTENTS

INTRODUCTION: pp. 1-8

Part One, p. 9
CH I: The Year of the Snake, pp. 10-12
CH II: The Family, Part One, pp. 13-22
CH III: Mish-mash of Head-flicks, pp. 23-39
CH IV: Chips off the Old Block, pp. 40-50
CH V: Tessa's Journal, pp. 51-61

Part Two, p. 62
CH VI: The Shell Game, pp. 63-77
CH VII: Story-time, pp. 78-90
CH VIII: I Want More, pp. 91-99
CH IX: Tyrants & Sycophants, pp. 100-112
CH: X: Choices & Chances, pp. 113-125
CH XI: Flashbacks & Consequences, pp. 126-139

Part Three, p. 140
CH XII: Game-dogs, pp. 141-151
CH XIII: Whitey & Rocco, pp. 152-168
CH XIV: The Domino Theory, pp. 169-183
CH XV: Pit-dogs, pp. 184-207
CH XVI: Shit-pants Joey, pp. 208-216

Part Four, p. 217
CH XVII: Meaning, Purpose, & Revenge, pp. 218-231
CH XVIII: Time to Wake Up, pp. 232-240
CH XIX: Girls' Night, 1st Party, pp. 241-247
CH XX: The Bridge to Nowhere, pp. 248-256
CH XXI: Mean Streets of C-Town, pp. 257-268
CH XXII: The Match, Part One, pp. 269-282

Part Five, p. 283
CH XXIII: Door # 4, pp. 284-294
CH XXIV: The Match, Part Two, pp. 295-304
CH XXV: Bobby-boy, pp. 305-312
CH XXVI: That Collective *Click*, pp. 313-326
CH XXVII: Fake it Till You Make It, pp. 327-335
CH XXVIII: Line in the Sand, pp. 336-351
CH XXIX: The Aftermath, pp. 352-368

Part Six, p. 369
CH XXX: 13 O'clock, pp. 370-388
CH XXXI: Girls' Night, 2nd Party, pp. 389-397
CH XXXII: The Arc Completes its Thrust, pp. 398-404
CH XXXIII: I'm Jack & I'm Back, pp. 405-429
CH XXXIV: The Family, Part Two, pp. 430-446

GLOSSARY: Glossary (Collinwood Definitions), pp. 447-449

Introduction:

July 29th was the first time I had been involved in a car bombing. Well . . . at least on the receiving end of one. Books have been written about gangsters, and Hollywood movies made about our 1976 Collinwood battleground, its warriors and casualties, but never about the untold pain and protracted loss that countless families suffered – that is, not until this book. My name is Jack, and this is my account of one Collinwood story:

The last I knew it was July 29, 2013, and then silence, a ghostly calm following devastation. I had questions but was forced to look for answers inside the same traumatized brain doing the asking. Yet I was aware of certain things, such as how timing surfaced to be the adjudicator of my every moment and master of self-inflicted fate. After all the gangster shit I'd been involved in for so many years – so very long ago, though none of it felt that far away – unconnected layers all led to one gnawing obsession. I needed someone to kill me, or someone to punish.

In the mid-1970s, while we were in our mid-20s, 36 car bombs exploded in C-town ending lives and forever altering futures of once secure Cleveland residents. Basements on the outskirts of our Collinwood neighborhood became bomb factories. A local Italian syndicate waged war against an Irish mob while we stayed high and networked with an MC of outlaw bikers, all of us headquartered in our Collinwood neighborhood.

From ages 16 through 34, I had swilled and popped, snorted and even shot, enough potent drugs to recognize what I was feeling other than excruciating pain. And at the moment I was powerless, with limited use of wrapped hands. Besides, no instruments of death within reach in that foreign room other than a quiet drip of ringer solution buffered with opiates. So I lay there, trapped in my own hell, in a year I thought I'd never live long enough to see. I woke burning and drenched with sweat, yet feeling high and somewhat numb, thinking: *Whoever did this to me, please believe I'm dead. And no matter who you are, you'd better hope I am.*

It was in extremes like those where I'd spent the first half of my six decades. When I had finally settled into an age I thought I'd never experience, I fooled myself into believing I had changed like other older people I saw. And once I accepted that myth everything looked different, at least to me – for a moment. I struggled to learn different ways and to adapt to various life stages. I thought back to that momentary idealism as I attempted to gauge the depth of my present situation in a cold dark room constructed to box in my darkest thoughts and feelings with me.

A nightmarish memory of a massive wall of concussive force woke me. A dream-roar too real power-vaulted me into an endless moment so I could plan to even a score. But that eternal wait stirred up sensations I hadn't experienced in many almost forgotten years while I got reacquainted with childhood dread bordering on panic and re-experienced that sweet rush of adolescent rage. Memories disturbing enough to wake me out of a coma-like nod rocketed signals of urgency to every nerve ending in my damaged brain and body. I felt paralyzed. That explosion happened on my 63rd birthday, in my car parked out front of our little farm nestled in Amish country. *Am I in one of those metal drawers at the Cleveland morgue? No way. I'm in too much pain to be dead.*

I struggled to rip blindness away from now when I felt the tug of restraints. Something was binding raw arms to metal rails. I began thrashing like a wolf caught in a leg-hold trap till more scalding waves crashed against my brain, till I forced myself to deescalate. *Easy does it… Wait awhile… But why won't my eyes open?* Instead of panic, I remembered the steadiness of so many game-dogs I'd shared life with. Their courage kept me relatively sane.

As a survivor of too many hard decades, I realized the choices we make, chances we take and rules we break are of our own doing. And just like her and him, we all create our own share or get sucker punched by the choices of others. It's all timing. Everything is. Like during bouts of extreme stress, rage binges, or moments during reckoning, the crush of time has a way of moving unlike most other parts of life. Fear-driven time moves along similar yet specific corridors as do times of illness or injury, hallucinogenic drugs or extreme violence, intense moments of love or hatred, sex or agony, when minutes drag like hours and years flash by like summer months. It's in that squeeze when time no longer fits conventional modalities. Then as soon as fears are faced, like viruses they morph along winding paths of coiled steel.

So meandering became a way of life, the path of a serpent, the flow of resistance. It took me till middle-age to realize Collinwood had become an opium den for rock & roll junkies priming ourselves with booze and testosterone. Pits and crests from that old life of violence and drug abuse hit like what I had imagined getting head from identical twins would feel like – a speedball running unchecked through hungry veins, caressing virgin receptor sites. But there was another side. There always is. A smother-fuck of depression followed, that remote valley of quicksand outweighed at times by sporadic blasts of synaptic explosions from more drugs, hot sex and the rush of violence.

1976 became symbolic with the self-destructive force of the ouroboros in mortal combat with itself, as well as the rebirth of a phoenix arising from its own embers. It had been the year of new beginnings and nerve endings. We had reached for maturity during a mini-version of Woodstock's peace and love era, synthesized by the bloodshed and bombings reminiscent of a Vietnam War. By the time we were 26, troops began returning from Southeast Asia while gangsters holed-up from their own bloody battles. An epidemic of Collinwood pregnancies resulted, culminating in a string of births to unmarried women.

And all the while, we became addicted to the concept of *more*. But as with most infatuations and appetites, priorities changed along with the calendar. There's a rumor that people change, too. That's what they say, anyway. But I'm not so sure about that, because *they* say a lot of things. I don't believe people intrinsically change. Things can modify us to degrees for short periods of time, like from drugs, extreme circumstance or from the powerlessness of age. That tells me things *appear* to change. And when they do shift, we pretend they really haven't while adjusting along with them. Like other mammals, we also adapt.

I did just that. I adapted while drifting through consciousness in that dark place in 2013, along a precipice of nothing. In that strange-smelling room where I woke, I found myself getting reacquainted with emotions covered by years' worth of cobwebs. Dredged up from an idealistic childhood of the '50s, a fledgling gang member from the 60s, that gun and drug shooter in the 70s, an existential thinker of the 80s, a student of human nature in the 90s, that college graduate in the 2000s, to a dead man when the ouroboros finally locked its jaws.

Because of that, I realized how life itself presented as the most addictive substance of all. Desperate to regain a toe-hold, I reflected on those transformations: from altar boy to gangster, criminal to counselor, dogfighter to citizen, counselor to killer. Fragmented scenes of sanity and tragedy bombarded me like a shattered mosaic. Visions of cartoon madness became my newest reality. Retribution offered a sense of hope. That purity of faith in justice showed reasons why I could be strong enough to climb off the bed, to move forward on my journey through nowhere.

July 29th, 2013 – The stakeout, last day: Settled in as family, the kids out on Rocco's chopper enjoying a warm summer breeze, Tessa and I sat mesmerized near an open window till a shrillness shook us out of our serenity cocoon. I sighed and picked up: "What's up, brother Hank? Tonight? Hmmm. Sorry, bro. I'll have to pass. We're on our way out. Any other night is cool. Okay, sure. So tell me now. Hey man, you okay? Then it can wait, right? Easy does it there, Horrible Hank. Everything's cool. I promise. Well if it's all that important, you and your ol' lady meet us at the Phish Pot in an hour. I'm not taking *no* for an answer. Jesus Christ, Hank! You're getting as bad as my daughter. No, we're not waiting here. We're celebrating. Come on, man. Well then just say it. Okay, bro, I believe you. I'm sure it is important. All the more reason you should meet us. If you aren't there I'm gonna feel bad. No, I'm hanging up now. Later, brother."

I told my wife, "I don't know what's up with that guy, Tessa. He was acting all spooky. I wonder if he relapsed on that white shit. You should hear how paranoid he is. I hope you're not disappointed that I invited them, but I'm a little worried. He was tense. That's not like him. You know how laid-back he usually is."

When the phone rang again I said, "Don't answer it. I have a feeling it's bad news. I don't want anything to spoil our night. The answering machine'll catch it."

"What if it's the kids or your mom, Jackie?" Tessa asked.

"Nope, baby, it's Hank. He knows where we'll be. If they want to meet us they will. Let's get in the wind before we can't."

"I'll be too distracted. Can't you call him back real quick, just to check and make sure, so I don't have to worry all night?"

"He's probably hassling with his ol' lady again. She's way too uptight. They need to go out more often. Let's go. I'm starting to get that bad vibe. You feel anything, baby-girl?"

"See? There *is* something! Call, bro, and get it over with."

"No, it's not him. I can't nail it down yet. But I'll get it."

"That was nice weed, bro. It's been too long, Jackie." Tessa pulled her long blonde hair, perfectly streaked with natural silver, away from her incredible face as she said, "Hank's was a sweet gift. Now I'm remembering back to the way things were."

I told her, "That stress drains right off. It's almost like when we dipped into that ice-blue, warm Bahamian Sea for the first time. Were we really just there, Tessa?"

"Yeah, I guess so. It really was amazing. It seems like a dream. You have your cell on you, right? Okay, let's go."

I said, "I put the pipe and baggie in a safe place where the kids won't find it. Because if they do, they'll figure it's community property. Since Rocco's been in treatment because of that ridiculous law, he needs to be careful – even with things like beer and weed. Cops don't care that the kids are both in their mid-30s. They don't give a shit that he had his script bottle at home. Rocco needs to understand we don't make the rules. But the only reason they fucked with him is because he's all tatted out. I've been dealing with that shit since I was 18. But the thing is he can't carry his medicine in his pocket. He's not a doctor. Besides, it's not a good idea for us to be get-high buddies rather than parents."

After checking windows and locking the front door, I stood on the front porch with my newlywed childhood sweetheart, holding hands, lost together in tranquility, as we watched a lone dark cloud hover. The top an ominous black, it was sprayed beneath with a fiery glow of a glorious sunset.

Tessa said as we walked toward our car, "I think I'm past blaming myself for my father drinking himself to death. Plenty of girls during the '70s woke up as unwed, pregnant daughters. And I no longer accept the blame for my mother following him to the grave. Cancer makes its own decisions. There's a special force that takes care of people like you, Jackie. You have a glow around you. I see it. It's the kind that lights up dark, dreary existences. Its light is a beacon to a new sense of purpose. That's why you're a great therapist, bro. I can never repay you for saving me from drowning in my own shit. But I can see to it that you're happy, Just don't get too cocky or I might punch those pretty hazel lights into a nice shade of black and blue. Hey! Are you okay, buddy?"

I was taken in by the power of the moment as I looked at the sky, as that shadow-blanket slowly crawled over us. The spell was broken by that familiar *Click*. "Something *is* wrong."

"Whoa! What's happening?" Tessa snapped out of her reverie. "I feel dizzy, like I might faint. Is it that weed?" A woman in wrap-around sunglasses sped past in a Hummer as red as the driver's windblown hair. "Was that who I think it is? What's that snake, Maureen Kelly, doing sliming around way out here?" Tessa asked, as she steadied herself against our front porch made of rough cut Wolmanized lumber and wall-sized screen panels covered by wooden lattice.

I dropped her hand: "That's the nice thing about living an hour from nowhere. Nobody just drives by on accident. She's a long way from Collinwood. Wait here, alright?" I moved toward our car. At the curb, I squatted as if inspecting for splattered bugs. A feeling not caused by the dense breeze ran clear through me. "Chilly, right?"

"What? I'm worried, Jackie. Maybe I shouldn't have taken that puff. We're way out of practice. It muddles my senses."

Then something else odd happened. Little Sinbad, normally quiet, began a tirade of incessant barking. Everything appeared to move in slow-motion, like in a dream sequence.

"It's like I've been here before, Tessa. But there's something else. Feel it?" With a raised index finger I said, "Hold-up. I need to look for something. You'd better go back inside. Make sure everything is locked up and check on the dog. That's not like him. I'll check out here. Get my gun. Okay, sweetie?"

"Don't, Jackie. Come back inside. Call Hank, please?"

I ignored her to scan the perimeter. She sulked her way back to our house, whining "You've never called me *sweetie* before... Are you hiding something?"

"Shhh… I wish that goddamn dog would quiet down."

Once inside the car I fiddled with buttons and knobs still turned off. I pounded my fist on my Forester's dashboard and muttered, "Ain't this some shit? Okay . . . I know what time it is." Then I yelled, "Make sure everything's off, baby-girl. Go back inside right now, Tessa." Our dog growled and bounced against the inside of the front door. "Alright, just bring it, motherfucker!"

Tessa looked from car to house, from me to where our so-called *Pit-bull* was locked inside: "You want me to go inside, Jackie? Or you want me to bring something? Quiet, Sinbad! Which one is it? It can't be both ways. Sinbad, NO! Talk to me, bro! Are you angry because I didn't rush to *make sure everything's off*? Is that what this is about? Sinbad, QUIET!" she cried out in desperation, as she tugged at her hair. "What's with you two?"

A wash of dread pushed through me. My heart pounded as if I'd just hit a stem full of crack or injected some primo dope. Eardrums roared; sweat dripped. All I could hear was that non-stop snarling from our little Yankee Terrier locked up inside our house, a pet who till that day had been worthless as a watchdog.

Tessa screamed, "SINBAD, GODDAMNIT, SHUT-UP! What's going on, Jackie? Please..." *Click* I saw it her freeze in face, suffocating panic. She clutched at her throat, constricted with terror. I read her eyes, darker green than usual from the fear. An overwhelming wave of nausea climbed over her. She begged, "No, Jackie. Please, baby. I won't let you do this! You promised you'd never leave me. I trusted you. Please, baby, don't do this to us!" Legs numb, paralyzed with horror, she wept.

I stretched out a hand, "No worries, baby-girl. I ain't goin' no place. And you gotta be here when the kids get home, remember?" Then I mumbled, "Yeah, just fuck-it…"

Tessa's emerald eyes reached across a lifetime. Her fear plunged through my heart. I watched, powerless, as that petite woman whom I loved more than life crumpled by our front door as a growl from a Harley motor grew softer and darker. She had no idea which type of glow and light she had a premonition of before I jerked the handle of our car door that one final time.

My last sentence was, "This can't be real." On reflex I kicked off the floor with all my might and dove off the seat, right before all the lights in the universe lit up the sky.

My last thought was: *I'm dead.* All the colors blurred from numbness to black as I shot through the air with other debris, the moment our car transformed into a smoking hunk of scrap.

My first thought upon waking was: *Why? It's been almost 40 years since I've been a coomba or brother, or some other fucking stranger…*

I re-woke confused, for what seemed like another first time, in that dark silence of old memories and new fears, as physical and emotional pain once again extinguished everything in my world. Then it hit me again: *Hold on just one goddamn second… Those dirty rotten cocksuckers!*

Evidently I had nose-dived into a concrete pit – minus an exit strategy. *Yeah, it's starting to come back like a flood.* The vortex I found myself floundering at the bottom of presented an endless climb, while armed with only the darkest corners of my mind to haunt me. I wanted to call for help, but I was numb from hitting too many bottoms for too many years. So I patiently waited for my turn at the diving board, above a dry pool filled with rattlesnakes. Something coursing through my veins carried me off on a cotton ball made from strands of heaven as I reminded myself over and over: *Stay vigilant. This is one of decades' worth of old wounds finally reopened to infect us all with the pus of consequence.*

I remembered something my father said many years ago. With his deep voice and piercing gray eyes he cautioned, "Jackie, guys like your friends don't learn. But you'll adapt – one way or another. You'll learn or become ugly to your soul. That's if the streets don't eat you alive. Because there's a final bottom waiting for your next move. You'd better realize that life is just one very short chess game." As usual, he was right.

My own turn at the board began in 1950 and seemed to crescendo during that decade of delicious decadence, from the mid-'60s to mid-'70s. My friend, Pazzo, warned me when I was a teen, "We pretend to be in control, to keep from losing a sense of control we've never really had. We're all slaves to it – the timing – while stumbling through webs of choice and dumb luck. Our lives seem interesting with the more reckless moves, till we box ourselves in. Usually we notice, but too late, that it's no way to live. If we're lucky, we break out like a bull in a corral to relearn and reclaim life. Choose wisely before you run out of options."

As an expatriate from a proud ethnic neighborhood laced with colorful characters and vibrant rationalizations, I found myself missing even the worst of times. Because on more than a few occasions I thought I had squarely hit rock-bottom.

But somehow I survived all that self-induced chaos to find myself trapped inside someone else's choices. *But I'm not dead yet. So that means it's my turn next.* As a retired addict, one who had indulged in the allure of hedonism and self-abuse for too long, a brand new type of slavery surfaced in 2013. As an ex-gang member with washed out dreams and faded physical graffiti stamped across me like travel stickers from a lifetime of colorful trips, I replayed distant memories while trapped at my newest version of rock-bottom.

Slipping in and out of awareness, I heard the ring of a land-line – muffled and far above me as I lay in a pit of emptiness. I realized: *I have too many questions. What I need are answers. Like where are my boots and my pistol, and who do I shoot first?* In silent darkness I came to terms with another startling fact. I was terrified for the first time since I'd been that shy little boy who looked at the ground and bought into the never-ending lies.

But the circle was not yet complete. The *Click* doesn't lie. *I'm a new man reborn with a renewed appetite.* The ouroboros still ravenous, the phoenix once again in bursting flight and flames, at age 63 I wanted more, more so than ever before. I knew I hadn't paid attention to the *Click* that day like I should have because I was high. That's a fact. But there's another truth much uglier. Just as sure as my name is Jack . . . I'm back, motherfuckers!

PART ONE

I figured I'd survived for two reasons: the *Click* & the *Bounce*. In Collinwood we had our own language. *Friend, brother* and *bro* became exchangeable with *paesano, coomba* and *coom*, names for camaraderie found in every Italian-American neighborhood.

The *Click:* ESP or collective consciousness expansion is the *Click* chemically induced by pioneers such as Albert Hofmann, Timothy Leary, Ram Dass, Aldous Huxley, Ken Kesey, Jack Kerouac, Ralph Metzner, William Burroughs, Allen Ginsberg, Anthony Russo and so many others. But there's no need to re-induce it with drugs. It's a natural instinct. It's an intangible piece that's everything and nothing at once, spanning time and space along an immeasurable continuum. It's part of an energy field permeating all dimensions, an invisible pool from where all things emanate and return. It's everywhere yet nowhere, detected by primordial senses. It's that unseen alarm soldiers in fields of terror become familiar with, that internal siren preceding savagery or escape which every urban gang member recognizes without exchanging a word. The *Click* proves things we do know, even when we can't. It's a sense belonging for all of Mother Nature's children, reminding us we are only one part of a vast animal kingdom. The *Click* is an irrational feeling of psychotic suspicion, only to find it was based in reality. Drugs only serve to dull it.

The *Bounce* is balls but has not much to do with gender. It's gameness to make one more *scratch* back into the face of adversity, to channel the pain into the place where triumph resides. The *Bounce* helps damaged souls draw a next breath. It caresses us away from the arms of cowardice and into a personal best. It's the faith to prevail, the will to endure at any costs; the perseverance to continue regardless of consequence; the gameness to reach the other side; to respond while temporarily trapped in another's hell. It's about fight, flight or compromise. The *Bounce* is a response to red flags thrown as warnings by our reptilian brains. It's a psychotic reaction, an instinctual drive that offers enough resolve to survive scarred yet wiser. The *Bounce* is a mother dying to protect her child, a child sacrificing freedom and life for family. It's being caught-up in an unwinnable situation yet persevering.

CH I: The Year of the Snake

According to the Chinese Zodiac, 2013 is Year of the Snake. There was a sense of transposed energy which filled what should have been invigorating air with a void of buzzing uncertainty, a feeling of dread, a promise that some life-changing event hovered just overhead – just within reach.

In the early 1980s, within a 12-month span of time, I lost my father, my job and a decade-long marriage. The healing began slowly. A 10th grade education at Collinwood high grew to be a Master's Degree with a chemical dependency licensure to be a substance abuse counselor. It all unfolded so easy once I quit abusing alcohol and other hard drugs long enough to swap getting high for a real profession with benefits and dignity.

    And that's how and where I met my son, as a professional counselor at a treatment center in early June of 2013, when he had randomly been assigned to my primary group. That year of 2013 turned out to be the absolute best and worst time of my life.

    Rocco, at 5' 11", 190 pounds of lean hard muscle, a well-trained mixed martial artist, entered my life angry. That was our first moment together. He had been court-ordered to a 28-day program in lieu of jail for having his own prescription medication in his pocket, but not in his prescription bottle. His mother, Tessa, and I reunited after 38 years during a Saturday visitation. It wasn't long after that when we introduced him to his sister, both of them born in 1976. It was on a day when Gina and Tessa rode out together to find they each had made a new best friend.

    Then it was my move. So I did what I had to do, which is what I wanted to do. That time it was to purchase four cruise tickets so Tessa and I could marry on a Bahamian island the same weekend of our son's July 4th discharge. The trip of blue sea and golden sun highlighted the laughs and tears of four grown children playing a game that had been postponed for almost four decades. Many *Clicks* had been ignored in '76 from being too drunk, compounded back then by a terminal case of the *fuck-its*, while the arc to continued its spiral thrust.

While trapped in that dark room, time became a roulette wheel of pain. So I distracted myself with thoughts from the 1950s, of how parents tried to mimic pseudo-life portrayals of *Leave it to*

Beaver and *Lassie Come Home,* sharply contrasted by things we were attracted to like electrifying blues from Jerry Lee Lewis and Elvis Presley or James Dean's broody darkness. A Marlon Brando film about outlaw bikers, *The Wild One*, introduced us to antisocial behavior in packs, along with another about juvenile delinquents titled *Blackboard Jungle*. Back then almost everyone complied with their expectations for awhile. Till kids from our generation became edgy, going through the motions with daily routines yet no longer having real conviction. The whole thing felt contrived. Existential questions burned off the morning dew of childhood fantasy to show a harsher, braver world at every crossroad.

By the arrival of the Woodstock era in 1969, most kids had stopped drinking the Kool-Aid of convention. Idealism metamorphosed to make way for budding pragmatism. We were in adolescence on the North Coast of America during that amazing era. Yet herds of submissive kids committed suicide, got killed in car accidents or Vietnam, while hired killers roamed the streets like packs of feral dogs heralded as kings. Lawmakers and enforcers became the common enemy. Racism, sexism, violence for personal gain, recreational drug abuse for profit, all in excess was all right there for the taking. We discarded old truths as easily as broken toys. We used fast and hard. The transitional decade of sex, drugs and rock & roll served up a buffet of sensations which led to enlightenment. And all that exploring and experiencing of *more* did was serve as a foundation for even more, all set in playgrounds built by cool characters, and plenty of willing warm flesh amid a cold world ruled by cannibalistic meat-eaters.

Something else as powerful as the explosion paralyzed me. I thought: *So this is how it happens? Okay, inhale one; exhale on two.* Curled to one side, I tried to hack up a gob of death stuck in my esophagus. *Can't breathe!* No air to cough out and no way to get any in. My eyes bulged chest heaved impotently from no oxygen.

One tiny gasp, just enough to hack up an obstruction. Remnants of a clogged air passage made its way to my soft palate. Thick mucus had gotten lodged while I was lost in what felt like a heavily drug-induced state. Labored breathing, heart pounding, raw arms ached till an unfamiliar pain coursed through my system. I timed breathing with my heartbeat to keep from suffocating, to keep the ouroboros from wrapping itself any tighter. Nerve endings in my brain burst into randomly vibrant strobes as a gyroscope of gray tones constructed its own reality. A rush of dizziness overwhelmed me. *In one, out two; in – out. Okay, I can do this.* At that moment I felt a strange sense of relief. Because of the pain and fear I knew for sure I was still alive.

I groaned as I asked myself: *Why do I feel so high? Yet I'm sore from head to toe? I think I read about this.* Mind-movies all too real weaved in and out of consciousness. *Dead or back in jail? Is this still 2013? And why do I think I asked myself these same questions before?* I tried not to think about a heartbeat banging off my eardrums. *It's the DMT released in the brain when you're dying. So I am fucking dying! I knew it! My whole body aches. Yet my head feels like I just shot up some really good dope. Where in fuck's sake am I? I can't even move...*

As an old man in my sixth decade, trapped in the bowels of a surreal existence, I dreamed of a chance to right some wrongs. *I've tasted death before, many times. But never like this.* The predicament in which I found myself was different than any other slice of insanity I'd ever doggedly pursued. *A price on my head. But why?* I was in no position to find out. That dance with death renewed my senses powerlessness and of purpose. I told myself: *Some stupid motherfuckers think I'm dead and will soon wish they were. Because someone's getting paid in spades for this shit. Bet on it. Just play this thing right and you're out. Yeah, timing – patience.*

I hovered mid-room till fully awake. *Okay, now easy does it.* I shifted for just enough wiggle-room to search for a less painful position so I could plan an escape strategy. But comfort no longer existed in my new world. I thought: *Alright, I need to concentrate on what I know. Okay, so what is it I know? I don't have many good choices at the moment. So in that case here's what I'll do: I'll just play along. Yeah! But I'll make it my rules. My game, or I go mad. Dealer's choice, baby – roll the dice and then we'll see.* But the worst pain was missing my family.

My father said, "Family is everything – that and integrity. Both are shaped by choices and weighted by timing. So once priceless things like loyalty and respect are damaged, they're gone."

Although I do agree, merely saying "Family is everything" rings like other phoniness people like to hear themselves repeat. The truth is we get stuck with relatives and choose family. Another *Immaculate Misconception* is when condescending people vow all knowingly, "Everything happens for a reason. There are no coincidences and no such things as accidents." Some insist, "God doesn't give us more than we can handle." *I'd like to put those experts in choke holds till they're pissing themselves and calling me God.* Another is, "We're powerless." *Fuck that! I'm not till I'm dead.* But I could choose to buy into limp excuses to be a perpetual victim.

CH II: THE FAMILY, part one

July 28, 2013 – The Stakeout, the 1st day: In a gray sedan, surrounded by trees on a peaceful afternoon, sat two villains from Cleveland's dark underworld. Unbeknownst to me or my family, two Collinwood men stationed themselves within view of the front of our old farmhouse. Fat Spuds talked, ate and made himself as comfortable as a grotesquely obese man can be in a new Taurus tucked away just down the road from our home. Skinny Vinny nerked around, repositioning his sports jacket and shirt collar in-between redefining pressed creases on the front of his cheap dress slacks.

Spuds, senior member of their crew, had Vinny equip them with tools for a two-day stake-out. Their gear consisted of a stolen car, a pair of unregistered pistols, binoculars, two dozen donuts, paper cups and a thermos of strong black coffee. Spuds, in the passenger seat as navigator, required much more stomach room. Vinny tightly gripped the wheel of a parked car. Having been ordered into the pilot's seat was more than okay with him, because from there he had more gadgets to fiddle with. A large white box rested on the bench seat between them. A plastic portable counsel with cup holders and a few other compartments fit over the car's transmission hump. Spuds and Vinny had to get this assignment right if they were to ever reach their goal of graduation within the Family.

July 28, 2013 – The Stakeout, the 1st day: Rocco's long black hair, fully sleeved tattoos and thick goatee gave him the appearance of a dangerous man. Friends of Rocco who hadn't seen him in awhile asked if he had gotten new ink because of his increased muscle mass. His training regimen was religiously conducted in a gray block basement with a cracked concrete floor. An unfinished, cobwebbed ceiling of hand-hewn beams and rough-cut joists full of dull ductwork, copper plumbing and outdated wiring shone from the glint of bare bulbs.

Rocco was over his pit weight from when he fought MMA at 170, but was stronger and faster than ever. As Rocco's arms and trunk grew heftier from doing bench presses with free-weights, bicep arm culls, triceps flies with dumbbells and extensions, as well as various strikes on heavy and speed bags, he became even more restless. He jumped rope for cardio and did hundreds of crunches per day. For a man in his mid-30s, he was cut like a college athlete. But he couldn't be mistaken for a jock on scholarship, not with all that pent-up rage and scars, facial hair and skin illustrations. He looked exactly like what he was, a retired Mixed Martial Arts fighter with a bum knee.

"Okay, I got a good story for you, Pop. I'll tell you and Gina about the day I rented the upstairs of that house from those two crazy old broads below me and Danni, right before I wound up in rehab. Ma already heard this one. And now, since you've met them, you should appreciate it. It's long but worth listening to."

"Why didn't you just stay with your mother?" I asked my burly-looking son.

"Come-on... You remember how it was. I was getting buzzed every day, pretty much all day long. Ma wouldn't put up with that shit. Plus I needed a safe place to stash product, because I was making moves at the time. Besides, I'm almost 37."

"Alright, sorry for interrupting. Go ahead, son. Tell your story. We don't have anything important to do till Monday."

"No wonder Gina's a smart-ass. Anyway, it was a beautiful Sunday like today. After I emptied out my pit-dog still at Ma's, I kicked over my scooter and proceeded to check addresses on wooden porches in the old neighborhood. I figured it was time for me and my ol' lady to get a place. Danni needed out of her house and away from her crazy alcoholic mother. So I putted real slow, past those old frame and brick Cleveland houses, separated by short driveways bordering thin strips of yard. You know the kind. All those Collinwood streets and houses look the same, old but tidy. Finally I spotted the right place, but a bit too late. I slowed and stepped my left foot to guide my scooter in a circle on that brick road, to get turned around. A woman sitting on a front lawn didn't look up when I snugged my back tire against the curb. I throttled slightly before flipping a toggle switch to silence my V-twin and closed the petcock before I un-straddled my hog to begin a new adventure.

After shaking the breeze out of my hair, so the curls across my shoulders could be smoothed back to make a slightly neater impression, I adjusted wraparound shades against the glare of a harsh noon sun. I even decided to fasten a few buttons of my sleeveless flannel shirt, to sort of spiff-up for my future landlady. I spotted an old woman rooting around in her front lawn. Kneeling on the grass, she seemed oblivious to my presence.

'Could you be Mrs. Downs?' I asked. Trying not to laugh, a warm breeze lifted a few strands of white hair off the top of her thin head like silver antennae. Still not looking up from her chores, I was able to inventory her gear. She sported a black wool dress and those hard black shoes with thick squatty heels like those gnarled *Zia's* (Aunties) in their widow uniforms wear on their morning walks to Mass. This woman even wore a black shawl wrapped over the back of her head, around her wrinkled neck and covering thin shoulders. But it was hot as hell out. 'Nice day for it,' I said, to break the ice. Bent over, she continued to work a pair of purple-handled scissors held parallel with the ground, staring intently at her handiwork.

So I tried again: 'Hi, I'm Rocco. Pleased to see you,' I said, as I stepped toward her. She ignored an offered hand to shake. 'I phoned yesterday about renting the upstairs.'

'Now how am I supposed to cut this grass after you went and flattened it all out with those stupid greasy boots?' the old woman asked, as she looked up at me for the first time.

'Oh, sorry. I thought maybe you were picking dandelions or something. I didn't realize you were cutting your lawn with those'.

'Well that's what people do with scissors, don't they? They cut things. What are you, some kind of city inspector or something? You sure aren't dressed like an inspector. In fact, you're dressed like a slob. Why are you questioning me? Is it a crime if a person cuts grass with anything other than a lawnmower? Is that some new law?'

'I'm not too sure, ma'am. There sure are plenty of strange laws. So I guess a law like that wouldn't surprise me any more than plenty of others people blindly accept.'

'Eeeee Heeee!' She squealed a toothless grin with ear-splitting shrill. 'So it's Rocky, is it? What a name! Do you dye your hair, or are you a *dago*? Because you look like a *dago* to me. My second husband was a *dago*. He had that black curly hair just like you. Well, are you or not? Speak up, Mister!'

'I'm Rocco, ma'am. My grandparents came from Sicily, if that's what you mean. So I suppose you could say I'm Italian. But no, I don't dye my hair. It's just black, same as my beard. I guess the same as your husband's.'

'My, my. Aren't you the one for the details? Well, Mr. Smarty-Pants, it's been my experience that a man's beard generally matches his hair. Unless, of course, he has one of those reddish beards you see every once in awhile on a Scotsman. You're a fella for details, it seems. I heard they call those redheads *gingers* now. Don't they, Mr. Inspector? Hey, Rocky, do you know any *dagos* with red beards? Because I've never seen one. Just coal black like yours. That is, if yours isn't dyed. But the fact is, all you *dagos* look alike to me. Now me . . . I'm Polish.'

'Excuse me, ma'am. But do you think maybe we could talk about me renting your upstairs instead of my beard hair?'

"My, my, aren't you the defensive one?" she asked as all five-foot-fuck-all of her struggled to stand, still holding those shiny scissors. "What would you do, Mr. Defensive, if I chop that black beard clean off?"

'I'd grab your arm before you got close. That's what.'

'Eeeee Heeee!" she cackled. 'You're a live one, aren't you? And you might even be about half honest. Me, I appreciate honesty more and more these days. Don't you?'

'Yes, ma'am, I do. As a matter of fact, honesty is something I can't get enough of.'

'Oh really? Then tell me, Rocky. Why do I dress this way on a hot summer day, sitting here cutting grass with scissors? You seem like some kind of expert on details. So tell me.'

'Well . . . at first I had you figured for a lunatic. But now I think you're trying to look about half-crazed so people around here leave you alone. No offense.'

'Ah Hahaha! You're one pretty smart *dago*, you are. But me, I'm a heck of a lot smarter than you. And do you know why, Mr. Smarty-Pants?'

'Because you're older than dirt under my boots, ma'am?'

'You're not even close, Rocky the *dago*. Now me, what I just went and did was get you to tell me why you have all that long hair, and those tattoos and muscles, without ever even asking – and without you even knowing you were being asked. That's why! Ah Hahaha! How do you like those apples, Mr. Smarty-Pants?'

'Well, then I won't bother to tell you about how maybe I had underestimated you. Because if I say it, that would mean you're a heck of a lot smarter than me. So instead, maybe I'll just defer to the truth in silence. You know, in the spirit of respect.'

'Well now, this is getting all sorts of interesting. But me, I'm here to call your bluff. Okay, so let's find out what it is you think you know. Go ahead. If you do, I'll agree to rent the upstairs today, as long as you have all the money on you. Go on. Say it out loud.'

'Well, ma'am, the thing is, I could tell that you were wondering what type of person would have all this hair and these tattoos. But since you had the courtesy not to ask I didn't want you to assume the worst. So I waited for an opening to let you know, and you gave it to me,' I grinned. 'So how about it? Am I right? Do I get the upstairs now?'

'Eeeee Heeee!" she cried out in joy. 'That's good! That's a whole lot better than I expected from a black-bearded *dago*! But you're only about half right.'

'Oh yeah? I see . . . okay. Which half is that?'

'I'll have to admit, you're right about me wondering if you were some kind of hop-head. But the part you missed is that Mrs. Downs is my sister. Ah Hahaha! She's in the house watching us right now through a hole in the draperies. I guess you did all your fancy turning around on that motorbike of yours for nothing, didn't you? And I'll bet you thought I wasn't watching. Didn't you, Mr. Biker?'

I turned towards the house, to their picture window, to see a large space between the curtains change from a shadow-covered darkness to a TV flickering from inside.

'Eeeee Heeee! I got you, didn't I? Go ahead. Just say it, Mr. Smarty-Pants. Even though you might have about *half*-tricked me, I ended up fooling you all the way with your own game. You can't admit it, can you, Rocky? Ah Hahaha!'

'Okay, alright, I'll admit it. You're good . . . *real* good.'

The front security door opened and Mrs. Downs shoved her white head with tufts of hair bent in odd directions through the bottom half opening of her aluminum screen door where a window should have been. It looked like she was on her hands and knees. It appeared as if she spoke with her head poked out from a pink igloo.

She called out, 'You quit your picking on poor Rocco. Leave that boy alone.' Then like a talking dog, she looked up at me and scolded, "You stood right here on this porch yesterday and told me face-to-face you'd have my money by noon. Well, it's quarter past and there's nothing in my hand but a filthy rug. You told me honesty's something you don't get enough of. Okay, where's my money? Did you bring it, or not?'

I smirked at the ancient women dressed in black and said, 'Oh, sorry. All you old ladies look alike to me. Excuse me while I

17

go talk to your sister face-to-face *again*, and give her the first month's rent. That is if I still have your permission to move in.'

'Eeeee Heeee! You're a pistol, you are. Yes indeed, Mr. Smarty-Pants. Now me, I think it will be good to have a man around here with half a brain, even if you are a black-haired *dago*. Go ahead now, hurry up and get a move on. And quit taking advantage of a defenseless old lady. And one more thing: My sister already told me you were here. I was waiting for you. That's why I was out here. Ah Hahaha! By the way, I'm very pleased to make your acquaintance, Mr. Rocco the *dago* biker.'

'The pleasure's all mine, Ms. Clara,' I grinned.

'*Clara?* Why would you use that horrid name on me?'

'Because I called your sister today from my cell phone. In fact, it was right after you walked outside to cut the grass. Mrs. Downs told me her sister, Clara, would be out front to greet me. Is it alright if I call you Clara?'

'Ah Hahaha! You're a pistol, alright! Yes indeed. And you may call me Clara. Why wouldn't you? It's my name, isn't it? What a silly question. Oh my! Now get along before we change our minds. That is if you really have the money, Mr. Cheapskate.'

As I climbed the porch steps, Mrs. Downs' pink igloo moved away from the broken screen and then their security door on the porch closed. I stood there for about five minutes waiting in the sun till I finally turned to Clara for direction. She was again seated on the grass, busy trimming the lawn with those scissors.

'Excuse me, Ms. Clara. I know your sister saw me, but now the door's closed again. Am I supposed to knock?'

'Well, it's a door isn't it? Now me, if I wanted someone to answer, I guess I'd knock. But I suppose you can just stand there and look stupid. It's up to you. Besides, there's something by the handle called a doorbell. Why don't you try that, Mr. Genius?'

I showed up to be interviewed as a prospective tenant looking like Charles Manson with muscles and much more ink. I wondered at the last minute if my appearance might seem strange to the landlady – first impressions and all. But I wasn't about to get a haircut just for a temporary address. And after seeing those two I felt at ease. I was feeling like the *normal* one.

Mrs. Downs answered the doorbell with the type of robe my mother referred to as a *house-coat*, but Mrs. Downs' was shiny pink and buttoned only at the neck. It flared out at her sides as if it had wires in it like an old-fashioned hoop dress. That explained the pink igloo while peering out the bottom of a broken screen door . . . if anything can ever explain the bizarre scene.

Because the landlady's stomach protruded so far, her robe was wide open except for that one button cutting into her turkey neck. Her stretch-marked, blue-veined belly almost covered a scraggly bush of white crotch hair. Her full cleavage of deflated breasts, the same texture and color as that rippled belly, hung down flat over her engorged paunch. Evidently, first impressions meant even less to them.

When she asked, 'Would you like to sit for milk and cookies, honey, while I make your receipt?' my stomach lurched.

With my head turned sideways I handed Mrs. Downs a wad of money – security deposit and first month's rent and said, 'No thanks, ma'am. I'm on a protein diet. I have low resistance. But thanks just the same for the offer. Maybe next month'."

Rocco paused to crunch his chocolate almond treat, shaped more like a banana slice than a cookie. Hard crumbs sprinkled across a paper plate. A few fell on his beard and chest. He carefully bushed them into the plate. He continued, "After that, I had Danni pay the rent for me. Forget all that naked, old lady action. I don't go for that.'

"That's very admirable of you," his sister mocked as she pet Sinbad's face with tanned feet and pink toenail polish. "Wow, such self-restraint. I'm really impressed, dude. You're a rock."

"Do you have to be an asshole your whole life, Gina?"

"There! See what I mean? It's always something to do with asses with you," Gina laughed. "You're obsessed, dude. Why didn't you ask your landlady to shit in a bucket for you? Or you could have dropped a deuce on her sister's head while Danni videoed it. Is that kind of like *anal retentive?*"

Rather than smile, Rocco crunched down the rest of his biscotti over a little plate. "Pop, did you know you were almost like a Robin Hood figure to some of us little street urchins in the Neighborhood? We heard stories about when you and Gus lived together, how you guys were in the Royal Flush *and* rode with the Wong Gongs. Both me and Whitey wanted to be you. Life must have been real different back then, huh? It seems like shit must have been cooler. People nowadays, for the most part, are shit."

"People are the same, Rocco. Some solid and most others are flakey." I said.

"So anyways," Rocco continued as he flexed his biceps, pulled back his elbows and rotated his head to ease the kinks from working out: those crazy old sisters were perfect for our needs at the time. Besides, the landlady had a great name."

"Mrs. Downs? Yeah, that's rich, son. I took a shit-load of *downs* during my career of abusing drugs. And I know you did."

"Yeah, but popping too many downers for too long eventually bit me on the ass. They went from relaxing me to wiring the shit out of me. But I guess you already know that part too, right counselor?"

"Hell yes, son! I lived it. Downs were my drug of choice, too. I didn't like downers. I loved them. But eventually I found out it was a one-way love affair. So I made adjustments."

"There it is, Pop. Yep . . .adjustments. Do what you did and get what you had."

I was left with my own dark thoughts to recall innocent times from a safe neighborhood of the 1950s. Tessa was my first girlfriend, at age five, although we didn't actually speak back then. We entered the world in 1950 and I fell in love with her in kindergarten, a fact she was unaware of till we were well into adolescence. The conception of our illegitimate child came at a moment when she was uncharacteristically drunk and reckless as was normal for me.

That one night in1975 Tessa and I had spent together, during a shared alcoholic blackout of flash-dreams and raw passions, was the night of our son's creation. My wife at the time, Butterscotch, was pregnant with Gina. I wasn't available for either. Back during that timeframe I ran through people's lives like a runaway train.

But even after a fuck-fest of hot days and torrid nights with countless women, the only one who ever really mattered was my Tessa. She was the same sweet girl I'd fallen in love with over a half-century ago, the loyal women who birthed and raised our son while outcast from her parents, yet never mentioning my name to her mad-dog father. Loving the idea of her love that when just out of reach was the worst pain of all.

The story Tessa related to a inquisitive boy about having a dead father rang true on various levels. Adult thugs struggled with our own turf wars. Fighting seemed the viable choice, even while I lay strapped down with a new type of physical pain, in a strange place compounded by confusion and the mental anguish of remorse. I never felt bad about anything in my adolescent life when I was out running and ripping, because I was a sociopath fueled by alcohol and driven by the prospect of *more*.

My son and I are alike in so many which have little to do with role-modeling a parent. Yet the similarities are striking and many. A major difference, however, is that as a child I had two parents at home, even if they did severely lack parenting skills. So did my Gina during her formative years. Butterscotch and I had taken our daughter everywhere with us, till the divorce.

From the first time Rocco and I met we sensed that familiar mind-meld. I felt it stronger than ever when I came face to face with his mother. After 30+ years of no contact he and I noticed we shared another dimension with her. Rocco was tuned-in but burning out at break-neck speed – just like I had. He was smart and knew better then to self-destruct and actually cared about many things life had to offer – just like I had.

Tessa did her best to instill proper morals and values in her fatherless child, the type she had been exposed to throughout childhood while in the safe nest of Collinwood. But her paradigm shift was extreme. Working fulltime with a mischievous young boy at home, even with some support from her Uncle Pazzo, her son gravitated to the same type of people he admired – the gangsters of Collinwood – just like I had.

A latch-key adolescent, just as many kids are who come from broken homes or single parent families, Rocco grew attracted to the familial bond offered by gangs and to the excitement and temporary escape found with drugs and their abusers. Tessa lost control of our son. Rocco became best friends with Ansel's son, Whitey. So in late adolescence he frequented the Wong Gong's clubhouse with Whitey – just like I had with Ansel. The weirdest part was that Whitey's mother was Maureen, the sister of Doyle Kelly. Rocco had connections with all of the Collinwood gangs – just like I had.

Rocco fought his way through school against tough ghetto blacks, like I had. Racial violence crescendoed from the mid-to-late-1960s in Collinwood high school for us and throughout the mid-70s till the blacks took over the school. From what I'm told, our son, Rocco, grew up fast and hard on those mean streets of Collinwood, just like I had. He hung out with bad-ass bikers of German, Irish and Slovenian descent, like I had. But fighting through all that pain seemed to only cause more, just like the way it had for me.

From what I learned, Tessa had been a single mother devoted to her only child. She supported him with no help.

Although Tessa and I knew one another all our lives, we spent our most important years apart and estranged. To Rocco, before we ever met, I was dead – back then and again now. Tessa had never married. An odd coincidence is neither of my middle-aged children ever married or had children, which could be another lesson I left behind in my wake of blackouts and wreckage.

      Rocco grew fast and hard, and in doing so acquired wings and flew his own way – just like I had. He was far from stupid and not even close to being a sociopath. But his ways were – shall we say – non-traditional, like mine were. He had a good heart and cared about many things. It's just that he didn't care enough – the same way I'd been. And now that I'm trapped in a punji pit with no way out, left with nothing other than my thoughts and regrets, now maybe I care too much.

Snapshots from one unforgettable year, of 1976 when Cleveland OH had been dubbed Bomb City, USA, led to an isolated incident years later. 2013 became another year which became every bit as memorable. It left my family and me with a cold awareness followed by a renewed sense of clarity, when life seems too real. Dying or dead, though of which I felt unsure of, I wandered through a mist of abstractions far from where my car had been parked that day everything changed, perhaps with the press of a cowardly button. I remembered a thundering blast and blinding light as bright as if the Sun were exploding our sky. Its searing heat must have melted clothes into my flesh as I soared like a superhero, rocketing from one nightmare to another.

***Okay, so all I need to do** is… Yeah, I'll just wait and then just do the next right thing. That's simple enough. Alright, so the smart move is… What exactly is the smart move?*

CH III:
Mish-mash of Head-flicks

GAME-TEST: A display of rare courage or bravery, deep or even dead-gameness, while engaged in mortal combat regardless of safety and consequence. Rare virtue manifested as resolve of perseverance. The integrity to win at the expense of life's most precious cost. It's survival at its most primal level. Determined composure and fixated dedication to the most extreme fervent struggle until the source of pain is no longer a threat.

The strange world of 1976 as seen through night terrors in 2013: I drifted back to the time when I had been married to a beautiful girl of mixed pedigree called Butterscotch. She delivered our daughter, Gina, in 1976, within two months from when Tessa, covertly gave birth to my son, Rocco, in California. The birth of my daughter ranks as one of the most glorious days of my life. The other birth serves as a reminder of why I no longer drink – blackouts compounded by serial fuck-ups. I never knew about that male child until I wound up being his counselor at a rehab facility. I guess stranger things have happened – just not to me. Well, just not lately, not counting the newest piece of insanity unfolding to forever alter my world.

I also thought of my first pit-dog. I could almost smell the beat-up tether snap dust into a new day during a mid-70s summer. A worn motorcycle tire dangled from a catalpa tree's limb, suspended by a thick length of cotton rope discolored from weather and use. Beading had been removed from an old front tire to make it more pliable in the little bitch's mouth. Gracie twisted in mid-air, emitting a low growl with each shake. The tiny dog squinted in ecstasy as she spun circles. Powered by fierce yanks and flips, the tiny Pit-bull watched me. She knew I wanted her to drop it but also understood that meant it was time for our walk. Crazy Gracie had been acquired fresh off the tit from a West Virginia dogfighter called Fatso who had mysteriously disappeared. I thought: *Yeah, if I live to be a 1,000 years old I'll never forget that dirty motherfucker. That one moment is when everything changed. But if I had to do it over…* The little red-nose fought that old tire as if it were death itself, as I listened for something I had felt.

Withdrawal sent shrillness in pulses. Dope-sickness filled my nervous system with non-stop buzzing from another all-nighter. One knee stoved-up, my right hand was swollen from an encounter with *whatever* during another blackout. *What's that noise?* A puffy fist shielded bloodshot eyes as I listened for that something still coming. From the backyard I finally heard its urgency, the desperate plea of an unanswered phone. *Just don't answer it.* Though I tried to ignore its impatience, I was drawn by a sick curiosity.

Why don't they just hang up? But it was time for her to let go, anyway. I caught that little red blur in midair and commanded, "Drop it." My head, knee and right fist throbbed. Thankfully, Gracie let go. Too sick to walk her, I carried her as I limped toward the house. The whole time she licked my face till I released her to zigzag throughout the front-room. Louder, shrillness tore through my skull. *Why doesn't it just stop?*

Dope sickness strafed across my head, embedded into my stomach and legs. I lifted the receiver on the second ring to hear a familiar voice, "Listen close." *I fucking knew it.* "Swear to Buddha, this is the last time I say it." *I could smell it.*

The voice warned. "Now let's see if you're as smart as you think you are. Understand what I'm sayin' to you?"

I told that dangerous guy in our crew, "I do," and I did.

I reached down and mumbled to our little red-nose, Gracie, "This Benny's a lunatic. But then maybe Ansel was on to something the whole time about a price on my head. But I don't know. Then if that's true, I wouldn't be alive enough to be thinking this, right? Shit! Check me out. I'm standing in the front-room asking a dog if Benny's crazy," I said, to a pocket-pit I respected more that any other friend I'd ever known. Besides, I promised my ol' lady, Butter, I'd take her to the grand opening of R-Bar. And I'm not a man to break my word – even if I do have conversations with dogs."

That night of the double date with our wives, we drove there with the toughest guy in Collinwood. Nobody picked a fight with our friend, Eggs, and walked away without a taking a severe beating. While at the R-Bar that eventful evening, when there was more electricity in the air than oxygen, Eggs and I left rosy-cheeked ladies at our table to blend with customers. Our club-brother, Fingers, still leaning on the bar, shook hands with a loose grip. His hair was so black it was almost blue like the color of paper wasps. He looked more mid-eastern than Italian. Dusky complexion accentuated simmering rage hidden within a gray sharkskin suit as he offered with a dark glare, "Come on. We'll go downstairs to the office so we can talk in private."

I mumbled to Eggs, "No shit. So Fingers is the one, huh? Maybe Benny ain't so nuts, after all. But I'm sure we can talk this out, right? I mean, we're all brothers. But I'm feeling real dizzy, *coom*, like I might pass out."

As we walked and waited for the other boot to stomp, Eggs agreed as we spoke inside an echo chamber, "Yeah, just stay cool, Jackie. Maybe we'll have a sit-down. Let's see what he has to say so we know how to act. I'll be right back, okay. Wait right here for me. I just wanna let my ol' lady know what's up so she ain't lookin' for me." Anxiety ripped me in half as Led Zeppelin's "You Shook Me" bounced from tile to ceiling. Eggs returned in minutes, all puffed up in the chest and red-faced, looking fierce with his piercing blue eyes and chiseled features: "Let's get this over with, *coom*."

I had taken Butter's advice and had been pacing myself with the booze so not to get sloppy. Yet I was high like never before. Rohypnol (ruffies); GHB; Ketamine; chloral hydrate, also known as "knockout drops" or a "Mickey Finn," all of them commonly hit fast and hard, producing slurred speech and lack of coordination. Powdered straight-jacket disguised in a drink of a drunk – one that disarms foolish victims just like me.

I slurred, "It's fucking weird, man. The slower I sip the higher I get, but a different kind. Everything's all fucked-off. And what's with these lights? See 'em? Dim, then bright. Check 'em out. Now look. Flared right back up. See it? The whole world's fluttering. Now listen close. Hear the echoes? You feel 'em too, right *coom*? Everything's spinning in slow-motion. Feel it?"

Inside the basement office, Big Louie from Little Italy posted like a sentry. Cagootz leaned on the butt of a rifle like a cane. Fingers stood next to the main man, Uno, who watched what was about to transpire through the cold eyes of a man dead. The room began to spin from what had been slipped from a drink into my brain.

My voice resonated a slow roar as if from another: "I know what time it is. You wanna showdown. Is that it?" *Fading fast.* "What? Now's too soon?" *Stay awake.* Jimmy Page electrified Robert Plant's moans as I stripped off my shirt and slurred, "It's slash-and-burn time, right Fingers? Yeah. It's all or nothin', right *coom*? I already dreamed about this night. But answer me this.

Which part am I supposed ta give a fuck about? Oops. Nobody's here but me. Okay. Fuck-it." I punched my friend and it was on.

During that test I felt what a game-dog lived in a pit – the pain of being isolated in a strange crowd of friends. My father told me many times in his deep voice, "Treat others the way they treat you." I did, but things went from bad to insane. The bridge of my nose went numb when I thumbed an eye socket. In self-defense I ripped an ear half off till my left cheekbone got wrecked by a decanter bottle. I could hear my father preach his familiar credo, "Fight and the pain will go away." I did, but that just made matters worse. Nothing made sense except attack and get knocked-out again. Tile slick with treachery offered another perspective to watch cigar smoke crawl across florescent lights, to fold in on itself till there was nothing but a stench.

As soon as Eggs intervened, Cagootz smashed a bottle over his head and jammed the broken end in his forehead. I couldn't tell my blood from his. Unknown to me, Eggs had been suspected of being an informant. When Fingers kicked Eggs in his bloodied face I growled through swollen lips, "Okay, motherfucker, my turn again."

Blood sprayed his new suit jacket when I fish-hooked his mouth with a thumb and yanked sideways. In turn, a fractured nose from a thick decanter spiked my brain. The pattern was simple: knocked-down, back up, knee and elbow, out again to dream I was home in bed. Knocked out four or six times in a row after I had been assured, "We can talk," consciousness illuminated a ceiling very different from my own each time I woke from a dream of sleeping in bed next to my wife.

A deep, familiar voice from childhood echoed inside my head: *Get up, boy. Do it now! Fight through the pain.* In survival mode, I had little choice but to obey.

I woke again on that same floor just long enough to get knocked cold beneath the maniacal face of Cagootz punching my eyes closed. But not before I saw my older friend, Pazzo, catch him with an elbow to the temple as he feigned an attempt to pull him off me. He shouted to him, "Hey, cuz! You okay?" In exaggerated gestures, Pazzo lifted Cagootz, slipped on that slimy surface, and then fell hard on top of him – more of a push than a fall. That big melon-head of Cagootz smacked the tiles and bounced after a dull thud. Pazzo said, "Here, *coom*. Let me help you up," as he pulled a dazed Cagootz upright by his straight black hair and flung him into a wall of that basement office.

Fingers said, "This ain't over. I'll be waiting. I'll be seeing you again, dead-man."

So it was him! It was Fingers after all, nursing a bruised ego after all these years? I guessed, with no proof.

PIT: (verb) Allow something, someone or oneself to engage in a gameness competition. (noun) Habitat for lost souls and doomed spirits; a miserable yet defining situation or place. A natural or artificial cavity in a body or the ground. A structure within a structure, enclosed or concealed, used for a specific combat function. A place used during a match which exposes degrees of cowardice or gameness. Tangible or indefinable trap.

I flashed to a scene of truly horrific imagery from 1969, when a heroic little dog was stuck in time with a worthless human called Fatso. As 19-year old *kids*, a club-brother and I had taken a ride to West Virginia to get a well-bred pup from a professional dogfighter reputed to have some of the best Colby blood in the world. My friend, Fingers, had long, blue-black hair and a dusky complexion. He was average size and built for a young Italian adolescent of that era, nothing much unusual looking about him other than his eyes which betrayed chronic simmering rage.

We prepared well, even though there were no cell phones or CDs. We loaded two wooden shipping crates in the Ford station wagon. 1969 also meant cops were still pretty much clueless about casual drug usage. There was a small box packed with 8-track tapes of modern music which years later became known as "Classic Rock." We passed a joint between us and slowly sipped warm, longneck Stroh's beers to cure the *cottonmouth* while Morrison warned, "People are Strange" on tinny speakers that vibrated when the volume was up. A 16-ounce bag of Johnny's potato chips lay on the seat between us. Tattooed arms dangled over the fake wooden sides of our car doors. Long black hair gnarled in the wind.

We pulled into a winding driveway full of potholes and large rocks to visit a breeder known on the fighting circuit as "Fatso." He was an older man in bib overalls, on his porch with another man.

He yelled, "Hey, bluebeard. Are you Jackie with all them daggone tattoos?" I nodded affirmative. He told us through a wad of chew, "Okay then, this here's yer lucky day, boys. We's about ta roll us some dawgs and game-test a young male we might ta sell ya. Savvy? Brung ya some cash ta get ya a good 'un, did ya?" I nodded affirmative again. He rose to spit a stream of brown slime off the porch. "Alrighty then, foller me."

    I caught the eye of Fingers watching the mountain man. He had a hammer handle sticking out of one back pocket. It had been shaved to a wedge to look like a long wooden duck's bill. We noticed a bulge in the other back pocket. *Click* Outlined was something more compact and looked heavy enough to be a metal object. Fingers grinned and lifted his black T-shirt enough to show me part of the wooden handle of his .38 Smith & Wesson, tucked under a thick leather belt against his wiry athletic frame. I palmed the material in a front pocket of my faded Levis covering a six inch switchblade and nodded.

    The fat man warned, "I don't let nobody up in these here kennels to see my secret breedings and such. We might sell ta ya a dawg, boys, but not the recipe. Savvy?" His partner he had referred to as "Ebb" came up out of a root cellar carrying by the scruff of the neck a small, scarred-up black dog with a graying muzzle. The skinny dog blinked from the rush of sunlight as Fatso announced, "This here's a schoolin' dawg. He ain't got no real name, 'cause he ain't got no talent. Savvy? All's this ol' worthless shit-eater is, is game. So we keep him chained in that ol' root cellar to kill rats. The onliest reason he's still suckin' air is 'cause I needs me a punch dawg now and again. That, and these boys think he might make 'em a good stud. So I'll take that stud fee every damn time." He said to me, "Son, hold on to this dawg a spell. Don't fret none. He don't bite."

    The old black dog dangled from Fatso's meaty fist when he handed him to me. I set him on all fours to pet him, wondering when the last time was he had actually gotten any affection. The little dog wagged its thin tail and lightly chirped, straining in the direction of Fatso's barn. I made up my mind to buy that old dog as a stud.

    We headed for a hill behind a dilapidated barn. Fatso's partner, a scrawny man named Ebb, also in bibs, ran back from what looked like an old tobacco barn carrying a large red dog tucked under a freckled arm roped with thick veins. The large dog seemed to be a yearling, yet already sported gray calluses on its elbows and hocks, evidently from laying on a wooden floor with no straw for bedding. Fatso called behind him, "Not in the pit, son. We's gonna roll 'em up on this little knoll right here, Ebb, so's we can see what the hell's goin' on. Savvy, boy?" Ebb nodded that he understood and followed.

They faced the dogs at the top of the hill behind the barn with its weathered and warped boards that faintly read, "Chew Mail Pouch." The young red dog barked wildly and lunged at the old black dog. The old dog with the grayed muzzle growled and lifted his lip to show small blunted teeth mostly broken off. It crouched down low in wait.

As soon as they were released, the bigger dog charged across at full speed. The old dog jumped up and caught the young one by an ear and danced him around in 360 turns. The old-timer's front legs were expertly tucked back and out of danger.

Fatso yelled, "Get a hold on that schoolin' dawg and break this sombitch off, goddamnit! I don't want that useless bastard teachin' this prospect here any bad habits. Let's just see if'n this youngster'll scratch back to 'im, Ebb. Savvy?"

"Okay uncle," said the emaciated younger man. Ebb pulled a parting stick out of his back pocket and easily pried off the nameless, toothless dog while Fatso held the younger one with a parting stick held between its shiny long teeth. Fatso walked about ten feet away, faced the young dog and released him. The red dog charged back and that time dove underneath the old one. Ebb held onto the old black dog while the young red grabbed a front leg, flipped the old dog half over and shook hard.

Fatso screamed, "Let that fuckin' dog go, you knit-wit!"

While the schooling dog's waist was still tucked between Ebb's spindly legs we heard a snap before Ebb let go. Because the little black dog couldn't defend himself one of the old dog's front legs flopped around like it was attached only by skin.

"Handle that black dawg, goddamnit! Now look what you went and did! I ought ta kick you up inside yer stinkin' ass, Ebb! Now take that ol' bastard down ta the bottom of this fuckin' hill. Savvy? Goddamn, this boy's dense!"

The old dog's tail wagged ferociously as Ebb did as asked. Fatso carried the big dog to the top of that hill. He pulled an automatic from a back pocket, the bulge we had seen, while the young dog bucked between his front legs, eager to get back into the action. Fatso yelled, "Now scratch that worthless bastard."

The old dog held still, conserving energy, till the moment when he felt Ebb had released him to make his scratch back to that younger, larger prospect. The *schooling* dog leaped toward his opponent but fell on his face when his leg collapsed beneath him. Regardless, the no-name dog was back up and stumbled up the hill just as fast as he could for a dog with a broken leg. Fatso chambered a round. Just before the old dog made a game scratch on three legs, Fatso aimed. **To be continued…**

BASEMENT or CELLAR: foundation or subterranean structure. A place for safety or secrecy; shelter for perishables; refuge or haven during a storm. A vault, mine, crypt or dungeon. Slang for a clandestine underground operation. An underlying formation at bedrock. The lowest part of ones life; a personal bottom. A killing floor or pit.

Where I was had the feel of a cellar. Regardless, a basement wasn't deep enough for me to defend myself or hide from whatever had been eating me alive. I couldn't scream. It had me pinned down, wrapped around my throat; choking the life out of me while devouring little chunks of itself, of me, one breath at a time. Hovering just outside of awareness, I woke covered in sweat and I felt as though my skin was on fire again.

Cleveland Wars of 1976: once a booming industrial town along the North Coast, became a nationally famous war zone during an organized crime power struggle. Collinwood, a neighborhood on Cleveland's Eastside, had once been a safe haven for morally grounded inhabitants having solid family values. Neatly manicured yards maintained by working-class families relied on an omniscient deity and a country which had at one time championed our own underdogs, made for a safe environment.

When most others were relocating away, Ansel's Wong Gongs boldly planted their MC clubhouse flag at the west end of Five Points. Adjacent to Uno's expanding turf it also bordered Mick's territory and Sonny Magic's hood. They convoluted that ongoing conflict when Ansel threw their gauntlet into the mix.

Ansel, a 1%er who had fervent backing from his own band of killers, was every bit as smart, vicious and relentless as Uno, the Mick and Sonny Magic. He was smart enough not to look for an all-out turf battle till his own club grew in numbers and the Cleveland syndicate grew weaker. Those Cleveland scooter tramps were younger, did more creative mind-altering drugs and cared less about having a future, kids or luxurious belongings. Plus, Ansel's ragged bikers had judiciously played both sides against a middle they had created to exploit, while Italian and Irish gang members kept killing off one another during the widespread bombings of C-town.

The ghetto of Glenville bordering Collinwood was a breeding ground for black power groups, the Black Panthers and the Nation of Islam. Sonny Magic laid low in his own jungle while he searched for opportunities as the cancer spread. Inner-city Cleveland became similar to a drag-pit from an Oklahoma cock derby combined with the stench from a Chicago slaughterhouse.

Basements have become a major part of life. One example was an incident when Irish gangster found himself at our mercy in 1976, beneath the first house I lived in as a married man. I answered a familiar knock at my backdoor, looking like the missing link with long black curls matted to my face. There parked a shiny new Cadillac near my garage. My closest brother, Fingers, carrying a cardboard box under one arm and holding Benny's neon blue aluminum baseball bat used for making collections and adjustments, stood at my door with my oldest friend. Benny held a familiar-looking man by his blonde hair, a gun pointed to his ribs. The man was wearing a shitty-looking suit that appeared to have been one of those cheap two-for-one warehouse deals. The man's mouth was duct taped shut. His hands had been secured behind his back. The middle-aged man, whom I vaguely knew, was a soldier in the Mick's crew.

Benny wore styled, medium length wavy brown hair. As usual he was impeccably dressed with expensive clothes and shoes. He believed in making strong first impressions. He asked in a hushed voice, "Is your ol' lady home, *coom*?"

When I wagged my head that she was not he explained, "We just captured this piece of garbage down Five Points. He beat and raped my mother last night."

Still quiet, I watched the dark eyes of those two men who had been my brothers for over a decade. Both were average height for Italians, with proportional weight. Each had athletic builds, not thick or skinny. Both were put-up very much like me but with less muscle. And both would not long after that incident become ex-*coombas* of mine, a fact still unknown to me at that moment. I watched their body language as well as studying cold blue eyes of the captured, duct taped man at my door.

Fingers asked, "Can we use your basement? We need an answer from this loser and we'll be out of your way before Butter gets back." Fingers' thick hair was longer than Benny's and much darker. Fingers was Sicilian, like me. He wore an old T-shirt and pressed dress pants with scuffed expensive black shoes.

I nodded my head that it was okay, still staring at the captive man. The three of them went downstairs, the bound and gagged man out in front. I closed and locked the door behind us and followed them. Benny walked toward a sturdy ceiling jack near a floor drain. "You remember Sean Greene, right *coom*?"

"Yeah. And that's a good idea for when he pisses all over himself," I chuckled.

Benny looked at me as Fingers said, "Yeah, *coom*, this pole will do just fine."

Fingers dropped the box and the bat. He pulled the roll of silver tape out of the box so he could tape Sean to that rusted pole extending from floor to ceiling beam. Benny said, "Okay, Sean, here's the deal. I'm gonna ask you the most important question of your life. If you get it right you catch a beating with this little bat as a warning. But if you lie... Well ... we don't need to get too specific about that part just yet. You're a man of the world. You understand how all this shit works, right?"

Benny yanked tape off the blonde haired guy's pockmarked face. He asked the dangerous Irishman, "Any last words, fuck-wad?"

Where the tape had been showed pink flesh beneath Sean's angry blue eyes. He answered, "Sure. I got somethin' ta say. Don't think fer a second nobody saw you two cunts nab me comin' out of the Shamrock Club. There's apartments, houses and cars all around, and lots of Celtic eyes watchin' ya *dago* cunts. Yep, that's right. All three a ya sawed-off cunts are in deep shit already. Count on that, boys. But I might still be able ta get ya off with a stern warning if ya step back and wise up."

Benny said, "Whatever... Okay, here's the questions: Did you molest my mother because you're a degenerate fuck of an Irish pig? Or did you hurt her because your scumbag boss, the one youse fucking faggots call the Mick, put you up to it?"

Sean laughed and spit on my old concrete floor with its spider web cracks reaching out to plain block walls. "You can lick me balls first then, Benny boy, whilst I think about this, and yer girlfriends here can jerk me off if they'd like."

Fingers reopened the cardboard box, put in the roll of tape and removed what looked like a folded travel bag for suits, a small white jug and a length of garden hose.

Fingers said, "Here's the thing: You'd better answer quick, tough guy. In case you haven't noticed, we ain't impressed with your boss, and we ain't got all day. You remember what happened to the Mick's brother don't you? He caught a one-way train to nowhere. Time's precious, Sean, especially for you."

"I'll answer ya. I didn't molest nor hurt yer mum. Alls I did was ta give the old gal a good fuckin' 'cause she's a horny ol' cunt. That's the sum of it, boys," Sean laughed. "I quite enjoyed her. Actually, I might consider making her me ol' lady. She gives some fine head. Did she learn that from you, Benny boy?"

From a front pocket, Fingers pulled out and unfolded a straight razor with bone handles and slowly stropped it across the inside of his tattooed left forearm.

Benny smiled and said, "Okay, thanks. We've heard enough." He re-taped Sean's mouth with the same piece of duct tape he had been holding and then went to work on him with his trusty neon blue aluminum bat, first arms and legs and then heavy body shots, till snot and blood ran from Sean's nostrils.

We leaned against a basement wall, out of batting range. When Benny grew tired from beating what had become a groaning bloody lump at the base of my metal pole, Fingers took over. He yanked up Sean's head by wet purple hair that moments before had been yellow. With a quick slice at the throat, Sean's whimpering became gurgling till a terrible hissing fell to silence.

I learned what my floor drain was for, although Sean had pissed himself. And that rubber bag was not for a suit, unless it contained a body. Benny connected the hose to a treaded faucet in my old washtub and sprinkled some liquid from that white jug on pools of Sean's dark artery blood puddled-up and coagulating. I helped them load the bag into a large Cadillac trunk. Then I returned to open two small windows and turn on a rusty fan to blow out bleach fumes. Watching a water stain slowly dry around the floor drain from an afternoon sunbeam shining through a small window, I smoked a joint that had been stashed behind an ear like a pencil. I thought about how quickly life permanently changes. I stayed down there till the water spots dried to patches of clean cement. I decided to clean the entire basement and did.

Payback... *But why the Irish? And that was 40 fucking years ago!*

MOTHER NATURE & FATHER TIME: masters of our universe. The perfect Mother composed of everything external and within, always was and always will be. Father, simply put, implies the when of occurrence in nature, before we were born, throughout our lives and long after we're gone. Timing: do the right thing at the wrong time and find out how much it's worth.

After our July honeymoon we were home again but as one family. When Tessa and I finally did marry, Rocco took my last name and served as our best man. My daughter, Gina, was maid of honor. The ceremony took place on a beach at a gorgeous Bahamian resort during a cruise so we could bond as family. That sunny day at Nassau's pale blue ocean sudsed by gentle waves, stands out as one of the happiest moments of my life. That and the birth of my Gina stand unequaled.

Our son had me by two inches in height and 20 pounds of muscle, at just under 200 pounds. And he and was about the same age as me when I got sober. Rocco's arms, like mine, were fully sleeved and interconnected from wrists to collarbone, inside and out. Shoulder caps also incorporated three back pieces laid out in triangle to symbolize mind, body and spirit, all touching each other. Also like mine, the front of the shoulder pieces wrapped around onto two large pectoral tats on either side. So technically, we had one tattoo each. The back pieces we went for together, at a friend's shop who specializes in fine lines and gray wash. We already had the other ink when we met.

It was almost comforting waking to memories of our own home. I remembered how Rocco and I had stationed ourselves on blue twin recliners while Tessa and Gina curled-up on our long, microfiber couch with its overstuffed cushions and pillows, where we attempted to untangle our jumbled lives settled into fixed positions in my mind. We'd spent part of almost every summer day in our small front-room sharing stories.

Gina matured into a tall slender woman with dense curls and tragic eyes reminiscent of her mother's. Pictures of her and Butterscotch at the same age showed the same features and body types. Two differences were: Gina's Sicilian olive skin and hazel eyes were mine, along with thick, wavy dark hair. But that's where our aesthetic similarities ended. Butterscotch had worn her soft strawberry blonde hair in an afro, fashionable back in the late-'60 to mid-'70s to highlight a creamy caramel complexion. Butter's one-fourth African-American heritage gave her an exotic look.

Tessa said she could pass for a Brazilian beauty queen.

I thought of my Tessa and recalled how one day she had quietly blurted out of nowhere, without looking at me, "Yeah, bro, me too." as if we had been engaged in a lengthy discussion. Che kept leafing through a dog magazine. When around strangers, although not shy at all, Tessa hid behind long blonde hair contrasting classic Roman features and watched.

Eyes closed momentarily, I breathed deeply. I knew that *she* knew exactly what I was thinking. "I couldn't agree more," I conceded to my childhood sweetheart as I looked down at my manuscript, to clear my throat – and my eyes.

Tessa had given me her cute, sultry half-smile: "Silly boy. Just feel what you feel." For a woman her age, she managed to be half girl yet all lady. It wasn't that she tried to act cutesy. She didn't act at all. During adolescence she carried herself with class and dignity beyond her years, even during her teens. She emanated a certain glow, like an aura. But regardless of enigmatic femininity contrasting toughness, there was another complexity. In her older years Tessa maintained a quality that was still fresh, although far removed from sophomoric or idealistic. If she was anything, Tessa was wise and sophisticated, but in a down to earth way that never appeared contrived or forced. As tough as she was, she despised any type of unwarranted cruelty.

I thought: *Yeah, I sure do, too. I like it just like this.*

She gave me a soft, beautiful smile while I reread my dog-eared, marked-up manuscript which was as close to being ready as I could ever get it to becoming a novel.

From our kitchen I listened to my middle-aged children get to know one another. They moved from being strangers, to family, to best friends, to soul mates. During one of our last days together I heard Rocco ask Gina, "I guess this is as good a time as any to ask. You figure we're in this alone, sister-girl?"

"The way I have it figured, we come into this world alone as frightened creatures, and eventually we'll all leave the same way. So it's up to me to be happy right now."

"Yeah, I agree. People in *The Program* are all the time droning on about a Higher Power, predetermined reasons for everything, how we gotta give up our willpower in order to be sober, and we have to turn everything over to God. Then they preach how we gotta be honest to stay sober. But when I admit I don't believe in God, they freak out."

"Some people are mindless robots, Rocco. Yet they have the nerve to try to invalidate others' opinions, those of us who dare to think outside their little security box."

"They don't push it with me too far though. The ones who know me know better. And the ones who don't . . . well, they find out quick enough that I have my own mind. But just out of curiosity, how would you handle a situation like that?"

"Handle what, little-bro? You mean if I got challenged about my ideas on entering and leaving life alone? Or do you mean about choices and creating my own destiny?"

"Yeah, exactly. But how would you say it to a person you sort of liked? You know; to people who don't realize they're insulting you and your entire belief system because they're so self-absorbed and deluded."

"I'd tell them we're powerless but only about being born and dying. That all the other stuff between those two dates on our tombstones, and choices of how we react to things we didn't cause, is on us. I'd say our life belongs to us, that we already own it whether we like it or not. So buckle up and deal with it," Gina answered.

"Cool. I kind of like that. I think I'll use that."

"What is it you say to those frothing *rebirthers*, Rocco?"

"You mean those AA Nazis battling the non-existent anti-Christ . . . meaning anyone who disagrees with them? I remind them that every animal on the planet is born from pain and dies alone. But we might be the only mammals aware of those gloomy facts. We're animals too, made in the image of primates. Most people try to use a bait and switch game with God as an inaccessible carrot on a stick. I remind them that spirituality always was and always will be. Spirituality is passion and love, integrity and creativity. It's the humanism to care enough about each other to risk money and freedom, injury and even our lives for one another – all based on secular freewill. It's making the next *sober* choice, and having the gameness to do the next right thing out of respect – with nothing to gain other than to reinforce our own worth – and then turning that choice into an action."

"That's pretty cool. You're smarter than you look."

"Thanks . . . I think. Anyways, I suppose I got a lot of practice about this stuff from being in rehab. Maybe not the way they intended it. But a whole lot of honesty and love can be found in treatment centers, even though those places have their fair share of pathological liars and sociopaths too – including staff. It's all that honesty I admire as much as the gameness, the integrity to stay straight. That's healthy self-love."

"*Love?* Now there's an overused word that's really lost its meaning. I thought I was in love one time, till I realized I was an idealistic girl stuck on a selfish and scared little boy who thought he needed a trophy chick on his arm to feel better about himself."

"Romantic love is real tricky. I'm not sure what it means."

"Codependency or insecurity, lust or infatuation, maybe symbiotic delusion? I just don't know, Rocco. I imagine it must be a beautiful thing when you find someone you're willing to put *everything* on the line for – but only if it's mutual. It would be like loving someone more than yourself, but without losing yourself. I guess true love transcends all fears and greed. Have you ever loved anybody that much?"

"Sure, but not the romance kind. I've always loved Ma that much. And now I love Pop and you that much, too. And maybe even my Danni and my bro, Whitey. But straight up, I'm still considering how much I trust those two. That's just being real. Anyway, I know this much about it: love and trust have to go together as if they're one thing. And it must be 100%, from day one on through for it to last."

"Same for me. I really do love you, and Daddy and Ma, and of course my mom, too. Butter's been cool in her own way, even if she is a psycho bitch. But that's it for me. I don't think I have any more love left in my heart to give. I'm not ready to squander anymore respect and loyalty on some one-way bastard. For me, gifts like trust and honesty mean way more than this mushy *love* talk we always hear so much about."

"You know the way people go on and on about heaven?" Rocco asked. "It almost sounds like they want to die."

"Those worshipers are the ones most afraid of death."

"I love life. But I'd give it up in a heartbeat to save us."

"I'm right with, buddy. Life is heaven. But I'd risk it all for us to all share a good life."

"Is your mom pissed when you admit you're atheist?"

"I don't know. Maybe. But at least I'm not a hypocrite like she is. Butter knows I'm like him when it comes to common sense – and a few other things. If anything, the only reason she might get pissed is because the older I get the more I'm like him. But she's learned to deal with it. She loves me. Even though she actually had the nerve to say that the only thing she loves more than me is God. Can you imagine saying that to your own kid? That's fucked up."

"Me and Whitey haven't believed in any of that mumbo jumbo since way before I knew I had an atheist father. Hey, maybe it's genetic!" Rocco smirked. "Ma doesn't care much for me telling people how I feel. But like love and trust are, to me politics and religion are really the same thing. Besides, Ma's a heathen, too. I figure she's agnostic, at best. She won't admit it, though. But I hear her talking to Pop about real things. She's straight with him about everything. But anyone else, even us—"

Tessa hollered out, "I hear you two mumbling in there. I don't talk about politics and religion because it's nobody else's business what I believe. Maybe you should learn to do the same instead of running your mouth, Rocco!" Tessa returned to her book to avoid any questions on those topics.

Rocco spoke loud enough for his mother to hear, "You know what, Gina? Speaking of love, we have a lot in common. If you weren't my sister I'd make you my ol' lady. If I could I'd marry you today. I mean, we're only half-related, right? And you're pretty awesome for a chick, the way you think and handle yourself. Plus, you're really hot-looking. In fact—"

"Jesus F. Christ, Rocco. Listen to you! That's a *schifoso* (disgusting) thing for you to even joke about. That kind of talk is even below your standards. What's the matter with you, boy?" Tessa shouted into the kitchen.

"Easy, Ma. I only said that because you're already taken. You know I'd marry you first. You were my first love."

"I'm getting a little jealous here," Gina said. "I gotta admit it. Since you've been hitting the weights in the basement, and now sporting this killer Bahamian tan… Mmm, mmm! And the truth is I've only ever been with one *real* man, and not since…"

"Stop . . . please!" Tessa moaned. "You're both very sick! You quit twisting your sister's head around, Rocco. You've infected her with your sickness. You leave that poor girl alone! Come back here, honey. Sit with me. Don't pay any attention to that filthy pig. He'll just get you in trouble with his crazy ideas."

We eased back into our old seating arrangement, Rocco next to me and across from Tessa and Gina. I could see Tessa getting upset so I asked, "Hey, Rocco, you have anything else to share besides boring subjects like religion, politics or incest?"

"I have something," Gina said. "The main thing for me right now is intimacy. I just can't seem to get enough of you. We need to make up for lost time. I really do love you, Rocco. I'd do anything for you. And I mean *anything*. I hope you know that."

"I feel you, sister-girl. We missed out on over 35 years of knowing one another on intimate terms. So that means I need to know everything about you, you inside-out. Just know this: right or wrong, I got your back every time – no matter what. But I do hear what you're saying about getting more intimate. I'm game."

Tessa raised her small hands as she said, "Please… This whole conversation is making me a little nervous. I know what you mean, but it just sounds weird. Okay?"

Gina beamed her dazzling smile at her step-mother: "You guys do understand there are other things every bit as intimate as sex. Right, Ma and Daddy-O?"

"Name one thing for me," Tessa asked.

"Like breaking the law or dropping acid together, or sharing each other's dark secrets or making new ones together."

"Of course we understand, honey," I assured Gina. "We're old, not dead."

Gina laughed: "So we agree that there are other intimacies, and there's so much more to life than sex. But just look at that hunk of a man! I'd go all the way with you, buddy."

"Ain't nothin' to it but just do it, baby…" he grinned.

"Why he does this to me I'll never know!" Tessa slammed her book on the wooden end table and stormed out of the room.

CH IV: Chips off the Old Block

I lay floating inside a shroud near the ceiling sometime in 2013, hovering above a hospital bed while I told myself: *I can't keep thinking about this family stuff. It's tearing my heart out. And it's my birthday. It's almost August already, for fuck's sake…*

July 28, 2013 – The Stakeout, the 1st day: Secure in our country home, cozied up in our front-room, eventually we found our way back to another segment of what Gina referred to as *story-time*. Tessa curled her tiny feet beneath her on our dark blue microfiber couch, posted behind a large black paperback with bright yellow lettering about the American Pit-bull Terrier.

Gina stationed herself on the floor, using Little Sinbad's doggie bed as a pillow, rereading my rough draft of *I'm Jack & I Want More* for the nth time with a red pen for reediting held between straight white teeth. I sat in my recliner, waiting.

My old line-bred mongrel, a Yankee Terrier, was considered to be a *Pit-bull*, although he looked like a miniature Rottweiler rather than either his Pit-bull or Airedale heritage. Sinbad flipped my hand off the arm of my chair with his snout, demanding attention. He made the rounds and did the same to all of us, commandeering our affection. In remote control, each of us took turns giving pats or scratching an ear. Unconsciously, we all did as our dog requested without interruption.

"Alright, Pop. When you hear the word *cheeks*, what is it you think of?" my son asked, out of the blue, as he pulled at his thick black beard with a calloused hand.

"Me? I guess I think of that song, *Patti Cheeks*. Remember that game we played as kids, Tessa?" I asked my wife. "How did it go again? *Patti Cheeks, Patti Cheeks, baker's man. Kiss her fat ass as fast as you can…* Is that it?"

"No. It was *pat-a-cake*. Not *Patti Cheeks*, you manic," Tessa laughed.

"I think he's right, Ma. Now that I think of it, it's definitely *Patti Cheeks*."

"Rocco, you and your father are both lost in Bizarro land. Ma's right again," argued Gina, as if her say on any subject made it final and indisputable.

Rocco continued, "Whatever… Anyways, what a coincidence. I've been thinking about cheeks and stuff. You know; like cheeks and asses? That *Patti Cheeks* song fits right in. Because come to think of it, that kids' song is really about cheeks and asses."

"Asses? You mean like donkeys, son?"

Gina butted in, "Shit… I knew it! Here we go again. Check this boy out. An ass thinking about asses? That doesn't seem so weird. Does it, Ma?"

"Oh boy," Tessa laughed again. "I can hardly wait to hear the ending – so it will be over quick. Because he's talking about asses and then says something *fits right in*."

"Relax ladies. This shit is deep. Okay, Pop. Say the first thing that comes to your mind when I ask this question. What's the first thing you notice on chick?"

Tessa said, "Yeah, Jackie. Please tell us. What's the first thing you notice on a *chick*?"

"Who me? I suppose I notice features on her face. Why?"

"Don't teach your kids to be bullshit artists like most of their other relatives. Be serious, Jackie. Because this topic could get real interesting, real quick."

"Okay. What I mean to say is I might notice the lips on her face . . . if they're in my lap. Know what I mean? Like if it's the mouth of some gorgeous—"

"Don't be a filthy pig around the kids, okay? Your son's already repulsive enough on his own. Don't encourage him. And Gina doesn't need to hear all this trashy talk."

"Hey! You asked. So that's my answer. Want me to lie?"

"Ma, give us a little break here. It's for college. Besides, me and Gina are in our mid-30s. Remember? Anyways, I always hear women saying stuff like this."

"Stuff like what, little bro?" asked his sister. "Please share your vast knowledge."

"They're all the time checking out guys behinds. You know; always talking about so-and-so's got such a cute butt, and check out those sweet buns."

"Wait a minute… You hear *which* women talking like that?" asked his sister.

"Don't let these two distract you, son. Go ahead. Say what's on your mind."

"Okay, Pop. So anyways, it's the ass that usually gets noticed by most guys. And on the real side, by most chicks, too. So that got me to thinking about asses in general."

"Ma, where does your boy dig up this crap?" Gina laughed. "As soon as I start to think I might know him… I think his eggs are fried from too many drugs."

"Okay then. What about you, Gina? Don't act all innocent just because Pop is listening, or because you're trying to impress Ma. What do you notice? Be honest."

"Alright, I'll be totally honest. I notice you're an asshole. Okay, Rocco?"

"Just talk straight for once, Gina. What is it about a guy's body you notice first?"

"I notice his penis, Rocco. I'm shopping around for a miniature one, but on a full-grown man. I think I'm regressing because I missed out on my childhood. Why don't you ask our sociology professor what that means and let me know, okay?"

"Just admit it, sister-girl. Partially, you're checking for firm butt cheeks. True?"

"How about you kiss my partially black butt cheeks?"

"Forget it. I should know better than to think you'd cooperate with a scientific experiment. How about you, Ma? Are you willing to help with my homework?"

"That all depends. What do I have to do?"

"Be honest and say what turns you on about a guy, okay? It's for an assignment. So humor me for once."

"Just get to the point, Rocco. I hate when you do this!" his mother scolded him.

"Yeah, Rocco," Gina chimed in. "Quit acting like an asshole again. No wait. Sorry," she smiled, "Maybe you're not just *acting* like an asshole…"

"See? That's one of my points. If someone does something wrong, right away it's got something to do with an ass. Just as soon as people say or do anything out of line, all the sudden they're accused of being an ass-*something*. Someone's being an ass or looks like an ass or is getting ready to get his ass handed to him. It's always the ass."

"Yeah, son, I see that now. It's like if someone says a certain thing smells or tastes like ass, a person automatically knows that something is pretty shitty."

"Oh my head! Stop it, both of you!" Tessa groaned.

The smell of gas wafted through the living room. Little Sinbad blinked a few times with a sheepish look on his face like he was embarrassed. Then he turned around and frowned at his butt as if his own body parts had somehow betrayed him.

"Jackie, can you please let this poor dog out before he shits the bed?"

"Okay, Tessa, in a minute. He's not pawing my leg yet."

"I'll do it. I don't want to hear this, anyway," offered Gina.

"Wait. I want you all to think about this part. Let's break this down into everyday stuff. Just listen. People have no problem with baby shit, right? They even touch it with their fingers like it's mud. Why? Is it just because the ass is smaller? I mean, shit is shit. Right? But let that same person walk into a bathroom after an adult forgets to flush and they come running out like there's a toilet bowl full of water moccasins in there."

I said, "In all fairness to Rocco, he really is making some valid points here."

"Don't, Jackie. I mean it!" Tessa gave me a concerned look that made it even funnier. "I can't believe what we're actually discussing now as a family."

"Alright then, Ma, let's go at this another way. It's common to see people blowing their noses or even snorting up thick loogies and spitting out juicy hockers. I mean it's *schifoso*. I'll admit that. But it's normal enough to see. Am I right?"

Tessa and Gina stared incredulously at Rocco, both of them slack-jawed.

"And besides that, it's not really that weird to take a leak in front of someone. It might be against some dumbass law, but it's common enough. We've all done it and have seen our friends do it. You've pissed in public before, right Ma?"

On that note we all sat like stone, no sounds or movements from any of us.

"Okay. I can see you agree. But did you ever notice how none of the ass functions are socially accepted? Think about it. As much as we all admire asses for their beauty – because there's nothing finer than a set of tanned buns of steel – you almost never see an adult take a dump in front of anyone unless it's in a hospital situation."

"What the hell kind of drugs are you on, boy?" asked Gina. "Are you tripping out, dude, or what?"

I cleaned wire rimmed trifocals on the bottom of my T-shirt. And tried not to laugh. We glanced at the screen door when a vehicle zoomed past at what seemed like about 90 MPH. As I put them back on my daughter asked, "Hey, Daddy. Not to change the subject, but what's up with the shades? Why are you wearing them in the house lately? Are you like your bad-ass son, or are you dibble-dabbling a little herbage?"

"Good one, honey. And I'm sure Ma doesn't mind you changing this subject. But the thing is I broke the nose pad off my clear ones wiping them off with a bath towel."

Tessa resumed as if there had been no interruptions: "Rocco?" His mother looked worried, "Why are you putting us through all this?"

Rocco held his palm up in the air as if directing traffic. "Hold up. We'll get to that."

Gina looked at her, sighed and said, "Oh well, nobody can say I didn't try."

"Yes you did, honey. But your brother is on a mission. He can't be stopped."

"It's just facts, Ma," he continued. "Most people think it's funny if someone belches out loud. Big joke, right? But if someone accidentally squeaks out one tiny little fart in public, right away everybody freaks out."

"Actually, he's making some valid points." I tried not to smile while my wife and daughter sat in horror. "In some cultures it's flattering to burp at the dinner table. We even had a rag-head friend named Shit-pants Joey. Remember him, Tessa? Bad timing made *Shit-pants* his official nickname all through school."

"Hold up one minute, Rocco. In which culture is it polite to fart at the table? I don't think they even do that in Afghanistan," Gina said, as she tapped her fingernails.

"Go on, son, I'm following this part so far," I encouraged.

"Jackie, please don't egg him on when he gets like this. Now he won't stop."

"I'm almost done, Ma. But Pop is right. In fact, in some places it's even considered rude if you don't burp at the table. It's supposed to be proper etiquette or some bullshit. I'm not too sure about the farting part, because this is just an intro class."

"Why the hell are we even listening to all this? What's your problem, *dufus*?" Gina asked. "And which backwards-ass countries are you referring to?"

"There it is," Rocco nodded. "See? *Backwards-ass*; *bullshit*; *ass*; *Shit-pants Joey*; *crap*; all the other words. Uh huh . . . okay... You're all proving my point."

"Really, Rocco? Then just what the hell *is* your point?"

"My point, Ma, is this: Why is it taboo to see asses uncovered, or to use them in a natural ways, or to talk about normal functions?"

His sister nodded her head: "Yep. You've finally lost it. You know that? You've gone completely over the edge, little bro. You're totally gonzo, man."

Tessa added, "Who would even think of something like this? You just wasted 10 minutes of our lives. Go let out the dog or we'll be looking at *his* natural ass functions."

"Is there more, son?" I asked, with a slight grin.

"Well, actually, my point has noting to do with asses."

"Why am I not shocked?" Tessa sat shaking her head.

"The point is cultural, Ma. Sociologically speaking, this shows how society determines what we can and can't do, even down to natural behaviors. These politicians have their noses shoved up our asses. And that's something I don't go for."

Gina shook her curls in disbelief: "Man . . . he's actually upset because he can't take a dump in the middle of sociology class. I mean, really Rocco?"

"Relax, Gina. It's just an observation. Maybe if you'd pay more attention to your surroundings, instead of taking things for granted like other *sheeple* do, you might learn something" Rocco said to his sister. "You might be more aware . . . like me."

"Not to change the subject, but I do have another question," Gina said, as she bolted upright. "This might sound stupid, but it's not nearly as far out as Rocco's stories."

"Go for it," I encouraged as I glanced at Tessa. "I can barely wait to hear this."

"No, Daddy. This one is for Ma."

"What? For *me*? Really? Wow, I'm flattered anyone even bothers to remember I'm here, even though I'm twice as clever as your father and more pleasant," she grinned.

"Okay, then here you go, Ma: a blast from your past. I saw that Maureen Kelly today down Five Points while I was at the drugstore. You knew her in high school, right? Isn't she like crazy, or some psycho bitch or something?"

"Why in there hell did you go down Five Points alone?" Rocco asked. "You could go to any drugstore in Cleveland. So why there, Gina? Stay away from those people!"

"Excuse me, but I'm not talking to you. And what makes you assume I was alone? I never said that. Besides, all those Irish pricks are long gone."

"It's not the Irishmen we're too worried about anymore, honey," I said. "Even other blacks don't go down there. Listen to me on this one. Don't ever go down there alone again, okay?"

"I wasn't alone, Daddy. I was with Danni."

"What!" Rocco yelled, in a rare show of emotion. "Are you fucking serious? Listen to me: Don't go down there any more. And don't *ever* bring my girl down there, either. Please pay attention. You're not like me and Pop. You get jammed up in some trick bag how are you gonna dig your way out? And how are we supposed to get you out of a shit storm down there? I barely go there anymore!"

"Okay. Easy. I won't, alright? We were just down there for a few minutes and now we're not. It's cool. We survived, right? Now can we please move on?"

"Pay attention to your brother, Gina," Tessa cautioned.

"They're right, honey," I said. "That's the most dangerous part of Collinwood, especially for us. And trust me, it's not just about nationality or color. Old grudges die hard. Besides, now it's all gangs and hard drugs. Promise me you'll never do that again."

"Okay, Daddy, I promise. Now can I run this other thing by you, Ma? Something happened that seemed innocent enough, yet weird to the point where I'm still thinking about it. It has something to do with an old classmate of yours."

"Hey! I wasn't finished with my story!" Rocco protested.

"You're never finished, Rocco. This is more important, so keep quiet. The whole thing just stuck a nerve with me. I think all of you will want to hear about this, even Rocco. The whole thing just stuck a raw nerve with me."

"I trust you," Tessa said. "If you say you won't go down Five Points again without your father or brother, then that's good enough for me. Go ahead, Gina. I'm sorry for cutting you off. What's the other thing you were going to tell me?"

"Well, it was really weird. I had to go down there to pick up a prescription, because the drugstore I usually go to was out of what I needed. They referred me to the store on the corner of St. Clair and E.152nd Street. Anyway, while we're at the pharmacist's counter I notice some redheaded women standing there staring at Danni and me like we have horns growing out of our heads."

"And that woman was Maureen Kelly?"

"Yeah, Ma. She used to be beautiful. Rocco showed me pictures of her in a bikini when we were at Whitey's house. You know she's Whitey's mother, right? And what's weird is the same thing that happened with you and Daddy, happened to Maureen and Ansel, them having a kid but not being together for all those years. Then they got back together just like you guys did. The main difference is Whitey always knew Ansel was his father."

"Go ahead, honey. What else happened in the store?"

"Well, then right out of the blue, Maureen shakes her head and says, 'What a picture this is! The two of you together? Damn! This is one for the history books!' Then she just walked away, laughing to herself. That woman is some kind of lunatic."

"What did she mean by: *The two of you together*? How does she even know who Danni is?" Rocco asked, with a worried expression as he pulled his curly black hair away from a rugged face. Usually unflappable, Rocco was breaking his own record for displayed emotion in one day.

"I know, right? That's what we'd like to know," Gina nodded a head full of curls. "I wasn't even sure she'd recognize me. But there she was, staring right at us. Danni was stunned. It was really creepy. So I just thought I should mention it."

I asked in as calm of a way as I could muster, "What else happened, honey? Don't leave out anything, alright? Did she look high or angry? Was she laughing or looking through her purse? Think about the small stuff."

"No, Daddy. Other than making that odd remark about Danni and me, it was all pretty much cut and dry. The whole interaction lasted maybe a few seconds at most and then she left."

"Okay, honey. Thank you. That's all of it, right?" I prompted my daughter again.

"There is one thing. As she was walking away, she mumbled something weird. I didn't mention it because I can't be 100% sure. But Danni and I thought she said, 'A family that slays together, stays together.' Weird… I have to be honest about something else. It's her looks. Because I noticed that, too. For being an older women who's about 60 pounds overweight, she looked almost perfect."

"Fucking cunt!" Tessa yelled. "I swear to Buddha! I'll pay that psycho bitch a visit right now!" Veins bulged from thin, pale skin on her forehead as she marched through the house headed straight for her purse. "Your big bad Royal Flush brothers should have taken care of that entire scum gene pool years ago, Jackie."

"I'll go with you, when it's time. But this isn't the time."

"Let me at least phone that crazy bitch, Jackie. We need to know what she meant by that *slaying* comment, and to make sure she stays away from our kids – or else."

"Don't make a bigger deal out of it than it is. She's just nuts," I assured my wife.

"Bullshit! She meant something or she wouldn't have said it. I find that comment really disturbing. I don't care if her ol' man is Ansel or not. That fucking Irish bitch is crossing a line here," Tessa said, as she fumbled with the keys.

"Before you start in with this, Tessa, let me say one thing," I interrupted. "Nationality and color have nothing to do with it. You play with snakes, you get bit."

Rocco looked unusually concerned, for a man who normally didn't show anything. I saw in his cold eyes that he was scheming. His eyes narrowed: "Speaking of biting, Pop, have you ever watched a hot chick eat a banana? You gotta admit. One of the sexiest things is a woman going down on a banana, even if she's not trying to be a prick teasing bitch for once. But you can always tell she's experienced by how she holds her—"

As I said, "Especially if it has peanut butter on it and she's trying to lick it off without breaking it." Tessa glared at me.

Rocco said, "Hey, Ma. Why is it these fat bitches with asses like a doublewide have the hairdo with not one strand out of place, and makeup that looks like it's applied with an airbrush? Why don't these fat pigs try spending a little time and money on a gym pass and a daily workout routine like pushing themselves away from the dinner table? You know, Ma, like *cumare*, Carly does. She's hot for an older broad, right Pop?"

Tessa stared, shocked that he would make a suggestive comment about his own auntie, as she unconsciously set her keys on our coffee table.

Click "You make a good point, son. Big girls are usually the ones who look like supermodels, but only from the neck up. But then, every once in awhile, there's the exception. Let's take Gina's mother for example. Butterscotch always had a beautiful face, with perfect hair and makeup. But even now as an older woman, Butter never needed to lose an ounce. In fact, right now at her age she's—"

"How much do your front teeth weigh? Because you're about to lose them," Tessa threatened, with a tiny balled-up fist as she finally set the keys on a thick oak coffee table and retook her spot on the large blue sofa next to Gina. "And you, you little bastard!" Tessa pointed at Rocco. "You'd better watch that nasty mouth. Since when do you refer to your auntie, my *cumare*, Carly, as old, fat or hot-looking? Besides, she's my age, you little bastard! You'd better watch that cocky mouth of yours, boy!"

I picked up her keys: "Now I'm hungry."

"Okay, who's up for a movie night and munchies?" Tessa said to no one in particular on that average weekend night with our new combined family intact. "But just not a dorky comedy, okay? I'm not in the mood for anymore stupid jokes tonight, especially after Rocco's disgusting conversation."

"I'm up for whatever!" Gina jumped to her feet.

"You know I'm game," Rocco said, in his gravely voice as he slowly stretched.

Little Sinbad bee-lined inside after sprinkling on his favorite tree in our backyard, let out one bark and began zigzagging through the house on his invisible figure eight track ingrained on a floor only he understood. Like a little locomotive, he serpentined throughout the house from dining room to front-room, back and forth, with the sound and power of his claws gripping the nap of the carpet.

"Looks like we might have a houseful of game ones, bro."

"Yeah, maybe. We'll see. Looks can be deceiving. I know for a fact you and Sinbad are game. But I wouldn't bet my life on these slackers just yet. If I had to guess though, I might agree with you. I'm thinking we have some keepers here. Meantime, let's go before it gets too late. Ma and I have an appetite."

Tessa set her book on the coffee table: "You all seem to like to talk a good game. But talk is cheap. Your father mentioned appetite. Let's all go out to get a half gallon of Spumoni, a 16-ounce bag of Johnny's potato chips, a couple two liters of Dad's root beer and rent an ass-kicking movie for tonight. Doesn't that sound better than all this philosophy? Who wants to go? Who's game here?"

"We can meet you kids at the video store. Get an action flick. Grab us an interesting one for tomorrow night, too," I said.

Tessa added, "As for our desert: just nothing with bananas. Okay? Not even banana cream pie or a banana split. I don't even want banana ice-cream at this point. The whole idea of eating bananas is off the list for right now – thanks to Rocco."

We watched the kids pile into Gina's Forester while Tessa and I basked in the silence of our home. Wordlessly, we walked out the front door. As we stood on our front steps I asked, "Remember that saying about the quiet before the storm? Look up, baby-girl. The sky looks really bizarre. Can you feel it? The air has been real heavy. And just smell it. It feels like fish. It reminds me of something from a long time ago, but I can't call it just yet. It's almost like—"

"We're gonna be late if we don't make a move. I don't want the kids to wait. Maybe something's wrong with them… Maybe that's what we feel."

I whistled the same signal I had used throughout Gina's childhood when I would call her back to the house for supper or to settle in for the night. She stopped the car and poked a head full of curls out her driver's window. "What's up, Daddy-O?"

"Let's not let them go alone then. Something's not right. I can feel it like a motherfucker," I told my wife.

CH V: Tessa's Journal

Tessa didn't share much with many. She trusted no one other than our little family. So instead of purging with a professional or gabbing to pseudo-friends, Tessa quietly journaled. At rare moments, Tessa exposed some of that pent-up darkness to our kids. Unbeknownst to her, I was painfully rehashing my own guilt while trying to find my way back, any way possible, to navigate to the winning side of a bad hand dealt to me. So as I schemed in pain, the love of my life wrote furiously to claw her way back to a semblance of sanity. Feverishly, Tessa processed some scrambled thoughts and her darkest emotions. That first night she listened to a song titled *Drunk and Lonely*, on a CD by a Collinwood girl.

Tessa's 1st journal entry – August 13, 2013:
 "Starting tonight, I'll journal every night to keep from entirely losing my mind. It's that trick Uncle Pazzo taught Jackie and me years ago, journal. A trick Dad's brother learned while serving time. It's the same pastime and passion that turned into a novel for my Jackie. He said it's a purging mechanism. I hope you will help me re-cross that point of no return. I'll write to you about how I woke on the ground when our car turned into smoldering shrapnel, that same horrible car that had my Jackie trapped before I lost consciousness. I knew something was terribly wrong. I could have stopped him, but it was like my legs were stuck in a tar pit. That last look still haunts me. Somehow he knew! Then a glow of unbelievable force when that explosion tore out my soul by its roots. Then another bizarre thing happened, journal, something I've never told anyone. When I woke-up, shattered and trying to deal with overwhelming emotions, it was in a different spot from when I blacked out. I know for sure I'm right about this! I was near our front steps – to check on things in the house – because Jackie insisted. But when I regained consciousness I was inside the house, and the door had been closed behind me. What the fuck? I woke up to Little Sinbad whining and licking my face. Am I crazy, journal?

    There's no way the blast could have knocked me *inside* of a locked house, keys still in my hand, and then closed the door while I was completely out of it. But I know for sure that's what happened. Whatever… I'll never forgive myself. No matter how many times I rethink that one tiny slice of time, everything stays the same. I try to change one word that might somehow make a difference, just one gesture that could maybe make things different. But my Jackie is still gone because I did nothing.

I was mad because Jackie demanded that I go back inside to *check on things*, to make sure everything was turned off and locked. But I didn't. Did I? No, I'm sure I didn't. I stood there arguing with him. I'm such a fucking bitch! So then how did I get inside the house? Fuck-it… Maybe I really am crazy. But none of that matters anymore. Nothing makes sense anymore. At first I wanted to kill myself. But now I know I don't deserve to get off that easy. Now I know I have to live so I can suffer even more."

Tessa's 2nd journal entry – August 14, 2013:
"Dear diary: the year my Jackie called the *Year of the Snake*, we lost him. Other than two grown kids and a grizzled Yankee Terrier watching our front door as if it were an empty food bowl, I have nothing. I lay awake till my tear ducts are inflamed from rubbing dried-out eyes. I'm desperate to hang on to that special something. To keep him alive I'll reread his manuscript, over and over, with our dog nuzzled against me. I so love this dog, even though he's labeled by the media as a killer – just because of the way he looks. But he's the best one of us. The harder and longer I cry, the closer Little Sinbad watches me with a tragic sadness in those deep brown eyes that only a game-bred dog can have. Because they, like us, are used to fighting for life in a ring of cheering strangers who smell very much like friends. Besides our kids he's my best friend. These tragic little dogs are forced to become too familiar with human concepts like abandonment, betrayal and premeditated cruelty. I'm too exhausted to do this. This isn't helping at all. Fuck this, journal! You wear me out – and for nothing. I'm done with this nonsense!"

Tessa's 3rd Journal entry – August 16, 2013:
"This journaling doesn't do shit. I had worse day today. So I sat hugging my dog's neck. I try to cry and scream. But what if I do? Everything is pure bullshit! Just a few handfuls of years ago I was a tiny girl playing school in my pink bedroom with dolls. Then I was that tough little teenager not taking crap from anyone during the Collinwood riots. I thought I was special; that I could handle well for a chick. I was Doc's daughter! But in another second I found myself knocked-up and disowned by a shameful father, all because he claimed I violated some bullshit Catholic rules, like he

ever gave one dry fuck about laws. Meanwhile, that hypocrite was out screwing his barmaid while my poor mother stayed at home worrying. And to make things even worse, I got knocked up the first time I ever had sex – and I barely remember it. Fuck him! All that stress Doc put our family through is what really killed my mother. Cancer takes over when a person is dealing with constant stress. It's a natural culling. And now I'm the one with the stress. I went from being a young woman without a family to playing the role of single mother – till that day Jackie miraculously resurfaced in our lives like some long-dead messiah.

Last month I was happily married to my first love, father of our boy and of a sweet girl I feel as close to as if she were my own blood. And now this… What the fuck? Yeah, this… Now I'm an old woman *and* a widow. All my son thinks about is finding the people who did this unspeakable act to his father. He wants to kill them. What next? Insanity? How am I expected to go on like this? Death? Why should I even give a shit? Because I can't do this alone. I just can't. I'm not all that tough, not like I used to think I was back in high school. The fact is I'm weak and scared. I cry out loud to this scarred-up old warrior whom I trust more than any person other than the little family Jackie and I made for ourselves.

My eyes are vibrating. Fatigue is crushing me into a pile of breathing dirty clothes that stink of disgust and failure. So I'll collapse on our bed, totally lost and so alone. Unfortunately, I think I'm on the mend physically. I'll close for now."

Tessa's 4th journal entry – August 17, 2013:
"Okay, journal. Doctor Joey told me, 'You're stronger than you think, Tessa,' when he released me from ICU. He said, 'You're lucky to be alive. Being close to a blast like that and surviving? It's God's miracle, plain and simple. You told us Jackie made you go back into the house *to check on things*. Everything happens for a reason. But you are still insisting you didn't go in. You say something made you stop, to turn around and watch in horror till you passed out. Somehow Jackie must have known something had gone terribly wrong, although there was no way he actually could know for certain. But he always had that strange 6th sense. You know? Anyway, you must have gone back into the house, because that's where you regained consciousness. You merely don't remember; that's all. But you will. Brain concussions do strange things to memory. With shock, temporary memory loss is

a defense mechanism. Temporary amnesia is a mental reaction to a physical condition – a way to deal with trauma. Yours was not *anaphylaxis*. But I believe what you experienced was sensory overload. Your body just shut down. God works in mysterious ways, Tessa.'

Joey's always been a good friend. But I wasn't in the mood for a sermon. I told him, 'I don't mean to be disrespectful after all you've done for me, Joey. But the simple fact is this: there's no way a loving God has my alcoholic father lose everything to bookies and loan sharks and then lets my mother get eaten up with cancer to suffocate on her own lung tissue, just so my kids and I can suffer even more. You're trying to convince me now that all the sudden I'm blessed because I was saved from the blast, so I could watch *my* husband get incinerated by a car bomb in *our* front yard? I'm blessed and then live with these haunting memories? Really, Joey?'

Joey assured me, 'God's looking out for you, Tessa. In more ways than you can know. He has plans for you. '

Even though Joey was a tired old man, I could still recognize the little boy in his eyes. Joey's swarthy middle-eastern complexion and black eyes seemed even darker with a full head of pure white hair. But even with all his college degrees and white hair he was still little Shit-pants Joey, the same little boy I'd known for almost 60 years.

'Okay, Joey, whatever,' I told him, just so he'd stop. 'I'm way too depressed to argue. Just write me a script for some good tranquilizers. I need some good downers. Because if you don't give me some high-powered stuff I just might do something crazy. Then it will be on your conscience and will be God's fault. See how this works? It's a double-edged sword. So if you do, I'll really feel blessed that I ran into you. Deal, Joey?'

What Dr. Shit-pants Joey didn't know was that I didn't feel blessed or lucky, not even one little bit. I wanted to die – but not with his drugs. The thought of going on without my best friend was too much. The softness of being in shock had been so comforting. But living with this crushing guilt, for not stopping Jackie that awful day, is my cross to bear. Besides, I can't put our kids through another family death. So I'll quietly lose more time while curled-up in a fog with my yummy Xanax and vodka. That's a good second choice to being in shock or dead. Maybe better, because at least I'll be able to feel the drugs. But I'm not sure if I even want to feel anything good anymore."

Tessa's 5th journal entry – August 18, 2013:

"In drug-dreams of lorazepam and herb I play one scene over and over. I run in slow-motion to him, desperately trying to reach him in time – to stop him and somehow prevent that explosion from destroying our lives. It's the hardest battle I've ever fought in my entire life. I wake covered in a sweat, determined that if I could change my tone of voice, or maybe even a certain eye movement, then we could wake up together. But the words to stop him still won't form in my mouth. And no matter how many times I replay that scene nothing will ever be different. It's always too late. I wake up and he's still gone. I know that no mater what, I'll be alone except for what I carry of Jackie inside me.

So emotionally, journal, I've hit rock bottom. I'm a train wreck. My nerves feel like what golf balls look like inside, when as kids we sliced off their skins to watch then unravel. Inside, I'm a tangle of rubber bands having no purpose or direction, just waiting to move anywhere at the fastest rate of speed possible. And now my Rocco is obsessed with revenge. I tell him I can't lose him. I just can't handle anything, anymore. So I quit my office job before I lost my mind. But now all this alone time is getting to me. Too much thinking; too much crying; too much of almost everything, yet not nearly enough of what I need. So I have to find a constructive diversion for much needed focus. I'll recall stories and songs Jackie and I shared in the dark. Our music CDs whispered magic to us. They still lull me into a false sense of security. In the dark I can feel him. I believe that somehow he's still here during these fragile hours between midnight and dusk. But respite is temporary. I cry myself to sleep during long mornings, holding a plastic jewel case Jackie used to keep his novel safe. It's heartbreaking to see his life's work fit onto one tiny computer disc. But it means everything to me."

Tessa's 6th journal entry – August 19, 2013:

"Jackie looked two decades younger than his 63 years. His hair, still mostly black, a flat stomach and firm muscles, added to his vibrant persona of pure electric magnetism. Not only that he was fit, his hazel eyes simmered with a hypnotic energy. During moments of anger, rare in older age compared to how he had been as a youthful coil of spring steel and testosterone, those same green eyes became wild with animal intensity that no longer fit the good man he had become. Yet even as an old man ready to retire, he had an aura of power that trailed him like a shadow. Maybe that shadow was because Jackie had an internal light to make a path for us. He didn't miss much, journal, even back in the days when he was in blackouts and on autopilot with some magic spell surrounding and protecting him.

     Jackie left us with his own brand of faith in spite of the pain – or maybe because of it. Plus he left me his story, a reason to continue to remember to breathe. I could almost hear the words his father taught him, the same wisdom Jackie repeated to us whenever we needed moral support from that man who wasn't very big on the outside but was a giant within. He assured us, *Fight and the pain will go away.* Jackie shared those words with our son when Rocco had been struggling with opiate detoxification. Jackie reinforced that same wisdom for his Gina when her boyfriend of almost 20 years betrayed her with another woman. And now my husband shares his pragmatic logic about gameness and loyalty with me, even after...

     I'm thinking more clearly now, journal, thanks to you. So I've decided to fight back, to be the things Jackie cherished more than anything other than our family. I'll try to be game enough to live and remain loyal to our kids' needs as well as to Jackie's memory. I'll fight to regain the toughness and integrity I once had as a carefree teen. I repeated those words today from Jackie's dad: *Fight and the pain will go away,* when I gamed-up and threw my pills in our toilet and poured my vodka down our kitchen sink. Now I have his obsession. When I retire for the evening I call Little Sinbad off his oval rug by the front door – still vigilant to catch a scent of his master. I have him accompany me into the bedroom for my fixation with rereading Jackie's thoughts on our computer screen. Then I curl up with his pillow on a beat-up leather sofa, a trophy from his earlier years, to rehash memories and to cry for him – anything to keep my Jackie alive a moment longer. I want more, even in the coldness of his absence, to help me get through the worst time of my life."

Tessa's 7th journal entry – August 20, 2013:
"Dreams hadn't always been restful for Jackie and didn't only occur while asleep. But that's one of those things you learn about a person only after you live together. He'd tell me, 'Life is a dream of a dream, Tessa, that slip of ecstasy between awake and asleep – a high that's pure magic.' He stayed up late and wrote almost nonstop to meet a self-imposed timeline, like he knew time was

limited. 'If I'm still awake at sunrise it's because I'm waiting for an idea to stay alive long enough so I can capture its meaning before it slips away.'

Fuck you, journal! I hate this. All you do is stir up shit I don't need to be thinking about right now. I'm going to pour lighter fluid on you and laugh as you burn up in my driveway. Good night, and good riddance you worthless piece of shit!"

Tessa's 8th journal entry – August 22, 2013:
"Okay. I might as well get to it. Alright. Here it is, journal: That last day, Jackie was so happy when he announced that his novel was complete. His eyes sparkled as we stood on our front porch to take in the stillness of dusk. I remember thinking he had the same composed expression of that boy I'd met over a half century ago in kindergarten; before he had developed a hard mask to keep people at a safe distance. Dusk was settling in. The sky was amazing. It felt like we were floating inside a magical moment when you're almost awake yet not quite asleep. But we were high. We shouldn't have smoked. We weren't used to it. I think that bud dulled our senses.

But Jackie said, 'I'm more awake right now, at this moment, than I've been in years'. Born in an idealistic time yet raised in a neighborhood full of violence and other drugs, Jackie was still the same torn child in old age he had been as a boy, a teen and a man. That last day, bathed in that glorious dusk, he squeezed my hand and said, 'I wish this moment could last forever, baby-girl. But you know me. I always want more. It's really too strange to think about, but sooner or later this little slice of heaven will have to be enough'. He swiped at a corner of a greenish eye as if to rid himself of a speck of cosmic dust.

Then as if he had heard a silent whistle, Jackie cocked his head of short-cropped gray hair to watch a lone dark cloud sprayed fiery orange, just as a woman in wrap-around sunglasses sped past in a Hummer as red as her windblown hair. He mumbled, 'Chilly, right? He stopped. But I knew what he meant.

When he shook his head with a look of disgust a rush of dread surged through me. Eardrums roared; heart pounded. All I could hear was non-stop barking and growling from our Yankee Terrier who till that day had been worthless as a watchdog. 'Sinbad, goddamnit, shut-up! What's going on here, Jackie? Talk to me, bro.' Frozen in suffocating panic, throat constricted with terror, a wave of nausea overcame me. I felt my eyes bulge as I begged, 'No, Jackie! Please, baby. Don't do it.' Legs numb, paralyzed with horror, I cried, 'No! I won't let you do this to us! You promised you'd never leave me! You said you love me! I trusted you, Jackie. *Please!*'

He stretched out a steady hand, 'You gotta be here when the kids get home. Remember? No sweat, baby-girl, I ain't goin' no place. You know that.' Then he nodded his head with that same disgusted expression and mumbled, 'Yeah, just fuck-it'.

All the colors blurred to numbness when our car transformed into a smoking hunk of scrap. My last memory was the growl of a Harley as my world grew darker. Sprawled on the ground I thought: *This can't be real. I can't do this alone.*

Tessa's 9th journal entry – August 23, 2013:

"I have our kids and this black & tan mongrel most people prefer to label a vicious fighting dog. But he's my most trusted ally, as loyal as our kids. So gradually I'm growing strong enough to realize that our kids, no longer children, and our old *fighting dog*, who hadn't had a scrap in a dog's age, were enough to help me battle to the other side of all this pain and loss. As I hugged our old dog I realize it's up to me to find the strength like Sinbad did when he had to, for me to find enough gameness to continue, to *fight and the pain will go away.* There are no other good choices.

My *cumare*, Carly, said, 'I'm not going to tell you he's in a better place, or that everything happens for a reason, or insult you by saying God doesn't give us more than we can handle. You know what though, Tessa? We figured we could do whatever, whenever, and still get another chance. We had that terminal *fuck-it* attitude'.

The longer I'm around, the more I understand how there are a whole bunch of things I don't want any more of but nothing I can do to change it. For example: I don't want to get a day older. But at the same time I'm not quite ready to disappear.

I despise when people come at me with their all-knowing religious bullshit, or when they try to get me to volunteer for campaigns with fake people even more corrupt than my father and uncle. But I'm probably not supposed to talk about religion or politics here either. I almost forgot. I guess I shouldn't be honest and open in my own diary – not about everything – because I'm not even supposed to think about these things. Yeah, fuck this! I'm done with this whole stupid journaling bullshit!"

Tessa's 10th journal entry – August 30, 2013:

"I did it. I added a chapter to Jackie's novel, one he never intended to be part of his book. But timing orchestrated that new chapter. So I ended his novel the way I thought would please him. He was going to call it *Collinwood Gray Areas*. I renamed it with a title that summed up his life throughout all its stages. It's called *I'm Jack & I Want More*. It seems fitting. That title has been a credo for his entire existence. No matter what he wanted: maturity or power, drugs or weapons; friends or loyalty; sobriety or women; knowledge or wisdom; family or safety; more was almost enough. Jackie talked a lot about the gray area, the *dialectic*. Maybe because when he was younger he went to extremes with everything. When he was a teen he went out of his way to create pain. I emailed segments of Jackie's novel to agents, hoping to find the right fit. Maybe there's a publisher willing to take a chance on an unknown's work. But I'm very tired. I need to crash. Goodnight journal. See you tomorrow."

Tessa's 11th journal entry – August 31, 2013:

"Looking back, I've learned a lot from mistakes and loss. I realize now how *our* people were wrong about so many things. Our fathers' methods were harsh, but their lessons imprinted like branding irons. The night before we did the Quaaludes washed down with Doc's homemade wine I asked, "Are there enough drugs and women to ever make you feel satisfied." He laughed and said, "Sure. But I might just want one more, later. You know?" When we got married I asked him, "Is it more passion you're addicted to, Jackie, or more wisdom?" His answer was, "Yeah." He even overdid it with tattoos. The last one he got took two hours of non-stop needles gouged into his back when he got an image of a snake eating its own tail, while he chatted with us and the tattoo artist as though he were getting a haircut.

We rode as a family so a Collinwood artist could scrimshaw that monster on their backs, as a reminder of life's struggles. Gina and I sat together discussing things women talk about when men aren't listening. Jackie went first. Then our son got that same image as his father had, a graphic representation of a scary-looking black and gray serpent. Instead of a circle, the snake was wrapped in the infinity symbol. Jackie referred to that shape as a *Lazy 8*. The inker called it a *lemniscate shape*. Gina called it a *Lorenz attractor*. I'd never heard of an ouroboros or any of those other terms till the day my husband and son got matching tattoos. I didn't understand its significance till Jackie explained its meaning. It was the last gift he gave to our middle-aged son, one that would last him the rest of his life, a thing to remind him to remain strong. It's also another sight to haunt me.

Jackie explained, 'The ouroboros is the vicious circle we hear about. It's eating itself as nourishment to sustain life while trying defend against what's killing it. This symbol signifies the end and beginning of a circle, of infinity, the eternity of the soul. The ouroboros transcends race, religion, age and culture. Like the fiery phoenix, the ouroboros represents resurrection and unity, the synthesis of death and eternity in an ever-changing now. It's the upwelling of daily life salvaged from the jaws of death. Yet that same struggle sinks us faster into the quicksand of life, killing itself for more nourishment to survive. And that struggle is about timing, Tessa, about making brave choices at correct moments. But either way, we won't last forever. Nobody does'.

He told our kids, 'This will remind us to live as if this monster on our backs is a reflection of what's sleeping inside you. It can sense your innermost thoughts. It gets stronger from the stench of fear and betrayal, excuses and regrets, and cowardly behavior like deception. The best way to defeat it is to stay strong, to grow from the pain, to get power from guilt, to use shame and fear for wisdom, to survive in spite of adversity, to thrive off challenges. If you weaken to the battle it's your own weakness that destroys you. You lose to you. That's how the killing snake can be you. Because we never do anything we don't really want to do, even when it's something we'd rather not do'.

Tessa's 12th journal entry – September 01, 2013:
"Dear diary, he was right. I choose to go down fighting, hanging onto what I still have. The last gift my husband gave us is when he saved my life – one I'm no longer sure I value. I almost missed the *Click* that day. But I did feel the depth of what Jackie felt. It was that same invisible thread of crystal that attached our minds that saved me, signaling danger even though we didn't know what or why. It was that same *Click* that took my Jackie from us. Since then I've become intimate, but with a truth so permanent – so dreadful – no words can ever express the purity of my anguish. Our kids and little Pit-bull show me reasons to *Bounce* from the dream-world where the dragon lives, but hopefully never again. I won't quit and won't allow our kids to forget. Not after all I've witnessed. Instead of curing out, I'll keep Jackie's spirit alive in us.

Then one day his soul will reabsorb mine. I need to believe that – no matter how crazy it sounds. I need to trust in our own brand of faith. I refuse to believe he's gone forever. So I won't!"

Tessa's 13th and final journal entry – September 11, 2013:
"Dear journal, my newest true friend that my Jackie talked to me and Rocco about for months, I finally get it. And because of this purging and self-examination I found out that I want more. Jackie always told us, "Fight and the pain will go away." Because like my man, my truest friend ever, I'll reinforce his tenacity with our kids to keep fighting long enough to make all the sadness worthwhile. And from that taste of gameness, an undeniable faith within reach, hopefully our kids will learn to devour rather than be destroyed. Thank you so much, journal. I needed you really badly. Jackie was right. Damn, I sure do miss him… But you've been a good friend, journal. Goodbye."

PART TWO

Please take me for granted, I thought, as I looked for a comfortable position that didn't exist. I thought back to memories struggling against the present. At times, psychotic delusions and psychedelic hallucinations spoke more genuine than traditional reality. In a mist of ambiguity we played in a Petri dish governed by rules where being free meant losing freedoms.

We enter the world terrified and make our departure the same way. In each case alone and terrified. So why should I give a shit about any of it? We buzzed and we banged to remain ambivalent about the inevitable. But what we have is the sweetness in-between those two dates on our tombstones – that hyphen – temporary and fleeting yet makes the tragic finality worthwhile. So I decided to make every choice count and to make sure they are my own. Facets like integrity meant more than traditional freedom, when living meant more than life.

Life for me had evolved from an idealistic childhood to adolescence, a product of the Woodstock Era. Those emotions in motion, hard boozing and other piggish drugging, at one time had appeared to define meaning while trying to survive a tidal wave of hormones and culture, ethnocentrism and bigotry. Zombie-like rigidity got dropped as quickly as a hot box of volcanic rocks. Unconventional truths blossomed and flourished as we grew wiser from earned loss. Pain became a survival mechanism during an existence by passions. Racing goggles of substance abuse illuminated a void created by blind faith and nurtured by disappointment. So we filled time with hedonistic options in dangerous playgrounds with cool characters and warm flesh.

Then I found myself at another crossroads filled with more uncertainty. In many ways 2013 was the most bizarre year ever. But it wasn't all bad. It was, however, extreme in too many ways for a man my age. Especially on that day of the explosion, when life seemed too real and madness just familiar enough.

I wouldn't have starting drinking *again after 30 years of being sober, would I?* Then I smiled: *No, that's right, I'm dead. Please be cocky enough to believe I got erased by letting down my guard – for finally allowing myself to be happy.*

CH VI: The Shell Game

Street wars of the 1970s: Bodies had been piling up as if Collinwood were a Nazi death camp. Those not yet murdered found new zip codes, unless they were safely off those cruel streets and tucked away in prisons. Fierce enemies were located right down Five Points, a location beginning where Collinwood High School's six floors towered into a gray skyline like a haunted castle. By then, Mick had become more of a threat to the Young Turks than the RICO Act. The Mick made several attempts to eradicate Cleveland of Uno. He did succeed with some *coombas*. And Uno missed a few attempts to behead the Irish crew.

Mick invented a persona of being a hero for the oppressed working-class citizen and it worked. A well built and articulate speaker who looked more like a movie star than a gangster, the Mick attracted attention from Cleveland newspaper reporters and television stations. A bare-chested Mick said to a Cleveland TV camera crew, "I need help from these Mafia scum like I need a fatal dose of lead poisoning."

Before he turned age 30, Mick took over remnants of his father's and uncle's Cleveland criminal empire and organized an army stronger than ever. Mick used local Irishmen and a few renegade Italians for muscle, and rich downtown Jews for financial backing. By the mid-60s, Mick Kelly had become the undisputed boss of Cleveland's numbers racket and drug trade in black ghettoes. Longshoremen and the Stevedores didn't move one crate without paying tribute to the Mick.

The Mick partnered up with an Italian in 1971 who had strong mafia ties with the Pittsburgh crew. That merger of Irish and Italians flourished till Fingers and Benny, both Royal Flush members, allegedly took out the Mick's Italian partner in a move not sanctioned by any boss. That killing caused internal friction.

That was a huge loss for the Mick, yet that hit gave him the momentum needed for some lateral moves with downtown Jews. The Mick used that friction to his advantage to ensure that the Irish legacy in C-town was far from over. That was till Mick's oldest and favorite nephew, Eamon Jr., was killed in 1975. Then Eamon Jr.'s best friend, Frankie Fazule, caught a life sentence in 1976 for killing an Italian bar patron at Mick's Shamrock Club down Five Points. The man was mistaken to be someone having had something to do with Eamon's murder.

Benny had been contracted to take out another of Mick's mobster nephews, Paddy Kelly. Benny did everything over the top. He marched Paddy out of the Shamrock Club at gunpoint, in full view of bar customers, the night Paddy was slaughtered. Benny's judgment came into question by the same people who had commissioned his services. The Cleveland Dealer reported that Paddy had been hacked to death with a sharp hatchet in his own car parked at a remote location, respect for Benny turned into suspicion, and even fear, by other *wise guys*.

So of the Mick's four surrogate children, two of the boys had been brutally murdered within one year. The third, Doyle, managed to stay alive and out of prison. The youngest of the three Kelly brothers, Doyle, moved into a power position in the Irish mob and arranged to have the Italian boss taken down by a skinhead. Benny vowed to kill Doyle in front of his family.

The fourth crazy Kelly child, Doyle's red-headed sister, Maureen, had become the live-in girlfriend of her brothers' best friend, Frankie Fazule, till Frankie caught a 1st degree murder conviction. Frankie was the maniac who shot my friend, Gus, three times in his chest at the Cheshire Club in downtown Cleveland a year after Gus shot him in a gang fight on Eggs' front lawn when we fought the Kelly Boys and Frankie Fazule.

Once the identity of Eamon Jr.'s murderer had been discovered an unspeakable act befell Toby while he lay passed out on Dago Red's floor. But getting beheaded while in an opiate dream can't be the *worst* way to die – just one of the more insane ways, and a grizzly way to be found by a best friend. That gruesome scene proved to be something too much for Dago Red to deal with. Consequently, drug abuse of those remaining No-Names sky-rocketed to addiction.

Fingers was addicted to power and recognition. That compulsion manifested as him being acting boss of Collinwood with Nino serving as *consigliere*. It was an unpopular move which forced Little Italy's Cagootz to be Fingers' right hand man and Big Louie his guard dog till such time when a more suitable arrangement could be found. But such a time didn't arrive because of internal maneuvering within the Young Turks' organization. Fingers, with the help of Cagootz and Big Louie, and a few others from Little Italy and Collinwood, Youngstown and Erie, PA, finally figured out a way to kill that lethal Irishman.

After that key murder things settled nicely, back to the pace of regular gangland war which lasted for another 13 years.

Cleveland's 1976 bombing wars, which began to escalate in 1975 and drastically tapered off in 1977, ended when the luck of the Irish finally ran out for the Mick.. Then it was over. That is till I got transported to my current nightmare in 2013, ejected from an exploding car while my wife watched in horror.

July 28, 2013 – The Stakeout, the 1st day: The sun was about to set. It had been a gorgeous day to be parked in the country. The leaves were brilliant shades of green. The sky, which moments before had been a bright blue, was being met with a dark gray the color of the Taurus stashed out of sight, yet close enough to be able to locate their mark.

A shiny new Ford Taurus, ominous dark gray, parked in a wooded dirt path. The new car squatted in unfamiliar surroundings, sharply contrasted by an array of colors catching the last of a rapidly setting sun. The car's two occupants parked off that make-shift, one-lane road, on an access drive which had once been used for commercial gas and oil trucks. Deep ruts scarred the ground from countless trucks to siphon oil from huge tanks pulled up by tireless pump jacks that squeaked so often their metal on metal groan became barely noticeable.

In the 30+ years I nestled on 10 acres of privacy, occasional loud trucks with the monotonous grind of diesel motors refilled steel bellies from lofty oil storage tanks. Even my dogs paid little attention, not since moving them and my daughter away from the turmoil of Cleveland's edginess to the serenity offered by rural Ashtabula County. My Pit-bulls didn't seem to mind the ritualistic intrusion by those invasive trucks dieseling across the road, other than irritating directional *piep-piep-piep* sounds mandated by the DOT, alerting any unsuspecting passersby of a vehicle's mission to back up to replenish an unquenchable thirst for more oil.

Other than wildlife indigenous to Northeastern Ohio generally seen at dusk and dawn, and vegetation months away from withering to bright golds and reds, something seemed odd and very much out of place. My first impression when buying my house was that the grouping of tanks down the road was a six-pack of beer designed for the Jolly Green Giant. Each tank had been painted a forest green and then sloppily stenciled with white block lettering from some long forgotten spray cans rusted over in the weeds. Over the years those green storage tanks, in a county once known for an abundance of shallow oil and natural gas wells, had faded and grown large rust spots on splotches where paint had chipped and worn from extreme Ohio seasons.

ATV's raced wide open on side roads accessing the homes of a mix of Amish, country folks and ex-city dwellers. Life seemed simple when compared with the chaos of Cleveland's manic vibe during the bomb wars of 1976, when I was only 26 years young, or with the desperation I felt as a 63-year old man trapped somewhere as a wounded prisoner, sometime in 2013.

July 28, 2013 – The Stakeout, the 1st day: Back from our uneventful mission of renting movies and buying non-banana goodies, a few moments of silence shared by us felt like a security blanket bonding us. We picked up Rocco's girlfriend, Danni.

A sting of remorse shot through me as I watched our son gaze outside. Rocco's Uncle Pazzo stood-in as a surrogate dad for a few decades till he relocated to Florida. Ironically enough, he had been a strong force in my upbringing. I regretted missing out on his childhood and adolescence but was grateful for finally being together. Once our lives merged as a family unit, Gina and me with Tessa and Rocco, life got real good real fast, as though we had always been together –like it was too good to be true.

Even though Rocco had grown up without even knowing he had a live father he reminded me of a younger me. We walked the same, sounded alike and even resembled in body type and facial features. Actually, he looked more like a middle-aged version of my father, only bigger and thicker. Once we got past the window dressing Rocco and I came to understand we had a lot more in common than cultural or genetic trappings. We both loved Harleys. Each of us, since childhood, had been a Pit-bull freak obsessed by the purity of gameness. Tessa and my daughter shared our penchants. Another thing we all had in common was a need for individuality, one which often came accompanied by heavy baggage. Throughout late adolescence and early adulthood, he and I had been accused of being lifetime drug addicts by straight people and even active junkies. They were right. We were addicted. But it was never to the drugs for either of us. It was the lifestyle – wild friends and crazy times while spun in the fast-lane.

Tessa and I discussed how back in the 1970s the movie, *2001: A Space Odyssey* seemed to have been set in an impossible timeframe. Yet we already were a dozen years beyond that benchmark film during a time when so many events reshaped our culture and revamped forever how our generation looked at things. We made room to watch the movie, where glasses of ice water and small plates for biscotti or *pizzelles* usually set. That space was on a narrow yet thick wooden table between the two dark blue recliners for Rocco and me. There was a matching natural wooden coffee table for those seated on the couch, also made of solid oak. Little Sinbad sat at Tessa's feet. He leaned against the couch with a sad expression as he snuck glances at his beloved doggie bed.

Like me, Rocco usually was bare-chested during mild climates, or we wore wife-beaters showing heavily tattooed arms and shoulders. That day mine was the white kind like my dad used to wear around the house. My son's T-shirt was black. Although I was in good shape for a man old enough to retire and he in great condition for being middle-aged, I appreciated a little elastic in the waistband once in awhile. On that day I wore plaid workout pants that looked like pajama bottoms, secured loosely at the waist with a tie string. Rocco had on a ragged pair of faded blue jeans with holes in the knees. He had been involved in various forms of martial arts since childhood – like I had.

I said, "I've never been older yet never appreciated so much," as I cleared my throat of emotion. Then I watched my black & tan Yankee Terrier study me, trying to pick up on my emotions. He thumped his tail and then eased down.

"Damn . . . listen to you, Jackie. You're getting a little soft and mushy in your old age, aren't you bro?" posed my wife, Tessa, in her cute yet sarcastic way.

"Appreciated what, Mr. Jack?" asked Rocco's girlfriend, Danni, in a soft, shy voice. She sat on the edge of blue recliner, dressed in all black. She slouched next to me, looking like a little girl, trying her best to look comfortable as the newest member of our family of misfits.

"Yeah . . . exactly that, Danni. I appreciate everything I still have and all the things taken or thrown away. So many priceless things taken for granted for so long."

"Excuse, me. I'll be right back." Danni slid her slight frame off the large recliner and quickly walked out of the room. She was a 35-year old woman built like a girl half her age. Short black hair and large clear eyes served to reinforce that illusion.

"Yeah, beat it," Rocco yawned, as he reclaimed his seat. "This is my chair, remember babe? Besides, this section is for men only. When you get back you should go over there on the couch to sit with the other girls and wait real quiet."

"Shut that mouth, Rocco!" warned his mother. "Don't be so crude. Why can't you ever be sweet like your sister?" Tessa wore black shorts and one of her usual black T-shirts that read, "Fighting for Life" in gold lettering. Those colors and long, natural blonde hair made a wonderful contrast.

"Rocco's a pig because he's a homophobe, Ma." Gina looked more like a painting than a real person, with dark auburn hair, honey colored skin and piercing gray eyes. Then she flashed a grin: "Just admit to what you are, little bro. He's insecure, Ma, so he has to put on this big sex-god act and pretend he's all bad-ass," she smiled, as she pulled thick, curly hair away from perfect features. "But the truth shall set you free, buddy."

Rocco asked, "Are you fishing? Maybe you're trying to tell us about your own secret desires, sister-girl. Are you and Danni forming a dyke gang? They're dressed exactly the same. Well almost. Danni's duds are a few sizes smaller." Gina's grin turned into a scrunched-up face when she stuck out her pierced tongue.

Moments later, Danni half-ran into the front-room, breathless with childish anticipation: "Okay, what did I miss? Hey, you big oaf, move it! I was sitting next to your dad having a very nice conversation. Go lay on the floor with the dog!"

"Come on over here and sit with the girls," Gina smiled.

"Too bad, so sad, baby. Snooze you lose." Rocco said to his girlfriend, while yawning and ignoring his sister. "Hey, Pop, let's change the subject and hear some of your rehab magic. It'll almost be like going to an AA meeting only better, because it'll actually be interesting and with less cliché."

"*Meeting*? You go to meetings, Rocco? Why? You're a pothead now, remember?" reminded his mother.

"*Now*," Gina laughed. "He's been a burner for years."

"Rocco only smokes in moderation," Danni assured them, as she nodded her mussed up head of short hair. She looked like she just woke from a nap.

"Ha!" Tessa scoffed. "What's moderation? Not smoking while you're on your bike? Or maybe not in *my* house while I'm here?" Tessa made a fist at our son. "Moderate this. Now move your ass off that chair. Kick him, Danni."

The phone rang. Tessa said, "You're closest, Jackie."

"Everybody I want to talk to is right here, right now. Let the answering machine catch it. It's probably spam, anyway."

"Answer it, Rocco. It's probably for you, anyway," Tessa said, as she threw a crumpled piece of paper from a legal pad at her son. The wad bounced off him and rolled across the blue carpet. Sinbad sluggishly lifted a paw to stretch a foreleg like a cat to set his black paw with its tan toes on the yellow paper.

"Pop's right. Let the machine catch it. We'll screen calls later. I'm ready to hear a pep talk about addiction and recovery, Ma. This is therapeutic for me."

"No, this is just more laziness because you don't want to move. You'll do or say anything not to budge off that chair."

"Maybe it's genetic. Being a thief could be back in my bloodline," Danni said, as she crawled to the dog, pretending she was stealing his paper ball. "Maybe I can't help myself because I'm addicted to stealing from family – like I'm powerless. Maybe it's in my pedigree, that I've been programmed to be this way."

Danni was on all fours and played a game with Little Sinbad. "What do you think, Sinbad? Am I a helpless creature? Because I'm gonna get your toy, boy!" She lightly smacked her palms on the clean blue carpet, reaching out slow for his toy, and then quickly jerked her hands away toward her. Sinbad kept one eye closed and tried to not wag his tail too much or too hard. The next time Danni reached for his toy, Sinbad jumped off the floor and sped into a figure eight pattern throughout the front-room and attached dining room. He made three fast laps, using the butcher-block table as a cul-de-sac. Then, just as quickly, he settled in the same place.

Little Sinbad, although graying on his muzzle, at times still acted like the same pup that had been born in my barn a dozen years ago. My grown kids, both born in 1976, still behaved like children, but not around outsiders. Danni was a bit younger. Tessa and I acted their age instead of ours. To us, being born in 1950 meant we had experienced enough to realize age is not determined by a calendar. Those mini-voyages we took without leaving the house were special times for us to share as one family of children.

"So go ahead, Pop. Lay a little of your profound rehab/recovery magic on us."

"Do you have to be so cocky all the time, Rocco?"

"Easy, Ma. I'm trying to chill. You're wound way too tight. Relax for once. You're not that old where you can't learn something. Besides, we should be able to talk about anything."

I butted in to postpone another quarrel: "Okay, son. I have one little nugget of wisdom for you. I figured out why so many people relapse! You ready?"

"We're listening," Danni said, leaning into me. "Say it!"

"But if most of you would rather not hear this…"

"Alright already, Jackie. Do we have to beg to hear this stupid work story of yours? I'm not into begging tonight, not for anybody. But you might be…"

"Ah man… Come on, Ma. Can we please do without all this parental sexual innuendo bullshit and just move on?" asked Rocco, as he cracked knuckles still red and swollen from hitting his heavy bag in our basement.

"What's the matter? I thought you wanted to talk about family activities. Is this subject too rough for you?" Tessa smiled. "Because your dad and I have a very healthy—"

"Whoa! Go ahead, Pop. At least two of us are interested in what you're saying." Rocco gave his mother a sideways glance.

"Okay, I have this theory about *comfort memories*. Would you like to hear it?"

"Anything's cool except that sexed-out geriatric crap."

Little Sinbad wandered through the house and stood at the backdoor, whining. Tessa looked at Rocco to let him out. I glanced over at Gina to notice she was ignoring me. Danni jumped up: "I'll do it. I want to. But please don't start without me. That's not fair." She returned within minutes to find that Rocco had abandoned his recliner for a bathroom break. So she quickly curled up in his favorite chair next to me and said in an excited sing-song voice, "Okay! I'm ready! Let's hear it!"

Rocco sauntered out, flexing muscles he had exerted from working out earlier that day. As he stretched he groaned, "No good. Go find yourself another place to squat, Danni. This is my spot. I need to get my batteries recharged. It's a recover thing. You should be on the look-out for me. Now clear out, sweetie."

"It *was* your spot," Tessa reminded our son. "Snooze you lose. Remember?"

"Whatever…" Rocco sighed, as he avoided the couch and loveseat and fell forward to a push-up position. He smoothly and effortlessly eased himself down on his flat stomach by thick biceps, then rolled over on his v-shaped back and put calloused hands behind his head on Sinbad's freshly washed doggie bed. His illustrated arms bulged as he encouraged, "Go for it, Pop. Tell us why people in active addiction crave loyalty and courage as much as drugs but are a bunch of one-way, codependent cowardly assholes. Or tell us just one pure truth, if there is one."

"Hmm . . . let's see. I'll try both. *Comfort memories* are parts and pieces of things we choose to remember, while conveniently forgetting all about negativity and consequence. And truth: I suppose truth is maintained with reliability *and* gameness. Together they comprise the foundation of every good relationship, right babe?"

"They'd better, bro," Tessa said, without looking up from her book. Tessa on the couch next to Gina who lay sideways with long, tanned legs stretched across Tessa's firm lap. Tessa pretended to read a book having the same name as the lettering on her T-shirt. The words "Fighting for Life" were in a strange font that made the shirt look Asian or antique. Little Sinbad, on the other side of me, watched Rocco monopolize his cushion.

Danni put her thin elbow on the thick arm of the recliner, her cute face on a small hand, staring at me as if I were about to perform a trick. That was probably the closest she had ever voluntarily entered my space. She asked, "Explain, please."

"Okay. Here goes: There are two kinds of truth. One is a version of reality we choose to believe, the stuff we want everyone else to believe. Then there's what's *really* true, based on hard evidence, tested with trial and error, and backed by facts and data. But an odd thing about truth, even if it's time-tested, is that it's still fluid. Arguably, there aren't many, if any, empirical truths. So that means even *real* truths can and do change. Once again it's the dialectic, Rocco, an upwelling of circumstance. When we're adults we create and then modify our own truths as we go."

"You totally lost me, Mr. Jack. It sounded like you just said two different things at the same time," observed Danni with a quizzical look. "Please explain."

"Okay. Let's look at the reality of Santa Claus. When that *Santa moment* was real nothing seemed more realistic, until a new truth emerged. But at that time, a fat guy sliding down every chimney on the planet, on the same night and being carried by flying reindeer, was a fact that was so real it was mystical."

"No good, Daddy-O," Gina said, shaking a head full of loose curls. "Little kids' truths don't count. Give us the adult version or I tune out."

"That one pure truth of whichever *comfort memory* or *Santa moment* we might hope to develop hinges on time. Just consider how reality has changed so often over the centuries, and how conventional traditions vary across cultures. Then just look at how drastically your own unique truths have grown or reversed.

It's almost funny now how the idealism of childhood and those extreme appetites of adolescence, even well into late adulthood, became nothing more a shimmering mirage on a dusty, deserted stretch of abandoned highway."

"I think I know what you mean, Mr. Jack!" Danni exclaimed, almost breathlessly. "But you promised we could talk about gameness," she reminded me with a childlike look of expectation. "Remember? You said truth is reliability and *gameness*. I was kind of hoping maybe you'd share an old story about when you guys used to make the dogs fight."

"Hmmm... I'm glad you just said that. Let me explain something real important. I know you didn't man it the way it came out. But this is a good time for me to explain this. Wording is vital. It conveys thoughts. You probably already realize what I'm about to say. I think the reason you said it that way is because you've heard it said that way hundreds of times since you were a little girl. Kind of like when somebody tastes something really good and says, 'Oh my God!' Or when someone is angry and shouts '*Jesus Christ!*' More than likely, that person wasn't thinking about God or Jesus, or might not even believe in a deity. It's just an expression.

Anyway, nobody I know of can *make dogs fight*. But even is some great trainer could figure out how to make things fight when they really don't want to, or when it's not about food or protection of their brood, that trainer would never be able to teach a dog how to willingly scratch back into the heat of battle. It's simply a fight or flight instinct. We *allowed* them to fight. We rolled and matched them. And I'm not any more proud of that than I am that I used to sell drugs, or that I smacked my ex-wife when she punched and kicked me, or other things I've said and done that I'm not proud of. But I've been able to learn valuable lessons because of mistakes."

"You're right, Mr. Jack. I didn't even realize I was saying it like that. I've seen rolls. If anything, the guys struggle to keep their dogs from getting back at each other. They love it."

"For me, gameness is loyalty to oneself. It's more than having multiple degrees or offshore bank accounts for others to piss away long after you're worm food. Money can insure popularity and protection, but it can't guarantee reliability, because loyalty is a non-tangible that's exceptional and priceless. Treasures like gameness and loyalty usually go underappreciated and underrated because of self-centered expectations of families or entitlements in society. So those rare gifts, more often than not, just go unrecognized."

"So if you admire gameness so much, Mr. Jack, then why don't you match dogs anymore or at least go watch?" Danni asked. "I don't get that. It's so exciting!"

"First of all: people, for the most part, are basically shit. I don't trust anybody outside this room. Dogs are true spirits like we aspire to be. But game-bred dogs don't have choices about degrees of gameness, Danni. Plus, they can't choose nurturing owners. Dogs can choose to fight, or to quit and end the contest. If fact, that's exactly what happens in every match I've ever seen. They're squirming and squalling to get at each other till one quits. But they don't get to choose their inherent blueprints or environments any more than children do. Nor can they choose what to eat, when or how much to exercise and rest. They're stuck with whatever they get. One pups lucks out and the next one doesn't. Gameness is hardwired with genetics, yet its depth is contingent upon things like age, management and health. Plus, they can't tell us they're not feeling well – to postpone it. So I guess it's appetite. Does that make sense?"

"No. But go ahead, Daddy. We're listening," Gina prompted without looking up from her self-imposed editing assignment of my manuscript which had no deadline.

"Okay. You all know I admire game-bred dogs. I have one here right at my feet." Sinbad gave one thump of his tail. "The only type I like better than a *game-bred* dog is a *proven* game dog. But along with proving the depth of a dog's gameness come things resembling premeditated cruelty and leaves the possibly of having to cull. Or worse yet stopping a yard accident, but then it's too messed up to take to a vet's office. So the dog dies because of bullshit laws. Rather than go to prison because your dog needs help due to a legitimate mishap, it has to die. When people *dog you out*, it's a deliberate act with premeditation. But because of dogs' immeasurable loyalty, some of them suffer the ultimate act of betrayal after they gave everything they had."

"Dogs don't *dog us out* on purpose like people do, right Daddy? Dogs just are what they are, and do what they do, and give all they have to give – whatever that is."

"That's right, honey. What game-dogs are, besides being products of breeders' luck or misgivings, while at times on the receiving end of torment and physical abuse, are by far the most steadfast and courageous creatures on the planet and mans' only true friend. So there it is, Gina, the one pure truth you asked for. It's the integrity of gameness. So it's really sad how ignorant or selfish most people are, taking for granted such integrity. It's that one truth, and some are on a mission to kill them because of it."

"Looks like you just went full circle on us, Dad-O. So now we're right back at the beginning, at the part about gameness and undying loyalty."

"Well, I guess loyalty is something all of us want but few actually give, although even the worst among us like to believe we are loyal. It's the thing we wisely doubt in most others, yet the same thing we expect from everyone. And loyalty usually changes just as fast as truth. Even memories change! But the weirdest thing about loyalty is what drives it. Loyalty is situational like truth. So I guess that brings us to how we rationalize convenient *excuses* into being valid *reasons*. Maybe next time we get all philosophical during our little *story-time* we can look at something as diverse as *appetites*.

"I'm not even asking you about that, Mr. Jack. My head already hurts from all that other stuff you just said. I need a nap."

"I don't need to hear it, either," Gina said, wagging her head. I've heard this sermon a zillion times, told in a dozen ways, ever since I was a little girl."

"Same here, sister-girl. He pounded our primary group every day with his integrity speeches till those addicts stumbled out of there tripping their asses off," Rocco chuckled.

"You said, *Same here*, Rocco. You mean you were a little girl, too? Wow, how cool. I've always wanted a little sister. Now we can sleep together."

Danni grinned, "Now the three of us can sleep together."

"Alright! That's it! I've heard enough!" Tessa warned.

Rocco said, "Well, I wanted to talk about addiction, but that was good shit, Pop. Gina wasn't even pretending to be not listening. I'm starting to dig philosophy, especially the existential stuff. It helps me not to get distracted by the trivial bullshit."

I lay in that basement remembering something Tessa said: "Nobody knows what type of surprises tomorrow holds. Sometimes, just when we think things can't possibly get any worse, the bottom falls out like an elevator with broken cables to expose a brand new bottom with another one beneath that. But every once in a while things get a lot better – despite the madness, or maybe even because of it.

July 28th, 2013 – The Stakeout, 1st day: Skinny Vinny said, "I mean it, *coom*. Not for nothing, but we should be looking at the bigger picture. Follow me?" Vinny resembled a human version of a cartoon weasel.

Shaking powdered sugar off king-sized treats for a jumbo-sized man onto that shiny black dashboard of that new Taurus, Spuds chuckled, "Vin, I know you wanna get all *phychosophical* about all this goofy shit of yours. You been goin' on for days. So just go for it. This is like a dinner show for me, you fucking nut-job. Go ahead, entertain me."

Spuds looked like a giant white potato with chubby hands and small feet popping out of his round body, and with a tiny head on top like a cherry on a sundae. His gruff voice exuded from a huge Ban-Lon shirt stretched tightly across *moobies* (man boobies). Spuds perpetually combed his slicked, greasy black hair with his right hand and smoothed it with his left. That whale of a man was a fanatic about perfect hair, not a strand out of place. Another quirk was his oral fixation. When he wasn't smoking, drinking pop or eating something with a napkin folded neatly across *Sansabelt* slacks straining to contain his ever-expanding gut, he was chewing gum and a toothpick.

"Whatever, Spuds. Just eat your other box of donuts. Everything's a big joke to you. Hardee-fucking-har..."

"Hey, Vin. I'm just sayin'. You know? Between that old prick, Danny Brown, and his over-the-hill gang of micks, if I was gonna get all hormonal and shit about this like you I'd be more worried about that other shit. But fuck-it. It's a done deal. But don't you think all this'll throw up a red flag? One of these fucks having an accident or a personal beef is life in the fast-lane. But three in a row could look like the type of grudge fuck that equals itself out with street justice. If more bodies keep popping up, it could be all-out war for everyone. And then, like you said, our heads get served up on a silver platter."

"Oh! Finally you're waking the fuck up? Yeah, Spuds. Those other *schifoso* from the Shamrock Club are only half our concern. This shit could turn into a real nightmare. I don't even wanna think about what could happen. Those Wong Gongs don't just kill people. Those sick assholes torture a motherfucker in their basement first . . . and then kill him."

Fat Spuds licked sugar and jelly off stubby fingers as he said, "I gotta say it, Vin. You got a bad memory. Here's us, part of one of the most lethal crews in America, and you're worried about a handful of old drunks and a couple dozen burn-out bikers? Fuck them! Are you growing a twat all the sudden?"

"No, Spuds. As usual, you're missing the whole point." Skinny Vinny said, as he swiveled his pencil neck around on delicate shoulders, all wide-eyed.

"Oh yeah? No shit. So tell me what is it I'm supposed to be missing." Spuds asked, as he wiped his forehead with a brown paper napkin from the bakery.

Waving thin arms around like he was conducting an orchestra, Vinny said, "The point is just this: if we stop now we might as well nail ourselves to crosses. I'm not talking about three hits here. I say let's go like 90. Let's waste all of them micks and bikers, just keep going like Sergeant Patton wanted to do to them Pollocks in the Ukraine. Chop of the head of the snake and the body dies. And then boom – end of story. Then we leave town till things cool off. That's when things get real interesting. *Capische?*"

Spuds flicked bits of crumbs off his white shirt and dark suit jacket with a diamond pinky ringed finger. He said, "Let's get this straight, just so I'm not missing this mysterious *point* of yours. First you wanna go after Doyle Kelly *and* Mr. Brown, so all those micks split town? Then you wanna go tip on Ansel and Filo, and even this Rocco kid who ain't even officially a part of any crew? And you think maybe that'll scare those Wong Gongs so bad they'll all leave town, too? Then whack Jackie. And you wanna do all this without the okay from the boss? Is that where you're going with all this, Vin?"

"No, Spuds. That ain't it. As usual, you got it all wrong."

"That's good to hear," Spuds said, as he inspected the inside of a white box and wax paper with one hand and drummed chubby fingers on his huge gut. "So what is it?"

"You got it all backwards, Spuds. First we hit this fucking Jackie. Get this shit over with now. *Then* we go take out Ansel and his kid, Whitey. Next we get Filo and this Rocco kid. And *last* we go after Doyle and Mr. Brown," Skinny Vinny said, as he straightened the lapels of his cheep-looking sports jacket.

Spuds looked deep in thought as he smoothed out the sides of his slicked back black hair with stubby hands. "You know what, *coom?* I was wrong. You're even crazier than I thought you were, you sick fuck," he grinned a big cheesy smile. "But you're too jittery. Easy, *coom*. You're making me all tired just watching you jump around in your seat. Relax. Let me handle the thinking, Vin. Just sit still and listen."

"No. You listen. This plan is flawless. The beauty of this whole thing is that those micks and bikers will all think Cagootz and Louie orchestrated those hits on Animal, Mr. Brown and Jackie. Meantime, we lay on the beach drinking Pina Coladas till the dust settles."

While Fat Spuds gingerly wiped powdered sugar off fat hands, he realized what it was his whacky partner had been talking about when the unexpected happened. A series of irritating directional *piep-piep-pieps* mandated by DOT. A tanker backed into the drive where Spuds and Vinny had been hiding to replenish an unquenchable thirst for more oil. Until that moment they had been enjoying a clear view of Jackie's old farm house – and it was almost dusk. Spuds whispered, "It's almost time. Now how we gonna act?"

They heard barking and growling. They hadn't realized Jackie still fed game-bred dogs. Both were afraid of dogs. Being blocked reminded them of the possibility that Jackie and Rocco might walk outside to investigate the disturbance. There would be no explaining. They would have to get the drop on them, kill the truck driver, and then figure out how to move that big truck before Tessa identified familiar faces to the cops – or worse.

Skinny Vinny jerked his head over to his partner: "Should we run them into the ditch? Come on, *coom*. What should we do, Spuds? Because we can't get trapped in here."

Spuds grabbed his piece: "Sit tight. I'll handle this. Just don't get too jumpy."

Years-worth of bloodstained lines I'd believed were indelible left a residual mark to blur all reason, mostly because I had been passive enough to allow drugs to use me for so long. So to compensate, for two decades we honed an edge so jagged nobody in Cleveland wanted us as enemies or friends. We became brutally fearless men who took reputations the way others take references for a *résumé* – in a reckless game of survival. We banged and bled together on those unforgiving streets of Collinwood, leading lives of dreams, smiling down that fast-lane into a nightmarish tunnel of abrupt endings and never-ending grudges.

CH VII: Story-time

July 28, 2013 – The Stakeout, the 1st day: "So how about it, Pop? Why don't we get back to what's new in the world of rehab since I left your group of AA commandos."

"New? Addiction is what it is. Nothing changes."

Gina plopped down next to Tessa: "Come on, Daddy-O," she asked in a fake whine. "Explain what a relapse is, because I don't get it. How come something *medical* like a *relapse* can't just be bad decisions made by sober people, over and over again?"

"Okay, little girl. You want the textbook DSM-4 explanation, or you want to hear what I really know to be true?"

"Tell us what you *think* you know," encouraged my wife. "Have you figured out why so many people who pray and work those Steps keep *relapsing*, counselor? Yet some other so-called addicts make changes in their lives out of necessity and willingness and get it the first or second time in rehab. Or others, like you, who've never had treatment get it. What's the technical term, Mr. Counselor?"

"That's an easy one, Tessa. We forget the severity and scope of the pain, yet we magnify remnants of long-gone euphoria. We choose to only remember the honeymoon phase but never the divorce. It's called *selective recall*."

"Right-on, Pop. Go ahead; explain this to these square-heads," Rocco smirked.

"Okay, son. Let's talk about something I refer to as *Comfort Memories*. For example: you've seen Gina's mother, Butterscotch, right Rocco?"

"What? Yeah, of course. Why?"

"What was your first impression of Gina's mother?"

"She's an attractive older lady. Actually, pretty hot."

"*My* mother? I can't believe what a dawg you are, little bro. You're even hot for old ladies now? Eww! That's pitiful," mocked his sister with a scrunched-up face.

I explained, "A potential relapse would be like me forgetting how much Butter and I argued during our last year together, and how we dogged one another out at the end of our relationship. Being in relapse mode, I'd only remember that heart-shaped ass and those full lips. The relapse would be me dating her again because I lied to myself to believe things could still be like the honeymoon if we got back together."

"Whoa, Jackie! You'd better back the hell up, bro," snapped Tessa. "I don't need to hear any more of this, not even if you're just kidding around. I mean it. Okay?"

"Easy, Ma. This is a sociological study I'll use for class."

"Oh yeah? What's your new class," asked Gina, "Cougars and Pervs – 101?"

"You chicks are too uptight. You need to lighten up."

"You refer to me again as a chick and I'll slap the cockiness right off that smart mouth of yours!" his mother warned with a stern expression. "Understand me?"

"Yeah, Rocco. And that is my mother you're drooling over . . . even if she is a total witch sometimes. So maybe you're the one who should lighten up," Gina advised. "Besides, our professor told us we have all weekend. Don't sweat it, little bro. I'll help you if you get in trouble again, because you're a little slow. What's the term for that learning disability? Oh yeah, I remember now. It's called *lazy*."

"Talk about *lazy*… What about you, Gina?" asked her brother. "All you do is fake sleep while we're talking story. Or you hijack stimulating conversations while everyone's ignoring you. What's really bugging you? You feel inadequate? Is that it?"

"You already know what's bothering me, so piss-off."

"What did I do now?"

"You let that ugly bitch smart off to me in class and didn't say shit. Where's your loyalty at, brother?" Gina asked.

"You kids aren't in trouble, are you?" I asked. "Because I know how that anger of yours can get, Gina. And your mother's already clued me in about your previous escapades, son. You two better be careful. Don't egg each other on. It could get ugly."

With a mock expression of disbelief Tessa asked, "Who, Gina might have anger issues? I have no idea how a child coming from you and Butterscotch could possibly have a quick and nasty temper. I'm shocked… It just doesn't add up."

I yawned, "Nasty temper? That's something nobody can accuse me of. If anything, I'm timid."

"Yeah, whatever, Daddy. Denial can be a wonderful thing. Anyway, I'm not finished. You should have seen how bitchy that fat tub was. I'm still steaming about what she said. I should have mashed in that turned-up, Pollack pig nose of hers."

I said., "I'm proud you didn't blow up again, Gina. Listen closely to me: I've already been your age but you've never been mine. I can teach you from experience how to better deal with situations like this. Okay?"

"Sure, Daddy-O. I'm all ears and good intentions. At least I can depend on one man in this house to have my back."

Rocco hissed at his sister, and then put his hands behind his head as I continued.

"Let's all look at this as a family. You're holding anger and resentment, right? I need to see it so we can help. Alright, so *show* us exactly what's still bothering you."

"What do you mean, Dad? *Show* you what? Like how?"

"I mean just show us what happened. Where is it? I need to see so we can fix it."

"Say what?" Gina asked. "I'm not following this at all."

"You mean you can't show me the past?"

"Ah, okay Daddy. I get it… It's only real in my mind, and only for as long as I allow it to be real. Hmm . . . Okay. I guess I totally stepped right into that one, didn't I?"

"Yes, my beautiful and smart daughter. You did just that. So now all of us understand that what's still bothering you doesn't exist other than inside your own beautiful imagination. So I guess we're in the present and now move forward, right?"

"What you're saying is if something doesn't exist in the moment then it's not there at all, so you really have no choice other than to just let it go. Right, Daddy?"

"No. You always have choices. But besides that, how can you let something go if it no longer exists? What I'm saying is, just face the facts. Whatever happened is over and done with. It's yesterday. It's history. What's already gone can never be changed. So learn from it. Grow from it."

"That's pretty good, Pop," grinned Rocco. "You're still in top counselor form. I suppose I'm pretty lucky to have you in my life, even if it did take you 3 ½ decades to come around."

"You're sure I'm your father, Rocco? You know the old saying: Momma's baby; Poppa's maybe. I might not be Gina's."

"Jackie, I'm giving you one second to say you're only kidding or we're going to kick your smart-ass from here to across the road. How would you like to wake up in some hospital because you're an idiot?" asked my petite wife. "I'm serious!"

"It's just jokes, kids and little *wifey*. Check me out: Hahahahahahaha. See? That was a seven *Ha* laugh. That means it's some really funny shit. I'm a great kidder, ain't I? But all kidding aside, I sort of like all of you strangers. Maybe not really a *strong* type of like. Perhaps just a casual *love*. You know?"

"I don't get it. Is there a punch line or something? Or is that it? Because maybe you're the one who should just learn to let things go, Jackie. Give it up, bro. You're not as amusing as you think. Nobody's laughing at your dumbass jokes but you."

"Right, Daddy. You're about as funny as a case of crotch rot on a hot day at Cedar Point. But there are two problems with your newest round of ball busting. First of all, I look just like Grandma when she was young. My *Italian* grandma. *Your* mother. And Rocco looks exactly like Grandpa. *Your* father, only a bunch of sweet-ass tats. So unless Grampa and Gramma really weren't *your* parents. I mean, Grandma's baby, but Grandpa's maybe. Right, old man? Hey, for all you know—"

Rocco reached his right hand out to Gina. "Good one, sister-girl. Here. Shake, pal."

Gina reached out a smooth hand. "What's this hearty handshake bullshit? Or are you asking for my paw?"

"Ahh. . . . not quite." Rocco pulled her up and then threw her over a thick, inked shoulder. "Come-on. Let's ride, you little, psycho drama-mama."

"You'd better put me down or you'll be riding minus front teeth!"

He did. I watched him kick start his chopper made of various parts from different years. Rocco's motor glugged that distinct Harley sound. Using one foot for balance and momentum, like on a kid's scooter, he cautiously guided them squarely onto the middle of our road and then roared him and his sister away into the wind.

"Okay then." I said, as I abandoned my comfortable recliner. "Come on, Sinbad, outside. I guess it's time for some air and for us to get away from this mean lady."

"Wow . . . that must be another funny one, right? You're really on a roll now, eh bro? So was I supposed to laugh right then, or is there more?" Tessa asked, through a sour expression as she drummed painted nails on the cover of her dog book.

The Basement – more flashbacks: No longer bound in wrist restraints, I was paralyzed by my own inadequacies. Heat beneath my skin grew unbearable, a thousand degrees – too much to endure, too real to be true. My back throbbed. The backs of my legs were on fire. *I need to refocus.* I did, long enough to see I was wearing a white hospital gown and no shoes. *Unless I have a private* *room at the Cleveland Clinic, I'm killing somebody.* My left arm tingled to numbness so I eased back to count the seconds for each of my breaths, facing a wall which housed a staircase leading to another mystery. Controlled breathing . . . in and out, slow and complete. When I inhaled I felt a restraint around my chest, which is when I began to feel a sense of panic. Heart racing, erratic breathing. *Where is this place? The morgue? No, I'm in too much pain. A hospital? No way . . . not this shit-hole.*

July 28, 2013 – The Stakeout, the 1st day: As a family at peace we settled in to watch *Valhalla Rising*. Not one word was spoken throughout the movie. Afterwards we sat in silence for a few moments, with credits frozen on pause from the DVD rental. The film had been stark and intense, brutal yet beautiful. It put me in mind of when I experienced my first dog convention where I saw my first professional dog match.

I cleared shatterproof blue bowls and plastic tumblers from our wooden dining room table into our dishwasher. Tessa and I had tri-flavored spumoni. The kids ate dark chocolate ice-cream. We killed both two liters of Dad's root beer and split the 16 ounce bag of chips, leaving a few broken ones at the bottom.

After shuffling around the rooms, upstairs and down, toilet flushing and teeth brushing, eventually all five of us, and our old dog, reclaimed comfortable positions to partake in or absorb more of our family *story-time*.

"Hey! Not to change the subject or anything," Rocco laughed. "But now I have an important question for Gina. Do you have any of that sweet hydro left, sister-girl? It's for a friend of a friend. I'll pay you back."

Tessa studied our shaggy-looking son as her lowered head wagged long blonde hair from across thin but muscular thighs. "I can't believe this. You're supposed to be in recovery? The thing with you, Rocco, is you overdo everything! I'm warning you. You get back on those goddamn pills and you can forget it! Please don't be an asshole your whole life. We love you."

Gina said, "Moderation, little bro. A taste once in awhile is no big deal. But you and Whitey must be sending up smoke signals again, dude. You can't be *chiefing* every day on super-bud and still keep your shit together. You'll melt your mind."

"They're right about this one, son," I agreed. "Swear to Buddha, you can't be out there doing all the dumb shit yet stay on task. Timing, remember? Because you've only been out of rehab for a few weeks you might want to think about something other than nice asses and sticky buds. Like I said, Chief Wahoo, you and your sister need to be more aware of subtleties and nuances to know what the bigger picture's like. But you gotta be straight enough to recognize it, or you'll be too numb to see the red flags shooting up. Ease off, son. Right, Tessa?"

"Goddamn! What's with all you people?" Rocco asked, angrily. "Right away everybody writes me off as a hopeless junkie, just because I might take the odd toke here and there. Let's move on, okay? But while we're on the topic, I do have this other question about addiction."

"Sure... Let's hear it," his mother sighed and lifted her book as a signal that she was about to tune out all of us.

"Okay, tell me: Is drug addiction physical or emotional?"

"Well, son, according to the DSM-5, it's—"

"Pop, I couldn't care less what those armchair quarterbacks say who never took real drugs. Straight business… Isn't it true that a person can get addicted to nasal spray?"

"Actually, that happened to me once," I said, petting my old dog next to me. "One winter I used a bottle of it a few times a day for a few weeks in a row and then could barely breathe without it for awhile. Yeah, it's definitely addictive."

"But once you get through the physical withdrawal from the nasal spray and are breathing right again, after your nasal passages return to normal, you can use the spray now and then as long as you use it in moderation – like Gina said. Right Pop?"

Tessa said with a sarcastic laugh. "I've never seen directions on a bag of pot. What is moderation with illegal drugs? In fact . . . what's your point, Rocco?"

"My point is now that I'm sober I'm figuring maybe I could socially shoot heroin on the odd weekend. It follows the same logic, right? I mean, it stands to reason that—"

"See what I mean, Ma?" interrupted Gina. "This boy has completely wigged out. No more rehab for you, little bro. Your next stop is the Looney farm. Have you and Whitey been hitting that other pipe yet? You smoking *A-bombs* yet, dude?"

"*A-bombs*? What the hell is that?" gasped Tessa. She stood up but sat right back down while gazing at our hard-looking son.

"An A-bomb's a *spliff*, Ma. It's just a joint dusted with smack. Where've you been?"

"Shut-up, retard," Gina snapped. "Quit torturing her."

"You're the one who started it, maniac. And the answer is *no*, Ma. I might have indulged in the past, but those days are over. I've moved on. I'm smoking *primos* now."

"*Primos*! You'd better explain, mister!" Tessa shrieked.

"Easy, Ma. It's just crack sprinkled on a blunt."

"*Really* Rocco? Are we back on this rollercoaster again?"

"Whoa . . . I'm just breaking balls here," Rocco chuckled. "It's just jokes, ladies."

"Hey, I have a good idea," offered Gina. "How about the next time you tell jokes, make sure they're actually *funny*? How's that sound?"

"Speaking of jokes, Ma, let's get back to that story about cheeks I was telling when Gina finally let us know about what that psycho bitch, Maureen, said to her and Danni."

Gina raised her voice: "Alright, I'm sorry. I forgot. And I said I won't do it again!"

"Anyway," Rocco continued, "try to follow this: If some stand-up comedian blasts multi-belches into his microphone, people laugh themselves breathless. But let that same guy bend over and crack the tiniest wet fart into his mike and that whole place would clear out as quick as if he was wearing a towel on his head and a vest strapped with C-4. Am I right or not?"

"Speaking of shit, son, you're totally full of it," Tessa said. "And you asked Gina what was really on her mind..."

"Hold up. One more thing. Admit it. When you look at all this for what it really is, we're just talking about the digestive process. Am I wrong? The first part, the ingestion or actual eating of food, seems okay. Right? I mean, it all goes back to having a slice of the pie in the sky – like, for example, eating a banana."

"That's true," I agreed with the most serious expression I could muster. "People do get together to break bread. It's a ritual. Some get all dressed up and go out, or invite friends over to share in the ordeal. Rocco's right about this. It really is the initial stage of digestion. Nobody seems to have a problem with that part."

"Exactly, Pop! Now here's the clincher. Let's take a serious look at the banana."

"Don't start in with that again!" Tessa warned.

"Alright. But tell the truth. One of the sexiest things a woman can do is eat is a banana – to a point – even if she's not trying to be a prick teasing bitch for once in her life."

Gina said, "I'm about to kick you square in the face."

"Yeah, right... Whatever, hot shot."

"What do you mean by it's sexy *to a point?*" I asked.

"Holy shit! You're as bad as your son!" Tessa slapped her thighs and mock-laughed at me.

"Good observation, Pop. I'm glad you asked. What I'm saying is this: secretly, during the meal or while sexily eating, we all know what the next step is with her and that banana."

Tessa said, "Please, Rocco, I'm begging you to stop this. I'm about to vomit."

"Okay, Ma. I'm almost to my main point. The thing is that every person around that table will eventually have to complete the food cycle. And no matter how sexy or wealthy the person is who's eating, no matter how fancy they're dressed or how expensive or healthy the food might be, ultimately the process ends up as a stinking mess in the toilet. And that's the part most people don't seem to go for. You know?"

"I gotta say it. Sometimes you're a real *schifoso*," Gina said. "You even go too far with jokes. That's the junkie in you."

"Hey, I didn't insinuate the Freudian stuff like last time. Gimme a little credit. And I'm not joking. This is serious stuff."

"How on Earth can any of this be serious?" Tessa asked.

"Okay, look at this part: One time I took this girl out for a first date at a buffet. She scarfed down three plates of food and a platter of dessert – banana cream pie, of all things! She was licking the custard off the bananas. Believe me. She knew exactly what she was doing. You should have seen the way she was moving her mouth and tongue."

Tessa scowled: "Rocco, I mean it! I want you to stop this right now! You promised you wouldn't go there."

"Anyway, she's sitting these yakking away like she's on speed, food all stuck in her teeth. All I could think about was the huge shit she was gonna take. You know; one of those dumps that fills up the whole toilet bowl and you need a plunger?"

"I'll admit to something," I offered. "When I was a kid and found out that nuns use the bathroom, I started to question my faith. That's when I transferred to public school. I figured the race riots in Collinwood were safer than me having to face those images in my head. I would have flunked out of every class."

"Yeah, I know what you mean, Pop. I broke up with my first girlfriend when her mother told me she was home sick with the diarrhea. In fact—"

"Please, Jackie. Don't give him any reason to continue. While you two are droning on about the digestive process, our poor Gina looks ready to upchuck."

"Yeah, both of you just give it up. I'm about ready to gag." Then Gina yawned, stretched and said, "Excuse me. It's time for me to take a potty break. And no smart remarks, boy. I just have to pee, if that's okay with you."

Tessa got up and padded her way into our little kitchen to pour herself a glass of water from a stand-up cooler. She returned carrying a chocolate walnut biscotti on a small white plate and asked, "Anybody want anything while I'm up? Jackie, will you please take this poor dog outside? He's still passing gas."

"And Rocco," his mother added, "Can you please stop being disgusting, at least while I'm eating something brown?"

"HA! That's a good one, Tessa," I said, with a loud and hearty fake laugh. "But you know what? That cookie looks so good. Let me have just a bite, okay?"

"No way, bro. Get your own, Jackie."

"Come on… Quit being such a Jew broad. Swear to Buddha, just one bite."

"Forget it. I know what your *one bite* look like. One bite and then nothing's left but crumbs. I'll be glad to get you one."

"Jeez, what a kike. Forget I even asked."

"Will do. Now what about what I asked you, Jackie?"

"Okay, Mrs. Ma." I scratched an ear to get Sinbad's attention. "Outside, old man? Come-on boy, let's go outside and leave this mean lady with her precious cookie." The muscular black & tan was a well bred mongrel, a carefully line-bred Yankee Terrier. Both his parents were half Pit-bull and half Airedale, both good dogs out of Ch Biddy. And like Little Sinbad, both were all Bulldog. He opened one eye to look around the room for a quick second and then returned to fake-nap mode. "Check him out, Tessa. This lazy bastard won't budge. He's pretending to be out cold. He wants back on that faggot-assed doggie bed of his."

"Okay, Pop, thanks for that insight about the dreaded nasal spray," Rocco yawned and flexed thick tattooed arms and his bull-like chest. "But just one more thing: Is it true that when people die they shit themselves?"

"I wasn't in Vietnam, Rocco. How should I know what people do when they die? Anyway, I'm a counselor, not a doctor. Besides, I've changed. I'm different now."

"I see. So what about shooting Toby? You're saying you couldn't go there again, Pop? Because you're the only guy I know who ever got that lethal while tripping balls."

"That was almost 40 years ago, son. Toby was very drunk and right up in my grill, fronting me off in front of friends. And I was young, foolish and on an acid peak."

Rocco smiled, "Good answer. Pleading the Fifth, eh?"

Tessa asked, "You don't think shooting him was an overreaction, Jackie?"

"Well, like I said, I'm a different person now. I've changed. Violence sickens me now, unless it involves willing participants – like MMA tournaments. I still love that stuff."

"Daddy, you're always straight with us. So don't go turning into a bullshit artist now just because you're a counselor. Drop the façade. You're at home with family."

"There are plenty of things I've done that I'm not proud of. That's one of them."

Little Sinbad stretched with rump up, tail curled over his back and forelegs flat on the rug while he enjoyed a huge yawn. He slowly lumbered to the back door, muscles moving side-to-side to cause a slight rolling motion. I gladly followed. He relieved himself on his favorite tree. I urinated on that same maple my dog marked for us. We had no neighbors to worry about and a wooden privacy fence for the occasional passing vehicle or walker. I could have pissed on every fencepost on our ten acres, or walked around nude if I felt the urge. Then Sinbad aired and rumbled a growl deep in pit of his chest. I looked around and listened, but there wasn't another soul in sight.

July 28, 2013 – The Stakeout, the 1st day: Vinny tapped fingertips to soundless music inside his thin head. While waiting for dusk, he loosened a thin black tie with a jerk and asked his partner, "I got a question, just between you and me. I'm sitting here trying to make sense of all this. Not for nothing, *coomba*, but just tell me this part. Why in fuck's sake would the boss wanna start this shit all over again with those lunatics down Five Points? It's been 37 years since the war ended. Why now? It's been peaceful, and now everybody's all edgy again. Even the cops are tweaked behind this bullshit. They remember how quick and high bodies piled up last time this fire had gas poured on it."

"How so?" asked Spuds, with a hunk of glazed sugar stuck to his bottom lip.

"How so *what*? What are you tripping, or what? Danny Brown might be old as mammoth turds but he ain't stupid or weak."

"Mr. Brown's a business man, Vin. That means he understands how something like this could happen," Spuds explained, as he spread cubby hands up with his palms upwards. "Sometimes there's accidents. What can you do? It can't be helped in this line of work."

"Oh, I see. And that's it? Thos Irish fucks are just gonna lay down behind this, because we had an *off* day?"

"Easy, Vin. Mr. Brown knows fuck-all about who did what. He probably thinks it was those sleazy Wong Gongs. Who knows? He might even suspect maybe those Five Points spooks running errands for that little *moolie*, Sonny Magic, had something to do with it. Trust me, *coom*, nobody knows shit about who did that except for you know who. Besides, Cagootz is the invisible man in this whole thing. It just looks like a local drug deal gone bad – plain and simple, because it was. Boom – end of story. But the important piece you keep forgetting is that the boss put all this shit together for a good reason," Spuds said, as he warmed up his paper cup of coffee from the large silver thermos. When I told Cagootz how this shit came down with that decrepit mick's shriveled ol' lady guess what he said? He fucking laughed… To me, that spells no problems," Spuds said, as he reached for another treat with a pudgy fist from the other white bakery box.

"Of course Cagootz laughed when you told him. Why would he give a shit? But you gotta keep something in mind, Spuds. Mr. Brown might be old as mammoth shit but he's still one of the most dangerous and powerful men in Cleveland. He's killed more *paesano* than cholesterol," Vinny said, as he pointed a thin, almost feminine finger to reinforce a point he had been trying to make. "And as far as that two-timing shine, Sonny, goes . . . that little spider monkey's always been just as crazy as the best of 'em. Not for nothing, but those black street bangers might even be stronger than us by now! I mean, just look at the kids of our big guys. They're a bunch of pussies. But the brothers are getting more powerful each generation."

"Look at you, ya trembling fuck!" Spuds said, laughing and briskly wiping his hands like symbols. "We're safe, Vin. No problems. We work for Cagootz. Everybody on the planet knows this. Am I right? We take orders directly from him. And he flies under the flag of Fingers and *la Cosa Nostra*. Nobody – and I mean *nobody* – fucks with the *la Famiglia*! We're untouchable. Know why? Because if the heat's on us, it's on them, too. So relax for half a second. Trust me on this one, *coom*. The boss has plans.

You gotta have faith, ya fuckin' bust-out."

Skinny Vinny tugged at his shirt collar. "Faith my ass... I deal in facts. Here's what the fuck I know as fact: Doyle's smart as a fox, just like the Mick was. If Doyle doesn't already know who put the touch on his calabash uncle's ol' lady, he'll figure it out sooner or later. And when he does, we'll be the scapegoats getting fed to those psycho Irishmen on a silver platter. You better have faith on that!"

"Hey *coomba*, calm down. Have a nice cruller. Besides, I hate those blue-haired old cunts, anyway. So it turned out to be one of them *what-cha-ma-call-its*. You know; collateral damage thingies. It happens in war all the time. We didn't mean it. And as far as those Irish fucks go: Fuck Doyle Kelly up his pink mick ass. He's probably got red hair and freckles on his ass cheeks, too. In fact, you know what? When we're done here, I just might take a ride down Five Points and ass-slam that punk myself – just for shits and giggles."

Vinny tugged at the lapels of a gaudy sports jacket: "Fuck Doyle. Whatever... But let's review a couple things, Spuds: First of all, you're the one that shot that old bitch, not me. I'm not saying she didn't deserve it, or that I don't have your back or any shit like that. But facts are facts. Am I right or not?"

"Well if you'd learn how to drive in a straight line, Vin, instead of tugging at you shirt and jacket all the goddamn time, this shit wouldn't happen. Besides, those Irish ain't shit anymore since their God the Mick got taken out," Spuds mumbled, while appraising their remaining inventory in the white box.

"You kill me, Spuds. You sit here stuffing your goddamn face like King Farouk. Meantime, if Jackie or his lunatic kid sees us parked across from their house, the party's over. In fact, they might be scoping us with crosshairs right now. They could pull in this drive any minute. And have faith in this, too: This Rocco kid's no pussy. He's just as crazy as his old man, only a lot younger and maybe as mean. They're *paesano* from the old neighborhood. Let's not forget this. Even though they hang around with niggers and hillbillies now, they're still crazy. And now this Rocco's tight as virgin pussy with those biker cocksuckers down Five Points. I don't know about you, but I ain't about to take Ansel and those other ragged fucks lightly."

Spuds, licking jelly off his thumb, asked, "Do I look worried, Vin? We're almost done here. Then we take out his spook buddy next. Once Jackie and Curtis are out of the picture,

Animal is down and ol' Danny Brown's shitting green bricks, we lay low. No big deal. The last person in the world Ansel suspects is us for taking out his brother. That fucking Animal has enemies all over the country. Ansel doesn't respect Cagootz, but if push comes to shove he'll back down from Fingers. So the moral of the story is: you need to fuckin' relax, ya whack-job."

"I don't know, Spuds. Maybe we should rethink this. What I hear is those Wong Gong's offered Rocco a patch. I say we grease this fucking kid too, before we run into a bunch of other crazy shit later on down the line. It's simple. We just take 'em both out. Boom! Save us some major league problems later on. Two fucks with one bomb, right Spuds? I vote we take a closer look at this situation. And if the broad gets in the way, we take her out, too. Make a clean sweep, right?"

"Take it easy, Vin. We don't need to solve the world's problems just yet. We'll come back tomorrow to finish this. Start this chariot up and let's ride back to the Wood. I'm fucking starving!"

Vinny said, "You take it easy, ya fat fuck. There's more to life than food. There's shit going on here we don't have the first clue about. And you just sit there like you're spaced out with your hand in an empty fucking bakery box. How much is enough?"

CH VIII: I Want More

July 29TH, 2013 – The stakeout, last day: During one of our last conversations I assured my wife and two grown children, "I've been doing some thinking about that other dimension, the one beyond our control. But I've also been thinking about choice." Seated in my blue recliner in our cozy front-room, elbows on my knees, I held my arms straight and studied my own tattoos as I spoke. "I figure if we do something – anything, whatever it is – it's because down deep we must want to on some level, or we simply wouldn't do it. We'd do something else – anything else, just not that. The simple proof is this: nobody can make us eat a pile of dog shit. You see the logic, right?"

"Is there something wrong, Daddy," asked my beautiful daughter. Her dark curly hair tumbled across her one of her intense pale eyes that contrasted dark olive-colored skin. She stared hard at me, searching for something. "I always know when something's wrong, sometimes even before you do. And you've always been straight with me so far. So if you need something, or for us to do anything just name it and it's done."

"I'd let you know if I knew. But I can feel it. Something's in the air. It's not always so easy to call, sweetie. Sometimes that ol' *Click* crawls over us like a live spider web of static electricity. It'll come to me, though. I just can't call it yet. Maybe it's that I love you all so much that I'm terrified of the day when a piece of our foundation crumbles into an emptiness of forever. But I apologize for being Captain Gloom & Doom. I'll stop now."

"No. Wait awhile, Pop. Is somebody fucking with you? Because I'm still young. I can afford to sacrifice a few years and still come out of the joint with a future. No offence, but your old. You might not have five years left to throw away for shooting more of these stupid motherfuckers. I'm not the shy type, so don't go politician on us."

"That's very nice of you to say, Rocco," Tessa said. "I'm proud of you for being so selfless. But can you please watch your language, especially in front of your sister?"

"Like you don't ever say the word *fuck*. Is that it, Ma?"

"I didn't ever use that language around my mother!"

"Well she probably didn't say it to you, either. Right?"

Tessa acted like no question had been posed to her. Instead, she looked at me. "You just seem off your game lately,

Jackie. I guess we're all noticing it."

"Thank you, son. That's real solid. I would have done the same for my parents and will for any of you. But I never want to be put in that position again. I really have changed. All the deliberate cruelty has really worn me out. But there's nothing specifically wrong with me. I'd say so if it was one thing."

"Okay, then just tell us what it is you think about when you drift off lately," my wife asked, looking concerned.

"It's just that we play out the remainder of our lives pretending there's not a monster sleeping inside us feeding on the stench of betrayal, excuses and regrets. We act like it's not teaming up with other inner-demons that grow stronger from things like illness and old age, and even pain and fears."

Rocco said with half-closed eyes. "Talk about me being Chief Wahoo… Whatever you're smoking, Pop, you might think about easing off just a tad. Because that spiel you just shared sounds like half of it is depression, and half is drug-induced rambling, and the other half is something else I can't call right now. But I'll say this much: You're one trippy guy."

Gina, added, "*Yeah* he is! Tell you what, Daddy-O. Whatever that crazy shit is you're chiefing, we'd like a little taster. Let's share that and our problems too, like family should."

Tessa expelled her usual Italian mother groan. "Jackie, you have these kids all jacked-up now. You promised before we got married you weren't crazy anymore, and that was only a little while ago. Now I'm in the same playpen as you. I went all these years being a single mother, not trusting one person on this planet after my mother passed, and raising a son by myself. And now I have three big kids to deal with? I don't know who's crazier between you three maniacs: your psycho babbling; our goofy son with his scumbag friends; or now this beauty queen of a space-case daughter we have. I think this old pit-dog has more brains than the three of you."

"Chill, Ma," Rocco said. "First you tell Pop to open up and now you're saying he shouldn't be so upfront. And as far as my so-called *scumbag* friends go, I have exactly two friends other than you three, which is only one more than you have. Whitey's been a brother since we were snot-nosed brats. But when you're right, you're right. The part about Gina is right on target. She is somewhat of a basket-case."

"Look who's calling the kettle metal. You got a lot of room to talk. Nothing personal, baby brother. But you must be allergic to rational thought, because you're breaking out in a bad case of obnoxious asshole."

At that, Little Sinbad yawned and panted a few times before resting his massive head on his thick, short front legs. Tessa said, "You're all going to be the end of what little sanity I still have. Aren't they, Sinbad? You're still my good boy." With his eyes still closed, he thumped his bullwhip of a tail against the blue carpet. Then Tessa's eyes sparkled, "So anyway, let's get to the nitty gritty here, bro. If you really do have a stash of some primo herb you'd best be sharing after these two leave. Then maybe I can understand all this jibber-jabber you're spewing."

"Ma! You smoke weed? Be honest. " asked our middle-aged biker son, affecting an exaggerated expression of shock while tugging at his almost blue-black beard.

"Just shut up, Rocco. Act your age for once," Gina said.

"Really, Ma? *Wow!*" Rocco leaned back his head and folded muscular arms full of brightly colored tattoos across a broad, hairy chest. He studied his mother as if he was meeting her for the first time. Gina and I, in some ways, still were strangers to him. "Don't you listen to FOX News, Ma, about the dangers of the dreaded *marihoochi*? It's illegal!"

Gina waved a tanned hand. "They're still newlyweds, Rocco. And Pop's on vacation. Technically, they're still on their honeymoon. So give them a break, dude. Although, I must admit, this whole conversation has been pretty bizarre," my middle-aged daughter said with a smile that had melted my heart from the day she was born. Then she turned that radiance towards me: "But Rocco's finally right. If you have an emergency stash you'd better let us test it before you two dinosaurs blaze up. It could be *laced!*"

"Yeah, right... We appreciate your generosity, honey. And I'm quite sure your brother would be more than willing to help you. But the thing is I'm a drug counselor. So what makes you think I would actually use such a dangerous and highly addictive drug? Do you think I'm trying to get Ma hooked?"

"Hey Pop, we ain't as stupid as we look. Well, at least I'm not. The jury's still out on one of us, though," Rocco chuckled, as he looked at his sister. "As far as Ma goes, I can't even imagine her buzzed. But I'd love to see it. Hell, I'll go score some green right now so we can pass the peace pipe – old-school, baby."

"Yeah, big Daddy-O and little Ma-Mo. This sounds great! Let's plan a party, like right now just for us. I'm pretty sure Rocco can access some *hogsbreath*." She looked at Rocco: "Bust out your stash, you *bogart*. Quit holding out, you cheap bastard."

Rocco grinned, "I'm in recovery. And you know this."

"Maybe you're the one should give us a break, son. Your mother and I aren't as old as we look. We know you still burn. And we know you do too, my sweet little innocent angel. Besides, marijuana is illegal. You and your brother have become partners in crime lately. I wouldn't put anything past the two of you. Tessa's a bad influence on the both of you."

Tessa returned to the large couch to sit next to my daughter: "*Me?* Look at you and your son with all those goddamn tattoos. You both look like walking coloring books. And you both act like total morons. Grow up! Gina and I are in a completely different league. We're classic beauties and sophisticates, with brains and elegance. So quit acting stupid."

"I got a news flash for you, Ma," she said. "Those two aren't just *acting* stupid."

I said, 'Yes, Mommy. Whatever you say, dear'. See that, son? The trick to being happy when you have women in your life is to make them think they're smarter than you. Let them believe they can outwit you. Allow them to be right every once in a while. And make sure you always complement them. Keep feeding that shallow ego. That keeps them distracted. It's sort of like training a puppy with rubber biscuits."

"Don't say one word or we'll both smack the dog piss out of you." Gina wrinkled her nose and made a fist.

"No, Pop," he said. "I think living with chicks is more like keeping a mean dog happy. You smother it with foolish baby talk and toss it little treats every now and then. But feed it with a long-handled spoon. That's how I trained Danni."

"Don't you have to be somewhere?" asked his mother. "Gina, you'd better keep in mind how clever they both are to always outwit us," Tessa laughed.

"Ma, I love you more than anything in the world," Rocco said, as he walked over to the couch to give Tessa a big hug.

Rocco's chopper was parked in the driveway, which was why my car had been out front. I remembered the drill. Bikes have priority for garage and prime driveway space.

Tessa said, "Why don't you and Gina go for a putt while Ma and I reminisce about our traditional upbringings, functional fathers and wonderful childhoods."

About 55 years earlier, an incident happened at a resort where my father recuperated from a near-fatal heart attack. He was an old-school Italian man of average height and build who had hair on every inch of his exposed body other than the palms of his hands and on his head. Because of his deep gravely voice, and especially because of those cold gray eyes, most people didn't dare call him baldy. But the fact is he was a hardworking family man who existed to care for his wife and two children. Rocco reminded me of his grandfather, minus the bald head. Even Gina was like him in some ways. Neither had ever met him.

But that ugly memory began to rear its ugly head for the nth time in my life. It was of a man named Homer who was smeared with bluish, faded tattoos. He reeked of stale body odor and whiskey-fume breath. That day, as my father watched from his high-perched stand while swimmers played in a manmade lake, something bad happened. Homer was a filthy, gnarled-looking man who tended the riding stables and ran a makeshift zoo. His face was covered with white stubble. Thin gray hair matted against a greasy forehead under a straw cowboy hat.

The foul smelling old man had promised to show us a trick and give us a surprise. Thrilled, Enrico and I eagerly agreed. We were in elementary school, back when most surprises were still good. Homer snatched away a prize bullfrog I just caught in a huge pond adjacent to the swimming lake where my father kept a vigilant watch over weekend swimmers. He dropped our croaker into a Cottonmouth's tank and then laughed at us with stank breath from cheap booze and rotted teeth. When we tried to protest, Homer committed the vilest act we had even seen. It was a day we learned about unspeakable acts. Some 55 years later, I still find myself hating that man and wishing I could hurt him the way he tried to hurt us.

I flinched and forced myself to refocus. *I need to think about family. No… That's just as bad.* Another vile image burned into memory was of Fatso of his dog while it valiantly attempted to complete his last scratch – to make the pain go away. Deep gameness like that little dog showed is what sets a game-bred dog apart from every other breed. But a game dog with no talent had no value to a waste of oxygen like Fatso. That deadgame dog without a name couldn't bite hard enough because his teeth had been broken off from previous outings to please his master. And a broken leg would have required the services of a professional. I winced thinking about that terribly sad day. I despised the memory of Fatso and his sycophant partner as much as I'd ever hated anyone. If it were at all possible, I would kill both of them.

While the old dog's waist was still tucked between Ebb's spindly legs, we heard a snap right before Ebb let go of the little black dog so he could defend himself. One of the old dog's front legs flopped around like it was attached only by skin.

Fatso yelled, "Now look what you went and did! I ought ta kick you up inside yer stinkin' ass, Ebb! Get yer ass up here and take that ol' bastard down ta the bottom of this fuckin' hill. Savvy? Goddamn, this boy's dense!"

The old dog held still, conserving energy till Ebb got him at the bottom. Ebb stood him up and let the little dog make his scratch back to the younger, larger prospect. Fatso pulled a large automatic from a back pocket and chambered a round while the young red dog bucked between his fat front legs, eager to get back into the action.

The *schooling* dog leaped toward his young opponent but fell hard when his leg collapsed beneath him. Regardless, the no-name dog was back up in a second and stumbling up the hill as fast as he could for a dog with a broken leg.

Just before the dogs made contact Fatso smiled brown teeth as he aimed. A bullet smashed though the old dog's trusting loyal muzzle. The little black dog's bottom jaw slammed into the dirt. He pawed at the air as if giving his paw, the last attempt to please his master. Fatso took more careful aim the second time and shot that little toothless warrior with its sad gray muzzle, by then wet purple, through its chest. The little old dog gurgled and seized. His legs stretched and stiffened before the nameless dog sighed. Its small body went limp and sluggishly tumbled back down the hill toward the smiling Ebb.

The great little dog rolled lifelessly back down the same hill that just moments before he had so gamely stumbled up on three legs, to once again try in vain to please his master – his God. Ebb picked up the dead dog by an ear.

When I said, "This ain't right," they broke out in laughter.

Those two *dogmen* both smiled but their eyes said something else. Although Fingers and I were still only in our late teens, we were pretty far from being kids. Still, that blatant disrespect for gameness was one we hadn't expected, even from those degenerates.

Still grinning, Fatso spit a huge stream of tobacco juice and then turned his gun toward us as he exposed a mouthful of crooked, tobacco stained teeth. He walked down the hill while he nodded at me, "Now let's just see how much money ya'll brung with ya in those fancy hippie pockets ya got there, boys. Savvy?" he drawled, as he spit some of the brown juice on the corpse of the nameless dog. Part of the tobacco spittle hung from his chin and dribbled on a worn pair of bibs that looked as old as he was. He wiped his face with the back of the hand that held a 9mm.

When I saw Fingers yank his piece I flicked open my bone handled switchblade and dove at Ebb while he fumbled for a .25 automatic that had been hidden in a front pocket on his bib overalls. We were young and fast. They were drunk and stupid. That day was the first time Fingers and I should have gone to prison for a long stretch.

I blacked out once I saw Fingers shoot. A rush of blackish purple hit my brain.

After the dust settled, Fingers shook his head full of long black hair, tied back with a white hanky around his forehead, and said, "I guess we fucked up big this time."

Like waking from a sound sleep I said, "Huh . . . what?"

"It was shoot or get punked, right Jackie? Now here we are. So now what, *coom*? Talk to me. How should act behind this?"

Things began to piece themselves together. I took off my belt and made a loop with it to use as a leash. "It'd be a shame to let this young red dog starve to death out here in the middle of nowhere. Let's take him with us. He's fucked if we leave him here. It ain't like we're dog thieves or anything."

Fingers chuckled, "Shit... The last fucking thing we gotta worry about right now is *stealing*. Besides, they sure as shit won't be needing dogs where they're going. They can keep that black one at the bottom of the hill." Fingers tucked away his pistol and walked back to the station wagon to put the young red dog into one of our crates. "Fuck this place. Let's split. We need to get back to the Neighborhood where it's safe."

"Hold up a minute, *coom*." I said. These local hicks out here are used to hearing gunfire. Besides, there ain't nobody around for miles. And I highly doubt those two fuck-heads invited any other company, not with the plan they had for us. That means we still got a quick minute to check inside that barn they didn't want us near."

"Who knows, *coom*. He might have bales of weed stashed. Let's do it," Fingers said, as he pulled the gun back out of its makeshift holster.

Ebb had left the barn door unlocked and cracked open. We crept inside to find it empty. Just an old building with a few wooden stalls. Then we heard a thumping noise from inside a stall. I crouched low and reached out to flip up a length of 2" x 4" set across a set of homemade wooden braces, used as a cross-bar lock. Fingers crept up to the stall, gun first, when we heard those thumping sounds get harder and faster, and heavy breathing.

Fingers jumped up, pistol first, and laughed. "HA! Check it out, *coomba*. You'll dig this, Jackie."

We found a scrawny bitch with a gray muzzle curled around one tiny red-nosed pup. It appeared as if she was nursing that thin pup or trying to keep it safe from the chaos outside of that dark wooden horse stall. There was no doghouse or whelping box. She panted and smiled at us as she thumped her tail on filthy plank flooring.

"Look at this shit, *coom*," I said. "Not even a fucking bale of hay for this old bitch and her pup to nest in. But check it out . . . that fat fuck's got bales stacked up to the beams right over there by the door – selfish rotten motherfucker."

"He's not selfish anymore, Jackie. He's got two things from now on: shit and nothing."

"I still can't believe that fat prick killed what was probably the gamest dog he's ever had," I said, as I unlatched the door to the stall. "Then he was gonna shoot us after we drove all the way from C-town to Hickville, West Virginia to buy a dog from that dirty cocksucker! My guess is this pup and that young dog they just rolled were sired by that no-name dog and out of this old bitch right here."

Nothing moved other than her tail. As we got closer we could see scar tissue formed from old bite marks on her front legs and stifles, shoulders, head and muzzle, and leathery-looking ears. Large patches of hair missing exposed sore spots. Fingers waited by the door, watching the driveway. I approached her, reaching out the back of my hand while saying in a soft monotone, "Good girl, old lady. You're a good girl, mama. Nobody's gonna hurt you anymore, girl."

Thumping from her tail got louder, as did her panting. I said, "Look at this shit, Fingers. No water bowl, no food, not bedding, no nothing. Motherfucker! But you're okay now, old lady. It's okay, girl. You're with friends now. Good girl."

Fingers said, "I oughta go outside and put another one in that greedy piece of shit. Meantime, now we got this new situation to deal with. I knew we should've split."

"These dogs would have been dead by tomorrow, *coom*. In fact, they ain't looking too sporty right now. She's all dehydrated and mangy and this pup looks weak as shit."

"Now what, Jackie? Should we dig a hole to hide those two from the buzzards? Those two pieces of shit are stinking up the whole place. I can smell them from here."

A shiny blade was still dripping in my hand when I regained my senses, standing over Ebb's limp body holding a gun and that no-named dog. "Takes too long. Let's drag them in here and cover 'em up with straw and a tarp. They'll make good rat food. I'll take a minute to bury this old toothless dog. He deserves some respect. He never even had a name, so he won't be needing a headstone. I sure wish I could've had the privilege to feed that old boy for his last days. What a cool animal."

"I can make a spot for that young male. But there's no way I can keep three pit-dogs in Collinwood. Should we put her and this pup down?" Fingers asked, holding his gun with a wild look still in his dark eyes.

"Nah, it's cool. We'll give the old bitch to Gus' mom. Her old dog just croaked. I'll name this runt Crazy Gracie. But before we go let's check that root cellar."

Fingers walked down first, gun extended. I followed with my knife drawn and opened. We spotted a metal trunk set on a wooden base propped up on top of a small concrete slab. Fingers laughed, "What the fuck is shit all about, the Holy Grail?"

"This guy got a rep of being a dogman, only because of that deadgame little dog he had. Real dogmen don't disrespect gameness like he did. I got a feeling. Let's check this place out."

When Fingers opened the chest I said, "Well I'll be double-dogged… Check out this…"

Fingers grinned, "Looks like we just became business partners, *coom*."

CH IX: Tyrants & Sycophants

July 29TH, 2013 – The Stakeout & last day: My wife still had the face of a young pretty girl, especially when she was concerned. She shook her long blonde hair out after she released it from the confines of a large silver clasp. Then she looked deeply into my eyes and asked in a sweet gentle voice, "Are you you're okay, bro? You can tell me anything."

"Yes, my friend. I'm fine. Just thinking about things."

"About what, Jackie? All or nothing, you know the deal. Deception by omission is still a lie, right, bro? Come on, buddy, let's have it. Are you depressed, angry or scared?"

"I don't know. It's just such a quick ride. I'll never again answer the phone to my father's voice. I haven't shed one wet tear since I was a small boy – not even at his funeral. It all seemed so contrived, like following some script, even though I felt a hole through my soul. As you know, he was the only person I respected and trusted on this entire rotting planet. He was 100% loyal. Then to know that one day we and our kids won't be able to spend not even one more second together. Just simple things like soaking up the sights, sounds and smells of nature together, to taste a meal, or share a movie, or for us to feel shared passions just once more. I can't handle the thought of losing any of you."

Tessa closed her book and padded barefoot over to my chair, stooped down and put a delicate arm around my shoulders. Her long hair wisped against my face, lightly scented with sandalwood. She pulled me against her small yet still firm breasts and kissed my forehead. "Thank you, Jackie. But now I'm going to ask that we not talk about this morbid stuff in front of the kids. It's making me sad and it's not good for you. Plus it would probably frighten Gina and disturb Rocco very much."

"Sure. Just let me tell you this while we're alone: In the last year of my marriage to Butter, if I would've said these things she would have yawned, ignored me or laughed. As pretty as Butter was, she was a hard woman, but not tough like you are."

"Okay, bro, I get it. Can we just shift gears now? Please?"

"She was solid in her own way and could handle herself well, but she has a cruel streak like a hitman. That meanness is what she tries to cover with religion and her smile. She makes people feel important and interesting so she can work them. With Gina's gene pool on both sides, after her ex cheated on her while they were engaged I was almost surprised didn't hurt him. I hope she and Rocco will keep each other out of trouble."

"Why are you talking like this, Jackie? I feel like you're slipping away from me, bro," my pretty wife said, wearing her troubled expression. "Do you see something?"

"I've been thinking about reputations. Our legacy can be making brave choices at correct moments, or curring out. But we all do exactly what we want to do, right up until we can't, or no longer care to. And then we simply do something else, sometimes even begrudgingly, even when it feels like something we'd rather not do – yet we do it anyway. And I know that you know why. But yeah, to answer your question, I do feel something."

July 29TH, 2013 – The Stakeout & last day: Across the road from our home Vinny said, "Easy does it, Spuds. You're getting powdered sugar all over these nice seats like 90 in here," complained Skinny Vinny, as he brushed invisible crumbs off his *glen plaid* blazer and into a small boney hand held facing up – cupped against his emaciated-looking frame. "Try to be a little more careful, okay *coomba*? This is a brand new ride. Show a little class. By the way, is this thing an '012 or a 2013?"

"Why do you give a fuck?" the fat man spat crumbs. "It's a hot car, for Christ's sake! Anyways, tone it down. When we're on stakeout you gotta learn to relax like me," Fat Spuds said, with the seat pushed all the way back and his stomach almost touching the dashboard. "I ain't a Ford Taurus kind of guy," he sniggered while he brushed the tips of short stubby fingers together. "This piece a garbage ain't my style," Spuds reminded Vinny, as he folded those pudgy hands over his huge gut. "I go more for a luxury sedan. I'm all about the class move, Vin."

"Oh really? Luxury sedan, huh? You don't even own a fucking car, Spuds. Which is why I'm stuck behind the goddamn wheel of this chunk a shit," Vinny said, jerking his thin head around to his grotesque partner. Skinny Vinny always gave the impression of having just done too much crank, with rapid speech patterns and jerky movements. "If you really don't like what we drive, maybe you should just take your complaints to Cagootz. I'm just sayin'. Who knows? The boss might be real interested to hear your input," Vinny said, as he rolled his dark eyes and rotated his head on a pencil neck thinner than one of Spuds' forearms. "Go ahead. Give it a shot."

"Try to relax for half a minute. You're new at this game, Vin. The trick on a stake-out is we make ourselves settle in. You gotta learn to adjust, *coomba*. Make yourself at home. And as far as a car thing goes: I got a Caddy at home in the lot. I just ain't got a license at the moment. But I ain't worried. Fuck-it. Just follow my lead here, Vin. You need to learn to unwind, like me."

"Are you for real? I'm fine. Look at me," Vinny shrieked, with a panicked expression. "I just don't need all this sugar all over my new pants. These are *sharkskin!* You know how I am about clothes," Vinny said, as he made sure his black shirt collar was neatly folded over the lapels of his loud sports jacket. "I always look sharp – just in case," said the stringy-haired man with a pale complexion. "You never know when you're gonna run into some horny bimbo, right? Plus, I dress for success. I don't plan on running errands forever, *coomba*. I'm making moves like 90."

"Look at you!" Spuds said, as he twiddled stubby thumbs on his stomach and smiled. "You're too amped out. Focus, Vin. This ain't got nothing to do with the boss. We're our own bosses out here. Now can I finish my story, or what?" asked Fat Spuds as he reached for his next jelly donut. "So like I was trying to say before you started whining like a little broad over powder sugar: I had this Rican kid shoved into my cell down at County. So here's me sitting on the shitter, minding my own business scratching my nuts and reading a Playboy when this *spic* crackhead decides to be a dickhead. Here's him: 'Listen up, fat man. I takin' this bunk, so move your shit off my bed.' Spuds paused to stuff the remainder into his mouth and then licked purple jelly off his fingers.

A siren grew louder. Both removed pistols from beneath their jackets, ones that had been wedged between their belts and right hips, and dropped them on the floor. Then with the heels of their shiny black shoes they scooted them under the front seat of that ordinary-looking gray car. To a passer-by, Spuds and Vinny, could pass for detectives.

"So which county we talking here, Spuds? Cuyahoga?"

"Of course, Cuyahoga County. What the fuck? We do live in Cleveland, right? You remember that much, huh Vin?" Spuds asked, as he combed his hair for the nth time. "Collinwood is still in Cleveland last time I checked." Spuds chuckled. The dark man smoothed the sides of greased-back black hair with fat palms. His gray suit jacket was large enough for Vinny to use for a blanket.

"Scuse me? Like we only commit crimes in Cleveland? Is that what you're saying? Are you fucking serious, or what?"

Skinny Vinny yanked at his collar. "Let's get the facts straight, Spuds. 'Cause we sure as fuck ain't in Cleveland right now."

"I guess not. But we ain't actually doing any criminal shit right at the moment. We're just on stake-out. Remember, Vin?"

"*Remember?* What is it with you . . . keep asking about my memory lately? You're the one with the fucked-up memory. You start out like 90, telling one of those never-ending stories of yours, and then just stop in the middle like you forgot all about it. So what's all that about, Spuds? Are you demented now, or what? I think all that grape jelly and powdered sugar is clogging your brain," Vinny warned, as he jerked the lapels of his cheap-looking jacket. "It's a disease. I saw it on a TV show."

"Suck-off, Vinny. I don't interrupt your stories! Show some couth for once, you fucking degenerate," Spuds said, pointing his short black comb at Vinny. "So anyways, I says to this scrawny *Spica-Rican* fuck with his jailhouse coveralls unbuttoned to show off his boney chest, 'Move *my* stuff? I got a better idea. How about I pack your shit with 10 inches of Italian sausage, you greasy little cocksucker?' Spuds enormous belly jiggled while he laughed. "Ah yeah . . . lots a good times down at the county. You know why I can say this? It's because I had to learn to adjust, to accept shit and make myself at home no matter where I'm at. Like for example being trapped in this tiny car, parked in these bug infested woods, with some twitchy little fuck nerking out next to me about nothing."

Skinny Vinny made a loud fake yawn while drumming thin fingers of both frail-looking hands on the steering wheel of a late model car they had recently stolen.

With a mouthful of deep-fried flour and pasty sugar Spuds continued, "So this little punk steps up, right? Like he's gonna make a play. So I stand up with my pants still around my ankles. Meantime, I think he was looking at the ol' *braciole* before I got it coiled up and stuffed back into my drawers. Now I'm lookin' down at him and says, 'Go ahead. Make a move, you stupid little fuck. I'll suck your eyes right outta your pinhead and swallow 'em whole. Now what, cocksucker? How you wanna make me act?' So he backs up and throws his hands up like we're in a boxing match. Meantime, he's got these little girl fists almost as small as yours, Vin. Can you believe this asshole, or what?"

"No, Spuds. I can't believe *this* fucking asshole, either!" Vinny answered, as he pointed a boney finger and stared a warning into the laugh-lined eyes of his obese partner. "Are you finally done with this goddamn, boring-ass story?"

"Wait. This part gets good. So anyway, this skinny little prick says, 'Touch me and you get your own drawer at the morgue, you fat tub a shit!' You should'a seen him when I—" Then Spuds began laughing so hard he almost choked to death on a mouthful of stale donut from a square of waxed paper on the floor. Wet crumbs stuck to the dashboard.

"Spuds. Do yourself one fucking favor and brush that garbage off your shirt. You look uncouth, *coom*," Vinny noted, while Spuds hacked up more pastry crumbs.

Still coughing, Spuds laughed, "You should a seen that douche when I grabbed a hold of my giant cock. You seen my cock before, right Vin? Anyways, I told that slimy fuck I'd make him my bitch so he could have my shit-baby!" Spuds held a hand over his mouth to muffle the laughter and the coughing.

"Hold up," said Vinny, holding up a thin index finger. "You know how I am. I notice things. I don't mind that every time you talk about sucking and fucking it's never the nice way. Instead, it's always nine-fucking-zero. But whatever… It's the other part that bothers me. I mean, why is it when you're talking about other guys it's: 'I'll suck this out, and he can suck me, and I'll fuck him up the ass?' What's up with all that?"

Spuds glared, wearing a gleam of perspiration.

"I'm just askin' out of friendship, *coomba*. Right?"

Spuds brushed his fat palms against one another. Crumbs fell next to where Skinny Vinny sat. "Jokes are one thing, Vin. I'm all about laughing as much as the next guy. And you know this. But be careful you don't cross a line here, Vinny. Because one thing I don't go for is remarks about me being a *finocchio*. I swear to Buddha, just back the fuck off with the fag jokes. *Capiche?*"

"Whoa, wait awhile, *coom*. I never mentioned fags!"

"No, Vin, you fucking hold up a minute!"

"Wait! I just saw a light go off. I think he's coming out."

Spuds' glare turned into a look of concern. The driveway they had stationed themselves on for the past two days was down the road from Jack's house. Their hot Taurus parked on what had at one time been a daily access road for tanker trucks and utility vehicles driven by weathered men who serviced a multitude of gas and oil wells scattered across Ashtabula County in Northeastern corner of Ohio. The farm sat adjacent to borders of PA and Lake Erie. Spuds and Vinny were tucked far back enough to not be noticed but still had somewhat of a view of the house.

"You outta your mind?" Spuds whispered to his partner, as he removed two sticks of Dentine from an inside suit jacket pocket and stuffed them into his mouth with short, stubby fingers. "It ain't even all the way dark yet. How could you see a light go off from back here?" he asked, while still staring at the front yard of Jackie's farmhouse. "And don't ever forget what I said about the *finocchio* jokes. Under-fucking-stand me, Vinny?"

"Easy, Spuds. I was just fucking around. Sorry. I didn't realize you were so sensitive in that area. I mean, a macho guy like you has no worries in that department. Right, *coom*? I didn't mean nothing by it, okay? But let's pay close attention. This Jackie guy's old now, but they say he's clever and can still be a sick bastard."

"Fuck me!" Spuds whispered. "Did you see that red car?"

"Who would drive a Hummer like 90 out here in the middle of *Stickville, Nowheresville*? Did you make the driver?"

"That big-ass red SUV was hauling balls. All I saw was she had wild red hair."

"Are you fucking kidding me? That lunatic cunt, Maureen Kelly, is out joy-riding past Jackie's crib like nine-fucking-zero while we're casing the place? Crazy bitch... What's she doing out here? She's gonna blow the whole thing for us, Spuds!"

"We're an hour from nowhere. If that happens, Vin, Cagootz is gonna be up *our* ass! Maybe we should follow her and take care of the problem. Know what I mean?"

"Are you nuts? What makes you so sure Fingers knows about all this? Or could Cagootz maybe be doing a little freelance moves on the side, and using us like throwaways? *Capiche*?"

"No way, Vin. Cagootz don't take a dump without asking Fingers how many turds in each pile. And Big Louie does everything like the boss. Believe me, I know what I'm talking about here," Fat Spuds assured Skinny Vinny in a hushed tone as he twirled the toothpick with his tongue yet kept it away from the two sticks of gum. Then he snuck another peak inside the large cardboard box, like somehow its contents might have miraculously changed. But Spuds only found sheets of wax paper and crumbs. "Why you asking about all this, *coom*? Straight business. What's on your mind?"

"Well, okay, a few things: First of all: Why do these guys have a world-class hard-on for this Jackie asshole? He's a fucking nobody! Besides that, everybody knows Jackie's wife is a cousin to Fingers. I mean . . . what if she gets hurt when we trigger this thing? Or what if her psycho kid gets in the car with Jackie?

Rocco's a cousin to Fingers, too. Then what?"

"Then we improvise, Vin. No problem. The bomb's already in place, right? So if Tessa's in the car with him, or their kid's in there, we follow and wait for the right time. See, this is the kind of shit I was tryin' to explain. Once you get experience with this you learn to adapt. *Capiche?* Okay, now that problem's solved. What's the other thing?"

"Well . . . now just hear me out for half a second. Okay Spuds? But just for the fuck of it, let's just look at a *What if* situation while we're sitting here, okay?"

"Vin, you're making me a little nuts here with all your games. Just say whatever the fuck it is you gotta say," Spuds said, while combing back his greasy black hair.

Vinny began twitching and tugging at his shirt collar, the whole time rolling his head around in circles on his pencil neck. "Let me collect my thoughts."

"We ain't got that much time, Vinny. Just spill it!"

"Okay. Let's just say – and I mean just for shits and giggles, okay – that this car bombing is the beginning a power move? Because that's how these things happen."

"*Power move?* Like how?"

"Okay. Let's just pretend for a hot second that Cagootz is making a move like 90 against Fingers and using this fuck, Jackie, as a diversion to throw everyone off track."

"Vin, do me one simple favor. Don't start in with your paranoid bullshit. You shouldn't even be thinking about this – let alone saying it out loud. This is the type of talk gets guys blown away. I been around too long to bring up shit like this. But okay, just for shits and giggles, what's your goofy take on this?"

"Well, it just got me to thinking. Not that I think our guys would pull any lowlife shit like this, right? But just *what if* Cagootz and Big Louie are using us like sacrificial lambs? Let's say we do this job. Now what? Boom – nine-zero. Here's us thinking maybe we'll score points and move up in the organization. But then Cagootz has Big Louie take both of us for the morbid drive."

"You're out of your mind, Vin. I told you before, you need to relax." Spuds lifted the donut box off the seat and tossed it behind him. It bounced off the backseat and its contents of sugar and crumbs tumbled onto the floor. "I know things like this can happen. But just for the sake of conversation, why would Cagootz wanna take us out when we're the ones he trusts to do him a big favor? It don't fit."

"Not that I think any of *our* people would actually pull any underhanded shit like this. Okay, Spuds? Let's get that straight right up front. But if Jackie disappears . . . then whether Fingers was or wasn't on board the logical move is we vanish. No witnesses, no threats. Nine-fucking-zero, *coom*. Too dangerous any other way. You been around. You seen shit like this before."

Spuds laced chubby fingers together, hands resting on his ample paunch, as he chewed his gum and thought about what Vinny proposed. He shook his head and said, "Nope, I don't buy it. Louie is loyal as a Pit-bull to Cagootz. And Cagootz knows better than to cross Fingers. Besides, this Jackie must have done some real bad shit recently to get the attention of the big guys. Or, he has something on them from the old days and now for some reason they're spooked. And since Fingers ain't scared of Jesus Fucking Christ himself, that ain't even a good possibility. Besides, all those guys are closer than brothers. No fucking way. So let's change the subject."

"Humor me for one more second, okay Spuds? Because we don't get any do-overs with shit like this."

"What now?" Spuds asked, irritated. "What else?"

"Okay. where's Cagootz and Louie from? Tell me that."

"Little Italy. You know that, you fucking scrawny prick."

"Now, remind me. Where's Fingers and Nino from? Just tell me real quick like but pretend like I don't already know."

"What I do know is you're gettin' on my nerves. They're from fucking Collinwood! Why you asking all this stupid shit?"

"Just think about it awhile. Uno was from Collinwood. He got moved up to Underboss. But that's been a position held by Little Italy guys since before Scalici. So then who does Uno move up with him? All the Young Turks from Collinwood, that's who. Pazzo and Auggie, and Jackie's ex-*coombas*, Fingers, Benny and Nino and a few other Collinwood guys. Uno made Auggie his main enforcer – another Collinwood guy. When Uno got whacked while he was inside who moved past Cagootz to take over? Fingers, that's who. Meanwhile, Cagootz and Big Louie are stuck running numbers and taking bets from The Inn like they're somebody's flunky. Because Fingers ain't got a son, all the sudden Nino's kid's runnin' around balls-out like 90, ready to step into the Family business. Cagootz and Louie are stuck selling draft beer like somebody's bitch, carrying packages and messages like hang-arounds, instead of being treated like the old-school *made-men* they are. Follow me?"

"Say what the fuck you mean for once," Spuds growled.

"Okay. What I mean is this: let's look at bottom lines, *coom*. Because once the shit hits the fan, it really don't matter why it happened. What matters is what *did* happen."

"Hey, Vin, I ain't stupid. Just fucking say what's on your mind!" Spuds almost shouted and almost choked on his toothpick. Instead he spit it out his window.

"Okay. Here goes: If Tessa or her kid get hurt in any way, we're dead. If Fingers wasn't the one to give the nod for this move against Jackie, who by the way is still close with Pazzo, we're history if he finds out. But even if Fingers doesn't find out who blew up his cousin's car, then Cagootz gets all paranoid and thinks we might leak it. Guess what? We get brand new toe tags. Even if Fingers really is a part of this he can't take the chance of anything getting back to Tessa's uncle. And Pazzo was Auggie's mentor. So guess what happens to us? Same ending like always. Like fucking 90. Boom! If Auggie finds out we hurt Pazzo's niece we're dead men. We're disposable."

"So according to your logic, Vin, no matter which way we slice it we're gonna get waxed. If what you're saying is true, then the best thing that could happen is if Cagootz disappears. I hope you ain't actually planning something like that. Are you?"

"Never that, Spuds. I'm all about loyalty. And you know this. All's I'm saying is for right now, we're still pretty much strangers to the Cleveland Family. These guys are *made*. We're drop-shots to them. They been together since they were kids. You're a Collinwood guy, but you ain't related to anybody in the outfit. Then here's me. I've been in the loop a hot minute, and I'm from fucking *Youngstown*. I might as well be from Mars to these guys. And don't forget: you're the one vouched for me. If things go sour we're both fucked. Family is everything to those guys, and you and me ain't Family just yet. Not for anything, *coomba*, but Cagootz and Big Louie can be real snakes. So that's it. Just between us, *coom*, can you see the logic behind this?"

"Whoa, let's freeze this bullshit!" said Fat Spuds, as he reached down for his .45 automatic that had been under the seat but was again hidden by his sharkskin suit coat.

A vehicle backed into the access drive in front of their Taurus. It was a red F-150 with a bumper sticker that read, "Real Men Love Jesus." Both doors opened. Two almost identically dressed, beardless men with ruddy complexions exited the truck.

"I smell rotten fish, *coom*. This is a set-up," Vinny whispered, as he yanked a .357 automatic from beneath his plaid sports jacket. "Which one you want, Spuds? I'm clockin' this fat fucker with the camo jacket and orange cap."

Spuds chambered his gun, released the safety and slid it under a napkin: "They both got Jungle Larry jackets and goofy orange hats like big game hunters. Keep quiet, Vin, and your eye on the guy wearing that little kid's hat. I got this other asshole covered. But no shooting yet, *coom*. You'll blow our whole deal if you do. Follow my lead. Don't shoot unless I do. I'm experienced. And you know this. I'll do the talking."

"What? They both got little kid hats," Vinny shrieked.

The man with the beaked cap met the other with a stocking cap behind their battered pick-up and together walked over to the passenger side of the gray Taurus. Both men carried 12-gauge shotguns, with bulges between bottom lips and chins.

Vinny chambered a round. He held the gun between his seat and the driver's door.

"Just shut-up, Vin, and pretend like you ain't scared." Spuds rolled down the window and asked, "Hey, ha you doin'? Youse kids lost or something?"

The man with the stocking cap spit brown slime: "Nah, we ain't lost, and we ain't kids. We was just wonderin' if you fella's was huntin' out here. This here is private property, son."

"No," answered Vinny, as he ducked his head to see the men. "We don't hunt. In fact, we're vegetarians. We just pulled over real quick to take a leak and check the GPS on my cell. But it's all dialed in now. Can you believe it? We thought we were in Pennsylvania! Yeah, we're going over to PA to see relatives. Thanks for asking."

The man with the billed cap spit: "Well, alrighty then."

Spuds shot his partner a look for him to keep quiet but Vinny continued, "Yeah, thanks for checking, guys. But youse might want to watch how you approach a man. It don't look right comin' at a man carrying rifles and shit. Follow me?"

The mustached man with the stocking cap bent down to get a good look at Vinny: "What's that you said there, bud?"

Spuds chucked and said, "Don't worry about him. He's never seen real guns before. You know . . . city-boy, first time out in the country. But if you don't mind, you got us blocked. I wouldn't want city-boy here to scratch up his shiny new car."

"You sayin' you ain't a city-boy? That it, big-guy?" The man smiled a big brown grin at his friend and shook his head.

Spuds began to sweat. Veins bulged on his temples. Color rose in his face. He started to hyperventilate.

Vinny said, "We're saying thanks, but we gotta go."

The man with the billed cap said, "No harm done, I reckon. We'll be on our way then," he nodded to his friend.

The man who had ducked down to look at Vinny added, "Be careful, son. There's bears out here of an evening." At that, they both laughed and got back in the old Ford truck. They blocked them for what seemed like hours, but was only a few minutes. As they pulled near the road the driver gunned it and kicked up gravel at the new Taurus, then roared away down the one-lane street.

"Dirty rotten motherless fucks," Spuds growled, as he slid his loaded gun into the glove compartment. "And you! I told you to let me handle it! You almost made me kill our way outta this!"

"Hey, I didn't say nothin' wrong! You were the one with all the smart-ass comments, Spuds. Besides, I told you we should've shot those hillbilly cocksuckers. And did he say *bears*? Is that really what he said? I'll show those stupid fucks what a bear looks like," Skinny Vinny said, "when they dig their graves with *bare* hands."

Spuds chewed two more pieces of gum: "Don't go lettin' your mouth get you in a jam that you're ass can't bail you out of. You're slimmed-hipped, Vin. Don't forget that."

"You think 1976 got ugly? If anything goes sour with this plan bodies are gonna pile up like in a Hitler death camp. It's not just us and those Five Points micks. These bikers are in the mix, too. And now those jungle bunnies are making big moves. Believe me, 1976 is gonna look like a poker game compared to if—"

"Okay, this is it, you stupid cocksucker!" Spuds hissed an angry whisper, as he pulled his piece out of the glove box.

"What did I say wrong? I'm agreeing with you, Spuds!"

"Can you just shut the fuck up for one minute, Vin?"

"You know what? I'm sick and tired a the way you been talkin' to me! I got a right to my opinions. I don't hear you makin' too much sense."

"Quiet! I ain't talking about that paranoid shit of yours. Look! While we're gossiping like two old hens, Tessa's already standing outside. She's right there! I can barely see the car from here, let alone who's in it! Is that her kid or her ol' man?"

Vinny squinted his weasel eyes as he said, "Whoa! Check it out. I don't think that's Tessa. I think it's that *shine broad*. Look closer, *coom*. See her?"

"What *shine broad*? Are you for real, Vin? It's dark out. How the fuck are you supposed to make a spook in the dark, even if she's a high-yellow spook?"

"No, really, Spuds. I think it's that what's-her-name. Crisco or Mayo? What the fuck do they call that fine-ass *moolie* chick Jackie used to bang? Hey! Maybe that old bastard's pullin' a *sangwitch* with both of his ol' ladies? Now that would be one sweet move, like fucking 90!"

"You mean Butter? She's his ex-wife, you fuckin' blind psycho. You need to get real, man. There's no way, Vin. First of all, that colored broad hates Jackie. Second: no way Tessa's gonna go for any three-way action. Period!"

"What? You think just because she's Fingers' cousin she wouldn't go down on some new carpet? Tessa's just like the rest of 'em. They're all dyke sluts. Believe me, Spuds. I know what I'm talking about when it comes to these whores," Vinny said, as he pulled at his lapels and swiveled his head around in circles.

Spuds chuckled as he smoothed out the sides of his hair: "When you're right you're right, Vin. But the truth is, you think that way because you ain't never been with anything except bitches you gotta pay to fuck. I got experience. But keep quiet now. Take this remote and go shimmy your slim hips over to the tree line to get a better look. Hurry up! If Jackie pulls away, just press the button and Boom! Then we can go home."

"Fuck all that, Spuds! I'm the driver! You press it."

"You fucking idiot. You think you're gonna be any less guilty if I press the button while you drive me here to waste this nutty bastard? Wake up, Vin. Now get your dead ass out there."

"Hey, I'm the one puttin' logic out here like 90! You the one that's the pro adapter, remember Spuds?"

"You're like a natural, Vin.. And I mean it. I'm gonna let the boss know you're A-1 for a new guy on a stake-out."

"You're the one has all the experience with stakeouts and shit. Am I right, Spuds? I'd feel better if you did it, *coomba*. I can watch a pro. I'm way too jittery. Go ahead. I'll even start the car."

"Leave the car off, you fucking dummy! We ain't got time to argue. Jackie's car's already wired-up to the gills, and we've been on stand-by for two goddamn days! If we don't finish this there ain't gonna be any *maybes* or *what ifs*. If we show up at The

Inn smiling like 90, and there's nothing about an explosion in the Plain Dealer, we're dead meat for sure. That's a fact, not a gamble. But I'm big-boned, *coom*. I can't crawl around out there. You're wiry like a natural athlete. You can handle this, *coomba*. Now hurry up before the car pulls away. Then we won't even know who's driving or who's in it. Get going! Take your dead ass out there before we gotta go tell Cagootz you decided not to follow orders from a senior member. Go on! Move it!"

It appeared as though people outside had been arguing. They could hear a woman's voice echo off the trees but couldn't make out her words, diffused by country sounds of dusk. "There he is! Jackie's near the car. He's alone. Tessa's still up by the house. Okay, now he's in the car! Let's go! Get moving, Vin!"

Skinny Vinny reluctantly exited the stolen car, his pistol in one hand and a remote detonating device in the other. He duck-walked behind wild brush and saplings, his knees carefully bent so as not to dirty his *sharkskin* pants or flashy sports coat.

"Here goes," Vinny whispered. "The moment of truth."

Vinny looked back at the Taurus, just in case there had been a last minute change of plans. He waved, hoping Spuds would wave him back in, like it had all been a secret *wise guy* test just to see if he'd really go through with it. Skinny Vinny smiled bravely at his fat partner to show he was willing to make his bones for the Cleveland Family. Instead of Spuds calling him back inside the car so they could share a funny story with all the guys back at The Inn, he nodded his head and gave Vinny a thumbs-up signal. Then Spuds folded fat arms on top of his huge stomach and waited.

This is it… I'm totally fucked, Skinny Vinny thought. *We're both dead and there's no way out.* He squeezed his eyelids tightly closed and held his breath while he slowly counted to ten. He inhaled that fresh country air so he could recite an Our Father out loud as he felt for the button on the remote, eyes still sealed. Vinny braced himself for a reaction that would forever change the quality of life for everyone involved. *Okay! Nine-motherfucking-zero! Here we go…*

CH X: Choices & Chances

About 55 years before the day I woke in pain beneath someone's house, I thought back to events from early childhood as a product of the early baby-boomer generation. After a near-fatal heart attack while living in inner-city Cleveland, my father took time off from micrometers and tolerances as a machinist for a recuperation job at a resort. It was owned by Uno's boss. Every morning we rode there in Dad's tank-like automobile with its thick cloth seats.

    Once in awhile he let me bring my friend, Enrico Colombo who was a big, muscular boy. Rico looked older than our 10 years. His hair was a cap of black ringlets. He was a natural athlete with dark skin and white teeth. With deft hands, we snatched-up horseflies off shiny split-rail fencing and bounced them off the long gravel drive. Although still young, we swam laps across a dug lake the size of a football field. A shaded pier stretched well into the swimming lake. It supported my dad's elevated stand which also served as a place to find darting salamanders hiding from a glaring sun.

    Besides that huge man-made lake, two ponds adjacent to it were home to snappers the size of garbage can lids and snakes as thick as a man's arm. There were heavy bullfrogs squatted on mud banks of algae-laced ponds that offered sanctuary to a conglomerate of insects, such as skittering water spiders and majestic dragon flies. My father had warned me about poisonous water snakes in there.

    I also remembered the stink of some old bastard smeared with bluish, faded tattoos, reeking of body odor and whiskey. Homer was a filthy, gnarled-looking man who tended the riding stables and ran a makeshift zoo at the resort where my father worked as a lifeguard for that one season. Homer's face was covered with white stubble. His thin gray hair matted against a greasy forehead. That disgusting old man had promised to show the Colombo brothers and me a "good trick," and to give us a "nice surprise." Enrico and his little brother agreed. Mikey said, "I wanna see that monkey!"

    The memory of that day caused me to flinch. I tried to think about other things. *I need to relax. Fuck all this sad shit. I'll think about family times. No! Fuck that, too. That's just as hard. I know! I'll clear my mind and think about relaxing my sore muscles.*

But as I drifted off to a dreamy place between consciousness and sleep I was drawn back to a familiar ugly scene from pre-teen years. The mini-zoo showcased an ocelot, a parrot and a tethered, neurotic monkey that pretended to ignore slithering creatures in glass enclosures. A crippled zoo keeper with homemade tattoos more like smears of axle grease hobbled over and said, "Go catch me the biggest bull in that ol' pond, yonder. I promise a nice surprise if ya bring back a trophy croaker. Go on ahead now; times a wastin' here, boys. Yer lil' brother can stay back and help with them rabbit cages yonder. I might could leave 'im touch one fer a spell ifin he's good."

So we left Little Mikey Colombo at that zoo to marvel at wildlife. Two years younger, a smaller clone to Enrico, Mikey was fascinated by the large French Lops. Rico and I bolted for the ponds. In record time we returned with a two-fisted bullfrog, the biggest I'd ever seen. Our pride faded when we noticed Little Mikey was crying.

Smiling a near toothless grin Homer said, "Don't mind that little one. I was a gonna let 'im touch a harmless snake and he went an got all scared like a darned little girl. Okay now a speakin' a snakes, you boys watch a spell." He shoved between us and snatched that prize bullfrog away that I had just caught in a pond adjacent to the swimming lake. The foul smelling old man took our croaker and dropped it in a snake tank. He said, "This here's a Water Moccasin," laughing putrid breath from cheap booze and rotted stubs for teeth. Shocked, I asked why he would do such a thing. He explained, "It's for this here frog to keep good company with this ol' snake. They's two of a kind, they is. Now they can be friends." When we asked him for our surprise he assured us, "Don't fret, boys. I done promised, ain't I? You boys is gonna be real surprised. You betcha you is!"

The snake glided effortlessly to the frog, slithering around it. Our frog froze like a lawn statue. Then the snake turned and glided away. That old man said, "See here, this ol' snake's tryin' to make friends, but that frog's darned rude, he is. What kind'a frog you boys brung ta me? This frog ain't no damn good!"

Then the snake struck so fast our bullfrog didn't have time to move. Its head planted firmly in the serpent's mouth; blindly it kicked further into death. The snake unhinged its jaws and pulled more of the frog inside, a little at a time – slow torture. I wanted to smash the tank to save him, but it was too late.

I screamed, "You old bastard! I should kick your gimpy leg." Then a new terror struck: *Dad will be super mad if he finds out I talked like this to an adult!* "Sorry for cursing at you, mister. But you shouldn't have done that to our frog."

The stink old man bared his rotted teeth and said, "Foller me in that horse barn over yonder. I gotcha a big surprise fer the three a ya'll boys yonder you won't never ferget."

Once inside the barn he smiled those putrid teeth at us. When he reached out for Little Mikey, Enrico shoved that crooked old guy in his chest and dumped him on hard-packed ground. I kicked dirt in his grinning face when Mikey began to cry: "He made me look at his thingy," Mikey told us. "He told me to touch it."

The old pervert squinted, dirt stuck to his sweaty face, "Just a little closer, boys. I got ya a nice surprise ya'll can play with. Lookie here at this ol' friendly snake." Homer unzipped his pants and with a filthy hand pulled out a shriveled, uncircumcised penis.

Enrico said, "We can kick him real good and hard now, Jackie. He won't tell. He knows Jack will kill him. I know for sure my dad will beat him to death. You're scared now, aren't you? You know better than to mess with Jackie's dad, you stinky fucker!"

Homer grabbed my arm and yanked me next to him. He was deceivingly quick, almost as fast as that venomous serpent still swallowing our frog. He yelled, "You boys shouldn't be swearing at elders!" He had me by the arm, pushing my hand towards his penis. "Touch this here lil' snake and I won't tell yer dad you been a swearin' and bein' mean ta elders." By that time his shriveled penis was swelling into an erection.

When Rico kicked the filthy old man in his good leg, Homer loosened his grip on me. I squirmed away, so he grabbed Mikey's leg. I booted him in the arm he had himself propped up with. He fell. I stood close to my friends. Laying flat on his back, the old man laughed even louder. "You boys is wild animals, you is. I got ya a nice cage fer ya'll. I'll pet ya real nice of a day and feed ya this here prize in my hand. This here's a good ol' snakey. See 'im? He don't bite. I'll take good care a ya'll with this ol' snakey. You can pet 'im real good. Come-on, now." Then with a frenzied expression the old man began to masturbate in quick jerks. His eyes rolled back.

Hyperventilating and wild-eyed, Enrico yelled, "You're in trouble, fucker. And I mean it! Let's go tell your dad, Jackie!"

The three of us ran away as quick as short legs could carry small boys. Little Mikey Colombo said, panting, "That man took my pants down and was touching my pee-pee. He stopped when you brung the frog. Let's get your dad, Jackie. We *gotta* tell."

My breathing returned to normal as soon as we resumed a walking pace. Instead of still feeling paralyzed with terror, I answered, "Hold-on. We can't ever do that. My dad really *will* kill him if he hears about this, and so would yours. That's means they'll go away to jail and we'll never see our dads again."

"What should we do then?" asked an out of breath Enrico. "We gotta do something!"

"Let's cool off in the lake. Come-on, I'll race youse."

We turned from that horrific experience, running to relieve ourselves of fear and to seek refuge. We ran giggling and snorting pig sounds till we ran ourselves breathless. We had heard about such things in the schoolyard but had never been personally exposed to anything remotely similar. Although stunned, we were too small and afraid to punish that perverted old man in a way so he would never again try to molest a child. Even though we still were devout Catholics at the time, we neither forgot what he did nor forgave him. We simply filed that ugly ordeal away as valuable experience. And we noticed a trend as we kept experiencing. A pattern showed itself. The smarter we got, the more confident we became and the stronger we grew.

But that day, running away from that makeshift zoo to the swimming lake where my father stood guard, we stopped to catch our wind long enough to soak up another experience. A young man from the Neighborhood walked, not swam, neck deep to the middle of that murky pond. His nickname was *Pazzo* (Pot-so), a word that means "crazy" in Italian. Pazzo calmly maneuvered on its silky, sucking bottom to retrieve a floating rubber duck for an unknown child. We hid among cattails to watch him return a cheap toy to a thankless mother.

His friend, Uno, looked detached. His boss owned the resort. Uno was a quiet man, dark and thick, who seemed to have an underlying rage which made him look even more menacing.

I do remember one time when Uno had actually spoken to my father while I was fake-napping on the pier. He said, "I'm gonna explain somethin' one time, Jack. The less you see and hear around here, the better. You seem okay, but you ain't our people.

I don't care about you one way or another. But Pazzo figures he owes you. He's like me; we don't forget a favor . . . or a backstabber. I'd just as soon deal with those snakes in this pond as I would one that wears quiet shoes. But my *coomba*, Pazzo, says you're not a man to play games. Just make sure your kid is deaf and dumb."

My father just stared at him through piercing gray eyes while Uno spoke. When Uno had his say my father explained, "Personally, I couldn't care less what anyone does. I'm here to take care of my family, not to play games. And as far as my son goes, I'm responsible for him. If he needs to be told something, bring it to me. I'll handle him myself." After that day my father didn't let any of my friends accompany us to the resort.

Enrico had been a friend since kindergarten. The first time he had my back was when I tried to squeeze out a sly fart in our 3rd grade classroom. Instead, I accidentally shit my drawers while seated in front of him. A kid named Joey next to me got blamed, thanks to Rico's glaring looks and a life-saving lunch bell.

During that walk of shame when Joey, all hang-dog, cried himself home, we passed him at full throttle as he lumbered all drooped over and bawling. Enrico sang, "Shit-Pa-ants Joey, Shit-Pa-ants Joey." Then Rico confided, "I knew the crybaby, fat kid would get blamed. You'd a done the same for me, Jackie."

From that day in 1958 and forward, Joey went from being an invisible fat boy of Mid-eastern origin to a Neighborhood kid with his very own nickname. Shit-pants Joey, being the good humored person he was, took the razzing in fun – happy to finally be noticed. And I skated from having to deal with that shitty nickname.

To reinforce his new name, while we were in the middle of a game of Jailbreak behind Holy Redeemer, Joey announced, "I can't play any more, guys. I got a stomach ache. I have to poop real bad."

Benny warned, "This is the middle of the game, fat-ass, and it's your turn to be in lockdown. If you leave before the game's over you can't ever play with us again."

Joey sat inside an invisible cell, clenching his teeth, till our parents whistled us in for supper. Joey was a neighbor on my street, so I ran home with him. When we got to his front door he found it was locked. We ran around to the side door. That door was locked, too. His mother's car was gone. Then the strangest thing happened. He sat down on the steps, crying, and deliberately shit in his own pants. The stink was overwhelming. As I backed away from him and down the driveway he begged, still bawling, "Please, Jackie, don't tell. Okay? I'll owe you one. Honest Injuns. I'm your friend, okay?"

"Don't worry, Joey. I ain't gonna say nothing. Besides, this sorta just makes us even."

By 1962 Joey publicly lived up to his moniker the day Benny literally blew the shit out of him. That occurred when Benny unleashed a homemade mini-bomb. The night before, Benny had dipped Cherry Bombs in glue and bee-bees. After school, Benny rolled one between fat-boy's legs. He scared that poor 12-year old boy shitless.

Over the years nicknames often mutate but remain in a cooler way. That didn't happen with Joey. Shit-pants became his only name outside of school. Shit-pants Joey wasn't a kid we ever hung around with. He was too square, too good of a boy for us to trust or accept with all our shady interests which eventually became criminal enterprises. Shit-pants, or anyone else, wasn't privy to details of illegal activity we engaged in as commonplace activity. Regardless, Joey seemed okay for a chubby camel jockey who had never broken a law or ever even been in a fist fight. He never got high or even smoked a cigarette. Joey was even too square for Enrico the jock.

Mid-'60s: Things between Collinwood and Little Italy had been tenuous for as long as anyone could remember, with the exception of a few higher-ups treated like royalty. But during the mid-60s, a conduit got established thanks to two teens named Louie and Cagootz. Louie remembered Cagootz from when his family lived in Little Italy. He remembered, from during recess at Holy Rosary, when Cagootz smashed a classmate over the head with a rusted metal garbage can to open his scalp like a tomato sauce can and then kicked him unconscious. But two years difference in primary grades was equivalent to four years or more in high school. Younger kids were pretty much invisible to those ready to transition to junior high, the preteens to those little idol worshipers.

Louie, a huge 15-year old from Little Italy, got caught in a brand new stolen '66 Corvette, drag racing through the town of Geneva-on-the-Lake. Cleveland's Detention Home is where Louie befriended a fat, loudmouthed 17-year old known as

Cagootz. The fast talking Cagootz, with black hair and eyes and very light skin was two years Louie's senior and light-years ahead.

Three of the No-Names and I also spent some time in Cleveland's Detention Home in 1966. That was after we beat a few kids during an incident where a teacher attempting to break up our little gang brawl in Collinwood high's basement dropped over in the middle of the skirmish from a massive coronary. The fight was me and a few friends knee-deep against Curtis and three other young thugs from Five Points. The post-fight rumor came back that the teacher died and one of those black kids had been stabbed. So my friends and I freaked out and devised a plan driven by hormones and panic. We pooled our money and split town, only to be nabbed in a stolen Buick Riviera in some backwoods shit-hole in Sapulpa, Oklahoma, eventually to wind up in C-town's detention home for juvenile delinquent boys till court.

Cleveland's D.H. was where I met the legendary street fighter, Horrible Hank. Although the blackest Negro I'd ever seen, it was Hank who stood up for me against *his own kind*. One of the people Hank went against was ol' *Flukey Doo* Curtis from Collinwood. So there Hank and I stood in 1966, side-by-side as brothers, to transcend a color line which had been so prevalent in Cleveland throughout the turbulent mid-1960s. I liked the way that nontraditional alliance empowered me. And I could sense he felt the same way. We became fast friends in what resulted as long-term brotherhood.

In 1966, at Cleveland's D.H., another life-long friendship developed when the abrasive Cagootz got jumped by four rough teens. The fight started while the short stocky supervisor known as Bossman was off unit. Bossman was taking one of his usual long breaks while shooting the breeze with other lazy fellow employees. Cagootz bravely attempted to hold his ground with those four rugged inner-city bangers but was quickly overwhelmed.

Cagootz got swarmed. What he lacked in size he made up for in brass balls. He was catching a pretty good beating till Louie jumped in. Louie soccer-kicked the biggest kid in his face, the one who had been on the ground pummeling Cagootz. Louie, a tall, dark and lumbering kid huge for his age, was bull-strong yet deceivingly fast and agile – a natural athlete. Louie crouched down like Two-Ton Tony Galento, with a low and wide center of gravity and growled, "Now I'm killin' everybody," and reached in a pocket. The tall black kid called "Foo" staggered back up, holding his eye so all four of those big kids could surround Louie to coordinate a better attack.

Foo said, "Ya'll made a mistake fuckin' wit da dawg. Dis *my* house, *guinea*-ass mah fuckas. Now yo flimsy ass pay."

Louie growled, "How youse *moolies* wanna make us act?"

Horrible Hank, the meanest looking teen in Cleveland's detention home who was built like a tall professional boxer, kept a close watch on Louie's pocketed hand. Hank was known to be the toughest kid in the D.H. But he remained on the sidelines, watching through slanted eyes from his American Native features, as Louie held what might be a knife. Hank, affecting the best ghetto jive he could muster, asked the lumbering 15-year old Louie, "Say whah, mah fucka? Look like you when an fuck up again, fool. Now you face da wrath a da boys. Now let's me an you dance, big gal."

"Wait awhile! We can't fight youse guys," protested Louie while eyeballing a ferocious-looking Hank. "It ain't fair!"

"Oh, look like we got us a lil' peep," Foo said, still holding his swollen eye. "Dis boy ain't no cock, son," he laughed as he high-fived one of his three co-conspirators. "Big gal here, she a dove – a luv dove," the closed-eyed teen sniggered.

By that time Cagootz was back on his feet and next to Louie. "No, youse don't under-fucking-stand nothin'. Know why? 'Cause youse spooks don't speak American. That's why!" Cagootz laughed. "Know why else? 'Cause youse ain't got no man-brain inside those fuckin' coconut heads, ya fuckin' porch monkeys."

"Say what, bitch?" asked Foo, who held a lump on his forehead the size of Louie's fist. "Say you wan 10 inches a black snake pumped up that *guinea* white ass? Dis zombie-ass bitch say *'We can't fight youse guys. It ain't fair.'* Ain't dis some shit, brah?" The angry teens mad-dogged each other as the circle tightened.

"No!" yelled Louie, hand still pocketed. "That ain't what we said. We mean there ain't enough of youse faggot cocksuckers to deal with the *men* from Little Italy!"

Big Louie's boulder-like fists had two of them knocked unconscious before he found himself trying to get out from underneath Horrible Hank when they all heard a terrible shriek.

Someone screamed, "He got mah dickie!" which caused scrambling teens to temporarily freeze in place.

Then they heard the supervisor swearing, "Motherless fucking little sons-a-bitches! All ya'll get shipped out in the a.m."

Foo pleaded, "Get this crazy-ass mah fucka off my dick!"

They turned to see Cagootz, his face a bloody mess, burying his teeth gums-deep into the upper, inside thigh of the kid with the closed eye who was making all that noise. Cagootz continued growling, shaking his head back and forth like a dog working a dishrag. Blood flew from Cagootz' head and mouth with each shake. Blood bubbled from under the lips of Cagootz as he bit down deeper and shook his hold even harder.

The lanky teen called Foo rolled on his side, punching Cagootz hard with rapid fire shots to the top of his skull. That melon dome of Cagootz is where his childhood knick-name came from. A "gagootz" is the Italian-American expression for a garden squash. His street name had been "Melon-head boy" as a kid, till he gave someone a concussion with repeated slams from a garbage can behind Holy Rosary church. Old neighborhood nicknames are like that. They can change meaning on the head of a pin. So after the rusty trashcan beating, *Melon-head boy* became *Cagootz*. That's also how fast reputations got earned, ruined or changed on the mean streets of C-town.

But in the meantime, while under supervision at the Cleveland D.H., Louie made his own reputation as being loyal and fearless. Because by the time the supervisor had stomped in the ribs of Cagootz, Louie was back up and crept around behind the stockily built man, short and thick like a judoka. Louie blasted Bossman in the back of the head with a roundhouse punch and knocked the supervisor out cold with one clean shot from his long arm driving a lunch box-sized fist.

One teen left standing was Horrible Hank, the one who had been going punch for punch with Louie till Bossman arrived. Hank said, "You boys went and fucked up big, this time. You're fixin' to do some real time now behind this stupid bullshit." Hank warned, "Now you best back the fuck off before Bossman wakes up and realizes he's gotta kill someone or send a few motherfuckers downstate."

Cagootz said, "Thanks for the advice . . . *nigger*." Big Louie and Cagootz rushed him. Horrible Hank dropped Cagootz with a straight left to his big potato nose and then fired a barrage of precise shots to Louie which left him doubled over till Bossman was back on his feet. Two other supervisors rushed to quell the disturbance. Hank and Louie both got knocked out with nightsticks swung like baseball bats.

All six, the two boys from Little Italy, and the four kids from Glenville, got shipped out to Boy's Industrial School (BIS) the next morning, with a warning for Cagootz and Louie to be kept separated from Horrible Hank and his jailhouse brothers.

Hank, like I did, turned 18 in 1968. He was given the option to engage in the daily wars fought in Mansfield Reformatory or those of Southeast Asian jungles. Hank opted for boot camp where he trained, competed and earned the coveted title of Green Beret, followed by hands-on application in Vietnam. He survived two tours of duty.

Hank told me, "Brother Jack, you got no idea how shit is out there in the real jungle. And believe me, you don't want to know what the Nam is like. The bad part is you start to like that wholesale craziness like killing motherfuckers with a license, tapping those fine-ass Gook chicks and scoring primo dope for the price of candy."

I answered, as ignorant as a person could who had never fought in an active military combat zone, "I hear you, brother. That shit don't sound all that bad, considering they're even paying you cash money on top of all that. Sounds awesome!"

"Sometimes, my brother. But only *sometimes*. Most of the time a man feels like he's drowning in that dense-ass jungle with motherfuckers booby-trapping the ground and squatting up in trees with AKs. That shit wasn't fun. Not even a little bit. What's even worse was when we learned why we couldn't use mosquito repellent on a relentless barrage of biting insects every goddamn night. It's because the Viet Cong could smell it! Those little dinks got noses like bloodhounds. So instead of bug spray, we learned to medicate with China White. It was a bad-ass pain killer for mosquitoes, fire ants, centipedes and all the other crazy shit they got crawling up inside your shit. And then we found out that a high tolerance meant we could stay alert while pulling night watch. But even after all that crazy shit, Jackie, sometimes I miss it in a way."

In serving his country during a war nobody was for, with the exception of politicians who had their kids tucked safely away in private colleges, Horrible Hank became a decorated soldier with the possibility of a new life – till he returned to his grandmother's home in a Cleveland ghetto with PTSD and an active heroin addiction.

Hank's three jailhouse inner-city friends got involved in another type of army before that, fighting a domestic war. They became Black Panthers. Two of his best brothers became C-town statistics in Cleveland's Glenville race riots. They were killed on the street by *unidentified police gunfire*. Foo devoted his life to drug addiction, a litany of arrests and prison sentences.

Hank settled in to being a loner, doing odd jobs for the infamous Sonny Magic. Hank liked having enough street juice to float above the sewage. But he was smart enough to feed Sonny Magic with a long-handled spoon. Sooner or later, Sonny fucked over everybody. It was his nature to be an unscrupulous sociopath. Even the Italian and Irish mobs stayed out of Sonny's territory. Too many people doing business with Sonny were catching cases or winding up inside parking lot dumpsters.

1968 became a milestone age. It was when we turned 18 and *eligible* and brought with it a dynamic not found in high school. The Draft Board's rules hadn't changed just for us. My *coombas* and I, like Hank had, became fair game for parts unknown, to do untold bidding for whomever about whatever. Prisons awaited our next charges. But down deep we knew that neither government and law enforcement nor the Church were in charge. Not in Collinwood, anyway.

By the mid-1970s, I began having vivid serial nightmares. I woke each time to the smell of kerosene and rubber from that realistic dream. It's strange the way dreams work. A few weeks later Ansel got arrested for the murder of his petite wife and accused of burning her remains in a metal trash barrel. Sometimes the *Click* was so strong I felt things before they happened or when I wasn't even present. It used to freak out my wife, Butter, when I would know things I couldn't possibly know – yet I did. Maybe it had something to do with me taking 28 tabs of LSD in one weekend.

Ansel had been suspected of being part of a hit squad that had taken down rival bikers and then of targeting one of Uno's Young Turks for the Mick. Ansel had also been accused of murdering one of Mick's men, allegedly paid for by Uno. 1976 was a time when I felt the squeeze around my throat. So I figured it was time for me to move my wife, Butterscotch, a gorgeous girl of mixed blood, and our baby daughter, Gina, out of Cleveland.

Drug abuse and affiliations had escalated from zero to 90. A drug deal almost caused a full-scale war. Horrible Hank and Curtis set up a deal with Sonny Magic. It was the largest we had been a part of since the pirate chest in Fatso's root cellar. Sonny put an order in for 40 bricks of *Acapulco Gold*, a kilo of cocaine, a pound of heroin and 10,000 hits of Brown Smudge, and said he needed delivery ASAP. Fingers and Benny went to Uno for a loan to invest in this deal. We used a New York connection for the smack, a Florida dog-fighter for the blow, and the Wong Gongs for the weed. We had to pay up-front for all the powder. Ansel agreed to take half of what was owed him for a deposit on a vanload of primo herb. The rest of the cash was used to buy the chemicals Rico needed to perform his colorful miracles.

Sonny insisted on dealing with "brothers only" at his nightclub called Sonny's Magic Spot located on East 105th and St. Clair. Hank and Curtis went to the meeting. Ansel insisted that Black Bart go with them and told me I was driving. What else Ansel also insisted we bring along a Cambodian RPG-2. It was a portable unguided, shoulder-launched, anti-tank and rocket-propelled grenade launcher. I didn't even want to be in the same neighborhood with that thing, let alone the same vehicle.

A physically weak, old scrawny man like Sonny didn't get to be top dog by being fair or shy. He got Curtis shit-faced on Stolichnaya while Hank was being entertained by his best two lap-dancers. When he got a phone call he jumped up and said, "Here go the cash," and threw a duffel bag full of money at Curtis. Where's my product? Let's go, man. Get your dicks back in your pants and get with it!"

Curtis said, "We got yo flukey out in da dukie."

Two thick teens named Willie Brown and Smokehouse, both of them already killers, dressed in black walking suits. They stormed into Sonny's office. Each looked like a black version of Oddjob from *Goldfinger*, wearing a black silk judo gi. They walked to the back door impatiently waiting to help move the goods.

Wille Brown said, "I just got a strange call. So let's do this and be done with it." They left the bar.

Click When Bart saw four men walking fast towards the van, Curtis laughing, Hank looking worried, and two ferocious-looking men dressed in black walking fast who seemed to be on a mission, he looked over to get a reaction from me. I said, "I agree, brother. This don't look good at all. I should've known."

Black Bart yelled out, "Nobody move! Hank, grab two stacks from the bag and bring 'em here. Just you. Quick, man! Do it now!"

Sonny's man called Smokehouse said, "We ain't some fuckin' hillbillies doin' business in da streets, mah fucka's! As far as you go, little man." he looked over at me, "Yo ass belong ta

Sonny now, Lil' Jack. Be seein' ya'll around, cuz."

Bart pointed the rocket launcher out the window and said, "I don't stutter, boy. And I ain't gonna say it again. Oh yeah, and by the way, this rocket launcher is armed with a nuclear warhead. And it's pointed right at Sonny's puny little ass."

Curtis and Smokehouse froze. Hank did as Bart asked while Willie Brown ran back inside the club. Hank dropped two thick stacks of $20 bills on the huge biker's lap.

Bart said, "Check 'em out, Jackie. I'll bet there ain't more than a few sets of serial numbers on all them goddamn bills."

Bart was right. Every bill in one stack shared one set of numbers. Each bill in the other stack all shared another.

The huge teen named Willie rushed back out, smiling, and said, "Sonny's glad you caught that mistake. I picked up the wrong bag. My dog and me were supposed to take that sack to get cleaned. Sorry, man. It's my fuck-up, bro. Sonny feels bad. He has what's yours inside. Plus, he's ready to give you 20k for that quality piece. No offense, man."

Bart warned, "My guess is you're smarter than you look. But if you come any closer I'm putting this thing right through your chest and it'll be on its way into Sonny's club. Everybody will remember Sonny's Magic Spot after this day."

The big young man said, "There's a new sheriff in town. His name is Downtown Willie Brown. This is just a mix-up. But I'll make this right. You'll see."

I told my friends, "Hand him back the bag, C. Come on, H. Hop in, brother. We gotta go. I mean like right now,"

Bart said, "Tell Sonny we're keeping these two stacks for gas, and that me and Ansel ain't gonna forget he tried to fuck us."

An 18-year old Smokehouse chuckled, "Bet yo sorry ass Sonny ain't neva gonna foget dis shit. We be da big dawgs up on block some day, muh fuckas. Den we gotcha. Bet on dat shit."

"We'll be around. You know where the clubhouse is. Look us up. Our prospects are in the attic with night scopes."

Smokehouse pointed his brick of a fist at me: "Me an Willie be watchin' yo slim ass real good, ya'll." Then he smiled a gold grill at Bart: "Sonny ready fo yo big ass too, big dawg."

There it is! *It's Smokehouse and Willie who did this to me.*

CH XI: Flashbacks & Consequences

July, 2013 – Our home: "Old-timers used to say, 'stick with your own kind.' But I don't trust anybody anymore, Pop, except for a handful of select people. I already told Gina who they are. Fuck all those cutthroat *paesano* down there. After Uno went down and then Ma's cousin got set-up on that racketeering charge, Cagootz calls the shots till Fingers' lawyers can figure out how to get his 10-year bit overturned."

"Cagootz should figure out a diet," Gina said. "And the only shot he should be allowed to call is which part of his melon head a bullet should enter. I hate that leering face of his," she frowned. "He's the stereotypical *guinea*. Nothing against *paesanos*. I love being half Italian. I don't even mind being part black. It is what it is. In fact, guys tell me my mixed blood gives me an *exotic* look." She pouted her lips and flipped auburn locks half across her face like a super-model pose from a fashion magazine. "What do you think, Daddy? Do I have that exotic look?"

"You're gorgeous. I love you exactly the way you are."

"Thanks, Dad. You're pretty special, too."

"Yeah, real exotic, Gina" Rocco said, as he raised his eyebrows. "You're a rare breed. But it's a little early for Westminster. Maybe there's a local dog show for you to model at. But I don't think they have a special mutt class."

"Did you hear anything just then, Ma?" Gina asked, as she nudged Tessa with freshly painted toenails on a tanned bare foot she had been petting the dog with.

"Nope, all I heard was a burst of hot air just then. But what you said about exotic I agree with. I can assure you, you're even prettier than your mother. And Butterscotch was one of the prettiest girls in Collinwood. Some guys must have thought she was even prettier than me." Tessa paused to give me the bad-eye. She continued, "I think you're wasting your looks in Cleveland, being around a bunch of losers. I wish I had the money and the clout to send you to Hollywood or New York to strut your stuff. You're the most beautiful woman I've ever seen, Gina. And that's a fact."

"Thank you, Ma. I love, too. But I like Cleveland, and love having roots in Collinwood. I don't mind that I grew up down Five Points around black folks and Appalachian Caucasians. Plenty of them are really nice. But what I do despise are thugs like Cagootz and Big Louie who make it bad for all the sweet Italians we know."

"You mean real sweethearts like me, sister-girl?" Rocco asked, with a big fake grin. "Don't be ashamed. You can be nice to me in front of them. You dig bikers, right?"

"No way. Ansel and his bros are as bad as my mom's worst nigger neighbors and those piece of shit Wops at The Inn. Look at Butter's cousin, Curtis, and those ghetto-ass pimps he hangs with. Curtis is as much of a shit bag as Cagootz and Louie, and those psycho bikers. I think Animal is the scariest of all of them. But they're all the same to me, all bottom-feeders. Those types pollute society as far as I'm concerned. I'm glad you got away from that life, Daddy, so now we have you all to ourselves! Now maybe we can get your idiot son on the right track before he winds up back in rehab, or worse. Because this boy's crazy! I've seen him in action. He has a really bad temper. He wanted to stab some drunk just because the guy was mouthing off."

"Easy does it, sister-girl," Rocco said. "Calm down. You might rupture something you keep getting all excited. That fancy ring through your lip might pop off and put somebody's eye out, or that pin in your eyebrow might shoot off and break a window. I guess all that metal in your face is sort of fashionable now, huh? But you could accidentally hurt somebody with all that cheap shit stuck in your face."

"How about your tats, baby Rocco? You look like a walking coloring book. I'm not sure if I need an erasure or a bottle of bleach when I look at you."

"Hardy har... That's real funny, Gina. You're almost like a comedian now, right? Meantime, who gave you permission to look at me? Anyways, Pop, like I was saying before we were interrupted..."

Gina moved up from the floor to stretch out on the couch next to Tessa. She draped her long legs over Tessa's lap. Gina said, "I'll go where I'm appreciated."

Tessa continued to look like she was reading the large dog book, as if there had been no interruption, but placed a hand on her step-daughter's ankle.

"Wow. Check out these two homos."

Without looking up, Tessa turned a page, flipped off her son with a middle finger and then set her hand on Gina's calf, who was scrunched-up on her side like a child.

"Like I was trying to say, Whitey's putting the bug in my ear about matching Bull. You know; to champion him out. But I still haven't firmed-up a decision. What do you think?"

"You should weigh-out your options and choose a lane."

"And do what? What's the move, all things considered?"

"There are two types of truths, son. I call it *truth-juggling*. One is something we want to be true despite all evidence and logic. The other is the way a person or place intrinsically is; the way a situation presents itself. Every once in awhile something can manifest just long enough for the *Click* to be felt, clear enough for you to know in your heart of hearts what the right decision is for that unique space of time."

"So what do you think the right decision is, Pop? You know the deal. You've matched way more dogs than I have. What should I do?" Rocco asked again.

A pair of four-wheelers raced past our house in a whine of Japanese technology: "I think there's an electrical circuit, an invisible wire that connects an intangible triple-beam in each of our brains, a connection to the heart and the gut. Put everything on that scale in your mind – one side positive, the other negative. Then decide, based on facts and instincts, rather than hopes and dreams. The *Click* doesn't lie, son. You'll know."

"I get that. So then it can't be wrong to match Bull if all things point to go. Is that what you're saying? I'm just asking what you would do if you were me."

Sinbad stood and shook as if he was wet, then walked to my recliner to settle next to me with a watchful eye on his doggie bed.

"I've been thinking about things. From all the way back to when I was a kid I've always looked for loyal and friendship with pseudo-brothers and inside drugs. Everyone outside of my loop believed I had all that brotherhood stuff locked up, like a guaranteed lifetime membership, and thought Butter and I had a perfect marriage. Yet I never trusted that guarantee and wasn't satisfied. I wanted more, even though what I'd been searching for had been with me ever since I was a wild teen. But I missed the blatantly obvious answer for all those years because I was too high and full of myself to see what was right in front of me the whole time. That's what I think, son."

"Okay, Pop, so then just tell me this: Is it wrong for me to match him? You know I love that dog. And you know it's never been about the violence for me. Because you're an old-school dogman, you also know a well-bred game-dog loves to fight as much as it loves to be babied by people. So is it wrong or not?"

"Which type of wrongs are we discussing here, Rocco? If you're not hurting yourself or anyone else with an isolated incident, or even with a broad set of behaviors, then only you can answer that question based on what suits your needs."

I scratched Sinbad behind his ears. He closed his eyes and gave a sigh of contentedness, wearing his contented Pit-bull grin. He rolled over on his back with his paws bent forward and did the gator crawl to rub his thick muscular back on the plush, dark blue carpet as he emitted a low grumbling sound. Then just as quick, he righted himself and returned to watching his doggie bed pillow.

"Alright, Pop, I'm gonna try this once more. Let's say this is about you, but it's happening right now and you're my age and still working the scams out in the streets like you did back in the day."

"Okay, here's the thing: and I'm not judging you or your friends, because I've done worse things than all of you. But the truth is I simply lost my taste for it. Granted, like you, the gameness is why I became obsessed with these dogs. At first I recognized gameness as being an amazing integrity piece, like loyalty and courage on steroids. And I have to admit, the excitement of the out of state game-dog conventions was something that kept it interesting. But now I see the brutality and the dogs' real value. It's a package deal: the intrinsic worth; their love and gentleness along with loyalty and courage; as well as their beauty and athleticism; the passion and gameness of these amazing animals. They're just regular dogs, only better at everything – including fighting."

"Straight business, Pop, I'm starting to feel the same way as you. I'd hate telling Whitey something like this. But Bull is like the brother I never had. At least I don't think I had…," then he looked over at his mother for a reaction. "The thing is: I love that dog. Damn! Listen to me. I swear to Buddha. I feel like a whiney little bitch saying this stuff out loud, even to my own family. Whitey would probably think I'm losing my balls. But yeah, what you're almost saying makes a whole lot of sense."

I added, "Besides me and your mother, and even Gina over there who's pretending like she's not listening to us, who else would lay down their life for you? Just name one person. Because I doubt that we have anymore family out there..."

Tessa said, "Let's change the subject, alright Jackie? No wonder your kids' heads are all twisted. And don't imply you might have more kids floating around in Collinwood, you pig. Taking advantage of us poor, innocent flowers of chastity... Shame on you! Go ahead, Rocco. What were you saying?"

When I reached down to pat a heavily muscled shoulder, Sinbad gave another of his vocal yawns and settled in closer. Flat on his stomach, big head rested on his forelegs, rear legs stretched out behind him like a frog, he seemed content for the moment but still sneaked occasional glances at his doggie bed.

Rocco sighed, "I can see the risks. It's not like I'm in a squeeze to decide any time soon. Anyway, Danni will help me puzzle though this. I know Whitey would like to see Bull make champion, but he's pretty much neutral about it. If I do decide to go for it he'll be my corner man and even put up some of the cash. But I'm just not feeling it..."

"You trust Whitey 100%, son?"

"Other than the people in this room right now, the only other people I trust are Whitey and Uncle Pazzo. Besides Ma and Uncle, they're all I had before you and Gina came into our lives. It's really strange, but even though I've only known Gina for a little while I believe she'd have my back . . . even though she's only a girl."

Without looking at us, Gina and Tessa both held up the middle fingers of their right hands at the same time, although it had seemed that one of them had been engrossed in reading and the other was dozing in the land of misty abstractions.

"Come to think of it... I guess I trust my girl, too."

"Danni said her mom is Christine Troia. Did she say if her father is from Cleveland, too?"

"Well, that's another thing we have in common. Danni didn't know her father. All her mother told her is he was a soldier – like Ma told me about you." Rocco glanced over at his mother, who seemed to be ignoring us. "Danni was born in 1978."

"I think I remember her mother. What's her other side? Did she say if her father is Italian? Not that it really matters... I was already out of the loop by then. But who knows? Maybe I know him. You never can tell who this guy could be, right? Hey, maybe you two are even related! I mean, stranger things have happened. Just look at us." I looked from him over to his half-sister for a reaction.

Gina still fake-napped while Sinbad longingly monitored his giant dog pillow from afar. She yawned and said, "I might have been tempted to let Rocco fall in love with me before I knew he was my little-bro. Luckily for you, Pop, I was with my idiot of an ex for longer than I care to admit." She looked at her brother: "But you said you do remember me from when I was staying at Auntie Carly's, right Rocco? What was that you said about us being at the same party and both of us being all loaded?"

Rocco tugged at his goatee, "Did I mention that to you?"

"Just what is it you're trying to say, Rocco?" Tessa asked.

"Well, me and Gina were starting to tell you guys about one time when we were at the same party, both shit-faced loaded, and we think we might have—"

"No! Stop teasing, you little bastard! Just tell us about what you were saying about Danni's father," Tessa said, almost in a panicked voice.

"Oh, that... Okay. Danni and her mom don't get along well," Rocco continued from where he left off. "Her mom's a bad alcoholic. When she's drunk she's a raving lunatic. Even when she's sober she's a hot-tempered, moody bitch. The sober part doesn't happen often. Anyway, you know how most of those old *dago* broads are."

"Yeah, Rocco," Gina said. "And we know what assholes most *guinea* guys are. Except for my daddy, of course." Then she beamed a smile to melt my heart.

Tessa, holding her book with both hands, drummed her middle fingers on it. She looked at Gina and said, "I think maybe your brother was on to something earlier about the word *ass*. Because there's no ass like a jackass or a dumbass. Right, honey?"

"Danni said that sometimes when the old lady's smashed she'll make sarcastic remarks about her Irish side. When Danni asks her about that when she's not all juiced, her mom says Danni's making up stories to squeeze information out of her. I gotta say it: her mom's a total nut-job."

I said, "I'm sure her mom has good reasons not to say more. Maybe it's a situation like with you and your mom, where it was in everyone's best interest that she didn't elaborate. But I'm sure it'll come out. Do you love this girl, son?"

"Danni's solid, and I'm starting to care for her a lot. Damn! Listen to me. This middle-age thing is making me all mushy."

"I didn't ask you that," I reminded him.

"I'm not sure what romantic love is. What do you think?"

"I don't doubt your judgment, son, at least not while you're sober. Just remember, either you choose people to be friends or they choose you as targets. Do you trust Whitey with your mother, your sister and girlfriend, or with your money or Bull and your bike?"

"I trust Whitey with my life. You remember how it was."

Fingers and I made our bones together while still in our late teens. That happened the same day I acquired that very same little bitch laying cold in the arms of my wife, Butter. My club-brothers and I had shared everything, from felonies to sweeties. But all that was in the past. He and every one of my other *coombas* would remain strangers – an awareness that left me cold at the time. Fuck the lacerations and fractures. Physically, I was on the mend from day one. But a cold realization showed I had lost something that hadn't ever really been mine. That game-test at the R-Bar served a few purposes. For one thing, I had raised the hurdle-bar on gameness for other kamikaze up-and-comers, left another indelible watermark for future wanna-be tough guys striving for sadomasochistic Hall of Fame status. I greeted a new morning, following my own game-test against former club-brothers at R-Bar, with the worst headache of my life.

I stumbled outside to find our little pet-bull, Gracie, dead on her chain. Evidently, she had been poisoned. Our neighbors loved that little red-nosed bitch. Finding our pet laying dead caused a terminal case of the "fuck-its" to inflame even worse.

Butterscotch heard me yelling and came out in a terrycloth bathrobe. "The neighbors can hear you! What the fuck?" When she saw Gracie, she sat in the dirt and cried as I went inside to make sure every gun in the house was loaded. I carried two of them out to our beat up old Ford. "No, Jackie! We have a baby on the way! Are you fucking insane? You'll be killed as soon as you pull the first gun," Butter sobbed, holding our dead dog in her lap while trying to revive Gracie with mouth to mouth resuscitation.

"Those dirty cocksuckers know I'd never be a rat. So what is it? Nobody ever got into trouble because of me. That's one of the reasons Benny bothered to send a word. He knew I wouldn't tell anyone he contacted me, not during his lifetime. We both valued our years together. Even the older guys know I'm solid. That's probably why Uno saved me from taking a killing. All of us despise cowards, snitches and double-dealers. So why?"

"If someone really wanted you dead, Jackie," she managed through gasps and sobs, "you'd have been waxed no matter who said what. You told me the only person who could stop a contract was a boss, and you no longer field that type of clout. Your wings got clipped. Now you need to stay away from the booze and be straight enough to puzzle through this. I can't handle finding you like this, too! Look at her! Look what those *guinea* motherfuckers did to our little dog – and for nothing!"

Once the dust settled on those long ago days, when I had transitioned from president of the Royal Flush to an untouchable, my entire life changed again with one more decision. Following that one-sided brawl at R-Bar against Fingers, the night my drink had been dosed with a powdered straightjacket, life flipped scripts like a bicycle frame with cards of cartoon drawings flapping against whirling spokes. I had metamorphosed from husband of Butterscotch and father of our little Gina to an unemployed, divorced asshole with nothing obvious other than bad habits.

Okay, Fingers is definitely still a suspect. *He tried to kill me in a fight in front of a room full of witnesses. So why wouldn't he blow the shit out of my car with me in it?*

I returned one gun to the house for Butter to access and stuck the other in the waist of my blue jeans as I went in the garage for a shovel. It seemed as though neighborhood people had been right about me. I did prove to be very dangerous. Yet the danger posed by me was to me, time and again. So I did my part to lessen disenchantment – I stayed fucked-up. Blackouts like fever-dreams matured to a real-life fantasy-world. Waves of dynamic tension pounded against bedrock. A frazzled CNS raged toward a line that once crossed would make return less than practical. I sought refuge in sanctuary offered by sedatives prescribed by an 80-year old doctor who liked my presence in an office inhabited by inner-city bangers looking to bully that old man for more.

Like a full-blown junkie, my head ached because my veins throbbed – but not from syringes. Internal shuddering came from vascular contractions of withdrawal. My system scrambled for *normalcy* with more drugs, to again plummet from synaptic assault. Ravaged neuroreceptors screamed, *FEED ME!* So I obeyed like a good boy. Mini-comas driven by addictive substances raped awareness. Enduring truths such as the *Click* and the "Bounce" helped cleanse off blurriness from being lost in the haze of abuse.

Fuck-it. Might as well shred my way through life. From lack of purpose I gradually lost myself. *What could be more honest than gameness to the death? Bite deep and shake hard, because life's one short-ass ride.* I wandered in that syrupy fog till I saw life through clogged filters. *It's all worth about one dry fuck, anyway.* I grew dizzy from walking that tightrope. Death filled the air and stank just like me. *So fucking what? Why miss out on the fun?* I asked a brain pickled with inverted logic. *It's just booze. What's the big deal? Besides, we all die anyway.* I repeated, as alcohol reared its ugly head to be one of the most dangerous drugs on the planet.

The bikers' buzz: temper flare-ups from crank and booze mixed with testosterone. And that miserable methamphetamines crash was nearly unbearable every goddamn time – time after time. Alcohol, stimulants and hallucinogens dogged me for as long as I allowed the cycle to continue. Inside a kaleidoscope of madness I'd smile when I almost heard whispering and nearly recognized figures in the dark edges of periphery. But somehow I managed not to violate a point of no return, though I peeked over its edge too often. *Remind me why I should give a fuck?* I asked an audience of one.

As it was with ex-friends and other ex-addictions, it was time to move away from a familiar hamster wheel of crack use. Compulsions came with pathological greed and suspicion as side-effects left to fester under the guise of *partying*.

Redemption struck a more universal tone once individuality had interfaced with a higher state of confidence, a truer sense of self, rather than the façade of arrogance which accompanies self-destruction. That transformation began through the collective, by mirroring myself by way of reactions. In the eyes of others I found two important factors. I had to be sober, and I had to find people I trusted enough to process the crazy thoughts bouncing around in my head like multi-colored ping-pong balls. The first part, the sobriety component, happened easily enough. The latter, however, the piece about trusting others, remained an ongoing issue and the most difficult part for me to adjust. It wasn't that I became incapable of trust or that I was unable to breech a dysfunctional value system. It's that I no longer felt the need. Family and friends gone, I entertained myself with false memories of trust as I grew even more pathological.

Italian and Irish underworld organizations paralyzed Cleveland till two Collinwood gangs became three. A couple dozen Wong Gongs fought and defeated twice as many fierce patch holders from an infamous black MC known as the Black Rebels in a knife and axe war during a night of public killings. At that venue, spectators and cops fled for their lives. After that, the Wong Gongs patched killer gangs from other states and networked with large-scale drug dealers from outlying areas.

The fourth gang was the Royal Flush, our young crew that gave respect to the older guys but feared no one. For over a decade of adolescence, back when Fingers, Nino, Benny, Gus and Eggs had been my brothers, we moved as one. As far as we were concerned: *fuck everybody else*. We blacked out on booze together, tripped out on acid, committed crimes, and never worried about a thing, awake or asleep. We kept each other's secrets and protected one another on all fronts. We were brothers. We would take a bullet for one another. We were the future. Any of us would go to jail for another of us. But that was back then, and back then has been long gone. We soon became menaces on two wheels, loaded with drugs and weapons. We reverted to childhood behavior, recklessly riding bikes in streets. Later we let a group called the No-Names ride with us, along with a select few periphery guys permitted inside our loop.

So then four crews became five. The last white gang to surface in Collinwood, before the Neighborhood was eventually taken over by African American families and black street gangs, was a band of junky brawlers who called themselves the No-Names. Like a railroad fussee burning from both ends, all six of them burned out fast and hard. Four of them were murdered or caught life sentences at young ages. Only two of them stayed alive long enough to navigate their way through addiction and into middle-age. Those two were Dago Red and Slick.

Regardless of what our families thought of our decisions, MC members welcomed Gus and me. But those bikers were wary of the same thing my ex-friends had mistrusted. I was a blackout drinker who stayed fucked-up day and night. Because of that fact I was considered unreliable by some. In those days, to me the word "party" meant non-stop substance abuse. For the two years Gus and I lived together we kept a half-gallon of tequila in the refrigerator for liquid breakfast, consumed around mid-day when we finally crawled off our beds. We woke up with the bottle and lines of crank, and then while on our bikes partied on beer and pills throughout the day. Whatever was available, uppers or downers, we consumed in mass quantities. The quicker the drugs hit, and the longer they lasted, the better we liked what we sought and procured. We used them to combat fatigue and internal strife. But for some odd reason the more and the longer we used, the worse our weariness and paranoia became, till our abuse escalated into the red zone. No more maintenance usage just to keep an edge. It became about survival.

My father disassociated himself from me. He told me I was weak. It didn't matter to him if mobsters' suits were tailored from silk or off the rack denim, clean shaven or bearded. To him they all were cut from the same cloth. He said, "You play with snakes, son, you get bit. It's as simple as that, so don't be surprised when it happens. And you can't always tell which ones are poisonous till it's too late."

The Cleveland Wong Gongs were just one chapter of a nationwide band of hitmen and drug dealers. All three crews had a few things in common: All were Caucasian; every member was lethal; and each gang wanted control over Cleveland's rackets. That third faction was a club of bearded scooter tramps who wore colors emblazoned across the backs of faded, denim cut-off jackets which served as vests to hold various patches and pins earned throughout their reign of terror over other bike clubs. Five years prior to the peak of Cleveland's war that had been waged throughout the city and surrounding suburbs, that outlaw gang of Collinwood-based bikers made their own reputation etched in blood. Led by the muscular, blonde Viking-looking man named Ansel, the Wong Gongs had made 1%er Hall of Fame history at a Cleveland motorcycle exhibition. Ansel, who allegedly killed three rival gang members in front of witnesses with a double-edged ax, established himself as a man to be feared and respected. He rose as a leader every bit as dangerous as Uno or the Mick. Perhaps Ansel proved to be deadlier, because his crew secretly worked in the middle, picking up contract hits from both sides.

Ansel, the #1 patch holder in Ohio and only president ever of the Wong Gongs, did contract hits for the highest bidder. He took a chance with me one day while we stood in the Wong Gong's garage that held chopped-out Harleys, as well as extra frames and motors on metal milk crates by a wall-length workbench. Ansel stood with his arms folded across his bull chest: "Some grease-ball pulled your ticket but I got it quashed. Don't ask who. That's all I'm gonna say."

"Now how the fuck am I supposed to act behind this?"

"Tell you what, Jackie: Take a ride to Tennessee to look over some property. Have your kid stay with your mom till you get back. Once that thing is done, we'll talk."

"I don't know, man… I'll have to think on this one."

"Whatever. But the way I see it, you got three choices. Let these chumps get away with almost beating you to death; or make a move against them by yourself; or make a deal with us. I know what I'd do. It's your call, man. Dig it?"

"Yeah, I understand But there's other things to consider. I have my little girl to think about. Plus, there could be a shit ton of debt from an expensive vacation like that."

"No big deal. When you get back from taking care of that thing for us, a two-timing whore and a traitor *coomba* will be nothing more than bad memories. Then you'll owe us. Cool?"

"I appreciate the offer, but I'll pass. Thanks, anyways."

"That was a one-time only offer," Ansel glowered. "And you know better than to mention our little talk to anyone."

"You don't need to tell me how the game's played. I'm not as stupid as I look. Besides, we're friends. I already forgot."

"Forgot what?" Ansel asked, looking down at me, all red-faced as he clenched and unclenched large knobby fists.

"I almost forgot why I came here," I answered. "I got a little a little something for you." When I reached for my back pocket, he dipped a meaty, scarred-up fist inside his ragged Levi vest. Slowly, I slipped an ounce of Panama Red out of a back pocket between thumb and finger and handed it to him. "Happy un-birthday, bud."

"What the fuck is this shit for?" he asked, moving away from the opened door.

"It's for awhile, for a buzz and for later. And on that note, I'm like yesterday."

I walked alone down his driveway, kicked over my shovelhead, flashed a peace sign with the back of my hand while looking straight ahead and blasted off for home. Naturally, if I had agreed, there would be blowback on my family later. Plus, I didn't like the idea of being indebted to a man like Ansel.

After that split from *coombas* at age 26, in 1976, I embraced the biker lifestyle more than ever. Gus facilitated my first ride on his first scooter, an orange '58 Panhead with a 21" over Springer front-end, ape hangers, forward controls, a solo seat and black spider webbing. It felt like sitting on a Brahma bull, hanging on by its horns. I was hooked. The power, sound and feel of that chopped-out piece of history seemed tailor-made for what I needed. My first Harley, a chopped-out shovelhead, was also acquired in the early-1970s. It was a "basket-case" pieced together in my parent's garage from various parts toted in bushel baskets. Gus had some wrench knowledge, but Slick possessed vast mechanical skills and the proper tools. The purchase was from my new friend, Ansel, a hot scooter with a rebuilt motor and new cases branded by illegal stamps.

Black Bart and Ansel became our new best friends. Gus and I dove into the biker scene. We spent time at Cleveland's clubhouse, got invited to parties and cautiously accepted trust sparingly doled out. We rode to and from local watering holes and rock/blues concerts together, as well as went with them to gambling dens, gamecock derbies and game-dog conventions.

Years ago there had been a rumor floating around the innermost circles of Collinwood that matched a vivid dream I had about Ansel's wife. That dream seemed as real as the one I had 37 years ago when I dreamed I had been intimate with Tessa, when I woke from another total blackout with her phone number clenched in my fist – my unchained bike parked in front of the crib. The dream of Ansel was more of what most people describe as being a nightmare, of screaming, seeing rivers of blood, a dream of a stench from which I woke choking with the residue of kerosene and rubber clinging to my lungs. That reoccurring nightmare began after Ansel's wife disappeared. Ansel had been arrested and accused of disposing of his wife's body. Not Whitey's mother, Maureen, but the chick Ansel was with before she came into the picture. She was young and beautiful, a natural blonde like him, a girl who needed to flirt.

I had ignored a warning from Benny who had been in a position to know things I couldn't, because at the time I was still a bulletproof, drunken asshole completely out of that loop. Drinking to excess used to define who I was. It became a companion and then a lover turned bitter. Drunk became a job I dreaded and hated every moment spent there. Because alcohol became so problematic I told myself I drank to relieve stress and because it was fun. But the truth is the booze set me on edge and made me angry. And the angrier I got, the more bitterness got dumped on whatever or whoever trusted me enough to forgive a drunk for repeated misgivings.

Pathological suspicion of the '70s had ensued far too long, just long enough to facilitate further damage. Lines of crystal meth to remain alert, dulled by mega-doses of booze to knock off the edge. It worked for awhile. More crank to counteract the stupor and hangovers. Then downers to crash off the speed. I told myself that because I didn't enjoy amphetamine, using those drugs in excess wasn't really addictive.

My skin shuttered from underneath as if my spirit were trying to simultaneously escape and reenter. Pretending to sleep, with a pistol on my orange-crate nightstand, my father's shotgun leaning on a paneled wall next to my cannonball headboard, I could hear blood gush and gurgle all night long through my arteries. CNS vibrated. Muscles ached from stifled rage, cramped from frustration. Nerves tweaked from too much buzz and not enough answers. Internal organs rolled in a boil. Something had to give. I wanted more, more-so than ever before. I packed heat whenever I ventured out on my scooter, or in my car to procure more of whatever was deemed appropriate at the moment.

Psychotic disorders manifested and magnified from frequent blackouts to drug-induced states of paranoid schizophrenia. Healing powers from "hair of the dog" bit as deep as a death hold and shook physical withdrawal from the body and into the mind. I repeatedly told myself: *Sooner or later everybody gives up the ghost. Fuck-it.* At the time I thought that statement bouncing around inside my head made pure sense, as if it was something deep and meaningful. Instead of thinking my life through and responding, I reacted with animal instinct and drug abuse. The objective wasn't the high. The goal was an ongoing orgasmic state of obsession and compulsion.

PART THREE

It seems weird how time swallows up even the most powerful men or the most revered women. It amazed me how there could be a living, thinking human one moment and just a slab of cold meat the next. It's almost unthinkable. It's so bizarre how the staunchest of people, from Presidents and Kings to beloved family members and life-long friends, all who had seemed irreplaceable, get forgotten almost as quickly as a great meal turns to fecal matter. It's the same for relationships as it is for reputations, one wrong turn and it's gone like a powerful storm that had already blown through. That strange void was the same when the invincible Uno got killed, and then when my oldest friend, Benny, got clipped. But the older we got the more we understood how infallible we are not. I've been so close to death so may times I almost gotten used to it. It was almost laughable.

Throughout childhood, Rocco had been told that his father was dead. Yet he stubbornly refused to believe it. Then one day, out of the blue, Rocco was assigned to my caseload where I worked as a counselor at a chemical dependency treatment facility. We sat face-to-face without ever suspecting we might be related. The old, thin man with short hair and thick glasses named Jack wore long-sleeved shirts, even on hot days, to cover fully sleeved arm tattoos peeking out from under cuffs. Rocco, normally an untrusting loner, felt a magnetic pull to his counselor, as did I to my son. I attributed that to sharing similar interests and originating from the same Italian-American section of Cleveland.

    Old habits dig in like deer ticks. Rocco remained cautious till everything changed with one visitation from his mother, my first sweetheart and only true love. Not long after, once a major truth had been revealed to him and me at the same moment during that surreal visitation, our lives forever changed. I suppose the entire ordeal was as strange for him as it was for me. Rocco began to tell me stories about me, once we were reunited as family. It was sad to listen to my son confess that he used to create scenarios about a father he had never met, and imagined what it would be like if they ever did meet. So, in turn, I shared my own stories. His favorites were about game-dogs.

CH XII: Game-dogs

August, 2013: Spuds pulled out his comb: "They say Ansel's right-hand man, that kid they called Animal, is the worst one of the bunch. I hear that maniac carries around some guy's finger in his pocket to pick his nose with. They say it looks like a shriveled piece of wood with an orange fingernail curled up and hooked on the end. See what I mean? Those guys are pure fucking *schifoso*."

"Can you believe that shit, Louie? What kind of person would do something like that? You knew that guy, right? So did you ever see that dried up finger, Louie? We heard it looks like a dried piece of dog shit. Does it stink, *coomba*?" asked Vinny.

Big Louie waved them off as if he had just shushed away a fly from his face and then went right back to watching a soap opera on the bar's television.

"Those Godless heathens still live like cavemen. But I got the big eyeball on them fucks. I got a couple a shines down Five Points keeping an eye on things. Know what I mean?" Fat Spuds smirked an all-knowing look.

"Yeah, Louie. No worries," agreed Vinny. "We got some spooks down there keeping an eye on things for us. Fuck these bikers. Are they looking for a war, or what?"

"Do youse two mind? I'm trying to watch my show. Stop talking!" Louie said, in his slow monotone voice.

"Okay, Louie," said Fat Spuds, through two sticks of gum. "We're gonna check with Cagootz. We'll be right back."

"Yeah, *coom*, later," parroted Skinny Vinny. "We're gonna go check with the boss in back. Be right back."

They might as well have been speaking to a totem pole.

The two walked in the backroom and stood at a closed door. "Go ahead, Vin, knock" Spuds said. "Then we can see what's up."

"Maybe we just better try later, when the door's open. Meantime, we take Louie's advice and relax. You look hungry, Spuds. We can have a nice lunch in the meantime, *coom*. How about some nice peppers and eggs sandwiches?"

"Quit fucking around, Vin. Knock and get it over with."

"I think he's on the phone, *coomba*. We better not disturb him. You remember how he likes his privacy, right?"

"I'd do it myself, but my hands are too big. You got those tiny fists. Know what I mean? Give a couple quick raps and boom; then we know. Right? Go on, Vin."

"I knocked last time, remember Spuds? And he was all kinds a pissed off, 'cause he was right in the middle a something. Let's go have a nice Bloody Mary. You know, one for the stomach. This way he can finish his phone calls. Makes sense, right *coom*?"

Just as they turned towards the bar the office door opened. Cagootz said, "I thought I heard rat claws out here. It's Mutt and Jeff. What are youse two fucking bust-outs doing snooping around my door?"

"It's just us, boss. We came back to see what's up, then we're gonna go have a nice heavy lunch. You hungry?" asked Spuds.

"Not me. I just ate. She's right there. See? She's still got her legs spread," Cagootz said. "You want a little taste, Vin?"

Skinny Vinny began laughing with a breathy hiccup type laugh, almost like a little kid. Then he peaked in real quick just around the door jamb and said, "Yeah, wow. Take a look Spuds. *Mingia*, the spread on this broad! Check it out!"

Fat Spuds walked in the office, looked the opposite way and said, "*Madonna mia*. We get to service that red snapper, boss?"

Vinny, all wide-eyed and slack-jawed, followed Spuds into the office. Cagootz and Spuds broke out laughing, pointing at Vinny for falling into his own trap.

Vinny turned red-faced and nodded his head at the floor, smiling. "Okay, alright. Hahahahahahaha. I really got youse guys this time, didn't I? Youse both thought I actually believed that bullshit, right? Man, I can't believe youse two really bought that."

"Not over there, you fucking dummy. The other side, in my chair." Cagootz pointed to his desk in the other direction.

Vinny's smile disappeared. He turned pale and whipped his pin-head around so fast he could have given himself whiplash.

Cagootz and Spuds starting cracking up all over again. Cagootz said, "There are assholes and world-class assholes, and then there's Skinny Vinny."

"Okay now. Alright, I'll admit it. You guys almost got me that time. Wow! Good one, guys," he said, as he pulled a white linen handkerchief out of a back pocket to mop his brow. He smiled a nervous grin and jerked at his shirt collar. Skinny Vinny wore black shirts, his good luck color, with loud print sport jackets and slacks.

Cagootz shook his head: "Un-fucking-believable… Okay, fun's over. Now what the fuck are youse two morons doing snooping around back here? Why aren't youse two scouting around, keeping tabs on things? Where's Louie?"

"He's just watching a little TV, boss. No worries with Big Louie," Spuds assured him, as he smoothed out his gay tie over his tremendous gut. "As usual, he's out there and right on point. Nothing gets past Big Louis, right *coom*?"

"Yeah, boss. Louie's on the clock – just checking out some tube, is all," agreed Vinny as he stretched his arms through his sleeves and rotated his fragile wrists.

"I don't need youse knuckleheads telling me about Louie."

"We know, boss," Spuds said, plastering his slicked back hair to his small head.

"Yeah, we know," Vinny said, as he fixed his collar and looked around in the office just in case a nude woman might really be hidden somewhere in that office.

"Youse two concrete heads answer my question."

"Which question is that, boss?" asked Spuds through two fresh sticks of Juicy Fruit and a mint toothpick.

"The other one. It's simple math, boys. Now answer me!"

"You know us, boss. We're here to see if you need anything," answered Spuds as he shifted his toothpick to the other side of his mouth while he smoothed down his hair with a pudgy hand.

"Yeah, you know us, boss. We don't fuck around."

Cagootz, very business-like, looked at his watch, "Oh yeah? Well, I want youse to check on that nigger, Horrible Hank. I need a full report on what he's doing these days."

"You mean that *melanzana* that used to run drugs with Jackie back in the day? What's up with him, boss? I thought he got out of the life after Jackie's *accident*."

"Yeah, boss, we heard that big *moolie* retired after Jackie had that car *accident*. What's this all about anyway, just so we know the best way to go about this? Know what I mean? 'Cause we heard that big spook settled down with some shine broad who shit out a couple *niglets* for him. That's what we heard, right Spuds?"

"I didn't ask what you heard, did I? I told you to find out what that Horrible Hank's up to. Can youse bust-outs handle this?"

"From now on that spook don't blow a fart without us knowing," assured Spuds as he unwrapped a stick of gum and shoved it into his mouth with short, stubby fingers.

"Yeah, we ain't scared of that big shine," Vinny agreed, as he rotated his head to loosen his neck from his collar. "Fuck him and Sonny Magic! We're all over this."

"Oh yeah . . . and another thing. That crackhead nigger, Curtis, is back on the streets. Those drugs fried his brain. He's a loose cannon. From what I understand, he's networked with that other jungle-bunny. Those two were out there making a payday with Jackie. So watch out for Hank *and* Curtis. Word on the street is they might both be doing work for Doyle Kelly now."

"I heard Curtis was strapped down on the nut farm in Lima. He flipped the fuck out so they had him all jacked up on Thorazine. He's probably all mellow now, boss," Spuds assured his boss as he reached for his comb again and ferociously chewed his gum.

"You mean they're both down Five Points, boss?" asked Vinny, as he yanked his own sport coat around by the lapels. "We heard Doyle don't mess with anyone had anything to do with Jackie. That's the word on the streets. It's supposed to have something to do with Jackie's *accident*. Know what we mean?"

"One more thing: I want you to keep a close eye on that kid, Rocco. Keep him under a microscope. I want to know everything he does with that pit-dog."

"Jackie's kid, boss?" asked Spuds, as he chewed his gum even faster. "Don't that Rocco kid match those dogs with those *schifoso* bikers down Five Points? I heard Rocco's best *coombas* with the kid of that psycho, Ansel. What's that kid's name? It's some hillbilly name. I know! It's that Whitey kid."

"Yeah, that's what we heard too, boss," agreed Vinny, as he yanked his white hanky back out of his pocket and dabbed his forehead with it. He laughed nervously again, almost giddy like an older woman would. "We heard those two bust-outs, this Rocco and that fuckin' Whitey kid, are tighter than virgin pussy. Oh boy! Listen at me. I crack myself up sometimes. That was a good one, right *coom*? Get it? Tighter than—"

"Yeah, Vin. That's real fucking funny. Meanwhile, speakin' of pussy, I guess I could go for a little something to munch on. Come on, Spuds, let's eat. I know you're always ready for a nice heavy lunch. You too, Vin. Let's go *mangia*. Then go do what I told youse slackers to do. End it. *Capiche*?"

As a child of the 1950s, my favorite show was *Our Gang Comedies*, featuring Pete the Pit-bull. I re-watched all 52 episodes over and over, obsessed with that dog. At age six my father presented me with what I considered to be the next best thing, a bob-tailed female puppy we named Toni. My uncle had phoned to ask if it would be okay. She came without registration papers from a Cleveland ghetto, but was said to be a "full-blooded Boxer." Uncle said he saw the dam and she looked like a boxer, only smaller. The people with the pups bred their bitch to a neighbor's stud to produce our pup's litter. She was the first great dog I had the privilege to share life with. Although Toni had the typical Boxer colors and markings, she was about half the size she should have been. Another thing was that even as a pup she loved to fight with other dogs.

That strange mini-boxer grew to be a lovable companion that welcomed everyone we accepted. Toni never bit anyone. But if I held her collar and sicced her on someone she would go ballistic. Pete the Pit-bull, Toni, and a dog fighting exposé in *Life Magazine* about Mexico all served as introductions to a life-long infatuation with game-bred dogs.

One night while I was out with my parents, my sister called the pound and had our dog hauled away because supposedly she urinated on the floor. When asked if she had let the dog out to relieve itself she replied, "That was your dog, Jackie, not mine!"

On Monday morning my father called the pound to inform them we would be driving there to get our dog. The man asked, "You mean that little fawn colored Pit-bull? Oh, she's been adopted."

He asked "What do you say when a dog's been put down?"

The man answered, "We tell them it's been adopted."

That day I learned it's not possible to put an eraser to all mistakes. I became plagued by nightmares of Toni being suffocated and then tossed into a pile of other discarded pet-flesh to be incinerated like trash. That day also spurred dreams of traveling to Mexico to purchase a dog like Pete the Pit-bull, and to match one of those brave and beautiful dogs here in America. In recurrent dreams I imported foreign gladiators to Collinwood, USA, where gameness co-existed with hardworking residents discriminated against because of our bloodlines. I knew that one day I would have a game dog.

Labor Day, 2013 – The Awakening: Life, as I had come to know it, had drastically changed as one average moment met head-on with evil. For the time being, I stayed quiet so I could piece together what was happening to me. A muted voice from a radio or TV above me announced that it was broadcasting a live show to commemorate its annual Laborfest Parade. I asked myself: *It can't be really be September already, can it?*

When I was 16 years old my father drove us to meet a famous game-dog breeder on Cleveland's west side. He had a full gray beard and a fat stomach barely held in by his well-worn bib-overalls. He instructed us to take a seat while he loaded and lit a corncob pipe, the first one I had ever seen other than in old movies. The tobacco reminded me of what my grandfather used to smoke, almost like a sweet cherry aroma. I wondered if that tobacco tasted as good as it smelled.

Then he began: "Well now, I've been an active dog-man for many a year. During the 1950s I associated with other legendary Bull-doggers like myself, from Cleveland, Erie and Chicago during a time when matching dogs was legal and still considered a gentlemen's sport. Alls a man needed back then was his word and a handshake."

Then the breeder showed us a UKC *Bloodlines* magazine that published flashy ads of famous game dogs during the 1960s. The glossy pages offered stud service to *winners* and registered game-bred litters out of *tested* stock.

"I need an address to get this delivered to our house."

The breeder ignored my comment: "Of course you wouldn't know this, but in the late 1880s Richard K. Fox was owner and president of the *Police Gazette*, a magazine that recorded dog matches and results, and even printed challenges from dog owners. Ol' Mr. Fox even sent out sanctioned referees to officiate the matches. How about those apples?"

"Do they still sell those books?" I asked the man.

"Not according to ol' Fatso down south. Only real dogfighters get these. But I might find my way to sell you one."

"How much you need for this one?" I asked.

"Anyway, it seems the police changed sides on us. Now these coppers are against us Bull-doggers. But back in the day, the

Police Gazette sent certified officials to referee matches governed by official *Police Gazette* rules." He relit his pipe and opened a man-door on the side of his garage to release a charge of muscle having wagging tails on one end and Pit-bull grins on the other. The puppies rolled and tumbled over one another, growling at each other, showing off for their audience.

"That's the kind I'm looking for. Are the parents of these pups that kind? What's the father look like? Is he here, too?"

Again he ignored me as he knocked out his pipe on the worn heel of his work boot and opened the backdoor to his house. We met the dam of the litter, a black brindle. She stretched and yawned and nosed her pups with a gentle nudge. Then she sat on one of the breeder's worn-out work boots. My father and I were impressed by the stable temperament of the bitch and tenacity of such small pups.

He said, "Well now, I'll take $600 cash for that smutty colored runt right there. But no paperwork. I'll sell you the meal but not the recipe. This litter is Purple Ribbon bred. Their momma and daddy's both got genuine UKC registration papers and all. These pups right here are from a pure Colby bloodline."

My father said dryly, "My son asked you a question."

"Well sir, my friend Fatso down in West Virginia owns the sire. He's a black dog with a rat tail, put together more like a terrier than a bulldog. He doesn't have one tooth left in his head from fighting bigger dogs. But I'll guarantee you he's game as the day is long."

"What's the sire's name?" I asked. "Is he famous?"

"Well, that's another strange thing. Ol' Fatso never even named that ol' dog. So's the fella's that know of that game dog just call him the no-name dog."

My father asked in his deep voice with gray piercing eyes, "Let's back up a minute. How do you have papers on these pups if the sire doesn't even have a name?"

"Well sir, all the fella's wanted to breed to that little toothless dog since we saw him get three-dogged at Fatso's place and never made one bad move. But the fella's wanted registration papers on their pups. So once all the fella's started paying him handsome stud fees, ol' Fatso filled out a breeder's certificate. Where it asks for the dog's registered name, ol' Fatso just put *No name*. Then UKC sent back his paperwork saying the dog was named *No-name*." the old breeder laughed.

"What about their dam? Does she have a name?" I asked.

"That ol' brindle bitch right there is named *Sinderella*."

My father lifted a fat brindle up by the scruff of his neck. The pup wagged his tail and yawned. When he set it on the ground the stocky pup ran over to me and grabbed the hem of my Levi's. My father said, "You'll take $300 for this big, mahogany brindle male tugging on my sons pant leg, with the papers, or we're done talking and this deal is over."

The man gave me a big, toothy grin: "Well, sir, you're a man who knows his mind, all right! You got yourself a dog." The old man went inside to get the pup's breeder's registration.

My father said, "How the hell don't they name a stud dog? That's something I don't go for."

I suggested we name the pup after his dam, *Sinderella*. Sinbad seemed like the right dog for me and the perfect breed: loyalty and smarts, beauty and grace, fun companionship and balls-out courage. My father respected gameness, too. He realized I required something other than the mundane. The owner of the no-named dog had recorded his name and address on the pup's registration papers. So I filed away that information in case later on I might want another good dog.

My mother supported our decision to bring home an old-school, game-bred pup, down from dogs like the champions I'd seen pictures of. My parents hoped I would become interested enough to be distracted from gangs and drugs. They knew I wasn't the type with patience for music lessons, or to be satisfied by joining sports teams. They knew exactly what I needed. From the beginning, Sinbad showed signs of intelligence and compliance. He matured to be one of the most loyal animals I've had the honor to befriend.

My mother not only tolerated a dog, she trained him as their house pet in one day and bathed him each week. Sinbad earned distinction as the son who could be trusted. They wondered if a Pit-bull would be just another *flavor of the day* for a fickle adolescent. But that proved not to be the case. Like drugs and motorcycles, I was obsessed with gameness and game-bred dogs and wanted more.

He matured fast and was a quick learner. When he did something wrong in the house it only happened once. He adapted to family eccentricities with voyeuristic enthusiasm. My mother still slept with her bedroom door ajar so she could hear. Sinbad would lay just outside her room. The only time he entered their room without being invited was the day he woke her, mouthing her forearm. He attempted to drag her off the bed.

Mom yelled, "Goddamn you, Sinbad, get the hell out of here before I kick you!"

Sinbad ran to the hallway window barking like a mad dog, then back into the room to again grab Mom's arm. She left the bed to physically chase him away. But when she got to the hallway she saw why he had been raising such a ruckus. The neighbor woman leaned out of her 2nd story window, surrounded by a funnel of gray smoke, house ablaze from a kitchen grease fire. The elderly woman was trapped in a room with no chance for escape other than to jump onto our concrete driveway. She choked from smoke inhalation, too weak to scream out for help and too scared to bail out the window.

Mom opened our hallway window and yelled, "I called the fire department. Please don't jump. Hang on just a few minutes!"

It was the same window my father had forced me to crawl through during childhood, wielding a 15 foot long bamboo pole in hand to knock apples off the top of our huge Macintosh tree. It was a day he thought he taught me not to fear heights.. It was also the same window I punched through during adolescence, because I was hung-over and didn't want to be roused back to reality just yet by a complaining mother. It was a window I had crawled underneath in a blackout to reach the sanctity of my childhood bedroom – my clothes wet with greenish-brown water from when I had overdosed in the Metropolitan Park on the outskirts of Cleveland and somehow drove back to reach the safety of youthful memories. It was the same window that stared into the neighbor's fire.

After the blaze had been extinguished, and our Slovenian neighbor had been rushed to Euclid General hospital, those firemen wanted to call a reporter from the Cleveland Plain Dealer to publicly commend Sinbad's heroic deed. My mother declined. She loved Sinbad as much as her own brood and that day was proud of him. Still, she passed on the offer. Even as far back as the early 1970s, owning a *dreaded* Pit-bull was frowned upon by the misinformed public. So my mom wisely rejected a proposition of public exposure. Old-school, Mom fried him a burger in a cast iron skillet. While grease sputtered and popped, he waited in a corner of her kitchen to see if that aroma might have something to do with him.

Our family accepted that Sinbad was my mother's dog. He navigated around the house with her but knew enough to keep out from underfoot. He could not rest until she did, which wasn't often. He watched her every move, to make certain she was not in harm's way. When she went to another room to clean or cook, or to our basement to do laundry, he followed to keep her within sight.

Once a week she hoisted his 65 lbs. of compact muscle up into her basement washtub sinks after she called him to stand on an old kitchen cabinet set on the concrete floor. Front legs in one tub and hind legs in the other, he stood like a statue till the bath was complete and she finished towel drying him. When she said, "Okay, boy, come-on," Sinbad would again step down onto that lower cabinet, jump down to shake off, and then wait at the bottom of our basement steps till she eventually called him upstairs when he was suitably dry. Sinbad didn't care for that part, because being confined in the cellar meant his hero was out of his sight. Although he let slip the occasional whimper, he complied. She loved that dog like another child, and he worshipped her as his only god.

Many people claim no love can compare to their first. In the case of that comical dog, my entire family fell in love with Sinbad. My infant daughter was raised with him in his elder years, even though he had been one of the better fighters I've owned. Our family is forever touched for having Sinbad, a once in a lifetime friend. He took pleasure in life as being a housedog with loved ones and eventually died of natural causes at age 15. He just fell asleep and never again opened those trusting brown eyes.

Countless Bulldogs became integral parts of my existence. They helped to define who I am. Sinbad was one of a multitude of great animals to share their lives. Unfortunately for most of them, I was too much of a drunken asshole to appreciate the qualities those animals afforded me. An organic buffoon under natural conditions has few equals in terms of being crude and caustic. Inexcusable, however, is the drunken asshole, a malady evidenced by repetitive mistakes and empty apologies. I was both.

Most of us forced ourselves to acquire a taste for adult appetites. Some of us acquired an unquenchable thirst for more. The first professional Pit-bull match I attended was in a Pennsylvania barn. I went outside for a moment to get some fresh air. But as soon as I got my legs back underneath me, I went back inside, gambled and won. Once the marathon matches concluded we made plans to hook-up the following month. The next time around it was like second nature.

Some of the biggest curs and culls I've ever met were gamer than most fools who doled out death sentences to such amazing courage. If I should choose to foster one regret in life it would be for insensitivity dumped on such noble creatures that give everything only to receive more abuse. Their unquestioning eyes allowed hands to clean fresh wounds we permitted to be inflicted, and stood obedient while Euthanasia was administered by societies paid by contributions to protect them. I'm not proud of my self-serving heartlessness or that of my ex-friends, or of disrespect doled out during the short and glorious lives of all the game-bred terriers I've had the privilege to encounter.

None of us have earned the right to stand in judgment of creatures better than us. I used the same tired excuse "I was drunk." I might have cried myself back to sanity but was too numb. Perhaps I should cry now, but I have no more tears. What I do have is atonement driven by anguish of betrayal, to memories of trusting eyes steeped in infinite faith as they comforted in approaching hands bloodied from treason. They were hands very much like politicians stained by soldiers, to kill and be killed in the name of greed and lunacy.

I morn the permanent loss of those who trudged toward anguish, forward into the jaws of extinction – merely to please us. Through abuse, they pleaded for us to understand. But we were the animals – drunk with narcissism, too self-absorbed to notice the hurt of animals too stupid to distrust human notions of greed, disloyalty or premeditated cruelty. So they paid the ultimate price, the type of loss from which one cannot *bounce*. Those little dogs taught us how to give all and asked for nothing in return, other than a little love and occasional attention.

What's that? I heard a muffled voice overhead saying something about a 12-year memorial of the Twin Towers. *Wait a minute. That shit happened in September. I got blown up in July. But I heard on a TV or a radio a voice saying it was Labor Day. Where the fuck have I been?*

CH XIII: Whitey & Rocco

Happy Halloween!: The unavoidable is where I found myself in 2013, buried in what felt like a cellar, listening to excited groups of children laugh and cry out "Trick-or-Treat!" I could hear the wind outside laying a thick wintry blanket against what must have been glass block windows. I thought about my own little Gina wearing her costumes over a winter coat and leggings. *Could that really have been 30 years ago? And now I heard a news story above me about the 12th anniversary of when those slimy cocksuckers attacked and destroyed the Twin Towers and killed thousands of our citizens for no fucking reason. That's September. But now I'm hearing kids outside calling Trick-or-Treat. That's October, right? Could three months have passed already? I got blown out of our car at the end of July. I know that for a fact. It was my birthday and the day I finished my novel...* I passed out again.

October 31st, 2013: The weather was unseasonably warm. Rocco and Danni stopped talking when they spotted old Clara and Mrs. Downs out in the front yard. They had strung a clothesline from a pillar of their front porch to a limb of a maple tree. Their line sagged almost to the ground in the middle. Mrs. Downs poised herself on a six foot high wooden folding ladder beneath the tree while Clara bent over an old wicker basket full of laundry. Clara had a few wooden clothespins sticking out of her mouth.

"Hi, Ms. Clara. Can I give you ladies a hand with that?"

Clara mumbled something incoherently in response. The skeletal lady was still dressed in her black wool uniform of a widow, even though she hadn't been married for decades.

"I'm sorry, ma'am, I didn't understand you."

She spit clothespins in a basket: "Excuse me, sonny?"

"What? Oh, sorry... I didn't understand you."

"I'm not deaf, dumb or stupid. I just don't get what you mean. Why are you always so *sorry* about everything? What do you keep apologizing about? I was the one with clothespins in my mouth, not you. Don't you know people aren't supposed to talk with their mouth full?"

"I don't think that applies when people are working, ma'am."

"Working?" clucked Mrs. Downs. "You call that working? I've been standing on this stupid ladder for over an hour watching her work." Mrs. Downs wore huge a pink sweat suit with shiny beads on the front of her shirt arranged in a pattern to look like an image of a rabbit. What she wore looked like a dirty child's outfit, only it was bigger than necessary to accommodate her generous girth.

"Why don't you let me move that ladder closer to the clothesline so I can tighten up that rope? Here, let me help you down, Mrs. Downs."

"She won't listen to me. I told her not to tie this rope to a tree. I told her if we tied it to this ladder, then we can move the ladder to tighten the rope. Doesn't that make better sense to you? What do you think, Ms Danni?" asked old Clara.

"Hmmm... I might do this in the backyard." Danni said.

"Why," Mrs. Downs clucked. "Does it look dingy?"

"Oh, no, ma'am," Danni said. "In fact, I was noticing the bright colors. It looks very clean. Did you do this load yourself?"

"I do the laundry," answered Clara. "Why? Are you saying there's something wrong with the whites?"

"I'll have you know, my sister does the whitest whites on the street," announced Mrs. Downs from her ladder, waving a blubbery arm. "Look around you. Do you see any of the neighbors with laundry any whiter than ours?"

Danni helplessly glanced at Rocco: "It's really impressive. I wish I could do laundry this well. Does she use bleach?"

"Ask her yourself! She's right there! I already told you, I don't care much for laundry."

"What is it, Rocky? Why are you trying to hide my laundry in the backyard? And why are you two so hell-bent on tightening this rope? You about to hang someone, are you? Eeeee Heeee! You Eye-talian boys have some tempers on you." Clara shrieked.

"Rocco is sweet and gentle," Danni said in his defense.

"What about you?" asked Clara. "Are you Chinese?"

"How do you mean?" Danni asked.

"You have heard of a country named China, haven't you? Well, people there are called Chinese. Are you one of them?"

"No, ma'am. I'm American."

"Well then, why are you so worried about laundry all the time if you're not Chinese? Are you sure you're not one of those Orientals? Because you look like some type of darkie to me. Or maybe you're Eye-talian too, like this big-shot, inspector boyfriend of yours. Well, are you or aren't you? Which is it?"

"Well, yes and no, ma'am."

153

"What? Yes *and* no? What on God's green Earth is that supposed to mean?"

Rocco said, "It means she's half Italian and half Irish. And her Italian half is Sicilian. If you don't need our help here, ma'am, we have some things to attend to."

"Ah Hahaha! Excuse me all over the place for even being born, Mr. Smarty-Pants *dago* with the Chinese girlfriend."

"Come-on, Clara. Let's get this laundry hung before it gets as wrinkled as you are," her sister advised. "I can't stay up here on this confounded ladder all day!"

"We would have been finished if it hadn't of been for Mr. Big-shot here and his little geisha girl interrupting us."

"Excuse me, ma'am, but geisha girls are Japanese. If you're referring to China, I think the term you're looking for is concubine."

Mrs. Downs said, "Chinese, Japanese, what's the difference? Does she have her papers, Rocky? Why can't you just admit it if you carried her back here from Vietnam?"

"I'm way too young to have been to Vietnam," Rocco reminded the landlady.

"Why?" barked Clara. "You're too young to get a plane ticket, are you? Or maybe you're trying to pretend you're too young to get you one of those mail-order dragon ladies."

"But I'm not even Asian, Ms Clara. Please believe me," Danni pleaded, almost crying. "I'm half Italian, half Irish and all American!" she announced with her best smile.

"Don't blame us! It's not our fault about your age *or* race, missy. Now if you'll excuse us, some folks have work to do. Now me, I've always been of the mind that when people are working, the polite thing to do is move on and let folks get to it."

"Kids today have no work ethic," agreed Mrs. Downs.

"It's been a pleasure seeing you two ladies. And you're right; we wouldn't want to stand in the way of progress. Come on, Danni. Please excuse us."

Hurrying to escape the two crazy ladies, Rocco led Danni by the elbow to the front door just left of the landlady's downstairs entrance. He slammed the door behind them and they ran up the stairs laughing harder with each step.

"Holy shit!" Danni said, between fits of laughter. "Is it possible that those two are actually getting crazier? Oh shit! I'm gonna pee myself. Hurry up! Thanks for getting us out of there,

Rocco. I felt like I was peaking on acid. Talking to them is like watching a Fellini movie!"

October 31st, 2013: A roach smoldered like incense in a thick glass ashtray while Whitey opened a fresh beer to a marathon of TV commercials. The set blared an historical bout broadcast live to decide the baddest man on the planet. Boxing's current WBA heavyweight champion was about to take on the UFC heavyweight champion in a televised mixed martial contest. He and Rocco had been waiting for this fight for months. The match was about to be enjoyed in Rocco's 2nd story crib above his batty landlady's house. She and her crazy sister, Clara, felt safe with Rocco and Bull there to keep an eye on things in a neighborhood that had quickly taken a turn for the worse. Collinwood had transitioned from an Italian and Irish bomb epicenter to a black ghetto of barred storefronts and gang-signed walls welcoming strangers into a gladiatorial arena.

Whitey left his custom Evo at the curb, chrome glinting off street lights. Once inside, he removed his colors from his thick riding leather. He slipped back into his faded, denim cut-off vest after he tossed his jacket on an empty front-room chair. The fringed jacket made a heavy thump when his riding pistol hit the chair. The back of his vest bore three large patches – their club colors: The top rocker arced down from its center read from shoulder blade to shoulder blade: "Wong Gongs MC." The bottom rocker arm, bent from his waist, read: "Cleveland, OH." The red lettering was outlined with white for contrast and then framed by dark blue. Those two arc shaped patches formed two segments of an uncompleted circle. In the center of them was the third one, a large red patch illustrating their "1%er" in flamed wings, also outlined with the white and dark blue, was centered in the middle of his denim vest – right in the center of his muscular back. Every member's colors were alike. The only difference between theirs and brothers in other states was the inscription of city and state of origin on the bottom rocker.

Rocco said, "I got something to run past you," as Whitey made himself comfortable. "When I was at rehab I was talking to a couple of guys about chicks. When you're confined in those places there are only two subjects: drugs and babes."

He and Rocco sat on an old nine-foot long couch upholstered in a rough pattern of earth tones, preparing for the upcoming pay-on-demand fights – now commercialized.

"Yeah, jail's the same way. All those guys talked about is pussy and getting high, the two things they can't get inside. Why, Roc?" Whitey asked, as he lit a cigarette.

"Thinking about something two guys in rehab told me."

"Okay," said Whitey, as he blew smoke through a nose that showed it had been broken a few times. "So what did those two assholes have to say that was so interesting?"

"First they started out talking about fucking, then getting head. Then they switched gears and were talking about ass fucking."

"Ass-fucking dudes or chicks?" Whitey asked, in-between blowing smoke rings.

"Chicks," Rocco said. "So when I asked them why anybody would want to stick their dick in some shit when that sweet gash is just an inch away, they both laughed."

"Oh yeah? What the fuck's so funny about that?"

"The one little guy said, 'Are you serious, Rocco? You really don't get it?' and they both started cracking up like I was George fucking Carlin, or some shit. When I told them I had no idea what the fuck they were talking about, this one real tall skinny dude with buck teeth said, 'It's about humiliation, man. It's to treat those whores like the pigs that they are, and then leave them laying there in pain with shitty cum all over their backs. It's about getting over, man.' And then they both laughed again."

"Why did you feel the need to share that with me, Roc?"

"I was sitting here thinking of all the reasons I never wanna fuck with high-powered drugs again and take the chance of going back to treatment. Plus, it reminded me of something my Pop said."

"What did Jackie say about ass fucking?" asked Whitey.

"He didn't comment on the sex. Gina was there. But he talked about addiction. He said, 'Drugs are a symptom of something else going on'. Pop said, 'Addiction is a thinking disease; a pattern of behaviors that linger because of twisted logic'. He said, 'Just because you stop using doesn't mean your brain automatically gets reset. That part is up to you'. And I see now that he knew his trade well."

"Yeah, dig it. Jackie was one smart dude. My ol' man always told me Jackie was the only *dago* he trusted in *WOP* town."

"I'm missing him real bad, Whitey. But I still feel him. I even look for him sometimes. I'm pissed and sad at the same time. And whenever I think about him I feel it even stronger. You know? It's like we get one chance and then it's all over."

"Yeah, man, I know what you mean. It's like that for me with one of the brothers I lost. It just don't seem possible."

Whitey had been raised by his mother, Maureen Kelly, till he turned 18, at which time he moved in with his father, Ansel. By the time Whitey turned 21 he became the only prospect the Wong Gong's vice-president, Animal, ever had.

Whitey, trying to ignore the loud TV ads, stubbed out his cigarette and asked, "Speaking of chances, what's your decision, Roc? You gonna take the bet or not?"

"I don't know, man. I could definitely use the cash. But there's a lot more to it than just money."

Whitey untied his long blonde hair and shook it lose over his colors as we settled in for a night of mixed martial fights. An advertisement for spray deodorant on the free segment of the show almost seamlessly segued into another commercial about the virtues of drinking manly beer.

"Come on, you pussy. Choose a fucking lane, Roc. Sack up, bro. Bull's a fucking Ace and still in the prime of his life. And you're a goddamn top-notch conditioner, you lazy prick."

"You've been hanging around you're ol' lady too much, white man. You ought to try not to curse so goddamn much, you crazy fuck."

"You're ol' lady's pretty far from Cinderella. And speaking of those two crazy bitches, Roc, where the fuck are they?"

Bull sat in front of Whitey and jammed him a few times in the thigh with one of his front paws. The large Pit-bull didn't realize his own power at times. When he did that pawing thing to get attention it felt like being jabbed with a metal poker.

"What, Bully? You gotta go outside? Tell your lazy owner."

"I just let him out before you pulled up."

Whitey asked. "So you don't think you owe this primo dog the chance to go for his championship? Is that what you're saying? He doesn't deserve to be a champion? Or is it the money? I already told you, man, I got you covered on that. No sweat."

"It's not just that, Whitey. Like I said, it's more involved."

"Really? Well, he sure the fuck ain't getting any younger. Are you Bully Boy? But you have to agree, Roc, he's still in his prime. Look at him. He's all muscle and balls. If he picks up his CH I oughta patch him – make him the first canine prospect."

"He is still in his prime, no doubt. Plus Bull loves the exercise and all that attention he gets while he's in keep. But I don't know, bro, probably not." Rocco stroked his thick black beard as a marathon of loud commercials continued.

"Fuck-it. You should go for it, Roc. This dog's like us. The onliest thing Bull likes as much as fucking is fighting. And he's the best pit-dog I've seen. My ol' man said the same thing, and Ansel saw some great dogs at the conventions. Plus, we can all get paid. Then you retire him and make a shit-ton of cash off stud fees and selling pups. He'll be getting paid to fuck. How do you beat that? Oh, by the way, Filo's little rednose bitch, Bella, dropped a small litter from when you bred Bull to her. Isn't that a good breeding on Jackie's CH Biddy through his Little Sinbad?"

"Yeah, that's a half-brother-sister breeding that Biddy bitch my Pop's bred that made an international Champion of Champions. That's the last of that blood from tested stock from the old Sinbad and Crazy Gracie line through Bella and Little Sinbad. Bull and Filo's bitch are all that's left. I sure hope those pups survive. I'd love to have a bitch from that litter for breeding. Maybe we could squeeze one more litter out of Little Sinbad."

Bull moved over to Rocco and began pawing hard at his leg. Then he ran one room over, into the kitchen, to knock around an empty metal water bowl on the linoleum floor.

"Okay, boy, I'll be right there. I gotta let him out. But I don't know, Whitey. I got a bad feeling about this. That Cagootz and Louie are taking over everything. You can't flip coins against a wall without those cocksuckers getting involved."

"Fuck those mob boys. Their day is over. My people got juice, too. Ansel ain't too impressed with those dudes. Besides, Bull should get a chance to pick up his third *W*. I say make him a champ, bro. Make him famous like Ch Biddy. That's my opinion, but that's what I'd do. This shit is history, Roc."

The empty water dish was being slid back and forth across the kitchen floor by that big, overgrown pup.

"I'd feel a lot better if Jackie, I mean if my dad… Never mind. Skip it. I can't even go there right now. AGH…fuck-it! But I gotta tell you something, bro. I'm not putting this behind me till I see a dead body. And I don't mean Pop's body."

"They never really found his body, cuz. Maybe he's still out there somewhere. You never know, right? Stranger shit has happened. He's one cagey old dude."

"I'd rather not talk about this. Let me go water this dog."

"I've never know you to be a quitter, Roc," Whitey yelled into the next room. "You got this hot chick slobbering all over you, so now all the sudden you're cunt-struck like some fucking teenager. Now you're bailing on Bull before he even gets a title shot. Don't give up believing your Pop is still out either, bro."

As Rocco reentered the front-room he said, "Nah, it ain't that at all. It's strange, but I still feel my Pop sometimes like I did when we were kids before I ever even knew him. It's like he's trying to connect with me. But I suppose everybody feels that when they lose a parent. I guess it's just wishful thinking, right?"

"Who knows, Roc?"

"But I'll guarantee you one fucking thing: if I ever find out who did that to my father I'm going to prison or dying. Fuck-it. And I don't give a flying fuck who it is or who they're connected with."

No worries, bro. If we ever find out who planted that bomb on your ol' man, some stupid motherfucker's getting greased. You can count on that shit, brother! Count me in for 100% of that action. I'm all over this," Whitey said.

"I don't know, bro. Maybe it's just me, but I can't believe he's gone *forever*," Rocco said, as he looked at the floor and shook his head full of curly black hair. "I don't know, man… I just know I'm all fucked up behind this shit. I sure do miss him. Then I go to The Inn to pick up Danni from work and those guys who knew Jackie all their lives pretend like nothing happened. It's like nobody cares. You're here and then you're gone. Boom – and that's it. Nobody gives a shit."

"Believe me, Roc," his oldest friend assured him. "That's the way these motherfuckers are, and you know this. They could care less," Whitey said, as he stretched long legs and rested his boots, one on top of the other, on a coffee table that held the remote and other necessary party materials for fight night.

Whitey was every bit as crafty and dangerous as his old-school biker father, Ansel, but appeared to be calmer. He repeated, "Yep. Bet on that shit. These ignorant cocksuckers could care less…"

Happy to change an uncomfortable subject, Rocco said, "Wait awhile. Back up a quick minute." He picked up what remained of the joint, hit it and passed it back to his friend. "Listen to yourself one time. Why would you talk like that?"

"What? Are you fucking kidding me? You gotta ask?" Whitey accidentally dropped an ash on his tattered Levi's. He ground it in to the material with his long thumb. "After all the crazy shit we've seen, you're still surprised by anything?" He tore the front cover off a book of matches, rolled it in a tight little tube and inserted the roach into one end as he added, "I don't know, man. Sometimes I wonder about you."

Rocco pulled his black curls into a loose ponytail and held it back with a hair tie from one of his well-worn pockets as he watched his best friend almost burn himself with a paper match. "Why? Just because I asked a simple question? All I'm talking about is the way you just said what you just said. Just back up and listen to yourself awhile. I'm trying to do you a favor here."

"Hey, Roc. Do me a small favor. Don't start in with your crazy shit again, okay? You want anymore of this or not?"

"Yeah. But just say that again. You know; the part about, *They could care less*. Listen closer this time." While gesturing with an index finger for effect, Rocco said, "It don't sound good like that is all I'm saying. It's the wrong *tense*, or some shit like that."

"Really? Just listen at you, dude. You're the one that's getting all tense. Fucking relax, cuz! Hey! Now look at this shit on the TV. They got heated condoms? Are they for real with this? Or is this like one of those fake commercials on Saturday Night Live? I mean, why the fuck would I want heated rubber over my cock when I'm about to ram it inside some hot juicy gash?"

"Yeah, really. And check out the dreamy look on this chick's face. She's probably thinking about sliding one of those hot socks on a big, fat dildo. Look at her eyes, Whitey. This fucking broad is scary, man. She's freaking me right the fuck out."

"Can you imagine a bull-dyke with a box full of those things? She'd be like Captain Big-Dick with porno nunchucks. Meantime, fuck these commercials. Let's get back to that other thing. Telling me I use the wrong tense… Are you for real? You're the one who's too tense. I could care less."

Bull zig-zagged throughout the house with his rump tucked, and then stopped in front on Whitey. Again he began gouging him in the leg with those drill-press feet of his.

Rocco said, "I told you this crazy bastard's gotta go."

The big red dog glanced at his giant black Kong toy and then repeatedly jabbed Whitey in the same spot.

"Why don't you just let him out and get it over with before the fights start? Hey, Bull, relax! Go fuck with your lazy owner. And what's with you lately with these English lessons?"

"English lessons?" Rocco asked. "Hey man, I'm just tying to help a brother out. It's really some simple shit, but we hear it wrong every day. Even though it doesn't make any sense at all, we just blindly accept it because we heard it before. Believe me. I know what I'm talking about. I learned all about this kind of shit in class."

Bull ran to his Kong and scooted it up against Whitey's greasy boot. He sat, all glassy-eyed barking at Whitey's hand.

"Hey thanks, Roc. Good looking out. So what are you now, a speech therapist? Hey man, you want this or not? I'm burning myself here." He passed the roach to Rocco and then reached for the Kong, as Bull's barking turned into vicious sounding growls. Whitey picked up the toy, commanded Bull to sit and then tossed is behind him into the kitchen. Bull took off like a shot to retrieve it.

"Okay, cool. I think there's maybe a hit or two left. But you'll be sorry you started that game with him," Rocco cautioned. "That fetch game doesn't have an ending unless he collapses or I put his toy up on the table. He won't mess with it up there." Rocco cherried up that tiny roach till he almost inhaled it through their homemade cardboard roach clip called a "crutch." He stifled a cough and then passed it back to his best friend. "Did I ever tell you the story about—"

"Quit being so wishy-washy, man. What do you think? You gonna let Bull get his title shot or not?" He shook his whitish-blonde hair back over his shoulders again and then carefully picked up the roach between the fingernails of his right thumb and index finger. "Besides, you're just trying to change the subject." Whitey inhaled the tiny roach so hard it got caught in his windpipe. "Goddamn, son-of-a-bitch! Look what you made me do? Talking all that nutty shit …"

"Alright, fuck-it. I'm just trying to help a brother out."

Whitey coughed again and chugged the remainder of his beer. "You're not gonna stop about this, right? So go ahead then. Just fucking say it and get it over with."

"First let me let out this maniac." Rocco let Bull out to piss on a fence post and they were back inside within minutes.

"Okay, first of all, let's recap. Here's what you said, Whitey: You said, 'They *could* care less.' Those were your exact words, right? Now just think about it. If they *could* care less, that means they *do* care but not all that much. Otherwise, you'd say, They *couldn't* care less. That's a whole different ballgame."

A commercial for erectile dysfunction came on as Whitey unrolled the cardboard crutch. "Oh yeah! Guess what? Who gives a fuck? Dude, look at you. You sound like one a them douche bags on the news. Just because you're taking a class at the community college doesn't mean you actually graduated yet. You're still in your first semester, killer. And you sure as fuck ain't no teacher. Do you even have your GED yet?"

Finally, that segment of commercials was over and two announcers were yelling at one another, standing about one foot apart from each other.

"I'm getting a cold one before it starts. You ready, Roc?"

"Nope. I told you I'm done drinking and finished with that other hard shit. But just hold-up a second. I'll explain what I was saying," Rocco offered, as he tossed the Kong for Bull.

"Be right back. Twist up another bomber."

As Rocco creased a paper and lightly sprinkled some sweet-ass hydro across its folded end Whitey yelled from the kitchen, "What time are the girls supposed to be here, anyways? They keep dragging ass like this, they're gonna miss the action."

"They don't care. They just wanna see the title fight."

"Yeah, no doubt. Fuck these loudmouthed announcers," Whitey yelled. "I'd like me and you to step in the cage with those two jerk-offs."

"But I figure the main match should be over in the first round. So we might as well watch all the fights. Hey, where's my dog?" Rocco licked the glue end and rolled the new joint tight enough to be packed but not so tight that it wouldn't burn. He wedged that *pinner* between the matchbook and remaining back cover, sealed the baggie and then let out a huge belch.

"What?" Whitey hollered. "I can't barely hear you!"

"See!" Rocco laughed. "You just did it again! You don't even know you're doing it, do you? You do too many drugs, man. Your eggs are getting scrambled."

"Save it," he yelled. "I can't barely hear shit with those assholes screaming at one another. Wait till I get back in there."

Rocco drained the rest of a sugar-free ginger ale while an old guy who had been around the boxing game for years tried to out-talk a UFC announcer who also did stand-up comedy. At the peak of mania, red-faced with glaring eyes, they laughed and shouted accolades into hand-held mics like they were on speed.

Whitey plopped down and slid a beer sideways to me with the back of his hand. "So what's all this about? What are these two maniacs on here going on about now?"

"They're saying if you didn't already purchase the fights to call now and shit like that.. But the freebee part should be good, too. I saw this Asian dude fight in Strikeforce. He's a little bulldog. This Mexican kid used to fight in Wrekcage. Even though this kid from WEC was a champion, I think this Jap will hand that *beaner* his ass on a platter."

The first pair of fighters' stats appeared on the screen just as the girls entered. Bull charged them and toppled Whitey's sweetie ass over elbows, and then licked her face.

Carrie laughed, "Get off, asshole! You made me spill my beer, you fucking goofball. I thought Pits were supposed to be guard dogs."

"Where did you hear they're serious guard dogs?"

"I read it in the newspaper or heard it on TV."

"Really, Carrie? And you believe all that bullshit?"

"Please, Rocco, don't start getting all political already. We've not even all the way inside yet. Give it a rest. Besides, now I have beer all over me."

"Why the fuck you gotta drink in the car?" Whitey asked. "You can't wait 15 goddamn minutes for your next fix? Go ahead; put the rest of those in the fridge. Hurry up. This could be quick, so keep it down. It's almost on, baby."

"Yeah, sure thing, *baby*," Carrie answered dryly, as she wiped beer off a red low-cut t-shirt stretched tightly across stand-up breasts that stuck out as if they were on a serving tray. Across her chest, printed in black lettering, read, "What Color Are My Eyes, Pervert?"

"Glad to see you, too," replied the blue-eyed blonde. Her freckled nose wrinkled as if she had smelled something foul.

Danni asked, "How about you, Roc? You need anything while I'm up, like stir-fry or a blow job?" She wore her usual black jeans and a tight black shirt to match short-cropped, thick hair and dark eyes. Her year-round tan contrasted the whitest teeth ever on a person who regularly drank tea and coffee.

They vanished into a bare kitchen just before the first set of mixed martial artists entered the octagon for their scheduled three round match – five minutes per round.

"Whitey, just look at this part one time. When you were in the kitchen you said, *I can't barely hear you.* If you *cannot* barely hear me, that means you would've clearly heard me. Get it now?"

"What? Hey, Roc, I gotta admit it. I could care less about any of this bullshit. Somebody please give this nutty fuck some hard drugs before his head explodes."

"There it is again… But okay, Whitey. Fuck-it. Go ahead. Take more hard drugs. Then we'll see whose head explodes."

"Hard drugs?" Carrie asked. "Who's holding out?"

Danni followed Carrie back into the front-room: "Drugs? Who has drugs? What do they have besides warm beer and this shitty weed? Do we have any blow to get drugs?"

"*Blow*? Fuck yes! I'll do some," Carrie smiled as she sat between them. "Who's got the blow? I mean, it is a party, right? So bust it out. Where's the candy?" She added, "Check their pupils, Danni. These fucks really did coke-up before we got here. Come on, man," Carrie demanded. "Don't be holding out, you two fucking tightwad pricks."

Round one ended. Whitey hissed, "Fucking unbelievable… Carrie, can we watch the fights? I can hardly believe this shit…"

Rocco put up an index finger: "You *can hardly believe this*, Whitey, or you *cannot hardly believe it*? Which one, bro?"

"Can you three maniacs shut-the-fuck-up so I can watch a fight?" Whitey asked, adjusting the volume with the remote."

"I can snit a line real quiet," Danni whispered, as she giggled and squeezed in-between Rocco and her best girlfriend.

"Come on, Rocco," Danni begged. "Carrie's right. This is a special occasion. Lay down some lines, buddy."

Just as Whitey turned to look at the girls in disbelief, the Asian fighter ran at his opponent with a flying knee and knocked down the ex-WEC champ on contact. The Mexican immediately pulled full-guard to clear the cobwebs from his brain.

Carrie begged. "Please… Just one line each. We'll do it real quiet and won't even ask for more."

Whitey said dryly, "Let me say this real clear. We don't have any coke or any other fucking hard drugs. All we got is what you see: beer, cigarettes and weed. That's it…period! Now can we watch this fight?" he asked, as Bull started barking and flipped his Kong toy up at him. "Okay, good boy, Bully. Go get your toy."

The boxing announcer screamed, "How do you knock someone out while they're on top of you! One elbow to the jaw and he's asleep! I've never seen this before!"

The UFC commentator yelled, "I've never even heard of this happening before! This must be some kind of record. And the night has just begun, folks!"

"What the fuck just happened, bro?" Rocco asked.

"Is the fight over?" Whitey answered, with a question.

"Thanks a lot," Danni said, while looking over at Carrie.

"Yeah. Thanks, Whitey. Now we missed out on the coke *and* the knockout!" Carrie said, as she turned her back to her ol' man and made a sour face. "Why the fuck did we even come?"

Whitey folded his tattooed arms: "I don't fucking believe what just happened…"

"Hold up," Rocco said. "Let me ask you two lunatics one simple question: Why would you think we have cocaine? I mean, where did all this come from? We don't even like blow. And you know this, Danni. When did you ever see me do coke?"

"Right… That's exactly the problem," she answered shaking her head. "We didn't *see* you do it, did we? Because you guys did it all up before we even got here. Fucking tightwads."

"And all because we were a few minutes late. Thanks a lot for sharing, Whitey," Carrie chimed in. "Nice party . . . fucking cheapskates!"

"Don't you mean, thanks a lot for NOT sharing?"

Carrie asked, "So you admit it, Rocco?"

"Jesus fucking Christ… Take a break. See, Carrie? That's why you shouldn't drink and drive. You get a split personality when you drink in the car. Besides, you know me and Roc could care less about that tweaky-ass nigger dope."

"I'll just bet you could care *plenty* less," she sassed him.

"See what I mean, bro? Even Carrie notices, and she's half-juiced. It's no good unless you say it the other way."

"I'm a little drunk. So one little line would mellow me out," Carrie slurred.

Bull continued to bark and growl, flipping his Kong around the house with his muzzle.

"Is that what you guys were whispering about when we walked in? Now you two are keeping secrets from us, like we can't be trusted?" Danni asked.

Bull growled, chasing his tail, ripping and running through the house with his Kong in his mouth. He flipped over and tossed his heavy rubber toy in the air. It landed on the wall by the TV and knocked the plug out of the wall outlet.

Carrie laughed, "Nice! Look at this, Danni. They even give Bull a line or two and can't give us one measly bump each? Real fucking nice. And now we miss the fights."

"It's just shit commercials. We can nurse this joint, sip on a brew, and by then Rocco will fix it so we can hear those dummies scream in each other's faces," Danni assured her friend.

Carrie said, "Why are you making us miss this. Is it over?"

Rocco bent the prongs back into shape and plugged it into the socket. "Nah. It's early. They got all this shit to sell first."

Whitey added, "Just look at these two nimrods. One's an old Jew and the other guy's an over-the-hill *dago* who still thinks he's a tough guy. Don't they have any white announcers?"

"That's a real nice observation there, Whitey. Maybe you should Tweet that in, bro. Oh, wait. You do have basic computer skills, right? Maybe they can dig up Johnny and Edgar Winter as announcers for the next card. Are albino's white enough for your neo-Nazi tastes? I mean, an Albino is *almost* as white as you, right?" Rocco asked, dryly.

"Don't take shit so personal, Roc. I mean, look at you. You could almost pass for a white man . . . in the dark . . . in Africa . . . if you'd shave that nappy-ass beard."

"My grandparents are from Europe, Whitey. What about your people? You look like those dudes from Star Trek. Are you about half Klingon, or do you have AIDS?"

"You have HIV, you fucking pig?" yelled Carrie. "How could you not tell me that? Real fucking nice, Whitey... Well, I hope you have a good memory, because that's the last time you'll be inside me, you fucking filthy pig."

"Yeah, Carrie, they probably got infected snorting all that blow they wouldn't share. I hope their dicks fall off," Danni said.

As if the girls hadn't spoken a word, Whitey continued without missing a beat: "Maybe so, Roc. But I'd rather be part Martian than bred down from stink-ass greasers and their nigger conquerors. Sicilians *are* niggers, right bro?"

"Well, at least my ancestors are human and not some fucking zombies. You look like those fucks from *Night of the Living Dead* that live on human blood."

"While we're on the subject of Africans, you remember that spook, Willie Brown, from Glenville who was running all that smack for Sonny Magic down Five Points?"

"You mean the one you and Animal did the Five Points shuffle on him and his gorilla buddy's heads? Yeah. Why, what about him?" Rocco asked, disinterestedly.

"That fucking mountain gorilla they call Smokehouse is one tough motherfucker. He's the only guy I ever knew to be able to hang with Animal for over a minute, till we put the boots to him. That sick bastard's nice with his hands. That's no shit."

"Is Smokehouse fighting MMA now?" Rocco asked.

"I passed Willie on my scooter. He was with a carload of other monkeys. He held his hand out of that lime green Caddie they cruise around in, pointing his black paw at me like it was a piece and yelled, 'There's a new sheriff in town. It's Downtown Willie Brown. See you soon.' They started laughing like a pack of baboons. I don't like that motherfucker looking at me."

"He's Sonny's grandson out of one of his whores, so Willie thinks he's all that. Why did you guys stomp mud-holes in their asses that time, anyway?" Rocco asked.

"I'm not sure, bro. Animal had a beef with him over some shit and we were together. You know how that happens. Why?" Whitey asked, looking at his friend's eyes.

"You pick up something weird from Willie or Smokehouse?"

"Yeah, man, I caught a bad vibe. Now they're in my head, and I don't like it. That's just not healthy."

"Not healthy, huh? For who, you or him?" Rocco chuckled. "Besides, Sonny's losing his power. He's too old. He'd never make a move against your old man."

"Yeah, maybe… Speaking of niggers, that reminds me of Bull's first two matches. So you gonna match him against white men this time?" Whitey asked.

"I don't know, bro. Maybe. I've been torturing myself over this. I sure could use some fast cash right now. But I don't trust the way this is moving. It feels all wrong."

"What about all those grease balls you're related to? What about that WOP, Fingers? He's got an ass-load of clout and money. Hit that *dago* up for the front money."

"No thanks. Related or not, I don't want to be indebted to those kind for anything. I'd rather do this alone or not at all."

Bull flipped up his Kong again, twirled his lithe body in a circle in mid-air and smashed one of his stifles into the TV plug in the wall. The screen went black.

Rocco jumped up to plug the set back into the outlet till he realized one of the metal prongs of the plug had snapped off. He turned towards his friend, holding the broken plug, and said, "Well, I guess we won't be getting our weekly ration of violence tonight. Not with this broke-ass piece of shit, anyway."

Carrie said, "Fuck me... No more coke, and now the TV's broken. So what should we all do now?"

Whitey groaned, "I'll be a motherless fuck! Let's go to the clubhouse, man. I'm sure Filo's tuned in to this." He grabbed his jacket. "Come-on, bro, let's boogie. I don't wanna miss this shit."

"Come on, Danni," Carrie slurred. "I'll bet we can score free drugs from your boss. He's got a serious case of the hots for you. All you'd have to do is flash him one of those cupcakes under your shit and we're set for the night. Roc don't mind."

Danni wrapped her legs around Rocco's waist: "You'd better fucking mind! Because if you don't, I might let them both fuck me and then you'll have to fight them. You're a tough guy. You can take them. Can't you, Mr. Tough-guy?"

"Two on one? I don't know... That doesn't sound like good odds to me. Maybe they'd better bring a friend." Rocco laughed. "Now unhand me, you little hussy."

"Go ahead, Carrie," Danni said, while she still clung to Rocco. "Tell them how you described Cagootz and Louie to me when you came to pick me up from work."

Carrie laughed and coughed, "I told her Cagootz looks like the retarded brother of Bobby Bacala from the Sopranos. And his shadow, Big Louie, reminds me of a *dago* version of Herman the Monster."

Whitey yawned as he walked to the door, "That's a good one. Okay, have fun girls. We won't wait up. Let's boogie, Roc. Maybe we can get a peak at those pups."

CH XIV: The Domino Theory

Gangsters trying to stay off the streets during 1975 went to "the mattresses." Tough guys were laying low. Not surprising, Collinwood had a wave of accidental pregnancies involving adolescents from that same generation we had grown up with. In fact, two of those children born in 1976 were mine. Nobody used condoms. We didn't need to worry about STDs back then. Getting the Crabs (pubic lice) was as ordinary as catching a common cold. The worst thing we had to sweat was the Clap (gonorrhea), which got cured by a shot of penicillin. Sex back then was more like throwing darts till it became a game of dice where we began crapping out in one big cluster-fuck, in a place where everyone was linked to someone – somehow or another.

My wife, Butterscotch, got pregnant in 1975 from my seed. So did Tessa, from a one-night stand. Rocco was born just two months after my daughter, Gina. Ansel, knocked-up the niece of the Mick, a fiery redheaded sister of our enemies, the Kelly brothers. That accidental merger of the Wong Gongs to the Five Points crew produced Whitey, who turned out to be the best friend of my illegitimate son, Rocco. Even the unmarried, alcoholic sister of Pazzo's wife got knocked-up that year by some mystery man. Allegedly, that daughter of Christine Troia was named after some mysterious relative on that side who Christine refused to discuss.

1976 hadn't only been unique in regard to car bombings, gangland murders and fatherless children in Cleveland. 1976 was the year when freedom as I knew it came to an end. I married Butterscotch, a gorgeous daughter of an unwed biracial mother, just as her own mother had been. 1976 also marked the death of brotherhood and the year in which I had passed what I thought had been my final game-test with flying colors. That night at R-bar, when brothers became strangers, all colors were shades of red, its stain all mine. 1976 had been the beginning of the end for other devotions. My obsession and compulsion with hard drugs like heroin, crystal meth and LSD, as well with other forms of self-sabotage, abruptly ended that year.

Uno, while behind bars for a RICO Act conviction in 1976, got shanked by a member of the Arian Brotherhood in a hit financed by Doyle Kelly, who by then was the lone surviving nephew of the Mick. But that one murder set off a chain reaction to a series of Collinwood killings between Cleveland's Italian Syndicate and Collinwood's Irish Mob. The driving forces for the ongoing power-struggle within Cleveland's underworld, money and power, took lives and destroyed Cleveland families.

    Even with Uno gone the Collinwood crew, reinforced by the Royal Flush, was still in control. By 1976, Fingers had interests in many enterprises. He had befriended the correct people to know in Cleveland's dark underworld, especially Ansel and the Wong Gongs. Those bikers had been a neutralizing force against a still powerful Irish mob down Five Points. So with the approval of Little Italy's then under-boss, Fingers was given the nod to fill a void at only 26 years old, to assure that what remained of the Irishman's mob didn't gain control of the Cleveland rackets. Fingers had been temporarily propped up as acting lieutenant at a very tricky time when it looked as though he would be killed by the still dangerous Irishmen, or the bikers who had become more powerful than ever, or his own kind from Little Italy, or at the hands of Sonny Magic.

    Fingers allowed his Uncle Doc to remain as manager of The Inn, which was still one of the central locations for Cleveland's gangland activity. Doc's rage red-lined when he couldn't find out who impregnated his only daughter. So he disowned Tessa during her pregnancy and never saw Rocco, his only grandchild. Doc, an old man more reckless than ever, finally killed himself via emphysema, cirrhosis of the liver, and a mind rotted from spirits used to self-medicate depression, anxiety and an intermittent explosive disorder. Not till after the death of her father in 1986 were Tessa and her bastard son able to return from California to Cleveland, only to watch her mother rot away from cancer of the lymphatic system. The elderly woman didn't last long. That death left Tessa and her son without immediate family in Cleveland, other than Fingers.

    In 2010, when Fingers had been convicted of racketeering conspiracy, extortion, bribery and fraud, he was fined $10,000 and given a ten-year bit in Marion, IL. In his absence, Cagootz became acting under-boss, with Big Louie, a cold-blooded murderer, as his main enforcer. Because Tessa's cousin, Fingers, was already 60 years old when his sentence began, and had been a heavy drinker and smoker since his teens, it looked like he would spend his few remaining years behind bars.

October, 2013: After the July explosion in our front yard in 2013, Gina spent most of her time with my wife. Tessa's best friend, Carly, had gotten herself impregnated in the mid-'80s by Butterscotch's mulatto cousin, Curtis. That produced a handsome biracial son, Junior. That same year of 1985 was also when, Horrible Hank's son, Little Hankie, was born. Those boys were raised as brothers and like younger siblings to my Gina. So those men, nearly 30 years old, became my calabash nephews. After my car *accident* they came around to keep an eye on her and Tessa.

Hankie grew to be a tall, dark and intimidating-looking figure. He was quiet and intense like his father, Horrible Hank. Junior was a charming young man of average size who looked more Italian than black. He looked like a male version of his mother, Carly. Hankie dropped off Junior at Tessa's temporary lodging, half of Carly's double-house, and yelled, "I'll be back in a half hour, cuz. Make sure you're ready for once."

Junior knocked on the front door and politely waited, even though he'd always known he could just walk right in. Gina came out and brushed right past him like he wasn't there. She plopped down on the stoop with her back to him.

"Where's Hankie at?" she asked.

Curtis Jr. sat down next to his cousin, my daughter, and said, "Hankie gone. What up, cuz? How Auntie be deez days? An where you be hidin' at, lil' girly-girl?"

"Stop it, Junior. Speak English. Besides, you're exactly one eighth black – just like me. You're not even dark, you asshole. On your blackest day you might be able to pass for Spanish. Get real! And you're half Italian, just like me. Remember?"

"Whatevers… I's here ta see how Ma's be doin' is all."

"Ma's not doing so well. Tessa mostly sleeps anymore. I try to hang around to help out, but it drives me crazy watching her cry and sleep all the time. It's like I'm just sitting there while she mopes around in some goddamn trance."

"Word-up. Mutha fucka's be in da Wood be sayin' dude be creepin' an shit."

"Cut it out, Junior. Speak American. And pull up those pants, you idiot. You're starting to look like those little *wiggers* you've been hanging with lately."

"Fuck all that. Ax ma baby-momma if I's be a *nigga*. She be swangin' on dis *nigga* drawers, fo sho."

"I mean it, Junior. If you don't cut that jive-ass shit out right now I'm going inside and locking you out here. Go practice your Ebonics all by your lonesome."

"What it? Now you gots sum Eye-talian brutha, all da sudden you's too good fo *niggas* up in da hood? Dat it, lil' cuzzy?"

"I'm warning you. Don't start in with your asshole act. Rocco is an amazing brother. So you'd better watch your mouth, or I just might tell him you're talking shit."

"Rocco be cool fo a *guinea* dawg. Where dat dawg be?"

"That's it! I don't need this bullshit today. Fuck off, loser boy! Go home and talk to the mirror. Leave me alone, asshole!"

"Okay, easy. I'm just trying to make you smile, is all. You need to lighten up, Gina. Laughter is the best medicine. Where's Little Sinbad?"

"Where do you think? He's on Ma's bedroom floor 24/7 like he's glued to her footprints. That old Pit worships her. He's the best medicine for her right now. Besides me, that old dog's the only real connection she has with my dad."

"True dat, lottie mama. Maybe wez goes in ta razz-ma-tazz the ol' gal wif some Junior jokes. Whatcha say, lil' cuzzy?"

"I say that this is the last warning, Junior. Then I'm locking your stupid ass out here. Besides, lifting her spirits is going to take a minute. She needs lots of time to wrap her head around what's happened to my dad. The only thing stopping me from imploding is trying to keep her from wigging out."

"I understand, Gina. I wish there was something else I could do to help."

"There might be. Stay close and quit acting like an asshole. And pay attention. Who knows? You might be next."

A carload of wanna-be thugs wearing sideways hats crawled by blasting a stereo worth more then their shitty-looking Suburban. Their ride looked as if someone had spray painted enamel over rust and dents. Scrawny white and brown arms dangled out windows against a black paintjob showing runs and drips in the sunlight.

"I know, Junior. Ma loves you as much as she does your mom. And it's good to know you're both so loyal. It's also good to give her some space when she needs it."

"No problem, cuz. This is what family does. So where do you go when she's got herself all barricaded in?" Junior asked.

"I read a lot these days. How about you? Are you still with that little stripper?"

"She's not a stripper, and you know it. Hey! I been here a flat 10 seconds and already you're on my ass like wet toilet paper. How about saying: 'Nice to see you, Jr.' That would be sweet for a change."

"Why don't you and Auntie come over for supper? I'll cook. How's that, Junior? That way Carly and Ma can bullshit. They need that bonding time. You know as well as I do, Tessa and Carly are the only two left from their old high school friends. Everybody else is dead or moved and gone away. It's just us and Rocco from now on."

"Don't count out, ol' Uncle Curtis. My crazy ol' man might not be much for hanging at the house, but he pays the bills and protects his own."

"I know. Daddy says Curtis is solid. He says that if your dad could ever get away from that smack he could accomplish anything."

"Yeah, he's still proud as a bald eagle because him and Jackie put in the patch back in the day. My ol' man said he made nothing but money working with your Pop."

"My daddy said Curtis took his bust quiet as a priest and did his time like a man."

"It's weird," said Junior. "You get a guy like Jackie who was one of the main bangers against the brothers during the Collinwood riots. Then he goes and marries himself my auntie, who's definitely a sister, and hangs out with two dope dealin' niggers from the hood. True enough, Auntie Butter and my ol' man can pass for high yellow spics. And you and me both look strait *dago*. But ain't nothin' mulatto about Uncle Hank and Little Hankie. Those two brothers are as black as that Suburban. Horrible Hank is pure African Zulu warrior and Uncle Jack's closest brother. How does that happen?"

"Don't trouble yourself about things beyond your comprehension level. Let it go, Junior. Anyway, Rocco should be here any minute."

Not long after, Rocco thundered up on his tricked-out bike that started out in bushel baskets as Harley parts. He backed it up to the curb, fist-bumped Junior and then grabbed Gina by the elbow to enter the house together. "Where's Ma?" he asked.

"Where is she usually? Barricaded in her room, I guess."

"Junior, thanks for dropping by. We won't keep you, cuz. We'll see you when we see you."

"Alright then, Hankie should be by any minute now. Later, cuz."

Then Rocco called out, "Hey, Ma, where you at," as he kicked off his boots at the door and led Gina into Tessa's bedroom with him.

Little Sinbad, old as dirt, jumped up till he saw friendly faces in a no-fly zone. He settled back down next to Tessa's bed. She flipped her long, graying blonde hair away from her face and paused to rub her neck with one hand while she pointed a petite finger: "Don't you dare brush me off, Rocco. I wasn't finished."

"I wasn't cutting you off, Ma. I just don't wanna talk about personal shit on the phone. You're old-school. You know that. But I came right over, didn't I? Look. I'm here now, right?"

"Like I was saying, before you brushed me off and hung up while I was still talking: Blood is blood. Whitey's allegiance is to his parents, no matter how long he's been your friend. Even though Maureen is a lunatic bitch, I'm sure he'd take a bust for his mother. And he'd kill anyone for his father, not that he'd actually have to. Ansel and their other brothers are as lethal as the worst *paesanos* and micks I've even known. I shouldn't have to remind you about their gang allegiance. You be careful what you say to Whitey, son. You with those stupid drugs again. And what the hell is Ecstasy, anyway? Why is your little Danni doing that crap? And why are you still getting high with her? Does she want you to wind up back in rehab?"

"You know I don't mess with that shit. All I do is smoke a little herb, and maybe have the occasional beer. I'm not an addict, Ma, and you know this."

"Oh really? Then why were you in treatment for a month? What was that, like a mini-vacation to get off work? Or maybe it was just to make me even crazier than I already am. Is that it? You're really full of it sometimes. You know that?"

"Here we go again. How many times I gotta explain, Ma?"

"Just say it so I can understand. And stick to the questions. Just because I'm old doesn't automatically mean I'm an imbecile."

"Okay, here's the thing: With opiates, especially like the shit I was doing and the way I was using them, you get a hook stuck right in the middle of your back. You wanna get it out, but you can't reach it. That hook hurts like a bastard, like a goddamn monkey with its teeth and claws dug right in. That's the *hook*."

"So then you get out and take Ecstasy? Are you serious?"

"Hey! That's not me. Can I please finish? You ask me a whole bunch of questions and tell me to explain, and then you cut me right off before I can answer. That's just rude, Ma."

"Oh? How does it feel when someone does it to you?"

"Please, Ma. I don't want to argue again, okay? I'm right here. Ask me anything you want."

"Go ahead, son. Explain it till it makes sense."

"Okay, so this hook, or monkey, or chemical anchor, is rooted in real deep and in a spot the user can't reach."

"I'm listening. But so far it all sounds like a crock of shit."

"Ma, you keep cutting me off because your mind is made up. Then you pretend like you really want to hear the truth."

"So far all I hear is hooks, monkeys and anchors. That's your version of truth?"

"Ma, please. Just try to follow this for a minute. When you've been using hot and heavy, every day for a few months, and then all the sudden you're not on the stuff, for whatever reason, the withdrawals are a living nightmare. Your whole body aches all the time, inside and out, like you can never get comfortable unless you pass out or take more. Using is the only time somebody who gets stuck with that hook can get any relief."

"Let me see if I have this straight, son. More than anything, you don't want those monkey hooks in your back. And the only reason they're there is because you abused opiates. So what do you do? You take more of the same garbage that puts those hooks into you in the first place, then take more dope so it digs in even deeper. And then because you're a big dope, you take even more till it's like a huge anchor instead of just a little sharp hook, till you *can't* get it out. And that's *relief*? Is that it?"

"Well, sort of. But you're missing something important."

"Oh really? Then humor me, son. What is it?"

"The point is opiate abusers don't only get real body-sick. They're also brain sick at the same time – like sickness of the mind. I was like that, too. Full-blown junkies and hardcore drug abusers tell ourselves the same big-ass lie while we're still caught in the middle of quicksand. And we all believe it, too. Because at the time craziness like that makes sense to a convoluted mind poisoned with drugs and full of dope sickness."

"I'm not a girl scout, okay? I get it, Rocco. Do you think your generation invented drugs and these concepts? Your father knew more about this stuff than anyone, so this isn't news. Okay? Lately you shut me out. Yet you seem to trust your friends more than family. What the hell is all that about, anyway?"

"Ma, you're making a big deal out of nothing. Easy does it, okay? The worst is over."

"Wow... What I'm asking you, son, is simply this: Why do you trust Whitey not to tell Ansel everything you say and do? Yet you don't trust me – your own mother! You just brush me off like I'm some addled old lady who was never a young girl."

"That's total bullshit, Ma, and you know it."

"Pay attention, Rocco. No matter how close you and Whitey are or how big of a bastard that Ansel is, that man is still Whitey's father. And when it comes to their club, at the end of the day you're a stranger to all of them – you're disposable and replaceable. Those Italians like my cousin are the same exact way. You'd better wake up and face what's real, instead of believing what you insist is reality but is nothing more that your own version of more bullshit drug dreams. Didn't you learn anything from your father? Just look what happened to him!"

"Ma, I'm asking nice. Please, take it easy. You're the one creating all this in your own mind. There's nothing to any of it other than what you're choosing to believe."

"Wake up, Rocco, before you wind-up at the receiving end of a final notice like your father did. There are certain things you can't apologize your way out of or bullshit your way through. Wake up, son, before it's too late. I can't lose you, too. Please... You remember what your father taught you and your sister about truth?"

Gina sat up straight on the edge of the bed: "Yeah, Ma. During one of our story-times Daddy told us there are two types of truths. He called it *truth-juggling*. Remember? Daddy admitted he'd done it with *brothers*, or adolescent *true loves*, or with *partying* while caught-up in adrenaline or hormonal rushes that for the moment helped myths seem to make more sense than health, well-being and freedom – and even life. Right, Ma?"

"I don't know this sermon," yawned Rocco. "Let's go."

"Daddy said, 'Truths are constructed.' Remember?"

"No, I don't. What are you, a human tape recorder? Let's boogie. My bike's out on the road." Rocco stretched and flexed.

"No, but I had an extra 35 years to hear him preach. He also said, 'At times we have to check that invisible scale in our brains and use dialectical reasoning to find which way the balance beams for logical reasoning tip and why. He said that can only be accomplished with an open mind in search of a higher, more usable truth. Not with a closed mind frozen in time by childish fears.' But that's all I remember." Gina gave a big smile.

"You coming or not? I gotta go see a man about a dog."

October 31st, 2013: At The Inn, Danni took a last look at herself in her compact, nervously mussing her short-cropped hair that was just as black and as thick as Rocco's, as he exited the car thoughtfully stroking his bushy beard. She wondered what was going on in that mind of his this time. In a way she hoped she was pregnant and figured that Rocco would come around to liking the idea. But the timing was all wrong. Still, she was tired of her life and fancied the idea of settling down. She was glad he had changed his last name to that of his father's, in tribute to him – which might soon be hers. Watching Rocco cross the street, she moved towards the front door and called out to him: "Hi!"

"Hi yourself, babe. Ready?"

As they drove home, she thought about today's events and blurted out, "People are saying you're bringing Bull out for his third. Why didn't you tell me?"

"People say a lot of things. That sounds like something that would come from your little friend, Carrie. Was she blacked-out drunk and shooting off at the mouth again as usual?"

"Maybe, Rocco. But the real question is, why does she think that? I'm just curious."

"Me and Whitey discussed it. He thinks I should do it. In a way I'd like to, to give him his chance at making Pit-bull history. But in the spirit of honesty . . . the fact is . . . I kind of lost my taste for all that. That dog is as much a brother to me as Whitey."

"If Whitey was determined to fight MMA like you did, would you be his trainer so he got the best *keep* possible?"

"Why are you asking me all this shit? Do you really want me to match our Bully-boy for a third time? Is that what this is?"

"It's not just that. It's . . . well, Cagootz wants you to stop in to see him when you have time. He's my boss, babe."

"What's that scuzz want this time?" Rocco asked dryly.

"There's going to be another one of those gambling things next month. It's going to be the weekend right after Christmas, on Saturday, the 28th of December."

"So? What's that got to do with me? I don't gamble, and he ain't *my* boss. Fuck the holidays and those assholes, and especially Cagootz. There's something wrong with that guy."

"He says he's got something going for you to make some real cash. He tells me it's juicy and it's right up your alley."

"I just don't trust that fat cocksucker. He has an aura of evil like a stink. Tell Cagootz to find some other chump to do his dirty work. Never mind. Don't tell him anything. I'll tell him myself. By the way, did you ask Mr. Big-bucks for that raise yet?"

"Yes, I did," she answered, not wanting to get in another argument about her boss. "That's when he told me about this deal. He said he would include my raise in this deal."

"Deal, huh? That guy's always got an angle. If it's that important, he knows our phone number. I still blame that fat motherfucker for our family losing The Inn and for grandpa's death. I'll tell you something, babe, this boy of yours doesn't impress me."

"Please don't start in again. And he's not my boy. He's a dirty old man. You're my boy. I'm just wondering . . . some fast cash wouldn't hurt right now."

She was sorry she mentioned anything about that, dreading a discussion over her presumed condition next. While Danni gazed at nothing in particular, Rocco slipped his arm around her slim waist as they passed through their gate. He was thinking what a shame it would be if she lost this perfect body due to his carelessness.

"I know what he wants. Whatever it is, it's some one-way shit where he profits and someone else gets fucked. That dude's poison, baby. Quit that dump and we'll move away from this neighborhood. We'll take Ma with us and get a fresh start somewhere else where there's jobs and real people. These people here are drowning, babe, and trying to drag us down with them. I can barely breathe here, anymore."

"I can't quit till I find something else. You already know this. And I'm not trained to anything else. Besides, there's shit for jobs in Cleveland right now."

"You want to own a champion that bad, Danni?"

"That has nothing to do with anything. I don't care about titles. But speaking of that . . . is he still young enough to pull it off? I mean . . . against top condition?"

"Who, Bully-boy? I guess so. Why? What's this obsession all the sudden with having a champion pit-dog?"

"Did I stutter? I already told you, Rocco, it's not that."

"Yeah, no shit. I knew that before I asked. So now maybe you're irritated enough to finally tell me what's really going on."

Rocco and Danni stopped talking when they spotted old Clara and Mrs. Downs out in the front yard. "Holy shit!" Danni said, breathlessly between fits of laughter. "Is it possible that those two are actually getting crazier? Oh shit! I'm gonna pee myself. Hurry up! Let's get upstairs quick to our guns and Pit-bull where we're safe!" she laughed while running upstairs.

"Those crazy bitches are nuts. But you gotta love 'em."

Still laughing in their house, she buried her face into his neck, as laughter gave way to what sounded like crying while burrowed into him.

"What is it, baby-girl? Did that fat fuck mess with you?"

"It's not him, and it's not that."

"Well, then whatever it is can't be all *that* bad. Right?"

She finally moved to face him. Her head slightly lowered, peering up through smeared eye makeup, she gave him a half smile and asked, "Wanna bet?"

She handed him two letters. He looked them over briefly and realized he still owed over $1,500 for custom parts on what just because his ex-Harley. If they repossessed it he would lose a main connection he'd shared with his brother for years.

"Okay, so that's a little more than we figured on. But don't worry, babe. We'll get by somehow. We always do."

"I'll tell you why those two old bats have seemed even crazier than usual. That crazy landlady and her batty old sister were up here earlier. They said if we don't get caught up and a month ahead by the first, we're out."

"I'll talk to them, baby-girl. I might be able to get most of it by next week, anyways," Rocco said, knowing full well that was most probably not the case. "Maybe I'll let her bake me cookies."

"Real funny, but I went to the doctor this morning. I was right... I fucking knew it! Can you believe all this bullshit?"

"Is that all? *She---itt*.... Watch me. I got this."

"There's more: Your lawyer called. He needs to talk to you first thing Monday morning. He's says it's urgent."

"That just means he wants money. That's the onliest time those pricks phone their clients. Well, he can get in line with the rest. Unless it's to clear it for me to get a CCW permit. If that's the case, my man bumps up to top priority. I'll call him first thing in the morning, bight and shiny," Rocco laughed.

"Oh yeah . . . and your pain management doctor called. He cut you off. There's a phone message he left for you, Rocco. Press the button. I saved it."

179

"He cut me off because I pissed clean. He's worried I'm selling pills. Fuck-it. I was getting off that shit, anyways. I don't need it. Weed works as good and won't fuck up my liver."

"You'd better not get strung out on opiates again. You'll be balled-up like a giant tattooed baby for a week, kicking the covers and begging me to get you fixed-up."

Rocco hadn't moved anything but his jaw muscles since hearing the bombardment of bad news. The last thing he needed at the moment was to be dope-sick on top of everything else. He forced out a little one-*ha* chuckle and offhandedly said, "No worries. You know I was never hooked. Besides, I'll just get strung out on Suboxone to help me detox."

Her lower lip trembled: "I mean it. This isn't funny."

"Fuck all that. I'm as clean as Mother Teresa's snatch."

"She's dead, Rocco."

"No shit! Sorry to hear that. When?"

"Sometime in the '90s. What planet have you been on for the past 20 years?"

"Hey, that reminds me! I got a great joke for you. Wait till you hear this one, babe. It's a seven-*Ha* joke. Ready?"

She started to shudder, making little sneezing sounds.

He looked closer at the beautiful girl by his side. Tufts of her short-cropped wavy hair stuck out while some of it matted by sweat to her forehead. Tears meandered down her cheeks, trailed by rivulets of eyeliner. She looked like a lost child who had gotten into her mom's makeup. He realized how much he loved this girl, and would do whatever it took to make her feel secure and happy again. He gently kissed the ringlets on her forehead and then her quivering lower lip as he wiped away tears from her cherubic face.

"What do I do now?" she wept. "I'm so fucked…"

"Dry your eyes, little girl. We're celebrating tonight," Rocco said, as he rumpled her already tousled hair. He then proceeded to tell her about his day. He was smiling while explaining how the three of them were a team, the Pit-bull rounding off their trio.

"So it's his turn now, baby-girl. Fuck-it. He wags his tail the whole time he's kicking ass. He squalls like a panther when you pry him off the other dog and then squirms around like a greased pig to get back into the action. If I could whip some ass to straighten this out, I would. Wouldn't you?" She hadn't said a word, just looked at him. "I did my best, and so have you. Now it's Bull-boy's turn again. I'll let Cagootz know after the weekend.

This is gonna be great, babe. You oughta come to watch. If we do this we're all in together, right? Thick or thin, all or nothing. There ain't nobody else except us, Ma and Gina, and they don't understand shit like this. My Pop would be here if he could." It's just us, baby. But just us is enough."

She started crying again, but this time for different reasons. She went to the door to let their dog in, feeling better than she had in a long time – maybe ever.

"If something bad happens I'll never forgive myself. Should I get an abortion, Rocco? Be brutally honest with me. I can take it. Just say it and I'll do it."

He laughed, "We're too broke for that, too. We can't make any money by you getting an abortion. Let's keep this in perspective. I love him, but he's a dog bred for centuries to enjoy fighting other dogs. This baby is our child. But before I agree to do this I need to see if I can get backers. There's a shit-load of cash we could split with people smart enough to get in on this with us. Maybe Whitey's bucks-up right now, or maybe he can ask Ansel. The Wong Gongs are always on the lookout to make some fast money. This deal could turn out to be a huge cash cow. Because for us, $2,500 just ain't gonna be enough to dig our way out of this mess we're in. I'll make a call tomorrow. Then we'll decide together what to do. We'll move together, like a family's supposed to do."

Rocco knew if he went to the loan sharks in Collinwood it would get back to Fingers, Uncle Pazzo and then his mother. So Rocco visited a man in Glenville he met in rehab and got plugged in with Sonny Magic – just for a short-term loan.

Rocco had been stretched tight as a drum skin for several weeks. But he kept cool for her, showing a calm preceding the storm she feared would inevitably follow. Danni dreaded all of her options, which made her feel even more sad and lonely.

"Cagootz asked how Bully's doing and how old he's getting to be. He asked for you to bring him when you stop by."

"That's a good idea. I'll let Bully bite off his balls. Maybe once Cagootz gets castrated he'll be nicer to people."

They opened the door to find the dog welcoming them with his usual gymnastic greeting of flips and zig-zags.

"Come on boy, outside."

Bull charged into their fenced-in yard, proving how well his name fit, snorting and pawing grass. He was a perfect specimen of a Pit-bull, still in the prime of his life and in perfect health. His reddish coat shone like polished copper in a patch of sunlight he located near the back of their yard.

Rocco held the window still as he watched his dog sniff around. "This guy's got crap squirting out of him, and he's going around real slow and sniffing like he's a bomb detection dog. Can you believe this? Why don't he just take his dump?"

She noticed Rocco was smiling, She also noticed how good her man looked. Being out of work had its benefits too, luckily. He had been working out with weights in their shared basement and lying in the sun with his extra time, which made his tattoos look bigger and made him look years younger than his age. His hair grew curlier and beard longer, which she liked. But his anger and resentments also grew from frustration.

"Well, Bully-boy finally found the right spot. What do you figure he's sniffing for, anyways? I'll bet he knows I'm watching and he's just showing off."

The next door neighbors' Doberman was growling. Bull ignored him, knowing he couldn't get to him with the fence between them. The Doberman obviously realized this, too. He had taken a severe beating a few months back, after foolishly hurtling their barrier into the Pit-bull's territory. Rocco had to pry him off with a *parting stick*, a tapered hammer handle. It was a piece of hardwood that amazingly enough was illegal to own in the State of Ohio. After that ass-kicking ordeal, the Dobie stayed well away from their partition while still acting ferocious. Bull, finally done relieving himself, turned and kicked dirt clumps in the Doberman face, then walked back to the house.

Rocco was curious about this deal brewing at The Inn, but didn't say so. He was already getting calls from Big Willie and Smokehouse, two of Sonny's main collectors and leg breakers. He even saw them ride past his house. The match with Bull would be a great way to get Sonny Magic off his ass, because he had no way to make the weekly Vig payments till he was able to repay the entire loan in one lump sum.

Rocco was content to honeymoon with his lady and forget the rest of the world for a moment. He watched her undress, getting ready to shower. He felt that twinge he always got when he saw her nude. Her body had the firmness of a teenager, with the kind of skin that begged to be caressed, yet with all the correct curves and ripeness of womanhood. He left his clothes where he had been standing but felt something was missing. Then he heard a familiar sound at the back door. So he shook the sex thoughts from his head. Bull was jumping at the door. Rocco walked down the back steps naked to let their dog inside, secured both bottom and top back doors, and then decided it was a good time for a shower. He unplugged the phone, and joined her in their tiny shower stall.

Danni mumbled, "Hey, it's too crowded in here." Her short black hair was neatly piled with a cone of white suds as she rinsed her face in the spray of warm water from a rusty shower head. "I need some room to finish up, bud."

"Yeah, I suppose so. But we're actually just getting started. Our bed's a roomy king-size, right? And we'll be under those cool sheets in a hot minute. Sound about right, my little cone-head?"

"I'm totally exhausted, buddy. A nice nap first, then some hot love for dessert. Sound good?"

"Whatever you say, sweet lady." Rocco was asleep as soon as he hit the pillow.

CH XV: Pit-Dogs

The match, Rocco's version: The wind caught Rocco off guard, whipping long curly hair into cold gray eyes. It was one of those autumn days when a bright sun warmed the wind just enough to where a person moving quickly didn't need a jacket. Though in his mid-30s, Rocco was still built like an adolescent athlete. As he and his dog, Bull, walked a brick pace, Rocco noticed a certain smell fouling everything. It was actually more a feel than anything else. It was a sensation he vaguely remembered from his past. The whole neighborhood felt it.

A handful of dirty cars passed by Rocco and his Pit-bull while a few random people moved aimlessly about in the fouled air. Neighborhood bars were beginning to open up while most local businesses drew iron grates across entrances for the weekend. The clocks were moving toward the end of a work week on what could be a last payday for some. And perhaps a stroke of luck for other players out hustling in pubs and on street corners. Local sharks would again surface to move purposefully under the veil of night. Soot encrusted smoke stacks, protruding like cancerous growths from dead factories, and archaic coal docks scattered along Lake Erie's polluted shores, stood vacant and dated. Those cold and deteriorating monuments of more prosperous times blended in with boarded-up, clinical smelling trap houses metastasized throughout Cleveland's inner-city.

Established neighborhood pros had plenty of new talent to contend with since closing of the downtown steel mills and the shutdown of Collinwood's railroad yards. Homemade *crack* and *crank* created a newer social disease which gradually devoured dreams in its relentless pursuit of misery and destruction. Cleaner prescription drugs led suburban youths like zombies down a path to a more perverse world dominated by heroin dealers. Plus designer drugs like *Spice*, *Bath Salts*, Salvia and MDMA helped to yank sane minds away from what had once been used as functional brains.

Rocco knew that kids would soon be out running wild at the end of their school day, enjoying sunshine and strong breezes caressing the last of nature's gloriousness with gentle kisses before an inevitable blanket of ice fell in silence for a long cold death called winter. Summertime's brazenness peaked in all its magnificence and intensity before autumn lulled inhabitants with its false sense of security, when landscapes became canvases of blazing colors whirling in defiance of winter's oncoming shroud.

Rocco adjusted his shades and continued to power-walk his large, well-made red colored dog, Bull, through an abandoned industrial area near The Inn where his girlfriend worked. His pistol was loaded in anticipation of the unexpected, tucked in the waistband of his faded and tattered Levi's. His .357, though somewhat uncomfortable with its bulky metal weight, reassured the middle-aged man in readiness beneath a thick flannel shirt.

Rocco said out loud to no one, "Unemployment checks can work for a minute. It's election time soon. Maybe the Governor's finally smart enough to understand we're all on to him, that we know he sold us out for corporate pay-offs on his way to being just another puppet. There aren't any real differences between the only choices those media pimps advertise as the second coming of a new messiah. What the hell's happening, Bully-boy? How come we all get ass-slammed by the same motherfuckers we elect to have our backs? Whatever happened to loyalty and gratitude? And why is it these street urchins seem to have enough cash to piss away on trivial bullshit? Who are all these assholes, anyway? Back in the day, when my ol' man and his crew ran the streets, these punks would have been exterminated like insects. But Jackie's out of the picture and his crew went down the same path as the politicians, corrupted by power and money. Oh well, fuck-it. Maybe things'll pick up. Yeah, right… These greedy fucks will keep bending us over, just like when they cheated Ron Paul out of the nomination. Then we'll smile and thank them so we can reelect these same cocksuckers, or more just like them. Fucking people… I hate 'em all, Bully, except our family."

Bull caught a scent and pulled towards a curb. Rocco stopped for a moment. While Bull sniffed around for what might be the perfect place to drop a deuce, Rocco leaned against a weathered telephone pole by a small illegible poster and waited, looking around to detect what it was he had been feeling. The old wooden pole he leaned on looked as if it were diseased. Rocco stared at an abandoned factory with broken windows while Bull relieved himself. They had been walking for the better part of an hour, watching remnants of their city's transformation from shit to nothing.

Rocco sighed, "Nobody cares. Look at all this. No wonder I'm on meds for depression. We all got our own problems yet expect everyone else to give a shit," he said to his intense dog. "Last year at this time I had a good paying construction job for a dozen years. You were eating like a fat hog, remember boy? Danni and me had it made. My nice ride and sweet-ass chopper helped make things almost perfect, till the bottom fell out. But that's okay. We're still in the game, son. I still have another check coming in. So I still got another move to turn this around before another trap door opens beneath us. Right, son? Yeah, we ain't done yet. So why is it I feel like a fly's buzzing at my face on a hot night and I can't move my arms? I feel like I'm choking because the only air I can get is thick with more of this same poison."

Rocco kept speaking out loud to his dog after he rounded a corner to find a small gathering of thugs in his way. One old man and two middle-aged men dressed like their heroes who played corporate America's games so they could cash fat checks. Rocco shook his head and smiled, thinking how pathetic it was that the obvious seemed to be invisible to most people. His smile quickly transformed. Those street bangers halted their exaggerated show of loud voices and wild hand gestures as they turned to face Rocco.

Two of them started walking his way. He mumbled to his dog, "Here we go again... See this shit, Bully-boy? What do these bust-outs want? They told me at rehab I'm supposed to stay off the hard shit. I promised Ma and Pop nothing but weed. But here they are, these drug-slinging cocksuckers on every other corner. Hey, I wonder if they take credit cards... Because I sure as fuck don't have any cash. Not that I want their product, anyway. I'm done with all that shit. Yeah, I'm retired from that life. But I ain't ashamed to shoot in a crowd. So fuck them and whatever they want. How are they gonna make me act here? Keep walking or get shot? That's really the question here. It's your call, motherfuckers," Rocco mumbled. As two of the men approached Rocco sounded a familiar alert to his friend: "Who's that, Bull! Watch 'em son!" which set the muscular dog on red alert, straining at his lead toward them.

Normally a lovable dog that had never offered to bite anyone, both Rocco and Bull were capable of defending themselves. The reddish fawn Pit-bull tensed-up well defined muscles and snorted when he heard those familiar commands. He rumbled a deep growl and curled his lips to bare long, white tusks. The heavily muscled dog pulled forward, straight for the approaching pair who looked like twins, but perhaps a generation apart. When those two players spotted the large Pit they stopped to discuss something with lowered heads and conspiratorial glances towards Rocco and his best friend.

"You see these assholes, son? This is the kind of shit I'm talking about, Bully-boy. Here's me, just trying to take a nice walk with my dog, and now this bullshit. This is why I gotta get out of this cesspool, before I get jack-potted again. Hey, maybe that's what I smell – a giant outhouse with a bunch of walking dead in this sewer we still call home. Nah, my skin feels strange like something's crawling underneath it."

When those two street hoods seemed to reach a decision and resumed their approach, Rocco jaywalked across the empty street in between street lights. He switched the leash to his left hand so he was free to draw his pistol, just in case those turf gangsters made a move to rob him or steal his dog. Rocco chuckled, "They probably think I'm scared because I'm white. They're used to all these pussies bowing down to these chumps. Why should I be afraid? The only difference between them and me is they got a better tan. That and they're about a hot minute from getting a led injection. Because I'll guaran-fuckin'-tee you, their blood's the same color as mine. And you know what else, Bully? What they don't know is I ain't the shy type at all – not even a little bit. This won't be the first time I had to shoot some stupid motherfucker. And if I keep living down here in this pit of existence much longer it probably won't be the last time. I need to relocate. But we can't move away without Ma. So for now, it is what it is."

Rocco walked faster and headed for safety, back to sanctity of The Inn where his girlfriend, Danni, worked and own kind congregated. But he still firmly gripped the well-oiled steel gradually warming from the tight grip of his bare hand. His Danni would be off work soon, and he knew they had some important things to discuss. So he kept his head down and continued their power-walk to a more protective environment.

That dangerous-looking posse stayed where they were but yelled out obscenities with animated hand signals. The largest of them, a tall slender man called E Z, stripped off his parka and dropped it on a grimy concrete sidewalk. E Z challenged, "Yeah, that's right! You best stand down, boy. Go on ahead. Stay yo ass up in dat mutha fucka. Yeah, you best cross dat street, bitch-made faggot, takin' dat lily-white ass and yo rank-ass cur back down ta guinea town, lil' uncle." He laughed, "Yeah, I know you hear me."

Rocco said out loud to his dog, "Well, at least they stayed on their side. Maybe these jerk-offs aren't as stupid as they look, with those sideways hats and their baggy pants sagging down to advertise punk asses. That's good, boys. Stay where you are. Just keep shooting off you're your mouths and maybe you'll live one more day. The last thing I need is to hustle up some money just so I can hand it over to another goddamn lawyer. We're almost back to the car anyways, son. It's only ten minutes till Danni gets off work, boy. I wish she could quit that job, Bully-boy. I hate those dirty motherfuckers at The Inn, too. I thrust those *dago* fucks at that watering hole about as much as I do these curb bangers. We're already months late on everything. So for now she's gotta work and we gotta keep walking. Fucking timing. One wrong move and then everything's different."

A darker man called Foo said, "I knows dat lil' chump. Hang tight wit da Wong Gongs. He be at dey clubhouse."

E Z said, "Fuck a whole bunch a Wong Gong ass. Dem filthy mutha fuckas ain't got shit fo us, brah. Dey be stayin' on dat side a da bridge. We run dis mutha fucka!"

Foo said, "Right on, brah. I feel dat. But check dat lil' fool wit dat Pit. Dat chup be a son a Lil' Jackie ass."

"I know dat Lil' Jackie. Who his ass belong to now?" a short, thick man with gold teeth asked. He was the darkest, shortest and stockiest of the three, dressed in black shorts, T-shirt and running shoes, as if it were still July. He wore a black doo-rag wrapped tightly around his thick, shaved skull. His skin was almost purple on his neck. 'Cause dat punk ass belong ta me he cross dis street. Bet on dat shit! I be tapping dat ass he bring it up on da *nigga* side. 'Cause we be da big dawgs up in dis mah fucka. An dat boy's white ass belong to da *Sonny*!"

"Yeah, Smokehouse, fo sho. Just keepin' it real, cuz. Thing is, Lil' Jackie run tight wit da Horrible Hank an dat crazy mah fucka, Curtis ass back in da day. I did a deal wit those wild-ass mah fucka's back when I was comin' up," Foo explained. "Horrible Hank and da Curtis is bowf a mah fucka. Dat ain't no joke, *Skippy*."

"Who da fuck you callin' *Skippy*, ol' man? You know my name, crazy ol' fool. You been suckin' dat glass dick too much, ol' man. So where da fuck Horrible Hank and da Curtis ass *now*?" growled the short, fat man with the gold teeth. "Look like everybody a mah fucka to yo old ass, Foo. You too old fo dis game, ol' man. Best be leavin' dis street shit to da young bucks like me and E Z. We da big dawgs now. Fuck all dem nursin' home mah fucka's ass! Where dey ass at? Tell me dat!" Smokehouse demanded.

E Z chimed in, "Horrible Hank a dinosaur like dis ol' fool," pointing to Foo. "Curtis still in da streets. Still crazy, too. But ain't no way da Curtis going against da home team fo dese chump ass mutha fuckin' cracka ass. I knows da Curtis too, ol' man. Da onliest mutha fucka's ass he sweat is Sonny Magic slim ass. An Sonny ain't much bigger dan a kid and black in a *nigga's* asshole. So dat make Curtis Sonny's bitch."

"Ya'll young bucks don't be listenin' too cool. Lil' Jackie ass used ta run with dem big-ass mah fuckin' *guineas* up on da lower Eastside, *Skippy*. And he still hang tough wit dem Wong Gong mah fuckas. So he think he all dat. So do his punk-ass kid." Foo said, as he unzipped his huge black parka and faced Rocco.

"You ain't listenin', man. Don't be calling my ass *Skippy*, crazy ol' fool. Dat mean fuck you, and all dat and all dem." E Z looked at the stocky man and laughed: "Doze days is ova fo dem smoove-ass mutha fuckin' *dagos*, brah. Day ain't about shit no mo. Dey is some big-ass nobodies, brah. Day noise went and got all dim an shit. On da real side, dey got no mo street juice, brah, not down in dis mutha fucka. We run dis shit," E Z assured his audience of two as he strutted around in a tight circle, waving around long arms and shouting at no one in particular.

Foo said, "Yeah, well da thing is . . . Lil' Jackie ass mobbed up wit dem big ass mah fucka's at dat beer joint down by da Five Points," Foo said. "You know dem two fat *guinea* mah fuckas run dat outfit up in da Wood? Lil' Jackie ass in tight wit dem fat mah fuckas, *Skippy*!"

"What up wit dis ol' fool, brah? He goin' soft of us, cuz?" E Z laughed as he asked the stout-built Smokehouse. "Fuck a mah fuckin' *guinea* straight up in dey fat ass. An I done toll you, ol' man. Don't call me *Skippy*, ol' fool! "

"Know dis: *dagos* don't care much fo a brother on da lower eastside," Foo explained. "An dem mah fuckan Wong Gongs kill a *nigga* quick as shit! Doze two fat mah fucka *guineas* and dem nasty-ass biker mah fuckas wen an fucked up a brotha when we was in da lock-down. Almost kilt his ass when we was doin' time in da Field."

"Mansfield? Fuck dat mah fucka," said the short thick Smokehouse, as he pulled a Glock from next to his spine and laughed. "We go bust dat ass right now . . . *boom*. Now what, ol' man? Tell me dat. Sonny got all deese cracka muh fucka's shittin' bones. Den we moves on dem slimy-ass bikers. I got somethin' fo dose racist, cracka muh fucka's."

"Not yet, brah," Foo cautioned. "I needs ta watch his punk ass.I got a paddle for Lil' Jackie ass. He and dem two *niggas* he run wit took me off back in da day. He owe me. Lil' Jackie need ta set-up doze two fat mah fuckas at Da Inn."

Smokehouse stood closer: "Who toll you dat shit, *nigga*? Why you say dat shit, Foo?"

"Dey fuck us up whiles we was holed up in da joint, is why. I needs doze mah fuckas. So's I let dis lil' mah fucka walk. Think he come up fo a quick minute. Now I see dis mah fucka routine. Dig? Him and dat cur-ass Pit he got think he all dat. I got dey ass now, *Skippy*! You mine now, bitch!" Foo yelled out.

"Easy does it, ol' man," Smokehouse chuckled. "You about to bust yo shit up. But ya'll needs ta stop flappin' dem big-ass boot lips, hear? Dat's Sonny Magic shit. Besides," laughed the thick man, "Da Curtis and dat Horrible Hank still think dey under Sonny flag. But dat shit over way gone. An Lil' Jackie went an got his ass fragged. So he gone. But yo ass need ta freeze-up on Sonny shit, ol' man. Feel me?"

Foo stripped off his parka: "Fuck dat *nigga* lovin' mah fucka punk-ass *dago*. I don't foget a bitch-made mah fucka or dat punk-ass ol' man he got! Yeah, yo ass better walk on home! But I be seein' yo flimsy ass again. Count on dat shit!" Foo yelled.

Rocco, his right hand on the trigger of his .357, said to his dog, "Those assholes have no idea how close they just came to checking out. But if they cross that street they'll find out quick enough if crackheads are bulletproof zombies or just stupid."

Danni scanned the brick street out the front window of The Inn, a Neighborhood bar owned and frequented by Collinwood gangsters and wannabes. The bar was run by a Cagootz and Big Louie, *made-men* in the Cleveland Syndicate, the two men Foo had cited as, "Lil' Jackie ass used ta run with dem big-ass mah fuckin' *guineas* up on da lower Eastside. Dig?"

Through the dirty front window, light up by a neon P.O.C. beer sign, she saw her man and their dog approaching and felt a rush of excitement. Rocco didn't look too happy. But then again, he wasn't much of a smiler. Rocco didn't like going to his grandfather's old bar, mainly because it should have been inherited by them. Like Danni, Rocco didn't trust those men any more than he did those street thugs who protected their desolate little patch of nothing.

Danni told Rocco, "I missed you, babe. And I love you. I'm so glad this day is over. I hate working around those WOPs. They're all scum. I despise them and detest my lousy job waiting tables for those grotesque pigs, serving them alcohol till they become even more obnoxious. But . . . it's green money."

"We don't choose our nationality, baby, so it's no big deal either way. What we do have is a choice about our own level of integrity." Rocco shared some concepts he learned in a college class. "So I'll opt for being careful over naive every goddam time. Or at least try to be cautious," Rocco said, as he rechecked to make sure his .357 was loaded. "You can't trust these motherfuckers, and you can't kill 'em unless it's a clean sweep. Extremes are what most street people understand, babe. I'm not about to drop my guard around any of these thugs, no matter which color they are, and neither should you. Home, with family, is the only place where I feel safe anymore."

Danni had been experiencing uneasy feelings all weekend, like something ugly was lodged in her throat that she tried to cough out. She got an early start the following morning. Danni had every other Saturday off, which gave her time to catch up to the long weeks filled with short autumn days. Rocco and Bull took their daily morning walk. The air was filled with colors and scents carried on a gentle breeze. On a last minute whim Rocco decided to visit Cagootz and would try to be as amicable as possible to the *made-man*, whose lecherous glares followed Danni's every move during her shifts.

Rocco rang the buzzer at the side entrance. Fat Spuds and Skinny Vinny didn't tale long responding. Rocco stood there with Bull held in his left arm. His muscles tensed as the door opened.

Spuds asked, while smoothing back his shiny hair with pudgy hands, "Something wrong, kid? Is there some problem?"

"Yeah, what's the fucking problem, kid?" asked the jumpy Vinny who was already reaching for a hankie to catch sweat running down his face like tears.

"Nothing wrong with me, fellas. How about you?" Rocco asked, with a furrowed brow as he looked closely at Vinny's beady eyes. "Why you sweating so much, Vinny? It ain't even hot out. You look like you're the one with a problem."

"No, kid, no problems here. I got the low resistance."

"Yeah, Vinny's got the high blood pressure," said the big fat man as he fumbled for his comb but dropped it on the filthy cheap vinyl tiles. He pretended that didn't happen and instead reached for and inserted a toothpick into his insatiable mouth.

"Really... Which one is it, fellas, low resistance or high blood pressure?"

"Both," they replied at the same exact moment, and then looked at one another as if the other one had just fumbled a play.

"I see... Sounds like you're coming and going at the same time. Maybe you should try smoking weed to level out. I can get some primo bud. You interested, Vinny? 'Cause I'll hook you up at friend prices. How about you, big man?"

"No thanks, Roc. Me and Vinny are gentlemen. We're whiskey drinkers like ol' Frankie Blue Eyes. We don't fuck with that nigger dope like youse crazy biker kids do," Spuds answered for them while shoving two more sticks of gum into his mouth."

"Yeah, kid. Me and Spuds roll like Sinatra. It's nothing but Jack Daniels for us, like fucking 90," Vinny said, as he swiveled his head around and repositioned an already perfect black shirt collar over the lapels of his garish sports coat.

Rocco looked at Spuds. "Well, good weed stimulates the appetite, just in case you go off your feed for a few days." Then he looked over at Vinny, "You know; keep up your resistance. But in the meantime, I'm here because Cagootz told my ol' lady he wants to talk about a business deal. So is he here or not?"

"You're one funny guy, Roc. No problem. You're okay, kid. Follow us," invited Spuds as he smoothed back the sides of his black greasy hair with fat palms.

"Come on. Just follow us," Skinny Vinny parroted his accomplice as he jerked his pin head sideways. "But keep that fucking monster away from me," the short thin man barked at Rocco as he wearily eyed Bull with a sideways glare.

"Relax, Vinny," Rocco chuckled. "You read too many newspapers. They aren't people mean; they're dog aggressive."

They brought Rocco and his dog to the huge dark man who resided within the inner circle of Cagootz and Fingers. Big Louie turned his massive back and mumbled, "I'll handle the kid from here. Come on. The boss is expecting you."

Quietly, Rocco and Bull made their way into the back. Louie leaned on a wall outside the still opened door.

With Rocco and Bull safely enclosed in Cagootz' office those partners went outside to light up cigarettes on that beautiful day that was still more like summer than fall. Vinny said to his partner, "He knows! I can smell it like nine zero."

Spuds laughed, "What you smell is shit in you pants. That fucking kid's on pot. There's no way he can know. But what makes you say something like that?"

"He looked right at me, Spuds. He knows it was us! I read it like 90 in those crazy gray eyes of his. Those fucking eyes don't even look human, *coomba*."

Spuds shook his head and smiled. "Okay, let's just pretend for a quick second that he does know. So what? What the fuck's he gonna do? You think that tattooed asshole can get anything past legends like Cagootz and Big Louie? They'll bend him over the bar and pump a gallon of jizz up his hairy ass if he even blinks the wrong way. Fuck this kid, too. We'll take him out while we're at it. No big deal. Believe me. That kid ain't half the man his father was. And we can bet green folding money right here and now we'll never see that Jackie fuck again."

Vinny stuck a claw-looking finger inside his shirt collar and pulled it for ventilation. "When you're right, you're right. Nobody gets anything past those two. So you don't think it's a set-up?"

"What the fuck are you rambling about now, Vin?"

Skinny Vinny looked over his shoulder: "You remember what happened with Benny, right? You know; after they sent him out to clip the Mick's nephew? You know, that crazy Paddy? Remember how that whole deal came down?"

"That's a whole different deal, Vin. They *had* to take Benny out after he wasted that Irish prick. It wasn't *what* Benny did as much as *how* he did it. Besides, it was the shit he was pulling before and after he zipped Paddy. Benny was a liability to our whole organization."

"That's bullshit. That's just the story they put out so we don't get suspicious."

Fat Spuds tightened his tie: "Everybody says Benny wasn't a rat. That much I agree with, Vin. But there was other shit going on, deep stuff, things they don't tell us because it's above our pay grade. No sweat. These guys love us. We're the future."

"Maybe so… But did you ever notice how just as soon as somebody stops coming around or gets whacked, all the sudden the same guy everybody agreed was cool and solid turns into some faggot-assed, snitch junkie, and it happens like 90?"

"Whoa, easy, Vin. You need to learn to relax, *coom*."

"I know the fucking story! They say Benny got clipped for a deal Fingers made through Ansel," Vinny stammered, as he yanked at his jacket with one hand and reached for his hankie with the other. "I mean, think about it. If Cagootz really wants this deal with Rocco bad enough, and if the kid tries to hold out, all he has to do is accidentally let it slip exactly who took the kid's father out. Boom! Then Rocco and his psycho biker friend, Whitey, clip the two of us – nice and neat. Then the kid's indebted to the boss. After a favor like that, he'd do anything Cagootz tells him. Am I right or not, Spuds?"

"Nah, Vin, no way. First of all, Benny was trying to take over the organization. He wanted the Royal Flush to pull a mutiny on Uno's Young Turks. That's why Benny had his *accident*. Besides, why would the boss pull some rat shit like that on his own people? No way. That story of yours just don't add up."

"Okay, Spuds, then let's look at it from another angle. Maybe the order came down from Fingers and it really was the plan. Maybe that's what this whole thing's been about all along. Maybe they needed a couple of patsies for when the time was right. Think about it. I fucking knew we got set-up! Remember I said it when we were sitting out there in those woods with all those big bugs and shit?"

"You need to learn to chill like me, Vin. See me? Look how relaxed I am. Trust me, *coom*, everything's copasetic. There's no way our own people make a move against us. You're way too paranoid, *coomba*. You need to notch it back a little."

"Swear to Buddha, Spuds. I don't really wanna believe this shit, but I just ain't ready to rule it all the way out yet. Back when I was a crazy teenager my ol' man taught me, 'Vincenzo, you can't be too careful. When something looks too good to be true, guess why?' Meantime, now I understand like 90 what the old man was saying."

"But all I'm saying is not *these* guys. These guys are *our* people, Vin. We ain't like those fucking jungle bunnies out there killin' one another. But you can't be too careful. So in the meantime, we keep our eyes open and our mouths shut. *Capiche?*"

November, 2013: "Hey! Look who's here! Good to see you, Roc." Cagootz greeted the younger man in an unusually friendly manner. "How's your mother these days, kid?"

"Stressed out, just like me. Times are tough right now. Lots of strange things happening these days."

"They sure are. Come on in. I see you got your famous Bull dog with you. Good. Take a seat. You know you're always welcome here, right Roc? Can I have my girl get you anything from the bar?"

My girl? "No. Thanks anyway." *This fat motherfucker...* "My fiancée, Danni, told me you had some business to discuss," Rocco yawned. "So here I am."

Cagootz was going through the ritual of lighting his cigar. First fingering, then licking, and finally striking a stick match under it, just to tease the end with a flame almost beyond its reach as he drew air through it. Rocco thought it smelled good as he watched the fat man roll the cheroot in his mouth, as he dabbed the match up and down.

"Cigar, Roc?"

"No thanks. I'm trying to quit everything."

Cagootz was a man who everyone in Collinwood knew and feared, but few liked or respected. He was a product of Cleveland's Little Italy, via Sicily as a boy, and had a tough upbringing. He and Big Louie seemed to be in contention with Fingers and Benny, yet all four had worked under the flag of Uno during their climb to the top.

Few people were foolish enough to stand in Uno's path during his campaign. The Mick became Uno's only serious threat. But eventually even he proved to be one of many to fall victim to the wrath of Collinwood's Young Turks. These men survived on their ability to sense strengths and weaknesses, using wits and instincts while swimming in a pool of other sharks.

Cagootz always maintained a reasonable politeness with Rocco, a courtesy Rocco figured had been extended because Rocco's Uncle Pazzo had been Uno's number one man. That, and his boss, Fingers, was Tessa's first cousin. Tessa and Fingers had been closer than brother and sister till Fingers acquired a newer, more powerful family which extended all the way back to the old country. Still and all, Rocco was blood. Plus, Tessa and Fingers shared history. The way Rocco had it figured, those were some of the very same reasons Cagootz didn't like Rocco. He felt Cagootz resented what little political juice he still wielded.

"I don't want to take much of you time, Cagootz. I know you're a busy man. I heard you have something important to say."

Cagootz fiddled with his cigar for a moment too long: "I got a proposition for you that could be fat for all of us. But how about a nice pepper and egg sandwich first?"

"I'm okay, I just ate. Thanks, anyway," Rocco answered, with a blank expression. Bull posted up on his lap, his eyes fixed on the ham-like fist waving smoke around in spirals. Rocco and his dog was line-bred on both sides of their bloodline from fast-lane players. They both watched closely and waited for subtleties and nuances. Rocco finally shifted his stone colored eyes from his black coffee to the dark glare of Cagootz.

Cagootz plastered on a grin: "Okay, Roc, let's get right to it then. There's these four rich fucks from Toronto and Montreal willing to come down to meet us next month. One's a retired sea captain with a shit-load of cash and no place to spend it. They have a dog they claim is a pit champion. They say he's won three fights for money over other champions ranging from 42 to 45 pounds. They heard about Bull and his win over that Detroit dog owned by the *melanzana*. They say that black dog was supposed to be unbeatable. By the way, did you have any trouble getting paid by those niggers? Because that was for big money, am I right?"

"No problems. Those guys were cool. They're serious about the game. Besides, I had Whitey and a few other bad-asses with me – just in case. You know?"

"I don't know who the fuck Whitey is. Hey, did you import that dog of yours, Roc? I heard that Bull dog you got's from some kind of *fancy* champion bloodline, or some shit like that. Did I hear wrong about this, kid?"

"He's out of some Cleveland stuff. I got him as a pup from some guy as payment on product. His pedigree is solid."

"Yeah, I heard something about that. I heard he's related to Jackie's Crazy Gracie bitch. I won nothing but money on her."

"To us younger guys back then, the Lorocco bloodline was the best in the world. And Jack was like a storybook hero to us. Anyways, my Bull is line-bred on some of Jack's best, his old Sinbad dog and Crazy Gracie that produced Ch Biddy before she got poisoned…" Rocco looked into the dark eyes of Cagootz. "I heard through the rumor mill he was plugged in with some of the wrong people here in C-town and that's why that bitch died."

Cagootz stared right through the younger man. "Let's quit playing games here. I know Jackie was your father. And you know we were acquainted. But I don't know the first thing about poison or dog pedigrees. I play the ponies. I study those bloodlines and racing forms like it's the fucking Bible. So that means I do know a little something about breeding and the bloodlines of certain people, too. Cur blood runs in certain families just like it does in thoroughbreds, game-dogs and gamecocks."

"What's that? Cur blood of certain families?"

Cagootz gave a rare grin: "Skip it for now, kid. Anyway, these fucking big-shots from up North are willing to match their champion with your Bull. They said they'll fight you at *catch-weight*, whatever the fuck that's supposed to mean."

"That means no specific weight. We just specify dogs."

"*Minchia*, sounds like you might know your shit, kid. Come to think of it, that's what that bust-out Frog said, too. They said you can come at any weight, as long as it's Bull. They said they picked all their matches with this champion of theirs, but they picked them from the top of the tree. By the way, your dog looks in good shape. You been working him for another match?"

"No, I work him three times a week when he's not in a keep. He loves it. But let's get back to that other dog. Is the dog you're talking about a brindle called Dickless?"

"I ain't sure what brindle means, Roc. But I think they did mention something about a big Dick."

"Dick's a big brindle, tiger-striped dog that won in Canada, the U.S. and Mexico. He's one of the few international champions in history. The only other dog I know about to win its title in three separate countries was one of Bull's aunts named Ch. Biddy, from his old Sinbad dog and Crazy Gracie. Jack bred her, too. But Ch. Biddy won her title on three different continents and against all champions. So that rare champion of champion gene is on both sides of Bull's pedigree, too. Just like you said, Cagootz, that's some kind of *fancy champion bloodline*. You're right on the money with that one. But there's no cur blood here."

"Whatever. Meanwhile, these Frogs got a few gripes. They insist we have to call which dogs we're gonna bring and make that part of the contract. They want Bull because they said he's rated as the best fighter in America for his weight class. And the fight has to be for at least $5,000 per side. Half as the forfeit gets posted with a neutral party. I'll post the lock-up money for us. They agreed to have Dago Red hold the forfeit. They said they know him from back in the day. You okay with that?"

"Yeah, I'm cool with that. They know Dago Red from back when Jack was still doing dogs. Dago Red's solid as stone in my book." Rocco said.

"I heard you were in the same rehab place with that old junkie. Is that true, kid?"

"Maybe. That was a long time ago. Why?"

"Yeah . . . whatever. He just better hope he ain't chasing the fucking needles again. Dago Red's a degenerate junkie. You understand that, right Roc? But he's not crazy or stupid. So he knows better than to ever double-cross us."

Rocco sighed, "Then there shouldn't be a problem."

"There won't be, kid. Bet on that, too. Meanwhile, Bull's the bigger dog, right? So this should be easy pickings for your dog. Am I wrong about this?"

Bull heard his name mentioned by this strange man more than once and was squirming to check him out. Rocco obliged him. He trotted over to Cagootz, stood up resting his front paws on the man's belt, and rammed his snout into the thick gut behind it. Then the dog walked around his chair sniffing, hiked his back leg and let out a trickle of urine, scratched at the carpet and walked back to Rocco.

Rocco shifted his gaze from the fat man's hands to those dark menacing eyes. "Bull's retired. Besides, I got the shorts right now. Even if I had that kind of *jing*, I wouldn't bet that much on a dog – not even Bull, and he's the best I've seen."

"I know you're short on funds right now. That's the reason I told *my girl*, Danni, for you to come over here today."

Rocco narrowed his gaze but kept quiet. He could feel his blood pressure climbing. He figured this was some type of test.

"The word on the grapevine is that Bull's the best at his weight. Plus he's a bigger dog than that piece of garbage from up there. I got a few extra dollars and plenty of confidence in your Bull dog since I won money on him against those shines from Cleveland. I heard their dog was imported from some top breeder in Texas. And Bull went through him like a dose of clap. So I'm willing to put up all the money and split the winnings with you 50/50. All you have to do is provide the dog, condition and handle him in the pit and win. Then you're ahead $2,500. If he loses, you're not out dime one."

"What about Bull? If he loses, he might be out more than just money. Look at the great boxers, guys like Ali and Frazier. They got greedy. They didn't know when to quit like Marciano. Besides, all these Canucks stand to lose is their win record. So far they're undefeated. They don't give a flying fuck about their animals. That dog is like a pair of dice or a deck of cards to them. I know about those guys. It's all about money and bragging rights with them. Not much else matters. And I've heard of their Dickless dog. He's supposed to be a killing machine. They said he bites so hard they had to put three different dogs in a row on him to test his gameness. Those Canadians are high-rollers, and their dog was bred by old man Andre in Montreal. Jack said Andre was rated as the top breeder in the world during the 1960s and '70s."

"I'll tell you what I heard, Roc. I heard that Dick dog fought a bunch of garbage up there. I heard he's a hard biting cur and won't hold up against a game-dog that's as talented as yours. And what kind of stupid fuckin' name is *Dickless*?"

"Well, like I said, they thought they had to three-dog him to check his dipstick. Even though when they tested him they brought him in fat and soft, he killed the first two in a row. But he was drag-ass tired against that the third dog."

"Oh yeah? What's all that got to do with anything?" Cagootz flicked his cigar ash and then blew smoke at Rocco.

Rocco tensed up but stayed seated, "I'll tell you what. That third dog shot up underneath him and bit off the tip of his dick. I heard he was bleeding so bad it looked like he was pissing blood. Good thing their vet was at pit-side."

Cagootz continued, "Fuck those cocksuckers. Those Frenchies ain't got shit for us. After this match they can change their dog's name to *nutless* – before they tag and bag his worthless ass. Because I heard some stuff, too. I heard that big motherfucker will quit. Dago Red said you got an ace, Roc. Those fucking assholes are in the minor leagues up there in Frogville, with their foamy beer and Canadian bacon. Fuck them! Read my lips: I could care less about their dog's dick."

Rocco wasn't about to give Cagootz an English lesson. He just sat quiet, smiling.

Cagootz continued, "Those bust-outs up there ain't got shit compared to the firepower we got. Believe me, we can take 'em down – no problem."

We? Hmmm... Rocco stood up. "Yeah, maybe so. But there there's no sure things in the big league. This is the fast lane. That's why they call it *gambling*. I guarantee you those Canadians aren't stupid. Bull has a solid reputation. I'm sure they know all about him and his great bloodline. So if they're picking their shots with him, it's definitely from the top of the tree. They know Bull's no easy mark, so they think they have an ace. And they just might have, if they're willing to go catch-weight for that kind of money. No, Cagootz, I appreciate the offer and could really use the dough, but I'll have to pass. I sort of promised my dad I'd retire him. This dog here is like my brother."

"I don't expect an answer right now, Roc. Sleep on it. But we got a safe spot right here in the bar's basement – plenty of room. Nobody'll fuck with us down there. We're not like those hillbillies from Canada or these burr heads down here in the ghetto. We're Italian! We take care of our own. Right, *coomba*?" He looked at Big Louie, who remained silent. "You're as safe as in your own yard when you're in my basement, kid. I even got the local pigs paid to sniff around at other places while we're busy."

"See, that's another thing. Even federal laws are goofy about this piddly-ass shit. The feds are busy locking guys up for smoking weed and fighting cocks. They're ruining people's lives behind this sport and then confiscating all their shit. The days of the big shows are gone. Those times were for Jack and his dog buddies back in the day. Besides, Bull has half a hanger missing."

Cagootz, still eyeing the dog, told the younger man, "Okay, look. I don't expect you to trust me with this right from the gate. I respect that. So I'm gonna share something with you, just so you know I can be trusted. Remember hearing about those *fugazi* pigs, Looney Lonnie and O'Reilly, when they got canned for monitoring a jewel heist from their squad car for the Mick and those Five Points hoodlums? It made headlines in the Cleveland Plain Dealer and everything. You see it back then?"

"I think maybe I might've read something about that."

"Did you know those cheap Irish bastards Down Five Points never gave their own pigs dime one to help them beat that case when they got popped for the Mick?"

"No, Cagootz, I don't follow politics. Why?"

"I'll tell you right here and now. It was Uno and Fingers helped those cops get their shields back after they were off for a whole year with no pay. That's why!"

"So what? What's that got to do with me?"

"Everything. Now that those dirty pigs, Looney Lonnie, and that Irish fuck, O'Reilly, work for us – that's what. Get it?"

Bull began whining and paced around in circles.

"I gotta get going, Cagootz. He's ready to bust a gut."

"If you change your mind by next weekend, kid, let me know. If not, I have some guys from Chicago with a dog that's been game-tested hard and ready to go."

"Well, there you go, Cagootz. See that? Timing. It all worked out for you."

"Not quite. The problem is those French bastards up there want the match with Bull. Not because they want an easy mark. It's because Bull has a big reputation. They want another notch on their gun. They want to beat the best plus do it in our back yard. Think about it, Roc. These fucks are insulting you."

Rocco thanked the hired killer again. When he turned to leave he saw Big Louie blocking the office door, just staring at him with emotionless shark eyes. Rocco walked around him and out with Bull as his heels. He could see his own old junker parked in their driveway so he decided to jog home, anxious to talk to Danni about his day. It was too nice to be cooped up in a bar, or a house for that matter. Rocco had already dropped off the dog at home so Bull could eat, drink and rest from his treadmill workout and their three mile walk. He left Bull in the yard and went inside.

Danni sat on the couch facing a cold, dark TV set. She wore the blank expression of someone hypnotized. Mail scattered across the coffee table. The phone was plugged in sitting next to her. Rocco didn't like the looks of this. He headed straight for the kitchen, pretending to be hungry. He banged around in cupboards and the refrigerator for awhile, checking inside unmarked containers. He found a small chunk of pepperoni wrapped in the wrinkled, white butcher paper. So he carried his snack out to the front-room.

"Hi, babe. Wannna bite?" He bared his teeth and growled.

He could see she didn't find him the least bit funny at that moment. She looked about as hungry as he felt. Mainly, he had asked for the sake of conversation. So he stayed quiet and waited.

"No thanks," she replied glumly.

Rocco wasn't exactly sure what it was she was declining. But he sat in his chair across from her, waiting. Then he began fingering the pepperoni the way Cagootz had used the cigar. He remembered the way the man bit off the end and did the same to his toy, trying to amuse himself. He was thinking of a funny way to tell Danni about his conversation.

He placed it in his mouth and looked at her to break the ice when he noticed tears. He removed his fake cigar and himself from his chair to sit next to her. She began to sob, hugging him fiercely, accidentally knocking the snack from Rocco's hand.

They played house that weekend. The only times they left were for their dog's long daily walks. He had already been in a preconditioning period due to extra time on Rocco's hands. It was time to begin to adjust the dog's body weight while strengthening muscles that had been unused till he had recently commenced their little routine of brief treadmill sprints and daily one hour walks.

Meanwhile, the underground population of Collinwood was humming with excitement. Everybody knew about it except the law. Anticipation of an upcoming event at the Inn, plus the rumor already circulating that Rocco's Pit-bull might compete, had neighbors prematurely psyched. Naturally everyone would back the home team.

Rocco knew most of the local big shots and many of their wanna-be gophers. Rocco tried to be a man of integrity. He never intentionally hurt anyone unless to defend himself. On the other hand, he had never cowered down when attacked. And when cornered he had proven to be as dangerous as the most feared.

Rocco was a loner, never quite fitting into any group. The straight citizens were too boring for his tastes. Besides, many were put off by his self-assurance and defiance of social norms. He felt more comfortable with outlaw bikers types and junior mobsters from the Neighborhood. When he hang around with anyone, like while he was in treatment, it was with offbeat non-conformist types a little on the shady side. He had been drawn to the energy of a free-wheeling lifestyle of brotherhood, substance abuse and violence just like his Uncle Pazzo and his grandfather, Doc, had been – just like I had.

As a single mother, Tessa had drilled a value system into her child from an early age. She stressed, "You're no longer a boy. That means there's never a reason for you to ever lie to me again. And remember, deception by omission is as vile as any other lie. If you want to trust me then I have to be able to believe you." She told her son, "A person born male can never really be a man without courage and personal integrity. Loyalty is the cornerstone of adulthood for women, too. So earn it and live it."

With his father gone, his Uncle Pazzo retired and in Florida, and his best friend, Whitey, all patched-up with the Wong Gongs, Rocco was faced with having to deal with people he was warned not to trust. He thought: *Who's left? Just Danni, Ma and Gina? That's it? So I won't trust these guys. I'll just take their money.*

Rocco knew what he would be doing was illegal, but that was nothing new. He had been to court on an assault charge after catching a junkie stealing from his mother's garage. He nearly beat the intruder to death, to set an example. Word travels fast on the streets. Rocco occasionally gambled, aside from the dog fighting. He had fooled with some illegal substances as a kid. But since his accident on his construction job, and then his layoff, Rocco dabbled more often with opiates till they became problematic and he found himself in drug court and then treatment. He view physically defending himself or getting high, gambling or selling drugs, far less criminal than the behaviors engaged and enacted by legislators and enforcers.

Rocco believed that humor was one of man's greatest talents. He stated the following in a report for his 10th grade English teacher at Collinwood: "Hells Angels and American Mafia and the 4th and 5th most powerful, lethal gangs in our country. Democrats and Republicans are 2nd and 3rd. But # 1 is the *Donor* Class. They are the puppet masters who use religion to hypnotize victims." Needless to say, Rocco flunked that class.

Rocco's confidence turned most people off, mistaken for being an arrogant braggart. Most seemed to prefer fake humility. He learned to utilize the triad of mind, body and spirit. He knew he was born with a good brain. And because he read a lot he got smarter. Plus he was okay being in his own skin, and could be alone with his thoughts. That frightened some people who alleged he was too cocky. Because he was a natural at physical things, like fighting MMA and conditioning dogs, many figured he was an egomaniac in that regard as well. And due to the fact that he was spiritual rather than religious, most saw that as an insult to their version of God. But his mother had raised him to recognize and properly ignore envy. He once asked me, "Why is it, Pop, I'm allowed to admit to my fuck-ups but not my achievements?"

Rocco's philosophy on the legal system was: "Victimless crimes shouldn't be illegal. They're invented offenses." He lived by his own rules, trying not to interfere with the space of others. But there were plenty to judge him for not being part of the herd. *Oh well, maybe I'll care tomorrow – after some mush needed rest.* He kissed Danni on her shoulder and wrapped a heavily tattooed arm around her firm waist. *I wonder if having this baby will draw us closer or make us like these other miserable couples we see.* He thought about those things and others as he drifted off to sleep.

"It's 8:00 a.m., baby. Time to get ready for another day for that fat hog at his pigsty. I'll make you coffee and some rye toast the way you like it, almost burnt and all buttery. How's that sound?"

"Go away," Danni mumbled into her pillow.

"You'd better hop outta that bed like pronto before I peel this sheet off you like a banana and eat you up for my breakfast."

She rolled over to face him, squinting the morning sunlight from her eyes while beaming a broad grin. "You mean peel it off me like a breakfast banana? Because I'm ripe and ready, boy. But you have to promise to eat it all."

He bent over to kiss her. Instead, he tugged on the mattress tumbling her onto the bedroom rug. She started to protest as he scooped her up and ran to the bathroom. Danni thought she heard the shower running and now knew why. She was in her nightshirt and he in boxer shorts. They stood laughing in the tub, dripping wet, half-clothed. Danni embraced him, her lips to his hard shoulder and asked, "Should we be scared?"

"Scared? Of what, baby?"

"Of…well…I mean, are you sure?"

"How sure can we be about shit we never did? Roll the dice and see what happens. What else is there?"

"I know, but . . . you know what I mean."

"This is our life to do as we please. We can fuck it up or make it the best thing since internet porn. Listen to me. First it's breakfast bananas and now cyber-titties. Am I hungry or horny?"

"Knowing you, probably both. But you can eat later, and I've got to get ready now."

They shed their soaked clothing and finished showering in silence. Each worried about their own problems, which were now, more-so than ever, each others.

The happy trio left their home apprehensive about their future. They noticed a peculiarity, like strangeness in the air, though neither of them mentioned it. It was like the staleness found in forgotten, uninhabited places: like abandoned houses, empty warehouses or unused minds. Danni was thinking about work. Rocco wondered what Cagootz might say to him.

"You coming inside, baby-boy?"

"Yeah, I guess so. Unless you see a door #4, I suppose we might as well settle this business so we can get to it. Cagootz is over confident because he doesn't know shit about real pit-dogs. But I got a bad feeling about this, baby."

Cagootz sat at a small booth with coffee and a newspaper. When he saw them he neatly folded his paper and sipped his breakfast. "*Buona sera.* Sit and have coffee."

"Good day to you, too. None for me," Danni smiled. "I already had some. More than one and I get all amped-out."

"I'll have mine black. Thanks."

"Roc, listen at this part: I talked to that guy last night. They said if your dog can last an hour with theirs, they'll pay off the bet but the match has to continue. They said, either way, they wanna see who has the better dog. If that isn't sweet enough, those assholes are laying 2-to-1 odds we choke. So if Bull loses in under an hour we lose. But if we have side bets, if he loses, the worst we can do is break even. If he wins, we win big. To me, that sounds pretty tasty. Meanwhile, pretty much whichever way we slice this, you make $5,000."

Danni was pouring the fresh coffee as Cagootz was explaining the options. Rocco noticed her steady hand and unchanging expression.

"I understand so far. What else is there?"

"Nothing. Just this: I decided to add a little sugar to sweeten the deal. I'll give Danni that two dollar an hour raise she asked for. Now how do you wanna act?"

"I've been doing some thinking. There's one thing: If Bull's unable to continue I'll pull him, even if it's under the hour mark. The money and the win are secondary to my dog's life. Bull comes first. Swear to Buddha, I won't budge on this."

"Sure thing, kid. Whatever…"

"No disrespect, Cagootz. I fought MMA as a pro. And I learned some important lessons. Even the best fighters have to tap out at least once during their careers. I didn't and destroyed my knee. Even the toughest can lose game and come back to win another day. That's the smart move. So if the time comes where my dog gets in a bad situation where he's hurt and can't continue, I'm picking him up. I don't care how much bread's at stake. Winning and losing money is all part of the gamble. If you agree to those terms, I'll consider it. If not, I'm out. No offense. I'm just being honest here. I'd rather we discuss these possible outcomes right up front. That way no surprises, right?"

"Easy, kid. It's just a fucking dog. What's the big deal?"

"Look, Cagootz. I've seen enough pit contests to know the score. When two evenly matched aces collide it's like a jiu-jitsu match of two masters, like when Royce Gracie fought Kazushi Sakuraba fight in Japan. All it takes is one move to change the outcome of an epic fight. Aside of a freak shot, gameness and conditioning usually determine the winner. But just keep this in mind: with two *unbeatable* champions anything can happen, and one of them will lose – that's a fact."

Danni was done pouring the hot coffee and glad of it. She held her breath, not wanting to move for fear of being noticed. Cagootz picked up an unlit cigar out of his ashtray. He placed the wet chewed end against his closed mouth, while leveling his gaze on a potential temporary partner, peering inside Rocco's heart.

"Oh, by the way, kid. Wait till you hear this ... I heard from that fucking burr-head, Sonny, today. He asked if I knew you. He said certain people are getting impatient. I told that *moolie* you're almost like family. So I went ahead and picked up that paper he had. *Capiche?* By the way, kid, how's your mother? I was just thinking about her and your sister the other day."

"What are you trying to say?" Rocco looked into the man's intimidating gaze. Bull was standing at Danni's side. The four of them, frozen in time, seemed to focus at an invisible spot.

"I'm not asking. I'm saying you owe me. *Capiche?*"

Rocco broke the ice as if nothing intense had just transpired, "Bull's in his prime. He's game, and I can have him in the best shape of his life." The silence had been interrupted, but not the stare-down. "My word is my bond. Just remember, this is between me and you or it's off. And if there's any blowback, it's all on me. So that means it's over when I say so."

Cagootz held the soggy butt in his mouth between yellow teeth. He took it back out and thoughtfully nibbled on the cold end till he finally spoke: "That's what I've been saying, kid. It ain't over till it's over. Now pay attention. You know my reputation. I can't let anyone double-cross me. Once I start something I see it through to its end. I know you're a finisher too, because I've seen you fight in the cage. And I hear you're a man of your word. That's good. If the dog starts to go into shock or some shit like that, we'll discuss it. Aside from that, he's in till it's over. He's a finisher, too. That's what the three of us have in common, and why we're in this together. If you agree to leave him in the box long enough so he can win, I'll do what I need to do."

Rocco stood up, still glowering. He looked over at Danni, down at Bull and then placed his hands on either side of his untouched coffee cup. "Then you've got yourself a dogfight."

Cagootz nodded, still stone faced, biting down and further mashing his mutilated cigar, again showing a mouthful of stained teeth in what looked like a snarl rather than a smile.

After work Danni asked Rocco, "What did Cagootz mean when he said, *I went ahead and picked up that paper?*"

That season was becoming a time for firsts. Rocco stroked his beard: "Oh, *papers*? Yeah, it's got something to do with dogs. You know how these guys are with wanting their papers." Rocco hid from Danni the fact that he had taken a $5,000 loan from Sonny Magic. That loan shark deal was the first time Rocco had ever lied to his long-term girlfriend. Then he found himself lying again to perpetuate his deception by omission trick – another thing he wasn't proud of at all.

Weeks got shorter, and days flew by like videos. Everyone was busy doing their own thing. Danni had her wages increased that same day, and her mind was put somewhat at ease. She enjoyed her walks to work, inhaling the fresh fragrance of grass and trees during the full blast of sweet summertime. The relationship between Danni and her boss couldn't have been better. Even bar patrons seemed somewhat less obnoxious.

    Danni said to Rocco, "You stepped up for me when I'm at my most vulnerable point, just like I knew you would. You're proving to be a true friend when loyalty is what I need most. So that means from now on I'm with you no matter what."

    "Really? That means you're cool if I fuck other chicks?"

    Danni looked shocked, as if Rocco had just slapped her across the face. She asked in a shaky voice, "You really want to be with other women, Rocco?"

    "Easy, babe. I'm just breaking balls. You're all the woman I can handle – and then some. I'm feeling pretty okay about this," he lied again. "Putting Bull through this *keep* will be good for me. Getting back to my own pit weight feels great. No booze helps my depression meds work better. I'm sleeping sound and waking up full of energy. And I gotta admit; the prospect of making some real money so we can dig ourselves out of this trap we're in is the jump-start we need. Our luck's about to change, Danni."

CH XVI: Shit-pants Joey

Winter Solstice, 2013: Animated thoughts of children, stoners, schizophrenics and dreams full of pain medication arrived like bed service to my gurney. Implosions of purple lightshows roared nonstop inside my skull to help me understand how something like an opiate high staggered me down there. Luckily for my tolerance I was already able to realize the gravity of what had transpired in my front yard – on that explosive day and concerning all the unknowns yet to form their own lines.

I woke to the slow and heavy thumping of footsteps coming down those green basement steps. I took a deep inhale and held it. For the time being I was at someone's mercy. I heard a familiar voice from my past, the same one I had dreamed about every night. That same voice that spoke to me, knew my name, had coaxed me back to a world of the living. More and more I had been resurfacing into starbursts of physical torment and mental anguish. The pain seemed almost unbearable. Those familiar purple implosions shot from brain to eyelids, then left a roaring sound against the inside of my eardrums. Evidently I had been heavily drugged. After finally regaining consciousness, from what I was told had been nearly a month-long voyage drifting through clouds of near-death, I groaned at what was so odd to me, a spark emanating from deep within me.

Because I was so weak and helpless, I also felt confident that my own killing days were behind me. I shielded my eyes from the lights to put a face to that evermore familiar voice. "It's me, Jackie. It's Joey. Remember me, *coom*? Shit-pants Joey, remember? Come on, wake up, my friend. It's Joey from Collinwood. That's it, Jackie. Good job. Stay awake this time, okay *coom*? You're safe now. It's Joey, okay bro?"

"Who? Joey?" The way he dressed, he looked like he belonged in a quartet from the 1950s. What the fuck are you doing here, Joey? You work here in this shit-box?"

"I live here, Jackie. You're safe, *coom*. You're with me."

"Why do you look so old, Joey? Hey, why are you here? Where is *here*, anyway? Where are we? Don't lie to me."

"You were in a terrible accident, Jackie. I found you in the woods across from your house. Do you remember any of that?"

"What? Where's my wife? Is she dead? Hey, wait a minute… You're not Shit-pants Joey! You're an old man. Who the fuck are you, and why am I here?"

"Tessa's fine, Jackie. She's at home with your kids. They're all fine. It's me, *coom*. It's Joey, your old friend from the Neighborhood. You're safe, Jackie. You're at my house. You've been convalescing. I thought I was going to lose you, bro. God saved you for a reason, Jackie. You're blessed."

I thought: *Okay, I see what's going on here.* "You're a doctor now, right Joey? Hey, is this a mental hospital? Don't you come near me. Because if I have to—"

I must have blacked out in mid-sentence. I felt stronger when I woke the next time, alert enough to notice my hospital bed, clean bandages, and an IV drip with drugs flowing through my system to soften everything almost enough.

The next time I woke was to Joey prodding me with more comments and questions. I pretended to be asleep, to watch body language through slits and to listen for subtleties.

Joey spoke as though I were wide awake: "It's Veterans' Day, Jackie." Then he turned away to leave me to my thoughts.

It can't be. I died in July. I became obsessed with the thought of death. Mine at first, each time I asked Joey to kill me. I watched my dark friend slowly shake his white head of hair and hiss between coffee stained teeth. Laying there helpless, weak as an orphaned infant, gradually I realized I might mend well enough to complete my mission. I'd track and murder them myself, whoever *they* are, rather than wrestle with an overpowering sense of shame and self-hatred. I remembered having a gun on my hip the last time I left my house – the last moment I can ever remember being a married man to my first and only love, my sweet Tessa, who was as loyal as a good pit-dog. But she must have given up by now, or lost a grasp on sanity. I could feel things inside of me had changed and knew they had in her, too. *She would still be that vibrant woman if only…*

I still cursed Joey for having saved me. I became a hollow shell that gradually filled with rage only to grow stronger from it. I heard a muted, one-sided conversation, as someone paced above my head. I could almost see through that small window up by the ceiling, two rows of three distorted glass block. Frustrated, I repeated, "I need my stuff returned, Joey…"

"In time, Jackie. There's no hurry. Instead of all this talk about killing and dying, use this time wisely to rebuild confidence by refocusing on workable strategies. That ass kicking you absorbed almost 40 years ago was baby stuff compared to what you've just somehow managed to survive as an old man. Right now, more than anything, you need time. You're a welcome guest for as long as necessary. I've had you on 10mg of *Oxandrolone*, twice a day for the burns. At the rate you've been healing, you'll be on your way inside of another month. Have faith, friend."

"Fuck that. You can't keep me locked in this basement forever, Joey. You've been a friend so far. I respect that and won't forget it. But right now I want my .357 and the shells returned. Plus I want my street clothes back, and I want them now. And if you're not willing to do that, then I'll know there's something else going on."

"Come on, *coomba*. I've known you longer than anyone, other than your mother. And she's so old now she probably doesn't even remember she has a son. And as to all this killing talk, just make sure your mind and body can match those lofty goals. While regaining your strength I'm sure that appetite for retribution will increase. And by time you're ready to leave it won't have you or me sighted in the crosshairs."

Locked behind an early winter storm called a "lake effect" that slammed the Great Lakes region fast and violent, snowflakes fogged a frozen block window and a wandering mind. An early snowstorm unleashed its fury with a carpet of frozen silence blanketing Northeastern Ohio. According to my childhood friend, an old man who claimed to be Dr. Shit-pants motherfucking Joey, an unseasonable Arctic front slowly pushed Southeast across the Great Lakes. Its icy winds, whirling around the perimeter of that strange room, almost matched a coldness locked tight inside my heart. I needed time to think and to mend, so for the moment I was content to just watch the storm.

"Is it really Veterans' Day, Joey? Have I really been here over three months?"

"Well, let me say it this way: Happy Thanksgiving, *coomba*. I'll bring home a nice dinner for us. You have a lot to be thankful for this year, *coom*."

"Hold up, man. You expect me to believe that you've held me captive down here in this tomb for four months?"

"It wasn't time wasted, friend. You're healing at a fantastic rate, considering you almost died on July 29th. Don't worry, *coom*. You'll have a plan. You've always been smart but about half-feral, always running on instinct. But I know you well, Jackie. You're a survivor."

"Yeah, I know you do. You remember me stomping a mud-hole in your ass when we were kids? And now you're stupid enough to drag me back into a world of the living, so I can flinch every time I imagine the terror and pleading in her eyes? You think this is how I want to live, to memories defined and weighted by all the tragedy I've caused? Besides, Doctor, what makes you think I'm not just playing possum?"

"Maybe because you were shitting and pissing in bags for a month, and have been intravenously fed by tubes? Those are pretty good indicators that this isn't merely a cat-and-mouse game, Jackie. Then there are your vital signs… You were slipping badly for a few weeks. I thought we'd lose you. You need to come to terms with a fact: you're not the man you used to be."

"Don't ever make the mistake to think I'm weak just because I'm a little burned out right now, Joey. I'm sure you're smart enough not to forget what I'm capable of."

"Yes, that's right. I remember you as courageous instead of a suicide or a bully. You're still healing, Jackie. And you're scared. You can admit it. That's natural. It's expected. In Nam I woke up to fear and went to sleep with it for a year. So no matter how much you try to intimidate me, I'm not budging on this. Get used to being here for a short while longer. You're in no shape to go anywhere – not just yet. Soon enough we'll cut off the wraps and leave them off. I need to get some things. I'll be back. Do you need anything?"

"Nope. I'm like the Tip-Top bread man. Can't you tell?"

"You are not there just yet, but you *are* headed in the right direction – and quickly. Don't lose faith, *coom*. As bad as all these different types of pain are they'll serve to make you stronger."

"My dad was really tough on me as a kid. And he used to preach to me: *Fight and the pain will go away*. But sometimes all that fighting ever did was to cause other kinds of pain. But no matter what, I gotta push my way to the other side of this."

"He was correct. He didn't raise you to be a quitter."

"I don't like to admit it, Shit-pants, but you might be right this time. Maybe I'm in no shape to be going anywhere just yet. I'm still pretty much defenseless like this. That's why you should get my gun, for protection, for when you're not here."

"Nobody knows you're here who would hurt you. What I mean is they don't even know you're still alive. Don't worry.

You're safe. So now you have the time to figure out your next best move."

"At least don't keep me locked up down here like some prisoner. I'm becoming my own worst enemy. What is this thing, Joey, a bomb shelter or a laboratory? And what are you supposed to be now, Shit-pants, some goddamn mad scientist? Who keeps a hospital bed hidden in a concrete bunker under his house, stocked with canned food and jugs of water, first aide supplies and goddamned IVs, and a shit-load of drugs?"

He grinned, "The smart kind."

"And another thing: Why is my asshole sore, Joey? Did you try to fuck me while I was in a coma? Just tell the truth, you fucking psycho. Did you try?"

"I won't even bother to answer that. Those four years of college haven't changed you all that much, have they? You're still crazy, aren't you Jackie?"

"You'd better know I am. So be honest, Joey, and I promise I won't come back after you. I just need to know the truth. Did you fuck me while I was unconscious?"

"I can't believe I'm actually having this conversation!"

"Just be straight with me, Joey."

"Did you forget about the bomb again, Jackie? Your rectum is sore for the same reason your thighs and buttocks are gouged and scorched. Your car was a burning hunk of scrap metal when I found you. That explosive turned your car into one big bomb. It was an unrecognizable heap of junk. You're blessed to be alive."

"Blessed, huh? So why didn't the blast kill me if I'm so fucking blessed? Explain that. And what did you mean saying: 'Nobody who would hurt you knows you're here.'? You're hiding something, Joey. I can tell, you sneaky Arab bastard!"

"First off, I've told you several times already, I found you lying face-down in the brush across from your house. Evidently you jumped out of your car a moment before the blast. I can't help it where my parents were born. And why do you insist on calling me an Arab? I'm as American and as Catholic as you are."

"Fuck you, Joey! Don't accuse me of being Christian, you fat Lebanese prick. I'm an atheist, not some twisted, two-faced *necrophiliac*. So quit trying to bullshit yourself, you fat cocksucker! And be straight with me about Tessa! Don't lie. Or I swear to Buddha I'll torture your whole family in this sick fucking basement of yours. I'll make your sorry ass watch till it's your turn. You fucking tell me everything right now!"

"Unfortunately, Jackie, I have no family for you to torture. They're all gone. And most of my old friends are gone. There's just you and our old friend, Enrico. That's it."

"What about Tessa? Why isn't she here? Why did you leave her out there?"

"You already know she was all the way up by your house, far away from the road, when your car exploded. She was face-down and well beyond the epicenter of that explosion. I checked her vital signs. She was unconscious but otherwise healthy. Except for a few minor abrasions from her fall, she appeared to be fine. Like I said, I put you in my car and then called 911 for her. Your worries are understandable, my friend, but are totally unfounded. I promise. She's not dead or seriously impaired. I put her in your house and made a call from that gas station near you. An ambulance brought her to the ER where I work. I saw her every day. She is safe and back at home with your children. The house was undamaged, other than a few shattered windows."

"Okay, Joey. Thank you. You know what you saw, whatever it was. You're real smart, Shit-pants, I'll give you that. But you didn't drop acid like aspirin like we did. And you weren't ever part of a brotherhood, so you don't live in that other dimension where I play. You've accomplished a lot and know the five senses well. But that's where your education ends. There's something else going on you're not even aware of."

"I'd better initiate a taper from your Diluadid protocol. You spend too much time lately drifting in and out of opioid hallucinations. Now that you're awake for longer than you're asleep the drugs are beginning to affect your mental state."

"Even though I haven't seen you for few decades you're right for thinking I'm still crazy. That is what you were thinking."

"Easy does it, *coomba*. You're in no danger here."

"I know it sounds like bullshit for a guy all wrapped in gauze, locked in some demented subterranean lab, to be issuing threats. But if you're lying to me about anything, or fucking me over in any way, Shit-pants motherfucking Joey, don't forget you'll be forced to kill me, or live in fear for the rest of your life. Don't believe I might have turned into somebody's bitch."

"I know exactly who you are and can imagine what you're still capable of. But I'm not doing this out of fear. Don't you forget that part, okay? I still remember Collinwood's rules, even though I wasn't a gang member or even allowed to hang around with your *Royal Flush*. But I know the code of the Neighborhood as well as you do. Think about it, Jackie. That's why I didn't take you to a hospital. That's why I put my career on a chopping block the day I put you in my car. I knew if I brought you to a hospital, whoever did this to you would find out where you were and finish the job. They'd have to, because they also remember how crazy you can get."

"Let's get something straight. How could we have let you hang around with us? You didn't use drugs, so that means we automatically couldn't trust you. Plus, you weren't involved in any criminal behavior. So that meant you'd have the goods on us, but we'd have nothing on you. How were we supposed to let some clean-cut pussy like you be around our dealings? Think about it, Joey. You're not making sense."

"Have you completely lost your mind, Jackie? You're saying you can only trust people who, for the most part, cannot be trusted?"

"Just tell me this then: Why, if I haven't seen you in over 30 years, and you don't live anywhere near me, were you on *my* street that day? How do you know where I live?"

"I ran into your old friend, Eggs. He was at the hospital for an outpatient procedure. When I asked him about you, he told me where I could find you. And you're lucky he did. You living out there, in the middle of nowhere – by the time someone called the cops and an ambulance arrived, you might have been too far in shock to be saved. And that's *if* they found you before the coyotes did."

"Okay, Joey, then how did you know it was me, and were able to find me that night? I mean, how did you even know where to look? It was almost dark out."

"First of all: who else out in the middle of nowhere would get their car bombed Cleveland style? It had to have something to do with you. Plus, I was in Vietnam in 1969. Remember? I was on a demolitions team. That means I saw plenty of vehicles get blown to hell. Things learned while in combat are the types of lessons one never forgets. It was easy to follow the clues. I noticed one flashpoint much longer than the rest from that scorched perimeter. That evidence told me a car door had been open *before* the explosion occurred. It also told me that because there was no body near the car, the logical conclusion was to follow that longest burn mark. The clues showed me that someone, somehow, ejected and left a door open before the bomb detonated – which to me is the most interesting part of all. I'm guessing it was a timer wired to the driver's door or a remote device. But how did you know to jump? What did you see, hear or smell? Why did you run from your car when you did?"

As I attempted to turn over to see him more clearly I asked, "Weren't you and Chilly in Nam together? I'm thinking I remember Chilly saying you guys got stationed together somewhere in that shooting gallery, fighting that bullshit war."

"Let's forget about Nam for now. How did you know to emergency exit your car? That's nit a normal reaction."

"This is the type of shit you can't understand. I sensed something. That *Click* strafed across my brain as loud as the blast that followed it seconds later. So now this is what makes me even more insane: Just as easy as it was to booby-trap me, that same bomb could have blown away Tessa or one of my kids. That *Click* saved us, Joey. And with the *Bounce*, some fucks are going down as soon as I'm back on these sore feet. If the code is still clear after all this time then you must at least intellectually understand the concepts of the *Click* and the *Bounce*."

"Of course I remember the unspoken language and gameness from Southeast Asia. And I do appreciate your simmering rage. I know that's why you want to leave. But I also know you're not ready – not just yet. I'll do what I can to get you healthy again, Jackie. And as far as the *Bounce* goes, *coomba*, you've been bouncing back at an incredible pace right here, taking into consideration your age and the severity of your injuries."

"So maybe it was the *Click*? Is that you found me, Joey?"

"Maybe initially. But I have to admit that finding you was dumb luck. The lighting was muted and dusk was already settling in, I literally tripped over your body in the high grass and fell right next to you. Even though you scared the living crap out of me, laying there in shock with your hair and clothes burned-off."

"When you tripped over me, did you shit yourself again, like when we were in elementary school? You don't have to be ashamed. It's not like it's the first time."

"Real funny, Jackie. How about I was scared shitless because I found my oldest friend lying near a smoking heap of junk that used to be his car? How about that?"

"You know how much I appreciate this, right? But why did you waste time going to the house to sniff around like a fucking coonhound while I was laying there burned-up and in shock? What's that about? There's a piece missing. I can feel it.

Why didn't you just load me up right then if I was about to die? And you're supposed to be a doctor?"

"When I saw Eggs in the hospital he related how you and Tessa had recently married. So my instinct, as a veteran and as a doctor, was to double-check the perimeter. I feared she or your kids might have been seriously injured, – or worse. I had to take a few moments to see if someone needed immediate medical care. I would have brought her here to my home. I've known Tessa for as long as you have. She's my friend too, Jackie. I never could have forgiven myself if she was in need of urgent care and I ignored her. Plus, I couldn't leave her defenseless out there to die. I had to check. What's the matter with you, anyway? Why are you so paranoid?"

"Why do you think, genius? Just look at me? This didn't happen on accident. It's not like my fucking car backfired or blew itself up. But no sweat. I believe you, Shit-pants. And I'm forever in your debt. Anytime, anything, just name it and it's yours."

"I'll tell you right now what you can do for me."

"Whatever, whenever. Just say it. As soon as I'm healthy enough it's done."

"You're already healthy enough right now for what I want. It's simply this: Don't ever refer to me as *Shit-pants* Joey again. Okay? I mean it. Besides the fact that I'm a respected physician. . . well, the thing is I'm an adult *and* one of your oldest friends. You should show more respect to a friend than that."

"Okay, you're right. But Joey Joseph? Really? No offense, but that's really a fucked-up name. If you're pissed at anyone it should be at your parents. When you think about it, Enrico and I did you a favor by giving you that nickname in elementary school. Nobody even knew who you were till then. You were just some fat-ass, *raghead* kid nobody even talked to. You were the invisible man. We made you famous, bro."

"How about that? We've been friends since kindergarten and that's the first time you've ever referred to me *bro*. Amazing!"

PART FOUR

Growing up as a bastard child, Rocco heard stories about a man who was in cahoots with big-time shylocks and high profile drug dealers. Like we had, Collinwood kids his age idolized the bad guys. Rocco heard that this Jackie guy allegedly parlayed profits from drugs to become an international dogfighter making shit-loads of cash and connections all over the world. People say it was Jackie who bridged the gap between the Wong Gongs and the Italian syndicate. Rocco heard Jackie opened that door by staging matches at neutral venues so organized crime outfits could pick up large bets when the Royal Flush couldn't cover high-rollers. Hefty wagers were won and lost against men from all over North America.

Rocco heard Jackie married a mulatto girl and moved his wife and daughter of mixed blood to a farm near the PA border to raise some of the best Pit-bulls in the world. Legends about him among Collinwood kids became larger than life. And the longer Jackie stayed away, the loftier those tales grew.

One common story was about a rift between Jackie and his brothers. A few old-timers said Jackie couldn't be trusted, yet nobody could say exactly why. Some said the problem was over money or a woman. Another version claimed it was a bluff; that Jackie had been freelancing for them on the sly. Some others said Jackie simply, but not easily, got out of the life to game-up in a different way. There were envious sycophants willing to set him up to get in the good graces with the Cleveland mob. But Jackie was confident that street-wise players steered clear of those back-biter types. All-in-all, Rocco figured this Jackie guy was someone he should meet. He guessed that they had a lot in common.

Rocco, raised by a devoted yet stressed-out mother, had fantasized about *what-if's* throughout childhood and adolescence. He wondered what it would have been like to be raised by a father who had been a straight peg in a crooked hole – just like he was. He wondered what if his father was alive somewhere and didn't even know he existed. A simple fact was that Rocco didn't know much about his own father, other than he was Sicilian and a soldier who had been lost in a war. He could see that his mother was ashamed so he didn't push her about it. Rocco had been close to his mother – just like I'd been so very long ago.

CH XVII:
Meaning, Purpose, & Revenge

2013, The Basement: Dr. Joey told me, "I've been trying to reconstruct the crime scene by what little evidence I have. Your burns are concentrated on your lower extremities and backside. Because the damage is almost twice as bad on the back of your calves than on your upper back, it's my guess you literally dove toward the woods across the street just as the blast triggered and sent you sailing through the air. That explains why I found you far away from the road, unable to talk and having injuries consistent with the toasted car, scorch marks on the ground and by the road. It's a miracle you didn't hit a tree. An impact like that would have killed you as quickly as the bomb."

"Very astute there, Joey. I'm impressed. Now find me a remote for this fancy flat screen. As bad as all this physical stuff hurts, it's every bit as painful for me to listen to these pimps and prostitutes 24/7 on this FOX News station. Man, I thought I hated these phony pricks before… But at least that fucking crybaby, Beck, with his magic underwear is finally off the air. Still though, these other two *scheeves* are just as sickening. And the two blonde-haired bitches on here, where did they dig up cunts like those two witches? Tell you what, Joey. I'd rather you overdose me right now on these tasty opiates than subject me to any more of this *compassionate conservative,* party-line redundancy."

"Now all of the sudden, just because you worked as a counselor for about a decade, you went liberal on us, Jackie?" Joey asked with his arms crossed. "Those left-wing socialists you like are the same people who back amnesty for illegal aliens, fund those killers at PETA and ignore church-burning organizations around the country posing as Americans. Your party's a joke!"

"Let me explain something to you: Fuck the liberals and those tea-bagger assholes. I've been fading in and out of opium dreams with really sweet cartoons playing in a cloud floating inside my head. And then the first thing I hear when the medicine starts wearing off is hatred spewed non-stop by these fascist, xenophobic lying cocksuckers doing their best to pollute our country with more lies. Divide and conquer, that's all they do and all they know. I admire real prostitutes more than I do these people who sell out their own countrymen and their souls. And you like these turn-coats? Yeah, that figures. What do you guys make these days, about 300 grand a year – at least? So now you're like the rest of these money grubbing *compassionate* dick gobblers, right? It's all about the money. I see how it is, you *raghead* fuck. Boy, some people sure do change. Don't they?"

"Yes, they certainly do. Wasn't that you who put a few black kids in the hospital during all that '60s racial unrest at Collinwood? But then you're the same person who married a woman of color, right? Weren't you the same kid who got expelled for dragging Curtis out of Mr. K's classroom by his afro and choking him unconscious with one of your judo moves right on the 1st floor hallway? But you were the guy who later hung out with Curtis and another black guy you met in jail called Horrible Hank – selling drugs with them throughout Cleveland. And now you're a drug counselor?"

"What? People can't change, Joey? Look at you with those faggot-assed clothes. You don't even curse anymore, all proper and stuffy now with all this phony-ass, reborn Christian bullshit. Wow! So what are you saying? You're the only person who can change? Is that it, Joey the fucking carpet rider? You're so terminally unique?"

"Some people do change. So what is it now, Jackie? You're one of those *progressive,* new-age atheists now? Don't tell me you voted for that hypocrite, Obama. Is that what all this is about? Did you assume the white guilt, too? Or is it because a few FOX newscasters are Irish? Because you've always been a racist."

"*I'm* a racist? I'm the one who married a mulatto chick."

"Why do you feel you have to quantify that by saying Butterscotch is mulatto? Why can't you just admit she's black? Or why even mention her race at all? I'll tell you why. Because you're racist; that's why."

"Suck off, Joey. Listen to yourself. You've lost your mind. Butter is ¾ white. So why the fuck would I refer to her as black?"

"Uh oh . . . looks like I hit a nerve. Sorry, Jackie."

"Hey, Shit-pants. How about this? You're pure *sand-nigger,* so you're blacker than she is. But I don't hold that against you."

"You're Sicilian, right Jackie? Wasn't Sicily invaded by the Moors? They were black, right? Or did you cut school that day?"

"You amaze me, Joey. For a smart guy you aren't too bright. All this boring-ass bullshit of yours just because I don't like those stupid Irish pricks on the news you idolize every night?

Besides, the Moors were Arabic – not Negroid. If they were black, then that means you're the nigger in the woodpile, not Butter or Curtis!"

"See? You're a big-time racist. You hate the Irish, the blacks and everyone from Middle-eastern derivation. Just admit it so I can go upstairs and get some sleep."

"I'm not racist at all. The only people I hate are fat-ass, Lebanese pants-shitters."

Joey's cell rang again. He checked it and put it away.

"Alright, Joey. You're gonna tell me with a straight face those Irish bastards from down Five Points don't hate Italians?"

"Thank you, Jackie, you just proved my point."

"Let me try to explain this to a little pussy who was too afraid to leave his mommy's house. If I'm not mistaken, 36 bombs exploded in one year. That was in 1976, between Irish and Italians. Am I right about this so far, Joey?"

"The Cleveland wars have been over for many years, Jackie. Bomb City, USA is in the past. The Mick and Uno have been dead since the '70s. The Kelly brothers down Five Points are out of business. The Collinwood gang wars are history."

"Oh, the Neighborhood war's over, huh? I see... So remind me. Why did I get car-bombed if the war's over? And I agree, all that insanity had little to do with race or nationality and everything to do with new insecurities, old grudges and territory."

"Those explosions occurred throughout Cleveland's Eastside. And not all of the killing took place during 1976. That was the year the kingpin, Scalici, died and the Cleveland mob went scrambling for power. I'll admit that many of those explosions during the mid-970s were in Collinwood. But like I said, that was years ago. You're living in the past. Granted, you were a victim of a recent car bombing. But it could have been anyone, and for a number of reasons. You've made lots of enemies over the years."

"Where was the last place you heard about an Italian guy bombed out of his car? Shootings and bombings did start before '76, and they ended way after. But how would you know any of that. You were too busy hiding. But I gotta crash. I can barely see."

"You should rest. You're way too excitable, and that's not good for the healing process. Try to unwind. This is your home."

"Okay, but just one more thing, Joey. How about instead of 'Shit-pants' I call you 'One-Dip'? You like that name better?"

"What now? I'm sure it's something else insulting."

"Well, because you're already a *sand nigger*, I'm thinking the term 'One-Dip' fits the bill. Evidently, your father was a three-pump Pete like you must be; if you've ever even been laid. So when your parents had sex that *one time* to get your fat-ass, if your old man could have held off and stroked it in for just one more dip, you could have been a full-fledged black boy instead of some dingy-ass sand-coon. See what I mean? One-Dip is a good name for a wanna-be nigger, right?"

"You never even met him, Jackie. So how is this right?"

"That makes two of us. You never saw the guy, either."

"I don't see how making fun of my family is appropriate."

"Take it easy, Joey. It's just jokes. Besides, fuck him. You don't owe him shit. You mother did a good job raising you. And you made it on your own, without him – without anyone. You don't even know what he looked like and don't need to."

The dogs next-door to Joey's house went crazy again. We heard muffled shouts outside. Then things quieted again, other than gusts of snow whistling and whipping against Joey's vinyl siding and triple-pane storm windows.

Joey pulled out his wallet to show me a faded black and white photo of a soldier: "I do so. This is a picture he sent to my mother while he was in Korea. He was a hero. See? Look right here. It's the purple heart. But how could I expect you to know that? I'm the one who served my country in Vietnam."

"Hero, huh? So where's this hero at now?"

"By now I suppose he's dead. My mother received a letter stating he had been *shell shocked*. He was never the same after he returned. He came home and stayed for a little while. My mother said he was different and very distant. Then he left the house one day when I was a baby and just never returned."

"Shell shocked? Does that means a nervous breakdown?"

"It's a form of PTSD caused from psychological trauma suffered on the battlefield, usually found in areas with high concentrations of intense shellings on battlefronts. Doctors at that time had little knowledge of this disorder. Soldiers were basically left to fend for themselves, very much like when our generation returned from Vietnam. It's very sad to think about all that. Actually, you could be shell shocked."

"Sorry, bro, just messing with you. I wasn't really gonna call you 'One-Dip'. I just wanted you to finally tell me about your dad. And it worked, didn't it? I got you, you fat fucker! All these years and you never said word one to me about him. So how long have you been carrying around that picture, anyways?"

"What kind of question is that?" he snapped. Then he lowered his head, "Sorry. This photo was the first item I put into my first wallet. My mom gave it and the wallet to me on my 16th birthday. I don't know why I've been holding that information inside for all these years. Maybe it's my own type of PTSD. I guess I'm still dealing with abandonment issues. A therapist once told me that's why I never married. I suppose he's correct. But we're from Collinwood. I guess we all have trust issues."

"Well, Joey, I just want you to know I admire what you've accomplished, and respect that you did it all on your own. I'm proud to have you as my lifelong friend."

"You're getting all gooey now, Jackie, and that's not at all like you. I like you better as a world-class ball-buster. Besides, even though we're the same age, I've always looked up to you as an older brother. You and your friends did the things I always secretly wanted to do. I guess I really was a coward."

"Fuck that! You're no coward, bro. You served in the Nam in '69 with Chilly when things were still hot and heavy over there. Plus those so-called friends of mine you mentioned were never half the friend you've been. I'm just breaking balls, Joey, and you know this. I don't have brain damage. I know who my real friends are."

"Get some rest, *coomba*. I really do appreciate you clarifying that coward stuff. I'll wake you later to have a look at what's going on under this gauze. Before I go up I want to ask this but give you time to think of an answer: I've been wondering about motives, like other enemies you made over the years. For example, do you still mess with those crazy pit-dog guys?"

"Nah. I've been out of the dogs for years. It was like with the booze. One day I just lost my taste for it. But most of those guys are okay. Besides, I had a good reputation. I do have a housedog, though – a *pet-bull*. Hey, Joey, don't believe that propaganda you read about that breed, and all that shit you gobble up on your mick TV channel. Those dogs have a fuck of a lot more class than people. A below average pit-dog is gamer and more loyal than most people who are considered to have integrity. But a weird part about this whole pit-dog thing is that my kid, Rocco, messed with the dogs before we ever knew we were related, just like my dad did as a kid. It's in our bloodline."

"Just thank God you're still alive enough to be thinking and articulating memories and feeling real emotions. How can you ever doubt the existence of our Lord again, Jackie. You're a living miracle. There's a reason He saved you."

"Fuck all that phony humility and gratitude bullshit. So tell me: if there are no such things as accidents or coincidences, I guess suicide bombers and terminal disease, raping and killing children, and cellular mutations called cancer are meant to be, right Doc? If everything happens for a reason like you diluted zealots claim, then why waste precious time praying? If things have been predetermined and we're all destined to our fates, why beg this Almighty God of yours to change his plans that already have been etched in time? I guess I'm supposed to believe that a bomb wired-up to our family car was part of a Divine Plan? Or if I survive this just to kill some stupid motherfuckers, then that's also part of His Plan? Oh no, wait… I'm sorry. I forgot. He only gets credit for the good stuff. That's right…"

"I'm asking you to rethink this with a clear head."

"I'm cool. One last thing: Who keeps phoning you this late? Are you running an escort service or selling blow?"

"Don't worry about that. Just someone I work with."

"Hey, Joey, you think I could be shell shocked?"

"Your damage is mostly physical. So you should be resting and either praying or meditating for positive energy."

I took Joey's advice. I did pray, to the cosmos, the great energy field, for the day when I could unleash my fury of wrath and retribution on those who did this. I felt gratitude for being alive to choose which type of payback best suited the occasion.

Joey slowly climbed his basement steps to living quarters so foreign to me it might as well have been overseas. He said, "Even though we are the same age you've always been like an older brother." Before he closed the door I heard his phone ring. *What the fuck? What does he do up there all by himself?* I also wondered how two fresh-faced kids so full of life during summer vacations that seemed to have lasted for years wound up reunited as old men clinging to bits of nothing.

I woke from another lucid dream to Joey standing over me, staring. I pretended I was still asleep, trying to get my wits before he engaged me in another narrative already prepared.

Fucking Shit-pants Joey… My most trusted ally. Maybe my only friend. Go on ahead, mad-dog, coom-boom. I love you, brother.

"Like I was saying, Jackie." He shifted gears as if it were a continuation from a conversation from the night before, or week before, like there hadn't been a lapse of any time. "I've always looked up to you as an older brother. You're the only family I have." While I slowly roused he added, "You're getting stronger each day, *coom*. Your vitals are strong again. Your skin is healthy. I can see all the signs. You're over the hump."

With my eyes still closed I asked, "How long have I been locked up in this shit hole? And where's my piece?"

Joey sighed but continued even though my eyes were still closed. "Use your head and walk away from this, *coomba*. You won because they think you're dead. You're free. Just walk away and get yourself a new identity until you can safely contact your wife and children. Don't go stumbling back into another trap. You might be able to win this by outsmarting them. Don't let a hot temper and the prospect of retribution allow them to push you into unwise choices."

"Fuck that. They don't make my decisions." I opened my eyes and continued. "Look how many years it took for those fucks to finally kill the Irishman. He stayed right there in Collinwood during all those shootings and bombings and did the same goddamn things every day like a robot. They knew his every move. His schedule might as well have been posted in the Cleveland Plain Dealer, yet they still missed about a dozen strategically planned opportunities to take him down. Mick was an FBI informant, which means he was weak and a fucking cur. And they're backstabbers. So fuck them all."

"See? That's just the drugs talking. You're smarter than this, Jackie. Those syndicate guys might be a lot of things, but what they're not is stupid or weak. And what they are is as game as the best pit dogs you've ever seen. Don't ever forget that."

"Yeah, I know. So what? So am I."

"Yes, but there is only one of you. No one man wins alone against an army. Like you always say, Jackie, timing is everything. The Mick was lucky right up until his luck ran out. Eventually pride got him. Taunting those *paesano* and being arrogant enough to stick to a daily regimen in public finally got his ticket punched. Don't go getting all cocky, my friend, or the next time you will be dead."

"I'm invisible. That's the beauty of all this. But you're right this time. I really am grateful and humbled. So I'll just walk away from this. All I care about is my family. Fuck those guys."

"Now you're talking, *coomba*. Just think of this as a life lesson. Consider yourself the luckiest man on Earth to have been able to live through a car bombing. Your pain is a blessing. Pain and fear are some of God's ways to instill survival mechanisms in us. This is your chance at a fresh start – a new life. Have faith that this is a God thing. He saved you for a special purpose."

"And you're such an intelligent person. Think about what you just said. It almost makes sense, babbling all that childish bullshit. Let me get this straight: I'm blessed because I'm burned up like a slab of bacon? It's a God thing because Tessa saw it and my Gina and Rocco think I was murdered? I've been saved so Tessa and my kids can continue to believe I'm dead? That makes sense to you?"

"You're putting words in my mouth. I didn't say that."

"Maybe, but that's what I heard. You're brainwashed by those buffoons on Fox News, and you subscribe to all their religious dribble like you're some mindless zombie. You don't have to be a herd member, you know. Have you forgotten how to think for yourself, Joey? Or is all this because you lost your dad at a young age? Is that what all this mind control bullshit is about?"

"Oh, I see. Thanks, Jackie. Maybe you're right. Maybe I wasn't thinking for myself when I broke laws and jeopardized my medical license the day I loaded your burned carcass into my car instead of phoning for an ambulance to take you to an ER."

"I'm sorry, bro. Even though I do think you're a fanatic when it comes to politics – you know, slurping up all that right-wing tea party, Christianity bullshit – it's not cool for me to attack you about it. It's your right to believe there are honest politicians and angels and heaven if you want to. I just feel miserable, Joey. I'm sore everywhere. And when I'm not floating on these sweet-ass drugs, I'm dope sick. But that's no excuse for me to be an asshole. I'll try to be more considerate from now on, Joey."

"Considering the trauma you sustained and the agony you're obviously in, you're doing better than expected. Since you came out of shock the emotional spectrum was concerning, till now. But let's be honest, Jackie. You've always been somewhat of a prick, even on your best days. So all things considered, I'd say you're doing fine. Your sarcasm tells me you're healing on the inside – you're getting back to your old self."

"You're right. Now can I have my gun?"

"HA! Even your twisted sense of humor is back!"

"Here's another good sign. If you don't change the channel I'm gonna throw my piss bag at that nice flat screen of yours. I can't handle another second of these arrogant fucks talking down to American citizens like we're a bunch of idiots."

"You cannot have your gun, or cell phone, or street clothes just yet. Soon you will have run of the house. And certainly you're healed enough to operate the remote. Put on anything you'd like, or turn off the TV. I left on some human sounds so you wouldn't feel alone, or like you were trapped in someone's basement," he laughed.

"Well this ain't exactly Cedar Point! But I appreciate you, brother. I really do. You're a good man, Joey, even if you are a sucker for *compassionate* conservatives and the bible. But don't mind what I say, okay? I'm not too sure of much right now."

"Tell me something, Jackie – anything. Go ahead..."

"Well, Joey, being alone down here offers me a luxury. And that treat is reflection. I see how my life is totally screwed up. And just like hers, his or theirs, mistakes are results of decisions belonging only to me. The choices we make, the chances we take, and the rules we break are of our own doing. Then we collect rewards or pay with consequences. Because just like her and him, we all get some of each."

"Wow, I'm impressed. You've been doing some critical thinking instead of wasting time. I see that your priority list is geared in another direction now, Jackie."

"As far as I'm concerned, fuck the pain. Feeling sorry for myself is the last thing I need. The fact of the matter is I'm still alive. I can move and think clearly enough."

"That's the spirit, *coom*! That's the old Jackie I remember."

I had managed to acquire enough cash and an unregistered gun to hopefully get what and where I needed – if luck stayed on my side. It had to. I needed to believe that. Even though I'd lost everything other than life and sanity, two specific things gave me the strength to keep going: revenge and being reunited with family. All the rest was bullshit. I'd been through too much to worry about window dressing. One thing this whole ordeal taught me was patience. And I was learning gratitude.

"Meanwhile, I'll just put one foot in front of the other."

"What else is it, Jackie? What else is bothering you?"

"I was dreaming of Dago Red, about when he woke up soaked in blood next to Toby's head. You remember Dago Red, right? Did you ever know about that night?"

"No. Once I went to medical school I saw very few people; although, Enrico and I did keep in contact."

"Cool. Rico was always a solid kid."

"I did hear some things. I heard you got to be pretty good friends with those kids who called themselves the No-Names. Where did they get that goofy name, anyway?"

"They named themselves after the gamest Pit-bull I've ever seen. They were okay guys. Maybe a little crazy for their own good. But they all became junkies. I think they're all dead now except for Dago Red, and maybe that burnout, Slick."

"How about you, Jackie? Do you ever hear from Enrico?"

"Rico saved my ass down in Georgia. He knew a cop down there who got me out of a bad spot. I always liked him, Joey. But no, I haven't seen him since then. Why?"

"Wasn't he a part of your crew for awhile?"

"No. Benny wouldn't give anybody else the nod. He said, 'No new members till one of us dies.' Then he got wasted. We all knew Rico was tough and solid, but he lacked the killer instinct."

"He always liked you, Jackie. He told me about how you and your Royal Flush spent the night at his parents' house, on the floor with guns drawn, protecting his family – waiting for some armed punks to return from Five Points. He said it was the Kelly brothers who threatened to kill his parents and then they shot up their house. Maureen was really a beautiful girl. Have you seen her lately?"

"Yeah. I saw her, alright. I saw her just before I got blown to smithereens. She came speeding past my house that night, hair all blowing in the wind, zooming by in a red Hummer. Then the next thing I knew, I woke up down here. Weird, huh? Hey, what's all that barking outside, anyways? You hear that?"

"Nothing to be alarmed about. It is the neighbor's St. Bernards. It's very windy right now. They're probably spooked."

"Yeah, maybe. But I'd feel a whole lot better if you go up and check. And while you're up there, bring me my gun."

"I have to put the laundry in the dryer, anyway. Be right back." He was back inside of five minutes, no gun in sight.

"So what's up, Joey? I got a bad feeling right now."

"It's just one of the next-door dogs chasing a plastic grocery bag, and the other one freaking out. Where were we?"

"Talking about that snake, Maureen. She was fucking that *dago* piece of shit, Frankie Fazule, till he caught a murder beef."

"The Mick and his nephews all are dead, aren't they?"

"Not Doyle . . . not yet, anyways. And now Maureen's with Ansel now. How about that shit?"

"Ansel? Who's that?"

227

"What planet do you live on? Ansel is president of the Wong Gongs and one of the most treacherous motherfuckers in Greater Cleveland."

"Is that my home phone ringing?" Joey asked himself.

"How would I know? I've never even seen your house."

"The answering machine just caught it. Okay, so you said Enrico doesn't have the killer instinct. What about you? Did they have killer instincts like those Wong Gongs?"

"Who the fuck are you, Joey? Do I even know you anymore? What's with all the questions? Do you have a hidden microphone and camera down here, too?"

"Yeah, Jackie. I film you jerking off with bandaged hands and then post it on YouTube. You're a superstar, now. World's smallest prick."

"I wouldn't be surprised, you homo. Especially the way you dress now. What is that style called? Retro dweeb?"

"What's wrong with the way I dress? I look like a distinguished doctor and gentleman."

"You look like a fag with that cardigan sweater. Hey! Maybe that's why you never married. You been biting the pillow down here, Joey? Is that why you have this all set up like a bedroom down here, like some fucking pervoid homo palace?"

"Real funny, Jackie. But I'm not the one jerking off in someone else's basement."

"HA! I wish I could jerk off. Maybe it would make this headache go away. Hey! Wait a minute. I got an idea. You're a doctor. How about you collect a sperm sample, just to make sure everything still works okay down here? Put it on a petri dish."

"You are one sick human being, Jackie. You know that?"

"Relax, fat boy. Youse *towelheads* ain't much for humor."

"*Towelheads* are East Indians. I'm a *raghead*," he chuckled.

"No you're not. You're a *sand nigger*, remember?"

"Tell me about your dream, the one about Dago Red."

"You still on that? Wow… you're like a Geraldo *wannabe*. I'll tell you about my dream if you bring me upstairs."

"Next week, Jackie. I promise. First we need to do some basic limbering and stretching before you can handle stairs."

Because the TV was finally off, we heard a doorbell. Startled, Joey asked, "Who could that be at this hour?"

"What are you, my mother? How should I know? Go see. But you'd better get my gun while you're at it."

He returned in a few minutes with two glasses if ice water. "No problem, really. Just some guy wanting to use the phone. He forgot his cell and got a flat tire right out front. I lied and said I don't have a phone; that I don't believe in all this new technology. So what were you saying about your Dago Red dream?"

"Okay. I'm gonna trust you with something really big. Dago Red became one of those daytime drinkers and a dope shooter. You know, like one of those nameless old bastards you see in bars during the day; sitting at the last stool all by himself, staring in his glass of flat beer?"

"That's wet brain syndrome, Jackie. It's called Korsakoff's Disease. Does he recognize you?"

"Nah, he ain't like that – not yet, anyways. But he's got advanced cirrhosis. So he's fucked . . . and he knows it."

"I'll pray for Dago Red."

"I'm sure he'll be giddy. Meantime, while you're praying, why don't you shag your ass upstairs to get my piece?"

"Let me outline something here, Jackie. I've proven that you can trust me. But so far I have little reason to trust you."

Joey's cell rang. He said, "It might be the hospital. Excuse me." He started for the steps when I heard him say, "Sorry, there's nobody here by that name. You have a wrong number." Then he came back near the bed and said, "That's odd. Someone just called asking for my mother. She's been dead for 20 years."

"What the fuck! Didn't I tell you I had a bad feeling? You never lived in my world, Joey. You don't even know who Ansel is! You're some ex-college boy who still thinks people are good."

"People *are* basically good."

"That's a crock of shit! You might know medicine, but you're clueless about these things. There are vampires out there that'll slide a knife under your ribs just to watch you piss yourself, and then laugh while you're gargling blood. Where's my piece, goddamnit? How many fucking times I gotta ask?"

"If I give you back your gun how do I know you won't start shooting the walls up if a dog barks or a phone rings?"

"This bomb blast made me temporarily disabled, not permanently stupid or some nutless wonder. Where do you get off talking to me like I'm a little kid?"

"I just need to be certain your brain hasn't suffered as much trauma as your body. It's for your safety too, Jackie."

"You wanna trust me? Here. And I've never crossed this line before. When my kid was in treatment and I wound up being his counselor. Dago Red was there, too."

"You and Dago Red worked together? That's great!"

"Relax, Joey.! That ain't what I'm saying. I could lose my license for this shit! You know all about HIPAA Laws."

"You don't have a license or a job. You're dead, remember? But if it's that big of a deal, why are you telling me?"

"It's because I want you to understand how trust is a two-way street. Right now you're the only person I *can* trust. Okay?"

"This isn't necessary, Jackie."

"Fuck-it. Just remember, I could lose my license over this. Okay? When my kid, Rocco, was in rehab and I was his counselor, Dago Red was in my group, too."

"I really don't need to know this. In fact, I'd rather not."

"How about this part? Ansel thinks I had something to do with killing one of his prospects. He thinks me and Chilly and maybe Dago Red might have wasted that maniac on some payback mission. He can't prove it unless someone talks. But Ansel won't let it go if he thinks somebody fucked him over, or if someone or something can come back to bite him."

"What does this have to do with a Dago Red dream?"

Joey's cell rang. We fell silent. He let voicemail catch it.

"This is about me, not Red. For awhile, The No-Names were a probate club for the Wong Gongs, and Dago Red was a striker. After some heavy shit came down Ansel yanked their patches. Most of them split town. Toby and Dago Red stayed. The Wong Gongs took their bikes, all their cash and drugs."

"You know the deal better than I do. That life is fun and games, right up until people go to prison or get murdered."

"There's more. Dago Red woke up from a drug stupor, dripping wet. He thought he had pissed himself till he realized the warm fluid he was drenched with was blood. He woke next to his closest brother's head. But Toby's body was in the next room."

"I'd rather not hear anymore about any of these things. But thank you for your confidence, Jackie."

"This whole thing is about loyalty, Joey. If you expect me to trust you then I have to feel comfortable with you. This is about dealing with and respecting brutal truths."

"Okay. Since we're taking honesty to another level, let me ask you an important question. Did you ever stop to think that maybe this whole thing is too good to be true?"

"*Good?* Are you nuts? You call this good, Joey?"

"I'm not talking about the bomb or your pain. I'm referring to the rest of it. Have you wondered how I could have loaded you in a car by myself, carried you all the way down these steps and lifted your deadweight safely up on this bed while you were charred like barbeque, without further damaging you? Look at me? I'm an old, fat man."

"Don't stop talking now, fat-man. Go on…"

"Enrico was so good at making that LSD he sold all over the Neighborhood and in Georgia, those sales helped pay for his undergrad degree. He really is a natural."

"Yeah, so what's Rico got to do with this?"

"After Enrico got his BS in Georgia he moved to Berkeley to pursue a graduate degree at the University of California. He earned a full ride to become a Ph.D. chemist."

"You'd better start making sense pretty quick, Joey."

"Well, the thing is, Enrico moved back to Cleveland years ago, after he got his post-grad degree and scored big funding. He's a top-notch scientist. He's famous now."

"Oh yeah? Good for Rico. Now you got one hot minute to tell me where you're headed with all this or I piss all over your basement floor and use you for a mop."

"Enrico's the top forensics man in Ashtabula County."

"Keep talking, motherfucker!"

CH XVIII: Time to Wake Up

Since that first day of waking like a newborn, to a strange world of tubes and gauges in Joey's basement, my existence developed around one purpose. Sleeping my way through good drugs and bad memories, physical pain kept me distracted till another type of agony took over. My vision, blurred from a tidal wave of heat and concussion, had in some ways improved.

Gradually, trembling and nausea subsided and my appetite increased. Paper-like skin on the back of my legs thickened but still impeded natural movement. Joey said I was lucky to have been wearing heavy boots which had extended almost to my knees. They were a Christmas present from my Gina, Thermolite lined and with construction grade soles and heels. They absorbed the brunt of the shock. Joey said those boots saved my feet and maybe my life, even though their heals were blown off. He cut and peeled what was left off like an outer layer of protective husk.

Carefully – ever so slowly – I slipped arms as sore as they were fragile in and out of a wind breaker, more for exercise than heat. My head pounded deep from within the core of my brain, emanating from that primordial nugget used for basic survival mechanisms within that reptilian gray matter, animal instinct at its most primordial level. Soon enough, unbeknownst to Joey, and after the bandages had been removed, I was going through my regimen of exercises while he fixed people at work. My legs grew steadier as range of motion improved.

December 25th, 2013: It was almost midnight: Sleep remained as indispensable as it was fruitless. When I wished upon a star my dream was comprised of livid, animated thoughts. From the first day I woke beneath Joey's house I lapsed into a deeply depressed state and looked forward to more drugs and sleep. Mind-flicks drifted back to relive a kaleidoscope of moments as I searched my mind for a missing piece.

My daughter and I had been best friends since the day she was born. I'd been Gina's rock for over 3 1/2 decades. I asked myself: *How can a sweet innocent girl handle something like this? How does she move on to live a normal life? How does Tessa, after all those years of getting used to trusting no one and then letting open the flood gates, keep her sanity? Or maybe she's severely injured too, or worse:* I worried.

Then I wondered: *How does Rocco come to terms with the idea that his long-lost father got murdered in the street like a stray dog? How does he live with that and stay sober?*

Visions of cartoon madness settled-in. A light-headed trip to an unknown sphere. Needed was that final nod, to let go just for an instant till it dissolved into the next, just a blink away and then reabsorbed. Fantasy blurred with reverie as I dreamed away countless hours, wrapped inside a throbbing skin of scar tissue. Switching from injectable Diluadid to Opana tablets helped somewhat with clarity; although, pain pills can only help so much. My skin no longer felt as if it would crack. And even though I ached everywhere I figured I was high enough to prevent chronic pain and smothering depression from keeping me pinned down.

At first, attempting to stand again without collapsing had been scary and painful. My arms throbbed as I stretched atrophied muscles on the bed. After a few days I was able to stand on my own. Not much else really mattered till I could move forward. When Joey was at work I hobbled around like a robot, a few steps at a time within a relatively short period till I was doing minor stretching and flexing, while holding onto the bed rail with white knuckles and cramped hands.

Headaches haunted me, even while I slept. Yet they helped me remember that only the sweetness of revenge could ever make the pain go away. I had to fight. A glaring morning sun pierced through a tiny slit between heavy drapes, searing like a lazar pointer into my throbbing skull. That mini-searchlight exposed a new day filled with more options. *Hello, today. So good to see you again.*

"Keep talking, motherfucker!" I warned Joey, even more infuriated because of being disabled.

Joey confessed, "Okay . . . he was with me."

"What? You fucking *lied* to me?" I yelled, as I flipped down the bed rail and dropped one sore leg over the edge.

"No! Wait! I'll tell you everything. Just please don't move or you *will* fall."

"I want everything, fat-boy, the whole truth and my gun right now. No more excuses."

"Here," he said, as he pulled my Glock out of his waistband, neatly hidden underneath a shitty-looking green cardigan sweater. Then Joey dug into a front pocket of his baggy, old man dress pants and handed me bullets which had been loaded in that *Glock* the last time I saw them. "Just promise me you won't do anything stupid."

"I'm not making any promises till I know what you did."

"Okay, Jackie, this is everything: Enrico drove out with me that day to see you. After I tripped over you, he carried you to the car while I went to look around the perimeter of your house. That's when I found Tessa and checked her vitals. It was Enrico's suggestion to not call an ambulance. He understands gang-related things much better than me. But he's married with children and grandchildren now, so his house for you was out of the question. I offered my place and agreed to look after you. He supplied the opiates and steroids. I already had the ringers and antibiotics."

"You're a brave man telling me all this shit while I'm pointing a .357 at your nut sack."

"I'm just being honest. So I'll tell you something else. Our old friend has big political connections now with the Chief of Police. So that's part of the reason why there's not a missing persons report on you. As far as Enrico is concerned, it's over."

"Are you and Rico out of your minds? The fucking cops actually know I'm here?"

"No. The cops think you got blown-up and dragged away by whoever did this. They figure there's no way anybody could have survived that blast. Nobody knows you're still alive, Jackie. I promise. So that means he's not looking for you."

"He? Who the fuck is *he*?"

"Enrico's younger brother, Little Mikey; now *the* Michael Colombo, City Prosecutor. You remember Little Mikey? Maybe you forgot this part, but they're cousins with Tessa on her mother's side. You probably never even knew this, but Michael stood up as Rocco's *padine*. Cleveland's Prosecutor baptized your son while Michael was still a criminal lawyer. And now Enrico and Michael each wield a whole lot of clout in both Cuyahoga and Ashtabula Counties."

"Well I'll be double-dogged. Little Mikey Colombo the Prosecutor? Me and Enrico saved that kid's ass one time. Karma is some weird shit."

"On top of that, Michael is best friends with Cleveland's Italian mayor, who I'm sure you know is half black. I heard he suspended your old nemesis, Looney Lonnie and his flunky, O'Reilly, when they got caught dirty in some bad dealings with that Doyle Kelly character.

"So why hasn't Rico been around to see me yet?"

"Enrico and I agreed not to have personal contact for awhile, other than daily phone calls spoken around things, till you were well enough to be moved. He asks me about how the dog is doing. I tell him it's getter better. I hope that explains the odd and late phone calls. But you're safe here, Jackie. And you're welcome to stay for as long as you need a safe place to regroup. Are you angry, old friend?"

I paused with a frown: "No, bro. I'm not mad. You saved my life and put your own ass on the line to do it. I'm just glad it was Enrico in your car and not some geek you work with. I trust Rico as much as I can trust anyone outside of my immediate family – as much as I trust you. You handled it the right way."

"Thank you, my friend. I'm quite amazed at how fast you're healing for a man your age."

"Yeah, Joey, I guess that's from all those years doing hard drugs and fucking lots of young broads. All that keeps a man fit."

"I wouldn't know anything about those endeavors. So I suppose I'm doomed. But when did you start walking around?"

"How do you mean?"

"It's not a cryptic question. Just tell me. How long have you been walking around down here without me to help you?"

"What kind of question is that?" I grinned. "Ever since I could, that's how long. I let my body dictate what I need and how far I can push myself. But I've been careful."

"So what now, Jackie? What's the next move?"

"The next move is the same move. We wait."

"Okay, good. Then that means the next move is upstairs. We'll step up the work, based on what I've seen being used with geriatric patients. The exercises will hurt at first. Are you up this, old man?" he grinned through stained yet strong teeth.

I didn't admit to Joey that at night I screamed silently from the pain in my legs. And I secretly worried he'd cut me off my drugs. What I did confess to was having a difficult time urinating. We decided to switch me from that numbing fog of opiates to a detox protocol consisting of a Suboxone taper and Tramadol for pain management. It was the reason he allowed me free reign upstairs. I had the run of the house, keeping his insulated drapes drawn at all times and not ever answering the door or phone.

His house was small yet had all the comforts, obviously a bachelor's pad. Not much furniture or decorations, but what he did have looked expensive and made to last. No carpet.

Lacquered hardwood floors shone throughout the first floor, except in the kitchen and bathroom with earth tone tiles. The theme seemed to be natural, if there was a theme at all. In his living room a long brown couch did not match the gold love seat or two tan recliners. A dining room table and its six chairs made of thick, solid wood sat in an otherwise bare room. The kitchen was also bare-bones, yet furnished with quality appliances and utensils. Same with the bathroom, scant but expensive hardware. Maybe his theme was pragmatism rather than aesthetics. The downstairs bedroom, my room, had a king-size bed with a headboard that resembled a raw slab of hardwood, a hefty oak dresser and a squat oak nightstand with a brass lamp.

Joey explained, "What seemed like confinement was for your own good, to keep you from injuring yourself or making mistakes."

I knew he was right. So while he did his magic with the drug taper, I watched TV shows and read online about healing. I created *Gmail* and Hotmail accounts with assumed names so I could entertain myself with *YouTube* videos and social networking sites. I became the invisible man, but was everywhere. I even sent *Facebook* friend requests to Rocco and Gina under a false name, but neither of them accepted. That pleased me.

Joey remarked, "I'm glad you're finally being agreeable, Jackie. You're regaining composure as well as confidence. That shows me you're on the mend."

"I'm okay now, Joey. I'm in no hurry to make any huge mistakes. Life seems more precious since I survived that blast."

When he was home and not sleeping away his late and long schedule at the hospital, Joey and I watched Hollywood and Independent films. DVD's arrived from online rental sources. Plus I had plenty of older flicks via satellite dish, as well as new releases on pay channels. Joey, looking old and gray, often crashed for the night in one of his tan recliners in front of a huge flat screen with surround sound, while I stretched out on his thick brown couch for marathon nights of movies and reading.

On his days off we discussed old times and recalled classmates we hadn't thought of in decades. Some of the kids he remembered I'd forgotten I had ever even known.

"When can I see Enrico?"

"That's too dangerous, Jackie. It's better this way."

"But I'd like to thank him, and to ask him something."

"No need, Jackie. He knows you're grateful. You would have done the same for him. Tell me more about your family. Your stories make me feel like I'm part of it."

"Well, Tessa's welcome back to Collinwood, after her father died, was to find nothing new other than that her best friend, Carly, had become a heroin junkie still living with her Butterscotch's crazy cousin, Curtis. You remember them?"

"I had the biggest crush on Carly, but she didn't even know my name. But I remember Curtis. He's that black kid you had all the trouble with in high school."

"Yeah, he's why I got expelled. We put in the patch years later. He turned out to be solid. But how would a pussy like you know about the Collinwood race riots? You were hiding in class or in your house while we were cracking heads. Hey, Joey, have you ever been in even one fight in your whole life?"

"No. But let's try to stay on topic for once. Sorry, but I just can't see you and Curtis being friends."

"Well, we aren't going steady. Let's put it this way: I trust him a fuck of a lot more than any of my ex-*coombas*."

"Wow, some things sure do change. You and Curtis were both racists, always fighting about nothing. You hated that guy."

"Even crazier, their son, Curtis Jr., is my daughter, Gina's, closest relative. They were raised like brother and sister."

"Butter was a classic beauty. How did her body hold up after she had your daughter?"

"Whoa, easy now, Joey. On topic, remember? Gina's mother and I got divorced in the mid-80s. They moved away from our little farmette near the PA border to move in with some old black guy."

"Where is Butter staying at these days? I must say, she really was extraordinary."

"Relax, you fucking horny prick. I'm telling a story here. Okay, so Gina's mother moved back to Cleveland after she dumped the old black dude. She's living in the Mentor-on-the-Lake area, cashing checks from a rich ex-husband. She hit the jackpot."

"Are you and Butter still friends?"

"*Still* friends? Fuck that whore. Tessa is my everything."

"The Lord wants you to have forgiveness in your heart."

"Don't start back in with all your Christian bullshit, okay Joey? I'm in no mood. You wanna hear the rest of this or not?"

"Yes. Sorry if I was being discourteous. Please continue."

"So besides Gina's newly found brother, Rocco, and his girlfriend, Danni, who've become best friends with Tessa, she's been close to Curtis Jr. His mother, Carly, and Tessa are still *cumares*. And Junior's best friend is Horrible Hank's son, Little Hankie. We're just one big, dysfunctional Collinwood family."

"I'm confused and tired. I need sleep. Goodnight, Jackie."

I returned to my latest novel, one of the Jack Reacher series, while Shit-pants Joey happily snored away up in his bedroom. I was on the sixth Lee Child novel in a row. I found his stories almost as addictive as my opiate protocol. He wrote clever and gritty men stories about a real man for real men. But women seemed to love them, too.

During our next conversation, when Dr. Joey had some leisure time off, he said, "I've been out of touch for too long. I like to hear about Neighborhood people, especially about your family. I'm getting to know them by proxy. That makes me feel like I have family again. Will you tell me more about Tessa?"

"Her father, Doc, was a psycho. And you know this, Joey. So it's best for all of us that he's gone."

"Even though he was a little scrawny guy I was afraid to look in his direction. And his friend, Uno… That guy reminded me of a bear, and not just the way he looked. I didn't like being anywhere near him. He gave off this vibe like when being too near a wild animal. He didn't need to say or do anything. People just knew he was dangerous. I could smell his ferocity."

"You know he got killed in the joint, right?"

"I'm still terrified of him, even though he's dead."

"I thought you *ragheads* were supposed to be tough."

"And why do you have to be such a jerk? I'm a sissy because I wasn't involved in the Collinwood race riots or fighting Pit-bulls? I'm a sissy because I never wanted to mess with mafia guys, didn't hang around with bikers or do a bunch of dope?"

"Yeah . . . right. I guess that sounds about dead-on."

"Let's recap. I'm the one who is making over 300k a year and can go anywhere to do anything. You're the one who's sleeping on my couch and can't leave my house. Is that accurate?"

"Point taken. Anyways, Doc sent Tessa to live with his drunken sister in California, on the condition she could return only after she put the baby up for adoption. To makes matters worse, Doc vowed to kill whoever was stupid enough to knock-up his only child. Doc's brother, Pazzo, is a man who looked out for me ever since I was a kid. If you remember your Collinwood history, Pazzo's best friend was Uno. More tangled webs, eh?"

Joey slowly shook his head: "My God, why did you ever get involved in all this?"

"I'm sure you remember that Fingers and Tessa grew up together like brother and sister. Right Joey?"

"Fingers? Isn't he that same closest brother of yours who sent you to an ER in the mid-70s with broken bones and multiple lacerations? Because that's what Enrico told me."

"Oh yeah? What else did Rico say?"

"He said Fingers stepped into Uno's spot as Captain of the Collinwood and Little Italy crews after Uno had been stabbed in prison by an Arian Brotherhood member."

"Yeah, financed by Doyle Kelly. Those nephews of the Mick got away with plenty. But after the Neighborhood guys got the Irishman it was open season. That also was the year my best friends jumped me and then I got tighter with the Wong Gongs. And that was the same year both of my kids were born. Meantime, I was in a full-blown alcoholic blackout the one night Tessa and I had sex. I don't remember any of it."

"If I didn't know you so well, Jackie, I'd think you were full of it. But this stuff is just crazy enough to be true. You've led a storybook life. You might have been a lot of things, but I've never known you to be a liar or any other type of coward."

"Thanks. Anyways, Tessa just disappeared one day and stayed gone for a few years. By the time she returned to Cleveland, Doc had pissed away The Inn to gambling debts and then finally drank himself to death. Then Tessa's mother became ill but wouldn't see a doctor. By the time she got diagnosed it turned out to be stage 4 lung cancer. She was a chain smoker. So she didn't last long, either."

"I feel so bad for her, Jackie. Plus after finally having a dad, your son thinks now you're dead. And your poor daughter. Gina… She must be devastated. As pretty as she is, her toughness must be quite a contrast. But I'm sure she wouldn't harm a fly."

"I wouldn't bet on that, Joey. She's as tough as she is pretty. I raised her like the son I thought I never had. She can be meaner than me and has a nasty temper. But I miss her so much. Being separated from them is killing me. I'd do anything to reverse this. So I need to think this through. There must be a way to fix this, right? I just don't see a way around this yet. Do you?"

To keep from going crazy, I eased into exercising for strength and incorporated slow *katas* from *Shito-Ryu* –

implementing dynamic tension with slow and measured strikes and blocks from a lifetime of martial arts training, to regain some ability. Yet I still devoted plenty of time to watching movies, reading novels and playing FreeCell to strengthen my mind.

Joey smiled, "Amazing! For a 63-year old man, you are recovering remarkably well. You'll be ready for your next move in another month or so, as soon as we figure out what that is."

"Thanks. I needed to hear that. Hey, do you ever hear from our old friend, Chilly? I've been thinking a lot about him."

"Hmm… We'll talk about that and other things when I get home. But I won't see you till tomorrow. Let me know if you need me to bring anything home. Meanwhile, I've been thinking about your dad, that he was correct when he used to tell us to fight back till the pain stopped. But you can't keep fighting all these battles by yourself, Jackie. You might not cur out or even get beaten down, but you will be worn out. Emotional injury can be as debilitating as physical pain. Both are bearable as long as there is hope. And working ER gave me a desperate need to believe there is something else – anything else."

"Now you're the Joey I remember, instead of a brain-washed news junkie. I tell families of my patients to put the main dysfunction on the table, the thing that's been hidden for too long, and then dissected it with the help of others to find what it is driving that, all the way to the bottom line. Self-reflection takes willingness and brutal honesty, followed by action. All that takes strength. Honesty begins within and builds outward. Pazzo taught me how to channel that with journaling. It's as a valuable tool."

"Well, well… And I thought you had become addled from the concussion of that blast and all these drugs I've had you on so you could properly rest and heal. From what I saw during my tenure as a physician, drug therapy helps providing two conditions are met: honesty and a burning desire to change. Healing from severe physical damage like you have also is twofold: the first part is cleanliness, drug therapy and lots of rest. The second thing is for a person to really, really want to get better and stay better. On the surface, most troubled people say something to the affect of: 'Of course I want to change. I hate my life'. Anyway, we had better call it a night. Don't wear yourself, Jackie. You are still very weak. Merry Christmas, *coom*."

CH XIX: Girls' Night, 1st Party

December 26, 2013: Danni invited Gina and her best friend, Carrie, who was Whitey's girlfriend, for a girls-only night. Rocco had gone out with Whitey to make some cash to wager on Bull. He couldn't trust Cagootz to come through like he promised. Rocco told Danni before he left, "I got a bad feeling. Only four things in the whole world mean anything to those *dago* pricks at The Inn. Those things are money, respect, fear and money. So with that in mind, and just to make sure I ain't getting ass-slammed by those bastards, I'll have Whitey get off all our bets before I climb into the box with Bull."

Gina pulled up in her trusty Subaru wearing ripped and faded jeans, a T-shirt and a brown leather jacket. She made her way up the front steps to the second story of the old frame dwelling above where their crazy landlady sisters lived. Rather than knock, Gina just pushed open the front door and yelled, "Up against the walls, motherfuckers!" She walked in to find Carrie already there, seated on a worn couch in their clean but old front-room. Carrie was well on her way to being loaded.

Danni yelled, "*Yes*! My other sister from another mister. Now the party begins!" She ran from the kitchen and wrapped her arms around her future sister-in-law. "My two favorite bitches in the whole wide world to keep me company. Yay Team!"

Gina said, "I just love you! You know that, you little slut?" Gina gave Danni a quick smooch on lips perfectly tinted with pink.

"Oh, okay…," Danni giggled. "This just might turn into a party after all." She danced around in a circle, dressed in her usual black T-shirt and tight black jeans.

Then Gina's energy surged throughout the rest of the house. She walked to the couch, bent over to give Carrie a firm hug hello, then asked, "What's up, mama? So you ready to get lewd, crude and brewed, or what?"

"Merry fucking Xmas, girlfriend. I'm already on my way," grinned Carrie. "Tell you what: grab a brew and cop a squat, beautiful, and I just might kiss you too." Carrie then stood to stretch and shake out her light blonde curls. She was dressed in a tight red tank top and even tighter black yoga pants. She had the body of an athlete, firm and strong – nothing too big or small.

Gina hugged her and smiled, "Yeah, no doubt. I mean, for fuck's sake . . . it's a holiday weekend, or at least it should be. I brought a DVD for us, just in case we wind down later. It's called *American Pop*. It's animation but geared for big kids like us."

"Is it porn?" asked Carrie. "Because I'm way too horny right now to watch any porn. Unless you two crazy bitches are in the mood to take a walk on the wild side!" she yelled, as she burst into a loud laugh which turned into a cough. "Here you go," Carrie said, as she slid over to one end of the long sofa. "Have a seat in my warm spot. Hey, you smoking Kools, Gina? Here you go, girlfriend, help yourself to these."

"No thanks, Carrie. I don't smoke anything . . . unless it gets me high. But what I need to do first, before I cop a squat here, it to go squat on the pisser and leave a quick pee. Be right back!" Gina dashed for the bathroom.

"Wow! That chick's gorgeous!" Carrie slurred, pale blue eyes already getting glassy. "She's almost as pretty as you, sista."

"No, Carrie, *you're* almost as pretty as me. Gina's prettier."

"Fuck you... I'll blow your shit away any day of the week, you no-tit bitch. In fact, I bet I can fuck your boyfriend," Carrie said, as she broke into another fit of laughter and more coughing. "I notice Rocco checking out my tits and ass. One time he asked me if I'm a natural blonde. Wonder what *he* was thinking about," she smiled.

"Whatever... Anyway, I'm kidding – and a little jealous. You're way prettier than me. You always have been. But this Gina might be the most beautiful woman I've ever seen. She's solid too, Carrie. You're gonna like her. She's way cool – just like you."

Gina rammed the door open, dashed back to the couch and dropped in between those two childhood friends. In her raspy voice Gina asked Danni, "Well, what the fuck kind of hostess are you? Where's my goddamn beer at, sweetie?"

"Your beer's next to mine, in the fridge. So while you're getting them get some munchies, too," Danni giggled again.

"Anything you need, sweets. How about you, Carrie? You ready?" Gina asked, as she started to get back up."

Danni slid her arm across Gina's chest and smiled, "Relax. I'm just breaking balls. I'll get it. I know where the munchies are."

"Bullshit. You just wanted to feel my tits. Admit it. You're bored with balling my brother so now you want me. Fucking gutter-slut whore."

"You're right about that one, Gina. This chick is about half dyke. The last time I spent the night here, she climbed in the goddamn shower with me and then accidentally on purpose bumped bare titties. Then later she crawled into bed with me!"

"You wish... But this psycho left out the most important part, Gina. We've been doing sleep-overs since the third grade and have slept in the same bed since we were eight years old." Danni added, as she turned a few shades of natural blush.

"Hey, you girls don't have to be shy around me. You start getting a little damp in the panty region, no need to find excuses to make it all the way over to the sheets. You can get down right here. I'll watch. Fuck-it, I'll even take pictures," Gina said, beaming her radiant smile, as she pulled a pink phone from her purse and laid it on the coffee table next to a thin baggie of light green buds and a new pack of E-Z Widers.

"I'll keep that in mind." Danni said, as she fired up a joint, hit it and passed it to Gina. "Meanwhile, I'll be back with two beers and a bowl of goodies. You need anything, Carrie?"

"Nope. Thanks, babe. I'm set. I'll just sip on this herb."

Danni was back in a flash with two cold *Yuengling Black & Tans* and a bowl of Gardetto's. She pulled the joint out of Carrie's mouth and sat down on the other side of Gina. With her dark eyes closed, Danni took another deep inhale. She slowly exhaled a plume of smoke, sighed and reached across Gina to pass it back to Carrie. "Hmm mmm, that's good shit!"

"Hey chick! Am I the invisible guest? What a bogart!"

"Watch out for this Danni. She's not as sweet and innocent as she looks. Did you see her yank that joint right out of my mouth and suck it like a stiff cock? Then this bitch gives you a dry-pass."

"Hey, Carrie, do you know how to have a conversation about anything other than fucking and sucking?" asked her oldest friend. I mean . . . seriously…"

"No, Danni, I don't. Why? What else is there worth doing? Oh wait, there is one more thing. I guess we could talk about drugs, even while we're indulging in some chilled *brewski's* and a little of this tasty *herbage* while we talk about threesomes."

Danni ran a hand through her short-cropped hair: "And you say *I'm* a fiend? Gina's going to think you're some nymph, drug addict lezbo with an itch that needs scratched."

Carrie made an expression of exaggerated surprise: "Oh no! Me? She'd be right on the money. I really am a fuck machine and a drug disposal, and damn proud of it! Hey! Did I ever tell you how many dudes I've fucked? About dozen, I suppose."

Danni said, "Holy shit! Are you serious? *Twelve*? Hey chick, we're not talking about in one weekend. A couple dozen dicks is a normal month at the corner bar for you, you fucking junkie pig."

"Okay, girlie, so I like sex. So tell us. What's better than sex and drugs? I gotta hear this one!" asked Carrie, wearing a wide grin with wrecked pastel eyes.

"Respect and loyalty are the only things that really matter. And solid, chosen family is all we ever have," Gina answered for her, as she took another drag off what was transforming from what had been a neatly rolled white joint to a damp yellowed roach. "Yep, that's it. Everything else is bullshit."

"I agree!" announced Danni, as she sat up straight and spilled some beer on her black T-shirt. "Shit! This top is new. Now I'm going to stink like a brewery."

"Well . . . seeing how we already smell like an ashtray, that might be a step up," nodded Gina in a thoughtful way. "If it stinks, take the motherfucker off. We're not shy around here. I don't even mind that you're not wearing a bra. In fact—"

Caught up in her own inebriated thoughts Carrie blurted out, "Besides, that looks like every other shirt she owns. So let's look at this part: Drugs these days are pretty much everywhere. Sex is potentially anywhere. Especially when you're a hot looking chick like the three of us are. I mean, honestly. Any one of us could walk out that door and grab the first dude we see, married or not, and get laid. Am I right?" Carrie didn't wait for a response. "But on the other hand," Carrie continued, "Gina's right. Loyalty and trust are rare commodities. No doubt about that. Just think about it. How many people in this entire world can you really fucking trust 100%, Gina?"

"Well . . . I'm guessing we're talking the real unconditional stuff, right? Let's see... I can trust Rocco and Tessa. And I think I trust my mom. And now I might trust Danni, too. And, of course, my daddy... How about you, Danni?" Gina asked.

"Hmmm... I trust Rocco and Tessa. But I definitely do not trust my mother. She's a lunatic drunk. Naturally, I trust Carrie. And I do trust you, Gina. I have a real good feeling about you. How about you, Carrie? Who do you trust?" asked Danni.

"Well, I don't trust Rocco, because he's best friends with my ol' man. Which automatically means I don't trust Whitey, either. I hardly even know Tessa, so I don't trust her. I barely know Gina. So I don't trust her, either . . . just being honest. Just you, Danni. You're the onliest person in this whole wide cesspool of a world I really trust. And that's it. And good weed. I trust that, too. And once in a while a stiff prick. But always a moist tongue! Besides that, I need another beer. Anyone else have a need or want while I'm up?" Carrie asked, as she wobbled to the kitchen.

"Well, we lasted about three whole minutes without talking about hard cock and hard drugs," noted Gina. "That's gotta be some type of world record for you two chicks. But I see what you like about this girl," Gina smiled. "She shoots straight from the hip, doesn't pull any punches." Then Gina yelled into the tiny kitchenette, "You're pretty cool for a girl, Carrie. You're so cool I'm about to roll more of these *gange* sticks for us."

Carrie returned with the frosty *Black & Tans*. She asked Danni, "Hey, sista, why do you buy this nigger brew? Let's go to a beverage store in Cleveland Heights that sells imported beer."

"Rocco likes it because Sinbad is a black & tan Pit."

"Yeah, whatever… it's still fucking nigger beer."

"Whoa, easy on the expletives. I'm part black, you know," Gina reminded Carrie. "Maybe just a smidgen, but still…"

"Gimme a break, Gina. I'm not talking race here. I'm referring to a total lack of class. Niggers, as you know, come in all the basic primary colors."

"Right on," agreed Gina. "That reminds me about our dog. Talk about loyalty and trust. He's the only other person I trust with my life. That old boy has been my dad's pride and joy, a best friend to me and the last of that bloodline in the country, other than my brother's Bully-Boy. Sinbad's got it all rolled up into one badass little Bulldog. And he's the sweetest dog ever! If that game-bred little dog of ours could talk, I'd bet my life he'd be honest to the bone, too. He's already reliable to his heart and game to the core!" exclaimed Gina, as she grinned and handed Carrie a freshly rolled bomber. "Blaze this up, bad mama."

"See? Take notes, Danni. Why can't you be nice like her?"

"Because you're a slut and I hate you. Any more questions?"

"Nope. That's about it. And that pretty much sums me up, ladies. Guilty as charged; I love sex and getting high. If I would have been born a man I'd be some fucking hero. But because I have a pussy instead of a penis I guess that makes me a sinner and a pig. And because I'm not some plastic, white bread, salad eating bitch acting all innocent, like I've never had a dick in my mouth, maybe I'd have more friends. You know the type: like we don't really know one another – like pretend friends?"

"One thing we three bitches aren't and that's phony," Danni stood and saluted. "We're goddamn freedom fighters!"

Gina smiled and shook her head: "You might want to have a seat, General. You're looking a little woozy there, hon."

"Yeah, sit down before your ass falls down," Carrie slurred. "Okay, so listen up. Here's an important test," Carrie said, as she exhaled a plume of smoke from that freshly rolled joint. "I have proposition. But this ain't gonna be so easy," Carrie nodded. "Okay, here's the twist: You two ever see those two WOPS that hang around The Inn? That fat pig, Cagootz, who resembles a demented brother of Bobby Bacala from the Sopranos, and then his shadow, Big Louie, who's like a pissed-off *dago* version of Herman Munster?"

Gina and Danni kept their full attention on a very loaded Carrie who lived with a member of the Wong Gongs. Gina said, "Go ahead, sweetie. We're listening."

"Okay, here's the deal: You gotta fuck and suck both of those ugly bastards all night, at the same time. And you gotta let 'em pork you up the ass first and then swallow cum off their shitty dicks. Oh yeah, and they can take movies of you doing all that grimy stuff, too. Only then would you get the million bucks. Would you still do it?"

Danni said, "Sure. I'd just pay somebody to kill those scumbags with part of the cool million I just made. Then have a long hot shower to get their stink off me."

"I'm calling bullshit," Carrie laughed. "You had trouble hiring an exterminator to kill the bats in your crazy mom's attic. Who you tryin' to bullshit, Danni? You're one of those fucking pacifists – and kind of a prude. Now me? I'd do them *and* their wives for half that amount. Social sex is like kissing. No big deal."

"There's no way you're crawling in bed with me, you little *dykester*, unless I can find footy pajamas that zip up to my neck."

"Don't flatter yourself, Danni. You're not my type. I prefer the type with a stiff dick."

"If I fucked those fat pigs for a million," Gina said thoughtfully, "there's no way I could live with myself after I went and put a hit on them because of my mistakes. Hiring someone to take human lives because I fucked up? No, that's just wrong."

"You mean you'd let those *scheeves* treat you like a piece of meat and let them post their little fuckfest on YouTube? Every time you saw anyone you'd have to hang your head in shame because a fine-ass chick like yourself fucked disgusting guys. I can't see a tough chick like you letting them pull some skuzzy moves like that."

"I didn't say that. I said I couldn't live with myself if I put a hit on someone because of my mistakes. I'd kill both of them myself," Gina said in a matter-of-fact way as she stared at Carrie who struggled to get beer in her mouth without spilling it.

"Yep, I'd fucking help you kill 'em all, goddamnit!" Danni slumped down. "Especially if it's those movie star bitches Rocco's got the hots for like the nut-job Christina Ricci, that old Halle Berry bitch, or that anorexic Natalie Portman chick. They're not real women. They look like plastic fuck-dolls."

"Dude, you're a wildcat. I love this new Danni." Gina hugged her future sister.

Carrie slurred, "Dude, you don't know the half of it. Everybody thinks *I'm* the crazy one, because I have a trashy mouth. But this Danni chick's a wild woman. I mean, think about it, Gina .Why else would I hand with her and be best buds?"

"Yeah, true that," Gina grinned. "Birds of a feather, and all that good shit."

"Okay, so check it out. I'm about half-dyke, and Danni's about half crazy. So what's that make you, Gina?"

"That makes me solid as the day is long. That's what. Trust, loyalty and integrity are all that matter, and a few solid family members if we're lucky. The rest is bullshit."

Danni smiled: "I say, fuck-it! No matter what happens from this point on, after all we've been through, it should be like rolling down hill. Right ladies?"

CH. XX: The Bridge to Nowhere

December 27, 2013: For the next few weeks Joey and I gradually increased the workouts. I could feel the strength filling up atrophied muscle tissue, and my skin becoming more elastic again from daily MEBO treatments. Weakness in my gut and limbs were being replaced with fire in my heart. Each day I grew a little stronger. The thought of dying dissipated. In its place, suicidal ideation had been consumed with the need for cleansing and healing to prepare for the final battle. I had nothing left to lose.

People were preparing to commit suicide across America due to long winters and unpaid bills, while Shit-pants Joey was on nightshift making rounds at the hospital and I made my move into darkness. I knew he wouldn't get in till after midnight. Dressed in black sweatpants and a black sweatshirt Joey bought for me as another gesture of kindness, I was about to set out on a new mission. But not before rummaging through a spare closet.

After nosing around I found a black goose down parka and a black insulated hoodie, things that had once fit Joey before he bloated into a fat, old man. Stuffed into one of the four oversized pockets of that parka were other good finds: a black knit stocking cap and a pair of black leather gloves with rabbit fur lining. I stashed a bottle of water and a few Granola bars from his kitchen in one pocket, a bottle of Tramadol and my loaded gun in another. I felt older yet readier than I had in many years.

I checked out my image in a mirror on his closet door and realized I looked like a gray zombie with no buzzed hair, a stubble beard, and splotches of pink scar tissue from flash burns. But I was feeling better than I had in a while – a fucking ninja on a mission!

On the closet floor I found an old pair of work boots. The leather was cracked, showing they hadn't been worn in years. Next to them was a rolled up leather belt with a chrome metal buckle that looked like a camera. *Fucking Joey…unbelievable! Why would anyone invest in a fake camera belt*, I chuckled to myself. *Man, this guy is all right angles.* I put on my square friend's belt anyway, to keep those pants from slipping during my trek.

Driven by the type of frenzied urgency that only emotions like hatred or love could nurture to such an extreme, I closed an insulated door on an incessantly ringing phone, making the cover of night safe for a walking fugitive. Unknown obstacles and hurdles lay in wait within the next few hours or days, if I lasted that long. I couldn't have cared less at the time, not for my own safety; not enough, anyway – not nearly enough to keep me from seeing my plan to fruition. *What's my plan, again?* I was way beyond the point of worry. I wasn't too sure about much other than I needed to move the fuck on, and that I had a *Click* screaming inside me, warning that my family was in danger.

"Not many people were as unselfish as, Shit-pants Joey, or as dedicated as our friend, Enrico," I told myself, as I opened the back door to Joey's house. A blast of winter's fury overwhelmed me. I held my breath and leaned against the door to make sure it locked behind me. "Okay, fuck-it. It's locked now. It's time to sack up and move on." I said, watching warm words form in frigid air. I was on the move again, in cloudy night air filled with frigid winds blowing sideways.

I laughed to keep from losing my nerve: "It looked kind of pretty outside, through the window while I was still tucked away inside that safe, warm house. It's crazy how every year we choose to forget the brutality of winter up North on the Mistake on the Lake. You're in the Snow Belt, genius. It's less than 20 miles from Lake Erie. What the fuck did you expect? It's windier in C-town than in Chicago," I said to myself as I trudged on.

"Sometimes it stays below freezing for a month at a time, you fucking dummy. Did you really think winter wouldn't be so cold this time? Alright, fuck-it, what's done is done. But at least I have my freedom again. Big goddamn deal… Now what?" I asked out loud, as I made my way down a snow-covered sidewalk with my head lowered to minimize wind pounding away at me like a sandblaster shooting fine ice pellets. The walks had been shoveled and the roads plowed – before temperatures dropped to minus fuck-all and the winds and snow kicked in again.

My lungs ached as I plodded through snowdrifts in the shadows of night, shivering from inside out. There was no way to keep my burned flesh warm. Winds blew hard powdered snow at my eyes. The cold began to numb my injuries but not the intensity of my dilemma. While still bandaged and with most of my hair and beard cooked off by the explosion, and then buzzed off by a doctor turned barber, getting a safe ride from a passer-by, especially in that weather was next to impossible.

I walked toward downtown, with no destination in mind. I convinced myself, "I certainly can't drop in on my family. If I go home I'll be putting them in harms way. I'm not doing that again. Whoever wired my car was aware that my wife or kids could've been with me when their timer ignited that charge of explosives. And whoever did that still thinks I'm safely dead. So I just need to put one foot in front of the other. I'll run into something. I'm not sure what just yet. But I'll know it when I see it. I could go to the City Mission as a last resort. I really am homeless. And right now I'd rather have bedbugs than frostbite."

I didn't notice the approaching headlights, because I leaned into the storm with my face to the ground and eyes squinted from the pelting of fine crystals. I didn't hear an engine, because I had that stocking cap pulled over my ears, the hoodie pulled over that hat, and then a nylon hood from Joey's parka covering all that. I couldn't hear tires on pavement, not in a blanket of deep snow. Fact is I didn't know anyone was close. I'd gotten lost in my own thoughts till I heard a familiar sounding CD blasting a muffled song from inside a closed up car. I un-squinted my eyes long enough to notice that headlights made the snowy air look alive. I trampled through at an old man's pace. I wasn't even sure if the driver had actually stopped till I heard a voice call out in that cold stillness. I froze in my tracks, my hand already on my gun.

    A man's voice asked in a hesitant and polite manner from a small white Saturn, "Are you in trouble, mister? Your car break down or something? You need a lift?"

    "Yeah, I'm sort of jammed up right now. But I don't have any cash on me. I don't even have a credit card. Which way are you headed?"

    "I live on the Westside of Cleveland, sir, not far from the zoo. I can take you as far as there. I don't want any money. I have to go there, anyway. I'm glad to give you a ride."

    "HA! How about that? That's right near where I was going," I said, figuring one place was as good as the next. The main thing at that moment was that I could hear his car heater blowing and it was set to high. *What a beautiful sound*, I thought.

    "Hop in, mister. This window's letting out all the heat."

    I moved a CD case that had the words, "The Black Keys," printed on it in white block lettering so I could sit down and close the door on that terrible night. As soon as I got in the passenger side I noticed the smell of oil. The interior light illuminated a thin-faced adolescent, maybe mid-20s with pale skin and a bad complexion. He looked tired and dirty enough to have just finished a second shift job. He wore dirty pants and boots, and his hands were grease stained almost as dark as his black fingernails and clothing.

"Just getting off shift?" I asked, to get a better look at my escort's face.

"You know. Shitty job... But you do what you gotta do, right mister? I saw how bad it was getting to be out the shop window, so I didn't even take the time to wash-up."

"When life gives us lime we eat Key Lime pies, or we dig a hole and use it to eat the evidence."

"Hey, no offense, mister. But I got two questions. Okay?"

"Sure, go ahead and ask away," I said, with gloves off while rubbing my hands together to jumpstart my circulation. I smacked my thighs to reduce the numbness in my legs.

"Why are you out walking around on a night like this?"

"My motor blew up," I answered as honestly as I could.

"Yeah, I know what you mean. That happened to me with the last beater I had. It sprang an oil leak. But I park outside – no garage floor or nothing – so I never noticed it. Besides, I'm all the time working on other people's cars. You know that old saying, right mister? It's like the plumber with the leaky faucets."

"Yeah, like it's the roofer with pots all over his floor."

"Well . . . no offense intended . . . but that brings me to my other question. You a cop or an armed mugger?" he inquired, as he pulled back stringy brown hair from his youthful face.

"*Me*? Not even close... Why?"

"Well, I'm of a mind that it's always best to check right up front. But speaking of pots all over the floor, you want some?" He reached towards his ashtray.

"I'll just take a hit or two to show you I'm not the law. Too much of this stuff these days and I'm too wasted."

"You ain't got a gun or anything, do you mister?"

"Take a closer look at me, kid. I'm an old man. Always try to look into a person's eyes to get the real answers."

"With that hat and hood and those glasses frosted over, I'm not even sure you have eyes," the young man laughed, nervously.

"Okay, fair enough. You can't look into my eyes right now. So the next best thing is to carefully listen to what I'm saying and not saying, and how I'm going about it. Usually, it's not what a person says but how they say it, or maybe what they don't say that counts most. Pay close attention, subtle nuances, voice and body language. But the most important thing, kid, is the

Click. You know what that means?"

"I can guess. You mean stuff you don't really see or can't hear, mister? You mean instinct? Stuff like when you're dropping cid or eating shrooms, or toking on some good bud like this?"

He reached into a clean ashtray, fished out a thin joint and cheap lighter. It caught on the first flick. For an instant all I smelled was burning paper. Then another aroma blossomed, like clean armpit sweat mixed with pineapples – a slightly skunkish yet sweet odor. The glow lit up the inside of that car, showing McDonald's bags and cups crunched up on the floor. I turned to face him as I danced a flame just beyond the tip of the joint. I could see he was even younger than I had first thought.

I took a slow, steady hit so that *pinner* didn't burn unevenly. I could smell that the kid had his pot double wrapped. Then I knew why. The herb was dense and sticky. Heated resin glistened through the papers. And because slightly moist marijuana burns slow, a single wrap would have torched quicker than the weed, causing chunks on unburned marijuana to fall as a burning ash. So he customized his doobie to compensate.

"This smells right, kid. Thanks." I handed him the joint, hot end facing me, like a person should hand over a knife.

He took a long, steady hit. "It's expensive but worth it. I can't smoke that Mexican dirt weed. That shit gives me headaches and sore throats. This stuff is magic. I buy a dub at a time."

"Weed like this, you should be using a one-hitter. Good pot gets wasted in the air with wraps."

"Yeah, I know that, mister. But the bust for paraphernalia is worse than getting caught with the *herbage*. Besides, I pre-wrap my *doobage* in case I get pulled over and have to eat it." He cherried the ash once more and then passed it back to me. "I have to drive through these drug infested areas in the middle of the night. It's all crack and heroin. The law sees some skinny white boy out here they gets suspicious."

I tapped out the hot ash with the tip of my thumb and returned the unlit portion to his ashtray. "Well, kid, at least you're not rolling blunts. I'll give you that much."

"I ain't no *wigger*, mister. That would mean I was embarrassed of my own mother. I don't understand all that nonsense. Let me ask you a simple question, sir. Why can't people just be who they are and forget about trying to be something they're not? Why is that so tough?"

"I have a question for you, kid. Did you ever see a snow beaver?" I tried to focus with eyes at half-mast.

"Snow beaver? You mean a mythological creature like an ogre or a leprechaun? Like that?"

"Nope, I mean a snow beaver. It's more like a cross between an ouroboros and a phoenix. You ever see one?"

"Mister, I think maybe you shouldn't smoke anymore."

"I'm cool. Legend says that snow beavers are these big, nasty things, all hairy with toothless gaping mouths. They feed on hemp but they're always hungry. And the more they eat the hungrier they get. I heard they live under bridges and swallow whole snakes in one gulp. Rumor is they hide at night and kill lost children and old people. And then after that, they just spontaneously combust. You know anything about of them, kid?"

"I'll tell you what I know, mister. You're pretty stoned."

"What I know is you should be going to school to do something with your life besides working a dead-end job. You seem smart enough, and you appear to have a type of toughness."

"Thanks, mister, but my mom's got the cancer. She can't work. I need to do this. She was a real hard worker and the best mom ever. She never smoked or drank, but she got that goddamn cancer. Now they have her on some strong pills. She don't like to take 'em; says they make her all *loopy*. But she's in bad pain. You know? So she does a lot of sleeping. But she ain't a doper."

"Yeah, kid, I understand. Sorry... Where's your dad?"

"My father's a worthless piece of shit. He's been in and out of jail my whole life. He don't even know what I look like. The last time I saw him I was 14, and that was the first time since I was a baby. He split town before I was one year old. Basically, they had sex and then I got born on accident. It's like I was a consequence of them being horny kids. That's about all there is to it, mister. No love between them, just sex and then me. He couldn't care less if me and my mom dropped dead. For all he knows, we already are dead. So that asshole's nothing to me."

He turned back up the volume on his CD of scorching guitar licks. We crept along, jamming to hard-edged bluesy rock.

I yelled, "These guys are great! Who the fuck is this?"

"This is The Black Keys, local dudes from Akron. These guys kick serious ass," he yelled, bobbing his head to the music.

"You mean kids today play this grimy blues with all the distortion and growling? Kids still buy this type of music?"

"Hell yeah, mister. These dudes are on fire. Not all of us kids are *wiggers*, dweebs or pussies. These bad boys lay it down!"

Leaning back on my headrest, I got lost in the kid's music and his pot. For as slow as we were going, by the time we got close to Downtown Cleveland that CD ended. When it did, I snapped back into reality: "Thanks, kid. This is where I get off."

"Right here? Are you sure? You're out in the middle of nowhere, mister. There ain't one soul out there."

"Ain't that the truth," I agreed with a half-smile. As we shook hands I looked into his youthful face having eyes damaged from too much pain and said, "Listen to me, kid. Do whatever you have to do to get into some type of school. Get a degree or license, or learn a trade and get certified. But do it right away, before you acquire any more appetites and anchors. Apply for grants, student loans, beg and borrow, but get an education before it's too late. No excuses. Just do it."

"I'll make you a deal, mister. You let me drop you at a friend's house or motel, I'll sign up for welding school come the new semester. I'll do it as soon as I wake up. I already got the admission paperwork at home. I can get a grant. I got those papers, too. So I'm all set. All's I need is the ambition to go. I guess I've been dragging my feet, feeling a little sorry for myself. But watching an old dude like yourself, out bulldozing through this crazy-ass night all by your lonely, and you ain't lookin' too healthy – no offense. Well, then I suppose I can game-up, too."

"Take me as far as the old High Level Bridge downtown, okay? We'll finish this *doob* and you can turn me on to another good band. You ever see that movie where the guy and the devil make a deal at a crossroads at the stroke of midnight? Well, if my boy keeps our appointment I just might take his damned soul. Do you understand what I'm speaking about, son? I hope so. Because that's as far as I'm going, and that's all I'm saying."

"You mean the Veteran's Memorial Bridge by Detroit and Superior? There ain't nothing around there, mister – not this late and cold, not even the devil himself. That's no man's land at night – especially during wintertime!"

"Yeah, kid. I need to fly under the radar. Understand now? There should be a car waiting at that crossroads. If they see anyone else they'll split. That means I have to be alone and on time. So put in another CD and hand me that lighter. Cool?"

He traded CD's. Similar to the last disc, this one also started with shredding guitar riffs. He yelled in that tiny car, "This is the White Stripes, dude! You ever heard of this crazy fucker before? He's a bad dude!"

Instead of answering, I relit the joint, took another steady pull and handed it back to him. "That's it for me, kid. I need to have my wits about me," I yelled back. "I'd better not get too stoned. I have a pet ouroboros at home I need to take care of." Then I reclined my head again to let that sweet hydro absorb the kid's electric blues.

I closed my eyes for a moment and got totally lost in the music. I was having a dream of being lost in an electric storm, strobe lit lightning blinding me, till I felt the car slow to a full stop. I jerked up my head to see a familiar sight. The kid was right. The old bridge looked deserted. But at least the weather appeared to be calmer than it had been.

The young man put down his cell phone and pulled over to a curb. "Okay, mister. Here we are. I'll be glad to drive you somewhere else. I ain't got nothing else to do. This bridge is over a half mile long. It's dead out here. This is crazy!"

"Nope, this is my stop. Black Stripes, right kid?"

"Nope. You got it all backwards. The first one was The Black Keys and this one is White Stripes. Hey, mister, what's a pet ouroboros? I Googled it on my phone but it didn't show any pets called that."

"It's just an expression. It's about doing the right thing at the wrong time and then finding out how much it's worth. It's about wants versus needs. It's about hitting yourself in the nose to get rid of an ass ache. Understand?"

I exited his warm car, into a white world of coldness and uncertainty. He watched me walk away through eyes that seemed to have gotten accustomed to disappointment, filled with dullness from chronic despair. So I called out through that icy wind, "Hey kid, I'll share with you what my father used to tell me: 'Fight and the pain will go away!' And I think he was right."

I watched the young man turn his ratty car around at the desolate snowy intersection and ease away into that white night. He waved through an open window. I turned from him to continue my voyage over the bridge and on to the next leg of my newest journey. I heard someone yell, "Hey mister! Watch out for them snow beavers! HA!"

Back at the hospital parking lot, Dr. Joey switched on his cell phone, psyching himself up for the treacherous drive home.

He checked for messages, as if there might be a sublime text to guide him through the trickier spots. He said a brief prayer, entered his 2012 Honda Odyssey LX, and closed his eyes. With the turn of a key he pushed frozen oil through a thankful motor. "Thank God…" A call came through while letting his engine get warm. He answered to a familiar voice, "I can't talk right now. Why do you think? Because I need both hands and all my wits. I'll phone you as soon as I get in. Don't worry. I told you he'd stay put. Besides, what type of maniac would willingly go out on a night like this? Don't worry; he'll be there. Where can he go?"

CH. XXI: Mean Streets of C-Town

"**Where is that Bobby now?** Is he hiding again?" the ancient nurse, Mildred, asked two elderly orderlies in her shaky voice. "Come out now, Bobby. This isn't funny anymore. Come out right now or you will not be able to brush your teeth tonight! I'm not kidding, Bobby. I'm phoning your auntie if you don't come out right this minute!"

Otis and Leroy, dressed in white uniforms, just stared at one another while the old woman continued to call out for a missing patient. The elderly man she called "Bobby" was their newest patient at a psychiatric facility near downtown Cleveland. Bobby, a mentally retarded man bankrolled with an unlimited trust fund, had been in the midst of being processed as a new admission. He was being guarded by an extremely overweight, ruddy complected man named Otis and his scrawny and hunched over partner, Leroy, who looked like an old piece of wood. Bobby was about to become a permanent resident at Turney Road Hospital when he disappeared. And that seemed to have occurred a couple of hours prior to the nightshift nurse finally realizing her new admission might have vanished.

Otis and Leroy had been taking turns trying to find Bobby, with one of them always in sight of Mildred. Otis, pink with sweat and breathing hard against the metal doorjamb from the exertion of brisk walking, signaled his sidekick to the stairwell: "Let me see yer key, Leroy," he panted. "Hurry up, son." Otis looked more flushed and pasty than usual. It appeared as though he were about to fall out.

"You don't need my key. You got our own." Leroy said through a heavily lined face that could have been carved ebony.

"I told you before, this damn belt clip's jammed. And my ol' belly gets in the way if-in I try. What's the big deal here, Leroy? Just let me use that damn key of yers now!"

"Lookie here, Otis. I've been sayin' it for years. You need to lose some pounds, boy. Lay off that candy before they lay you out in a box! You got the sugar diabetes and the cholesterol. I'm worried about you, is all," Leroy said, as he grinned a big toothy smile at his fellow orderly.

Otis wore a perpetual expression of the terminally concerned about everything: "I got the hypertension, too. So I don't need ta be hastelin' here, son. I don't have enough air to argue about this right now. By God, all I'm askin' is just show me yer key, Leroy."

"You don't need to curse the Lord, boy. And my key is my key, just like yours is yours," nodded Leroy with a serious look on his long, dark face like that of a tiki mask. "You know how Mildred is about sharing work property. She wants us to use our own equipment. She's strict on that one. Just take your belt off, Otis. You can carry all your keys in your pocket just the same as I do."

Mildred softly paged through the overhead, more of an amplified whisper, not to wake any of the other patients, "Otis and Leroy to the head nurses station, please."

My pants is kind a tight right here, son. I'm thinkin' strong on a real diet real soon. I went and popped the top button clear off these here pants, Leroy. What the hell am I supposed ta do if my pants go a fallin' off whilst ol' Mildred walks in? Get fired; that's what. She'll think we went and gone queer, by God! Now give yer key here, son."

"Please, Otis, don't take the Lord's name in vain. Besides, if ol' Mildred walks in and sees that Louisiana snake of yours, you just might get a raise." Leroy let out a loud laugh to hide his panic. His creased face appeared to be made of varnished wooden facial features, even when he was smiling his insincere grin.

Louder than before, Mildred paged through the overhead, "Otis and Leroy, you will both *please* report to the head nurses station on the double." There was a hint of urgency in her voice.

Leroy shrugged, "What's fair is fair, Otis. That's what I've always believed. That's what my mama always taught me. She always said, son, what's fair is fair…"

"Don't give me that business. It was yer turn to watch him, Leroy. I ain't gettin' fired because you were too damned lazy to do yer job and stupid enough to leave yer key layin' around *again*! How many times did I warn you, son? If I've told you once, by God, I've warned you a 1,000 damn times!"

"*My* turn? My turn was up. And I've asked you not to curse the Lord. I was hunting *your* big ass down to relieve me, Otis. Alright, so I had to piss. You know I got the weak bladder and now this prostate went all haywire on me. What do you expect a grown man to do once he's got to piss? My daddy always told me —"

"I expect you to not keep losing yer damn keys *and* patients – that's what. You better hope we find that Bobby-boy's crazy ass. If we don't locate him soon, I ain't covering fer you again. You're on our own this time, Leroy. Old Mildred suspects foul play here. I can smell it! I know that ol' bag only too well, by God..."

"Lookee here, Otis. This whole thing is half your fault for not being back. You know I got the weak bladder and this prostate thing. Lord knows when a man has to piss, that's that. You been feeding me coffee all darn night. Now you expect an old man to hold onto his piss like it's liquid gold? This is your fault for not letting a man take a proper break. And stop cursing our Lord!"

"We've been searching fer this nut fer hours, Leroy. He ain't nowhere to be found. What is he, the damned invisible man? If that Bobby-boy was here, we would've already nabbed him. I think he might have unlocked that door and wandered outside. That's what I think! And if that happened, we're up Shit Creek without an oar. What we both need to know is exactly what happened here. So I'm askin' fer the last time, Leroy, let me see yer damn key ring, son!"

Mildred paged for them even louder. She sounded irritable. "Final call for Otis and Leroy. And final means pronto!"

"You worry about your own darn key, Otis! I'll worry about mine!" Leroy grumbled, as he headed for the nurse's station – shuffling even more stooped over than usual. Otis lagged behind, mopping his shiny forehead with a thick, ruddy and freckled forearm. When they reached the nurse's station Leroy stood at attention facing Mildred, wearing a broad smile that creased his black face.

Otis, who towered over Leroy, stood behind and gazed at the floor. Still breathing hard, he rubbed a pink chubby face from head to chin with both hands, trying to wipe away nerves.

"I want the truth, and I want it right now," demanded the tiny lady with the white hair tinted silver-blue. "And I don't want to hear anymore bull from either of you."

"Well ma'am, truth is we're close," Leroy grinned.

"Is that your story too, Otis. Because if it is, I'm phoning and waking up our supervisor to further discuss this matter."

"If that boy's here, by God, we'll damn sure find him."

"Watch that language, Otis! And Bobby is a grown man just like you and Leroy. We're all adults, so let's act accordingly."

"It was a mix-up, ma'am, and it's partly my fault, Ms. Mildred. I'm willing to take half-responsibility," offered Leroy.

"Oh really?" Mildred asked. "And that solves what?"

"Ma'am, I sure didn't mean to imply that," Leroy answered, as he scuffed a thick soled black shoe across a shiny tiled floor. "But it's half my responsibility is all I'm saying, ma'am."

"Responsibility? Here are some facts: Bobby-boy's mother abandoned him as an infant. His auntie raised him as if he were her own son. Now since the aunt died, and because Bobby's trust fund is in Mr. Shapiro's care for his life-long stay here, do you two have any idea how serious this is? What do you think will happen when Mr. Shapiro's law firm finds out we *lost* Bobby, and on the very first day, and with all that money transferred to the company account? I'll be forced into retirement and the two of you will be fired on the spot, probably with criminal charges filed! Oh my goodness gracious…"

Otis called over his shoulder as he headed for the cloakroom, "I'll look around outside, ma'am. Leroy, I'll speak to you later."

"Bring a trash bag so you can carry my coat and boots with you just in case you find that boy wandering around out there in this blizzard," suggested Leroy. "He's in flimsy hospital clothes, is all. That boy's probably chilled to the bones by now."

"I've already told the both of you not to refer to our male patients as boys, haven't I? Take a flashlight, Otis. If you don't locate Bobby by the end of your shift then I'll suggest to Mr. Shapiro he terminate you both as of this morning, just in case you decide not to turn in your resignations! Are we clear?"

"Yes, ma'am," they harmonized like a duet.

Leroy walked with his soon to be ex-colleague to the lunchroom: "Otis, we darn well better find that boy, or a retarded twin brother of his out on those streets, or we'll be scraping trays and wiping down tables at the food-court over at Tower City Mall. This is serious this time!"

"Leroy, I think it would be a good idea if you don't talk to me. Since *I'm* the one going outside in this damn icy crap I expect you ta double recheck every room in this damn place, by God!"

It was three days after Christmas. Veteran's Memorial Bridge in Downtown Cleveland is the length of ten football fields. The long section used for driving and walking spanned about 100 feet above the Cuyahoga River, which is wide and deep. During midwinter the river looked frozen in some parts, especially on that late night in 2013. The Cuyahoga, used by tugboats to access and unload cargo from ships docked in Lake Erie, didn't look too serviceable that wintry night. Snow blew across that iced-over river as if it were a winding stretch of iced-over road beneath that bridge. It had been a drop-off point in 1976 where many people weighted with chain and concrete blocks got dumped straight down into the pits of hell. Thinking of those deeds led me to remember a couple of titles by AC/DC as I squinted to look at that mysterious highway beneath me.

Some people say winter is clean and beautiful. Many of those same people say they become energized in the brisk air. But that night in downtown Cleveland, invigorated was not what I felt. To me, winter always seemed to be a death trip. And on a night like that one, the possibility of remaining outdoors for too long hung in that frosty air like the Sword of Damocles. I thought: *timing and choices. I could have been as snug as a crab in a bush if I would have wintered it out at Joeys.* But the fact is I didn't. And another one is that sooner or later we usually get what we want out of life – providing we persevere. What I wanted at that point in my life was to keep moving before I froze, while I tried to figure out my next move during the trickiest chess game of my life. So far, my first move looked dismal.

I could see Cleveland's Terminal Tower all lit up in the distance, glowing a colorful aura thanks to blasts of snow-filled wind between it and me. After about 20 minutes of a bone-chilling walk, with downtown's winds howling off the lake at nearly gale force, I panted out loud to myself to keep from losing what little sanity still appeared to be intact.

In puffs of foggy breath I said, "Okay, here we are. So now what? You've done some stupid shit in your life. But this one really takes the booby prize. You made the decision to take a long walk to nowhere on a night like this? And that was even *before* you got high . . . you fucking dummy. So now what, genius? I might be better off getting attacked by some goddamn snow beavers, instead of slowly freezing to death out here in the middle of goddamn nowhere. There's not even a fucking dog in hearing distance, let alone a person. What an asshole I am…"

As I argued with myself the wind slowed and abruptly changed directions. Those new gusts of frigid air carried not too distant sounds with it. "It almost sounds like voices," I said to myself. "But from where? What kind of maniac would be out and about on a night like this, wandering around talking to himself? I should just turn my ass around right now. Yeah, fuck-it. I'm going back. I'll turn up Detroit Ave. I'm sure I'll run into some crackhead zombies or other dope-sick junkies out sniffing around like hungry rats – or maybe even some cops doing their jobs for once. Wait awhile... What's this?"

Too tired and cold to be rational, I began to hear *and* see things. I blinked: "Wow, if I didn't know better, that looks just like a naked guy standing up on the guardrail of this bridge. What the fuck? I need to make it back to Joey's basement. I'm cracking the fuck up. Now I see *three* people. Fuck-it. Is that a gun? This shit just ain't my problem. But wait a minute. Goddamn son-of-a-bitch! Why didn't I just turn around back there? Better yet, why didn't I let that kid drive me back to Joey's? In fact, why the fuck did I even leave his house tonight? Man, I'm a world-class asshole sometimes," I said to myself to keep from completely losing my mind, while I headed for what was either a hallucination or a whole bunch of brand new trouble.

I came up behind two tall figures facing a nude white man standing at the edge of the bridge over the frozen Cuyahoga River. The tall men were dressed nearly identical. In fact, they were both dressed very much like I was. One of those two thin men pointed an automatic, yelling something at a naked man teetering on the edge of the bridge. The tallest man wore wraparound shades. The other man next to him appeared to be laughing. I was close enough to hear what was being said. The two men standing were clueless of my presence. And the nude guy teetering on the edge had yet to notice me. I stopped to listen. *Don't get involved. You're on the run. Keep moving.*

The naked man was elderly and bald. I could make out his face. He looked Jewish, an older man about my size. But there was something wrong – other than the obvious. The old Jew nodded his head constantly, like a nervous tick. Holding onto a support with one hand, he faced me but seemed oblivious to my presence. He appeared to be hiding his lips inside his mouth, as if in an attempt to protect his teeth from the cold. It looked like he might plunge into the river and had managed to capture a small audience. *This is one bizarre sight.* What looked like a white plastic bracelet on one wrist glowed off a nearby streetlight. Clothes were piled on the ground. I thought: *This might be the craziest shit I've ever seen.*

The potential jumper said to the cold night air while nodding, "Yeah, 'cause Vah Vee Voy got vuck teef on. See 'em? *Gnang Gnang Gnang.* I'm Vucky Veaver."

"Fuck a whole bunch a buck teeth, retard mutha fucka. You ain't got cash, E Z. about ta help yo dumb ass jump – teeth or no teeth. Dig?" said a tall emaciated-looking man who appeared to be the younger of the two street bangers. They could have passed for father and son. "Foo, go ahead push dis crazy mutha fucka ass on over."

"Yeah, 'cause I'm Vucky Veaver. Vah Vee got good kind a vuck teef on. See 'em? *Gnang Gnang Gnang.* Lookie Vah Vee Voy's teef. *Gnang Gnang Gnang.*" The man made weird chewing sound while looking at the ground, bragging about buck teeth. Yet, not one tooth was visible.

The man with the automatic chambered a round and held his gun straight out at the nude man standing on the edge of the bridge: "Last chance, Bucky Beaver mutha fucka. Give up da bread Bobby Boy, or we bust a cap in dat stank ass. Dig?" said the man called E Z, as he leveled his weapon at the man teetering on the iced-over bridge's edge.

"Ease up, E Z. Dis stupid mah fucka ain't got fitty cent fo da first clue," laughed the older man beneath a huge parka. He was every bit as lanky as his partner. "Let's pitch deese cheap-ass clothes in dis river an leave his ass dangle in da wind. Be fun, *Skippy*. Deese phony-ass mah fuckas drivin' day asses ta work find dis buck-toothed fool froze to dis pole in da morning like a big-ass mah fuckin' fish stick."

"Nah, Foo. I'm about ta drop da hammer on dis bitch made retard. An I toll yo dumb ass 100 goddamn times: don't call me no goddamn *Skippy*, stupid mutha fucka. Now watch dis lily ass try ta swim fo a quick minute wit some lead up inside dat bitch if he don't give up da jing. We need dat money. Fuck dis buck-toothed fool." E Z fired a round right at the naked man through that stormy night, but he missed.

I shook my head in disbelief as I stuffed freezing hands deep into Joey's large parka pockets. That's when I felt the gun.

The man who referred to himself as Vah Vee Voy, continued with his insane dialogue, as if no danger were present. "Vucky Veaver. See 'em? Wanna touch 'em? I got vuck teef on. See? *Gnang Gnang Gnang.*"

"Come on, brah. Let's split dis scene" encouraged the older man. "This chump ain't got dolla one. Dis crazy mah fucka don't even know he ain't got buck teeth. Let's slide on over to da crib befo da po-po curb our ass. Ain't no money here fo nobody, brah. We don't need us another case, specially fo dis retard ass."

He adjusted his sunglasses: "Tell you what, blood. You in or out, Foo? 'Cause I'm shootin' dis fool, green or no green. If you out, I save me one a deese here lil' caps fo yo chicken-shit, punk ass. Now which way you goin' with dis, crackhead mutha fucka? Tell me dat?" E Z asked, as he pointed the automatic sideways at his friend.

Through the blustery wind I heard a fourth voice, one that sounded exactly like mine. Then I noticed a .357 in my gloved hand, pointing at the armed man. The new voice, my voice, hollered in a matter of fact tone plenty loud enough to be heard, "Drop the piece right now or I shoot you where you stand. This isn't a debate. Just do it right now, or you die right now. It's your choice, big man."

"Yeah, vuck teefner. I got 'em. See 'em? *Gnang Gnang Gnang*," the nude man announced to the howling, frigid wind blowing across his white body turning blue.

Foo spun around to face the new voice: "Oh, lookie here. We's got us a *new* toy. An dis mah fucka ass think he all dat. But no sweat, brah. I got yo back, *Skippy*," he assured his partner as he slowly approached me.

"Oh, so das it, *nigga*? You let a mutha fucka creep me whiles I's at work? Punk-ass ol' mah fucka. Dis how you got my back, crackhead? An I done toll yo dumb ass neva calls me no *Skippy*!" The armed man pivoted into a quick 90 degrees turn *Blam*, but instead of firing at me he shot his friend at close range. The bullet struck Foo's left shoulder and spun him completely around before he hit the snowy ground. He lay groaning between me and the shooter, almost covered in powdery snow.

"I'm hit, *Skip*!" Foo moaned, while writhing on the ground. The snow around his left shoulder turned a dark purple and steamed as it bled into the fresh white snow.

I yelled, "Freeze! Let me make this real clear. I don't give a flying fuck about you or your friend! Unless you plan on shooting yourself next, you'll drop that gun right now, you grimy mother fucker. But who knows? Maybe I'm all bluff. So go ahead. Test me."

"I'm Vucky Veaver. I got good kind a vuck teef on. Wanna touch 'em? Lookie, vuck teefner. *Gnang Gnang Gnang*."

E Z paused long enough to weigh his options. "Ya'll mutha fucka know fo sho I ain't bluff. It be suicide yo ass lookin' fo? I be da man oblige yo ass." As he began the 180 degree arc, a move that would turn him into me with his gun still raised at shoulder level, I saw the end of my level pistol jerk up three times in a row. *Bam Bam Bam*. Each time it barked, puffs of smoke filled the frigid air with the stench of gun powder. Temporarily deaf from the rapid fire blasts I watched the naked man on the edge of the bridge talking to himself, with lips stretched tightly over his teeth to cover them while he nodded and rocked back on forth on the small and icy ledge. I couldn't hear a word.

E Z loosely held his automatic as he coughed up blood. His eyes widened as he clutched at his chest and struggled for breath, drowning on dry land 100 feet above the frozen Cuyahoga River. His last words gargled in blood were, "Mutha fucka…" Death in real life is never as easy as what gets portrayed in movies. I reached down remove the automatic from his lose grip while he seemed to be stuck between an inhale and an exhale, making gargling sounds as he tried to speak. I watched the terror build in his eyes, the horror of his new reality, as it pinned him down and drained the life out of him. He eyes bulged. Soundless words sprayed mouthfuls of blood over his face. Those agonizing moments which seemed to last a lifetime gave way to horrible gurgling and hissing sounds till his spark began to glaze over.

I forced myself to focus. I turned E Z's automatic on the other downed man with the shattered shoulder, a man I recognized from my drug associations as an old-time junkie and professional crackhead from Collinwood named Foo. "Kill him, you cock-sucking junkie!" I ordered. "Put your piece of shit friend out of his misery."

"Fuck dat cold-blooded muh fucka. Drown, bitch."

"No, fuck you! Strangle him with your good hand, or I shoot. You know I'm not afraid to shoot in a crowd."

Foo struggled to his knees. "Let's see yo ink, mah fucka. You best be showin' me some colors, ol' man. 'Cause if you ain't bangin', *Skippy*, you ain't hangin' wit me up in dis mah fucka. Dis my hood, baby boy. So you needs ta show me you connected."

"Just shut the fuck up and do what I say or you get yours next. I'll leave your punk ass to freeze to death next to your chump friend. You two faggots can hold hands waiting for an ambulance that's never coming unless I call it in – but I won't."

With his right hand in the snow, supported by his good arm, Foo crawled over to the dying man. "You mean just choke his ass out right up on da bridge? Like *now*?"

"That's exactly what I mean. He shot you, didn't he? He was planning on killing you and the naked guy. You must owe him money, right? It was almost perfect till I showed up. Now I'm done talking. Kill him or I kill you. Do it now or you die, too! Or are you a coward?"

E Z ripped open his parka as he emitted terrifying sounds a man makes while drowning. "Aaaggghhh…" His eyes nearly popped out of his face as he tried to cough up enough blood to clear his air passage for just one more breath. But the blood was filling his lungs quicker than he could possibly choke it out. He was in full panic mode, struggling for each snatch of air till he completely bled out or choked to death on his own blood.

Foo grabbed his get-high partner by the throat. He grimaced and squeezed as hard as a man could with one good hand. "Die, mah fucka! It's you got me strung-out on dat stem, chasing goddamn ghosts all mah fuckin' day and night! I was cool wit da *heron*. But it's yo mah fuckin' ass make me do da dumb shit, while you up profilin' and actin' all bad like you somebody. You ain't shit! Yo bitch ass is mine now, *Skippy*!"

E Z tried to rip Foo's hand away from his throat. His eyeballs strained even larger, both in disbelief and suffocation, till his hands gradually fell away and his head tilted to one side. A last gush of blood puddled-up in new snow next to his gaunt face, leaving a black pool steaming in night air on that frozen bridge.

Foo glared at me: "You gonna kill my ass now, mah fucka? Do it den, honky-ass mah fucka. You ain't nobody," the injured man said, crying while still on his knees.

"You talk a lot of shit for some piece of shit that just choked out his own brother. Guess what? This ain't over," I assured him. "You just don't get it yet, do you? Because you're all whacked out on base is why. You fucking crackheads are all the same, all paranoid about nothing, seeing shadow-men and hearing sirens. But then you're clueless to real dangers right in front of your faces. Now put your good hand on the top of your head." I frisked him and found an 8' switchblade in Foo's right sock.

"What you waitin' fo, cracka-ass bitch?" Foo asked, as he wiped tears off his face with the back of his right coat sleeve.

"Get that hand back on that nappy-ass head! You move one muscle and you'll be stretched on top of your bro. Look at his pants. He pissed all over himself. You wanna be found like that, too?"

"I ain't goin' nowhere just yet, mah fucka" he said, still on his knees and looking at the ground. Then Foo mumbled something emanating from an expression of pure hatred.

I put E Z's automatic in my left coat pocket, secured with my hand on it. I approached the nude man who was still clutching the support beam with one arm. "Come on. You're gonna let me help you down off that ledge so you can get dressed. We'll get those nice warm clothes on you. You are cold, right?"

"Yeah, Vucky Veaver. See 'em?"

"Did you say *Bucky Beaver*? Is *Bobby-boy* is your name? Okay, Bobby, you're safe now, friend." That's when I noticed an entry hole in him, small and bloodless, but the exit hole was a mess and the man was losing a lot of blood.

"Yah, I'm Vah Vee Voy," the strange nude man said in a voice trembling from cold, with his teeth tucked safely behind lips that had turned blue. He began to sway. "I got vuck teef on."

"Buckteeth, is it? Yes, I see them. I like buckteeth, Bobby. Now let me help you down so you can tell me all about those fine buckteeth you have. You're hurt, Bobby. Please, let he help you. I'm your friend, okay?" I braced myself and kept my center of gravity low, so he couldn't pull me over the rail in case he grabbed onto me and then jumped.

I turned around to the wounded man still on his knees and warned, "Just remember: I can draw my piece and shoot a lot faster than you can stand and run through deep snow with a slug in your shoulder. You'll never make it in time, man. Don't even think about trying. Don't make me kill your dumbass, too. You know now, for sure, that I'll do it. So just stay put and be a good boy and everybody goes home tonight, except for your piss-pants friend you just killed. Are we clear?"

Instead of answering, Foo glared the most frightening and hateful look I've ever seen on a human face. I had that tingling sense of alarm, like when too close to a carnivore filled with bloodlust – its instincts set to devour. Menace and frigid air drained me. The threat of another life or death showdown became inevitable. His blast of hatred washed over me colder than the near gale force winds whipping across an unforgiving wintry lake. His evil crawled across me, from my aching head to frozen toes, to seize and my heart and lungs as it squeezed my throat. I couldn't swallow my own saliva.

I began to feel weaker. I forced myself to sound convincing: "So there it is. It's all over." But my own animal instincts were in high gear. That *Click* warned me just as it did him. We both knew this game wasn't over. I shivered from the bitter cold, and from terror, while trying to look as mean as I sensed he really was. I knew he wouldn't stop till there was another corpse. The smell of frozen blood sickened me. It reminded me of the unmistakable odor at a wintertime match, when dog blood soaked the combatants' coats and got absorbed by an ice-cold carpeted floor to help the dogs have surer footing to better wreck each other for the amusement of gamblers.

CH XXII: The Match, Part One

In the 1980s my older friend, Pazzo, told me, "Pay attention, Jackie. This life isn't what you think. Gangsters are as bad as those scumbag businessmen and politicians out there throwing each other on the tracks to save a buck or some discomfort. *Wise-guys* are every bit as disloyal. It's just that they screw you over for different reasons, plus faster and much more final."

"Maybe," I grinned. "But we're in the Wood! We don't cave-in or set each other up. So maybe that's the difference."

Pazzo said, "Don't hand me that *maybe* bullshit. I know. You don't. I've been your age; you've never been mine. I've been in your situation; you haven't been in mine. Either way, squares or *wise-guys*, the bottom line is *more*. More power or highs, more money or toys, more pussy or booze, or to feed some other insecurity. Squares are punks, so they can't be trusted. They'll do anything to save themselves a little discomfort. And the major flaw of a criminal is his nature – because most criminals can't be trusted. *Most*, but not all. Still, it's a bad bet. Use you head for something besides drug storage before it's too late, kid. And remember this part: everything is timing. Get an education while you still can, and then a decent job before you can't."

"I got all the education I need. I'm ready!" I informed my mentor. "Maybe I'm exactly where I need to be."

"Here we go again with *maybe*... I'll tell you where you are. Nowhere. You need mileage. In your life, you learn from mistakes that make you smarter and stronger. And once that happens they're no longer mistakes. But in my life there's zero margin for error. One wrong turn can get you a shallow grave in my world. Have a family and forget about this life. Nothing is more important. So when is the best time to begin a family? And when is the best time to appreciate what you have?"

"Do you regret any choices, Pazzo?" I asked the only man I respected after my father died. "I mean, would you do it different if you had a chance at a do-over?"

"That's crazy talk. Haven't you been listening? You can't change history. Why even think about it? It is what it is – all of it, like it or not. You'll drive yourself nuts trying to rework the past. It's done and that's that. You pick yourself up and move on."

I shared knowledge gathered from my father and Pazzo with my kids. Gina had been raised with stories since she was a child. Rocco knew his Uncle Pazzo well. So he heard them, too. Ravenous, he wanted anything he could cling to from grandfathers he never saw. Doc's alcoholism was why Rocco never relapsed. Although in conventional AA traditions he had – but only is he was a true addict. Rocco had to go to treatment in lieu of jail. While in treatment he saw what a slippery slope opiates actually present, a pastime he had taken way too lightly.

When Rocco asked the difference between abuse and addiction I told him, "Basically, it's needs versus wants. Words are just noise unless they match behaviors. Addiction is about slavery, it's an inability to stop and a *need* to continue." Rehab provided a broad education and a well timed wake-up call before he got in over his head and couldn't get out. When he asked for a bottom-line definition I said, "True addicts must go to treatment and work a program. It's the only way. But abusers just stop one day, for one reason or another . . . or they continue and become true addicts. So the bottom line is this: if a person requires intervention in order to quit, that person is an addict. If a person cannot be trusted to have substances around when no one else is watching, that person is an addict. If people continue to use daily, eventually they'll have severe physical, financial, emotional, legal, family and mental problems." Rocco proved to be a good student who wanted more, just as much as every true junkie does. But which *more*, and when, make all the difference in the world.

December, 2013: Bull was already a two-time match winner. His first win was over a Cleveland star named Blackie, a local dog going for his grand championship. Blackie had beaten a handful of rough alley fighters. He picked up a few wins on Hough Ave. and his championship down on Kinsman. His fourth was against Sonny Magic's people in the Glenville area for big dollars. But that contest against Bull staged in a Pennsylvania hay barn had proven to be a total mismatch. It featured a game amateur that had been schooled on curs with wins over average talent, against a natural pro. Bull had some of the finest pit-dog blood in the world flowing through his veins. He easily won against a deadgame dog and stubborn owners who refused to pick up a great dog and bring him home for breeding. Bull became a local hero, but Rocco figured Bull's reputation stayed in C-town.

The black gang-bangers from Detroit met Rocco on neutral ground for Bull's second match. They brought their red-nose champion named Red Dog and an entourage of rogues and gamblers coming from New York to Chicago. Red Dog proved to be a serious contender. Plus, the men from Detroit were top conditioners and handlers. That same trip to Pennsylvania had also proven Bull's gameness and ability against a worthy opponent in a hard fought battle that lasted nearly two hours. The Detroit team gave it up. But they wound up losing their money and a magnificent animal, while Bull defeated his second champion en route to his own title.

Rocco knew about their tentative Northern competition. That Dickless dog they were bringing down to Cleveland was purely a beast with a well-established record as an International Champion having a well-deserved reputation. Those Canadians even had people on the payroll to condition dogs and had been known to cover some outlandish wagers. They would be willing and able to cover all bets against them.

Cagootz was planning to lay a sizeable sum on Bull's match, which would be a lot more than he had admitted to. Plus, he would be charging spectators $50 per head, per fight as an entrance fee. There were two great matches scheduled to take place. The event would be staged in the basement of The Inn. Cagootz could probably squeeze 200 people down there, plus sell drinks at twice the normal price. The gate alone was worth 10 grand. So even if Bull lost, which was unlikely, Cagootz stood to make plenty from bar and gate proceeds and possibly the other contest scheduled for that same convention.

That week before the show Cagootz treated Danni with respect. He tried to make his leering less obvious. He didn't try too hard to contact Rocco after tossing out the bait. Cagootz was over confident they would win, even though he didn't know anything about real pit-dogs. He told Rocco, "No sweat, kid. It's just a fucking match. What's the big deal? They're just dogs."

Rocco explained: "I've seen enough pit contests to know the score. When two evenly matched Aces collide, just like with a jiu-jitsu match of two Masters, all it takes is one good hold to change the outcome. In the short run it's all timing. Then the timing factor changes. In a marathon match, depending on how it goes early-on when both are full of energy and still can bite hard, usually gameness determines the winner. But that depends on endurance. So that brings us right back to timing. Just keep this in mind: with two *unbeatable* champions, anything can happen – and one of them will lose. Many times physical condition is a huge factor. This much is for sure: It ain't over till it's over. So if we do this thing, let's not count our winnings just yet. Meantime, I'll do my part the best I can."

Bull had already been put into a pre-keep before the deal was even made. Then Rocco rigorously worked his dog twice a day. Long walks, running a treadmill, tugging on a hide, and chasing a tennis ball were all parts of daily routines switched up with two days of work and one day rest – break down and build back up. Bull was five years old, which was still prime time for him but nearing its end.

If Bull won this third match against the Canadians, he would be declared a Champion of Champions and officially retired. Bull would have made an indelible mark in history and would be valuable as a stud dog. Still in his prime, the warrior was diligent in his routine. He had a great work ethic. Because Bull had been down this road before, and loved it, he sensed that his reward was just a short time off.

Rocco jumped out of bed at sunrise every morning. He was feeling less bitter. He had committed himself to Danni and would do his best to make things right. Rocco felt he had been cheated in life, not having known during childhood what it was like to have a father. But he wasn't the type of man to lay around whining, wishing or praying for things to happen. He was a mover and a shaker. Regardless, he seemed to come up about a moment too late and a quarter shorter about half the time.

Rocco's bad luck didn't break him, though. In fact, it made him more determined. The failure of his first relationship conditioned him for one that would thrive. The loss of his construction job, after a decade of diligent service, honed his survival instincts. He hoped his past experience with exercise and nutrition, along with mind-tuning and self-discipline, would continue to benefit both him and his dog.

Rocco never faltered with their schedule. They hadn't reached their peak yet, and were already in the best shape of their lives, mentally and physically. Win, lose or draw, Bull would be retired after this flight. Nothing could change his mind. Rocco just hoped everything went smooth. If Bull was in bad trouble, he would throw in the towel.

He figured Cagootz would have some serious cash bet on the match, a lot more than he was admitting to. Rocco knew if it came to a major confrontation between them, it could also be a flight to the finish. He had managed to survive for over 30 years and remain solid while on the mean streets of Cleveland. He would not relinquish his manhood to anyone. So it was his job to make sure Bull was fit in order for the match was to run smoothly, for their financial problems to be ironed out, for Bull to remain alive, and for Rocco to stay out of prison or a shallow grave. He must do everything perfect – zero margin for error.

Bull gradually reached his peak. The timing of his *keep* was just right. Leading to the big day that lay, relatively speaking, just a few hours ahead, Danni was busy finishing her duties at The Inn for the week. She slowly walked home with her paycheck, a wad of small bills, in a front pocket of her jeans, not focusing on the depressed area they lived or her own fatigue. She was distracted and had been daydreaming, walking home on remote control.

She entered the house to find Rocco stretched out on the sofa, Bull next to him on their oval shag rug. Bull thumped his tail against the floor. They both lifted their heads to acknowledge her presence, then went back to their originally positions.

"Those people from Canada were in this morning, Rocco. They got in yesterday. I met one named David-something. He seemed nice. They were downstairs mostly, helping Fat Spuds and Skinny Vinny set things up for the morning. "How you feeling, babe? You okay?"

"Cool, calm, and dry." Rocco yawned while flexing. He sat up. The dog stayed where he was, wagging his tail while gazing at some invisible object.

"How's Bull doing today? Did he peak-out too soon?"

"No way. He's ready. This week went perfect, and his weight's good. He's hydrated. He's not flat mentally. He's as ready as he's ever been. But this'll probably be his toughest fight. Those guys seem awful cocksure. Every dog's as good as his last match. That makes these two both aces. When two dogs of this caliber meet, which isn't too often, well . . . it's not unusual for both to croak off. You still coming, babe?"

"Of course I'll be there. We're a team. Right, my knight in white satin armor?"

"How about you and your knight in white satin armor pull up stakes after this? You can give numb-nuts your two-week notice tomorrow, after Bull wins. We'll move out to my Pop's farm house. This place stinks, baby. It's starting to choke me. It's like I need some fresh country air. Know what I mean?"

"Let's see what happens. We can think about it awhile." She was dreading leaving her best friend, Carrie. Danni only saw her once in awhile lately. But the assurance of knowing they were near each other helped them both get through their struggles. "Maybe it would be best. Give me till tomorrow to think it over, okay? Oh yeah, that David guy said they brought two dogs. The other one's a female."

"Yeah, I know, a 28-pounder. They're matched to the Keystone bunch from PA. I'm betting the Canucks get their clocks cleaned both times. That little bitch the Keystone boys have is nothing but bad news. I've see her. She's a fast-forward mini-monster. She moves like a goddamn blur and bites like a big male. The bitches always go last so their scent isn't on the carpet. So if we win – I mean, *when* we win – I'll bet a wad on her, too."

"Rocco, I love you. If you want to move back to your dad's place we'll go. It's only an hour away. Is it too late for us to change our mind about this match?"

"I can't forfeit. The lock-up money came from Cagootz. There's no way we can repay him. Like it or not, we're in now."

"Okay, then just be a good boy. Keep your cool. Please?"

"Danni, I've been thinking… If this crazy motherfucker tries to screw me over I'm gonna cut his head off and run it up his big ass. Maybe I should be, but I ain't afraid of those guys."

Danni was anything but a religious person. Still, she silently said her own type of prayer to the universe that night, wishing for a collective energy to embrace their dog so he would be alright. Money no longer seemed to be a factor. She regretted being responsible for this coming to a head. Now she had valid concerns about their loyal housedog. And on top of that, her hot-tempered yet gentle man tangling with killers. She thought back to the talk our family had about dogs fighting. She shivered.

December 28th, 2013 – The Basement Pit: before and after prison, more cautious than ever, Fingers lived in the suburbs and stayed off Cleveland's radar screen as much as possible. So he wasn't available to monitor day-to-day operations. As a result, most of the real power fell into the hands of Cagootz and Big Louie. And they liked what they felt.

Rocco woke before dawn to meet the men who ran Cleveland for Fingers. Danni was still in dreamland, all curled up like a little girl. One of her breasts was innocently exposed.

He smiled and slowly shook his head and laid out his clothes, to quietly begin his day. He loaded their little coffee maker with extra grounds of dark roast espresso and let it steam while he sat at their kitchen table in his boxers, thinking about all the possibilities. After he sipped down his cup of strong, black coffee he got dressed and walked Bull out for his last time before the match, watered him and brought him back inside their house. Rocco left to run some errands before Danni roused.

"I'm back. Wake up, baby-girl. It's almost time."

"I was up, did some things and came back to bed. But I've been awake since you got back, just laying here thinking. I don't feel well – my stomach. I think our baby doesn't like stress. But I'm coming. I just need a few minutes."

Whitey and Filo roared up in a black Corvette, parked it and they all rode together in Gina's hatchback. He was called FILO because his toughness and reliability in gang fights. FILO is an acronym for "First In and Last Out." And Filo was exactly that.

"Hey, that Russo kid's here with that beast of his," Nino said to some henchmen from Little Italy. "I won money with this kid before, and on this dog. If this old hound can still scrap half as good as this kid, we're in the chips."

"His name ain't Russo anymore," reminded Spuds as he combed his hair. "He's got his father's name now. Remember?"

"Yeah, he's got Jackie's last name now. You remember now, right *coom*?" Vinny asked, as he rolled frail shoulders.

Cagootz waltzed through the crowd dressed in a black silk suit. He ushered those three friends and their almost too calm dog downstairs to the site. It was a dark, musty-smelling basement large enough to accommodate a small bowling alley. One spotlight, which hung from the 8 foot tall ceiling, cast a revealing light over all of their futures.

Gus was already there. He stood pit-side, guarding empty beer cases which would be used for seating. Heavily tattooed arms folded across his bull chest, tats displayed as proudly as the colors emblazoned on the backs of their ragged Levi vests. Evidently, he and Filo had reserved seats in Rocco's corner behind Whitey. Yet there was empty space surrounding them.

Although men in attendance came from different backgrounds, everyone there had at least one thing in common. It was strange to see those two hard-core bikers standing next to old-school gangsters like Big Louie and another tall, well-dressed man at pit-side called Auggie. The slender man stood emotionless with shark-like eyes. He looked more Eastern European than Italian, perhaps like from the Balkans or even Albanian. But he was pure Italian. That was certain, because he was *made*.

The pit had been positioned in the center of the basement, beneath the bar. It had been constructed of plywood with a two-by-four frame. The open-topped box was 16-feet square and stood two feet high. Old carpet rolled over the floor was held down on its perimeter by the weight of the wooden walls and had been duct taped to the concrete floor. Two dozen empty beer cases had been set around the pit to serve as reserved seating for the front row of spectators. There was one 5-gallon bucket in the center of the pit, half full of water. It held two large natural sponges of the same shape and color. More than one bucket would leave temptation for a disgruntled gambler to poison the other's water used to sponge out the dogs' mouth and cool off their bodies while in the heat of battle.

Near the steps was a makeshift wet bar, fashioned from the same material used to construct the pit. Two old men from Collinwood tended bar. Those crazy cousins had moved to Erie right after Benny took Paddy Kelly for the morbid drive and hacked him up like a spiral ham in his own car while he was still alive. That bold move even made the big boys nervous. So his car *accidentally* got blown to smithereens not long after he took the Mick's nephew for that one-way trip to hell.

Because Sally-boy and Nicky had been at Mick's Shamrock Club the night Benny escorted a smiling Paddy out the front door with a chromed .45 pressed against his back, they changed their zip code. After that, everybody in Collinwood found themselves under a microscope. Uno's people, along with Mick's crew of Irish mobsters, as well as the gang of Wong Gongs who took work from both sides, were being watched by each other, by local cops and even the feds. So those whacked-out cousins, Ice-cream Nicky and Sally-boy, stayed away till long after both the Mick and Benny had been safely dead and buried. Both Nicky and Sally were wannabe gangsters.

With the matches about to begin in The Inn's basement, Sally-boy yelled to Rocco, "Whoa! You too good for us now, ya little prick? Now you're some big-shot, you can't even gimme a hug hello, ya fuckin' bust-out. Look as this kid, Nicky. All the sudden he's a big man. He don't even know us anymore, like we're fuckin' strangers ova here. Come-on, kid, have a drink."

Sally-boy picked an 8-ounce clear plastic cup, one from their stacks of hundreds behind the homemade bar, and filled it with cold draft beer. "Get ova here!" he called out to Rocco. Sally was dressed incognito with thin gray overalls and a "Vito" nametag on the chest pocket which he wore as his usual disguise.

"Are you kidding? You givin' the kid tap beer? He's a star tonight. Come on, kid," Nicky offered. "I'll make you a nice highball. It's a gentleman's drink, *coom*."

Rocco walked to the bar to greet them. "Good to see youse guys. No thanks, Sal. I'm good, Nicky. I might be stuck in that box for a couple hours. Booze or caffeine is the last thing I need right now. I'll be in there having to piss like a rhesus monkey if I drink this. But thanks, anyway." Rocco nodded to the other bartender. "So how you doing, Nicky? You're looking sharp tonight, as usual."

Ice-cream Nicky, still dressed in his faggot-assed, white ice-cream uniform with that goofy-looking hat like the skipper on Gilligan's Island, curled his finger back and forth as he head-signaled Rocco closer. He whispered, "See those motorbike kids you got with you? They got any reefers on him? It's not for me, kid. 'Cause for strength, *coomba*, I ain't like these other fuckin' bust-outs. I ain't hooked on the pot like these Five Points shines and them Irish pigs. And you know this. I'm lookin' for some smoke for some gash and her girlfriend. They wanna do a sangwitch with me, but they says I gotta get 'em stoned. So those kids got any reefers on 'em, or what?"

"Relax for one fucking second Nicky. This kid just got down here, and he's got shit to take care of. Let 'im move around a little, get the feel of the place, before you start in with your same bullshit again. Besides, are you blind? This poor kid's trying to fight his dog, for Christ's sake! Give him a little space before you start in trying to gouge him for joints."

"Whoa, Sal. Why you gotta talk to me like this in front of company? You're supposed to know better than this. We wasn't raised like that. I'd never lean on this kid. He knows us *good fellas* take care of our own kind, Sally. So how about showin' some fuckin' class for once in your life? Ya bust-out!"

"*Class? Me* show some class? Is this how you talk to me in front of these kids? Where's your respect? How you wanna make me act in here, Nicky? Don't pay attention to this manic, kid. You know how he is. Meantime, I was gonna ask you something. Why is it youse kids like to fight these dogs? I seen some fights before. It's kind a boring if you ask me. So why do you do it?"

Rocco paused for a moment: "Well – for one thing – it's out of respect for the purity of the gameness. It's a spiritual experience every time I see one that's got no business scratching

277

back into its opponent go flying back into the source of the pain."

"Really, Sally?" Nicky laughed. "You mean you didn't know this?" Nicky smirked while he clinked ice cubes in a plastic cup full of Canadian Club and ginger ale. His pinky was extended as if he were holding a crystal martini glass.

"Nicky, did I ask you? I'm talkin' to the kid. So kid, you said '*For one thing*,' like there's more."

"Check this out, Sal: What else can you bet on where you win as much as you bet, and the odds are always 50/50, and the house doesn't have the advantage or take a cut? Sweet deal, huh?"

"*Minchia*! You mean if I bet 10k, I win 10 large, Roc, and the house don't even take a piece? No shit! But I gotta say it. This sounds too good to be true." Sally raised his eyebrows.

Nicky downed half of his whiskey and ginger: "You sound like a rookie, Sal. This shit's old news.. Try ta keep up with the times, *coom*, like me."

"You know what, Nicky: You'd just better—"

Cagootz interrupted the wacky cousins: "Fuck all that noise. Come here, Roc," he laughed. "This guy here's David Hinton. He's Mr. Big-bucks. And these other three characters are his *corner-men*..." Cagootz shook his head in disdain.

David, the spokesman for their camp, said, "It's truly a pleasure to finally meet you and your marvelous dog face-to-face. I've heard you're an honest man with a one in a million dog. May I look him over, Mr. Russo?" Dave squatted down to get a closer look at Bull. He looked like a shiny copper statue.

"It's Lorocco, not Russo. But call me Rocco."

"Look all you want, man." Whitey scowled, "Just don't touch the merchandise. Same rules go for Roc's ol' lady."

David looked up with a grin, till he saw the patch on Whitey's back and that he wasn't smiling. "My mistake, friend."

Rocco added, "Whitey's my corner-man."

David quickly averted his look from those light blue ice-balls set deep in Whitey's hard features. Rocco noticed the other Canadians staring at Whitey's patch when he entered, his colors partially covered by his long blonde ponytail. In fact, everyone there saw two of Whitey's club-brothers flying the same patch at pit-side – in Rocco's corner.

Good, Rocco thought. *Everything seems to be on the up-and-up.* "How about we weigh now, Dave?"

David looked down at the dog: "If it's all the same to you, sir, we can waive the weigh-in. But we will wash them whenever you like. Mr. Cagootz can choose someone to wash my dog, and my son here will wash yours. Nothing personal, standard procedures. You know the drill."

"My wife washes your dog. I don't care who washes mine."

The bitches had already been washed, weighed, and put in airline crates which had been covered with sheets in an open anteroom where everyone could see them but nobody could get close enough to put a rub on one or slip something to another.

David's dog, Dickless, was a thick-made brindle with well-bent muscular stifles. That meant lots of driving power. His light fawn undercoat contrasted black tiger-like stripes. Shoulder muscles bulged and relaxed as he shifted his feet in the large galvanized washtub. Danni sponged the monster down like she was washing a car. The dog loved the attention and gave her a lick across her face to show his gratitude.

Finally, it was Bull's turn. He had been this route before and seemed indifferent to the whole procedure. He yawned as David's son washed and rinsed him. Well-tended muscles rippled beneath a rich red color that gleamed of good nutrition, as well as from a strict regimen of alternating strength, endurance and rest days. He looked like a mega-version of the little red-nosed Crazy Gracie bitch acquired many years ago from a West Virginia dogman called Fatso.

David said, "As Mr. Cagootz agreed, the referee for both matches will be old Walter of the Keystone Combine. He's a well-respected man in the Pit-bull community, as I'm sure we agree."

"Ol' Walter's cool. He reffed Bull's last match in PA."

"Then I presume we're ready to commence, sir?"

Cagootz shook his head as he stared at the temporary bartenders: "I had these two bust-outs come down today so they could build that piece of shit bar and string some lights up in these rafters. It was too dark to have all these unscrupulous motherfuckers in one place with all this cash floating around. You never know who you can trust these days, right Roc? Anyway, these old fucks begged me to let 'em bartend too, 'cause they wanna watch the fights but don't wanna pay the gate. Look at these pathetic old fucks."

Cagootz hollered over to Ice-cream Nicky, "Hit the light switch so we can see who's betting against us before it's time to collect from these tight-fisted pricks."

The ceiling lit up with stringers of red, white and green Christmas bulbs. Gangsters in silk suits and bikers in ragged denim lit up like Santa Claus ornaments.

Whitey said, "You gotta be kidding me… Is this shit for real, Roc? How the fuck are we supposed to fight dogs in Disneyland?"

"Wow, this makes for one bizarre-ass scene." Just as Rocco said that, overhead Christmas lights began to blink. The entire room began to breathe. One of the bitches let out a howl from her kennel.

Danni said, "Aww, poor baby. She's all confused."

"A dogman can't handle in these shit!" Rocco protested.

"I don't know," Danni said. "Bull loves Christmas."

Vinny shouted, "Turn that off before I have a seizure!"

Fat Spuds added, "We don't go for that faggot-assed bullshit around here."

The black biker from Five Points named Curtis, laughing and high-fiving Horrible Hank standing next to him yelled, "I be one stank-ass mutha fucka! Ol' flukey-doo wen an put da flukey to da dookie up in dis ma fucka , fo sho… HAHAHAHAHA!"

My intimidating-looking friend, Hank, mumbled under his breath, "Be cool, brother man. This ain't home. We're out of our element down here. Go with the flow."

"It's all good, baby," Curtis giggled.

Cagootz hollered, "Nicky, turn that shit off! That's it! No more dogfights for youse two clowns. Youse bust-outs gotta go home now."

As the two cousins moved from behind the bar and towards the steps Sally-boy asked, "What the fuck did I tell you, Nicky? Didn't I say, don't go for the blinking lights? But no… Right away you're like some fucking *finocchio* decorator."

"*Me* a fag? You're the one wanted Italian flag colors. I wanted blue, remember? If they was blue and all the same, nobody notices. Meantime, now it's all my fault, right?"

Sally-boy dejectedly walked up those rickety basement steps, "I said it once; I said it a hundred times. No fucking blinkers. Now look what you went and did…"

Nicky, right behind him, argued, "Maybe next time you'll listen to me for a change. When I say all blue, I mean it. Blue's a man's color. Dogs love blue. Right away you start in with this exotic bullshit, it freaks these faggots down here right out."

Whitey asked Gus, "Where the fuck are those two old bastards going? It ain't safe to let anyone leave now. I don't like this at all."

"Don't sweat those two, bro," Gus assured him. "Those guys are world-class assholes, but they're okay. The one I'm worried about is this Cagootz. I wouldn't put it past him to hire a couple of shines to rob this thing at gunpoint. You got any idea how much cash is floating around this place tonight?"

Whitey asked, "You packed extra heat, right bro?"

"I got two guns and a knife," laughed Gus. "You think I'd walk into this *guinea* nest without being strapped to the nuts? Besides, these goons know if they rip us off they better kill us."

Fat Spuds and Skinny Vinny came back downstairs with two hanging trouble-lights and extension chords. They hooked one in each dog's corner, hung from rusty nails on weathered joists, so handlers could better see their dogs.

Cagootz yelled, "Okay, Spuds and Vinny, good work! Now get over there. Youse two are bartenders for the rest of the night. *Capiche?*"

"We gotcha covered, boss," hollered Spuds "No worries."

"Yeah, no sweat here, boss," Vinny agreed. "We ain't like those other two dummies. We're sophisticates."

Whitey asked his brother, "Is that who I think it is? Those two idiots work for this Italian crew now? No wonder the Cleveland mob ain't shit anymore."

"This is one strange world, bro," agreed Gus. "Now all the sudden these two jerk-offs are dangerous men? What did they do, run a spot for prospects in the want ads?"

Curtis started singing to himself, "Fat and Skinny went to bed. Fat blew a fart and Skinny was dead. HAHAHAHAHA!"

Hank grumbled in a low growl, "Easy does it, brother man. I don't want to have to kill my way out of this motherfucker. Let's concentrate on us getting off some bets."

"Okay, flukey doo. We cool as snowballs, Massa Hanky."

As the dogs were being prepared, one after the other in the same tub, spectators in the reserved beer-case row stood to watch. First was the washing in a large galvanized tub with a baby shampoo and a clean water rinse from a 5-gallon bucket, half on each dog. That was followed by rubbing alcohol sponged over the dogs' coats, a rinse with gallon of milk spilled over each dog, with more fresh water for a last rinse. The dogs were tasted by Walter.

As soon as Walter stepped into the pit the crowd hushed. "Ladies and gentlemen, there will be no yelling during the matches. There will be no talking while a dog is stood-up to make its scratch. Any violators will be ejected. No warnings. One time and you're out. The first match is between Rocco's Bull and Hinton's Dickless, both fighting at catch-weight. You've agreed to Cajun rules with ten seconds to complete scratches. Your dogs will be handled only when out of holds, unless I instruct you to handle your dogs or if either party concedes. The dogs will take turns scratching into their opponents until one refuses his turn or is counted out. I will count out loud, 10 seconds for each dog to cross the pit and mouth its opponent. Nobody, other than the two handlers and me, are allowed in the pit once the match begins. If either handler commits a foul I will call a foul and the contest ends. At that time I will declare the other handler and his dog the winners. Once a decision is made, or if a dog does not complete its scratch, the match is over and my decision is final."

The man trying to get off some early bets was a drug dealer from down Five Points who had been in and out or jails and prisons half of his life. Already seated, he stood again waving a fist full of one hundred dollar bills, "I got my man, Roc, all da way ta da bank. Now who want some a dis flukey? Who wan ta looz day money, come see ol' Uncle Curtis – da dawg man – put dat flukey straight up dat dookie."

A Canadians called out a $500 bet, immediately covered by Curtis who grinned, still fanning his wad. "I got plenty mo flukey fo yo dookie. Whole else wan mo a dis, get ya some."

"I've got a cool thousand to lose right here on the Bull dog. Who's got me covered?" asked Horrible Hank.

David snagged Hank's offer. Whitey took a $2,000 wager with another from David's camp, and then Auggie took a $5,000 side bet from the Canadians. Handfuls of smaller money were being pointed at one another, nodding heads in acknowledgement of wagers just made before the action began.

PART FIVE

Like a train whistling through the blackness of sleep, people crash through our lives linked-up like a string of locomotives blasting through night air. All that commotion, of us stepping in and out of each other's situations in a storm of randomly colliding moments, brought me right here, right now. Those paradigm shifts of happenstance spin at maddening paces till an arrangement is reached to merge, collide, or avoid being blind-sided again. Similar to burning gyroscopes whirling through space and time at a frantic pace of manic frenzy, we mini-tornadoes eventually get absorbed by a breeze of inevitability set in motion by all the choices we've ever made, multiplied by those of all others already dead and still dying. And while we're tumbling throughout space and time, we teach and hire people to invent truths like predestination, preordination, predetermination and providence, all in place to decide my fates however I choose.

If door #1 is first up, is it there for me to choose which way I turn using the five "W's:" who; what; when; where and why?

So then door #2 must be for if I'm determined to go straight and how I proceed; or if I stop, go backward, alone with whomever, whenever I feel like I can.

And, of course, there's always door #3, the open-house invitation for the good old-fashioned *fuck-its* to supersede all other window dressings; or continuum items like common sense, moral sustenance and enough pragmatism to prioritize affairs.

So the way I had it figured, I'd probably be forced to opt for door #4. It guarantees that my life has been determined from living as a free-thinker. Door #4 is comprised of all the doors combined from that one, leading to a hallway of others, to reinforce how my destiny is to re-synthesize. The faith to embrace enough courage to do the next right anything. The gumption to scratch back into the face of adversity despite popular opinion and regardless of consequence.

Or we simply could pretend not to choose and then dump it on anyone else. Or, what else we could do is to take it as it comes, one way or another, whether we like it or not.

CH XXIII: Door # 4

When I reached my left hand out to Bobby he didn't respond other than to say, "*Gnang Gnang Gnang*. Vuck teefner." By then his whole body shivered. His breathing had become more erratic. He appeared to be hypothermic. I had a few more minutes at best to get that poor soul off the ledge and clothed before he bled out or froze to death. But I needed to be vigilant, because Foo watched my every move – just waiting like a vulture.

I took off my gloves, tucked away the pistol and reached up to take hold of one of Bobby's wrists with both of my hands. Bobby-boy screamed and jumped. The only trace of him remaining above the viaduct was that plastic wristband wrapped around my numb fingers. To make that experience seem real, I stuck his ID in one of my pockets and then looked over the edge of the bridge at the frozen river. All that remained of Bobby's existence was a hole in the ice.

I turned to the kneeling wounded man and could see the pain's imprint, that his natural endorphins were wearing off and he was finally softening somewhat. "Okay, you still got a choice. Actually, you have three choices. It's up to you how we do this."

"Talk, mah fucka. Dis a free-ass country."

"First choice is I put a bullet in you with your friend's gun and then leave it and your body up here."

"Or I call my partner and we haul your sorry ass away for the murder of that scumbag there in a puddle of blood. I'm a witness. It'll all go in my report. I'll also note that I caught both of you taking turns ass-slamming the retard, and that's why you threw him off the bridge. The way I see it, that's why you killed your friend, too."

"The third choice is I can simply let you walk – providing you wise-up and do the next right thing. Up to you, man."

"You da man?" Foo asked in a not so tough voice, clutching his left arm. "I toll dat *nigga* we was tailed. I knew you was 5-0, soon as I saw yo shiny ass." His face contorted in pain."

"So it's that time, Foo. Me and you are gonna make a deal. I don't like you. And you know this. But I don't want to have to kill you, either. All that paperwork and an investigation… Of course I will if you make me. You know this too, don't you?"

"Okay, man. Let's see door # 3," the man with a bullet through his left shoulder asked in an even weaker voice.

"Door #3 is actually four things. One: You're gonna help me lift your friend's body and throw it over the side and into the river. You're gonna give me your wallet and all the ID and money you have, and everything from your friend's pockets and wallet."

"Cool, baby. Yeah, let's do dat."

"Shut up. I ain't done. Two: I need you to pose and smile." I stepped back, lifted my parka and pretended to take a picture with the stupid looking chrome belt buckle of Shit-pants Joey's. "Now I got a nice night vision picture of you next to a body with steaming puddles of blood around it. Maybe I'll sell this to Cleveland Magazine. You'll be on the cover. This is huge, *homes*. You finally made the big-time. You're famous, bro."

Foo grumbled under his breath but didn't argue.

"Before you go bitching and moaning again like some little girl, listen to the rest of it. I'm not done yet. Three: We already know you're a snitch, which is why you're still on the streets slinging poison. But I need you to learn to be solid for once in your pathetic life. If you ever say one word about any of this to anyone you'll find this picture I just took with my surveillance camera on the front page of the Plain Dealer, along with all the others I snapped before either of you geniuses even knew I was standing behind you with your naked boyfriend."

"Fuck you, faggot-ass mah fucka! Yo ass gonna bleed befo you leave out dis mah fucka. Yo ass gettin' reborn."

"Oh yeah, thanks for reminding me about the last thing. Four: You will admit yourself into rehab *today*. I'll make calls later to check recent admissions of all nearby treatment facilities that accept Medicaid patients. And because I'm a Cleveland detective, I can do that. So if you don't comply with all my demands you'll be arrested by this afternoon and be known throughout Cleveland as the R&R Killer . . . the *Rapist of Retards Killer*. Now give me your wallet and then go frisk your friend, crackhead!"

"How da fuck I know you a cop? How 'bout *you* da one show some ID, pig-ass bitch? Fact us, you know what? We changin' deese mah fuckin' rules. Here go #1: You show ID. I get da cash. Den you call my ass a cab or yo dumb-ass in fo a real surprise!" he threatened from his knees.

"Okay, fair enough. Here's some ID." When one of Joey's construction boots made contact with Foo's mouth, his lips exploded as if they had been filled with raspberry syrup. "You need to see more ID than that? Because you might still have a tooth left I can help you extract." I said, as I raised my piece to pistol-whip his face. "Now hurry up, Foo-foo boy. I'm getting bored with your all whining."

He spit out a tooth and slurred through a mangled mouth, "I'll be seein' yo ass again – cop or no cop. Bet on dat shit, *guinea* mah fucka! Yo racist ass down on *nigga* homeboys gonna get yo own drawer up da County Morgue. Honky-ass punk bitch! 'Cause I done made yo dumb-ass. How's dat? Huh? Just tell me dat?"

"I'm real intimidated by your threats, especially while you're kneeling. And I'm equally impressed with your proficiency of the English language. But in the meantime, shut the fuck up and do what I say or you'll die on your knees, *homeboy*."

"You da big man now. You got da piece, so dat make you all rough an shit. Ain't dat right, *Skippy*? You da big dawg now."

I smiled and answered, "You're finally right about something." Then I smacked him across the forehead with the automatic. His big head jerked as he fell backwards into a fresh pile of snow. Foo quickly regained consciousness and struggled back to his knees. "And don't call me Skippy. You got anything at all of value to say?" I asked, smiling.

He said, "Oh yeah, mah fucka. Deys somethin' else, all right. Bet yo sweet ass on dat shit, baby!" He handed over a black Velcro wallet and a slim pack of $20 bills secured by a cheap chrome money clip. From his dead partner's pockets he fished out a leather wallet and a thick wad of $5, $10 and $20 bills held together in a roll by a thick, tan rubber band.

"This is it?" I laughed. "This is what you're chancing going back to prison for? This is all youse two fake gang bangers are worth? Damn… Hey, man. I heard they're taking applications for potato peeler over at Royal Castles. You oughta give it a shot. Because you ain't much of a thug – that's for goddamn sure…"

"Here you go, baby boy," he sprayed fresh blood at me through mangled lips. Let's me an you swat dis stem. You know; blood brothers an shit." He handed me a baggie with a few dozen tiny, clear Ziploc bags, each holding what looked like a piece of rock salt. He had a tire air pressure gauge with black scorch marks. I knew it wasn't rock candy. I had smoked my share of freebase when the No-Names and I lived in Florida – back when our jobs were manic runs with dancers, from Miami to Cleveland.

I shook my head: "Nah, you keep that shit, *homie*. Smoke it up real quick good before you get to treatment, because this will be your last hit. Hey! You know what? I got a good idea! Load all that shit up at one time. Can you imagine the rush? That way, maybe you'll luck out and your heart will blow up before you have to sober up – you fucking pussy. Now crawl over here and hand me those wallets and ID, nice and slow. I'll be needing all the cash. Did you pat your boss down for weapons?"

"You got all the heat he pack, lil' man."

"How about you, *homeboy*? You got heat on you?"

The wounded man grabbed his crotch: "Yeah, baby, I got all da heat yo ass need. Check it out. I'll tap dat ass fo real."

"No thanks. I'm not a *bottom dog* like you. I prefer women. And it's not that I doubt an honest gentleman like yourself. But I'd better check your partner for weapons, just in case you might have missed something on accident."

"No, baby boy. Ain't no accidents up in da hood. We keeps its real up in dis muh fucka here, *Jack*."

Out of nowhere sirens blared. I saw flashers off in the distance. It looked as though a squad car was heading our way. With a loud, exaggerated three-Ha laugh I looked at my wrist: "Well, it looks like my partner called it in just as planned."

"You mind I calls yo ass *Jack* stead a *Skippy*? 'Cause we friends, right dawg? I'm wit yo ass all da way, baby. We cool as twin Eskimos, *Jack*. We do it yo way, cuz."

I said, "Ahh, finally! Here's help right now!" I hunkered down before the speeding cop car's lights crossed our path to pat down E Z's long thin body that felt more like a mannequin than human. I let out a sigh of relief as a deafening siren and blinding lights passed. "He's clean. Now stand up real slow, *homie*. You're gonna help me. Nice and easy, or you catch a bullet in your spine. Remember what I said. It's up to you, man. Even though you're flying high as that streetlamp post, you clearly saw what happened. That means I have no qualms about killing again."

"Yeah, we cool, baby. Gwan ahead, dawg. I don't need da man findin' dis stupid muh fucka layin' his dead ass up in here. Just bring heat in on da hood, cuz. Let's do it fo real."

"Okay. Now you're making sense. I'll take his feet and you grab him up top. We're gonna lift him up and then lean him right where that retard was. I want your friend to have the same view that other poor bastard had when he panicked."

"I's da one shot. You take da mah fucka up top."

"No way, player. I only have one hand. And I need to hold onto this piece. So move your big ass before I toss both of youse cocksuckers in the drink and watch you drown. Move it!"

"No can do, pig. You done shattered my shit all up. I can't even move dis mah fucka." Then he pointed a longer finger at me from the hand on his good arm. "You want dis stank-ass *nigga* over da wall? Den you needs a new plan, baby. Dig?"

"Okay," I said, as I stood up, the raging patrol car no longer within earshot. "That's fair. We'll use a different strategy. We'll each grab one of his arms and drag him to the wall. Then just wrap that lanky arm of yours around his chest and prop him up while I push his piss-wet ass up and over. We'll just both keep pushing till he's airborne like a giant turd getting flushed."

"Yeah, you ass is funny fo a pig, mah fucka…"

It was a struggle for two handicapped men and a sack of deadweight. But after some effort we got him up and over. The dead man smacked on top of the ice-covered river, right next to where Bobby-boy had hidden his teeth and everything else. The impact made the hole twice as big as it had been.

"Good boy, *homie*. You do pretty good work for an old fag. You're strong for a junkie. And this whole time I was thinking you were completely useless. Hey! You have any skills other than selling drugs to kids, raping the handicapped, sucking off drug dealers and making deals with cops? I might have a job for someone like you, someone with a strong back and no brains. You do know what a *job* is, right *homeboy*?"

"Yeah, and so do yo ol' lady wit dat stank-ass pussy, be up on dis bridge wit da brothas suckin' big black dick."

I smiled, "Tell you what: You mention my ol' lady again and I'll shoot out one of your eyes. Go ahead. Test me, Foo."

"Fuck you and yo trick-ass bitch. You a cop mean shit ta me. I got yo strong back, bitch!" he said, as he grabbed his crotch again and glared with the meanest, most hateful look yet. When he growled, smoke came out from the sides of his large remaining teeth. His hot blood-tainted breath mixed with the frigid air.

"I'm sick and tired of your trashy mouth. All you do is talk a long line of shit and make faces. Make your move."

"Naw, you da big dawg wit dat piece, right boss-man? You remember da boss-man back in da day, right cuz?"

"Yeah, whatever, *homie*. Just keep your back to me and lean against the edge of the railing. I'll pat you down with one hand. My gun is pointed right at that black snake you're so proud of. You make one fast move you'll be wearing a Kotex where your empty nut sack used to be. That should make a huge impression with those *topdogs* inside the big house, right *homeboy*.

Because that's where you're going if you fuck this up. I'll bet you like *pitchers* better than the *catchers* anyway, right? You probably like it rough, too. Am I right? No pussy for you, right *homo-boy*? I can tell just by looking at you. I'll bet you're a *man's* man!"

As soon as I began to pat him down, Foo spun to his right with a quick elbow-strike pointed at my throat. I tried to turn and duck. His elbow smashed my nose and shattered the eyeglasses Joey got for me. The blow knocked the gun from my hand. I knew my nose was broken because my eyes filled with tears and blood flowed from both nostrils. I squinted and dove for where the gun might be. But the snow was deep and my vision blurred enough to make that an arduous task. He was fast for a wounded man. Foo leaped on me with a barrage of one-armed punches, wildly missing. Some of them punched into that thick layer of snow to smash iced-over concrete underneath. His left arm dangled uselessly while he crashed punches down at me with bloodied, broken knuckles.

Foo yelled, "Ah shit!" He shook out his hand and then repositioned himself to mount me. He sat up tall on my stomach, grabbed my throat and straight-armed down hard on my neck, choking me. "Now you my bitch, mah fucka! I choke yo dumb ass out, den toss yo flimsy ass in da drink wit dose fools. Foo the mah fucka in charge now! 'Cause I'm back, *Jack*."

What? Dizzier by the moment, a familiar voice from childhood echoed through a brain rapidly losing consciousness: *Fight and the pain will go away,* warned inside my head. My air supply had been cut off.: *Never quit. Attack the pain!* Because I was much shorter than Foo, I was able to get my left leg between us and tucked a knee between my stomach and his in order to take in a half of a breath. *All or nothing. Do it now!* I worked more by feel than sight, shifting my position to twist hard to the right to loosen his grip on my windpipe. *I'm blacking out.* I tasted another sip of cold air mixed with my own coagulating blood. With all the strength I had left, I extended my left leg and laid it across the right side of his face to create a little more distance.

Foo laughed and said, "Yeah, dat's it. Leave yo little peg post up dey so daddy can fuck yo ass real hard, baby – just da way you likes it. Punk-ass faggot, you best spread 'em wide fo big daddy. Get ready *Jack*, ol' Foo gonna bust yo sack."

Jerking my head from side to side enabled me to get a quick exhale and inhale and then turn to my right. On remote control, from years of martial arts training, I flipped up my right leg to knee into the bend of his long arm, then up-kicked him to the face and axe-kicked him on the way back down. He hunkered lower to avoid the kicks and to apply more pressure on my throat. I was being suffocated in a pile of snow, in a dream world turning dark and warm. I laced a leg behind his head to apply a figure-four. I had my legs locked. His arm lay across me. With my last traces of energy I secured that forearm with both arms and thrust my pelvis against his elbow, pulling and pushing as hard as I could, I cranked on that arm bar with all I had left.

He growled again, more interested in getting me off his arm than choking me out or hitting me. Breathing in quick gasps, I axe kicked his wrecked shoulder with my heel of my left boot as I tugged at that arm bar. Because I still held his forearm trapped against my chest I was able to thrust my pelvis up higher to hyperextend the elbow on his good arm till it bent the wrong way.

Foo hollered when his elbow snapped in a position no human arm should ever be. I released him. He sat in a daze, breathing heavy. Dumbfounded, he held up his arm to stare at the unnatural shape, trying to comprehend why his jacket sleeve bent the wrong way. Fierce winds kicked up, swinging the broken arm as if it were on a two-way hinge – back and forth like a broken hand of a large clock swaying aimlessly over the six. He watched in shock as his arm swayed while I slid out to reclaim my footing.

That's when Foo began to sob. I actually felt sorry for him at that moment. So I helped him regain some dignity. I chambered one of Joey's thick boots and kicked up and out as hard as I could, smack into his chin. I was amazed to find that he was still alive, let alone conscious. But at least the crying subsided.

Foo's shredded lips resembled pulled pork soaked with purple sauce. Along with a nasally groan, head down and slightly bouncing, he used a split tongue to push out chunks of white teeth, one at a time, like babies do when they first eat hard foods.

"On your feet! Quit whining, you fucking crybaby. Your legs still work fine. Or do you want me to fix those for you too, *homeboy*? Because, swear to Buddha, I'll do it."

"Gwan ahead, badass. Fix me up good, cuz," he slurred through a crushed nose as ragged lips spilled fat clots on snow.

"Okay, *homie*, let's talk. I'm still willing to offer you a deal. But this is your last chance. First, struggle your big ass up here. Up against the wall so I can pat you down. Don't make me arrest you. Do the right thing and you're free as a bird."

He moved slowly. "Say yo gonna fix me good. Dat right, boss-man? Yeah, I pays what I owes. 'Cause I knows da Horrible Hank ass. I seen yo ass befo wit dat *nigga* mah fucka. So dat mean I get da ID now and I get dat cash. Dat shit mine now, baby. Las chance, *guinea* mah fucka. Dig it, *Jack*?"

" I can dig it. I'm a man of my word, *homes*. I see now who holdin' the cards up on the bridge. I'm cool, friend. If I say I'll fix you up, then no worries. If I say you're free as a bird, you'll fly. I just need to make sure you aren't holding. Cool? But hey, why do you keep calling me that name? Who the fuck is *Jack*?"

"Hell yeah, baby. We boph gangsta to da mah fucka. We some street runnin' hoods cool as Biggie and Tupac – long as I get paid. Den we cool, *friend*. Den we foget dis shit. Be bros, right *nigga*? You da big dawg now, right Lil' Jackie? 'Cause I know dose cold-ass gray eyes pierce right through a mah fucka back from da D.H. Yeah, dat yo ass, Lil' Jack, gangsta in a mah fucka. I done made yo ass," Foo laughed, spraying blood on me.

"What's this Jack guy to you?" I asked, quickly scanning the snow for my glasses. "I'm trying to cut you loose. I admit it. I violated all kinds of citizen rights with this arrest. I fucked up. So stand up so I can pat you down, *Super Fly*. But we're cool now."

As soon as Foo leaned against that blood-stained edge where Bobby and E Z had been, he laughed through mangled lips while his chest pressed against the bridge wall: "Stupid-ass muh fucka," he chuckled. "I get lawyered up, take yo ass to court – tell da judge you a racist mah fucka. Da jury ear dat shit up."

"Come-on, friend. There's no need for all that."

"Yo white-ass went all limp, Lil' Jack. Dat's why dem *guinea* mah fuckas squeeze yo punk ass up out da hood. You was munchin' dem sista's while yo boys was out makin' moves. Looks like yo ass fucked up again, Lil' Jackie! You ain't made fo deese streets, baby. You ain't up to da game. You don't get it, man."

"Yeah, maybe you're right, Foo. Maybe I don't get it."

"Ya'll ain't shit, mah fucka. Who da man now?"

"I'll tell you who. *I'm* Jack, motherfucker, and *I'm* back!"

The last sounds Foo ever heard were: *Bam Bam Bam*. Then I jammed him quickly with my body, to keep him from slipping down to the ground. "Check it out. After 63 goddamn years of talking shit, I've turned out to be the ruthless killer so many people used to think I was. HA! How about that? But nobody can ever find out about this," I said to the dead man as I held him into position. I lowered my center of gravity. "How do I ever let my wife know I'm a cold-blooded killer? I could never look my kids in the eyes again if they knew what I did this night. So I need to be precise and quick. Okay, so the smart move is to clean up here real fast and then move on down the road."

With long arms draped over the side of the bridge from when the three shots had entered his back, I laced my right forearm beneath a wet groin for a high crotch lift. His fresh urine was already cold in that cruel wind. I locked my hands together and squatted down to lift and toss him over the edge and into the river in one attempt. Then I groaned out load, straining every muscle in my body. Yet somehow I managed to heft him up and over with one fluid motion.

Adrenaline is my new drug of choice, I thought. With gloved hands, I tossed the shooter's automatic smeared with their prints and blood into the small but hungry mouth in that frozen river and then replaced my own pistol in the parka. Because the 100 foot span had been such a far drop, each body had plummeted completely through the thick layer of ice and vanished towards Lake Erie with the help of a powerful undercurrent.

I stripped off bloody gloves and dropped them. Then I stopped to look around, to check for clues. Using work boots as mini-plows, I kicked drifts of snow over purple puddles which moments before had been a precious life-giving circuitry for two powerful forces now gone – both game and dangerous, both extinguished with a few puffs of hot smoke in that brutal cold.

I slid down with my back against the wall, to sit in snow while I tried to regain composure. I convinced myself, "I'm out of the woods. By daybreak those holes will be iced over like a skating rink. Then this never happened. Fuck-em both, anyway. If they hadn't of done what they did to that defenseless, disabled man they'd still be alive. I'm not a killer. The only thing I do feel bad about is that Bobby-boy. He couldn't understand any of this. Fucking crazy Bobby… In some ways he was the happiest of all of us – just a big child. I wonder who he was, anyway."

I spoke out loud again: "If anyone from Collinwood finds out what I did they'd think I'm a hero." But as far as I was concerned, the bravest thing I'd done that night, on the long span of a frozen bridge, was when I stripped down to my boxers in that frigid weather and kicked off those bloody boots. That biting wind was made of ice crystals and pure torment. Almost instantly my skin went from freezing to hot to numb. I put on the mental guy's clothes and shoes and then wrapped my bloody clothes around the stained gloves and boots like a hobo's pack. Then I slipped back into Joey's black parka just as quickly as I could move. I fished around in the deep snow for my eyeglasses. "I can't see too good, and I can't allow anyone finding eyeglasses up here with my blood on them." I washed my face with snow and packed snow into clotted nostrils till the blood stopped.

But I was stiffening up fast, numb turning to a prickly feeling. On the verge of frostbite, I fished out of a deep pocket of that ninja parka the bottle of water and a granola bar. I chugged a half bottle and devoured that protein bar with trembling bloodstained hands. After I washed them off in a mound of snow I remembered the ID bracelet. The last name had been smudged.

Robert. "Yeah. He was referring to himself as Bobby-boy. So what was this Bobby doing wandering around on a night like this? There's a hospital name and an address on here, too." I squinted in the reflection of a street light. "Let's see… Maybe this poor bastard managed to escape from a mental institution. I guess he thought he'd be safer out here. If only those two bangers hadn't of fucked-over that poor old guy, none of this crazy shit would've happened. This creates even more distance…"

I sat back down before I fainted. "All I did was just respond to a bad situation. That's it. Fucking timing… I didn't mean to hurt anyone. But all that's for another time – if ever. Because all this is done and over with. So now what? What's the next move? Because I sure as shit can hang around here."

I felt around in the snow till I came across an odd shaped lump. It was E Z's wraparound shades, packed with ice but unbroken. I picked ice clumps off them and put them on. "If any locals find me it won't be good. If the cops grab me I'm even more screwed. But I'll freeze to death out here. Gotta move. Time to go somewhere – anywhere. I'll figure it out when I get to wherever it is I end up. Just move away from here as fast as possible – starting right now!"

"I shouldn't have smoked that kid's weed. It made me even weaker than I am. I'm so tired and cold right now I could just curl up right here and… No! Stay vigilant. I was getting way too cocky back there, like it was fun. But this isn't a game…"

During the late-1950s, we Neighborhood kids didn't play regular games. Instead of "Cowboys and Indians," we played "Jailbreak." In our game, killers and thieves eventually escaped. In our world, "bad" guys were always the good guys. So, of course, the inmate team was a preferred side to be on. Prisoners were named after local heroes, some of them names police were yet unaware of the depth of their involvement. But we knew, because everybody in the Neighborhood who was anyone was in the loop. The cops in our games were villains, and given disgusting names like lard-ass; ass-wipe; dick-head; jizz-bag, all who suffered fatalities from imaginary guns shooting invisible bullets. The warden was a psychotic homosexual. His guards were on the take from the inmates while taking it up the ass from him. The real game was to keep common knowledge from our all-knowing justice system.

Many inner-city kids got involved with gangs because of dysfunctional home lives. Although most Collinwood kids had a sense of family, teen years during the late-'60s was a time when innocence faded from chronic disarray. In spite of what had appeared to be conventional values, other juvenile delinquents having voracious appetites like mine role-modeled our own personal gods. We knew we were safe around the gangsters and safe because of them being around our neighborhood. They had money and friends; nice clothes and cars; pretty girls hanging on them and other dangerous men who respected them. So throughout adolescence, besides pro boxers and Pit-bulls, we worshipped them till *we* became C-town's wise-guys.

We played games with the *Click* and the *Bounce*, while boys and girls worried about reputations for gender specific reasons. Collinwood guys held only a few things sacred – most being intangible and irreversible. We aspired to be loyal and game; to maintain the courage and willingness to throw down to the last man; to learn how and when to keep quiet; to maintain and nurture a costly reputation. As students of life, we grew to realize how knowledge comes from things learned and wisdom pays off from things earned – how experience must be lived to be shared.

The animated picture presented to us by the opposition looked clear and simple. Governments and religions invented rules to make money from and to control others with – and they're tax exempt. Evidently we paid little attention to those constructs. But that didn't mean we were strangers to fear and passion or that we lacked morals and values. We made our own rules and adhered to our laws as if they were sacred scripture.

CH XXIV: The Match, Part Two

December 28, 2013: The handlers started towards their respective corners. Rocco couldn't hear any sounds except his own breathing and his dog's rapid heartbeat. But he could tell by the fervent motions of the crowd that some heavy wagering had already begun. He watched as David climbed over the wall with his magnificent specimen in perfect condition. When old Walter signaled to Rocco and David with a wave of his huge hand, all the animated spectators stopped moving and appeared to hush, in anticipation of watching the primal exhibition about to unfold. This was game-dog history in the making. Even though most of the people in attendance weren't typical *dogmen*, all were gamblers and thrill seekers. Nobody in Collinwood who was anybody wanted to miss the match. Everybody who was anybody knew.

Walter waved his huge hand across the room to get the handlers' attention and silence excited onlookers. Rocco's hearing returned like a wave crashing against a break-wall. Everything was too loud and intense. Dickless was in the pit first, tearing at the carpet with his claws, jerking to free himself from restraining hands. He was snarling like a wildcat, showing Bull every tooth in his head. David held his dog by the scruff of the neck with both hands, while keeping the dog's waist secured between his knees, facing him toward the center of the 16' foot square pit.

Rocco held his dog the same way, in a corner behind a line marked with silver duct tape stuck to the short fibered carpeted floor. Bull stood deathly still, facing his raging opponent, slightly crouched and set like a coiled spring. He was emitting a low rumble from his deep chest. His tail whipped the back of Rocco's legs.

Rocco heard whispering and savage sounds emitted from the opposing corner. He was thinking how lucky he was to have a 10-second scratch rule. The handlers would pick up their dogs while out of holds, alternating turns. Some preferred 20 seconds to cross the pit and continue the battle before one got counted out. But he and David agreed on 10, which gave the advantage to the gamer dog. Ten seconds for $10,000.

Deep gameness was usually more prevalent in the smaller weight classes. Generally, very much like MMA fighters, the smaller dogs on average were gamer and faster, while the bigger ones, like pro fighters, were more body-strong and packed more powerful punches. Rocco felt sure Dickless would quit if taken into the deep end of the pool. He just hoped Bull could withstand the terrible onslaught that was coming in the first few minutes. Dickless was known to have a punishing mouth and had inflicted plenty of damage to top competition from the initial release. All his rolls and matches had been quick stoppages.

"Handlers get ready. Release your dogs!" Walter instructed with his bellowing voice.

Both vaulted dead-to-center, a head-on collision of teeth and raw courage. Dickless grabbed a front leg and flipped Bull to his back. Bull set his fangs in the brindle's muzzle, content to stay in holds, to conserve energy and stay out of trouble. Dickless was shaking that leg wildly. Bull bit deeper into his muzzle. Dickless was shaking so hard he was doing as much damage to his own face as to Bull's leg. Dickless let go to move up into a shoulder. He bit down hard. Bull was caught in a bad spot. Blood flowed over his chest. He tried to stand, but found his right front leg was becoming useless. This brindle was a horrible biter.

Rocco feared he might soon be permanently injured. Bull was desperately trying to regain his footing. Dickless braced his long legs, straddling Bull. He bored in deeper, savagely damaging the shoulder. Bull twisted just enough which enabled him to seize the bottom jaw that punished him so. Dickless let go and lunged for a back leg. A stifle joint was where he aimed, but Bull swung away just in time.

Now Bull had the brindle's stifle. He took it right back to his grinders. He bit down with everything he had. Dickless whirled around, catching an ear hold. They kept spinning like a huge pinwheel, each keeping their holds.

Rocco looked at David and said, "I see why you bet this wouldn't go an hour. That dog's a killing machine. Is he game?"

"I'm not sure, because he's never had to make even one scratch yet. But he's the hardest mouthed dog we've ever seen in Canada. Everything we put him on quit in short order."

Whitey heard what David said and called out, "I got another $2,000 on the down dog." His bet was immediately covered.

Curtis yelled, "I got 5 Gs. Come get ya dis befo da ma fucka get his ass kilt. Uh oh, ol' flukey takin' a killin' now."

David turned towards Curtis and said, "I'll take that, sir."

"Ol' flukey gonna take it alright. HAHAHAHAHA! Ya'll about ta take it up in da dookie from ol' flukey!"

"A beast like that shouldn't have to be game. But he's got a dead-game one glued to his ass this time," Rocco assured David. "Come on, Bull, take this poison-mouthed cur out. Shake it out, son." Bull shook hard and the brindle started growling.

"Uh oh, Davie," Whitey laughed. "I think your boy's getting his game test right here in C-town. Shake it up, son. Good boy, Bull. Show 'em how we do it in the Wood."

The pinwheel stopped in a corner. Bull was trapped. Dickless dove into that same shoulder and shook Bull off his feet. Shaking madly, Bull's leg flip-flopped in those massive jaws. David was down on his hands and knees yelling, "Now, son! Finish him!"

Bull was wedged in a corner. Dickless buried himself in Bull's brisket. Bubbles formed on the edge of his lips. Bull was in serious trouble.

The room took on that unmistakable nauseating odor of a dog fight, of fresh blood mixed with wet dog fur and saliva on that filthy carpet. The entire room reeked of death.

Cagootz motioned to Rocco. "We're not beat yet, *coomba*. That brindle bastard will quit. I see it in his eyes. Have faith, kid."

"He can't take much more. I've never seen him this bad. I've seen him two hours before with a good dog on him, but not like this."

"Wait till we get a handle, Roc. If the brindle scratches hard we'll throw in the towel."

"What if we don't get a handle?"

"Hold off and we'll see. Your dog is smart. Faith, Rocco."

"Faith my ass. If Bull's going into shock this is over."

"Do me one favor, Roc. Let me know before you pay them off. Remember, we're partners on this!"

The crowd roared. Bull managed to position himself around. He had Dickless across the forehead and was hanging on for dear life. The brindle dog was still driving the curled up red dog around the pit floor like a Boomer Ball. So Bull changed his grip and took a firm hold of the eye sockets. He was biting down for all he was worth. The Canadian dog let out a loud howl.

"Sing to yo papa, flukey missa mah fuckin' dookie," Curtis giggled. "Make dat nutless ma fucka sang da blues, baby. Bull put da flukey right up dat ol' dookie. I done toll yo ass!"

Danni leaned over the pit wall. "That's my good Bull. Pretty boy, Bull-boy. Shake him out, son. Bring that little bitch home, son."

"Get ready to handle your dogs," the referee directed.

Dickless flipped over his opponent and dove underneath, finally free from Bull's hold. They were both free of holds, but would remain so only momentarily. David, proving to be a good sportsman, snatched up his dog to make a fair handle instead of waiting till Dickless took another bite. Both handlers simultaneously grabbed their dogs and went to their original corners to receive wet sponges.

Rocco sponged off Bull's face and wounded shoulder and then held the cool sponge against Bull's stomach to bring down his body temperature and slow his breathing.

"No turns were called. Red dog's turn to scratch back to his opponent, being the red was bottom dog."

They had 25 seconds facing in their respective corners to sponge down, 5 seconds to face around and get ready before the *scratching* dog used his 10 seconds to continue or be counted out.

"Face your dogs. Red to scratch. Release your dog!"

Bull flew out of his corner, catapulting half way across the pit. When he landed, his right leg gave out and his face smacked the floor. Dickless was growling and bucking in his corner. Bull quickly regained his footing and stumbled on three legs to meet his enemy. Bull flew into Dickless, right side first. Dickless grabbed his mangled leg and shook unmercifully. Bull found the black nose and tried to touch his teeth together in its center. The brindle complained even louder. The audience was ecstatic.

"Flukey crazy in a ma fucka! HAHAHAHAHAHAHA!" Curtis shouted. "Dat crazy ma fucka game in a som-bitch!"

"Keep it down or we'll clear the room," Walter boomed.

Curtis let out a loud, exaggerated whisper while grinning: "Shhh... Okay, now. I be givin' 2-to-1. Who wan some? Come get ya some flukey for yo dookie. How 'bout you, Canada man? You still backin' that chump?" Curtis giggled and whispered.

Bull was finally doing the driving. Dickless was frantic to get away. Bull kept steady on him. He was everywhere Dickless tried to go. He had the Canadian champion pinned in a corner. The brindle looked confused. Bull switched from nose to throat. By then Rocco was laying on his stomach, his face inches from the dogs. He was careful not to touch either dog.

"Shhhhake it up, son," Rocco encouraged. When Dickless howled Bull worked his hold even harder.

Horrible Hank beamed a glowing grin as he said, "I'll lay a thousand to a hundred that your big-time champion won't even make his first scratch."

Dickless back-crawled up the pit wall and flipped Bull over. While they scrambled for top position Whitey yelled, "I'll lay a thousand to a hundred that brindle rides home in a garbage bag unless you pick his cur ass up."

Bull trapped the champion securely in a corner and was burrowing in. He bit down with everything he had. He seemed to be trying to crawl into his opponent's body through its windpipe.

"Shhhake son. Shake it out, Bully-boy," Rocco continued.

Bull rattled the brindle's head off plywood pit walls.

The referee walked over to David and said, "I believe your dog is finished, sir. You ought to pick him up now. He's been a good one for you, but he won't win this day."

"He's on his own!" David snapped like a little cur. "I can't use a stud for breeding without a penis, especially if he's a cull – champion or no champion! So I choose to leave my dog in. I think that Bull dog's minutes away from being dead, anyway."

"Suit yourself," Walter answered. "It's your champion."

Rocco said, if you don't have enough class to save your dog I'll do it for you. "Drop it, Bull," Rocco ordered. "Drop it, son! Come here, boy. Come on, good boy. Come here!"

Bull's glazed-over eyes came back into focus. He looked at Rocco. "Drop it, Bull. It's okay, son. Come here, boy."

Bull released his hold and turned to face his master. Rocco quickly grabbed his dog and headed for his corner. David waited. When Dickless didn't get up to chase Bull he reluctantly handled his dog. They were sponged off while in their corners by their handlers and faced-off for another scratch.

Rocco expected Cagootz would be rubbing it in his face about how right he had been. But surprisingly, not a word…

"Brindle's turn to go," Walter bellowed. "Release your dog. One… Two… Three… Dickless just stood there. Four… Five…" Dickless looked away from Bull and to a pit wall. "Six…." He started out of his corner, but not towards Bull. "Seven… Eight…" Dickless walked to a side of the pit and put his front paws on the top edge of a neutral pit wall.

"Nine… Ten! Winner and new champion, Rocco's Bull."

Horrible Hank shouted, "If you're planning to cull him I'll take him and give him a good home."

Curtis, laughing like a madman, toppled over into the pit. Laying on his back and holding his stomach he asked, "I knows where you ma fucka's can buy a real dawg, wit a dick *and* balls!"

Spuds and Vinny held up their high-balls in plastic cups.

Gus and Filo slapped each other on their colors.

That memorable night of Bull's Championship match staged in The Inn's basement was the night it became evident that five Caucasian gangs in Collinwood had all along been six.

Dickless hurtled the wall. When he landed, a loud crashing sound was heard throughout that huge dingy basement. Those trouble lights in that musty ceiling blackened for a moment. The only lighting came from those blinking holiday bulbs, casting eerie shadows across the large, dark room. Then floodlights seared everyone's vision. Pupils were fighting to regain focus while brains tried to process all that new information.

A shrill bullhorn blared static and almost inaudible commands throughout the basement, echoing off concrete walls: "Don't anyone move! This is a raid! Up against the wall, motherfuckers!"

This was like saying, "Everybody go crazy." People ran over each other, going nowhere.

Danni came into the pit where Rocco was, so Rocco jumped over the wall with her under one arm and Bull in the other. Dickless saw Bull and jumped back into the pit.

Spuds and Vinny were raving like lunatics at the uniformed policemen. They broke ranks and made a dash for the door with a frenzied mob at their heels but were beaten back with nightsticks and pistol-whipped by drawn revolvers.

Dickless jumped back out and staggered over to an officer. He sat on O'Reilly's foot and wagged his tail. O'Reilly shot Dickless in the chest. The dog lay down, wailing a gurgling, nightmarish howl as he profusely bleed from his bullet wound. O'Reilly walked to the two airline crates and shot both little bitches who sat trembling in their cages.

When David scolded them, O'Reilly's partner, Looney Lonnie, shot David in his foot. David cried from the floor, "You can't shoot me! I'm a Canadian citizen, for fuck's sake!"

Rocco stood frozen till Lonnie snatched Bull out of his arms. As a knee-jerk reaction, Rocco struck the officer with a right cross to the jaw – knocking the cop down and his dog free.

O'Reilly drew a bead on Bull and squeezed off a round. Whitey caught the cop with a side kick to his chest – a second too late. O'Reilly folded on the ground next to Bull.

When Whitey and Rocco tried to take the pistol from O'Reilly, a slug of Lonnie's grazed Rocco's left shoulder. So Gus broke Lonnie's shooting arm with a metal folding chair.

Bull, severely injured, lunged up and grabbed Lonnie's thigh. That was the first and only time in his life that dog ever offered to bite a person. But more dead than alive, he let go of his hold and crumpled on the concrete floor, bloodied and panting from a bullet hole pouring blood from his ribcage.

O'Reilly was back up. He clubbed Gus across his temple with his nightstick. Then he put two more slugs into the critically injured dog's chest. Bull's eyes rolled back. His eyelids fluttered. Blood oozed onto the floor even after his final wheeze, till his legs stiffened. Then he just deflated – limp and lifeless.

Rocco dove head-first into O'Reilly. By then Lonnie was back on his feet. He beat Rocco off O'Reilly with a stick and then kicked and stomped him while he was down. When he aimed at Rocco's stomach with his pistol Filo clobbered the cop over the head with a 2" x 4", hard enough to crack the pine board.

O'Reilly staggered back up and stumbled toward the staircase. Hank swung Lonnie by his hair right into Filo, who waited with a chambered fist that caught Lonnie square behind the ear. Lonnie was knocked cold by that brick of a fist.

O'Reilly caught Danni with a fist to her jaw. She went down hard and looked like she had literally pissed her pants. Horrible Hank lifted O'Reilly over his head in a fireman's carry and power-bombed him onto the concrete floor. O'Reilly lay unconscious. As Hank reached for O'Reilly's pistol, Lonnie fired from the ground with his weak hand and grazed Hank's thigh.

Looney Lonnie staggered back up to his knees, held his gun with his left hand and steadied himself against the pit wall as he leveled his aim at Filo. He announced, "Okay, the party's over! Everybody line against that far wall right now, nice and slow so nobody else gets killed. You bikers stand on this end with the two niggers. You too, baby cakes," he waved his pistol at Danni, "over there with your sorry-ass boyfriend and those other scumbags. Help your coon buddy that got shot, Rocco, or you get it next. All you assholes know who I am. And you know I'm crazy enough to do it!"

"You point that thing at my ol' lady again I shove that gun up your ass and shoot through your neck! Understand?"

Lonnie yelled back at Rocco. "You're not built for this game. Your father was a low-life piece of shit, and you're not half the man he was. You got no balls, kid. Open your mouth once more and I shoot your slut of a girlfriend in her flat tits, you bastard of a whore!"

Rocco slowly faced him and smiled: "Go ahead, cocksuckers. Just one finger on my ol' lady and you're gonna have to kill me in front of everyone. Come on. Just say one more bad thing about mother. Go ahead. Then we'll see who's crazy…"

Lonnie hollered, "We don't have time for this bullshit! But we know where you live. We'll be seeing you again – soon!"

O'Reilly was back on his feet: "You *guineas* kill me… You're almost as smart as this scooter trash and these ghetto niggers. Your simpleton Royal Flush flunky now turned head grease-ball in the grease-ball Cleveland mob, Fingers, turned on one of your own just because we said so . . . fucking asshole."

Lonnie laughed, "Yeah, you dumb fucks believe cops! All you cutthroats turned on your own brother, Eggs, when we lied about him being a snitch. You assholes are always talking about loyalty. Shit… As for you greasy bikers, one of your own flea bitten scumbags is feeding us information after Church every Thursday. How do you think we knew about this little show?"

O'Reilly laughed, "These two greasy shines here are still bending over for that little spider monkey, Sonny Magic. What a pathetic crew… No wonder Cleveland organized crime is such a joke in the other states . . . bunch of fucking losers. And these two blow-boys here, Spuds and Vinny—"

"That's enough, O'Reilly! Drop it!" Looney Lonnie ordered. "You losers line up next to those fatherless bastards, hands on the wall, nice and easy and nobody dies tonight. Everybody drop your weapons, wallets and money on the floor right next to you, nice and slow, right where you're standing. Do this right and we let you walk – no arrests. Anybody holds out goes straight downtown. Run and you're dead."

David whined from the floor while holding his foot, "You bastards! You killed our dogs?"

"We fucked your mother, too. So what?" O'Reilly laughed. "Any more questions?"

"We demand to call to the Canadian consulate," David shouted. "We demand our rights as Canadian citizens!"

"Okay, no more Mr. Nice Guy," Lonnie threatened. "From now on it's hardball. I'm gonna shoot another of you

*Canuck*s if you don't hand over all the cash. Hey, I heard you knuckleheads up there named your dollar after me. Is that true?" Looney Lonnie smiled with fresh blood smeared across his face.

While Lonnie collected wads of cash from Canadians and the guys from Pennsylvania, Whitey said, "Hey, O'Mickly, next time you kiss your wife let me know how my cum tastes." He stood and aimed at Whitey. Filo broke ranks, growling as he charged the cop. O'Reilly fired just as old Gus tackled him.

Big Louie fired a shotgun into the ceiling. He screamed, "EVERYBODY FREEZE! That means youse fucking cops, too." All movement stopped. "Put down those guns. Spuds and Vinny, make sure they're unarmed. Then stick 'em back in their squad car. Youse Frog cocksuckers get your sorry asses moving before you wind-up in an American prison gettin' ass-fucked by a tribe of hard pipe-hittin' gorillas – but not before you pay-up. We're doin' this Cleveland style. Now out of Collinwood!"

A man from PA asked, "What about the forfeit money on our bitch; the one you maniacs killed for no fucking reason?"

"Hillbilly piece of shit…" Lonnie chuckled as he slapped the man in the face with a revolver and dropped him. Louie pulled back his suit jacket to expose a chromed, pearl handled automatic. He pulled and held it in his left hand. "I got enough for everybody. Any more questions? You Canadians get lost!"

One of the Canadians was already warming up their van out front. David's son helped him up the stairs.

Whitey phoned Ansel from his cell phone. Lonnie knocked his phone on the floor and stomped it to pieces.

Curtis was told he would be taken to Downtown Cleveland, to the Justice Center, on a parole violation. He laughed, "Hot damn! Here we goes again wit deese muh fuckas. You gots da dookie, baby, 'cause I gots yo flukey right here."

Horrible Hank said, "No worries, bro. I got your back."

Big Louie said, as he pointed a sawed-off 12-gauge that looked like a toy in his huge fist, "Okay youse two cops. Beat it!"

Lonnie and O'Reilly left The Inn with only on prisoner – Curtis, and a bag full of money they had confiscated.

Louie ushered everyone outside and then locked The Inn before local street thugs helped themselves to the spoils of war.

Rocco and his fiancée walked home with Bull's body draped around his neck. Rocco was shoulder–shot from the scuffle with those cops, but the would was superficial. More painful were vague memories of lost dreams, feeling emptiness and uncertainty, though nether of them mentioned it.

Louie, in a new black Cadillac, pulled alongside them. *Click* Rocco had the strongest feeling he was about to be killed. He unwrapped Bull's body from over his shoulders and stepped to the car. Instead, Louie said in a calm tone of voice, "Call Cagootz tomorrow. You'll need to make restitution. He has some work for you. Remember. *Tomorrow*. It's important. Get a hold of him early." Then that long shadow of a car slithered down a side street and vanished into a black hole of nightness.

"Do you need to go to a hospital for what happened to you?"

"No, just as long as I don't get an infection I'll be fine. It wasn't much more than a blood clot – just a heavy period, is all."

"You were brave enough for one day, baby. You can cry now. You're allowed to act like a girl," he smiled.

"We don't have health insurance or money, Rocco. Remember? Besides, I took some of Bull's Baytril pills from when he had that infection in his lungs. Remember you refilled it and then he got better? You said you'd save it for a rainy day. Well, we have a whole script. He won't be needing them…"

"That's dog medicine! Let's wake up, Ma. She'll be super pissed if she finds out we didn't get you someplace right away."

"No, it's people medicine that sometimes is given to dogs. I'm fine, Rocco… Go to sleep."

"You're not allowed to get sick in this country unless you're one of those welfare mamas shitting out a kid a year, or you're one of those rich pricks with the special benefits who works in Washington. You know . . . the ones we hire to make sure we have things like jobs and health insurance…"

"Please, Rocco, not now. We'll talk in a few hours, okay?"

"You sure you're alright? I can get money from Ma. I'll take you to the hospital right now. I'm gonna phone Gina."

"It's almost light out, Rocco. What I need is rest. Please, I'm begging you. I have to sleep now."

CH XXV: Bobby-boy

I stood and sighed as I looked around the area and again over the edge of that deep drop-off. I said to myself, "I'll just keep going the same way I was headed. Why not, right?"

I walked for about ten minutes, carrying my bundle of soiled clothing away from that unmistakable odor of fresh blood pooled up in a purple slush. Their life-force frozen in time. Head down while lost in thought and distracted by my newest physical pain, I thought I saw the glare of lights behind me, lights I hadn't noticed before. A feeling of dread washed over me.

Someone saw me! The snowy air in front of me seemed illuminated by floodlights, just like it would be if I were being tracked by a hunter's spotlight – or worse yet, a cop's flashlight. *I'm getting way too paranoid. It's just a car...* I tried to calm myself with a deep breath. Instead, I got sick to my stomach from the taste of blood in my nose and bile in my throat. That old rush of fear returned like during adolescence when Fingers and I had faced the prospect of being robbed at gunpoint, or killed, or some mega-serious problems with the law. That sick feeling of dread hit my stomach with a wave of nausea. I leaned over and puked thick crumbles of wet granola and water into a mound of clean snow.

Then I thought I heard a new noise, like maybe the slow but persistent sound of tires crunching my hopes on that icy bridge – straight at me. *I should run for it. Somebody really did see what happened. Someone set me up!* But there was no way I could run. I was having a difficult time even walking. *I'm totally fucked.*

A voice called out through the howling wind, "So you're the one! You really went and did it this time, didn't you?"

What's he asking me?

"You're the one. Just admit it!"

I kept walking, head swimming, trying to remember my last moves and figure out my next one. *What have I missed? I have to ditch this gun in that river. But what if it just lays on top of this goddamn ice? Fuck me! There's tons of evidence on me! Double homicide! Hell, they'll even blame me for the naked guy. Jesus Fuck! I even have that mental guy's ID in my pocket! I'm so goddamn screwed. I know . . . I'll just shoot!*

A white fender aimed its headlight at me, reminiscent of countless detective cars I'd seen. It pulled right next to me and stopped. Its lights glared on me like a spotlight, like I was on stage. *No big deal. Just relax. I look like a bum, anyway. They'll ask a few questions and I'll be on my way. If he tries to radio anything in I can shoot him. What have I got to lose? There's no way I'm going to prison for murder – not at my age. Fuck-it...* Hand already in my pocket; I reached for the pistol. *Even if it's two cops, I can get the jump on both of these cocksuckers. There's no witnesses up here at this hour. Not even street cameras can pick up details in this weather.* But I felt all tapped out of bravery for one night. My breathing quickened, heartbeat raced.

That same voice yelled from the car, only much closer this time, "Up against the wall, motherfucker!" All the blood in my head sank along with the same gravity of the situation. I was ready to pass out from exhaustion and fear. I thought: *This year has dished out the two absolute worst nights of my life. Yeah, just fuck-it...*

Someone yelled from a car now parked at my feet, "I said, up against the wall, motherfucker."

I gripped my pistol tighter. Then everything returned to dead silence. Not one sound. I froze like a statue – just waiting. My index finger already putting slight pressure on the trigger, I gradually eased it out of an oversized pocket of Shit-pants Joey's ninja coat. I was breathing fast, getting dizzy.

That same voice called out again, "Hey! I'm talking to *you*! Did you see them, or not? Tell the truth! You did it, didn't you? Just fucking admit it, man!" Then I heard loud music blaring from cheap tinny speakers: "I like Marijuana. You like Marijuana. We like Marijuana, too. Mara – Marijuana."

I turned my head to witness a truly amazing sight: "Well I'll be a motherless fuck!" I muttered in a daze. The pistol was out of my pocket, dangling from a limp arm.

The voice laughed and said, "D.O.A."

"Huh? D.O.A.? Me?"

"The song, mister. It's called 'Marijuana Motherfucker.' You should be able to remember that one. It's from back in your day. It was done by some freak named David Peel in the late '60s. It's a classic, man! You gotta remember that one! But this version's by an old punk band called D.O.A. You like it, mister?"

"Kid, you realize you were a cunt hair from getting shot?"

"You're funny, mister. Besides, I know you couldn't really shoot anyone. You're too nice of a guy for any crazy shit like that. Besides, we're friends. Hop in, mister. The heater's blowing hot as cougar pussy in here. And I dug out another CD you'll like."

"Be right back. I feel like I might puke. Wait right there, kid." I walked off sideways and then hung my two arms over the bridge, pretending to vomit, as I threw the gun down at the frozen river as hard as I could. Then I turned my back on that bridge and stepped into the road to find an open door blowing heat into the harshness of that extremely brutal night. I kicked bloody snow off my boots, got in and closed the door on a chapter of my life that would be best to leave shut and forever locked. "I thought I told you I needed to be alone, kid, that I had to make a deal. Isn't that what we agreed on?"

"Yeah, but you said a deal was coming down at midnight. It's already 12:30, mister. Why are you wearing shades at night?" he laughed. Then he looked concerned: "You mad at me?"

"No, kid. Why would I be angry with my good friend?" His idealistic face reflected a smile lit up by a bluish streetlight.

"Okay then, friend! You know where the roach and lighter are. Blaze up while I put on more scorching blues. Hey, is that the package you had to get, mister?"

"What? This? Ah . . . it's just some dirty laundry, kid."

"Sure thing, mister… But before we blues-out again I wanna say this: I stopped off for a coffee and phoned my mom. She said you could crash for a night. Tomorrow I'm off work. I'll drive you wherever you wanna go. How's that sound, mister?"

"That's real kind of you and your mom. I really appreciate the offer, and it's tempting. But I'll have to take a rain check. I already did make a deal, which means now I need to be someplace else. But that also means I have money for gas now. I need a ride up by the old Cleveland Developmental Center. They call it the CDC. You know where that old place is, kid?"

"Ain't the CDC the hospital for retards and crazies that was near that huge insane asylum up on Turney Road? Ain't that the nut ward folks used to call *Turney Tech*?" The kid laughed.

"That's probably not funny, kid. The mental patients at Turney and the MR people at CDC didn't do anything deliberate to get the way they are. Their conditions didn't stem from bad choices like regular people. They just caught the stink end of a gene pool. Just bad timing is all, when that one wild sperm hit that wrong egg having an extra chromosome. Then boom!"

"My grammy told me that the old mental ward got demolished back in the '70s because workers were torturing and raping those crazies locked up in there. Is that true, mister?"

"Maybe so, kid. I heard the same story."

"So what about that CDC, mister? Mom told me that nursing home for retards got closed down 10 years ago."

"The City of Cleveland condemned the place and sealed off the main buildings. Most of the land got sold to condo developers. But there's still a wing open, rebuilt by private investors. It's for mentally retarded patients who, for one reason or another, can no longer stay with their families. It's very sad."

He looked tense. "Really? Wow... Why do you know so much about nut houses, mister? What's the deal with that?"

I looked over at him as I reached for his ashtray: "The reason I know something about those places is because I used to facilitate group therapy before I was involved in a car accident that almost killed me. I asked if you know how to get there because I'm going to a friend's condo right out by there. I've been off work since I got hurt in a car accident." I shifted the bundle of clothes as some type of evidence to prove my case. "While I was studying to be a therapist I found something real interesting. In the old days addicts used to get sent to mental institutions. As recent as the 1970s, alcoholic women got institutionalized in psych wards for addiction. Pretty wild stuff, huh kid?"

His posture and expression relaxed: "Wow, dude. Really? That's some freaky shit right there. So folk's wives and moms were getting suited up in rubber rooms just because they drank too much? No shit? Goddamn! That really is wild! Let me ask you a question, mister: Do you believe this stuff is really addictive?"

"How many people have you known who absolutely cannot begin their day without at least one cup of coffee? And how many people do you know who might commit pretty serious crimes if they couldn't get a cigarette or a dip?"

"Okay . . . I hear you. So it's up to the individual. I get that. I used to drink coffee, and smoke and dip. But now I hate caffeine and nicotine. They started making me feel like shit, so I stopped doing it. Hey, not to change the subject, but how about if I give you my number, just in case you get jammed up again?"

"You have a pen and paper anywhere in this shit-box?"

"Reach in the glove compartment. Help yourself, mister."

I found a 3" x 5" spiral notebook with a pen stuck in the wire. "Okay, shoot.. I mean, fire away. Never mind... Go ahead."

He said, "If you don't mind, mister, fire up that *doob*."

I set the pad next to me on the seat and lit the roach, took a tiny sip and passed it to him. The weed tasted ashier from being lit and stubbed out. Still, it was as good as the fourth of an ounce of hydro that Horrible Hank gave to us, and a one hitter, as part of our wedding present.

The kid gave me his cell phone number. "Now I'll throw on this ass-kicking blues CD if that's cool with you, mister. But first I'd like to ask you a question, okay?" he said as he faced me beneath a streetlight. Then his voice changed. "Wow! What happened to your face, mister? Damn! Are you okay?"

"I'm like the Wonder Bread man. I just had a little mishap, kid. Didn't you notice it when I was in your car the last time? This weather is treacherous. I slipped and fell. But I'm good to go now. So what was it you were going to ask?"

He hit the joint and asked in a strained voice of little fragments as he was holding in the smoke, "I hope I ain't out of line with this. You don't have to answer. Well… So did you see them out there on that bridge or not? You really did, didn't you?"

I held my breath. *What did I forget? He drives past here every night. He sees these locals out here. What's visible from the road? What's he know? He drove right past blood stains on the bridge and the red snow mounds on the sidewalk. There must be some evidence. And if he noticed it… I need to go back! But what about the bundle of clothes on my lap?* I thought, as I moved them between my leg and the door. "See what, kid?" I slowly exhaled and closed my eyes – waiting.

"You see 'em out there? The snow beavers? You run into any, or not?" He let out a whoop of laughter.

"Ha! Funny… Nope. I didn't see anything or anyone worth mentioning, except for the meeting I had at the crossroads. You were right, kid. It's as deserted as unicorn pussy; a real no-man's land out there. Now if you don't mind, I need to think a minute so I can write an important note. Between it being so dark and me being so zoned, it's tough for me to think straight."

The CD began with some major shredding. That guitarist, whoever it was, was amazing. But there were two singers. One I recognized from years ago.

"That one guy sounds like John Mayall singing . . . but that isn't him playing. Who the fuck is this, kid? This is nice!"

"It's Walter-fucking-Trout, man! He's the fucking bomb!" he said, as he pulled a long dragon hit that cherried the ash which glowed red on his thin face. The weed was drier already, being heated from the last time we smoked. It was able to be smoked like a cigarette, only with much different results. He exhaled a plume of serenity and yelled over the music, "But you called it, mister! You know your blues, too. That *is* John-fucking-Mayall. He's doing a guest bit on one of Trout's CDs. Tell the truth, mister… Do I know good music, or not?" As he laughed, his thin face shone a pale blue from the streetlights. He looked dead.

"Hell yes! I swear to Buddha, kid. You're a bonafide bluesman. You know your shit when it comes to good music, good weed and good people. Right-on with the right-on, kid!"

I opened the pen and paper at hand, squinting to write between alternating extremes of blue streetlights and pitch darkness. I felt like I was having a seizure. The kid carefully tapped out the beat on his steering wheel as he navigated his way through a night in which nobody should have been out driving, let alone walking. I tried to fix my attention on composing a note rather than listening to the hard-jamming electric blues. Quickly, so I didn't lose my train of thought, I scrawled a few words. Then I placed the note in his ashtray, shut it and left his lighter on his counsel, at which time I briefly closed my eyes.

The next thing I knew someone was saying, "This must be your stop, mister. It's the only condo complex out here by this mental academy. But the invitation's still open, friend. You're welcome to come to Mom's for the night. Just say the word."

"I appreciate your offer, my good young friend. But this really is my stop. Thank you for being solid, kid. You're a good man. I do have one last favor to ask of you."

"Shoot, mister. If I can do it, I'll be glad to."

"*Shoot*? HA! I left some notes for you in your ashtray. But I don't want you to look in there till you get home. Promise? Because timing is everything. Right kid? I know I can trust you if you say you'll do it. So do we have ourselves a deal, or what?"

"Sure thing, mister. Mom says I'm the most trustworthy person she's ever known. You got my word. And I want you to know something: It's been my pleasure to be able to help you. I'm a people watcher, so I consider myself a petty good judge of character. I see two types of dudes your age. The first type is a bunch of crotchety old bastards that forgot what it's like to be young, or just too bitter to want to remember. Then there's the other kind, pure assholes because they're trying to *act* young."

"Oh yeah?" I laughed. "I wonder which category I'm in."

"Nether one. You seem to be a cool guy, mister. My guess is you were a smooth younger guy that just happened to get older along the way by accident. Like you said – timing. It's everything, right mister? I see that now. Thanks! I won't forget you, sir."

"You're a stand-up guy, kid. I respect that. It's a rare quality these days. But be careful out there, son. You might be a good judge of character for your age, or even a great one for any age. But there are some real motherfuckers sliming around out and about. Stay vigilant, my friend."

"Right here's my mom's number too, just in case you run into any of them damn snow beavers!" he laughed. "Don't hesitate to call. Hey, I don't even know your name, mister."

"That's true, kid. Thanks again." I exited the car, toting my bundle of laundry as if it were treasure as I approached the strange complex. I ducked behind a row of hedges and hid behind a dumpster, hoping residents at those condos wouldn't see me. *No new lights or sounds. So far so good.* Quietly, I lifted the lid of a large blue container just enough to deposit the pile of filthy laundry wrapped around bloody boots and gloves. *No headlights on the road. I hope that kid is as tired as I am and he goes home.*

I headed for Cleveland's oldest psychiatric hospital. I wondered why the lights were on. But nothing seemed all that surprising to someone stoned who had been blown up and was nearly frozen to death. Especially not to an old man who just killed two gang bangers in a black ghetto while clutching the wristband of a naked mental patient. *Let me try to see this thing under the light.*

While I was hopelessly trying to read that ID bracelet, a brilliant plan came to me like a flash from a camera. It was the type of epiphany to appear during an LSD peak, when one stores it away for later but is too high to remember. I had what seemed like a cagey scheme to get me out of the cold, off the streets and away from anyone wanting to cause me any further problems: *Okay, so how do I break into a mental institution, in the middle of the night, yet blend with all those nuts in there? It says right here, if I'm reading this right, that Bobby was admitted today! And I hate to admit it, but with my hair buzzed and beard gone, that old Jew could pass for my retarded brother. Who knows? Maybe my father was out doing the same shit I was...*

Whoever this Bobby was, the hospital must be frantic to get him back inside. And because I was wearing Bobby's institutional clothing and had his plastic ID bracelet, I figured that if this worked it would be the safest place in Cleveland for me to be. Nobody would look for me there. Although I trusted Shit-pants Joey as much as I was capable of trusting anyone outside of family, his phones constantly ringing bothered me. And that at least one more person knew I was alive, even if it was one of my oldest friends, freaked me out. That made two too many.

I paced back and forth, trying to figure a way to get myself inside a mental institution, what appeared on that night to be a safe haven. I kicked around near the dumpster till I found a rock. I figured I'd break a window. Just as I was almost to the main walkway I got startled half out of my wits. A huge man hollered in a deep voice, "I gotcha now, by God, ya crazy bastard!" A flashlight temporarily blinded me.

My first thoughts were: *One of the crazies escaped! Why the fuck did I ditch that gun? I can't fight anyone else. I can barely walk.*

The strange man's voice asked, "Bobby-boy? Is that you, son? What the hell happened to your face, boy? And why did you make a run for it with ol' Leroy's keys? We didn't even have you all the way processed in, son. You trying to get us fired, boy? *Hmph*! I don't even know why I'm wasting any oxygen on a darned fool like you! You ain't much of a talker, besides braggin' on those damned invisible buckteeth. Come on, boy. Foller me! We're going inside right now!" the big voice ordered.

My response was, "Yeah, I got vuck teef on."

"Yeah, yeah, we know. We heard all about your damn buckteeth when your ol' auntie's lawyer dragged your pitiful ass in here." Then he finally redirected the beam away from my face. As soon as my eyes readjusted to the dark I saw a large overweight man with a brown buzz cut. He said, "It's just Otis, boy. I ain't gonna hurt you none. Not yet, anyway… You'd better not make another run for it! Hear? Damn… I never thought I'd be so happy to see another damn retard. I could almost hug you!"

"Yeah, I'm Vah Vee Voy. I got vuck teef on. See 'em?"

"But first I need to frisk you. I need Leroy's keys back, boy." He patted me down quickly but found nothing. "No keys? Damn-it! That old bitch of a nurse might still take our jobs, after all! Well, let's get a move on before you turn into some damn *Heebsicle* out here. So come on, Jew-boy. Get your dumbass back inside before you catch your death. Hear me?"

"Yeah, vuck teefner," I replied, as I allowed the obese man to nudge me forward with his flashlight. I wondered: *What the hell am I getting myself into now?*

CH XXVI: That Collective *Click*

December 29th, 2013 – pre-dawn: Rocco and Danni showered together in silence inside their tiny bathroom after one of the worst nights of their lives. She put bloodied panties in a freezer bag, remnants of their two-month old fetus, and dropped them in the trash. Normally a fastidious person, Danni towel-dried her short hair, dumped the wet towel on their bathroom floor on top of her dirty clothes and quietly followed her man into the bedroom. She brought a clean, dry towel to put under her.

They lay with their backs pressed together, each looking at opposite sides of a cheaply paneled and skimpily furnished room. Danni looked at her graduation picture on an old chest of drawers as if it were a TV show of an old corny movie. The color 8'x10' photo was framed in fake wood and had been set on a low white dresser which held most of her clothes – black jeans and black T-shirts, small black under-wire bras and skimpy black panties. The happy 18-year old girl dressed in white in the photo, bravely smiled into the camera. She was still full of life and determination. She exhaled a slow, deep sigh, curled up in a fetal position while pretending to sleep. She tried not to time her breathing with Rocco's or she'd be awake all night. She lay there completely still, trying not to think about current events.

Rocco stared through their small digital clock with its glowing green numbers, quietly glaring 01:11 a.m. It was almost New Year's Eve of 2013. But his thoughts drifted to happier times when life was simpler for him and his mother. His vision blurred out of focus. Almost lost in childhood thoughts, he listened to Danni breathe in sync with his every third heartbeat. He knew she was wide awake by her breathing pattern and wondered if she was ready yet to talk. *I fucked-up, big-time*, he thought, as he remembered Bull's faithful Pit-bull grin. *Dogs can't read. They don't have Bibles. My dog had a concept of God and it was me.*

"You sure you're alright? I can get money from Ma. I'll take you to the hospital right now. I'm gonna phone Gina."

"It's almost light out, Rocco. What I need is rest. Please, I'm begging you. I'm going to faint. I have to sleep."

"It's amazing how everything changed so quickly. Just one bad call is all it takes. All this violence," he whispered. "I can't do it anymore. First my father, and now the best friend I've ever had. Bully gladly laid down his life for me. And I let all this happen just because of some motherfucking money we didn't even get! Now my car won't start and I might need a lawyer. I should have listened. Ma and Pop warned me to stay away. Uncle Pazzo warned me, too. I knew better, but I did it anyway!"

"We need sleep, babe. We have another big day coming up. But the worst is behind us. You'll see. Everything will be brighter under a new sun. Goodnight, Rocco. I love you."

"Pop told me in his own way not to ever match Bull again, but he left the decision to me. What an asshole I am. Now I'm indebted to this fat fuck, Cagootz. I'm so stupid. The signs were all right there. Pop even warned me in treatment, 'Put it all on that intangible scale in your mind, negatives on one side and positives on the other. Then see which side weighs more. Do the right thing at the wrong time to find out how much it's worth. My father said to make sure you start the way you plan to continue, the way you want to finish. He told us to pay attention to the subtleties. I knew the timing was all wrong, Danni. That *Click* was gonging inside my head like electric symbols. But I totally ignored it. I deserve all this and more for what I did to you and Bull."

Danni began to weep: "I'm so sorry, baby. All this is my fault. You never would have done any of this if it weren't for me. I hope you can find it in your heart someday to forgive me. I shouldn't have been so selfish. And now our Bully-boy is gone. *Agh*... I can't even stand to think about him trying to protect us, even after what we did. That look in his eyes when the first bullet hit him. *Fuck*! I'm so, so sorry... I'm even sorry about crying so much, and especially for having to keep saying I'm sorry. That word 'sorry' isn't even close to being the right one. I fucking hate myself for making you do this."

Rocco wrapped a firm tattooed arm around Danni's slender waist. "Listen real close, okay? Nobody can ever make me do anything. I did exactly what I wanted to do, just like always. I could have called Uncle Pazzo, but I was too proud. I could have asked Ma for help but I didn't. I could have robbed a bank, but instead I let Bully put *his* ass on the line. I hate everything about this – especially what a coward I am."

"Our dog is *dead* ... and now I lost our baby! What the fuck were we thinking about, Rocco?"

"You know what? You were right when you asked me to forgive you. And I do. Now I'm asking for your forgiveness. We can't blame each other, and there's no sense torturing ourselves. It's done, and that's that. This is the worst thing I've ever done.

So this is as good a time as any to learn. We can't beat ourselves up for the rest of our lives. It's history, and that's it. Instead of picking on each other, or killing ourselves for what can't ever be undone, let's grow from it. In the morning we'll make a plan. Let's make today the first day for us making better decisions?"

She placed both of her hands on his protective arm as she whispered, "It can't get much worse, can it?" She voice quivered like a lost little girl. "Somehow I'll make it up to you. I promise."

He hugged her closer and softly kissed a flawless shoulder. "One more thing, Danni. I've been laying here thinking. How come Cagootz wasn't down there when all that shit jumped off? And why did the cops back off when Louie pulled and fired an illegal weapon? Something stinks like dead fish around this whole so-called bust. There's something else missing."

"Whoa! Really? I didn't notice. I was too scared. Are you absolutely sure?"

"Yeah, baby, just as sure as I'm Jack's son. He knew."

"Fuck me... So what's next, Rocco?"

"I guess we'll find out. Good night, baby. I love you."

The phone woke Rocco from a dead sleep. He tried to open eyelids stuck together from dryness, squinting to find Danni's half of the bed already empty. He heard his answering machine catch an incoming call. He dipped the tips of a thumb and finger into Danni's water glass on her nightstand and dabbed water on his eyes to moisten them enough to be opened. Then he sat on the edge of the bed, hands on his face, and shook his head in disbelief. "How the fuck could I have been so ignorant to walk into that trap? Like those greedy fucks can actually be trusted? My father would have seen this coming a mile away. I'm such a coward, weakling pussy motherfucker." Slowly, he stretched and walked into the front-room to check the caller ID.

Danni, in new black lace panties, staggered her way back to their bedroom like a zombie. He watched and thought: *Even when looking sexy is the furthest thing from her mind she's still amazing – maybe even more-so.* Rocco looked at the message to see his mother's number. He phoned: "What's up, Ma? You okay?"

"Your father's friend phoned last night. We need to talk."

"Now, Ma? I got some real important shit to take care of today. Can't it wait till we come by for supper? We'll come over later to eat with you and Gina, okay?"

"Of course. But I need you here. Just for a few minutes."

Tessa hung up. Rocco knew better than to call back to haggle when she ended a conversation like that. He put unfrosted cinnamon Pop Tarts in their little white toaster oven. The aroma drew a sleepy Danni out of the bedroom like she was under hypnosis. Slumped over at the table, her small, firm breasts rested on crossed forearms.

Gina arrived within 10 minutes, wearing tight jeans and a white T-shirt with a thin brown leather jacket. Rocco came out with Danni. All three dressed similar. He set his 4 lb. lump hammer and construction grade crowbar in back.

"Has Ma cooled off yet? Because I got shit to do."

"Sorry, I'm still half-asleep. But you know how she gets."

"I'll drive, Gina. Did she say what she wants?"

"I'm okay. She wouldn't discuss it, and I know better than to push it. It is what it is, little bro. So let's get this over with."

"Okay, fuck-it. Let's go. But I gotta hurry."

Gina pulled into a cracked cement driveway, up to an old frame double house owned by Tessa's best friend, Carly, bought from drug money earned by Curtis over the years. Tessa was staying on the first floor. They walked in without knocking. All of them left their shoes on a clean plastic tray by the front door.

Gina said, "She's in her bedroom, bro. Danni, I apologize. Ma said just me and Rocco. I'm really sorry, honey. You know how she is."

"That's cool. I'll sit by the sun." Danni padded barefoot to a wooden rocker while Rocco and his sister entered the room.

"What's up, Ma? Why you want us here so early? You okay?" Rocco looked worried when he saw her.

"Rocco, Daddy's friend phoned last night." Tessa said, in a slurry voice as she sat in bed holding a newspaper. She was dressed in shorts that used to be sweat pants and a large black T-shirt that had the words *I'm Jack & I Want More* printed in bold red lettering.

"Which one of Daddy's friends?" asked Gina.

"You know who I mean. Quit being cute."

"Are we're talking about Chilly again?" Rocco asked.

"Shut up and listen! Lonnie and O'Reilly were still on unpaid leave, even though they were in uniform. They were both out of service from monitoring a jewel heist with their squad car radio for Doyle Kelly."

"That's old news, Ma. Is that why you called so early?"

316

She continued as if he hadn't spoken: "They claim last night was a citizen's arrest. Your godfather gave a statement to the Cleveland Plain Dealer. It's all right here."

"Who, Uncle Mike? No shit! This should be good news!" Rocco said, looking at his sister and finally seeing what Gina must have looked like as a frightened little girl.

"I'll read it. Sit down, both of you," Tessa ordered. 'A professional dogfight was stumbled across late last night by two off duty Cleveland policemen. It was reported that men and dogs from as far away as Canada and Pennsylvania were present. City Prosecutor, Michael Colombo, stated 'All dog fighting and assault charges have been dropped because of countless violations committed by the arresting officers who both were out of service at the time of the raid. Each officer will remain on indefinite suspension pending results of a thorough investigation'. Come in, Danni. I know you can hear us. Rocco's Uncle Mike is in tight with all the big-shots in Cleveland and Ashtabula County."

Danni stood in the doorway. Her eyes welled up with tears. "What's that mean?"

"That means the worst part is over," Gina laughed, hugging her future sister-in-law.

"Rocco, he told me they sent men to kill Daddy."

"Uncle Mike said that in the newspaper, Ma?"

"Of course not, you idiot! You know what I'm talking about! Don't you start with me!"

"Why are you doing this, Ma?" Gina asked, crying and stroking Tessa's long blonde hair.

"You keep quiet too, Gina. I'm not finished yet," Tessa said, while patting Gina's leg. "Chilly said Cagootz isn't done."

Gina began sobbing: "Ma, please, we've been through this whole Chilly thing before. You promised you were better."

Tessa screamed, "I know that! I told you to shut up and listen, didn't I? He said it was those same men who killed Mr. Brown's wife. And the same ones who killed your biker friend, that Animal. You can remember those incidents, can't you?"

"Of course. Everybody remembers these things. But that doesn't mean someone named Chilly said it. Ma, I'm gonna take you back to the hospital for a check-up later today, as soon as I get back. I want you to talk to that nice doctor again, okay?" Rocco asked, over his sister's sobs, as he touched Tessa's hair.

"Listen to me, you little mothering bastard! I'm not going anywhere near that hospital. Quit running your mouth till I'm done! And don't you dare condescend to me!"

"I'm not, Ma. We're just worried. Look at poor Gina."

"Auntie Carly called. They found Uncle Curtis."

"They *found* him, Ma? I was just with him last night!"

Gina cried, "Some kids found him in a trash bin. His face was all shot up. This part is straight business, bro."

"*This part?* Just what the fuck is that supposed to mean, Gina?" Tessa screeched, moving her hand from patting Gina's head to tightly gripping her wrist. "Are you saying I'm making up all the other stuff?" Tessa's eyes were bloodshot and glassy.

"No, Ma, of course not. I'm just very confused right now. And I'm really very scared and sorry, okay?"

Rocco yelled, "Ma! You're hurting her. Let go!"

"Both of you get out of my sight! No! Gina, you come here and sit. I'm really sorry, honey. I didn't mean to squeeze your arm so tight. I'm at my wit's end. Are you okay, sweetie?"

"No worries, Ma. I'm fine." Gina smiled through tears.

"Rocco, I'll see you and Danni for supper. We're having macaroni. Danni, have you told my son about losing the baby?"

Danni avoided Rocco's look and began to cry. Gina stopped crying and appeared to be shocked.

"Is she right, Rocco?" his sister asked.

"Okay, Ma. Just get some rest. I'm real sorry about Uncle Curtis. I'll go visit Auntie Carly tonight if she wants company."

They walked out of the room with their heads down. Gina gently touched Danni's shoulder and then carried her tiny boots to her. She said, "I'm not about to try to tell you everything happens for a reason. I do believe in bad luck and coincidences. And I also believe we all love you, more now than ever."

"I'll tell you what I believe. I believe I finally feel at home somewhere. I've been looking for this place since I was a little girl." She grabbed Gina and hugged her as tightly as she could while she wept with her face pressed firmly against Gina's chest.

Gina drove, all three of them still in a daze, to The Inn to help eradicate the aftermath of that surreal night of the match. Rocco knew it was his responsibility to get rid off any evidence.

Danni confessed, "I should have told you, Gina. I was going to say it. I'm so sorry for all this. Then just now I heard all the yelling and screaming. I wasn't trying to listen. I couldn't help but hear some of what was being said. Is Ma getting *sick* again?"

Gina ignored the question: "We'll hold supper for you two. Ma's making her baked rigatoni with the ricotta, and using that extra lean Italian sausage from the butcher. Your favorite, little bro. Nothing better to liven up the spirits than a bowl of Ma's homemade pasta. I'm helping her, meaning I'll be doing the work and she'll be issuing the orders," Gina laughed. "Oh yeah, and Ma said for you to take this. That's why she told me to stay. She said Daddy told her that he wants you to have it... Fuck!" She handed her brother a loaded pistol. "Be careful, bro."

"I won't be hungry for awhile. I'll bring Danni by if we can catch a ride. But don't wait, okay? As to Pop's piece: I think I'm gonna pass for now. I'll be tearing things apart and it'll just be in the way. Besides, if they see I brought a gun it could cause problems. Anyways, I'm so sick of all the violence, Gina. I can't do it anymore. This did something to me. I'm a changed man. You'll see. I've learned some important lessons from all this."

Gina tucked the pistol in her waistband and hopped in her car with them: "Okay, whatever... But Ma's having some psychic vibe like daddy used to get. And I can't just ignore it. I've seen Pop do weird shit like this too many times. Ma said to make sure you take it. That's why she wanted you here, besides to tell you about Uncle Curtis. But she got so pissed off at me she forgot to give it to you. Maybe there's something to what she was saying. I think you should take it, bro. Those mob guys don't give shit if you've changed or not, unless you're one of them."

"I'm cool. Besides, I can't afford to catch a fresh case."

"Well, if you need anything, whatever it is, Ma said for you to call and we'll be right over. Don't think you're imposing. You're not. The only thing keeping Ma alive is being useful to us. We've become her sole purpose. And I gotta tell you: I don't like the way this whole thing feels, either. You know what Daddy calls the *Click*? Well, I have it and so does Ma. How about you?"

"Yeah, sometimes it's clearer to me than words and actions. I feel it big-time, too. But we're all hyper-aware from all the crazy shit that's happened in the past 12 hours. There's a lot of static in the air, bro, lots of negativity closing in."

"What about that intangible scale he talked about for weighing possibilities and looking for *hypotheticals*?" Danni asked.

"No worries. If I sense anything looks dangerous I'll get you out of there." He's insisting you be there because you work there. And you can't afford to get fired. With that said, Rocco and his tools headed away from that warm car. Danni tentatively followed a few steps behind. She mumbled, "I feel it, too..."

It was that awkward day, December 29th, a Sunday wedged smack in-between Christmas of and New Years Day. The front door of The Inn stood closed. Rocco had a sudden ray of hope till he tried the handle. He let out a heavy sigh as he and Danni entered. They went down those horrible steps to find Louie and Cagootz dressed in gray work pants and white T-shirts. That was the first time they had seen either of them without expensive suits. Christmas lights still dangled from cobwebbed rafters. He felt like he was in a dream of a weekend acid peak.

"Good morning, Louie. Cagootz, do you guys need any coffee?" asked Danni in a timid little child's voice.

"Morning, guys," Rocco said, as he got right to work. With his hammer and crowbar he tore off a two-foot high, 16-foot long section of pit trimmed with 2" x 4" pine studs top and bottom. Their ends had been nailed to other walls forming three parts of a pit difficult to look at. He was in a hurry to transform it into a harmless pile of lumber. He unscrewed the top and bottom rails with an electric drill, separated that into two 8-foot lengths, and then unscrewed that into four reinforced, 4-foot lengths.

It had been deigned with shorter plywood sections screwed together on long headers and footers so when not in use it could be disassembled and stacked in a small storage area without it looking anything like what it was. The pit had been Sally-boy's design. Rocco saw that sobriety treated Sally-boy well. His brain was working almost normal. Meetings were paying off, and being a lead speaker at AA leads gave his life meaning.

Each 4' x 2' section of plywood had been trimmed with chunks of Wolmanized lumber. The pit had been made to last. But Rocco knew he would never use it again. Although that experience had been a valuable lesson, he had a bad feeling school wasn't over just yet. "Any news about last night?"

"Fuck all that, Roc. Drop that and pay attention for once. We got some serious questions of our own," snapped Cagootz.

"Questions, huh? I have a few. But go ahead, you first."

"It's okay, boss. The kid said go ahead," Louie baited an irate Cagootz. "That means you can talk now. Rocco just said so."

"First of all, gimme that fuckin' crowbar and drop the hammer. We ain't ready for all this pounding. We need to talk."

"Sure. Communication is the *doorway* to making a bad situation better." He looked at Danni and glanced at the stairs. She inched closer to the steps but moved her eyes from side to side to let him know she wasn't leaving without him. Rocco looked edgy. He set the tools next to one of the 4" x 4" support posts to face Cagootz. "Okay, what's up?"

"We lost a lot a money last night, kid. Plus, you were already into us for a chunk. You know what that means, right?"

"I saw Louie collect from them. Everybody saw."

"Oh? Then you must be saying I'm a liar. Or maybe you're saying Louie here's a rip-off. Which one is it, Roc?"

"Forget it. Maybe I made a mistake during all that confusion. But the bust was bogus. It's in the newspaper and everything. I saw it. Those cops did everything wrong. They're fucked. We can all *walk away* from this." Rocco eyed his fiancée.

Danni started to cry. Rocco looked at her and snarled, "What did I just say?" He glanced again at the steps leading upward and out of The Inn, then back at her.

"We don't have any money, Cagootz," Danni said, her head held bravely up high but her face wet from tears. ". We were in bad shape *before* the match, which was the only reason we agreed to do this. And now were totally screwed."

"Shut her up, Rocco," Cagootz warned, as he tossed the short thick hammer towards Louie. It bounced off the concrete. Louie had to sidestep to keep from getting hit. "It's simple. You owe us. So you pay with money or favors. One way is as good as the other for us. We're not trying to be hard to get along with. It's just business, kid, and you know this. Ain't that right, Louie?"

"What's on your mind, Cagootz?" Rocco asked, as he puffed out his chest. Veins popped on his neck and forehead.

"Okay. Let's get right to it then. First of all: you were so scared you missed the most important piece. Those fuckin' cops walked off with all the money. Now they're making out like we have it. Our reputation went right down the shitter."

"Are you serious? The cops scammed the scammers?"

"Oh, is that funny? Well, then you should like this one: You're gonna bring that hillbilly biker kid here for a late night party. It's time. *Capisce*? This shit should've been cleaned up years ago with those grimy cocksuckers."

The Wong Gongs would kill me if I did that. No way. Besides, Whitey's my best friend. So never that. It's gotta be something else . . . anything else."

"*Anything*? We're trying to be fair. Okay, whack Doyle."

"Come on, guys. You know I'm no killer. Besides, nobody can get near that guy. He's protected better than bin Laden was. Anyway, I'm no gangster. I'm a college-boy dogman"

"You turned us down twice already. We'll offer you door # 3, but that's it. I've been thinking about giving my girl, Danni, a promotion and raise to thank her for all the pleasure she's given us, and so she can work off the loan I bought from Sonny."

"Careful, Cagootz," Rocco said, raising his voice with a dark glare. His thick tattooed arms flexed as he clenched fists hardened from years of training on a 70 lb. leather bag.

"Easy does it, kid. It's not what you think. You're too touchy. This kid reminds me of somebody. Don't he, Louie?"

"You know what? Now that you mention it, he reminds me of some bust-out," Louie nodded his long face in agreement.

"Let me guess," Rocco said, with a disgusted look. "I'll bet it's Jackie. Am I right?" Rocco glanced at Danni.

"Maybe. First things first," Cagootz said. "So let's get back to that other thing – the thing about the side-job. You know; the part about how she'll be dancing nights here in the basement so she can work off the weekly Vig. Sort of help out with bills and shit, since all this is her fault anyways."

"Let me explain something right here and now!" Rocco growled through gritted teeth. "You stupid fucks even touch her the wrong way and you'll be forced to kill me. Are we clear?"

"Hey! You were right, *coomba*," Louie sneered. "This fucking kid not only looks like that dead guy. He even acts like him. Genetics is pretty amazing shit when you stop to think about it. Like those *shit-bulls* of his this kid thinks are so game."

Cagootz hefted the large crowbar: "Yeah, but I gotta admit it, Louie. That fucking Jackie had mega-balls for being the low-life, nigger loving piece of shit. Okay, enough fun and games here. Let's get back to work."

Rocco heard what sounded like a series of sneezes. Danni placed her hands over her face and sobbed each time she inhaled, making strange noises bordering on hysterics.

"Excuse me, guys. But I gotta get her home. Danni don't understand this humor. I'll drop her off at her mom's and be right back to help out."

"Hey, Danni," Cagootz called over to her. "Your mom's Christine Troia, right? We all used to hang out together back in the day. You remember Chrissie Troia, right Louie?"

"Who? Chrissie Troia? Oh yeah. That fucking whack-job Sicilian broad from Five Points that used to fuck the Mick?"

Danni stopped crying. Mascara smeared across her cheeks when she wiped her eyes with the backs of trembling arms.

"What?" she asked, all wide-eyed, still on the verge of hysteria.

"Oops! We thought you knew about that Irish piece."

Danni and Rocco looked stunned, staring at one another, almost as if all the other madness up until that point had been overshadowed by this brand new piece of insanity.

"You might've made a mistake here, *coom*," Louie chuckled as he slowly shook his huge head. "I think maybe you let the cat outta the bag."

"You see, Danni, we're your friends," Cagootz grinned a mouthful of crooked teeth yellow from years of chewing on cigars. "These other people in the Neighborhood know, but nobody bothered to tell you. If it was me that was a bastard kid, I'd want to know who the stud was. Of course, *my* mother wasn't out whoring around. She was married. So I know who my father is, unlike youse two little bastards."

"What do they mean, Rocco?" she asked in slow motion as if she were in a trance. "What's happening, babe?"

Rocco felt true terror for the first time since he was a child, not so much for himself as it was for his girl being trapped in a basement with angry killers. And the quicksand was getting thicker by the second.

"Enough! Chicks don't understand these kinds of jokes."

"Yeah, the kid's right about this," said Big Louie. "There ain't nothing funny about today *or* last night, when we lost all that money from some punk who's already asshole deep into us."

"You know what, kid? I kind of liked you. You had quality. We could have used a young guy like you in our organization," Cagootz said, while looking from Rocco to Louie, still holding the crowbar. "It's too bad, really. What a waste."

"Yeah, too bad," Big Louie agreed. "It was the same way with his old man. Jackie had everything going for him, except one thing. If it was me, I might've been able to overlook it. But you know how Fingers is. He don't forget anything. Yeah, *coom*, genetics is pretty amazing what kind of shit runs in families."

"When you're right you're right, Louie. But for truth, *coomba*, even the Mick had potential. Too bad your father wasted his talents being a double-dealing scumbag, honey. He was a natural for the rackets, a born leader with a good business mind."

"Are you really saying the Mick was my real father?" asked Danni in staggered disbelief. "Does that mean those creeps, Doyle and Maureen Kelly, are my cousins?"

Cagootz laughed: "This fuckin' broad kills me, *coom*."

Louie proceeded like she hadn't asked a question: "I have to disagree about the Mick being a natural leader," Louie wagged his long head. "Unless we're talking about being the head of a pack of rats. That piece of shit was giving information to the Feds the whole time he was running the docks. He didn't get whacked soon enough, in my opinion. In fact, I think his whole rat bloodline should be exterminated. Know what I mean, *coom*? When you think about genetics and all, the turd doesn't fall too far from the asshole. Like some other asshole I can think of."

"I know exactly what you mean and couldn't agree more, *coomba*," Cagootz said, as he studied Rocco's every move. And while we're already on the subject of fathers: Kid, do you know why we never came after Jackie for all those years?"

"Yeah . . . of course I do…" Rocco sniggered and nodded his head-full of wildly blown-out, long and curly black hair. His cold gray eyes penetrated defiantly back into the fat man's dark glare. "That's just common sense. Even a mole knows when an old tomcat's watching. Even a bat knows when there's a wall."

"What the fuck are those smartass remarks supposed to mean?" growled Big Louie, as he moved in even closer. "You got something to say? Get it off your chest!"

"Nothing. Skip it," Rocco said, as he looked over to Danni and frantically jerked his eyes at the steps leading out.

Cagootz continued, "Yeah, I suppose you're right, Louie. We needed to take a closer look at that fucking Jackie. He had real potential. That crazy motherfucker was game right to the bitter end. Am I wrong about this, *coom*? I mean, from what I hear, he never even flinched. And the best part is: we think he actually knew! Ain't that what you heard too, Louie? You figure Jackie knew what time it was that day his car turned into a piece of charcoal? Yep, that Jackie was a natural."

Big Louie chuckled as he wiped a huge hand over his face, "You crack me up, Boss. You're the one who's a natural, a natural born comedian. I gotta let youse two kids in on a secret. Cagootz is a world-class ball-buster. You never know when he's kidding."

Rocco walked closer to Cagootz, tilted his head back and asked, "Hold up now. Wait awhile. Are youse two saying what I think you just said? Let's back up. Tell me again, okay? What's this you heard about my dad and his car?"

Louie took a few large strides to get behind Rocco. He breathed down the top of Rocco's head, "You're the one that better back the fuck up, kid. We're just speakin' *hypothetically* here.

You remember what that word means. Don't you, college-boy?"

Rocco turned to face him, "Sure, Louie, no problems. Youse guys know me. And I know what that word means."

"Is that a fact? Then why don't you tell us what *hypothetically* means since you're so fucking smart, college boy," snarled a pissed-off Cagootz. He was insulted that Rocco dared to defy two killers, and in front of a witness.

"Well, what it means to me is what my Pop used to say. Youse guys just remember him as a crazy Sicilian kid from the old neighborhood. But he's very smart. I remember him as being the greatest man alive and coolest guy I've ever known. Anyways, he shared these nuggets of wisdom with me and my sister."

"You mean that colored broad with the great ass? You actually admit to that thing being your sister? Aren't you ashamed, kid?" Louie chuckled again.

Danni froze in horror at what Rocco's reaction might be. Rocco looked at her pleadingly and back at the steps leading out.

Rocco snorted and hockered on the floor. "Okay, fuck-it. You know what? Keep it up with this type of no-class bullshit. I promise you're both gonna look like you've just been in a fight."

"Sorry, kid, but I got a better idea. *Hypothetically*, we can just fuck both of youse little bitches up the ass."

Rocco ignored the comment, which shocked Danni even more than what Louie just said. "One of the things my Pop tells us is, 'Hypothetically, everything is timing.' I learned a lot from my father. He's my hero, and nothing you can say will tarnish that." Then Rocco beamed an uncharacteristic smile and looked over at his girlfriend. She noticed his eyes didn't match the smile. *Click* "When we were kids we used to figure the word *hypothetically* was a fancy term for someone being in cold water for too long. Then our cousin, Fingers, told us it's a stairway to new ideas. You remember, Danni, when I told you what Ma's cousin, Fingers, said about other ways of getting shit done?" Rocco asked, as he again looked at the steps leading up to the bar and freedom. He refocused on Cagootz: "Isn't my cousin, Fingers, your boss?"

"Who me? I never had a boss, kid. Sometimes I work *with* people. And I agree," Cagootz said. "*Hypothetically*, timing really is everything. In fact, you got no idea just how right you are about this," he laughed, as he glanced over at Louie. "Look at this fucking kid… I swear to Buddha, *coom*, I'm gonna miss having him and his mick ol' lady with that fine ass around here all the time. No shit, kid, you got some brass balls for a bastard child.

That must have come from your mother's side, right?"

"Yeah, *coomba* . . . no shit. Their bust-out cousin, Fingers, would've even been proud of this kid," Big Louie grinned. "That's if Fingers ever found out about how this kid handled himself under real pressure. You know what? I like this kid, *coom*. I mean it. He's no bust-out. He's solid. You know what I'm thinking, *coom*? I'm thinking we give this kid a pass, take him under our wing," Louie said, while grinning large horse teeth. But Big Louie's eyes were anything but smiling.

Danni felt even more powerless while trapped in the bowels of The Inn, at the mercy of two of Cleveland's most dangerous men, than when as a child trapped with her manic mother during drunken rages while she transformed into a stranger. But that paled in comparison to the degree of fear she experienced below The Inn with two known mafia killers. What made things even worse is when she saw something she had thought couldn't ever be possible. Her man, her hero, Rocco, was *afraid*. And that terrified her to the core. But she refused to budge. Those steps might as well have not even been there.

Danni shivered as she recalled Gina's words and the strangely intense look in her eyes during their last sleep-over. Gina had said to her and Carrie, "Respect and loyalty are the only things that really matter, and solid family is all we ever have. Everything else is pure bullshit!"

Danni recognized that statement as powerful as well as genuine the night Gina articulated those words. But beyond that, their meaning ended up becoming what perhaps was the one pure truth Danni had been looking for.

CH XXVII:
Fake It Till You Make It

December 29th, 2013: "No way! Fuck this! These meds are way too strong. I ain't taking this shit anymore!" a younger man said, as he crossed the large room to sit next to me by some wire-meshed windows at the Turney Road Psychiatric Institution. I can't even get wood behind this stuff. I'm way too young to be impotent. I'm a goddamn stud!"

Old Mildred said, "We won't stand for that gutter language, especially taking of our Lord's name in vain. I'm a good Christian, young man!"

"Oh, yeah? I guess you have no problem with priests ass-fucking little kids then. So let me ask you this, since you work with mental disorders. When a man of Jesus is raping boys, does make him a fag, a pedophile, or just a goddamned twisted motherfucker who needs to be killed?" The younger man moved his plastic folding chair next to mine.

"Please cease with such horrible blasphemy," Mildred said, in her haughty way, while reviewing and organizing patient chart notes. It's uncalled for and won't be tolerated!"

The cursing man looked at me and said, "No fuckin' way, man... I knew it! I knew I did way too much acid back in the day. I feel like I'm in a Cheech & Chong movie. Hey, are you for real, or like some goddamn hallucination? Can I touch you, dude?"

"Vuck teefner," I mumbled my best Bobby-boy masquerade.

"Oh no you don't... Because I know things. Hey, can I touch you, man?" he asked again.

"Yeah, Vucky Veaver. See 'em? Wanna touch 'em? I got vuck teef on. See 'em? *Gnang Gnang Gnang*."

The irate man whispered, "See, the thing is, I know things. Like for example, I know everyone of your tattoos like they were my own. Even the tips of those on your wrists, almost peeking out from beneath those long sleeves. I even know why go got 'em."

"Yeah, see 'em? *Gnang Gnang Gnang*. Lookie Vah Vee Voy git vuck teefners on. *Gnang Gnang Gnang*."

"Don't go handing me this buck teeth bullshit. I might be an OD'ing asshole, but I ain't all the way crazy just yet."

I covered my face with scarred hands and said, "Vucky Veevner got vuck teef on." Then I turned just barely enough to peek through my fingers, to see what felt like I was the one having hallucinations. A rush of dizziness ran through me.

"Quit playing dead. You're freaking me out. Don't do this shit to me. I mean it! I'm way too fucked up right now." the cursing man said, with a frightened and trembling voice.

"Yeah," I answered. "Vuck teef," lips curled over my top and bottom front teeth.

He looked ill. "Okay . . . Maybe I am nuts. "Wow! And I thought I only got stuck in this place because I overdosed. Uncle paid big bucks to put me in this ritzy-ass place for *observation*, or some shit like that. But I wasn't trying to kill myself – straight-up. I was just tying to get really tuned-up with all this crazy shit's been coming down. You can dig it. So are you dead?" he whispered. "I need to know."

I answered loudly, "I got Vucky Veevner. See 'em?" which is when I looked directly at him.

"Because I've been looking at them tats since I was a baby. That is you, right? You know I got your back, Uncle Jack," Junior whispered, even quieter than before. "But I'm guessing you don't even now about my dad yet, do you?" The cursing man was someone I'd known since he was born.

Old Mildred said, "Curtis, you leave Bobby be now. You're upsetting him."

"Ah shit! Okay… You got your own scam going on. Alright, I can dig it. Catch you a littler later. But check it out: There's a 72-hour window for observation," he explained with urgency. "Once we're in private rooms upstairs, security's a lot tougher. So if we're gonna make a move it better be tonight," Junior said, barely audible, to a man staring blankly outside, grunting and breathing noisily through an open mouth.

I stayed silent. Mildred asked over the microphone in a quiet and reassuring voice, "You're home now, right Bobby? You're safe here with us now. Isn't that right?"

I gave a toothless smile to Mildred. "Vuck teefner."

"One more thing, Unc. Don't take any more meds. Cheek 'em and spit 'em out when they ain't looking. We need to stay awake. I'll fill you in later." Junior said, as he moved away under close scrutiny of Mildred.

As soon as Curtis' son walked away, a tall and very thin older man with stringy brown hair took the seat next to me. He looked like a doctor but was dressed in hospital scrubs. He folded his hands in his lap and elevated his long hook nose while he evaluated me: "I am Edvard, sir. I am in charge… Is there anything else I can do?"

"Yeah. Vuck teef," I answered. My lips protected my teeth from inspection, just as Bobby-boy had done.

"Sir, there is no need to be coy. I can read minds. I know exactly what it is you need." Then Edvard began laughing a loud phony laugh, clapping his hands and looking up at the ceiling. "Oh boy, we have a winner here!" followed by more loud fake laughter.

I responded, "I got Vucky Veevner. See 'em?"

Edvard waved his arms in the air, braying like a jackass. "Well okay then! I guess that settles it. But I knew about your tooth phobia before you arrived." He sat with his legs crossed like a woman. Head tilted up, he switched from mania to condescending depressive tones in an instant. "That is because I am Him, sir. I am *the* one. But I could not expect a person like yourself to be privy to such advanced information."

Mildred encouraged, "Go ahead, Edvard. Share with us how you know which day the world will end. Have you a strategy yet?" she asked the pompous string bean.

"Please, do not give it too much credence, dear ma'am. It is nothing quite as illustrious as that. It is much more ergonomic with quite less the flair of dramatics, dear Mildred. You know I abhor redundancy!" He sniffed and sat straighter.

Junior asked, "Hey Ed, how come if you're so important and shit you're locked up in a nut house with us crazy motherfuckers?"

Edvard turned his back to Junior as he spoke, "Excuse me kind sir, but gutter-snipes are not required in intellectual discussions. Even if I am the only intellectual involved in this particular dialogue," he said, with raised eyebrows.

"Now gentlemen," chuckled old Mildred, "Let's all try to focus for a moment. Shall we, Edvard? Because we all have bigger fish to fry, don't we?" she winked.

"I do not indulge in carp or sheep head, if you do not mind," Edvard answered, looking at Junior. "My family happens to be of a refined nature, culturally as well as historically."

Junior paced the room: "You got something against blacks? Say it, and quit acting like some faggot-assed bitch!"

"I had not noticed your race, sir, If fact, I had not noticed you at all. But now that you have invaded a topic I shall venture to say you do look rather Latino." Then Edvard sniffed the air again, as if it were somehow tainted.

"Oh yeah? Well I'm mostly Italian, Ed. But I got a little dose of black in me, just enough so I got one of them big fat dicks swingin' between these legs."

Edvard started in again with the laughing hyena bit, long arms waving around like they had minds of their own. "I am quite sure I am not interested in *your* penis, one way of another," Edvard glanced a little too long at Junior's crotch.

"So why don't you do like Mildred said? Clue us in about when the world's gonna end, and all your other bullshit."

Trying to change the subject I said, ""Yeah, 'cause Vah Vee Voy got vuck teef on. See 'em? I'm Vucky Veaver."

"My goodness gracious, yes!" exclaimed Mildred. "Bobby-boy has such beautiful buck teeth!" She clutched a tissue to her breast and smiled like an old movie star.

I glanced at Junior and then to an empty seat in our circle. He took the hint and sat on the other side of me, away from Edvard.

"Okay, Mr. Rogers. Let's hear what you got, Ed."

"No, not Rogers, although we do know the Rogers' of Hilton Head. But I can tell by skull shape and set of eye that these men come from more primitive stock. At any rate, I shall begin by saying no one here has any breeding to speak of, other than Robert," Edvard looked down at me. "It is rather unfortunate that he has been a victim of devil's trickery. Poor thing…" Then he picked invisible lint from the front of his hospital scrubs. He sat as if he were being painted.

"Come on, Ed. Shit or get off the sink, man." Junior bobbled his heels up and down on the balls of his feet.

"During my post-grad education, Mother insisted I take one summer off to read the *Dead Sea Scrolls* and the *Books of the Apocrypha*, the *Pseudepigrapha* and all ten manuscripts of the *Book of Enoch*. And it was then I began the brewing of Salvia and smoking Bath Salts, when it all began to gel. I do not expect you to follow this, young man. You may be excused if you find this a bit too heady," Edvard said to Junior.

"I was thinking about crashing till you mentioned Salvia and Bath Salts," Junior laughed. "That shit explains a whole lot. Go on ahead, Big Ed. I'm listening."

"Yes, Edvard, please proceed," smiled Mildred. "We're all very intrigued."

"Well, it was then I began to see holographic geometric shapes and abstract patterns alive in my living room. This one specific abstraction, this thing you see as life, is real – but only for me. None of you exist outside my own realm of creativity."

"Oh, man. I'm so glad I chilled. Thanks, Bobby-boy. If it wasn't for your crazy ass and all those goddamn buck teeth hanging out I might a missed this shit," Junior chuckled, with the back of his hand over his mouth. "Tell me more, Eddy."

Edvard sat rigidly like a teenage girl at a Miss America pageant. "If you can handle un-blunted truisms, sir, I shall continue! The world as we know it began exactly on February 21st, of 19 and 62. And that, my good people, is precisely the date when all life will cease to be. But no one here is capable of tracking this. I think not," he said, and broke into another phony laughing fit. "Oh dear goodness me!"

"Yeah, Vah Vee got the good kind vuck teef on. See 'em? *Gnang Gnang Gnang*. Lookie Vah Vee Voy's teefner."

"Yes, my dear Robert. I concur completely with your assessment."

Junior held his head in his hands, shaking it back and forth: "Jesus fuck! I almost missed this shit. This is *great*!"

Mildred said, "Hush, Curtis. Then she encouraged the very tall, very thin man, "Maybe you should explain how the world just began a little over 50 years ago, Edvard, yet will end on the same day it began. Not all of us follow that line of reasoning. Some believe only our Creator knows that information. Wouldn't you agree, Edvard?"

"You still don't recognize Me, do you? Have I not been answering your prayers, Mildred? Yet I can see you mock the pure logic of my oral dissertation merely because you cannot realize what it beyond human comprehension. Might I surmise that this was all of it?" Edvard let out a loud, long moan, resting the back of his right hand against his thin forehead.

"Yeah, man, something like that, but... You know, Ed, there's always those nasty little things that get in the way of bullshit stories called *facts*?" Junior smiled a wide grin.

Edvard stood: "The reason the world will end on my birth date is because I will die on February 21st of 20 and 14. Now is this making any more sense to you mere mortals? Those objects you call God and Devil are returning home on the day I turn 52. I saw it in a vision while I was being born. Don't you see the connection? Oh boy! Never mind then. If you do not wish to be enlightened then there is nothing more I can do for you until you accept me into your heart as your Savior." Edvard began to cackle and wave gangly arms above his head as if he were summoning spaceships.

"Go on ahead, big Ed. I think I'm following you now, loud and clear. Enlighten me. You might be our only hope," Junior grinned. "Save us, brother man."

"Okay then! Finally a voice of reason crying out from a forest of ignorance. Here's why: The 52nd year of my birth? The 52nd day of the year? Get it? The number of white keys on a piano. 52 Americans held in the Iranian Hostage Crisis which lasted for 444 days. Coincidence? The number of cards in a deck. 52 weeks in a solar year. *Azariah* reigned for 52 years in Jerusalem. The 52 treaties of *Nag Hammadi*. It is an untouchable number, never the sum of proper divisors of any number. The Mayan Calendar moves through a complete cycle every 52 years. Understand? It has been 52 years of this pitifully transient world, one created for me to walk among men. The 52nd word of the King James *Genesis* is *The* word of *God*! It is *My* word! It is both trans-spiritual and shape-shifting! See it yet? The 52nd *Book of Enoch* assures you, 'the *Elect One* shall appear before the face of the Lord of Spirits.' Because I am Him! Because there are exactly 26 letters in the alphabet, which is only half of the story – half of 52! Understand yet? Because when you assign the numerical value to each letter of my name, the numbers total 52! Coincidence? I think not! Because this entire world exists only in my mind and only for my entertainment!" he shouted. "And when I take my leave of this flat dimensionless animation, this entire flimsy imagery of your pitiful existence will dissipate on that very moment of that same day! All of you! No Prisoners!" he screamed.

"Okay there, Edvard, Easy does it now, son." Otis said, as he and Leroy entered the room, Otis pushing a yellow mop bucket steering it by a long-handled mop inside of it. Leroy limped in carrying a yellow shammy and a white feather duster. "Okay, gentlemen, fun's over for the night. Time for sleep. Let's go. You too, King Edvard. You need your rest come Judgment Day." Leroy said. "Be all nice a fresh."

Later that same night: "You don't have to say anything, Unc. Just listen, okay? And don't worry. See this? The ringer's turned off but the battery's good. I smuggled it in. That big Otis is as dumb as a stump. Check it out: You know that retard, Bobby, they think you are? Yeah, well anyway, they think this dude, Bobby-boy found Leroy's keys and split while nobody was watching. This weird-ass Bobby's the same cat they're pretending is you. But I guess you know that, because you showed up wearing his clothes and ID bracelet. I don't even need to know how that shit came down. But I heard those two dummies, Otis and Leroy, talking in a panic. His auntie died and her lawyer put him here with an ass-load of money in a trust fund. So if they admit you're not him, they have to admit Bobby's gone. If they lost him they lose out on all that cash plus wind-up getting sued and losing their jobs over this."

I just stared at my nephew, trying to digest all he'd just told me, plus trying to figure out if he had suffered a nervous breakdown. Perhaps that explained why he found himself as a patient at the Turney Road Psychiatric Institution. I heard what he said about the overdose, and that story was believable enough. As far as I knew, Junior never lied to me before. But I had to keep in mind two simple facts: Junior currently was a patient in a mental hospital. And if Junior had flipped-out like Edvard had, but I just didn't know it yet, then I couldn't hold much stock in anything Junior said.

"You know what's freaky, Unc? You see me a shell of who I was. And I see you being more paranoid now than ever. But what's really freaky is that with your hair short and your goatee gone, you being about the same age and size, and all pale and shit instead of tanned and buffed like you usually are, you guys could pass for brothers with your tats covered. But all us honkies look alike anyway, right?" chuckled the handsome mixed-blooded man whom I helped raise like a son.

I walked over to a window covered with heavy wire mesh that was facing a brick wall, carefully waiting to make an important decision. Being a CD counselor for a decade meant I got paid to read some of the best liars and con artists in Ohio.

"Okay, Unc, here's the scoop. Earlier, I found a set of keys. Once it got dark, and as soon as I had an opportunity, I unlocked one of the side doors to this place. I guess that retard, Bobby, saw me. I figured if any of these mongoloids saw they were too stupid or crazy to know how to open a door, anyway. Then, before I knew what happened, Crazy Bobby's ass vanished – no coat, no nothing. He just slipped away unnoticed – like I was planning to do. But his crazy ass beat me to it."

Quietly, I continued to watch Junior, not only to hear his words but to study him as he told his story – to see if he had flipped out and was just rambling some gibberish.

Junior continued, "Anyway, I phoned Little Hankie." He held up his little cell phone again. "Because I heard old Mildred telling those two stooges of hers that I was getting shipped out to some top of the line drug rehab in Ashtabula County, way out in *Ass-fuck, Nowheresville*. Uncle Hank paid for my stay there, too. But fuck all that. I don't even use drugs." Junior spoke softly and sat very close. "I'm not like my parents. Both of them are full-on junkies – well, they were..."

Being raised in Collinwood for a quarter of a century and then working with addicts for a decade in rehab, I knew when someone was lying about drugs.

"Okay, Unc, so here it is. It's the part that there's no way for you to have known about." Then Junior moved closer to me and began to weep. "It's my ol' man… He got whacked. I had to identify the body. It's been so cold out, so he was preserved pretty good. But his face was like Spam. He ate a lot of bullets. He's gone, Unc."

He paused to wipe his eyes and nose on a corner of my freshly cleaned, stiff white bed sheet. He took a deep breath and resumed: "Okay, so after that I guess I freaked. But I ain't crazy, Unc, and for sure I ain't suicidal. I see the way you're looking at me. But I'm cool now. I wasn't too cool at the time, not when I found out my father got murdered and then saw what his remains looked like. But I'm okay now . . . I guess."

We heard some noise outside the dorm, so Junior rolled off the bed and ducked down. Someone stood in the doorway, peaked in, and moved away loud enough for us to count footsteps. Then he again sat quietly next to me. "The first thing I did, after screaming and crying like a maniac, was to rip apart Dad's room to see if I could find an IOU or something, anything. I needed a clue to help me find out who did it. I wanted to shoot somebody. But instead I shot me, when I found his dope and works. I tied off like they do in the movies. I had no idea about dosing it right, but I did what looked about right, then shot up for the first time in my life and overdosed. I guess my mom found me, went berserk and called Uncle Hank. But the good news is Little Hankie's on his way." My eyes shot back towards his and for the first time focused.

"Don't worry, Unc. Hankie don't know shit about you being here. Not yet, anyway. But he's solid. And he loves you like a father. So do I. And you know it. So fuck this place. You saw that, Edvard. And he's one of the saner ones in here. Some of these other whackos hemmed up here are swacked out of their skulls from Thorazine or pinned down with bed restraints because they're dangerous. You know how much of a nut-job you have to be for a doctor to tie you down in restraints?"

I almost smiled, but focused on his steady brown eyes.

"Oh yeah, that reminds me of another thing, Uncle Jack. I heard that old nurse out there talking to those other two idiots. They said Crazy Bobby's lawyer will be here in the morning. That means we need to get in the wind before daylight. Cool?"

I looked into his fearless eyes and nodded.

He said, "Alright! Now you're talking. Little Hankie will be here in a few hours. Get some rest, Unc. I ain't about to sleep one wink. I'll wake you up. See this right here? It's our key to the highway, Uncle Jack. You'll see. Hankie won't let us down. He's to me like your brother, Uncle Hank, is to you. Both of them dudes are stout. They're all about loyalty, just like my dad was and Rocco is, and just like we are. So we're about to bounce up outta this motherfucker – together. No worries. I got your back, Uncle Jack."

CH XXVIII: Line in the sand

The basement pit, December 29th: Danni shouted, "Gina was right!" She said, 'Respect and loyalty are all that matter. Integrity and family are all we ever have. Everything else is pure bullshit'. And I don't see anything *hypothetical* about that!"

Louie said, "This bitch is nutty as her lunatic mother."

Cagootz laughed: "I think she's tellin' us *hypothetically* means *maybe*? So *maybe* youse kid ain't so stupid after all. Yeah, *maybe* you're about as smart as your fathers. Wait… Where are they again? Oh yeah . . . I almost forgot. They're dead. By the way, did you know your bust-out cousin, Fingers, retired? Look at this kid's face, Louie. You didn't hear about this yet, huh kid? Yeah, well, *maybe* that's because he hasn't, either – not yet, anyway. But he will. So guess who's callin' all the shots in Cleveland from now on – starting with you? And you know what else? *Maybe* that cur old-man of yours is better off dead."

"My father's better off *dead*? Really?" Rocco took a slow deep breath. "Try to show some class, Cagootz. Even you should know better than to talk shit on a man's deceased family. Even dead, my Pop would be twice the man as both of youse fucks lumped together into one glop of steamy shit. If Jackie was here you'd be singing a different tune. You figure that *maybe* he's changed? He has. And in a way he still respects youse guys. And *maybe,* in a certain way, he might even fear youse guys. But both of you've known him long enough and well enough to understand that once you put him in a corner with only one way out, you'll have to kill him to stop him."

"Kill him? Hey! That's a good idea, Roc! Why didn't we think of that? Louie, you know this breeding for gameness thing this kid's always going on-and-on about with all that dog pedigree bullshit he talks about? Do you think *balls* are hereditary, *coom*? Because I'm wondering if this bust-out has half the *coglioni* his ol' man had. He talks a good game. But *maybe* it's just talk."

"You ask me, *coom*, I think they're all curs. All that genetic shit really don't matter anymore, anyway," Louie answered, with a noise almost resembling laughter.

"I'm wondering how either of youse geniuses would know anything about having heart, one way or another. Because I'd bet my life Jack's smarter and gamer than the two of youse soft motherfuckers put together. And since my Pop's not here to defend himself, I'm happy to do it," Rocco said unwaveringly, standing eye to eye while trapped on enemy territory.

Cagootz gave a wide grin, exposing a mouthful of crooked teeth. He chuckled, "I'm glad you said that, kid. You do got some brass balls for a bust-out. Louie's my Rottweiler and closest *coomba*. So he's the one that takes care of my personal whacks. But Louie ain't the one tipped on your ol' man. Swear to Buddha. Meantime, right now me and Louie could use a tough kid. So I'll tell you what: all ball-busting aside, since you showed so much heart, I'll really let you slide this time. Straight up, Rocco. But it can only happen on our terms."

Rocco didn't say one word and never lowered his gaze.

"Here's the deal, all bullshit aside: You agree to do one thing for me, to show how deep your loyalty is, and not only will I let you two walk out right now, I'll make you a part of the crew. I'll put you in charge of lower-end guys like that Skinny Vinny kid from the Heights and Fat-ass Spuds. And then you forget the weekly Vig. Just pay what you owe me and we're clean."

"I'm listening closer than I have to anyone in my life."

"Bring me Ansel and you've got it *made*. Then I find your father's killer and make things right. It'll all work out. Because if you're one of us, your father's killer becomes *our* enemy."

"Rocco let out a long, heavy sigh. "Man… If I'd set up a brother or a brother's father, even for another brother, that makes me a low-life who can't be trusted. After a move like that, *hypothetically* speaking, you'd have doubts about me. Youse guys started to look at Benny a whole lot different after the crazy shit he pulled, and he was solid as gold."

"You ain't Benny and I ain't Uno. And I ain't got all day. Yes or no? We ain't got the time to play *Patti Cakes* with you."

"Cagootz, swear to Buddha, this is the absolute toughest thing I've ever had to do in my life. But I gotta say no. I couldn't even trust myself if I did a thing like that."

"Okay, last try: You take out those two rogue cops who fucked us out of our money and made us look bad. Final offer."

"Look, Cagootz. I'm no tough guy. I'm not like you and Louie. It broke my heart to see a *dog* get hurt. I'm no killer."

"Too bad, kid. But you never know, just *maybe* we'll let you slide anyway," Cagootz chuckled, looking at his bodyguard.

"Yeah kid, you're not like us." Louie said, as he looked at his partner in crime. "So we decided to *maybe* let you slide. But then you gotta ask yourself: What the fuck does *slide* mean?"

Rocco tried to watch Louie's advance as Cagootz swung the crowbar sideways into Rocco's left forearm, the same arm that was shot. He said, "This is for Looney Lonnie." A sickening metal on bone cracking sound of a compound break in that quiet basement was followed by Rocco tripping into the pit. Everything turned purple and then black as he slid to the floor. He reeled and puked, desperately trying to balance himself on a 4" x 4" stub, to keep himself from passing out and choking on his own vomit. Danni screamed in hysterics. Rocco sat, leaning against the pit wall. His good hand was on that wooden post to balance while the room spun at a dizzying speed. He knew he had to stand.

Doubled over, Rocco fought to not lose consciousness. Danni frantically shrieked while he braced on that chunk of sturdy 4" x 4", attempting to regain his footing. Then it was Rocco's turn to scream: "RUN! . . . NOW!"

Louie charged with a balled-up left fist, the maul in his other, his huge bulk illuminated by blinking festive lights strung in those old basement rafters. Quick as anything the nail Louie had palmed got slammed down on the back of Rocco's right hand just long enough to get pounded through, nailing Rocco's right hand to the Wolmanized post.

It was like getting hit with the hot wire from a live electric line. Excruciating pain dropped Rocco. He groaned. His head twirled in dizziness. A throbbing of paralyzing pain came in terrific surges. Then he began to lose feeling though his entire arm, from neck to fingertips. Yet that strange numbness hurt more than anything he had ever experienced. Both of Rocco's arms had been rendered useless within seconds.

Danni sobbed uncontrollably, stumbling away, falling up those filthy steps, mumbling incoherently. Gasping in terror, she floundered on the stairs for another moment. Needing to be sure of what was happening, to make certain her eyes hadn't betrayed her. The new information was not being processed as reality.

"KEEP GOING" Rocco pleaded with her, as he tried to find the strength to stand. But he was in agonizing pain while still attached to a short length of wooden pit wall, holding him prisoner like a wild animal caught in a steel-toothed trap.

Cagootz yelled to Big Louie, "Go get that little cunt and bring her back down here! She ain't goin' no place!"

Louie hesitated long enough to look up at the stairwell. Rocco looked at the hammer and then up at Big Louie. Rocco fought through the worst pain of his life. He stood and snarled,

"Youse stupid fucks don't get it yet! My father ain't dead... And I ain't, either. You fucked up big-time. Jackie'll hunt both of youse cocksuckers down like rats in a cellar. Now go ahead, Louie, you dumb fuck." He moved closer. "Follow her. Go see who's waiting up there for your big dumb ass. Jackie'll be real glad to see you, you stupid motherfucker! We knew this was a set-up."

Louie gave his partner a puzzled look, just long enough for Rocco to jump into a head butt, exploding the bridge of Louie's big nose like a Roma tomato. Blood streamed over the front of Louie's white T-shirt. Louie hopped out of the pit. He dropped to one knee, using the pit wall for protection, while he wiped broken nose tears away to regain his vision.

Rocco heard the sound of running overhead and then the front door slammed, which meant Danni had made a clean break. He yelled at Cagootz, "Hear him? I told you!"

Cagootz hollered back, "Then you pay double!" He charged with the crowbar over his head like an ax. The timing was perfection. While the crowbar was still chambered behind his head, Rocco caught him in an ear with the toe of his left boot. A tremendous roundhouse kick spun Cagootz around and put him to sleep. Cagootz stumbled over the pit wall. His forehead bounced off that thin carpet stretched over a concrete floor, which snapped his neck backwards. He lay there out cold.

Louie got back up but wisely kept the pit between them. He drew the hammer back like it was a throwing axe. Rocco lifted the four-foot section of pit he was nailed to and used it as a shield. But the maul hit hard enough to punch halfway through it.

Rocco, in the worst pain of his life, growled, "AGHHH" and pushed forward as fast as possible for a man attached to a quarter sheet of plywood trimmed in pine. He used his shield like a battering ram, driven by the nailed hand wedged between his ribs and the bicep of his crushed arm. Louie tried to deflect the wood with a wild swing. But Rocco's frantic thrust, as he belly surfed in mid-air, slammed the mini-wall past Louie's fist and into his neck. A solid wooden corner crushed Big Louie windpipe. He fell backwards, his eyes glassy and round. He gave an expression of disbelief as blood gurgled through those huge hands covering a torn open throat caused by a gash from a bent ten-penny nail.

After that huge adrenaline dump, the smallish wooden wall became a lead anchor. Rocco's arms trembled. *I have to rest*: he told himself. He puked again. When he caught his breath he thought: *Not yet, you fucking pussy. Do it like Grampa taught Pop. The harder I fight, the quicker the pain gets extinguished. I ain't done yet!*

Cagootz struggled to get his bearings. He tried to pull himself back to his feet using the remainder of the three-sided pit, still unaware of Louie's condition. He was clueless about who had taken control of the situation till Rocco attacked him again. Rocco held the wall against his chest and slammed a corner of the framed edge of with every ounce of crazy-man strength he still had onto Cagootz' spine. Cagootz wheezed. Rocco screamed in pain. The obese body of Cagootz draped over a full section of the pit wall. Rocco front-kicked him squarely in his temple, over the wall and inside the pit. Face-down, Rocco stomped in his ribs. Cagootz' work boots rested on the top edge of the pit.

"Oh shit... I fucked-up big this time." Rocco spoke out loud to himself. "These are fucking made-men I killed!" Then he froze. He heard something on the steps. He felt an overwhelming sense of dread wash over him as he grimaced and lifted his little wall, balanced on his head as he waited.

"Baby?" she spoke in short breathless sobs, "You *okay?*"

"I told you to run, didn't I? Why didn't you listen?"

"You didn't say all the words, so I wasn't positive."

"Bullshit. I'm really fucking pissed about this. You could have gotten hurt real bad, or even worse. Why the fuck can't you just listen?" Rocco groaned in pain.

"I'm sorry. Please don't be mad. I just can't take anymore. I thought this would be a better day. What happened?"

"Just listen to what I say from now on, whether I say it or not. And stop the fucking sniveling. Go get that toolbox in the corner before I pass out. Hurry up."

"Are we in serious trouble now, Rocco?"

"These guys are *made-men*! What do you think? Now do as I say. Okay, good girl. Bring it here and open it. See that one with the yellow handles? Right over there. Good! You're doing good. Get that small claw hammer, too. Yeah, that one. Good job, babe. You do realize I can't use either hand right now, right?"

"I'll call the police before they wake up. Okay, Rocco?"

"NO! No cops, Danni! We still have options here – good ones, too. The law is one of the last fucking things we want here."

"What's the other last thing we don't want, babe?"

"Well, we sure as fuck don't want any of their friends walking in on us. So we'd better move fast," he groaned.

"I left the front door open, Rocco. Should I go close it?"

"Fuck that door. I need you to do something right now."

"What if they wake up? What should we do?"

"Take a good look, babe. They ain't never waking up."

"Really? They're dead? Are you serious? You *killed* them?"

"I didn't have any better choices. But I can't sweat that."

"Dead? Really? Good! Fuck them!" Danni started for Cagootz, holding the claw hammer with both hands in front of her like a sword.

"Whoa, easy! I need your help, okay? I'm in a whole bunch of pain. And we have to be real quick, alright? I can't see shit. Take that sponge and wipe the sweat off my forehead, okay? It's going in my eyes and blurring my vision."

"The water is all red and yucky from blood. You sure?"

"A little dog blood is the last of my worries right now."

"Okay . . . anything. I'm your girl, right?" Danni asked, as she fetched a sponge out of a water bucket and squeezed it out. Brownish water pooled up on the filthy basement floor.

"Yes you are, baby. You're my girl. You're the best ever. You're doing a great job. Bring me a hammer and those snips."

"Like this? Okay . . . what now?"

"I'll brace against the pit with my legs while you pry that nail head away from my hand, okay? We just need to make a little more space first. Sound good?"

"I'll do it. But it doesn't sound so good to me, Rocco."

"Please, babe, just go ahead. I can't do it myself or I would. Yeah, there you go. That's it. Just slide the nail head between those prongs. Push it in a little farther or you'll strip the head. *Agh*! Shit! Fuck! Okay. You're okay. Go on. Tap it in."

"Oh! Is that what these yellow ones are for, for tapping?"

"Yeah, tapping. Whoa! Go easy. That's it. Nice and easy."

"Am I still doing a good job, Rocco?" she asked, as black tears streamed down perfect features. Her tiny nose was running.

"You're doing really good so far. Fuck! Okay, here goes. Now I'll spread my fingers real wide on this post. I'm gonna want you to pull on the handle. Rest the hammer head *between* my fingers, not *on* them, or you'll crush them. Make sure the hammer head is on the wood for leverage. Remember: not *on* my finger. On the wood. Got it?"

"I think I have it. Okay. Ready?"

"I'm as ready as I'll ever be. Do it now, Danni."

"Okay. Ready… Set… Here goes!"

"AAAGGGHHH… FUCKING MOTHERFUCKING COCKSUCKING MOTHERFUCKER!!! Okay… Wait. . . .

hold-up. Let's stop. Just rest a minute," Rocco panted, out of breath and ready to faint. He dry-heaved and spit bile.

"I'm so sorry, baby," she cried even harder. "I didn't mean to hurt you. I know I'm fucking up everything!"

"No you're not. You're right on the money, Danni. You're saving my life, plus keeping me from catching a case for a double murder beef. So fuck all that *sorry* bullshit. Just get me out of here, and I'll owe you – forever. Okay? Okay, now please wipe off my head again with the sponge before I pass out, and then go upstairs to the bar and bring down a bottle of tequila or whatever – anything strong."

"You're in recovery, baby. You sure? Plus, what if—"

"Stop! There's something at that homemade bar right there. Remember where Ice-cream Nicky and Sally-boy were working last night? Right over there. Look. See it in the corner? Can you go over there by yourself?"

Danni used forearms rather than dirty hands to wipe her runny nose and tears. She lifted the first bottle she reached and asked in little breathy sobs, "Is this kind okay, Rocco?"

"Yes, baby, that's better than okay. Just get booze."

She didn't want to be too far from her man. "Am I still doing it right?" she asked, as she offered a bottle of gin.

"Straight gin? HA! Okay, fuck-it. Why not? Open it and hold it to my mouth. Keep it tipped till I turn away. Then you can set it on that stack of lumber over there by the tools, okay?"

"Oh, shit! It spilled some you… Let me get that sponge."

"Fuck that sponge! You're already a pro at this, babe," he said, after he had drained a good portion from that new bottle. "Okay. That's a little better. Now get those snips. Wedge them between the bottom on the nail head and the back of my hand. I'll flatten my hand out real close to this post. Get it in as far in as you can, like a scissors, so the nail is at the back of the snips, and then squeeze with both hands as hard as you can till it cuts through the nail. But don't twist them. Okay… Ready?"

"I can't do this," she cried, with a lowered head.

"Can you please just do this one last thing for me today?"

"Okay. I'll do it. But I'm sorry if I'm hurting you, okay?"

"Wait, sweetie. One thing first. I have to piss real bad. If this hurts as much as I know it will my bladder might let go."

"How will I be able to help you upstairs to the toilet with a wall stuck to your hand? Or do you want to pee in that bucket?"

"Just pull down my zipper and take it out for me."

She asked, "You sure you don't need that bucket?"

"The floor's cool. Piss on this whole fucking place."

"I have to go, too. Can I pee on the floor?"

"You, my precious baby, can do whatever you want. You're amazing! I love you so fucking much, baby. Hey . . . I got a good idea. You know how to do mouth to mouth, right? Maybe after we get this wall off me you can revive Cagootz. Then he'll rehire you to sling more drinks for these fat cocksuckers."

"Fuck them! I hate those pigs! I'm glad they're dead."

After they relieved themselves on the floor she put Rocco back inside his worn Levi's while her own pants were still down. *Thump . . . Thump . . .* They turned in horror while Danni struggled with her jeans. Terrified, Danni looked at him, her pants and black panties somehow tangled in a knot around her knees. In a panic, she pushed and pulled material at the same time while her pretty mouth fell wide open to a deathly silent scream. *Thump . . . Thump . . .* that terrible sound of footsteps, one at a time, nearing the steps. Rocco nodded to a dark corner. Somehow she succeeded in getting her legs untangled from her pants but left them unzipped. She froze, staring above her head.

Thump . . . Thump. Rocco lost his ability to breath. He was being strangled by those ominous sounds, seemingly coming from one set of determined footsteps *Thump . . . Thump.* Slowly and steadily someone descended stairs into their pit of hell. *Had that fucking Big Louie been able to make a call from his cell?* His windpipe constricted. He felt as though the ouroboros on his back had slid around his neck. His eyes, normally gray, bugged out black and insane. Everything began to fade. His chest heaved in vain, because there was no air left in that basement. He growled as he struggled for that next draw of beautifully putrid air fouled from when Cagootz' bladder and bowels released.

Thump . . . Thump. Rocco whispered, "Go in that dark corner behind the lumber. Real quiet, but move fast. Go!"

Rocco lay on the concrete floor, curled up behind the piece of plywood wall still firmly nailed to his bloodied and badly bruised hand. Danni, as compliant as a frightened puppy, scrunched up in a corner of their trap – her eyes squeezed shut. *Thump . . . Thump.* Footsteps stopped at the bottom of the stairs.

Someone mumbled, "Jesus Fuck! What's all *this*?"

Rocco lost his ability to breathe, frozen in terror. He tried to muster up some strength, yet tried to conceive how he could possibly keep going. *Fight and the pain will go away.* He bared strong teeth in a grimace as he looked over at Danni, who was curled in a fetal position, knees against her forehead. Breathing returned in gasps, then panting. He thought: *I'll pretend I'm dead till he gets close. Then I'll smash my wall in his face so Danni to make a run for it.* Rocco took more deep breaths. *I need to lure him in.* He peeked out from behind his attached barricade till he thought he heard stirring from where Big Louie had fallen. *Fight harder to get to the other side faster and forever.* Footsteps on the concrete floor, coming closer. He heard another rustle from where Louie was. *I'm surrounded. We're totally fucked.*

Rocco recognized a raspy voice say, "Holy fucking shit!"

"Gina??" Rocco asked, in disbelief.

"What the fuck's going on here? What have you done, little bro? And what's with the Christmas lights?"

"Get your ass over here and get down!" Rocco hissed.

Gina squatted down and whispered, "Ma went crazy again. She said I needed to get over here right away to check on things. She said she had a bad feeling, for me to make sure everything's off! What an odd thing to say! I thought she'd lost it. Swear to Buddha, I'll never, ever doubt her again. What the fuck's going on, bro?" Gina again asked.

"Stay down and keep quiet!" Rocco whispered.

"Have you finally lost your mind completely? Did you forget who these people are, dude? And why the hell are you holding onto that little door? Put that thing down and let's split! Jesus Fucking Christ… I can't believe my eyes! Who's that fat guy laying in the pit? And what's that awful stench? Is it that Shit-pants Joey guy?"

The gin bottle shattered and hit both of them with shards of glass. Gina picked splinters out of one of her leather jacketed arms while Rocco noticed something odd. The bottle's neck still rested on the stack of lumber next to a reciprocating saw, exactly where Danni had set it. Then something ricocheted off a wall.

Rocco leaned up to see a huge fist wrapped around what looked like a .357 automatic. It rested sideways on top of the pit wall. *Zipp…* Another round fired from a silencer. The bullet went through Rocco's shoulder muscle and slammed him backwards. It hit the same arm that had been broken with the crowbar.

"DOWN! HIT THE FLOOR! HE'S SHOOTING!"

"Who's shooting?" Gina asked, and then dove through that thick air into a crawlspace beneath the stairway, completely hidden from anyone other than her brother. "Who else is down here? Who's that stinky guy? Is it Shit-pants Joey?"

Rocco stood, slipped and fell into a giant puddle of warm piss pooled up at one end of the pit. His section of pit wall covered him as if it were a coffin lid. "Shit!" He whispered, "That's not Shit-pants Joey. That's Cagootz! Stay where you are," he winked, as he kicked the mini-sledge hammer into a slide over to her. Then Rocco motioned with his eyes to the other end of the three-sided, 16-foot partial square. The only thing in the entire world separating them from Louie's gun was the U-shaped plywood structure, only two feet high. Gina hadn't even known anyone else was there, because the only other person visible had been Cagootz sprawled on his face, his work boots still draped over the edge of the pit. Underwear full of excrement stained through the seat of new gray workpants, with a white price tag affixed to a back pocket. Ricocheting bullets were burying themselves into old concrete walls and wooden beams.

All five of them, including the dead Cagootz and a still very dangerous Big Louie, were down on The Inn's cold basement floor. Rocco heard wet sucking and gagging sounds coming from where silenced shots had been fired, from the same spot where Louie had fallen. Terrible wheezing and choking came from that same place where he had been sure Louie died. Nothing made sense anymore.

Danni was curled up and as still as Cagootz. Rocco raised his eyebrows and with a wide-eyed look at his sister he yelled, "Okay, Louie, you win. Two of us are dead, and I'm hit. I'm gonna die if I don't get help real quick. I'm bleeding real bad, *coom*. So I'm coming out. It's all over now, *coomba*. You win."

Instead of an answer, they heard a growling, gurgling sound. Another round fired and ricocheted of the concrete floor.

Rocco said, "I finally got my hand out from underneath that nail, Louie. So now I got my boot gun ready. It's not too accurate, but I'm real fucking close. Don't make me kill my way outta this motherfucker. You already know I'm not ashamed to kill a motherfucker if I have to. But I don't want that, Louie. Not here. Not now. There's no sense for all of us to die. Toss your weapon into the pit and I'll do the same. We'll both throw them in on the count of three, okay? Here we go . . . ONE!"

Still hidden beneath the steps, Gina went from being curled in a crouch position to stretching out on the floor with polished nails. Unsure if the shooter could see her, she extended an arm towards that heavy hammer just out or reach. Rocco saw in her eyes that she wouldn't stop till she had it secured. Gina had no idea why, but was willing to risk everything to accomplish that one goal. Rocco saw his sister had committed herself to the task, that the hammer was hers; that to her nothing else mattered other than possessing that hammer. When she felt the tip she smiled. Her tanned knuckles whitened when she grasped the edge of its thick wooden handle. Slowly and as silently as she could, she began to draw her prey into her cavern.

Rocco began coughing loudly as a distraction. He yelled, "I'm dying here, coom. You hit my lungs. He rooted around beneath his plywood till he managed to kick off one boot with booted foot, and then struggled with a stockinged foot trying to take off the other. "Come on, Louie. Use your head, *coomba*. Cagootz is already dead. You know this. My girl and friend are dead. You killed them. There's no reason for everybody to die. We still have a chance, *coom*. I'll call a hospital. You tell me which one. Okay, Louie? We need an ER right away or we ain't gonna make it. I'm gonna count to *two* now. Let's do the smart thing, alright? Rocco kicked off his other boot. Okay . . . TWO!"

Gina had the hammer. Silently she rolled to her hands and knees with a big grin, as if the last one to possess the hammer is declared the victor. Smiling her dazzling grin, she looked to Rocco for approval and advice. What she saw was her brother peel off one sock with his other stockinged foot. Then he grabbed those yellow-handled snips between his big toe and the second toe, like a monkey would take a third banana.

Rocco made eye-contact with Gina and gave a short series of slight nods with a stern look. She nodded enthusiastically back at him. He shouted, "Okay, Louie. This is the moment of truth. This is our last chance. I'm gonna stand up like a man and drop my piece in the pit, just like I promised. You know I'm a man of my word, right *coom*?"

Rocco stood up his section of the pit wall to look like a four-foot tall door and yelled from the floor, "You listening, *coom*? Here it comes, Louie. I'm tossing my gun into the pit. You do the same and we're out of here." Rocco glared at his sister with the most bizarre look she'd ever seen in the eyes of immediate family.

Click Gina, with a terrified look, took a deep breath and wildly nodded back all wide-eyed. Her beautiful smile had been vanquished by emotions and instincts much more powerful than joy or fear. With the stoic look of determination, she set herself into a low sprinter position with one foot back ready to spring.

She looked at her brother again, just to be sure. But she already knew the answer. It was the thing she dreaded most in the world. Yet, at the same time, it was the only thing that made sense. Adrenaline rushes felt as if they were shooting up and down her spinal column, into her extremities and through major organs, straight to the top of her skull. Nothing else existed but that one moment. She had lived her entire 37 years for this one brief sequence of time that was about to unfold.

Rocco saw Danni watching Gina set in her sprinter stance, so Danni grabbed the jagged neck from that shattered gin bottle. Eyes locked one last time. Gina smiled again. That time it was for her new best friend, for the sister she never had. Danni returned the sentiment with a hard, fast nod of her head and a wild-eyed grin as Rocco yelled, "Okay, *coom*. Here I come with the gun! I'm tossing it in the pit. Ready? . . . THREE!"

With a bare foot, Rocco flipped the yellow handled metal snips into a corner of the pit farthest from him or the girls. The heavy metal object made a metallic *thunk* when it hit the carpet flooring of the pit. He yelled, "There's mine, Louie. I'm all in."

Zipp... Rocco saw a hole appear in the bloodied plywood. Then he heard the empty click of a firing pin. *I fucking knew it!*, he thought. Now it was Rocco who was smiling. He yelled, "NOW!"

Gina scrambled around one edge of the pit holding the raised hammer as Danni rounded the other corner wielding the rough-necked stem of glass from the broken gin jug. Rocco stood with the flimsy wall positioned in front of him and screamed, "Kill me!" The next sound he heard was a sickening squish of a *thud*. Then he heard Danni screaming manically – like a wounded animal being eaten alive. She shrieked wildly, yowling otherworldly, inhuman guttural sounds of anguish.

"Motherless Fuck!" Rocco hollered, as the wall section balanced on his head. With one bare foot he hobbled over to find Danni still screaming. With a downward thrust, Danni kept stabbing at Louie's back as if she were using an ice pick on a bag of melted-together and refrozen cubes. Gina continuously pulverized Louie's head to an unrecognizable pulp using a two-handed grip on that large and heavy hammer, as if she were splitting wood. Chunks of skull and meat clotted them like a macabre Jackson Pollock canvas made in a haunted house.

"Holy shit!" Rocco whispered, as he let out a long exhale. "Okay. Wow, nice job. Easy, sister-girl. It's cool now. No more danger, girls. That's it. It's all over now, Danni. Good job, baby.

Just drop the maul, okay? Yeah, that's right. The hammer, Gina. Just put it down. Yeah, just let it drop at your side. That's a girl. You too, Danni. Just let that bottleneck fall. Good. See? Look around. Nothing else can hurt us now. I promise. It's all over. See us. We're safe now. It's just us here."

Gina paused, the bloody hammer still raised over her head. Pieces of bloodied bone were falling from her dark thick curls. Her beautiful face and tanned hands with their pink nail polish were splattered with clots of dripping blood. Danni threw the jagged bottle end at Louie and ran over to Rocco.

"This is important, okay girls? Stay behind me. We need to check to make sure that fat fuck is really shut off for good."

Gina stood, almost robotically. She lowered the hammer but did not drop it. Then she said, "Shit! I forgot I had this," Gina said, as she pulled out her father's gun.

"Okay, cool," Rocco laughed. "Tuck that into my belt, nice and easy. I don't have any kids yet, so go easy. Now I just need you to stand by, Gina, while I check. Okay, sister-girl. Can you do this for me?"

Mutely, and with slumped-over shoulders, Gina nodded affirmative with a blank expression. Her eyes, which normally were full of light and wit, had transformed to a menacing darkness during her frenzy. But life gradually began to return to the light pastel eyes he recognized as belonging to his sister. Rocco sat on the edge of the pit and said as calmly as someone could who had a bloody wall on the top of his head, still nailed to his right hand, "I need a little favor, sweetie."

Danni jerked up her head with a petrified look on her pretty, blood-masked face. Her short black hair was mottled with small white chunks tinted dark purple.

"I need someone to put on one of my boots." he held up the foot with a sock still on it. "But get both for me, Danni."

Like an automaton, silently she did as asked. When Danni started to put on his second boot Rocco said, "Not just yet."

Rocco hobbled to where Cagootz lay, his construction boots still draped over the top edge of the pit. Gina stayed close behind, tightly gripping the pistol. "Check him out. Don't be afraid. Look at his back. It's as broken as my checking account. And that ain't water he's laying in. His bladder let go, too."

"Can we go now?" Danni asked in a little girl's voice.

Gina finally spoke: "Bladder? Then what's that stench?"

"His bowels dumped, too. That means he's totally fucked," observed Rocco, as he stared at his own disfigured hand.

"Danni's right. Let's get the fuck out of here, bro."

"Rocco nudged Cagootz with his boot. Then he touched his face with a bare foot. "This fat fuck's still warm." Next, he moved his toes over to the neck: "I feel a weak pulse."

"What's that mean, Rocco?" his sister gasped, trembling.

"That means we can't afford to take any chances."

Danni wrapped frail and bloodied arms around herself to calm her tremors. "Will he come after us?"

"No, honey. We won't ever see him again. Hold up the end of this board behind my head, okay? Alright, good job. Now I want both of you to take an end. Very important: keep it level so it doesn't move! Okay? Gina, you come on this end, alright? Now I need both of you to face the other way for a quick minute. You can close your eyes. Trust me. If you have to look at anything, then just pay close attention to this wall on my head. Make sure it doesn't slip. Just trust me one more time."

They did exactly as directed. Danni scrunched up her face, squeezing her eyes shut with all her might, like that force would stop any unwelcome images from intruding. Gina tilted her head back and focused intently on the little wall over their heads – the one still attached to her brother's hand.

Danni said, "Okay, they're shut. I won't look till you say."

Using the foot with the boot, Rocco stomped the neck of Cagootz with his heel, over and over, until his neck permanently bent at an unnatural angle. Then he stomped one of the temples of Cagootz till his big melon head was shaped more like an oval.

"Okay," panted an out of breath Rocco. "This fat bastard ain't going anywhere. That's for sure. Now for the hard part…"

Gina gave her brother a blank stare and dropped the pistol. "What do you mean, *hard part*? Let's just leave right now."

"Good idea. We'll make a quick plan and scoot. Pick up the gun and slip it in my waist like I asked. Danni, get that claw hammer and those snips. Let's get this wall off me so we can get our lucky asses out of here before something else happens."

"What's *before something else happens* mean, baby?" asked Danni, her eyes still scrunched closed. "Worse than this?"

"Open those beautiful eyes, baby. It just means this ain't the movies where someone just falls down and goes to sleep. I'd of given odds both of these guys were stone-cold dead, right up until they both came back to life. And this ain't even close to

Easter. So who the fuck else is gonna raise his ass up from the grave? I sure as shit don't want us to be trapped in a basement when it happens. Please hurry and get this goddamn wall off my hand. I want to get back home to Ma, to make sure she's okay. Grab those snips in the pit."

"Fuck those snips." Instead, Gina fetched a Sawzall from on top of the lumber pile where Danni had been hiding. She plugged it into one of the extension chords from the previous night. "Let's do this before we get fucked up our lucky asses."

Danni asked, "Smell it? You should see what he eats," as if she were hypnotized. "It's stuff that's really bad for you. That's why he's so fat. Do dead people all poop themselves like this?"

"See, sister-girl? I told you. It always goes back to ass functions. I was right after all, wasn't I? Just admit it."

"What?" Danni asked robotically, steeped in a daze.

"Don't listen to him, sweetie. You can open your eyes now. It's okay now."

"What's that do?" she asked Gina, as Danni blinked to get reacquainted with twinkling Christmas lights strung in that foul-smelling basement. Odors of fresh urine and excrement mixed with pools of coagulated blood next to the cooling bodies.

"It fixes and destroys things. But don't worry, sweetie. My daddy raised me like a boy," Gina said, as she test-started the reciprocating saw with a quick whir.

"Can we please go now? I don't like it being down here like this," Danni whined. "So why is it we need that thing, Gina? And what's all that noise for?" she frowned.

"It's the sound of freedom, little girl. In just another quick minute Gina will have me cut me loose from this goddamn wall. That means we'll be on our way home to Ma's pasta kitchen like nothing ever happened. It's finally over. We're finished with this."

Rocco held the top of the boot between his teeth. He growled to keep himself from passing out again while his sister sliced the nail away from his hand with the vibrating saw blade.

"Stop! Goddamn-it this nail is fucking hot! Okay. Wait. Just hold-up. Let me catch my breath," Rocco said, as Gina set down the saw. "Quick! Put that wet sponge on my hand."

Danni did as asked. Gina buried her bloodied face into smeared hands and cried. "I don't think I can do this. I can't hurt you like this, Rocco. Please don't make me do this."

"That's it. Let it cool off for a second. You're already more than half-way through, and this thing ain't getting any cooler. So fuck-it. Let's just do it. We gotta get out of here, and this is the only way out. Come-on, sister-girl. Don't cur out on me now. But please do it quick…"

"Can we please get some fresh air," asked Danni. Then she puked on the floor in a puddle of their urine.

"Sure thing, honey. We'll roll all the windows down once we get to the car. Okay, bro, let's get this over with. Ready?" Gina restarted the saw and put all her body weight against if. She was completely through the nail within seconds. Rocco's eyes were as tightly closed as Danni's had been. Rocco screamed. Gina dropped the saw. The heavy metal tool thunked against the floor in finality. She slid Rocco's hand up off the spike that had been nailed between metacarpals, a trap holding him captive through that entire fiasco to a 4" x 4" support brace of a piece of pit wall.

"Thank you, my friends," Rocco whispered, weakly.

"Okay, I'm a little better now," Danni said.

"YES! Okay, then let's boogie!" Gina said, as she and Danni lifted Rocco to his feet and helped him to the steps.

"You both look like used maternity panties with all that blood and nasty gunk all over your faces and hair. We can't drive around like this – not even in Collinwood."

"What about our clothes," asked Danni. "They're nasty."

"Yeah, you're right. But let's not get too sidetracked. We'll be hunkered down in your car. Just remember: not one word about this – ever! We can't even talk about it to each other. This shit never fucking happened. And eventually, when we do hear about it, act like you're not shocked or pretend you're indifferent. Just don't overdo it, that's all. Just act the way you really feel about it – minus the paranoia. Got it?"

"Hey man," smiled Danni for the first time that day. "Haven't you heard the news? My father was a famous gangster. It's in my pedigree to handle stuff like this."

"Mine too, bro," Gina laughed long and hard with a blood spattered face. "So how about you, boy? You up to this?"

"Oh, yeah… I got this. Bet on that shit!" Rocco groaned, doubled over in pain.

CH XXIX: The Aftermath

December 29th, 2013 – The Inn: While looking over the carnage in and around that pit, spatters of dog and human blood unrecognizable from one another, random purple splotches formed as creatively as a Rorschach inkblot test.

"That was really something the way everything came down so quick. Wow… Just one wrong decision and your whole life turns to pure shit in an eye blink. But before I forget, there's one last thing we need to discuss."

"No way. You've said this before – a few times. Let's just boogie," Danni encouraged her man.

"Okay. First let's just take a minute to think this through. Because once we turn our backs there ain't no coming back."

"Good. Because I'll never step foot in this pigsty again."

"That might not be the best idea, Danni. Let's talk about that, and some other things. First things first, though."

"I agree with her, little bro," Gina said. "Fuck this place. Once that door locks behind us, we need it to stay locked. No second chances here, ever. That time is gone. Our time is now. That's what Pop would say."

"Okay, Gina. I think you're on the right track. So let's look at this from another angle. You've known our father for more than 35 years longer than I have, back when he was still a young buck riding Harleys and hanging with 1%ers and wise-guys. Can you remember what he was like? You know, like the vibe he threw off, or certain patterns of behavior for typical ways he might think and respond."

"I don't know . . . I guess maybe a little. I'd have to think about that awhile, but we just don't have that luxury at the moment. This isn't the time or place for cruising Memory Lane."

"I have to ask you one question, sister-girl. Put yourself in Pop's shoes. We need you to answer the way he would, okay?"

"Let's go. I'm getting the creeps just thinking about this."

"Hold up. Let's pretend for a second Pop's here with us," Rocco said. "Just like when we all responded to the *Click* today. So, what's the next *Click*? Think about it hard; feel it; be part of it; live it; react on that mind-meld level; do it like Pop would. Let's do it together right now, just like he would. Be him! Do this!"

"Well . . . yeah, hmmm." Gina nodded her head with half-closed eyes. "Let's see… How about we begin with all the tools we touched with our bloody hand prints."

"Okay, good thinking! Grab the Sawzall. Danni, get the maul and crowbar. Hand me the claw hammer and those snips."

"What about that bottle neck you told me to drop? We want that one, too?"

"Yes! Good stuff, baby-girl! You're all over this. Get it and drop it into my front pocket. Okay now, Gina, what else?"

"What about this nail in this post? It's still covered with your blood."

"Right-on, Gina! Back out those screws holding the post to the wall. Can you use that saw to slice off the top of this post with the spike in it. Then drop it in that Dollar Store bag over there, the one from Nicky and Sally-boy's lights. Sound good?"

Instead of answering Rocco, she removed the post, sawed off the nail and then the end of wood, and dropped the stub into a yellow bag that held a string of blue lights. She dropped the bloody spike into her brother's pocket and felt it clink against the bloody roughneck Danni put in there. That clinking sound, a physical connection of two items in one pocket linking their dilemma, created a small jolt to help him feel that things were finally coming together for them.

"I know! The wallets! I need their wallets!" Rocco announced, as if he had just experienced an epiphany on a celestial level. "Grab the wallets and check their pockets."

"Why?" Gina frowned. "It's not like these two goons can't be identified just because they're not dressed in expensive silk suits. Everybody in Collinwood knows these two scumbags, maybe everybody in Cleveland."

Danni volunteered, "I'll rob them."

"Gina, you actually think I'm worried these two *schieves* won't be properly ID'd? Fuck them. I couldn't care less if we dumped these two pieces of shit in the sewer out front," Rocco said, as he watched Danni pat down the pockets and body of Cagootz. She took his wallet. "Phew... This guy is really getting ripe down here, babe. This whole basement smells like ass. Hey, Gina, remember my story about asses?" Rocco asked.

"Which story? You never told me a story about asses."

"Well, Danni, it's like this—"

"Are you for real, Rocco? What happens if some of their friends decide to drop in? Then who are the real asses?"

Rocco spotted a thick roll of bills in another pocket of Cagootz. It turned out to be all hundreds. Gina walked over to the remains of Big Louie and did the same.

Gina said, "Bull lost his life in this same pit. No way we leave without this money – our money – for the local animals and cops to find. Whatever these two pricks have on them, plus what we find in the register upstairs, is ours. We split four ways."

"Four?" asked Danni. "Where did you go to school, Gina, Collinwood? There's only three of us here, honey, unless one of these butchered guys turns zombie on us."

"Four, meaning Ma gets a cut. We'll tell her we went in on a $20 scratch-off. Put all the wallets and cash in there," Rocco said, pointing to the Christmas lights bag.

"Now you're gonna start lying to Ma?" asked his sister.

"Okay, Gina, then we won't give her anything. Or you can tell her the three of us just murdered two mafia men and then robbed their corpses. Is it better like that?"

"Let's just hurry. But no lies after today – not ever."

"Danni, you're familiar with the register. And your prints are supposed to be on it. Go up and take all the folding money, no checks or change, and make sure you look underneath the drawer for the large bills. Then leave it wide open, okay?"

"Can Gina please come with me? I'm still shaking."

"Okay, come-on, honey. Let's clean these bastards out and split," Gina said as they headed for the stairs. "I hate to admit it but Rocco might be right about this."

"Hey, another thing," Rocco called out. "Use napkins to lift a few full bottles from the bar. Set them at the top of the steps. Put the napkins in your pockets. We might need them."

"Are you serious?" asked his sister. "I think we can buy our own booze, you cheap bastard! Besides, you're supposed to be in recovery. You can't drink. First you're trying to lie to Ma, and now you're stashing booze? What the fuck, little bro?"

"Just do what I asked, Gina. We can argue later, once we're tucked safely away in the car. Just do it!" Rocco groaned.

While the girls were upstairs, after all pants and jacket pockets of Cagootz and Louie were thoroughly rechecked, Rocco went back to where Danni found the bottle of gin she had used as a pain killer against the claw hammer. He winced when he thought about her trying to yank that nail out of his hand.

Rocco held two opened bottles of booze between his knees and carefully with his smashed hand he carried one of them over to Big Louie and spilled it from its pour top across him as if he were basting a rotisserie pig. The other bottle he used to saturate the carpet of the pit floor, artfully on and around the perimeter of Cagootz' body, like he was making a liquid chalk drawing at a legitimate homicide scene by an illegitimate cop. He was careful to pour straight booze into their open wounds. He said to himself, "Not even Robert De Nino can play dead thought this pain. These assholes are as gone as yesterday."

Rocco lifted two more fifths of booze, their necks secured between almost dead fingers, lifted them over his head and dropped them on the concrete floor next to the wooden pit, where three of its 16-foot long sides were somewhat intact. About half of them broke. Two bottles at a time, he dumped glass containers on concrete near the three-sided basement pit. Rocco shattered two more by the lumber pile where Danni had hidden.

With shaky legs he went upstairs for the first time since they had arrived at The Inn. Evidently, the girls made a quick pit stop to freshen up. Their hair was dripping wet. Their shirts were damp and wrinkled. Rocco noticed neither was wearing a bra. He quickly looked away and said, "What, no make-up?"

Their shirts must have been stripped off, washed and rinsed in the women's bathroom sink, and then squeezed out by hand before being put back on. Rumpled and damp, they looked like lost orphans – huddled together near the rest room, holding each other's hands like frightened children. When they saw him they beamed dual smiles like winners at a wet T-shirt contest.

Danni ran up to her man and snuggled him. "When we heard footsteps coming we didn't know what to think! I knew I loved you before, dude. But now? Shit, man! You're the fucking Z-bomb! I'm never leaving you, buddy, not for anything in the whole wide world. You're the best friend I've ever had or ever will have. And I know this. Plus the bonus plan of our friendship is we have mad sex."

"I love you too, baby," Rocco grinned. "But it's no big deal what any of us did here today. It's just the way true friends do. But I will say this: If I can't have Whitey at my back, youse two ladies are just as game and maybe even deadlier."

"And to you, Gina," Danni said. "I'll tell you something right now. If I ever start digging on bad-ass, beautiful chicks, I'll be calling on you, sexy mama. You're my fucking hero, you crazy psycho bitch!" she giggled. "And in the spirit of honesty, I gotta say it. I snuck a few peaks when your shirt was off just now in the bathroom. Chick, you might have the nicest tits I've ever seen!"

"Ditto on that, sweet thing. Tell you what, Danni. If my brother ever dumps you, look me up. We'll move to Washington and I'll marry you're sweet self and serve joints at the wedding if his dumb ass won't commit," Gina grinned and shook wet curls all over her face as she laughed out loud in relief. "FUCK YES!!! We did it, didn't we?"

"Before you two *dykesters* get too invested in your twisted little daydream, just know I ain't going anywhere. That means both of youse nutty bitches are stuck with me, for better or worse – forever. Swear to Buddha, we're all bonded for life now."

Gina said, "At least we don't look like used sanitary napkins. Why didn't you tell us we had blood clots and pieces of bone all over?"

"He still gazed down the basement stairway, like in a trance, hoping that was the last time he'd ever see a pit. Did youse dry off with a cloth towel in a machine or paper?" asked a pale Rocco who looked weak as he leaned his back against a wall.

"Paper," Danni said. "Why, is there paper stuck to us?"

"Where did you put the used towels?" Rocco inquired, as if his new calling in life was as a private investigator for the Collinwood fashion police.

"Where do you think? We threw them in a trash can. Why?" Rocco's sister asked. Then she rolled her eyes at Danni. "Come-on. Let's boogie our bad selves out of here."

"Go get 'em. Hurry up." Rocco said to his sister and girlfriend. "In fact, bring the whole trash can here to me, right here by the top of these steps."

They came back out dragging a medium-sized metal trash can that sounded full. When they got it to the top of the steps, Rocco removed the lid, kicked it down the steps and said, "Both of you get two bottles of booze in each hand. Do it quick!"

"Do you want more tequila?" Danni asked with a frown. "Maybe you should ease off for awhile, buddy. It's early."

"I don't care what kind. Just fucking do it!"

"Hey! Don't yell at us, asshole!" his sister snapped at him. "We've been through a lot here, okay? Lighten up, Rocco…"

"Sorry. My hand and arm are killing me. I apologize for being short with either of you. I won't do it again. But we really need to step on it. We're hanging around here like there ain't two dead mafia guys in this basement, and like we're not saturated with their blood. Look at us. We need to move like pronto, so let's do this really quick. Get two of each – of anything that contains alcohol. No beer or wine, please…"

"Don't worry, honey," Gina assured Rocco's girlfriend. "You didn't do anything wrong. When Rocco gets tired or hungry, he acts like a fucking asshole and picks on the people feeding him and providing a bed. You're doing just fine, sweetie."

Danni ran to the bar and back. "I'm sorry for being a bitch. Here's the tequila. You want a glass too, babe? I trust you."

He stared at Danni, like meeting someone odd for the first time. And in some ways, he was. No hysterics, not even anymore tears. She was as steady as a rock – just a bit ditzy. But considering what they'd just experienced, she and his sister were handling amazingly well, almost as if murder was old-hat. *Maybe composure under duress is a genetic component.* Rocco made a mental note. He considered the, "You want a glass too, babe?" comment. That was an odd thing to ask. He wondered if she had suffered a nervous breakdown or was slipping into shock, or maybe she was one of those rare people who didn't panic during extreme stress.

Gina said, "Give her a break. We've been through the most traumatic event of our lives, and it isn't over yet. What's the plan, little bro? Just say it quick so we can scoot."

"Throw three of those bottles down the steps by those towels, Gina. Let them crash on the floor. Then split. Leave the front door open, but try to look normal. *Walk* to your car, don't run. Then pull your car onto the next block, right behind the bar. Take the Sawzall and big hammer with you. Me and Danni will hightail it out the back and be waiting for you. She'll help me. We'll meet you with the other hand tools. Cool?"

"Laters, bro. I'm already there."

"See you in a flash. Love you, big sister."

Gina rushed toward the door, awash with confusion by the newness of so many firsts occurring all at once in her life. Then she remembered their plan, so she took a deep breath to slow her roll so she wouldn't look panicked.

"Okay, baby-girl. It's your turn, Danni. You got a match?"

"I have a lighter. You need me to find matches?"

"No. A lighter's better. Open this tequila and then take out the driest paper towel you still have in your pocket. Twist it like you're rolling a joint. But make it tight. That's it. Good girl. See? Even drug abuse pays off sometimes. Now stuff that paper tube about half-way inside. Great! Okay, just light the wick you just made and toss the bottle. Then we run like hell to find Gina."

Rocco's legs still worked fine, although wobbly from pain, blood loss and trauma. Regardless, working on adrenaline, he and Danni dashed away from The Inn as fast as two people half in shock can flee, to find Gina parked exactly where they expected to find her, with the engine running and both passenger doors partially open. She maneuvered her little all-wheel hatchback through side streets, driving the speed limit. The sky behind them changed from a blustery blue to a torrent of filthy gray smoke.

"Damn! All this being solid stuff must run in the family," Gina laughed and hollered from the front seat. "I have the coolest goddamn brother and sister-in-law in the whole fucking world!" Then she said, "Nope, no way. Fuck this! I'm pulling over on this one!" Gina braked and slid into a parking spot in front of some random house a few blocks away. She jumped into the back to ferociously hug them. "AGH! So this is the meaning of life! I finally get it!" She kissed each of them on the mouth, hard and quick, still laughing. Then she hopped back behind the steering wheel to slowly and calmly drive back to Tessa's as if she were an old maid bus driver transporting a precious cargo of children after a strenuous day of play at their schoolyard.

Three damaged, middle-aged kids pulled up in Tessa's driveway, psychologically traumatized, physically spent, and one badly damaged. Gina parked all the way back in her step-mother's driveway near the garage and turned to face her brother and new best friend. *Click* The three of them nodded, wordlessly they cemented their newest pact before navigating their next difficult hurdle. They slowly exited Gina's inconspicuous-looking car, trying to pretend that the shocking day they had just experienced was part of another normal Sunday dinner about to unfold in Tessa's cozy dining room. But they stopped at the door as if it were electrified. Rocco finally knocked. Little Sinbad barked his "Someone's here but it's a friend" alarm and ran to the greet them.

Danni paused and shuddered with her head lowered. He wrapped his good arm around her and tenderly kissed a flushed cheek. Danni returned a nervous smile. Next he put his forehead on the top of his sister's cluster of dense curls and kissed her wet hair. "Stay cool. We got this."

Gina pushed herself away from them to open that dreaded passageway, took a deep breath and then reached back to grab a collar of each. As they awkwardly struggled through the

36" doorway into Tessa's domain Gina laughed, "Can you believe those assholes? There should be hunting season one day a year for jerk-off drivers like those two idiots we just had to deal with!"

Click "Wow! You're not kidding!" Rocco chuckled loudly, uncharacteristic of his usually subdued, laidback style. He quickly reined in his composure. He was aware that his mother was nobody's fool, so he switched back to dialogue she would recognize as a tone more typical of his ever-vigilant macho persona and sarcasm. "Yeah, I've seen some world-class dip-shits in my time, but those poor bastards are Hall of Fame. I mean, how does anyone get through life being that much of an ass-wad and still be allowed to come out of their attic without helmets?"

"No shit! Those types scare the crap out of me!" Danni blurted out. "I'm surprised they weren't wearing tinfoil hats." She took in another deep breath. "But you two are nuts! You know that? I just have to say it out loud. There's no question. You two are definitely related."

Gina watched her step-mother shake her head. Tessa smiled when she heard them laughing and talking loud. As they entered the next room, still laughing, Tessa asked, "What is it now? What did I miss this time? Oh, and since when do you knock at your own door, Rocco? You too, Gina. Go ahead. Tell me this funny story of yours." She watched their eyes.

Gina dropped her large purse with a thud and a few contents spilled onto the thick rug. Little Sinbad was there in an instant, nosing things to inspect for goodies. In one deft motion, Tessa's attention already diverted, Gina swept a few items and the pistol back in as she lifted her purse and slung it over a shoulder. Then the beautiful woman with an olive complexion charged through the house, speaking fast and loud: "Some freaks nearly killed us out there, Ma! They ran us right into the curb and then were yelling and flipping us off. So my idiot brother hops out and decides to fight these two guys by himself, like he's some tough guy. Look at his hand! Plus, I think his arm is broken!"

"Oh my aching Christ!" Tessa gasped. "What the hell happened to you, son? Let's go. You need to get to the hospital."

"Easy, Ma. It's just surface rust. I knocked off a little bark, is all," he assured her with a serious look and his usual smirk. "And because those punks in that custom hotrod were totally in the wrong, there won't be any blow-back with cops from any of this. It's cool. Really…"

"Just surface, Rocco? Really?" mocked his sister. "You're arm is broken, dude. That's pretty far from surface, you maniac! Danni's right about you with all the tough guy bullshit. That's why he had a problem with drugs, Ma. This fool thinks he's bulletproof. You think it makes you look soft if you say no or reach out for help. Don't you, Rocco? Maybe use your head and learn to step back to process once in awhile before reacting. You could have put us all in danger, crazy boy."

"Gina's right. Did they hit you with something, Rocco? Tell me right now!" his mother demanded, with dainty fists firmly planted on slim hips. "Don't you lie to me!"

"They had some metal thingy," Danni said, wearing a worried expression, "It was like an iron rod or some type of tool. But Rocco is game as hell, Mrs. L. You should have seen him! Mr. Jack would have been proud of his boy." She turned to her boyfriend, "Even though you're a pressure cooker, babe, your dad would've been proud. I know Gina and I are. I'm even more in love now, if that's even possible. You can't believe the terrible things those two guys said to Gina and me! And I really believe they were thinking about hurting us if Rocco didn't step-up like he did. This guy's a hero!"

"Yeah," smiled Gina. "You got some brass balls, little bro. That's straight-up. You're my new hero. Pop would be acting all concerned but bursting with pride. You did good, buddy. I have the coolest brother in the whole world. He's so brave, Ma!"

"*Mama mia*! How many times do I have to tell you about that road rage of yours, Rocco?" Tessa raised her voice with a trace of a half smile. "I'm serious! One of these days you're going to run into someone you can't beat up with all that judo stuff of yours. Or worse yet, someone will try to kill you. Someone just did try! You're about half crazy, you know that?"

"Hey, don't look at me. Talk to these two whack-jobs," Rocco laughed, holding his injured arm. "They double-teamed one of the guys. Holy shit! You should've seen it, Ma! It was so goddamn funny."

"Really? You two helped Rocco beat up two men? Seriously? Come on, don't try to bullshit me."

"Honest. You should a seen 'em, Ma. They were amazing; incredible; awesome; dead-game! We're gonna start a gang, wear colors and get matching tats. These are two bad-ass mamas."

"I don't want to hear anymore about it," Tessa sighed. "It's your fault these girls got involved in whatever kind of trouble you're in now. What's the matter with you, boy? Why are you corrupting these two angels? First you have them cursing like you and talking filthy, then you coax them into getting high with you. And now you have them fighting with men? You said all this was over traffic out in the street? Wow... What a foolish thing to do, Rocco. You really are a little nuts and very immature."

"Okay then. Hold-up, Ma. Let me explain. I'll tell you everything right now," he said, glancing at his sister and girlfriend.

"No, Rocco! I already told you. I don't want to hear it. Just drop it and go have a shower before we take you to the hospital. You smell like a wet dog but worse, and like booze! Are you wearing underwear? What makes you so sure those guys didn't take down your license plate number? Do you have any idea how many people get hurt in traffic? Some of them end up going to jail or even get killed. *Madonna mia!*"

"Well, Ma, hypothetically speaking—"

"That's enough! Just go! You're stinking up this whole house. And put on some decent clothes . . . and some underpants! Now hurry up and shower so we can leave. You go help him, Danni. He wouldn't let me or his sister in there, even if he was dying. But I'm sure he won't mind you in there..."

As Rocco and Danni entered the bathroom, Gina went into the kitchen and got a glass of ice water. She leaned on the counter to take a few slow breaths to control her rapid heartbeat. Then she asked in a more controlled voice, "You want anything while I'm in here, Ma?"

"No, honey, I'm fine. But grab a beer and come back in here. I need to tell you something while they're still in the bathroom. So hurry up, okay? It's important."

Click Gina took a deep breath and shook out her hair. Then she beamed her brightest smile ever before she returned to find out exactly what her step-mother wanted to talk about, although she had a pretty good idea. "Here I am, my *favoritest* step-mom and very *bestest* friend in the whole world! What can I do for you? Just name it, Ma."

They heard the shower stop beating against the tub surround. Tessa answered with her own beautiful smile as she looked affectionately at her step-daughter: "Look at you! That face of yours gets me every time. You really are the prettiest girl I've ever seen. I think that smile of yours could stop wars. You should patent it. We'd be millionaires and our problems would be over." When the shower turned back on Tessa asked, "Do we need to go back to make sure? I need to be sure about some things. Has everything been cleaned, honey?"

Gina cleared her throat and examined her toenail polish. She wiggled her toes as she asked, "You mean his cut, Ma? I guess we'll see in a quick minute, huh?" Gina laughed. "Well, unless those two love birds are in the shower together. That could take a whole five minutes. But who knows with those two?" she laughed. "It might even be healed by the time they get dressed," Gina said, as she again flashed her dazzling smile.

"What color was that custom hotrod those two guys were driving, Gina? Because Rocco already said a color, I want to see how good your memory is. Go ahead, tell me."

Gina shifted her stance but smiled. "How do you mean?"

Tessa gave her a disgusted look and with a big sigh she put her hands on slim hips again and said, "Okay . . . enough already. Just stop right now with all this. Please."

"Stop what, Ma?" Gina said, but with a much weaker smile as she again avoided eye contact and slumped a bit in her shoulders. "I'm not exactly sure what you mean."

"Tell me what happened. It's okay, Gina. You're safe."

"I did, Ma. Rocco was in a fight with two guys and we helped. I promise! That's what happened."

"Oh, I see. What if I was a cop and you can't even tell me the color of the car? Well, let's continue with the memory tests. At least tell me this: Who was my father?"

"What? Doc, of course... Why would you ask me this?"

"Good. Now just play along. And who's my uncle?"

"You mean Pazzo? Come on, Ma. What does Pazzo have to do with anything? Anyway, can we get ready to go?"

"Okay so far. Now tell me who my godfather was."

"And I'm not sure where we're going with this."

"Yes you are, Gina. You're positive. Now talk to me."

"Okay... Let me guess. Uno was your godfather. Am I right?" Gina attempted to beam another of her blinding grins at Tessa, with milk-white, perfect teeth. "I'll go knock at the door."

"Hold on. That's pretty good so far, honey. But the water's still running. Only a few more of these type questions. Who's my cousin? You know, a guy who was more like a brother while we were growing up together? What's his name?"

Gina sighed, "You mean his real name or his nickname?"

"Yes . . . whatever!

"Everybody knows him as Fingers. Okay? Have I passed the memory test?"

"Almost. And now for the last one: Just humor me, okay? Just remind me of who my husband was, the guy who trusted no one in this entire world other than you till he finally married me a few months ago? What's his name again?"

Gina whined even louder: "Geez... This is really silly. Okay... Your *husband* was my *father*, and also the father of Rocco. His name is Jack. Why are you doing this, Ma?"

"After having all those lunatics in my life, all the way back since my earliest memories till now, do you really think I'm this naive? Oh, and by the way, I saw on Channel 8 about a big fire down Five Points. Were you anywhere near it? I smelled smoke when you came in."

Gina stood still, staring at the carpet, thinking of the best answer. Other than the shower running, the only other sound came from ice cubes clinking in Gina's water glass. She finally looked up at Tessa, but that time with a frightened expression. "I don't know what to say about any fires. I didn't see a fire. Okay, Ma? Please?"

"Okay. So I'm going to ask you one last time. Has everything been cleaned to the point where it's as spotless as a blank domino?"

"Yes, Ma. As spotless as a blank set of dice, okay?"

"Don't forget: I know where you took your brother and Danni. You left from here. And I know why you had to go there and who you had to meet. So that means, based on what I already sensed, what I heard about on the news and now what I see, I can guess what happened. So do we need to go back or call someone in for help?"

"It's over."

"Do I need to worry?"

"Never., Ma. I swear to Buddha. Like I said: it's done."

"I see... Can we trust her?"

"Yes. Implicitly."

"You're willing to bet your freedom on that?"

"Yeah ... I am."

"I sure hope so. You're 100% certain on all this?"

"I'll bet my life on it. Pop would be very proud. Rocco stepped up, but at the right time. His head was clear. No drugs."

"Okay, I trust your judgment you, honey. Your dad would be proud of you, too. That's for sure. And speaking of fathers, do you know who her father is?"

"Yes, Ma. But I'd rather not get into details now. Okay?"

"You don't need to. I've been around this madness all my life. I've seen it too many times not to recognize it."

"I'm so sorry, Ma. I really, really am. I feel bad in a way."

"May worms rot in their eyeballs, those dirty motherfuckers! I'm not concerned about them in the least. Are you sure you're alright, honey? Come here. Give me a hug. Tell me true. You can be real with me. Are you really okay?"

"Yes . . . I mean, I think so." Then Gina burst into tears and ran into her step-mother's outstretched arms. She leaned her head down on Tessa's shoulder and sobbed till the shower turned off again. Then she ran back into the kitchen to wash her face and dry her eyes. She silently swore at herself, thinking she had betrayed her brother, and fearing she was weak for crying when Tessa needed her to stay strong."

When Gina came back into the front-room carrying a blue plastic tray she said, "Okay, Ma, here we go. Nice glasses of ice water for everyone."

Tessa handed her a pair of sunglasses. "Gina, I told you to grab a beer. Why did you only bring water?" She stroked Gina's face and hair as she said, "You know something? It's really amazing. You remind me so much of your father. You're one tough chick – a real Collinwood girl. I know I can count on you, honey. Now with Daddy gone, I hope you understand that no matter what happens you always have a home. I'm your mother, too. This terrible day only drew us closer."

"I really do love you, Ma, and of course Rocco . . . and now Danni, too. But I sure do miss my daddy." Gina broke down in tears and held an arm over her eyes as she wept.

"Do you ever dream about your dad? I mean, like realistic dreams?" Do you understand what I'm asking?"

Click "At times I actually hear his voice. Sometimes I remember the words after I wake up, like he's talking to me while I'm asleep. I've been afraid to tell anyone. Why? You too, Ma?"

"Yeah, honey. Me too. He tells me things while I'm asleep. This other thing is really weird. Almost every night since he's been gone I dream I'm being suffocated by something. Your dad rescues me in my sleep by pulling something off my throat. Then he tells me he's coming home to take care of us."

"Whoa! Swear to Buddha, that's the same dream I have. Is it a dream of a snake choking you?"

"Yes, it's a dream of the snake tattooed on his back – that ouroboros smothering me."

"The one like Rocco has! What the fuck, Ma? What does that crazy shit even mean?"

"We've discussed his *accident*. But the thing we never talked about is that they never found a body. All the police found was left of some burned up clothes and boots in the woods. On them they found hair, skin and blood. Forensics was able to match the blood type to your dad's. But not one body part was ever found– nothing. Don't you think that's odd?"

"You saw the car, Ma. You were there. It looked like someone crushed a ripped up beer and tossed an empty into a bonfire. Nobody could have survived that explosion – not even Daddy. Even the cops weren't surprised. It was like a cremation."

"Yes, I know. But why is it they could retrieve clothes but not anything more solid? I mean . . . well . . . what about dental matches?"

The coroner said if the blast and fire were hot enough to melt solid metal, then it easily could dissipate bones, teeth and even fillings like in a crematorium. And the explosion itself could have scattered tiny parts of him all over the woods for birds and critters to run off with. I know it's totally gross to even think about, Ma. But you heard those cops talking about it, too. All of that's on the report, right?"

"The coroner is good friend of an old friend. The words he used were '*could have*'. But that's only if we assume your dad was still inside the car during the time of the explosion. None of them ever considered other options; at least not in front of us."

"But you said you saw Daddy in the car! You gave a statement to the cops and everything. You told me and Rocco that same story! You said he was sitting in there pressing radio buttons, talking to himself and pounding the dashboard. You told us you were paralyzed with fear and then passed out, Ma, and you said that's the last time you ever saw him. That's exactly what you said! I heard you say it! We all did. I was in the hospital when you woke up. Did you forget that?"

"No, honey, I didn't forget. The dreams of him telling me he's coming for us began while I was in the hospital, in a coma, or shock, or a breakdown, or whatever the hell happened to me."

Gina looked at the floor again just as Rocco stepped out of the bathroom with Danni trailing behind him. He said, "Ahh, that feels a little better. But I gotta say it: Okay, Ma. It's official. My arm's probably broken. I'll have the girls drive me to a hospital. That way they can look at this hand, too."

"Not without me. Just give me half a minute to double-check, to make sure everything's turned off. Gina, honey, please let the dog out for a quick pee, sweetie. And then we'll all go together. I need to show my insurance card, anyway."

"Give us the card. The girls can take me. This way—"

"Save it, son. I'm going, and that's that. Danni, you help him into Gina's backseat and sit back with him. Okay, sweetie?"

"Rocco protested, glancing at his sister. "There might be people there trying to make some bullshit reports. You know how they are, acting all important with their stupid little questions. Gina will phone you when we're leaving the hospital so you can start boiling the *gnocchi*. This way it'll be all ready when we finally get done with those bust-out doctors and cops."

"*Cops?* Why would there be cops? I don't understand. You said there would be no blow-back, didn't you?"

"Well, *hypothetically* speaking—"

"Stop with that bullshit! Listen real close! I'm saying this once. I thought I saw moisture around the chimney. Rocco went up on the roof to see if there's a leak. This same idiot son of mine stood up on a snowy roof, trying to shovel it off when he slipped, fell off backwards and broke his arm. What's even worse is he hit a board that had a big nail sticking out. It went through my idiot son's hand. Things like this happen all the time when people have been drinking – people who are in recovery…"

He stood up straighter: "I don't drink, Ma. Today was six months," Rocco said, defensively. "And you know this!"

Gina pulled a cold can of P.O.C. out of her purse and handed it to her brother. "Here, drink this. They'll test you for booze, just as sure as we aren't about to win the lottery anytime soon. So the next time you open your mouth, keep quiet and pour this piss-water in your big yap."

"I can't," Rocco said, with a shit-eating grin. "Besides, why would you get involved in this? I already told you. It's cool." Rocco tried his best not to look down at the rug for too long.

"Whatever… You smoke almost every day," Gina hissed. "Now all the sudden you're in recovery? Give us a break. Just slam this little beer! Quit being such an asshole, Rocco."

"Why am I involved? You're my family, that's why! Like I was saying," Tessa continued, just as calmly as Gina was riled: "You girls were in the house fixing dinner, so you missed it. Only I saw what happened. You poor thing, Rocco. You're still all shook up from that nasty concussion, You're confused about the whole incident. The only parts you remember, since I'm the one who found you laying unconscious in the snow with a board attached to the back of your hand, are climbing onto the lower roof from your bedroom window and waking up laying on the ground. You're such an idiot! So that's why I need to be there. I'm the only one who found you. Understand?"

"You sure about this?" Rocco asked, in obvious pain and stern gray eyes to mask his fears.

"Danni, where were you when this happened to Rocco?" Tessa demanded. "And don't you dare lie to anyone about this! Tell the exact truth . . . the same truth for everyone."

"You mean when you found out that Rocco fell?"

"Don't you concern yourself about what I mean... My kids and I need to know exactly what you think about this, and we need to have your answer right now."

"You already know all this, Mrs. L. Gina and I were in the kitchen stirring the sauce like we do every Sunday, talking and boiling macaroni, when we heard commotion outside."

"Stop! I won't listen to any more of that *Mrs. L* bullshit. You hear me, Danni? Are you family or not?"

"Sorry," Danni said, looking away from Tessa's piercing green eyes. "Yeah, I'm family" she grinned. "It won't happen again, Ma. But I really did tell the truth the first time. What I said is exactly what happened. And I'm willing to wager my life that my story will never, ever change. Why should it?" she asked, while quickly looking at Gina, then over to Rocco, and then directly back into Tessa's penetrating gaze with her own beautiful smile that gradually relit that darkened room. "So can we eat as soon as we get back, Ma? The smell of this sauce is almost killing me. I'm just in the mood for some *gnocchi* and some of Gina's killer antipasto. We'll handle the cooking when we get back. Gina and I can be killers with simple kitchen gadgets."

"Yeah, Ma, that's the goddamn truth right there. My big sister-girl will make someone a *lethal* housewife. I mean . . . when you got it, you got it; and that's that." said Rocco, as he dipped a chunk of fresh bread in the pot of tomato gravy and stuffed it into his mouth. He wiped the remnants of sauce off his moustache with the back of his still useable tattooed arm and nodded, "Gina's a *killer* cook! She ain't too bad of a driver, either. In fact, as soon as I inhale a little more of this, I'm gonna let her haul my sorry ass to the emergency room to see what else I injured from that fall off the roof."

"Maybe we end this circle jerk long enough for a little nourishment before we're riders in the storm again?" asked Gina.

"Just a quick slice of bread dipped in sauce. Hurry up!"

Rocco tried to flex thick fingers sticking out of his wrapped hand. Danni had used gauze and a new ace bandage to combat the throbbing till he got professional help. He starred at his red, swollen fingers as he said, "I sure wish Pop was here."

Without looking up from her plate Gina said, "He is."

"Whoa… Are you getting religious on us all the sudden?"

"I've been feeling our father stronger and closer every day. I'm not sure why. But that *Click* has been pounding inside my skull for days, especially during sleep." Gina said, while stuffing her mouth with freshly baked bread dipped in sauce.

Danni rose from her seat to put an arm around Gina. She smoothed Gina's mussed-up curls and assured her, "Don't worry, sweetie. It's okay. We're here for each other. We all just need a good meal and a good sleep so we can get back to normal."

"Yeah, sister-girl. I feel him. He's real close."

Tessa tilted back her head to allow her long, silver blonde hair to drape across her back as she smiled and said, "So . . . I guess I'm not the only one then, huh?"

"Well, well," Rocco responded, as he shook his head, "I'll be goddamned. And this whole time I thought it was that hydro putting the zap to my brain." He painfully stroked his thick beard.

Danni said, as she returned to the pot of simmering sauce with her little saucer and another slice of fresh Italian bread, its golden crust topped off with sesame seeds. "This whole day, without a doubt, has been the craziest experience of my life."

Gina agreed with a vigorous nod of curly hair, "No doubt. But I have a weird feeling this isn't even close to being over."

Rocco had Danni pop the can of P.O.C. He gently held it between thumb and fingertip and grunted as he chugged half of its contents. "Ugh! This is horrible! Do I have to finish it?"

"Gina, put another one in your purse and let's go."

PART SIX

I woke to a searing baseline pounding dream-lyrics through a throbbing brain. It was something I'd heard before, from a dream I could almost remember, while drifting in the periphery of life.

With a child comes a vision. From that struggle unfolds how
From adults grow more childish ways alive in dreams of madmen
Off blind eyes reflecting a past too real. Its present all too far
Away, gone as quickly as right now.
Constricted in its death grip, shredding itself with passion.

Living dreams out of focus, passions almost within reach.
Of carefree moments until the nightmares settled in, a time
Before that final breach.
Weightless transparencies from a moment much like me,
To meditate and ruminate that this loop will cease to be.

But that serpent's in my brain. Shredding logic, who'll I blame?
Ain't no place to run or hide; now it's burrowed deep inside.
Ain't nowhere I can go. Tearing me insane, apart because I know.
Savage thoughts still flashing through these snake eyes from
Which I view.

Lucid dreams; distorted passions; courage in pathetic rations.
A past and present all too real, a future I could all but feel.
Weightless transparencies from that moment I'd expired,
Idealistic dreams forever lost in those two I sired.

Still that serpent's in my brain. Poisoned madness, who'll I maim?
'Cause that thing's inside my head, no more rest until I'm dead.
Face the fear; fight the pain; six of one – still in my brain.
These snake eyes with which I view are still looking inside you.

I felt the *Click* as clearly as anything I've ever experienced with those five traditional senses we've come to understand as reality. My future, the fate of my family, a final resolution, as always all rested on my next decisions, as usual all beginning with how I navigate the first and next steps or when I decide to—

CH XXX: 13 O'clock

December 29th, 2013: Rocco had Danni pop open the can of P.O.C. He gently held it between thumb and fingertip and grunted as he chugged half of its contents. "Ugh! This is horrible! Do I have to finish it?" Tessa slipped his black leather jacket over his shoulders. Gina pulled out of the driveway and headed for a nearby hospital. Rocco winced as he finished the cheap, watery beer: "Damn! This shit tastes just as lousy as I when I was a kid. Why do you buy this crap, Ma?"

As Gina sped across town Tessa answered, "We keep a six-pack of it around for company."

Rocco asked through gritted teeth, "*Company?* Are you serious? Why would you give this garbage to your guests?" trying to mask his pain with a forced laugh.

"Because I don't like to be around drunks. And nobody I know will drink too much of this piss water. So I keep a six-pack in the fridge since Daddy's gone. Just in case a visitor asks for a beer I don't want to be rude, so I give them one of these."

Gina laughed, "You're a little on the nutty side, ma'am."

Danni asked nervously, "You have another one in there, Gina? I'll drink it."

"Sure thing, right away. I always carry around cans of the Pride of Cleveland in my purse. Would you like chips and dip with that, too?"

"You don't really have munchies in there... For real?" Danni asked, excitedly. "Because I'm starving!"

"Ma, I apologize. I said *you're* a little nutty? This Danni chick, with all her innocent looks and quiet act, might be the craziest one of us."

"She might be a close second. But her boyfriend's the gold medal winner. You, my favorite son, are hands down a certifiable lunatic."

Rocco looked at Tessa, then to his sister and girlfriend as he noted, "Shit! This is really hurting bad. The numbness went away to make room for more pain. Gina, you got weed on you?"

"No, little bro. We smoked all your shit up. Carrie sure liked it. She has this neat trick she does with good weed. You'd probably enjoy it. Ask Danni if Carrie can teach you, too."

"Keep talking, Rocco, to keep your mind off the pain," his mother suggested.

"Alright . . . shit... Yeah, okay, well all of us have these unique gene pools to draw from." He let out a slight growl and whistled out some air. "Okay, let's see: Ma, you're sired by mad-dog Doc who was so volatile even those killers from Little Italy didn't mess with him. And his brother, Uncle Pazzo, is no slouch in the crazy department, either. But he has class, and that goes a long way. So I inherit my insanity from Pop and from *Vamprilla's* family," he said, nodding to Tessa. "Gina, you get your madness from Pop and Butterscotch. That double stat right there should qualify you for the #1 spot in Bizarro Land Hall of Fame, considering how nuts all you are on your own merits. And then, as if Danni's wacko mother isn't bad enough, now little Miss Innocent over here finds out her father was the Mick? Holy shit! No wonder we're all such a mess."

"Keep quiet and drink that second beer while I talk. I wish you would have met your grandfathers," Tessa said to her son. "Those stories you heard about Doc are all true. Even the craziest gangsters in Cleveland were afraid of that little skinny guy. He'd just as soon shoot someone as argue. Your dad's mild next to the way my father was," Tessa said, as she wrapped her arms around herself to fend off nerves. "Yeah, we're all pretty lucky. Jackie's a special guy. He's just as tough and gritty and he is gentle and loving – game-bred to the core. He's a keeper, alright."

Rocco and Danni finished the beer. Gina let out a little gasp as she swung into the lot. She stopped at the front. They headed into the emergency entrance "Hey!" Danni said, as she pointed a gloved finger in the air, "Have you noticed whenever we refer to people who've died, it's always in the past tense? But when any of you mention Jackie, it's like he's still alive."

Automatic doors opened a gush of warm air for them. Lights at the Collinwood Clinic seemed way too bright. A young brown-haired nurse in a starched white uniform and wearing no make-up, rushed to them with a clipboard and a slew of questions. After taking Rocco's demographics and insurance information she paged a doctor and ushered them to a waiting area. Tessa had her face buried in her hands, elbows on knees.

A stooped-over, heavyset old man with a thick shock of white hair and a dusky complexion didn't take long to respond. The doctor extended a hand towards the mutilated hand of Rocco's. Rocco ignored him, winced from pain and said, "Dirty rotten motherfucker..."

Instead or shaking hands or even shocked by the language, the ER physician, while reading the chart, put a hand on Rocco's shoulder and said, "Well I'll be a monkey's uncle! You couldn't know me, son, but I have known your mother since she was a little girl. And I can remember you when you were born, Rocco. I believe it was California, was it not?" The old fat man with dark skin turned to the women and smiled slightly yellowed yet healthy-looking teeth at them, "You must be Gina. Your mother came for a check-up during her first trimester here at the Collinwood Clinic. I must say; you have matured into a stunning woman, young lady – truly stunning."

Gina eyeballed Tessa, "Who's this old perv? Am I supposed to know this guy? Because I don't recognize this character at all."

Tessa said to her hands, "That's all very nice, sir. Your memory is impressive. But we're here for treatment, and we're in a hurry. My son is in a great deal of pain. I'd like to speak with the physician on duty right now to address his injuries."

The old doctor asked, "You don't remember me, Tessa? We went to school together. It's Joey, from the old neighborhood. I used to live on the same street as Jackie. I had a *funny* nickname back then. It's Joey from Collinwood. I just saw you, when you were here after the *accident*. Remember now? That was nearly a half of a year ago already. Wow, time flies."

Tessa looked up. "Holy Toledo! Joey? Of course! I'm so sorry, and thank you! Yes, you took good care of me." Tessa gave him the type of hug where the woman leans forward at the head and turns one shoulder into the man's chest, so their chests are not close and their bodies are even farther apart. She lightly patted Shit-pants Joey on his shoulder with a flat open hand.

The only people other than Jackie who got real hugs by Tessa, the warm kind that amounted to more than just an air-hug, were their two kids and now Danni. But she was so relieved to see a friendly face on such an ugly night, she left both hands on his stooped over shoulders for a moment. "I'm really sorry. Please excuse us. It's been such a crazy day. How have you been, Joey? Hey, Rocco and Gina, this is a childhood friend of your father's. Danni, this is Dr. Joey, an old and good friend of ours. He was the doctor who took care of me after Daddy's…"

After they exchanged pleasantries Joey said, "First of all, let me say how sorry I am for you loss. I heard Jackie is still missing. Is this true?"

"We're pretty sure Jackie's dead. The coroner said nobody could have survived a blast like that. The only reason I'm alive is Jackie made me go back to the house. And the explosion nearly killed me, anyway. The detectives said they think Jackie's remains got dragged away by the people, or maybe by coyotes or raccoons or fox or… And it rained really hard that night… I'm sorry, Joey. I'm not strong enough to talk about all this just yet. I'm sure you understand," Tessa said, as she wiped her eyes with a tissue from her big black leather purse that was more like a saddlebag.

"Yes, Tessa, I do understand. But I want you to know that God works in mysterious ways. I have known Jackie longer than I have anyone. Even longer than you have because as you know, he and I were neighbors before kindergarten. I have a good feeling that somehow he is with us. I really do believe that."

Rocco groaned, "Dirty bastard, rotten motherless fuck!"

"Excuse me?" Joey inquired as professionally as possible.

"I can't fucking stand this pain much longer, Doc. I need help fast, and I need something strong!"

"Thank you, Joey. I'd like to believe that. But that brings up a host of other things to worry about. Sorry, I can't do this right now. So let's concentrate on my son for right now, okay? He's really is hurt very bad."

"Please excuse my thoughtlessness. You are right. My apologies. I was just so happy to see that you are okay. Alright, let me see what we have here, son. Umm, okay. That does look ugly. We need to run tests right away. While we are working you can tell me how this happened. We need to file reports for injuries."

"Hold-up, *Doctor*," Rocco hyperventilated. "Let's back up a second to something you said before. What did you mean by you had a *funny* nickname? Was it something like *Dr. Demento* or some whacked-out shit like that? Just be honest here," Rocco asked the old man. "Are you one of those creepy old dudes who puts people to sleep and then does some twisted shit to them? What are you, like some *Professor Perverto*?"

"Rocco! Shame on you! That's inexcusable. You be nice. This man is one of my oldest friends, and he's always been kind to our families. So you curb that nasty mouth of yours. Being in pain doesn't give you a license to act like an idiot."

"I'm not offended Tessa. Actually, I would prefer those names over the one I got stuck with in grade school. Tell you what, Rocco. After you tell me exactly what happened to you, and I get you patched back together, I'll tell you what my childhood nickname was. Deal? Now if you ladies will wait here, I will bring Rocco to meet with our trauma team."

After Rocco told his story to Dr. Shit-pants Joey and his wary medical staff, about him falling off a snow-covered roof and onto a pile of lumber with an old spike jutting upwards out of one of the boards, Joey began running tests.

"Do you have an allergy to opiates, son?" asked the doctor. "You do understand the language I'm speaking here, do you not?"

"Who me? No, I'm cool, Doc. But I do have a high tolerance. So spike me with something good and quick or it'll be like shooting me with ice-water."

Rocco's puffy fist, more like a paw or an MMA glove, turned a nasty yellowish purple around that ugly dark red puncture. And his arm was pretty much useless.

"You have some very serious injuries, and you will be in pain once I begin to work on them. If it is okay with you, I will administer a shot of Diluadid. How is your pain right now, son, from 1 to 10 – 10 being the worst? Is it bearable?" Joey asked.

"Pain? Oh yeah . . . it hurt's like a motherfucker, Doc. I'm an easy eleven. I'm thinking suicide and shit it's so bad. So can I get a double hit of that Diluadid?"

After Dr. Joey did a wound culture, the nasty hole through his hand had been thoroughly cleaned out and sewn up with just a stitch on each side to allow drainage. Joey gave him shots of *nafcillin* and tetanus and then tightly bandaged his hand with breathable material. Joey handed Rocco a small brown bottle containing 10 Percocet and wrote him two paper prescriptions to be filled with a druggist. One was for 60 *Unipen* for his infection. The other, for 30 *Percocet* 5/325, were like aspirin compared to the high tolerance Rocco had acquired from his long-term abuse of high, daily doses of *OxyContin* and *Opana* used for emotional pain.

The nurses and radiologist finished up their work while Dr. Joey re-read the X-rays in his office. "There seems to be a problem, son. X-rays show a stress fracture on the second metacarpal bone in the meaty part of his hand, between and behind your right thumb and index finger. A blow of high impact to drive a spike through one side and out the other could easily have shattered your finger bones into useless fragments, yet the wound is precise. Even though some dirt and a small wood splinter pushed into the wound, most of it went all the way through. There will be a lot of bruising, swelling and soreness."

"Yeah, I kind a figured that, Doc. I'll just take it easy for awhile. So that's it? Okay, thanks."

"Not really, Rocco. There's something else."

"Now what the fuck? Do I have cancer of the dick or some shit like that?" Rocco glanced over to the office door.

"I certainly hope not, for the sake of that lovely young lady of yours," Joey chuckled, making his best attempt at humor. "You are blessed. God was looking out for you. He must have a plan for you, son. He saved you for a reason. But an odd thing is you were just as lucky with regard to the severity of your arm and hand injuries, yet your legs and back appear unscathed. It really is amazing how a fall from a rooftop could result in pinpoint accuracy, each injury isolated from the surrounding areas. That is unusual from a high fall onto rubble. More of your body should be broken than just those exact points of impact."

"Speaking of points, Doc, what's yours?"

"I guess what I am saying is that even though you seem to have isolated injuries, do not be surprised if you wake up to find out this whole thing is worse than you thought. By the way, I fought in Vietnam in 1969. How about you? Are you a veteran?"

"Nope. Not from foreign wars, just domestic shit. Okay then, Doc, thanks for the heads-up and for taking care of me and my mom. So we're all done here for the night, right?"

"Not quite. You are in a great deal of pain. That is obvious. Yet you took the time to shower and change your clothes. Who does that, Rocco? I'm just curious."

Rocco tried to stroke his beard with his bandaged hand that looked like a boxing glove. "Well, Doc, it's like this: When I fell I ripped the crotch right out of my pants, and I wasn't wearing any undies. And then, on top of all that, I shit myself when I got knocked out from the fall. You know how mom's are, right? Since I had to change anyway, she insisted I just rinse off real quick. You remember the way mom's get about this stuff. But the funny thing is, as old fashioned as she is, she made my girlfriend help me in the shower," Rocco laughed. "Alright, so I'm glad we got to the bottom of all that. Okay, later."

"One more thing, Rocco: Actually it is your report concerning what happened that I find even more disturbing than the shower and change of clothes. You have a good story about slipping off the snowy roof to explain a fractured humerus, and also a semi-believable account of how you acquired a dirty nail hole through your hand. But for some reason you completely omitted explaining why you have a hole creasing through that muscular shoulder of yours."

"You gotta excuse me, Doc. I had a concussion, and I can't remember shit. Plus I'm not used to such powerful drugs. I used to be, but that seems like another lifetime. I guess they made my head a little numb. But yeah, that happened during the fall off the roof, too. Okay then, so I gotta get back out there. You know the way mom's are."

"I see. Besides the fact that you never even mentioned such a bad injury, which evidently is nearly as fresh as the other two, that brings us to another issue. The thing, Rocco, is that third injury. As I mentioned, I am a veteran of Vietnam. I was there for one year and saw a lot of injuries similar to this one. The hole through your shoulder is deep yet clean – not counting the burns on both entry and exit. And that's puzzling. There are only a couple of explanations for a wound like that."

"Entry and exit? What's that mean, Doc? Like I said, I had a concussion from that fall. Sorry, but I can't remember shit. If you have anymore questions, ask Tessa. My mom will be glad to straighten you out on whatever seems to be bugging you."

"No, that won't be necessary. You remind me a lot of your father. It might interest you to know that my report says another spike went through your shoulder."

"Whatever you say, sir. You're the doctor. But you seem cool, so I want to come clean with you. You shared with me about being a soldier, so I'll tell you something personal."

"Maybe you should just rest right now, son. Sometimes opiates affect people like amphetamines. Some get real talkative while under the influence."

Rocco smiled: "Yeah, now I can see that you and my Pop are friends. That's cool. But the thing I'm about to say is this: I fought MMA in the octagon for awhile. So I'm no stranger to pain. I know how my body reacts and how long it takes me to heal. So I guess that leads me to a question that's just between me and you. Can I get about 180 of the 30mg single ingredient *Roxicodone* IR's instead of this Girl Scout cookie bullshit?"

Joey raised his eyebrows: "Not yet. And be careful with these. Even though they are relatively weak compared to what you could get from a follow-up visit with your PCP, any opiate can begin the onset of a short climb up a very slippery slope," Dr. Joey said, as he put the pills and paper prescriptions in a jacket draped over Rocco's shoulders.

"I understand why you would want single ingredient *Oxycodone*. Because even more physically dangerous than the opioids is the high concentration levels of *acetaminophen* when taking a high dose of prescription opiates to manage severe pain. But I don't want Tessa angry with me," Joey said, with a concerned expression. As you said, 'You know how mom's are'."

Tessa stopped her son in the parking before unlocking the doors of her black Outback encrusted with road salt and inner-city grime. "Let's see your medicine and prescriptions, honey."

"They're already in my jacket pocket. I'm cold, Ma. I'll show you at home where it's warm and we have lights."

"Show her," encouraged Danni, with her sweetest voice.

"Hey, I'm injured here. And I'm freezing my ass off. It's dark, anyways. Let's get inside, start the car and the heater and then flip on the interior lights so we all can see."

"Just show her now, little bro," his sister insisted. "We're cold, too. What's the big deal, anyhow?" Gina asked. "Just do it and it's done."

"That's what I'm saying. What's the big deal? Here, gimme the keys. I'll fucking drive," Rocco snapped, as he reached for his mother's keys with his bandaged hand.

Tessa yanked away the keys and gave them to Gina. "Here, sweetie, you drive again. But not just yet. Not till your brother shows us what that doctor gave him."

"What the fuck, Ma? Why are you being such a bitch?"

"Watch that filthy mouth or I give you a slap in this parking lot, you little bastard!?" Tessa glared up at him.

Gina started the car with a remote starter. "Yeah, Rocco, quit being such a fucking baby. Just show Ma what you have and get it over with."

"Thanks. Maybe he'll listen to you," Tessa smiled at Gina.

The mid-size hatchback cranked right over and purred warm exhaust into the freezing air. Rocco covered his bandaged hand with his good one. He breathed on it to create warmth, but the temperatures were well below freezing.

"Just show her, baby. I'm getting tingly and numb all over," Danni encouraged, as she wrapped her arms around herself and pressed her thighs together. Her protection from the elements was an unlined, fringed suede jacket the same color as their dog had been. "Show her so we can get in the car, okay? Look! The windows are already defrosting and the light's on. Come on, babe. I'll bet you want to see what you have, too."

"What the fuck, Danni? You're my ol' lady! You're supposed to have my fucking back here! Now you're going against me too, you fucking bitch?"

Tessa lifted her hand as if to swat her son across the face. "What did I just say about using that type of goddamn language around these girls? Now give me those pills and prescriptions before I knock you on your ass, boy! I mean it!"

"Jeez oh man! What's the big deal? They're just bullshit *Percs*, Ma. They're like M&M's to me. This Dr. Joey guy is a friend of Pop's. He wouldn't give me anything that would mess me up. But go ahead! Take them! They're in my left jacket pocket. I'd have to eat the whole goddamn bottle to feel anything."

"Yes, son, we know. And that's what we're afraid of. Because your injuries will be throbbing like bass drums tonight. I know what these are he gave you. The acetaminophen in them will kill you if you take enough for the dope to break through pain like you're dealing with. So that's why you're going to give them to me. We're worried about liver damage or you overdosing because the pain really is severe. I'll dole them out to you."

"Okay, Ma! Here you go. Happy? Can we leave now?" he said, shoving his heavy leather jacket at her. "Everything's always gotta be a big fucking deal!"

Tessa stomped from one foot to the other, trying to keep warm, as she dropped the pill bottle into her black leather purse. "Now the slips, Rocco. Hurry up. Where are they? You're going to make us get sick out here in this freezing weather."

Rocco sighed, "Jesus fuck! Two written prescriptions are in the other pocket. Satisfied?"

Tessa ripped up the script for *Oxycodone* and deposited the scraps into her purse, then handed him back the other for his antibiotics. "I'm sorry to be such a bitch, son. But we've had enough drama and chaos for one year. I don't need to worry about this. Come on, let's go home. A nice bowl of homemade macaroni on a cold winter night cures all ills. Plus I have some nice wedding soup in the fridge. We'll heat that up, too."

"This is pure bullshit… I'm a grown-ass man!"

"Trust me, son, please. So this way I can trust you. I need yo to do this for me. I'll make it up to you. I promise." Tessa said, using a gloved hand to wipe away a frozen tear.

Gina pressed the remote door opener. The car beeped twice and the interior light came on with a glowing invitation to warmth and home.

They piled inside. Gina navigated through snowy side roads with her step-mother seated next to her. Rocco and Danni huddled up together in the backseat. She nuzzled up on his left side. Her delicate frame seemed to melt against him.

"Sorry, babe. I do have you back, always – promise."

"It's okay. I understand."

"It won't happen again, okay?"

"Yes, Danni, I know it won't."

"Please, baby. You're my best friend. I love you."

"I know, babe. It's cool. Sorry. I love you, too."

Gina laughed, "Listen to you two love birds cooing!"

Most of the house lights glowed through the snowy blackness of that clouded-over night of no stars. They reentered the toasty house to find Little Sinbad seated near the door. Instead of his usual rough-housing with Rocco, the old Pit-bull sniffed his legs while they all deposited boots and shoes on a plastic mat with a rim to prevent melted snow from running onto the floor. Wherever Rocco went the dog stayed close, but not too close. He sat next to his feet at the dining room table.

The three women disappeared into Tessa's big, bright kitchen. The kids always told her that it was her fault they still believed in miracles because of the magic she performed in that kitchen. It wasn't long till four small bowls piled full of steaming, homemade potato *gnocchi* with a heavy meat sauce, simmered in front of them on the dining room table.

Since I vanished, thanks to a car bomb, always set an empty place setting at the head of the table where I sat. Rocco had the other end, which had become his spot. Tessa and the girls were up and down. Two of them changed seats during the meal.

Gina brought the salad while Danni carried a black cherry *Gazoza* for each. Tessa retrieved a block of aged pecorino wrapped in a damp washcloth from the small refrigerator, unlike the huge side-by-side still at home. She set it and a small shiny cheese grater next to Gina's bowl as Tessa wore her serious expression, which meant she had something important to say.

"We can have the soup before we turn in for the night, unless you'd rather have it now instead of the *gnocchi*. Don't eat fast, Rocco, and just have a little bit for right now. Oh, and one more thing. We're going to prioritize. This is something Doc taught me. He used to call it 'Going to the mattresses.' That means we're sticking together and staying here till we find out more about what's in the wind from this nasty business. Nobody leaves unless it's necessary. If one of us really has to leave, two of us go and two stay here. That way nobody is ever left all alone. After supper we'll inventory our weapons and ammunition and keep them within reach so any one of us can grab a gun during the middle of the night if need be. Then the girls and I will clean up the table and kitchen while you get comfortable. You need lots of fluids Rocco, and lots of rest. Understand, big-shot?"

"Ma, you're amazing! You're the coolest mother ever. I mean it. Give me two of those bust-out pills before I eat or they won't do shit."

"Okay, here's three so you can sleep. But don't expect three every time. And another thing… Thank you. You're the bravest son ever. I'm so proud of you, risking everything to protect your fiancée and to defend your father's honor."

Rocco let the fiancée remark slide. But she was right. He wasn't about to let Danni get after the way she stepped up. She held her mud better than most guys would have. So if getting married was the way to keep her happy, then that was a no-brainer. Instead, Rocco asked Tessa, "Ma, you got any of Pop's weed laying around? You know; just for medicinal purposes so I won't need so many pills."

"Yeah, Ma," Gina jumped in. "I have aches and pains all over the place. Plus I'm traumatized as shit. Look at me! And now look at poor Danni. She's trembling like a lost puppy. We just need a little herbage, not to get shit-faced stoned, but so we can decompress from the craziest thing that's ever happened. The three of us will go outside for one quick toke. Swear to Buddha, we'll be right back."

"Bullshit!" snapped Tessa. "What did I just say?" She drummed her fingers on a manuscript. Her kids recognized how she had begun to cradle the unfinished book like it was a stuffed animal whenever she missed her husband the most. "Unreal…"

"Honest Injuns, Ma," Danni said with a hand raised in oath. "We'll be right back. We're going right out to Gina's car, real fast for one quick puff, and then—"

"Are you kids deaf, dumb or stupid? I said *Bullshit*, didn't I? First of all, what did I say about going to the mattresses? Nobody's ever alone, right? Now, right away, you're bailing out on me? Don't any of you big-shots know what *bullshit* means?"

"Lies?" whimpered Danni.

"Does this have anything to do with ass cheeks, Ma?" Rocco grinned. "Because if it does, I have this theory—"

Tessa ignored him when he acted like an idiot.

Click "I know!" beamed Gina. She pointed an index finger in the air as if Tessa was a teacher asking her class a question. "It means incorrect information, doesn't it?"

"Yes, honey, that's exactly what it means – *Incorrect information*! Okay, let's see if you're as tuned in as your dad. I'm sure Jackie would know. So tell us. Why is what Rocco and Danni are talking about pure *bullshit*? Do you know why, honey?"

"Come on, Ma, don't start," Rocco grumbled.

"I think I know," Gina grinned in a sing-song tone.

"Please do enlighten us." Tessa said, staring at her.

"What's *incorrect* is we won't be right back. Am I right?"

"Maybe... Go on. Explain to us why."

"We won't be back because we're not going outside."

"Come on, Ma. Don't be such a Jew. I know Pop had a little stash from the wedding. Little Hankie told me Uncle Hank gave it as part of your wedding gift."

"It's not like that," Gina assured her brother, her grin widening and eyes twinkling.

"Ah, okay..." Now Tessa smiled for the first time that day. "You really *do* have the gift that your dad calls the *Click*!"

"Ever since I was a kid. I used to think everyone had."

"Come on! Just say it, Gina, please!" begged Danni, as if Gina had just decoded the meaning of life and was misering it.

"We're not going outside . . . because we're going to smoke right in here. And that's because Ma's going to blaze up with us! Am I right, Ma?" asked a giggling Gina.

Danni's big dark eyes widened. Rocco watched his mother's expression change.

"Just one puff for right now, for each. I don't feel well."

Gina laughed and yelled, "YES! Fuckin' ay right! Ma, you're the absolute best!" She fist-bumped her step-mother.

Rocco shook his head and grinned: "I'm feeling lucky again, Ma. The pendulum is swinging the other way for us."

In tarot readings, the number 13 represents a closing of one portal to signal a new beginning. In the 13th year of the 3rd millennium, my spiral hit bedrock and then rebounded. That *Bounce* presented a opportunity for me to transition from being a devoted father and husband, a renowned dog show judge and addiction counselor ready to retire to pursue my dream of being an aspiring author, only to become a broken dead man hiding in a basement and a mental institution.

Timing: Tessa had become acquainted with darkness while in her mid-20s. She thought she had hit rock-bottom after being disowned by her maniac, drunken father who partied like a rock star throughout middle-age till both Doc and Tessa's mother died in close proximity of one another. Then having to birth and raise a child while in her mid-20s, on her own in a strange place. She had her aunt to lean on for awhile, till she was killed in a car crash while Rocco was still a toddler.. Tessa's aunt, just like Doc, was a raging alcoholic. In California, not Tessa's first choice, her young boy had never met his grandparents – nor did he know one thing about his own father. They returned to a home where their only close relatives were gone. Doc's brother, Pazzo, retired to Florida with his first and only wife. Tessa'a cousin, Fingers, turned mafia chief, could no longer afford to trust anyone. Then another new bottom opened beneath Tessa, in the shape of a remote device, to carry her to a new depth of darkness she had never imagined possible. Tessa understandably became jaded. She trusted no one, other than me and the two kids. Her *cumare*, Carly, became a full-fledged junkie, till Carly couldn't even trust herself.

    Before my *accident* that forever changed our family dynamic so drastically, a whole lot of luck determined by timing taught me how to ease into the lifestyle of a middle-aged man who had lost or pushed away everything and everyone. From living fast and hard for far too long I had smacked into too many walls and bottoms while still looking for another slice of *more*. So I did the best I could with what I had till it caught up with me. We can't outrun things like vendettas, age or illness. What already happened is etched in stone. What will brings consequence. So that's how we learned to adapt. Another thing Tessa and I found after acquiring enough frequent flyer mileage is why some old people become bitter and hateful, still wanting to be young yet knowing it's over. We also saw the other extreme, kids who had never really lived and then in old age desperately needed to arrear to be young and cool. Then there those like Tessa who were cool but just so happened to get old along her perilous journey of life.

    A few who survived that onslaught of obsession with alcohol and other drugs, without too much lingering damage, managed to gather wisdom along the way as a result of mileage. But no matter which way I sliced it, I recognized one simple truth as a recurring concrete fact. We all end up getting pretty much what we ask for, one way or another – sooner or later. Call it karma or providence; timing brings us the best and the worst of opportunities and ongoing costs. As a result, survivors take positive lessons learned from negative consequences and synthesize. In turn, we get through life with ways we've earned.

The four of them sat on the long blue couch, as if Rocco and the three women were contestants on a quiz show panel. Danni held the joint for him. They took one puff each of primo sticky bud, to wash away compiled stress and insane trauma. The fresh bud was veined with purple threads to stitch together carefree and youthful times past. We didn't dare take a second hit. All of us were old and wise enough to recognize the covert rush of *creeper weed*. The type of hydro where the high just keeps building and two dragon hits could be one too many.

Staring at Sinbad, Rocco said, "Filo's bitch had pups."

"I wanna play puppies. Can we see them?" Danni asked.

Gina said, "I've been drinking and smoking too much. I'm thinking about quitting again. But not right away."

Tessa said, "Okay, we've shared the peace pipe. After all we've shared; this is the least of it... But ash that, Gina. I'd like to run something by you. I've been thinking about some things puzzling me. And it's finally starting to gel into a moving picture."

"Ma, you're stoned. Ease back and chill." Rocco chuckled.

Tessa continued, "You relax. I don't mean like now."

"Rocco's right this time, Ma. You're not used to this high-powered bud. You and Daddy used to smoke that Mexican headache weed when you guys were young. But this stuff—"

"You relax too, Gina. I'm making an important point here. Pay attention... Okay then. Now just listen: Hmm, alright, just give me a minute. I just misplaced what I was going to say."

Danni burst out laughing. She rolled off the couch, onto the blue carpet. Gina joined her.

Tessa said, "Oh, I see. *I'm* the one who's all stoned-out?"

Both girls rolled back and forth, cracking up.

"Damn, what lightweights! Look at how goofy you get!"

At that they laughed even harder. Rocco winced with pain from all the laughter and all his injuries, yet he smiled.

Sinbad started his snorting and running in circles routine. By then they were holding their stomachs, laughing hysterically.

Tessa sat still until their crazy laughing stopped. Sarcastically she asked, "Can I talk now?" She waited for sporadic bursts of laughter to die down till she continued. "Well . . . hang on now. I'll think of it in a minute. Till I do, I'll tell you something your dad taught me about drugs."

"Sweet!" Rocco stopped laughing and perked up.

"Daddy admitted that any drugs, but especially psychedelics and marijuana, really do open windows to heightened perceptions. He said that drugs were a symptom, not the problem; that obsessions and compulsions were. He said once the window is opened, it's opened. He explained that if a person keeps trying to open a window that's already opened, it will jam, or it might even break. Your father said that's why people get so broken from drugs; because they continuously try to open a window that's already been opened as wide as it can possibly be."

Rocco, Gina and Danni stayed as still as stone, waiting for the rest of her story.

"Oh! Okay, I just got it! I've been thinking about what happened to Jackie . . . I mean Daddy. And I might know why happened when what it… I mean… Shit! Just listen, okay?"

Everyone sat up. Smiles frozen in place. All three middle-aged kids were stoned yet very much attentive.

Gina said, "Go ahead. We're listening. Remember yet?"

Tessa smiled and wearily shook her head: "Yes, I do. Thanks. And yes, this is powerful. Wow! Alright, one of the reasons I smoked with you kids is to reinforce how you can implicitly trust me. Another is I appreciate that you're not kids. Plus, now you have something on me. And who knows? By the time this whole ordeal is over with, you might know a lot more about me than you'd like to. But I'm done hiding my thoughts, feelings and emotions. Jackie opened me up that way. Besides, we're at home and we're way beyond facades with one another."

"No sweat, Ma," said Tessa's son, as he leaned his back against their dark blue couch. "I'd take a bullet or a prison stretch for you. And you know this. Plus I can vouch for these two little ladies 100%. Other than you and Pop, they're the only people on this entire diseased planet I'd trust with my life. It's funny how that works out. Out of all the bad-asses I came up through the ranks with, of the four people I trust most in this whole world three of you are women. Who'd a thought?"

"Thanks for sharing that, son. You girls have anything to say before I continue?" Tessa asked. Her eyes looked glassy. But she seemed coherent enough. Gina and Danni looked at each other, then back at Tessa and just shook their heads signaling no questions or comments.

"Okay. The first thing is *why*. Why in the hell did anyone come after Jackie? He's been away from that lifestyle for almost four decades. And he hasn't screwed anyone over. He's become a well-respected man. So do any of you have a logical answer?"

"Wasn't Pop suspected of being one the guys who whacked that Wong Gongs' prospect, Erby? Rumor is that Erby's hit was a payback from when Pop's friend Benny, from the Royal Flush, got wasted. That's what I heard from Whitey before he was a striker for the Wong Gongs, and before I knew Jackie was my father. That's when me and Filo were getting dogs from Pop's bloodline that went back to some of Jackie's most famous sporting dogs. But if it's that thing about Erby is true, and if there's indisputable proof, those kinds of grudges don't ever go away – kind of like hitting a *made-man*. With certain lines crossed, even after 40 years of good behavior, time doesn't change shit."

"It's possible, son. But I doubt it because your dad still did business with the Wong Gongs long after Erby was found dead in his apartment with his old Airedale. Jackie's alleged involvement was never anything more than speculation. One of the main suspects of Erby's murder disappeared till city workers smelled something putrid beneath a manhole cover."

"I heard that Pop might have gotten in too deep with Ansel, even before that, something about his ex-wife. So there's another good possibility with those guys."

"Yes, Rocco, it's possible. But that brings us right back to the same answer. Your father and Ansel had been doing big business with weight for years after the cops found her charred body in that rubbish barrel. So evidently, Ansel trusted Jackie enough to allow him to remain in the loop. Large deals like those leave even the toughest of people vulnerable. So . . . no."

"Okay, Ma," said Gina. "Let's get this out in the open. What about your cousin, Fingers? Daddy had plenty of shit on those Royal Flush guys, because he was their president for 10 years. That's means Daddy knew everything on everyone in their crew. Plus there could be lingering resentments from other things. Who knows with those *guinea* maniacs, anyway? I can't stomach any of those arrogant assholes."

"No way. I don't buy it. If Fingers and those Young Turks from Collinwood were paranoid enough to make a move against your father it would have been 30+ years ago. Why wait?"

"But I heard Daddy pulled a knife on Fingers and put it to his throat one night when they ran into each other at a bar. Supposedly, it was after the big fight they got into at the R Bar. Then I heard after that happened, Fingers pulled a loaded gun and put it to his head in front of everyone at a dog convention."

"Believe me, Gina. If those *paesanos* were coming after your father it would have been when Jackie was still boozing. Everybody knew he was a blackout drinker. I know how those guys operate. Too much time has passed. None of it adds up."

Danni asked, "What about those Irish mobsters from Five Points? Didn't Jackie and his friends mess up the Kelly brothers a few times? And he's supposed to have some raw shit on Doyle, about catching Doyle getting head from a fag retard when they were teens. Excuse me if I don't refer to them as my cousins. Wow... I still can't believe the Mick was my father. Listen to me... Don't feel bad, Ma. I'm zoned out, too."

Tessa responded, "Jackie and Fingers beat up Doyle and his brothers after a high school dance, too. But that's all kids stuff. Gus is the one who shot their friend, Frankie Fazule, in that brawl in front of Eggs' house. And then Frankie shot Gus at the Cheshire Club in front of hundreds of witnesses. All your dad did both of those nights was jump in and get beaten up and stomped for his trouble. And when Nino and Daddy caught Doyle getting a blow-job from a mentally retarded boy behind the school, was in junior high. So that was almost 50 years ago."

"There's other stuff after that, Ma. I heard Daddy and my mom talk about it years ago," Gina reminded her.

"You mean Benny? Yeah, Benny killed Paddy Kelly. Everybody knows that. And that maniac, Toby, was the one who clipped Eamon Jr. Jackie didn't have anything to do with those murders. Granted, all those guys were friends with your dad. But Jackie wasn't directly involved, and they all know that. Besides, your dad even shot Toby one night after that. Since then, those other guys have been trying to land bigger fish. So they have more recent enemies to concern themselves with."

Rocco's black curls, from drying without a towel, twisted in long sausage locks. But his eyes were made from stone. "What's your point, Ma? None of this is going anywhere."

"Alright, let's look at the bigger picture. That crazy stuff you all recited happens to be facts. It's all a part of Collinwood history – ancient history. After years of no violent conflict between all those Collinwood gangs, just in the past five months the shit has hit the fan like it hasn't since the 1976 Cleveland wars. So the question is: *why*, out of nowhere, does this whole thing get inflamed all over again?"

"Great question, Ma. So who's got the answer?" asked Gina, as she unconsciously twirled auburn curls around a tanned and polished index finger of her right hand.

"Well, there's something else. And now I remember it."

Danni, with knees against her chest, scrunched up her face and ran fingertips through her short black hair as she asked, "Is this next part gonna make us sad again, Ma?"

"Yeah, really... Let's talk about movies and books or politics and religion. You're gonna bring us all down with all this heavy shit. Let's enjoy the buzz." Rocco tried in vain to find a comfortable position.

"Humor me. Within half a year, my husband gets blown up; your friend, Animal, gets shot off his motorcycle; the Mick's oldest friend, Mr. Brown, watches his wife get gunned down in a car with him; two *made-men* are burned to death when The Inn exploded; and then Uncle Curtis is found with a face full of bullets. Uncle Hank, who is fearless and can be very dangerous when need be, is afraid to leave his house. All those events occurred just within the past few months, not necessarily in that order. Have I missed something?"

Rocco yawned: "You missed having a point."

"Okay, big-shot. What do these things have in common?"

"What do you mean?" he asked, stroking his thick black beard with the back of a bandaged hand that looked like a mitten.

Danni put her legs across Rocco's. She raised her hand like a schoolgirl, "I know! They're all from Collinwood and they all know each other. Am I right?"

Rocco bent over to bite one of her legs and then sat up against the couch: "Nice try, babe. Wow... that's some real genius deduction there. Nice going..."

"Leave her alone, punk. I think I know. They're involved in Cleveland criminal activity and all do business together."

"Bullshit, Gina! Pop hasn't even been over the speed limit since the 1980s. So no, you and Danni are both wrong. The only thing they have in common is that they all know one another from back in the day; back when men were men and women were glad of it. Not like all these drop-shots now, running around with baggie pants half-way down so they can advertise their bitch asses like rental property. And not like those little fruitcakes with their skinny jeans and girly make-up. No. What's happened is obvious. It's just another power grab. They just want more."

Gina asked, "What do you think, Ma? Does any of what we said make sense to you?"

"Yes. In fact, all three of you are 100% right. And that's the whole problem," Tessa said, to her best friends lined up against the couch like the three wise monkeys.

"Whoa. Back up a second here, Ma. These girls are pretty cut right now. They don't understand what you're trying to say. So maybe you oughta slow it down a little for their sake. Explain it to them so they can follow you." Rocco said, all glassy-eyed from pills and weed.

Gina laughed, "Ha! Go ahead, dude. Then why don't *you* explain it to us girls."

"No, no. I don't wanna steal Ma's fire. She's on to something here. Out of respect, let her go ahead and finish her theory. She's not too high to finish."

"Good try, little bro. But nobody's *that* high."

Tessa unwrapped a dark chocolate egg and passed a small crystal bowl of them to her audience: "I was talking to Uncle Hank about this. He sees it, too. The problem is there's *too much* evidence. That doesn't happen with career criminals. Something stinks to holy hell and back about this whole thing. It's a set-up."

Danni unwrapped colored foil off chocolate eggs and dropped one each into the mouths of Rocco and Gina: "What about those other *WOP*s from The Inn?" Danni asked.

"Cagootz and Louie were stone-cold psychopaths," Rocco reminded his mother. "Those *guineas* down there are as bad as jailhouse niggers and toothless hillbillies. And that fat tub, Spuds, and his skinny girlfriend, Vinny, are even more dangerous. They're trying to impress those mob guys, so they'll do anything. They're like prospects for *The Club*."

"There's just so much evidence it's overwhelming. We're tripping over all of it." Tessa said.

"Yeah, Ma, you're tripping all right. But you just might be tripping over what might finally lead us to truth." Rocco suggested with eyes at half-mast.

CH XXXI: Girls' Night, 2nd Party

Armed with her best smile and the most jovial tone of voice she could dredge up out of that pit of anguish within her, Gina counted those long steps for the last time above Rocco's crazy landladies flat in sync with choppy nervous breaths. Three girls were about to again congregated at Rocco and Danni's, hopefully to chill and decompress. They had forever been changed by one recent incident. The girls got together for another girls' night. Gina and Danni felt relatively safe that two of the bad guys were no longer a threat, Besides, Rocco's house was a known hangout for the Wong Gongs. Even though Irish and Italian gangs had lost most of their membership due to killings and life sentences, along with the RICO Act and old age, political clout and street juice waned but they still were powerful. They were respected organizations with very dangerous members, but not enough so for notorious Reds and Blues to fear them in everyday business affairs. The Wong Gongs grew stronger than ever, because they had merged with other MCs and patched over entire chapters. Street thugs knew if they molested family members of hard-core bikers or mob guys, then high profile, old-school players of all varieties took those culls out of the game.

But Carrie didn't feel safe anywhere. Because no matter where she went, her potentially worst enemy was right there with her. She came storming into the house dropping loose cans of beer she had been carrying in a torn and damp, brown paper grocery bag. She kicked off fur trimmed boots at the door and dropped her leather jacket next to them. She was dressed as if it was autumn, with big holes ripped out of the knees of her faded, skin tight jeans and a black tank top contrasting her very blonde hair that showcased a rack of firm cleavage. She lit a cigarette, picking up a full can of beer: "Motherless fucker. I got the worst goddamn luck on the planet! Son of a bitch!"

Danni stepped out of the kitchen wearing her usual uniform of a black T-shirt and black Levi's: "You're not even all the way inside yet and already you're motherfucking someone or something. What happened, sista? What is it now, mama?"

"I lost my goddamn cell phone. The last one I had dropped in the toilet while I was putting on make-up. I just got this one! And now it's lost already?"

Gina asked, "It's lost? You think maybe you're partying a little too much lately, my good friend?"

"Tell me straight. Do you think I'm addicted to sex and staying buzzed due to my insecurities? Because that's what some shrink told me. But he said he couldn't say for sure until I handed back him the gram of coke and took his dick out of my mouth."

Two of the girls laughed while Carrie dumped her purse onto the hardwood floor. "Straight-up, though. He said I'm codependent and maybe histrionic. But I know neither of you are judging me because I like to get off. So I have a really serious question for you ladies, okay? Tell me this, Danni: I already know your favorite actor is Leonardo DiCaprio, because I've only heard you drone on about him about a million times. You think he's some kind of sex god or some shit. So be honest. If you could spend the weekend with him and have him be your drug infested fuck slave, would you do it? Tell the truth."

"My guess is there must be more to life other than sex and drugs, right? Although Carrie, you do make an interesting proposition. I'm curious about your answer too," Gina said.

"Clarify what you mean?" Danni asked. "Are we talking straight fucking and sucking? Or are we including anal, too?" she said, with an earnest expression and furrowed brow.

"And *I'm* the slut? Listen to this nasty bitch. She'd fuck other dudes while she's your brother's ol' lady, providing it's not up the dirt road. You still trust this little whore?"

"Implicitly. In fact, I don't blame her. I'd fuck Leo, without condoms or reservations," Gina said. "I'd fuck Johnny Depp, too. Nobody can be blamed for having sex with superstars. That doesn't count as cheating. Anybody would do it."

"Anyway, I was just kidding around," assured Danni, still serious. "I'd never cheat on Rocco. And I know he's the same way with me. He's different than most guys."

"Sure thing, Danni . . . whatever you say. Hey, Gina, have you ever been married or anything? You know, like a steady ol' man? Or are you the only smart one of us?"

"I'm free as a bird now. But I was with the same jerk from junior high till last year. I spent over half my life with that selfish bastard. We were engaged when I found out he was fucking some skank at his job. And this hose-bag he was tapping weighed in at about 195 and had a face like a boar hog. You know; one of those big-boned bitches with the Pollack pig face and turned-up nose, and a gut as thick as her fat ass?"

"Yeah, I know the type," Carrie said, as she shook very blonde hair over her face. "Then these fucking pricks act all innocent. They pretend like they're doing us some kind of favor by being with us during their precious spare time. I hate men. They're all little boys. Dudes are all just cur dogs on two legs. The only difference is that even cur dogs are loyal and cool. But dudes are disloyal by nature."

"I have to agree with you on that one, too," Gina nodded. "Most people are shit. But the best part of my heartbreak break-up story is that as soon as I broke up with that asshole his pig-faced bitch dumped him. HA!" Gina laughed as if she was hearing her story for the first time. "Then he came crawling back, sniveling like some little cunt, telling me everybody makes mistakes, begging for forgiveness with those puppy dog eyes."

"That chump has no idea," Danni reassured her.

Carrie set a joint, still burning, in the metal ashtray with a Mack Truck bulldog in its center. The chromed dog stood on a pedestal for holding cigarettes. "Fuck-it. Let's go find that punk right now and kick the dog shit out of him. I'm not one of these liberal, anti-violence salad-eating bitches. Let's go kick that ass."

Gina laughed and turned to Danni, "Thanks, buds! But getting back to that movie star thing: You think my brother wouldn't fuck one of those primo bitches like Charlize Theron or Beyonce' if he had half a chance? You ever see how he drools over them?"

"Are you serious? You really think Rocco would want them sexually? You're only joking, right Gina?" asked a shocked-looking Danni. "It's just pussy!"

Carrie chugged her ice cold beer, burped and said, "Hell, that's quite a thought. I'd even have to give that one some serious consideration. You know what? I might do those bitches myself. I don't necessarily mean all at the same time. *Although...*"

Danni just shook her head. "I think you might want to slow down a bit, Carrie. You've been here lass than a half hour and you're already shit-faced to the gills and still going strong. And now, because you'll be all gooned out, you're going to have to sleep over again. You're too loaded to drive a tricycle tonight, let alone a car."

"I shouldn't have taken my meds, huh?"

"What other twisted stuff can we discuss?" asked Gina. "You have any more crazy shit you'd like to talk about, Carrie?" she asked, as she looked deep into Carrie's glazed-over blue eyes.

She, by then, was slumped over, melting into the couch.

Carrie seemed to snap back into focus upon hearing her own name mentioned. She jerked up straight. "Huh? Yeah, I sure do… But first I want to ask you a question, sista," Carrie said, looking at Danni. "You ever see that movie *Indecent Proposal* with Robert Redford and that little fox, Demi Moore?"

"Isn't that the one where she's like this straight-laced, married chick who winds up on a cabin cruiser with this rich fuck and he's got the mega-hots for her?"

"Yeah. I saw that one," Gina said, trying to shake the fog of too much hydro from her mind. "This smooth talker has mega-bucks and offers a happily married woman a million if he can spend the night with her. Right?"

"Yep, that's the one," Carrie nodded. "Okay, now let's all be honest here. I have a question. But think it over, because this isn't gonna be as easy as it seems."

"It's easy enough for me," Gina laughed. "I'd fuck and suck Robert Redford all night for a cool million. Who wouldn't?"

Carrie slurred, "Did you ever see what that asshole really looks like? First of all, he's old as mammoth turds. Besides that, his skin, without make-up and minus all those camera shots taken through silkscreen, looks like somebody poured battery acid on his face and tried to neutralize it with an ice pick. That ugly bastard should be making monster movies instead of playing some international stud."

"I'd fuck him!" Danni announced, with a look of resolution, as if she were still dwelling on the possibility of Rocco having sex with other women.

"Fuck-it," Carrie mumbled, as she lit the new joint with a shaky hand. Her nail polish matched her very tight shirt. "Ask me if I give a shit about any of it. I'm just a worthless, filthy gutter slut, anyway. So who cares…"

Click "Carrie, I know we're still getting to know one another, but something's going on. Can I ask what?"

"Is something wrong, sweetie?" asked Danni, as she knelt in front of her childhood friend and took Carrie's free hand into hers. "You can tell us anything."

"*Us?* You're my sister, Danni – always and forever. And you've never, ever given me a reason to doubt you. You say you trust Gina, so that means I trust her. If you're wrong, we're both screwed." Carrie pulled away her hand, passed the joint to Danni and set down her empty beer to light another Kool – trembling.

Gina stood and collected her phone and purse. She smiled, "Wow, I can't believe how late it's getting to be. I really shouldn't stay much longer. I need to get back to check on Tessa before I get too stoned to drive. I'll phone you as soon as I get home, Danni. It's been fun again, Carrie. I enjoyed it. We three need to get together more often."

"Nope, Gina. You need to be here. I'm afraid this concerns you, too. Goddamnit, I hate this fucking shit!" Then Carrie's light blue eyes welled up with tears.

"Tell me, sweetie. What is it?" Danni again asked her oldest friend. She hadn't seen Carrie shed a tear since childhood.

"Okay, let's get back to that loyalty piece we talked about the last time. Here's the deal: I was at Whitey's, sort of passed out on our couch. I'd been asleep but woke up feeling like warmed-over cat shit, all dry-mouthed from too much booze. You know the feeling, right? Anyway, I was just laying there in a kind of in a daze. I heard Whitey talking on the phone. I'm pretty sure it was to his father. At first it was in his usual code language I've heard a million other times when he's talking to any his club-brothers. Then he said something really weird. It sounded like he said something about, 'that *dago* dogman getting himself a good tan', or something like that."

"That's not a big deal, sweetie," Danni assured her old friend. "Whatever it is, everybody in the Neighborhood has been talking about the same thing. It's been Collinwood headlines for months. I wouldn't concern myself too much about that."

"Let's let her finish, Danni. There's more, right Carrie?"

"Of course there's more. Isn't there always? Anyway, Gina, I'm getting the feeling from the way Ansel and Whitey were talking that they think your father's not dead."

"How would you deduce that from a one-sided conversation?" asked Danni. "That's not much information, especially if they were talking in code language. Maybe we're all too high to be talking about this stuff right now, sweetie."

"Fuck that. I'm fine. Anyway, they switch back and forth from their secret code language to normal talk. And like I said, I heard that shit a million times. Plus he thought I was passed out."

"Okay," Gina smiled. "Evidently you have some strong feelings based on some things you saw or heard. Sometimes it's not easy to put into words, because sometimes the feeling is based more on body language or what's not been said."

"You hit it right on the head. I'd been having that feeling for awhile. Whitey's been acting like he was hiding something."

Gina said, "I know you can handle. But you are pretty wrecked right now. Wow! I sounded like my father..."

"It's cool. Anyway, the feeling I got was Ansel wasn't happy that your dad might still be alive, even though I couldn't hear him. I don't get that part at all. Ansel hates those *guineas* from The Inn. And Jackie was his friend. Am I right, Gina?"

"Yeah, that's true. My dad and Ansel were good friends. But that was a long time ago. Things change super fast in that world. So tell me. Bottom line: whether they're sad or not, what makes you believe those guys think my dad might still be alive?"

"First of all, there was no body. Everybody knows that."

"Yeah, but all that got explained. The explosion was so big and the fire so hot, and it burned for so long out in Bumfuck, Ohio with those dumb ass volunteer fire department morons. When those jerk-offs finally showed up with their ancient fire truck it was completely out of water because they had filled up some guy's cistern earlier that day. And then it rained hard right after that – all night long," explained Gina, as though for some reason she needed to convince Carrie of something she had never been able to believe. "Are you afraid to say it? Because I swear on my mother's life, this is between us."

"I'm not done... Whitey said one of *'the old dogman's'* old friends had some pull with whoever conducted the investigation in Ashtabula County. He said it was some other *guinea* named Michael. They think this Michael guy's withholding evidence."

"Man, that's just crazy!" added a skeptical Danni.

"That's nuts alright. Cops never liked my dad."

"Okay, now check this part out," Carrie continued. "From what I could make out, it sounds like some kid recently picked up a hitchhiker who could fit Jack's description. I guess this kid liked this hitchhiker guy so much that he told his mother what the guy looked like and some things they talked about."

"What description is that?" laughed Danni. "He's under six-foot-tall; dark hair; Mediterranean-looking; medium built but looked strong; intense eyes but seemed smart and a little crazy? That's almost every Italian guy in Collinwood."

Carrie said, while lighting another Kool, "Well, for one thing, the guy mentioned to this kid he was a therapist. Why would a therapist be out walking around in a winter storm? Plus another thing is he said the guy looked all banged-up.

"Hmm... That's pretty odd but generic stuff," Gina said.

This kid's mother who picked up the hitchhiker is friends with Maureen Kelly. You know; that redheaded cunt who's Whitey's mother? That's how they know about this."

"Yeah, I know about Maureen and her family. We appreciate the heads-up, Carrie. That's very interesting and all. But none of it really means anything," said a disappointed-looking Gina as she blankly stared at a clean but worn hardwood floor.

"There's more. While this hitchhiker was nodded off in this kid's car, he took a picture of the guy with his phone. The image is dark and just a profile – more like a silhouette. But the kid's mother thought she recognized him. She said it looked like an older version of some guy named Jackie she used to know."

"Whoa... Now that is pretty heavy," Gina mumbled through thick curls twisted in ringlets across her face.

"As you know, Gina, here in C-town everybody who's anybody is known by everybody else. I know some stuff I'd rather not know. So I'm faced with this loyalty check. Do I tell my closest friend something really serious that concerns her fiancée's dad? Or do I keep quiet for the sake of my boyfriend, if he's involved? If I say anything, I betray Whitey. If I don't, I stab Danni in her back. I wasn't sure on this. So I stayed high and talked about a bunch of other crazy shit to keep my mind off how screwed-up my life is. Ether way I go with this, I'm fucked!"

Gina asked, "What else is there? It seems like you have a healthy suspicion that Ansel might have been involved in my father's car bombing, or that he at least knows about it. That's the feeling I'm getting here. Am I right, Carrie?"

"Yeah, you're right. I don't know on what level. I'm not sure if he was directly involved. But I'm pretty sure he at least suspects who did it and knows why."

"Did he say anything about a guy named Fingers?" asked Gina, jaw muscles rippling. By then she wore the same expression she had when she punched out her boss for *accidentally* touching her ass at the copy machine the same day Gina got fired.

"Nope, never that. Whitey talked to Ansel about two losers he called Whale-ass and Slim Jim. But I'm sure those names are just part of their bullshit lingo."

"Is there anything else, Carrie? Even if you don't think it's important. Anything at all that sounded odd or out of place?"

"Yeah, one more name that was really strange – even for Collinwood. They talked about some guy they called *Shit-pants*."

"So that's it, right sister? That's all of it?" Danni asked.

"And cops are piecing together clues about what happened to some guys in a band called the *Young Turks*. And he mentioned something about some pigs missing and that something was *Looney*. Whitey sounded worried when he said it's starting to look like '76 all over again. Does that mean anything?"

Gina nodded her head with a stern expression comprised of both fear and anger. "Yeah, Carrie. It means we shouldn't get involved. I don't even want to see those people. They scare the shit out of me. But I have just one more question, if that's okay."

"Sure, sister," Carrie relit the joint, hit it and passed it to Gina. "I've already said too much. So fuck it now. Go for it."

"Is my brother in any danger with Ansel?"

"I wish I knew. Whitey tells me dick. I don't trust him because he doesn't trust me. And fuck his psycho father, too."

"No thanks. I'll pass on that offer," Gina smiled.

Danni said, "That reminds me. Do you really think Rocco would have sex with those movie stars? Tell the truth. Because now I can't get that image out of my head."

"Tell you what, Danni. I'd much rather have *that* image in my head than some other shit I've been flashing on lately. How about this? If Rocco's slick enough to get all those chicks into bed, then I hope it's at the same time. And speaking of images, if he can pull off that move then I hope he takes pictures of them getting it on with each other. Because even though my little bro is my new hero, if he could pull off that move he'd get elevated to the coolest motherfucker on the planet for eternity. Especially if he gave me a disc of the JPEGs. Or better yet, a USB drive with an MPEG for action scenes – but only if he's filming, and his hairy ass isn't in any of those images. How about it, Carrie?"

"You're pretty slick for a girl, Gina," Carrie grinned, with watery eyes set at half-mast. "In fact, you're so cool I'm about to roll another joint for us to share – even though it's your brother's weed. By the way . . . you sleepin' over with us tonight?"

"*Who me*? Fuck yes I'm sleeping over! I plan on getting crude and unglued tonight and acting all out of character. But I'll pass on any more smoke for right now. It'll just put me to sleep. We have a really cool movie to watch. You up for a movie now, little sister?" Gina nudged Danni, both of them wearing very concerned expressions.

"After that I'm up for anything. Whatever's clever."

"Same here," Carrie slurred, "Fuck-it. I'm down."

"Okay, then it's movie time!" said a grinning Gina, as she high-fived Danni and Carrie and then carried the DVD over to her brother's surround sound system. "I changed my mind. I'll take one more for the movie. Give me a shotgun, sweetie," Gina asked. Carrie wrapped pouty lips around the middle of the joint, but with the lit end inside her mouth. She moved her face to Gina's, her lips almost touching as she blew a stream of smoke into Gina's mouth. When Gina finally pursed her lips together that meant her lungs were filled. She pushed Carrie away and began to cough and laugh at the same time. "Goddamn! That hit blew the back of my head off. Dude, I'm fucking wasted. Holy shit! It's been years since I've done that."

"How about me, you stingy bitch?" asked Danni. "Where's mine? Why can't you be nice like you are to Gina?"

"Because you're a cunt and I despise you."

"Oh, okay. You want me to be nice? How about I give you a shotgun like the way we used to during high school sleepovers? We called them *hot-guns*. Remember?"

"Sure . . . I'm game," Carrie smiled. "But I'm so fucked up already, one of those will do it for me. After that, you might as well leave my ass stretched out here on the couch for the night. But yeah, fuck-it, let's go for it. I'll sleep like a baby after that. No demons in my head tonight."

Danni took several small inhales in a row without exhaling, till her dark eyes were bulging out of their sockets and she looked about to explode. Then she dropped the joint in the Bulldog ashtray and put her lips against Carrie's. She exhaled slowly into Carrie's mouth as Carrie inhaled, their open mouths pressed tightly together, till Danni was completely out of air and Carrie's lungs were full of that same marijuana smoke Danni had just given her. As soon as they separated Danni took a huge inhale of fresh air while Carrie trickled out sweet smoke in a thin stream as if she were whistling a silent song comprised of colors. Both of them fell back onto the couch at the same moment.

"Where the fuck have you two maniacs been hiding all my life?" Gina laughed, as she tried to rub the blurriness out of them. "Danni, you have a whole other side to you I never saw till recently," she said, still laughing and clapping her hands on her knees, "and I like really it. You're a fox in sheep's clothing, chick. You're a little demon, aren't you? Meanwhile, let's celebrate."

CH XXXII:
The Arc Completes Its Thrust

December 30th, 2013: After that holiday week, when The Inn caught on fire and police were out looking for suspects for arson and murder, Gina and Danni began drinking more beer and smoking more bud than usual. That extraordinary day when The Inn went up in flames, Gina felt not much other than anger followed by numbness, then fear. Then she self-medicated in hopes to once again be able to feel anything other than a fear which penetrated so deep that drugs seemed to be the only remedy. Plus, Gina still hadn't fully recovered from her ex-boyfriend's infidelity. She feared she might never again trust enough with a powerful type of complete love she felt a desperate need to share with a soul mate. She forced a smile, calculating chances of escaping what seemed inevitable.

Every time Gina barged through the front doors of Rocco and Danni's or at Carly's where Tessa had been staying she yelled, "I'm back!" It was the same cheerfulness she used while trying to fool herself into believing she had not been a part of such brutal violence, as twinges ran through her every time a scene from that horrific day flashed back to haunt her. Because her life seemed empty without a steady presence she had grown accustomed to since birth, she felt exposed and frightened. Regardless of all her father's flaws, Gina always felt safe with him around. Bravely, she tried her best to continue living a life which no longer held much value. But she didn't share that dread with Tessa, or even Rocco, not those innermost thoughts of despair or her overwhelming feelings of hopelessness. Although she had committed acts beyond her wildest imagination and was terrified of retribution, she felt nothing related to remorse. That bareness of Tessa's new lodging reminded her of a gnawing emptiness inside her. Gina loved her immediate family, plus Sinbad and Bull. But that was it. Everyone else was a stranger. She realized that by losing her Daddy-O and then Bully-boy, her passion for love and familial closeness had a giant hole ripped from its core.

Danni would never again be greeted at the door by their dog. She could never watch that overgrown pup race through the house with his butt slightly tucked, running in circles in front of the couch, smiling that goofy Pit-bull grin he wore for family.

And to her dismay she found that her small world was rapidly shrinking. She tried to convince herself that with losing their baby and their dog in the same night, she might not have anymore love to share. But she knew that wasn't true. She understood she could never feel the same, and that enraged her to the point of numbness. At the same time however, she also saw how foolish it would be to squander any love she might still able to muster up and share with her new family. Danni felt torn in that empty room, half of her somehow more attached to those already gone and the other half adhered to the few needing her more than ever.

Gina pushed through her brother's front door and charged through their front-room: "Hi everybody! I'm back!"

Danni called from the bedroom, "Is that you, babe?"

"No, Danni. Rocco's not back yet. It's just me..."

Danni came running into the front-room: "I know that, silly. I was talking to *you*! I just hung up with Rocco. He called to say he's on his way." Then she gave her future sister-in-law a big hug and a quick peck on the lips. "Sit. I'll get us some beers."

The two girls had been hitting it hard since The Inn. It was to the point where even Carrie was beginning to worry.

"Danni, I want you to know something. I really love you."

Danni began crying. She took one of Gina's hands and put it against her neck to feel Gina's warmth and steadiness. "I really love you too, sweetie, with all my heart – forever. Before Carrie gets here I need to ask you something real quick," Danni said in a shaky voice. "Who are you more worried about, the cops or those fucking lunatic *dagos*?"

Gina twirled her curly dark hair around a finger as she said, "I'd have to say the pigs, because we can't kill them. Well, I suppose we can, but I'm pretty sure we won't get away with it. How about you, Danni? What's been keeping you up nights?"

"Even though I despise cops and have never trusted any of them, especially since that Irishman and that Italian pig shot our dog and our Rocco and then stole our money. But even with all that said, I'm still less scared of those pigs than those Italian gangsters. Especially now since I know that those mad-dogs *guineas* from The Inn all know the Mick was my father and that I'm with Rocco. That part makes my stomach flip-flop."

"The Inn? There is no more Inn. Remember?" Gina said, as she fussed about and rearranged things on a thick coffee table made by her father. She began the ritual of rolling a joint, the first of the day. She anticipated the sweet smell and how it would tickle her senses as soon as she opened the baggie. "My dad made this table the same weekend I was born. It was in my bedroom from my earliest memories. I used to play dolls on it, and set up my little plastic tea set right here," she said, pointing to the bag of buds. "When we found out Rocco was my Daddy's son and my only sibling, I gave it to him. It's hard to believe all that, and a whole bunch of other stuff, happened just within the past few months. I mean what the fuck? Has the whole world gone completely off its tits, or is it just me?"

"I wondered at first if you were angry at your dad or jealous of Rocco or Tessa. You know; after all those years of being an only child, and then BLAM . . . instant family! I think I might have been if I were you. But you seem to have taken it all in stride. You're one cool chick, Gina. I sure am glad we're sisters. But the truth is that now, after all that other stuff happened, we're closer than any two blood sisters can ever be. Aren't we?"

They embraced, both sobbing, each finally able to drop the pretense of toughness, to expose the frightened little girls hidden deep within. They plopped down in unison on the cold hard floor, sitting as close as two people can be without one being on the other's lap. Their legs tangled with one another's; arm-in-arm, leg around leg. Danni opened ice-cold *Black & Tans* on that old gray linoleum kitchen floor. They toasted and drank till they both thought they heard a noise in the front-room.

"Maybe it's the wind," Danni said, almost silently.

Gina whispered in a child's voice, "Shit! Didn't I lock it?"

Gina unwound herself from Danni to slide open a narrow drawer. She extracted two bread knives. They held one each and flattened themselves against cupboards next to a narrow arched doorway. From there they listened intently to their own heartbeats and to someone rummaging around in the next room.

Danni missed their Bully-boy more now than ever. As friendly as Rocco's game-bred dog was, he knew right from wrong. He never would have allowed anyone to abuse his adoptive family. That thought caused her to momentarily lower her head to ease the pressure of immeasurable heartache from guilt and shame. She whispered, "Yeah, it must just be the wind."

Gina's green eyes sparkled and widened. She held a tanned and polished index finger against pursed full lips tinted with glossy pink lipstick. Then she held out a strong but feminine opened hand against her as a gesture for Danni not to move.

Someone yelled in a garbled, gravely voice, "What's that? You thought I wouldn't be back? Is that it? Well here I am, bitches. So where the fuck you at? I need to come hunting? That's how you're gonna make me act up in this mutha fucker?"

Shocked, Danni looked wild-eyed at the expressionless Gina, while gripping a long, shiny knife. Danni puffed up her narrow chest and said, "You won't need to search for us too long, motherfucker! Here comes your worst nightmare!" They both charged into the tiny dining room, knifes over their heads, prepared for a new living nightmare. Sister and girlfriend, entrenched and bonded in a new yet familiar blood lust, a frenzy driven by animalistic survival instincts, both of them seemed to have adapted all too well to their new roles.

He smiled at their fears mixed with savage aggression. A light film of perspiration shone over their exquisite features.

The women gave each other looks of pure relief when they saw Rocco. The hospital-looking boxing glove was gone, but his left arm was still in a cast from just below the bullet wound in his shoulder to his wrist. A thickly bandaged hand dropping a crinkled paper grocery bag onto an old oval wooden table with signatures carved into it by famous bikers and dogmen from across North America who had passed through his life. The bag lay tipped on its side next to stacks of banded packs of $100 bills. Rocco's oiled .357 revolver looked even shinier beside all the dry paper money and that wrinkled-up tan paper sack.

Gina hollered, "Thanks, fuck-head! Make sure that door is locked behind you, you little asshole! We almost had a heart attack! Where did you get all this cash, boy? We need answers."

"Put that shit down before you two dummies cut yourselves," Rocco said. Gina and Danni set their knives on the table to inspect the stacks of large bills tumbled out of the bag.

Danni asked, "Is this the real thing, babe?"

"It's real alright. Real fucking handy. Me and Whitey made a little business transaction, is all. No big deal. You likey?"

"Is that all yours?" Danni asked, in amazement.

"Of course not…" he said to his girlfriend, smiling and kissing her all over her neck and face. "Sometimes you ask such stupid questions for such a smart girl. You burn too much."

"Wow! I didn't think it was all yours," Danni smiled, carefully setting down a pack of hundreds as if it were a set mousetrap. "So when do you and Whitey split this up?"

"Oops, wrong again. We did that before I came home."

"Who else are you involved with?" asked his sister. "Are cops looking for you, too?" Gina tossed a stack back on the pile.

"*Cops?*" he chuckled. "I highly doubt that... I'm involved with two other dangerous characters now. But I wouldn't have been able to pull this off if youse two manic bitches hadn't of saved my ass. So we're gonna cut this up into three neat piles."

"Fuck you... *Really?* Or are you breaking balls, as usual?"

"Nope, straight business, Gina," he said, putting his knotted fingers through his sister's thick curls and kissing a flushed cheek. But first things first: Come on, ladies. We'll have plenty of time to play with this paper. None of us are in a big hurry, right? In fact, I have a taste for one of your famous *Caffe Coretta's*, Danni. Hey, Gina, did Ma send those biscotti over with you the other day?" Gina was in shock at the sight of all that money and the news that one third of it was hers to keep. "Let's have a nice espresso with a little *anisette* and some nice *biscotti*." Rocco said, shaking out long black curls over his broad shoulders.

Still talking, the three of them entered their sparse little kitchen. Danni scurried about getting a tarnished espresso maker, an almost empty bag of Starbucks finely ground coffee and a greenish mason jar half full of lumpy white sugar. She said, "I'll make the espresso, but you don't need *anisette*. You're in recovery, remember? We'll just have it virgin. You don't need to get into anymore trouble, you sick maniac." Danni laughed, as she set up their little silver and black machine.

Gina took three small black cups from an end cupboard when they heard a door slam. *Click* It was the front door. The one Gina forgot to lock. The same one Rocco evidently hadn't locked, either. They looked at each other: *All that money, the pistol and those carving knives are still out there on the table.* Rocco handed the girls small steak knives with white plastic handles from the silverware drawer and gently lifted a wooden rolling pin and as a rapid approach of stomping came straight toward them. Each footfall shook the house harder with every step, quicker and louder.

Someone charged into the kitchen. "Hey! You fucking cunts were supposed to call me!" laughed Carrie with her throaty voice. "And what the fuck's with all the kitchen gadgets? What is this, a Tupperware party? Or are you sawing beer cans in half and then slicing tomatoes? Hey, what is it you guys are making? I want some too, whatever it is." She gave Rocco a peck on the cheek and then pulled both of the girls into her for a group hug.

"*We're* supposed to call *you*? Bullshit, lady. I told you Gina and I would be waiting right here for your lazy ass, as usual."

"Well, you could have called . . . or at least texted me."

"Oh. So do you have your phone on you, Carrie?"

"Of course I do, you addled little mick. I always have my phone on me. What kind of burn-out question is that?"

"Cool. Can I make a quick call, Carrie?" asked Danni.

"Anywhere in the world you want, babe."

"It's not long distance. Gina just wants to phone your mom's house real quick," Danni assured her.

"Damn! Are you guys burning without me again? You couldn't wait five fucking minutes?" Carrie asked. "Pass it this way, *sista*. I need a quick toke to chill the fuck out."

"Is it turned on?" asked Danni, in her little girl's voice.

"Of course it's *turned on*. Everything that gets close to my ass is turned on."

"Okay, hot mama. Then check to see if I texted you."

Carrie sighed, pulled a pink smart phone out of the small denim purse on her hip to notice a black screen. "What the fuck! I know for a fact it was on."

"Maybe you forgot to charge, girly-girl," Gina said to her new friend. "I do that at least once a week. I hate that shit."

"I'll be double-fucked! This piece of shit battery…"

"Give it here, space-case. I'll charge it for you," Danni laughed, as she snatched the phone away from her numb friend.

While in the kitchen, the three girls heard someone roar from the front-room, "I'm back, motherfuckers!" a man snarled.

"Shit, shit, shit…" Danni whispered, as she crawled towards the knife drawer. Carrie had no idea why her girlfriends were so paranoid. When she saw Rocco looked worried, reasons no longer mattered. She chose a meat mallet from the drawer.

A look of realization washed over Gina's face. She smiled. In one smooth motion she opened her suede fringed purse and unholstered her other new friend. Slowly and quietly she chambered her father's gun, thumbed off the safety and with two hands aimed at the center of the open doorway.

The man in the next room growled, "Dirty rotten motherfuckers!" as something hit a wall. In a low, gravely voice he grunted something else as he rumbled for the open doorway to where the girls' legs shook along with the kitchen floor.

By the time Danni reached the railroad brakeman's club leaning against the outside of the doorjamb leading to the dining room, Carrie had armed herself with a steak knife in one hand and a mallet in the other. Danni stood flat against the kitchen cupboards nearest the doorway, with the long wooden club over her head. Carrie positioned herself next to her oldest friend. Rocco stood closest to the door – waiting.

The man yelled, "I guess it must be open house up in this motherfucker. Maybe I'll just take this cash before I—"

Rocco dropped the rolling pin. It crashed to the floor as he lowered his head and folded his better arm across his chest.

"Babe? Is that you?" Carrie asked, in a half-whisper.

"Any asshole could just barge in here! Who's the dummy left the door unlocked?" Whitey asked, as he entered.

Carrie insisted, with corrugated knives held down at her sides, "I swear to fucking Buddha! I locked that piece of shit door. You girls heard me slam it, right? Holy shit! Am I that burnt?" She dropped the knives in a stainless steel sink and leaned on the blue Formica counter, shaking very blonde hair.

Whitey scooped up Carrie in his thick illustrated arms and twirled her around in a tight circle. "Me and you are going on that vacation we talked about after all, you little fucking psycho bitch."

Danni still held the brake club on both ends like Bruce Lee's nunchakus before battle. Parallel with the floor, on outstretched arms, hands out in front of her shoulders.

Whitey asked Danni, "Roc teaching you how to use the bo staff now? He's good with all that Jap shit. I watched him compete. Ol' Roc was a contender before he blew out a knee."

Gina ejected a shell into her lap from her father's gun, reset her piece to a safer mode and replaced it into her purse as she said, "You guys are such assholes sometimes. You know?"

"Of course. I ought to. I'm the one who's the asshole, right?" Rocco grinned. "If I didn't know, I'd *really* be an asshole."

"Nice to see you too, Gina. What did I do now?" Whitey asked. "Why you always giving me a case of the blues? Or are you three little girls snitting lines of crank off each others titties again and getting all paranoid while Roc here takes the video? Because I sure as fuck didn't expect an armed welcome from friends."

"It's a long story, bro. But it's all good," Rocco said to his puzzled-looking ally. "It's been one hell of a weekend! But at least we're not broke anymore! Salute! Here's to good drugs, stupid laws, true friends and depraved junkies who sell their souls."

"I hear you. I guess motherfuckers get what they ask for."

CH XXXIII: I'm Jack & I'm Back

So Neighborhood legend goes: Fingers called for a sit-down to be held on New Year's Eve of 2013, with the leaders of C-town's criminal empire. It was to be hosted on neutral territory, to get to the bottom of some recent killings of high profile underworld figures and the disappearance of two dirty cops. Recent events were putting heat on anyone in every crew. Plus, some mortal sins had been committed. So someone had to pay the ultimate price.

Fingers used excuses for their historic meet. He claimed he wanted to get to the bottom of who killed Tessa's husband. Fingers couldn't care less, and everyone knew that. He said that his cousins, Tessa and Rocco, could have been in the car when that bomb detonated in front of their farmhouse. But a move against his family without at least some effort would make him look soft. The other thing is if Fingers was the one who did do it, then that was a great way to take the focus off him.

To get the other crews interested, other reasons for the meeting were to find out who was responsible for the murders of prominent leaders since Tessa's husband had been taken out. A shocking incident had occurred when the wife of a notorious Irish gangster was shot and killed in a car with Mr. Brown while arriving at St. Joseph's Parish for Mass. A man's family is never to be involved in business. A concern of Fingers' was that he needed to clear his crew from suspicion of killing a pious lady who had never harmed a soul or publicly spoken a curse word in her life. For a deed such as that crime was, everybody turns against the guilty party. Enemies become allies to irradiate the world of that disease. So Fingers immediately sent a message of condolences and got word to Doyle Kelly that by the time of their meeting the identity of the murderer of Mr. Brown's wife would be revealed.

Another shock killing happened that same weekend. The Wong Gong's vice-president. Animal, who was also Ansel's closest brother, got assassinated while putting through Five Points on his way back to their clubhouse. He was gunned down in daylight and in his own territory. Fingers got word to Ansel and claimed light would be shed on whoever the guilty party was who had shot-gunned Animal off his Harley as he cruised near Doyle's Shamrock Club. The Wong Gong's suspected that Little Eamon might have something to do with their brother, Animal, being gunned down by a rival drug dealer slain on a known Celtic block. Doyle swore on the eyes of his children that he had nothing to do with killing of Animal. As with the Mr. Brown incident, each hit was an unforgivable act for which an individual or group would he harshly and quickly dealt with as soon as proven truths rather than speculation surfaced as facts.

Then the buzz on the streets became about what transpired at The Inn to Cagootz and Big Louie. Word was that the slayings and arson had been the handiwork of Doyle Kelly's hit squad. Police on the scene reported that the inferno had burst all the bar's hundreds of liquor bottles, which in turn inflamed everything even quicker due to how fast and hot alcohol burns. Fingers guessed the guilty party or parties were clever enough to attempt to cover their tracks, which they seemingly had done quite well – so far. No witnesses and not much evidence as a result of good luck and timing, along with extreme temperatures.

Fingers suspected that the story about Doyle being the guilty one might have been generated as a diversion to throw him off the real scent. Two of Fingers' top men had been brutally murdered at the same location where illegal dog matches had been staged the night before. Both *made-men*, Cagootz and Big Louie, went up in flames with his tavern. Because at those dog matches being raided a handful of hours before Cagootz and Big Louie had been butchered or possibly burned alive, the Wong Gongs had been cheated out of a large sum of money during a fake bust believed to have been orchestrated by Fingers' men. War seemed unavoidable.

Every boss has bosses, even the President of the United States has them. Fingers had angry bosses in other states urging him to diffuse an ugly situation in his hometown before Cleveland developed another full-scale conflict like the 1976 war.

During the Irish/Italian bombing war of '76, everybody lost – except the Wong Gongs, who used that opportunity to fortify their power base. Escalated shootings and bombings meant more intensive scrutiny from local and federal agencies in all states, more arrests and prison sentences to weaken existing gangs, and ongoing loss of profits. A void is created when big dogs are forced underground while law-dogs do their sniffing around. Even worse, while established crews like the Young Turks, the Celtics, and the Wong Gongs scaled down operations and took to the mattresses, hungry criminals rammed crowbars into hairline fractures to exploit openings to their fullest potential.

So the heat would fall on everyone, even cops. But there was another type of heat for those reckless enough to commit those crimes to consider. A move against *made-men* was an unforgivable transgression, whether Irish, Italian or outlaw bikers. An attack on innocent family members exponentially increased the pay-back factor. Confession wasn't necessary; absolution unthinkable. There was a price to pay, and that debt would be marked by at least one more death. It was the law of the concrete jungle. Fingers had the bar insured and no money was lost at the matches, so money wasn't his main concern. The Feds harassed him, insinuating he had arranged to have his own bar remodeled by fire to collect insurance money on an old building and a failing business in an area no longer known for having prime real-estate.

Fingers was determined to get to the root of the mess which had begun in my front yard and escalated with my son's dog. Although he had been contemplating retirement, a plan only Nino knew about, Fingers was still in charge and the bar had been his property – even though he had planned to sell it, anyway. This became an issue of pride more so then anything else, other than he might be next on the list. So Nino brainstormed a twofold plan. He advised Fingers to have two meetings. The first, a small talk with Cagootz' boys, Spuds and Vinny, was to delve into day-to-day Family operations and recent business transactions, all of which had been gradually and cleverly taken over by Cagootz.

The second part was for a history making sit-down, one comprised of grizzled old men and younger enforcers who hadn't mingled together since adolescence, unless it was inside prison. When locked up, gangsters in silk and/or denim made truces in order to defend against extremely powerful black, Latino and Arian gangs running American prison systems. Mafia men and even the hardest core of the big six U.S. motorcycle gangs were nobody in prison due to simple math – the sheer numbers of bangers willing to kill a known gangster to be accepted as a brother inside those cold walls where they felt secure.

Nino sent the word to be whispered throughout the streets, that echoed one simple message: whichever crew doesn't show proves their guilt. So the meeting was set for New Year's Eve at 11:00 p.m. and was slated to take place at Dago Red's house situated in the outskirts on Collinwood, on territory as neutral as one could get without involving law enforcement. His house was in a neighborhood near Lake Erie, which although recently becoming predominately black was kept immaculate, with well-kept houses and yards, and home owners brimming with neighborhood pride. Nino also had pride. He set four ground rules for the summit about to take place at Dago Red's.

    Rule #1: No guns, but knives are permissible.
    Rule #2: Nobody shows up without an invitation.
    Rule #3: No physical altercations – period.
    Rule #4: No exceptions.

    Dago Red had been chosen as moderator because he was still relatively trusted by all factions summoned to the meet. In view of the recent mayhem and slaughter involving members of all three of Collinwood's most notorious organized Caucasian crews, Dago Red knew every man invited. He was a former member of the dismantled bike club, the No-Names, as well as being an ex-striker for the Wong Gongs. And he was a longtime friend of the Royal Flush, later absorbed by the Uno's Young Turks. Also, Dago Red went to Collinwood high school with Doyle Kelly. That made Dago Red a likely candidate as host for such an unusual gathering. Nicknamed because of red hair and baby face and his passion for homemade red wine, years of hard drugs had aged Dago Red before his time. He no longer had one trace of red hair. And that baby face had been lost many years ago to heroin and crack addictions. His heavily lined and scarred face, crowned by a head of white hair, made his pasty complexion look even older and sicklier.

    That once in a lifetime conference of Collinwood's elite professionals was to be held in a vacant 2 1/2 car garage which had windows on its front overhead doors facing the road, as well as on the side man-door which would be used as both entrance and exit. The building was fairly clean and empty because Dago Red didn't have a driver's license or a car. What he did have was a police record littered with drug offenses and DUI's. So he depended on his old No-Names brother, Slick, to run errands with him and to get them to AA meetings clean and sober. Still brothers, they helped to keep each other with recovery.

    That garage was an old structure, sided with wooden panels of chipped white paint. The roof was solid but sagged a bit. It didn't leak and its floor was stout enough to keep out the moisture. But the weather that year had been as volatile as recent Neighborhood events. According to local forecasters, that night promised to be brutally cold – even for late December in Cleveland. As timing would have it, the blower on Dago Red's Torpedo heater went on strike at the last minute, shortly before the big event was about to commence. Stores were closed for the holiday. Dago Red couldn't change plans on his own, so he placed a call to Nino. A tactician, from menial problems to complex matters, Nino had been appointed *consigliere* in Fingers' Cleveland Family the same day they seized control after Uno was assassinated in prison.

Nino implemented Plan B which was to move the meeting into Dago Red's home. But the old house didn't have one room large enough to accommodate all those anxious people invited. A wall between the tiny front-room and dining room would have to be removed to fit everyone in the same area. But the little frame house was a rental. Nino advised Dago Red to hire his old friend, Slick, to knock down the partition and they would pay him for materials and labor to rebuild it after the meeting. But because of recent landlord problems and nosey neighbors, Dago Red wisely passed.

Out of necessity Nino suggested a third strategy. Plan C arranged for them to convene in Dago Red's musty full basement. But that proposition posed yet another set of problems – the worst of all being suspicion. Those fearless gangsters were feeling paranoid about meeting off their home turf. Nobody from Collinwood was happy about being trapped in anyone's basement, not after what had recently transpired at The Inn.

Even though everyone was aware that Dago Red was a recovering junkie, he was old-school and respected. He pulled some serious time without anyone else ever being implicated. Being dope sick in a holding cell in the Cuyahoga County Jail was anything but fun. Even when he had been faced with a deal for time served if he *cooperated* by giving up remnants of the Mick's old mob, Red held firm. After he took a bust for the team, he conducted occasional business transactions with Doyle Kelly who came from a long line of psychopaths. Doyle was the youngest brother of redheaded siblings Eamon Jr. and Paddy, and brother of their fiery carrot-topped sister, Maureen, the mother of Whitey (best friend of Rocco) and live-in ol' lady of Ansel. So she became an integral person able to confirm that members of the three crews had all been invited to the secret rendezvous spot for some of Cleveland's most dangerous men.

Dago Red was a true yet unique junkie. His addiction never interfered with integrity. He never robbed family for a fix or set-up friends for the cops or a deal. He didn't shit where he ate and didn't go out of his way to make new enemies, because he had been around long enough to realize bad enemies last longer than friends, and have better memories. That bit of personal history was only a portion of his legacy. He had been a trusted brother of the No-Names. He did deals with Ansel and Cagootz. He knew Fingers since he was a kid and did time with Big Louie. He grew up with Paddy Kelly from Five Points, Fat Spuds from the Neighborhood and Filo from the Wong Gongs Being solid in an unconventional way left Dago Red in an awkward position.

Dago Red was one of the few individuals from the heart of the Neighborhood who attended school or did time with men from all of C-town's syndicates. He had managed to maintain a long-term, working relationship with Fingers' crew, as well as with Italian mobsters from Little Italy. Those credentials left him responsible to properly network with all three power gangs in Collinwood, without any backup of his own. Dago Red managed to keep on fairly good terms with Ansel and his Wong Gongs, the Cleveland-based biker gang which enlisted the most feared scooter tramps as patch-holders on the North Coast of America. Good terms in that world meant he might not be an immediate mark to get ripped off or be killed. Dago Red understood that if he was being set-up there was nothing he could do to change it.

Individuals of the crews summoned to Dago Red's *casa* represented Cleveland's most treacherous Caucasian outfits. All were organized crime figures monitored by local, state or federal law organizations as closely as most normal men would watch bisexual tongue-in-cheek action featuring pretty women. Nino selected handful of delegates from each crew to represent each syndicate. Fingers guaranteed a safe right of passage for all, for that one night.

Doyle had been given a personal invitation by Nino. Allegedly, Doyle planned to attend. Not because he feared reprisal, but rather to prove his lack of fear.

The Wong Gongs would attend to show that they respected nobody beside other club brothers.

Then Fingers sent word he would be undergoing emergency colonoscopy surgery but insisted the meeting take place and appointed Nino to preside. The only person invited not in a crew was Rocco. And that one detail left him sleepless.

New Year's Eve, 2013: Everyone expected the Wong Gongs to be the last to show. It was an unwritten biker code to be rudely late and disruptive. So they arrived early. In fact, they were the first to arrive. The Viking-looking Ansel sent his son, Whitey, in his place, when he found out Fingers would not be at his own meeting. Ansel sent along two other club-brothers. Allegedly, Ansel had been picked up for questioning on a drug conspiracy and was being held in Cleveland's 6th district in Collinwood.

Rocco's oldest friend, Whitey, drove with Filo to the meeting place. Those patch-holders arrived in a new black Ford Econoline with stolen plates. Unkempt hair and matted beards, clothing deliberately left dirty as another sign of disdain, the Wong Gongs also flaunted a big *fuck-you* statement by flying their club colors to the historic meeting. The center patch proudly proclaiming "1%er" rested in the middle of their blazing colors on faded and ragged cutoff vests worn over stained T-shirts. Torn Levi's along with nonchalant attitudes merely added to blatant disrespect held for Cleveland's other elite gangsters. They were greeted at the door by the personable but cool Nino and a nervously standoffish Dago Red.

The Italian contingency arrived next. Fat Spuds in front with Skinny Vinny driving a black Cadillac that had been the property of the late Cagootz. Dago Red met old acquaintances and ushered them into a kitchen just above his basement steps.

Spuds took out his tiny black pocket comb to smooth perfectly plastered down, greasy black hair tightly to his small skull atop of an immense body. He chewed gum quickly as he said, "Hey, how the fuck ya doin' there, Red-man?"

Skinny Vinny, who looked like a human version of Biggy Rat cartoon character, repeated, "Yeah, how the fuck you doin', Red-man," as he jerked his topcoat collar up and with a nervous tick rotated his head in circles at the same time. "So who the fuck's here, Red-man? Everybody here already, or what?"

"Some are already here and a few others are on their way," answered the weary-looking Dago Red with his slow and measured voice. He looked old and tired, his red eyebrows also long ago consumed by white, his eyes were heavily creased from a lifetime of heavy drug abuse and long stretches of prison time.

Nino rode in the spacious back leather seat with Auggie, a man rumored to have killed more people than any two triggermen from their crew. Auggie stood well over six feet, almost a head taller than the short, stocky Nino. Auggie was slender yet the second tallest man there. He moved around like a small man. He had straight, light brown hair, pale skin and dark circles around dark eyes. Auggie didn't look old or young, he looked dead.

The son of Doyle's oldest brother had become his right-hand man. Little Eamon, who was anything but little, had driven Maureen's red Hummer fast yet arrived last. Little Eamon became the most feared man in Cleveland's Irish Mafia. He was big and muscular with close-cropped red hair and chiseled features. His rugged features, size and built favored his mother's Ukrainian side. Eamon looked and was built like *Samooborona Bez Oruzhiya* fighters with broad shoulders, a thick neck and fists like rocks. Rumor was he trained in Russian SAMBO fighting. He looked the part with high cheekbones and light almond-shaped eyes.

Doyle also brought along Mr. Danny Brown, a pioneer who had been a close associate of the Mick back in the formative days. Mr. Brown, a cold-blooded contract killer, had somehow managed to see old age. His glass lenses were so thick they made his eyes appear beady like those of a rodent.

Every man invited was fearless and extremely volatile. Each had made his bones long ago. But another plain and simple fact is that all were intelligent enough to know that nobody wanted to be stuck underground without windows or doors, especially after what had recently happened when two untouchables went up in smoke in another Collinwood basement. In light of those recent murders it became common knowledge that as it was in 1976, nobody was immune – no matter whose flag they flew or how closely connected they were. None wanted to be stuck underground, but no one was willing to be the first to admit it. So one by one, men slowly descended into Dago Red's basement, with its cold, gray block walls and dingy cement floor.

Rather than one entire crew to be left at a possible disadvantage, stranded down there or left upstairs, an unspoken deal had been agreed to. An individual from each of the crews took the initiative to filter down while some bros, partners or *coombas* remained topside till things unfolded and made further sense. Others plunged down into Dago Red's basement to face the unknown and to deal with well-hidden paranoia. Half up at a time, so not to drop all their soldiers from a single camp into one foxhole, they moved like unmonitored cars at a four-way stop. Too quick or slow of a move might have proven to be less than advantageous. Those up and down scanned their surroundings and assumed positions like it had been rehearsed. As if using invisible walkie talkies, one by one they slowly descended. Within a few minutes it appeared as if all were downstairs and had found what they considered to be key locations for whatever came next.

With greasy boots up on rented chairs, the Wong Gongs smoked joints, spoke loudly and laughed. They gave the impression of not being impressed or concerned.

The Italians, dressed in dark silk suits, huddled in corners to speak in whispers. They could have been at a funeral with their mannerisms, pressed shirts and silk ties.

The Irishmen stood in a line against a gray block wall and watched everyone. Polo shirts and expensive slacks made them look like retired athletes at a game.

Every man present had done a contract hit, and most had served time. All had criminal records and current ties to Cleveland's vast underworld. None could afford to show any signs of weakness, so attending that meeting was a must for all who had been invited. Yet Fingers and Ansel were somehow exempt from that stigma, just as the Mick would have been. Doyle Kelly, also one of the big dogs, made a show of it. His gregarious style and loud mannerisms made sure everyone noticed he was the only one of the big three who had been ballsy and recklessness enough to tempt the fate of the gods.

But no matter who sat slouched into random folding chairs or who spoke loud enough for others to pretend they couldn't hear, nerves were raw all the way around the room. Tempers had been set to hair trigger and were one blonde pussy hair away from blowing the roof through the upstairs living quarters in which people suddenly and audibly were walking over their heads. Everyone stopped in mid-sentence or stride, mid-laughter or whisper. Silence fell over Dago Red's basement like a smothering fog. Fear or anger, just as closely related as love and hate as are envy and **sycophantism**, no one dared move.

The lack of stealth from above was maddening. Loud shoes and boots clomped down the wooden staircase. Disrespect for their collective ferocity rose from insult to outrage, till they saw the source of those loud footsteps. It seemed like a lot of noise for the three who descended. To everyone's amazement it was a woman, a stooped-over old-timer and a longhaired hippie.

Tessa walked on the railing side. She wore a black sweat suit, black running shoes and carried a large black leather purse over her free shoulder. Attached to Tessa's other shoulder in the center of the staircase was the short old man who had a thick shock of medium-length white hair. The old man was dressed impeccably yet casual, with a cream colored silk shirt worn out over an expensive pair of perfectly pressed tan pants. The old

413

man's shoes reflected the way people used to polish Stetsons back in the mid-1960s, with hard toes spit-shined and buffed out to a mirror finish. He wore a camelhair topcoat. Mr. Brown took one step forward to squint behind thick, horn-rimmed eyeglasses to have a better look. Then he leaned back into the shadow of his younger and larger accomplices whispering something to Doyle.

The unidentified old hippie held the right arm of the old-timer, guiding him down from the other side of the steps. All the 1%ers who had been seated, stood to puff up and glare at what somehow looked dangerously familiar. Perhaps a rival from another outlaw motorcycle gang? The hippy-looking older man ignored them through wrap-around mirrored shades, as well as everyone else in that basement. He wore his straight brown hair, obviously dyed, well past shoulders also covered by fatigues. His long full beard, also dyed brown, blended in seamlessly with unkempt hair. He was dressed in camo with a patrol cap stenciled "Vietnam" in white lettering, an ACU jacket, paratrooper pants and Vietnam jungle boots. He wore thin, tight brown leather gloves. The hippie crab-walked through the intimidating bikers to lift two chairs, one for Tessa and the other for the small old man with the snow-white hair. They sat facing the center of Dago Red's old basement. Standing behind the two who accompanied him, the old hippie placed one gloved hand in a front pocket of his military jacket and the other rested on the old-timer's chair.

As Dago Red descended, to keep an eye on things, Whitey asked in more of a growl than a question, "Who the fuck's this asshole?" nodding towards the old hippie.

"Whoa, wait awhile," Fats Spuds said to Dago Red, with a pudgy hand up as if to halt traffic. "If *these* guys don't know who this hairy freak is, and *we* sure as fuck don't, then why's he here?" He looked over at Doyle: "This thing belong to you?"

Mr. Brown answered for Doyle with a chuckle. "Does he look like one of ours, laddie?"

Skinny Vinny chimed in, "Yeah, Red, who's the long-haired freak and this old dude? And what's with this chick? What the fuck you runnin' here, a retirement home for old junkies?"

Dago Red deflected the left-handed insult at his own drug history with a hiss and a slow shake of his head.

"I'll tell you who they are. They're guests of mine," Auggie said. "Why? Does anyone have a problem? Because if so, I'll ask the boss so you can clear up this and any other problems."

Filo laughed out loud, snorted and hocked up a wad, and then spit on the floor while looking at Skinny Vinny. Filo had been a kid when he first met Auggie, both of them from Collinwood but members of different generations and affiliates of separate crews. Fat Spuds was also from Collinwood. But the fat man's partner, Vinny, grew up in Cleveland's Little Italy.

Vinny tugged at the lapels of his coat while jerking his head sideways. "Okay, real funny. But I'm talking to you, Redman. Tell me something. You off the wagon again, or what? Because this hairy bastard looks like a hop-head to me."

Little Eamon broke away from his contingency to confront Dago Red. "We ain't here for social call. What's this shit about? 'Cause we ain't got all fuckin' night to socialize. Get to it!"

"No worries. We're on time, Eamon" he assured him.

Eamon yelled, "I ain't worried, motherfucker! I ain't got time for all this bullshit! In fact, you know what—"

Little Eamon stopped in mid sentence when an upstairs door slammed. He quickly refocused on the noise coming from above their heads as he reached into his full-length leather coat. All the men looked up at once as if the ceiling rafters had begun making noises exactly like loud footsteps. Then all eyes cut into Dago Red at the same moment, looking at his tired eyes for signs of betrayal. In the next moment those same footsteps were on top of that staircase, clomping as something large made its way down. Dago Red raised his hands "Don't blame me. I guess someone was in the bathroom."

After a few excruciating seconds, every man's gun was drawn and aimed either at the steps or the ceiling, except for one. Mr. Brown trained his piece at the center of Dago Red's body. "If there's shootin' here, laddie, you're be the first one gets it." Dago Red nodded his head to acknowledge he understood. Crows feet spread out from the outside corners of dark fearful eyes.

Whomever or whatever had been upstairs was making its way into the belly of that cold gray basement, into a firing squad of killers. The men down there watched as a pair of spit-shined shoes appeared, followed by four scuffed boots making a slow descent into the pit of Dago Red's arranged meeting place.

A dark-skinned man with dyed black hair was the first to appear, casually yet immaculately dressed in an Italian knit sweater and pressed silk pants. He wore a full-length cordovan leather coat with its buttons open and its leather belt dangling at each side. But he was at least 60 pounds heavier than the last time I had seen him, many years ago. As he reached the bottom Spuds hollered, "*Coom*! You made it!"

Skinny Vinny said, "Hey, it's *coomba* Fingers! Now we can get to the bottom of all this bullshit." Then, looking over at Filo he added, "Now who's got somethin'—"

Auggie, with long strides, walked over to greet Fingers. "Hello, *coom*. Even I'd a lost a bundle on *this* bet. But I'm willing to make wager right here and now, as crazy as this spectacle is, I got a gut feeling this isn't even close to being over. In fact, it ain't even started yet. Am I right? No, don't tell me. Let me be surprised. Meantime . . . what do you need, *coom*?"

Vinny stopped dead in his tracks when he saw Fingers was followed by none other than Ansel himself. His long blonde hair and full beard had turned more than 50% white. Ansel was still built like a fighter. He pulled his hair back and snorted deeply, as if to clear away any residue from a cocaine drip. Ansel's Levi's were clean. The front of his Levi cutoff vest was loaded with small patches and pins like that of a military veteran of foreign wars. Cleveland had been the first Chapter of the Wong Gongs. And because Ansel had been one of its founding members, he was known across the U.S. as the biker's biker. Ansel still rode a raked and stretched yellow chopper during the nicer months, a beast that was bored and stroked for the fast lane.

An old Royal Flush club-brother, Gus, stomped down those wooden steps behind Ansel. His blue jeans were covered with motor oil to make them look like black leather pants. As Gus strutted through, giving the Irishmen bad looks, the musty air filled with the odors of gasoline and oil. His black engineer boots shined, but not from polish. He walked over to where Dago Red had positioned himself, leaning against his natural gas furnace, towards the opposite side of his basement. Dago Red stuck out his hand. Gus grabbed it with a firm, quick shake.

Filo chuckled, "You were saying?" as he looked over at the Italian crew, watching Skinny Vinny tug at the collar of his shirt and twist his head on his pencil neck. Vinny's forehead broke out in a film of greasy sweat, reflected by the bare bulbs in ceramic bare-bones fixtures affixed to old wooden beams.

Ansel strutted over to his crew. With his back to a wall he posted next to his son, Whitey. Filo made a bad attempt at stifling another laugh, still shaking his head of short-cropped dark brown hair on a thick muscular neck. "Welcome, brother," he said to Ansel. "Things just got real fucking quiet– real quick-like."

Gus piped in with his gravely voice, "Yeah . . . right? Quiet like little mice. I almost dozed off for a hot second. But shit's about to get interesting now." He stood, thick arms crossed over his massive chest, and positioned himself on the other side of Whitey, and behind Filo, who was seated with his boots up on a folding chair – still chuckling while looking at Vinny.

Then everyone remembered there was another pair of black scraped-up boots at the top of the steps. The person stood in the dark, just up enough to still be out of sight.

Skinny Vinny's left eye began to twitch. He rubbed his temples in an attempt to calm the spasms and in hopes that no one noticed him nerking out more than usual.

Fat Spuds snapped, "Everybody just relax!" He twirled a toothpick around while chewing a mouthful of gum at the same time. He smoothed the sides of his greased back black hair with fat hands that looked more like bear paws. "Don't youse guys forget whose party this is. We're callin' the shots tonight!" Spuds said loudly, as he broke out in beads of sweat.

The second pair of scuffed-up boots slowly took one step at a time . . . a pair of jeans . . . something thick and white, like the man was carrying something wrapped. It was Rocco. The thick white thing was his cast. Rocco walked over to stand in front of his mother and Uncle Pazzo, and by that quiet old hippie with the scraggly long hair, full beard and wrap-around shades.

Mr. Brown said, "Well, well. May the baby Jesus, the Virgin and Joseph all be nailed to the same goddamned cross. Just look at the conglomeration of fine gentlemen in this one room. Shall I clean my glasses? Or have me eyes finally done failed me?"

His own calabash nephew, Doyle, said, "Nothing wrong with your eyes, Uncle. You always told us if we live long enough we'll see everything. I'd bet 10-to-1 the Mick would have wagered green folding money we'd never see this day – no matter how long we lived," Doyle said, as he looked around to apprise the congregation of killers; drug-traffickers; high-stakes gamblers; a hippie and a women; all packed into Dago Red's basement.

"Yeah, no fucking shit," agreed Fat Spuds. "Now what?" he asked, smoothing back the sides of his hair with sweaty hands. "Red, you got coffee and donuts for your guests, or what?"

Skinny Vinny, tugging at his collar with a curled finger to loosen his red tie and shirt from his throat said, "So now what the fuck? Because this just ain't smart, us all being trapped in one spot – donuts or not…"

Spuds asked, "What the fuck happened to your hand, kid? Looks like you been jerking off too much again, huh? These fuckin' kids kill me…"

Rocco answered, "You remember when all of us got raided at the matches? Anyway, those lunatic cops broke my hand *and* shot my dog, and then they took all our money. I was so pissed off I didn't even realize my arm was broken. Cagootz and Big Louie were real lucky they didn't get busted, right Spuds?"

"Yeah, whatever… Let's get to the business at hand and move the fuck on," Spuds said, as he shoved two more sticks of gum into his mouth. "We're all supposed to be businessmen, right? So let's get to business and cut the bullshit."

"I agree," Vinny chimed in, as he tugged at the lapels of his cheap jacket and pivoted his head in tight circles. "Let's get this over with. We're professionals. So let's quit acting like a bunch of broads."

Auggie spoke up again: "Rocco, Nino asked you to be here because we think you have some information for us."

The old-timer shifted in his seat. Tessa hugged her purse. Rocco didn't blink, as if his face had been chiseled from stone.

Fingers stood in the center of the floor. Nino posted next to him on one side and Auggie on the other. Fingers finally spoke: "I got somethin' to say."

Everyone, standing or seated, quieted to listen while Fingers addressed the meeting. Whitey picked his fingernails with the tip of a bone handled switchblade. The quiet old hippie, dressed in his Army surplus battle gear, stared at Dago Red's chipped concrete floor through dark wraparound shades. All other eyes remained on Fingers.

"I invited a few people here I believe are solid. It's not that I'm stupid enough to trust most of you farther than I can piss. That is, other than my *coombas*."

"Well, something we finally agree on," Doyle sniggered.

"We've all suffered huge losses," Fingers continued. "I don't pretend to know all youse guys personally and couldn't guess what anybody's thinking right now. But I do know this much: all of youse guys are stand-up individuals when the heat's on and none of us is a rat. Everybody; even my cousin, Tessa – or she wouldn't be here. And the reason she is, is the same reason Ansel's here and Mr. Brown is here. And the same reason I'm here. We've all been trying to deal with some heavy losses."

Danny Brown cleared his throat: "That's all well and good, Fingers. And I appreciate the left-handed pat on the back. But I lost my wife. And I won't rest until I find out who the soon to be dead men are foolish enough to pull the trigger and to issue that order for a hit on me! I'm old and sick, boys, so that makes me the most dangerous man here. I have nothing to lose, lads."

"I hear that," said Doyle Kelly, as he stood to give everyone else bad looks. "I ain't as old as him, but I'm plenty sick. My auntie took a bullet for being in the right place at the wrong time. She was the sweetest woman in the world. That means somebody else has to die for the sins of the wicked."

Rocco spoke up: "I'm really sorry for your loss, Mr. Brown. And like Fingers said, we've all suffered grave losses. My father got blown up in our front yard. My mother was standing outside at the time. The only reason she wasn't in the car is . . . well, I'm really not sure why. No one is. For some odd reason Pop made her go back to the house before the explosion. But she just as easily could have been in the car with Jackie, or my sister, or my girlfriend, or me when that bomb went off. Then Curtis, my auntie's husband, gets found down Five Points with a ventilated face. And then Animal, a good brother to my friends right here, gets blown right off his bike – again, down Five Points. So yeah, someone's gonna pay. Bet on that!"

Filo stood next to Rocco: "Tell you what: These speeches we're all giving are real moving and shit. I'm sure everybody's speaking from the heart. But this ain't no fucking funeral home or acting class! Some stupid motherfucker took out a Wong Gong. My brother, Animal, got ambushed. And let me tell you, he was respected by the gamest sons a bitches in the country. He didn't have a cur bone in his body. Animal was the biker's biker, the grittiest motherfucker I've ever known and loyal to his core. I got a feeling somebody here in this house knows what happened. So fuck this little circle jerk we got goin' on. Here's the rest and the last of my speech: Somebody's paying for my brother's death before I leave here, in person or with an IOU that will be collected and paid in full. That's a promise."

Fingers lifted a wooden crate off the floor and said, "One of my rules was no guns. Even I violated that. But I see willingness in this basement tonight. So as an act of faith I'm putting my piece in this box to show you guys this ain't no set-up." He walked over to Skinny Vinny and Fat Spuds. "Here, youse guys do the same. It's the class move, and we're all about class. Go ahead, right in here." Spuds smoothed back the left side of his hair with one hand and did as he was told. Vinny nerked around for a moment but then reluctantly followed suit.

The old hippie stood and looked at the steps when he finally spoke. In a hoarse, gravely voice he said to Dago Red, "Excuse me. I need to use the facilities. I can piss outside if you don't want me wandering around upstairs."

Doyle shouted, "Just hold up right there, you hairy bastard! You ain't goin' no place till I fucking say so!"

Eamon Jr. growled, "Who's this old bastard? Why is it none of us gentlemen know this hobo?" His eyes went cold.

Whitey took the switchblade out of Ansel's hands: "You try to go up those stairs, old man, you'll be a pile of chopped ham by the second step." When he moved to grab the strange man, Ansel placed a callused hand on his son's arm.

Rocco said, "He's an old friend of the family. His name's Chilly. He was my father's best friend. And my Uncle Pazzo right here will gladly vouch for him."

Fingers wheeled around at Ansel: "You mean to tell me this guy's not with your crew?"

Pazzo turned to look at Fingers. He assured everyone, "I'll stake my reputation on this man. He's a *Friend of Ours.*"

"I don't give a flyin' fuck who he is. He ain't going upstairs because nobody is." Fingers growled. "There's a bathroom in that corner behind the furnace, right over there," as he pointed to a dark area farthest from the steps. "Anybody's gotta take a leak, Dago Red goes with him. Same for me if I gotta piss. Same rule for everyone. No exceptions, unless it's Tessa. And the only reason her and her kid are here is I have questions!"

Ansel agreed, "Cool by me. Go on ahead, old man," the Viking-looking biker chuckled to the old hippie. "There's only one way out of here, and that's through all of us. And like you already saw, everybody's packing heat – even though we weren't supposed to. That's one thing about guys like us. We ain't too good at following directions," Ansel smirked, as he reclaimed his switchblade to nonchalantly inspect his fingernails.

"Yeah . . . sure . . . fuck-it, old man. Go ahead and take your piss," Doyle said, red face matching his hair while grinning like a madman. "We're right here waiting for you."

Then, stooped-over with an odd-like crab walk, the old hippie cautiously limped his way through the small gathering, side-stepping a roomful of sharks looking for an excuse to attack.

The bathroom was two plywood walls in a basement corner.

After a few minutes of silence the plywood bathroom door reopened. Where one longhaired freak had entered, three other men exited the tiny stall. Everybody redrew their guns with the exception of Fingers, Pazzo and Rocco, who looked calm. Spuds and Vinny were no longer packed. Tessa glared at the sight of the new men, shifting a large black purse on her lap.

One of the three mystery men was older but in solid condition, tall and very black, dressed in a black silk suit and white shirt with short-cropped gray hair. He had another black man, an old man dressed in a red leisure suit with a yellow dress shirt, in front of him. That old man was even blacker; a short, skinny player with processed white hair slicked back tight with grease to his thin skull. That old man's hands were behind him, silver duct tape covered his mouth.

The third man walked behind the tallest. His clothes looked identical to what the hippie had been wearing, but he had very short gray hair, a wore a close-cropped goatee and eyeglasses. He looked like a burned-out schoolteacher.

Mr. Brown chuckled, "Put away those heaters, lads."

Doyle hesitated, but then complied with the odd request.

Ansel told Whitey and Filo, "Do the same, brothers."

Auggie hid his but clocked every move with hawk eyes.

Fingers announced, "Here is my gift to you. This well dressed man is a friend of Tessa's. His name is Horrible Hank. Some of you older guys might have heard his name mentioned as being a partner of Jackie's. Take off the tape, Hank."

The large black man did as asked. He ripped the duct tape away from the old man's white moustache and a soul patch growing beneath his thick lower lip. The old man hung his head, quiet and shamed. Hank shoved him to the center of the room.

Mr. Brown said, "Allow me to make the introductions. This gentleman, who is about to stand trial, is an old colleague. You younger bucks only know him by name, because he doesn't get out much – for obvious reasons. This man is Mr. Sonny Magic himself – old-school gangster from back in the day."

Ansel said, "I'm impressed. This is quite a catch."

"Yeah... So what the fuck's the deal," asked Doyle Kelly. "Why were we all called out on the worst night of the year? Just to stare at some old nigger tapped up in some shitty basement?"

"Why don't you tell them yourself, Sonny? You always prided yourself as being a class act. Go ahead. Let's see what you got left, old man," prompted Fingers.

Sonny slowly raised his head to stare at Spuds and Vinny. "I threw some money at those two cut-throats right there, and these boys decided to do a little freelance work."

Doyle said, in his usual sarcastic tone, "Good for you, old dude. You're a real humanitarian. So what else, or is that it?"

Sonny raised his head up even higher, "Cagootz and Big Louie sent them to hit Jackie, to cause a diversion. The plan was to whack Fingers, Doyle and Ansel, and then Cagootz take over C-town. They got to business and picked up contracts on Danny Brown and the Animal, and then on Curtis. But that wasn't enough. It never is, is it? They wanted more. So they thought they'd try to play me, because Cagootz thought he was playing me. So their next move, according to what those two told me, was to enlist my services to help them take down Cagootz and Big Louie. They thought I was stupid enough to believe we were partners. These two are a joke. I'm saddened to see what's happened to the empire Uno built. I made my bones on street hoods a lot tougher and smarter than you two ass clowns," Sonny Magic hissed at them.

Everyone was left speechless except Mr. Brown. "That's real interesting. Which one of those two shot my wife?"

"That weasel-looking son of a bitch right there," Sonny nodded his head at Skinny Vinny. "I've done a lot of bad things in my life, things I might have to pay for in the hereafter. But I've never killed a man's wife. Even I have a value system and a sense of moral decency, unlike these two."

"Let's everybody cool it!" commanded Fingers, as he stepped forward. "I got a few questions for these two snakes. So let's all of us just remember whose party this is and why."

Mr. Brown moved fast for such an old man. He pulled a straight razor and sliced Skinny Vinny's neck wide open. Vinny's eyes bulged in horror, jerking his head around in panic he yanked at his collar as he sat drowning in loud gasps, spraying dark red bubbles over a cheap sports jacket. Finally he slumped sideways onto Spuds, bleeding completely out on the fat man's lap. Spuds didn't budge, like maybe nobody would notice him if he held still.

"Don't fool yourselves into thinking I put my only piece in that box!" shouted Fingers. "I have three questions for the fat man and then you can have him, too."

Filo walked over to get a closer look at Vinny: "Excuse me, Mr. Brown," Filo said, making his way around the old

Irishman. "Wow, I've never seen anything like this *inside* a house. Goddamn, what a fucking mess! You've got one hell of a clean-up job on your hands, Red!" he laughed. "Now watch this…"

"Wait just a goddamned minute here!" commanded Fingers, as he put his hand in his jacket pocket. "We all have questions, and they'll all get answered. Right now I have an important question that pertains to all of us! Just hold still, Filo! First of all: we got cops crawling up every one of our asses since Looney Lonnie and O'Reilly vanished. Rocco, you're the reason all this shit jumped off inn the first place. They threatened you and your ol' lady and shot your dog. What happened?"

Filo interrupted again, "Hey, Sonny. Just out of curiosity, was this shifty-eyed, scrawny fuck the same nutless piece of trash that blew my brother off his scooter?"

"Nope," Sonny wagged his head at Filo. "You're pissing on the wrong tree stump, my man. The shooter of the Animal would be that fat tub right there, right next to that dead boy."

"Filo, don't make me sorry I trusted you. I still need to question him!" Fingers bellowed, just as Filo made his move.

Fast as a bullwhip, Filo threw a reverse punch to the fat man's throat. When Spuds grabbed at his own neck, Filo grabbed him by both ears and drove his knee as hard as he could into his nose. Spuds and Vinny both fell off their chairs onto the cracked concrete floor, by then saturated in Vinny's warm blood. Filo side-kicked a folding chair out of the way and stood over Spuds, holding the fat man's head in his meaty hands. He said, "He's still alive. You wanna ask, now's your chance."

Fingers said, "I should have known better than to think I could trust any of you…" He grabbed the other chair and flung it into a block wall. He pulled a snub-nosed .38 from his jacket pocket. "I need to know who killed my men!"

Filo pivoted thick shoulders as he twisted fast and hard. A crack could be heard throughout that run-down basement just before Fat Spuds fell limp. Filo laughed, "Stupid motherfucker," spit on Spuds, and returned to stand between Ansel and Whitey.

Ansel was still busy cleaning greasy fingernails with his shiny switchblade. His son, Whitey, stared expressionless at the bodies piling up on Dago Red's floor like a pile of used clothing.

Mr. Brown wiped his razor on the loud jacket of Vinny, whose limp body looked tiny lying next to the corpse of Spuds. He folded his straight razor and put it back into a jacket pocket before he took a seat next to a grinning Doyle.

Sonny looked at his host: "I did my part, Mr. Fingers. I gave you these traitors on a golden platter. I can't help it if you lost control in your own block. Now release me!"

Nino said, "The only reason you *gave* us anything is because we've been paying your crackhead whores to set you up, old man. We're the ones who sent them to you in the first place. Now we want more names and warm bodies. Who took out Cagootz and Big Louie? That's the only way you walk."

"It was a lot of time and money, but well worth it. Who gets to waste this old fucker? I'll be glad to volunteer," Auggie smiled. "I'm sort of a collector. I enjoy killing famous men."

"I deserve this," growled Rocco. "And I don't need two good arms to take down a legend." *Nothing...*

"Go ahead. Head butt that old fuck," Whitey laughed.

Fingers pointed his chromed .38 with pearl handles and yelled, "The next man to attack will be me! Nobody makes a move till I get my information. Two of *my* men got taken out – two *made-men*. Nobody wastes a *made-man* and gets away with it, not without the nod of the commission – not here or anywhere."

"You want information?" Sonny asked. "I know for a fact these two wired up Jackie's car. They sat in the backroom of my bar and bragged about it. They got drunk on my free booze and then starting mouthing off – thinking it was code language…"

"That doesn't make sense, old man. Jackie's been out of the loop for over 30 years. He was nothing more than a *used-to be*," Fingers reminded Sonny. "You better have more cheese than that, Sonny, unless you want to leave here in a garbage bag. Besides, why would Spuds and Vinny tell you anything? They wouldn't. Not unless you were in on it. That's how this adds up."

"Mr. Fingers, nobody knows for sure. But the educated guess is these two traitors stretched out on this floor did it." Sonny, with his head up high, said loudly. "That was the plan. I might have known a little something at the beginning. But they all got greedy. Nothing is ever enough. You know that. Cagootz wanted everybody's cut. He needed a distraction so he could take over. Smart money says these two took out those cops, too."

Fingers hissed, "They'd never have the balls to cross me."

Sonny continued, "Your boy, Cagootz, told these two idiots on the floor you got old and soft. Those boys said that to me, themselves. So they went and took Jackie's ass out to make it look like someone was creeping around with old grudges, to get everyone guessing, to keep everyone paranoid. I agree with you about Jackie. He was nothing more than a *used-to-be*. And even then he wasn't anything but a crazy-ass drug addict. So when these two went after Danny Brown and that Animal, it kept the Italians and the Irish, and even these bikers, all off balance. But they went too far. These two got scared and took out their own kind. So let's not forget the facts, Mr. Fingers. It was two *Italians* that took out Jackie. We African-American folks in Cleveland don't move like that. We take care of our own kind."

Like a trap door slamming, Sonny Magic went flying, face forward, to the floor. Behind him a shiny shoe retracted from a front kick to Sonny's spine. Horrible Hank said, "Yeah, motherfucker. That's how we take care of our own kind. Because Jackie's my brother. But you ain't shit to me, old man. And that's how we move in Collinwood."

Sonny rolled over, away from the two corpses, onto his back. Groaning from the ground he said, "I'd bet my last dollar these two were behind the killings at The Inn. It only makes sense. They couldn't afford to leave any witnesses. *Dagos* fucking *dagos*. That story is as old as organized crime. Even the Irish and these nasty Wong Gongs don't pull unscrupulous shit like that. They're *your* guys, Fingers. This is *your* shit! They were *your* people. So fuck you and Jackie! This is *your* mess!"

That's when I stepped around Hank and held a combat boot on his stomach: "*Fuck Jackie*, huh? Well guess what? I'm Jack and I'm back, motherfucker!"

"We never lost faith, Dad," Rocco said, quickly wiping at an eye with the back of a bandaged fist.

I continued: "Sorry about your loss, Mr. Brown and Doyle. That act was one of the worst things I've ever heard. And I really do feel bad about Animal getting taken out," I said, as I looked over at the Wong Gongs. "He was a man among men." Then I looked at my family. "And you especially. I'm sorry for not getting in touch with you sooner. But there was no way until the time was right. It was all or nothing. Because the taller the stack of lies gets, the easier it topples. So the timing had to be perfect. I couldn't afford for one piece to shift, even though I'd wager my life none of you would talk."

Pazzo finally spoke up: "Well, I guess somebody better shoot me. Because I might have *accidentally* said something to my niece," he said, hugging Tessa's shoulder. "But that's only because I know she's as solid as any man in this roomful of mad-dogs."

"Fucking Jackie... if it was anybody else I wouldn't believe it. You're the *onliest* motherfucker I know ever stepped back from the grave," Ansel said, in his low aggressive chuckle. "You need to teach me that trick, bro. By the way, man, you look like shit. Looks like you ain't been tanning much lately," Ansel laughed, "or maybe too much, by the looks of things. And who knows? Maybe you really were dead. Because you look like some fucking retarded zombie or some shit. The truth is you're freaking me the fuck out. I feel like I'm tripping balls."

Tessa ran to me, hugging me around the waist as Rocco had an arm hooked around my head, kissing me on the cheek. Tessa cried, "Ever since you came down those steps I've been wanting to do this so bad!"

I hugged him back, kissed my wife and then pulled away. I wasn't too comfortable getting too happy in front of those people, or having my family trapped down there while two bodies lie cooling on Dago Red's basement floor. "Thanks, Ansel. Fact is: I ain't been doing much of anything, other than healing and planning for this one day. I apologize for all the drama. But we needed to get this motherfucker down here," I said, pointing down to Sonny. "Thanks to my brother, Hank, we still have a live hostage full of information. And we needed these other two cocksuckers unarmed, thanks to Fingers. This whole thing just slid right into place."

Doyle yawned, "I've seen some crazy shit in my time, but this even tops sweet Jesus peeling his ass off the cross. You go from being an asshole to a college boy, and then from a dead man to a hippie and then back to an asshole. I'm almost impressed." He looked at his Little Eamon: "This is that fucking Jackie. You know; the dead guy."

"Nothing changes between us, Jackie. This ain't Easter; it's New Years," Fingers said, simmering his dark glare. What I need is to find out what the connection is with you getting blown up and my bar burning to the ground. Too many bombings and dead guys lately, huh Jackie? Or maybe not enough? What's the correlation, huh? What else is it you know?"

I nodded with a stern expression, "Speaking of too many dead guys: I heard about Cagootz and Big Louie. Bad luck... But you know the old saying: *Three rats can keep secrets a lot better if two of 'em can't talk.* This time was a bonus. You got rid of all of them for the price of one trap."

"What the fuck's that supposed to mean? You talkin' about my *coombas,* Cagootz and Louie? You think it's funny that two *made-men* got whacked? Is that why you're laughing?"

"Easy, Fingers," I answered. "I meant these two snakes laying right here dirtying-up Dago Red's floor. And I'm talking about this other old fuck right here who thinks he's smarter than everybody else. I said three, right? Two and one makes three." I turned to Filo and Whitey: "For those of you younger guys who don't know me, I'm Jackie. Like Doyle said, I'm the dead guy. And I'm the motherfucker that—"

BLAM! A gun firing in a basement is deafening. Everyone jumped just a little, yet no one really moved from where he had been before the shot fired. Smoke still wafted from the muzzle of Jackie's gun, held firmly in both of Tessa's delicate hands. Her large purse lay open on her chair. The bullet entered the side of Sonny's head and took away part of his skull. Bits of purple and white bone and brain scattered across Sonny's red walking suit.

Horrible Hank said, "Well, I guess that's that. Now all we need to do is dispose of this garbage."

"Not quite," Fingers yelled, as he smashed the wooden box, containing the pistols of his two recently deceased soldiers, against a block wall. Wood shattered like shrapnel. Miraculously enough, none of the guns in the box accidentally discharged. "Goddamnit! I should have known better than to allow a woman to be here – cousin or not. All their fucking emotions and bullshit. Uncle Pazzo, I can't believe I let you talk me into this shit. I should have my head examined! Now what the fuck am I supposed to do? Maybe I should try to wake up Vinny and Spuds and ask them about who whacked my men? Or maybe I can revive this slimy old spook so I can threaten him? FUCK!" Fingers roared, as he picked up a folding chair and smashed it over Sonny's limp body. "Now what the fuck? Tell me that!"

Doyle said, "Now me and my crew leave. That's what."

"Yeah," agreed Ansel, as he folded and put away his switchblade. "It's about that time. It's been real fellas, but all good things must come to an end."

The Irish mob and Wong Gongs headed up and out.

Rocco said, "I don't know how much I can do handling two big men while working short-handed. But I'm willing to try my best." *Again, nothing…* "But if you need any help cleaning up this messy basement, I'm willing."

Fingers kicked a chair: "This ain't got nothin' to do with you! Just take your mother home where she belongs!"

Hank said, "I brought Sonny here, so I'll take him with me. I know just where to plant him, to send a message for a brother. Because I know for a fact Sonny is the snake who put the hit on Curtis." He lifted Sonny with one huge hand and tossed him over a broad shoulder of that new suit, and then gingerly walked up the steps and outside.

When everyone had gone other than Finger's crew and my family, Pazzo spoke: "If Uno would've been here, Fingers, this never would have happened. I left you in charge as Acting Boss, but you got cocky and lazy. I trusted you to be my eyes and ears, but you were too busy gambling and playing the big shot. Then you got too paranoid. You've made quite a mess of what the Old Man in Little Italy built up for us in the '30s, and what Scalisi nurtured for us till the War of '76, and what *coomba* Uno lost his life trying to keep. I've hung on this long so all the spilled blood of so many solid men over the years wasn't all in vain."

Pazzo wiped his eyes with wrinkled hands. "But while I was in Florida getting old, you handed my empire over to that melon-head, Cagootz, and his stooge, Louie. Why? Because you got too arrogant, Fingers. You thought nobody would dare fuck with you. Well guess what? Now I really am retiring, and making a new appointment before I do. No offense, Nino. You're a good man. You're as loyal as a Pit-bull, too. And that's exactly why I can't give it to you. Because if I did, it would be business as usual. Fingers would still be in charge. Nope, those days are over. This town is in enough of a shambles already. This never should have happened. So now I'm left with two choices." He sighed and looked around the room.

Pazzo stood, with the help of Tessa. "Go upstairs, Red." Trance-like, Dago Red made his way up his rickety staircase. and closed a door at the top of the steps.

"I know I'm out of line saying these things in front of *strangers*. But in light of all that's happened the past few months, and with three public murders within a few minutes inside this basement, I'll speak my peace. Besides, I trust Jackie, my niece and her son, even though they're not *one of us*, they are *my* family. Those two opportunists lying on this floor were *Friends of Ours*, and so were those two traitors who went up in flames in the basement of The Inn – of my brother's bar, not yours! And I know for a *fact* that both of your men were traitors."

Tessa said, "We'll wait for you, Uncle Pazzo. Just call us when you're ready to come up and we'll help you with the steps."

"Stay right where you are. Like I said, now I'm left with two choices: I can stay in power, or I can really retire this time. It's my decision. But if I go I must have this one thing as a pledge: I don't care who killed those two in that basement, whether they were *made-men* or not. They were as low as informants. They were turncoats. Whoever it was did our Family a great favor. And I couldn't care less who burned down that shithole of a bar. Business tanked. It was a loss to keep it open. Collinwood even got dangerous for *wise guys* like us. So we take the insurance money and move on. And now, Jack, I'll ask you to take your family outside with Dago Red. Call me tomorrow. Auggie, I'd like to speak to you now. Fingers, you stay put."

Auggie said, "Sure thing, Don Pazzo. Whatever you need. Then I'll help you upstairs and take you where you're going."

Our son kept his good arm on me to help me navigate those stairs. My wife walked behind me with her hands on my waist. Once outside in that frigid air I let out a foggy sigh of relief. Finally, I was able to return home with my family, to be reunited with my Gina. I silently wept in Tessa's car on the way home. Then I breathed deeply and said, "It's past midnight, so it's a new day. Happy New Year, family. I love you more than you know."

When Pazzo's family was safely upstairs he walked towards Auggie, his left hand in a jacket pocket till he reached him. Pazzo stuck out his right hand to shake. Still holding firmly onto his hand, Pazzo opened a silver straight razor. He pulled the blade across their clasped hands. They watched the blood run as he said, "I kiss your hand, *Capo Don Augusto*. May you rule in peace and prosperity. Okay, that's it. I've given my last order, Auggie. Now it's all yours. I only ask that you honor my last request and leave dead dogs lie. *Capiche?*"

Auggie embraced the tiny old man and kissed Pazzo on both cheeks. "I never expected this." Auggie came close to what looked like a smile: "The thought crossed my mind I might be getting whacked in this basement along with those two. And then I saw the razor… But of course, Don Pazzo, I will honor your last request with my life and guard your honor to my grave. I hope you don't mind if I keep in touch now and then, *coom*.

CH XXXIV: The Family

January 1st of 2014, as soon as we got home my daughter screamed. She and Little Sinbad jumped on me as if she were still a child and knocked me down on that dark blue carpet. Gina sat next to me on the floor, punching me, crying and yelling, "I fucking hate you! Why didn't you call us? How could you put us through all this? Please don't ever leave us again, Daddy."

Sinbad stuck his nose in my ear, snorting. He knocked Gina over onto my chest, running in circles, growling. Danni rolled out of Rocco's chair and joined us on the floor, sobbing. Tessa and Rocco fell down, laughing and crying at the same time, while Sinbad hurtled over us, growling and yipping. We all stayed up late, crashed right there on the floor and woke up early.

Tessa said, "We're moving back out to the farm. Gina and I have been packing for two days. Everything is in boxes. Oh, and I hope you're in the mood for company. If not, too bad. It's a combination Xmas/New Year's party. Dr. Joey is coming for my baked macaroni and pizza. It will be great to see old friends. Hank is coming with his family. He's bringing *cumare* Carly and Junior. They love your pizza, Jackie. I even invited Christine. This will be so much fun! I can't wait to get back to our home!"

"*My mom?* You're kidding, right?" Danni asked, shocked.

"Nope. We're moving back to the country and having our own little Collinwood reunion out there. Gus said he'd stop by with Whitey and Carrie. Filo invited himself," she laughed.

"Ma, slow down. You realize what we're in store for with Christine Troia and Carrie at the same table," Gina laughed.

"Hide the booze," Danni said, with a half-smile.

"Is that all, Ma? You mean we won't have the Collinwood Safety Patrol coming over, too? Maybe Sally-boy and Ice-cream Nicky can do a cameo?" Rocco said, grinning.

"No. But you just reminded me. Of course, Uncle Pazzo will be there. Oh yeah, and *padine*, Michael, might stop in for cassata cake and cannoli. He's bringing Enrico and Dr. Joey."

"Tessa, that's a lot of people for this little house. Are they coming in shifts, or are we having a January barn dance?"

"No worries, Jackie. I have it all figured out. You remember those huge folding tables against the wall and that stack of folding chairs, don't you? But the house has been empty since August. So we're all going down there with the vacuum, dust rags, mop and buckets. I even found some blue Christmas lights here in a Dollar Store bag to hang in the ceiling. And we have some movie posters to hang on the walls. It will be great!"

Rocco asked, "The *basement*? Are you serious? I'd rather get my teeth pulled out with a spoon. I don't feel real comfortable in basements right now, Ma. How about we—"

"Sack-up, boy. Face your fears, remember? This will be so much fun! I can barely wait! So come on you slackers. You better get plenty of rest, you lazy bums," Tessa grinned like a teenager.

The next morning I read in the Plain Dealer that Sonny Magic's body was stumbled across by a homeless man picking through garbage, in the same Five Points dumpster where the body of Curtis had been found. There was a picture of Cleveland's Mayor, flanked by City Prosecutor, Michael Colombo, and the Chief of Police, in an article assuring Clevelanders patrols had increased.

I read out loud, "The Mayor stated, 'We're closing in on perpetrators. There will never be another war fought in this city, not while I'm on the clock.'" *No one word of missing police.* The Mayor, half Italian and half black, was a no nonsense kind of guy to synthesize the extremes of Cleveland's 3rd millennium gangs.

Rocco yelled, "Anything about Lonnie or O'Reilly?"

I smiled as I folded the paper and set it down so I could scratch my old dog's ears. "Horrible Hank still has a sense of humor. The same Five Points dumpster, eh? That was a nice touch. Looks like 'ol timing went and stuck us with good family, eh boy? HA! How about all this?" Then I said to my wife, "Life is some strange shit. Of all the people in this big beautiful country, we lucked out and found each other at a moment when all the planets were aligned. For as old as we are, we're pretty goddamn lucky to have what we have and to be where we are. Timing really is everything, because without you, baby-girl, I'm nothing."

Rocco said, as he walked in from the kitchen, "What?" He took the recliner next to me. Gina plopped on the couch next to Tessa. Danni sat on the floor near Little Sinbad. Rocco said, "Pop, I just threw those comments out to Fingers about taking on a legend short-handed and a basement clean-up so we could study his reactions. But you already know that. I mean, we saw nothing in him, did we? Either he doesn't know the first thing about that *other* basement, or he's in the running for an Academy Award. But this whole basement thing is over, right Dad?"

That was the first time my son ever called me *Dad*. I smiled inside as I continued to talk to my old dog: "So what do you think? What's this boy talking about? Which basement? Ma's party? But I guess this whole dark mess has a silver lining. My son proved to be a game one when he got tested, just like you. Now let's hope he can be as quiet as you, Sinbad." Then I looked at Gina and then at Danni: "Do you girls know anything about some bullshit legends or a clean-up job down in some basement?"

Tessa answered for them: "You must be getting old, bro. How do you expect any of us to keep quiet about something we don't even know what it is we're not supposed to know, or talk about something that's non-existent and pretend we're pretending when we aren't? You know? Now let's go clean *our* basement."

Gina yawned and stretched her feet near Tessa's legs. "Hey, Daddy-O," she smiled. "I have a question. Do you think you're the only person to ever hear of and embrace the concept, *omerta*? It's really not a guy thing, or even an Italian thing."

"No, Gina," I said. "But not everything should be kept a secret, at least not to everyone. And it's not always loyal to keep quiet. But maybe we'll get to that part later."

"Hmm . . . okay . . . interesting" she smiled. "The mystery and intrigue continues. Alright, Captain Daddy-O. It's your call. This is your day, so we'll play it your way."

We laughed and joked about a variety of topics, talked about a strange assortment of off-the-wall subjects until the phone rang. *Click* We all pretended to ignore it but laughed a little quieter, the spontaneity of the moment replaced by trepidation.

The smile on Gina's face was replaced with dread. Tessa set down a book she had been pretending to read. Danni curled up in a ball next to our dog. Rocco, wearing an expression of hatred, folded his good arm across his chest to embrace his cast. I watched the phone. We all pretended to ignore it yet laughed a little quieter, the recklessness of the moment gone. The answering machine clicked on. *Silence.* I wondered if someone had turned off the volume before we crashed.

Rocco said, "It's probably Whitey and Filo about the truck," but he didn't move.

The second call brought with it a spattering of residual sounds and expressions from us, followed by short bursts of nervous laughter. Again, as before, no message. By the third call, those who had been seated stood, and those standing walked to that black and silver machine of surprises and secrets.

I said, "Okay, fuck-it. I can get it." I walked to the phone, staring as if it were an unknown object from another planet, hoping it was about to fix itself from making that terrible sound. All of us were way too paranoid. Our nerves were wrecked.

On a frigid January 2nd of 2014, well after my car *accident*, I was almost good as new other than some new scars and a few tattoos that needed to be retouched. The women had everything packed and ready to go. We rented a large box truck to haul Tessa's things from Carly's double house to the home where Gina had been born. It was the home where Tessa and I lived as a newlywed couple, the same yard from where I'd been blown out of existence for five long and very confusing months. Because Rocco and I were both out of commission, Whitey and Filo offered to drive and do the heavy lifting. Rocco moved out from above his crazy ladies. He and his girlfriend were moving in with us. I put in for retirement/disability. I wasn't sure of how much time any of us had left. I just knew I was done working.

The kids had somehow acquired a bunch of wealth and insisted Tessa and I take half. We didn't ask how, nor did we argue. When they offered to tell us if we needed to know Tessa said, "That's so nice of Filo and Whitey to help us move. Those guys usually don't go out of their way for anyone. And as far as this cash goes: it seems green enough to us. Thank you for holding us steady while Dad and I are off balance – as it should be. We love all of you with all our heart – and you too, Sinbad."

Danni got down on all fours in our front-room like a child, playing her usual game with Little Sinbad to chase away the blues so she didn't start crying again. She patted her palms on the clean carpet, reached out slowly with creepy-crawling fingers for his black Kong toy, and then quickly jerked her hands away. Sinbad kept one eye closed and tried not to wag his tail too much or too hard. The next time Danni reached for his toy, Sinbad jumped up and ran figure-eight patterns throughout the front-room and its attached dining room, under the table and around chairs, and then dropped exactly where he had begun.

"Dad-O, tell us a crazy story. We're bored. So entertain us," Gina whined. "Come on, old man. Don't be such a Jew."

"If you're bored, honey, it's because you're boring. That's why we still don't have grandbabies to play with like other old farts our age. You and your brother aren't cooperating. Ma and I need a baby. That tiny addition would go full circle to make us even more complete."

"Yeah, I know." Danni sighed and stood. "Family really is awesome!" she said, as she reached her arms out as if to hug the entire house and all of its contents. "Promise, we'll try again."

"Danni, I'm happy you finally know who your real father was," I said, as I stood to put an arm around Rocco's girlfriend. "If it were me, I'd want to know. From what I understand, the Mick was quite a guy. I didn't know him personally. But I can tell you from Collinwood history that your dad was one tough son-of-a-gun and a real clever guy, too. But things back in the '70s were more than just crazy. And the Mick got in too deep, way over his head with the law and the *coombas* from the old neighborhood. But because he had no quit in him, he found himself in a real bad spot with some real bad people."

Gina said, "How about all this crazy shit? In just a half of a year Rocco finds out that my Pop is his father and then you learn who your father was. That's pretty amazing right there. I mean, I love the fact that Rocco and I are brother and sister, even if it's only half. And it's way cool that you and I are soul sisters. Plus, we're both half Italian. That almost makes us like blood related or something. But sometimes I wish I knew who my mom's father was, just so my pedigree could be complete."

"Why would it make any difference, honey?" asked Tessa. "It wouldn't change anything. You're still you, either way."

"I guess... I think he was white. But I don't even know that for sure, or what he looked like, or what nationality he was, or what kind of person he was, or anything... And that kind of sucks. What about if I have kids?"

"Come on, let's all sit down," I said, as I nodded to my wife and then eased back into my recliner. I clasped scarred hands over short, thick gray hair. "Go ahead, Tessa. This is as good a time as any. We're all adults here. And we're way beyond secrets. There's nothing but love, truth and trust between the five of us."

Gina eased onto the blue couch next to Tessa and Danni, all wide-eyed and open-mouthed, as she asked, "What the fuck now? You mean you knew who my grandpa was this whole time and kept it from me? You know how I feel about this stuff. I can't believe you'd do such a thing. You've always been straight with me, all the way back since I was a little girl – even about Santa and God and the rest of that happy horseshit . . . for Christ's sake! And *now* you're gonna start lying to me? *Really*?"

"It wasn't Daddy who knew, Gina. It was me. I'm sorry, honey. Jackie and I were going to tell you on his birthday, the same day he vanished. Then so much bad stuff came crashing down on us all the sudden. We had planned to sit and have a talk as a family, without any of Rocco's goofy stories. That was our plan. But as you know, our plans got changed a few times about a whole bunch of things. Not that it isn't still important, mind you. But it sort of got lost in the shuffle for awhile once people started . . . well, started *disappearing*."

"Okay, Ma. I understand. I might have handled it the same way. But it's a new day. So let's start the way we plan to continue. Go for it. Lay some heavy truth on me. I'm tougher than you might think."

"Even Rocco's about to hear this for the first time," Tessa assured her step-daughter. "I told your dad. But we need to keep in mind that the marriage and so many other life-altering things happened in the past few months. So I guess somehow, that one really important piece of information kind of got sidelined by all the fresh chaos our family's been trying to deal with. I really, really am so sorry, honey."

"Jeez! Okay. You're sorry. I believe you. I forgive you. Can we please move on? What exactly are you telling me? Just say it. Please, Ma? I promise. I'm a big girl now. I can handle – well. And you know this."

"Well . . . I'm not sure if your mother knows about this."

Rocco said, "No shit… Better yet. Okay, who is it?"

"I can guarantee that Butterscotch didn't have a clue while we were married, Gina, or she would have told me. We told each other everything. Well . . . right up until she forgot to tell me she had a new boyfriend. Anyway, I doubt that your mother knows his identity. Maybe your grandma was ashamed."

"Why would my mom or grandma care?" insisted Gina. "Obviously they both went out fucking around and got knocked up. And everybody knows Grandma wasn't married when she had my mother. So what's the big goddamn secret all the sudden? Who does she think she is, the fucking Virgin Mary or some shit like that? This doesn't make any sense at all, Dad."

"Well, maybe your grandma didn't say anything because the guy didn't want anyone to know," I said, to hopefully help her process what she was about to hear. "Maybe the guy gave your grandmother a bunch of money to take care of your mom. Maybe she and the guy figured child support worked like hush-money."

435

"The guy? Why do you keep saying, *the guy*? What guy? Come on, goddamnit!" Gina shouted, as she bolted up off the couch and began pacing around the front-room tugging thick loose curls away from her beautiful face. "I have the right to know who my own grandfather was, don't I? So who was this old pervert, anyway?"

"Not *was*, honey," said Tessa, as she looked back to me.

"*Not was*? What the hell does *that* mean? You're saying he's no longer a pervert? Why would I give a shit about that?"

"Those words, '*not was*' means your grandpa is still alive. He's old, but he's healthy," I answered for Tessa, trying to relieve some pressure mounting between my daughter and my wife.

Rocco finally spoke up: "Okay. Fine. We get it. He's alive, old and healthy. So what is this, a fucking game show? Can she buy a goddamn vowel next? How about you two finally answer Gina's one simple question? Who is this asshole?"

"Rocco, I'm about to smack you in your filthy mouth," Tessa warned with a pointed finger. "Okay, honey. Just humor me, Gina. You remember me asking some redundant questions about my family that night Rocco's hand got injured in his *accident* . . . the night he *fell off the roof*? I was asking some weird questions. Remember I even asked you, 'Has everything been cleaned to the point where it's as spotless as a blank domino?' And then you answered something like, 'Yeah, as clean and spotless as a blank set of dice'. Remember that?"

"Of course, Ma. I remember every word from that day. How could I ever forget?"

"That's good, honey, because so do I. Partly, I said those things so you knew I was aware of what had happened. I didn't want you to think I'd just dropped off the side of the meat wagon. I didn't want you three believing I was stupid enough to buy into that load of crap you con artists were trying to feed me."

"Yes, Ma, I remember. I promise. You are quite the little detective, aren't you? Now will you *please* just say it?"

"So then you also remember when I said, 'Good, Gina. Now just play along another minute. Who's my uncle?' You remember that part too, right?"

"Yeah, I do! And then I asked 'You mean Pazzo? Come on, Ma. Okay, so we get it. We both have amazing memories. Now maybe you can give me a break here. Can you say what you mean? You're getting almost as bad as your son – no offense."

"She just did, sweetie." I offered as another distraction.

436

"She just did *what*? What's with all the cryptic head games? Just say it! I'm sick and tired of these games. Not tonight, of all nights. I'm way too fragile right now for all this."

"*Holy shit…*" Rocco mumbled. "Un-fucking-believable."

"Can you please watch that mouth?" Tessa asked.

"What the hell's everyone talking about. I'm totally lost," Danni said, holding her forehead with both hands while running slender fingers back and forth through her short-cropped, very thick, very black hair. "Can someone please speak English?"

"Yeah, really! That makes two of us," Gina agreed, still pacing. "What's the big fucking secret everybody seems to know about except for me and Danni?"

"I think they're telling you, sister-girl, that you're more Italian than you think." Rocco said, looking at his mother.

"What the fuck? You're going to mess with me, too?"

"No," Rocco said, calmly. "I think they're saying you're also a blood relative to Ma. Isn't that what you guys are saying?"

"Yes, son. That's exactly what we're saying," I sighed and stood again, that time to calm Gina, who by then had been doing laps across the carpet. She squirmed at first but gained enough composure to absorb what was about to be said.

Tessa tried again: "Okay, honey. My dad's brother, Pazzo. That's all of it. But please don't ask your mother about this," Tessa pleaded, as she took both of Gina's hands into her own.

"What?" Danni asked, as she shook her head in disbelief. "What do you mean by *Pazzo*?"

"Exactly that," I said, trying to hold Gina still.

She pulled away: "This is really fucked up. I mean; I think it is. Isn't it? Well, is it fucked up or not?" Gina asked Rocco.

"Nope, not even a little bit. It's cool," Rocco assured her.

Tessa continued: "What I'm saying, Gina, is that sometimes people make impulsive moves when they're young. In fact, sometimes when they're middle-aged, too," she said, looking closely at Gina, then Rocco and Danni. "And sometimes even when people reach the age of me and your dad. You know why? Because we're all flawed creatures – even the best of us."

"Whoa… Wait a while. Just back up one stinking minute. You're telling me that you and my *mulatto* mother are 1st cousins? Is that what you just said to me, Ma?" Gina asked.

"What?" Danni repeated, still holding her head.

I sat back down and flipped up the foot portion of my recliner so I could appear to be relaxed. "We did the math. Your grandfather was only 15 years old when your mother was born," I offered, as some type of consolation. "And your grandma was only 16. They were only 14 and 15 when your mom was conceived. They were babies themselves! What were they supposed to do? Besides, it was a different world back then. Back in those days, whites and blacks didn't *mingle* all that much – even if they were only part black."

"*Mingle*? Holy shit! You think fucking qualifies as *mingling*, Daddy-O? Because in my book, having sex and making babies is most definitely more than *mingling*."

"I didn't mean it like that, baby. I just meant—"

"Wait." Danni said, shaking her head. "What is *mingling*?"

"Things were different back then. But we're way beyond that," Rocco assured his sister. "Related or not, we're family."

Gina gasped, "Fucking aye… So let me get this straight. Your gangster uncle, Pazzo, was screwing my half-breed grandmother. Then my *dago* father here knocks up my *high-yellow* mother, who I just find out is half-Italian. Then my mother's out fucking some old black dude while she was still married to Daddy, which is why they got divorced. Then I find out after all these years that I have a half-brother. And now I find out I have a stepmother who's also my cousin? Are you sure that's all of it? Because so far it sounds like I come from a long line of inbred whores! Is there more? Maybe I'm part Mormon or Amish, too."

"Ah, okay, I get it," Danni said, smiling. "Actually, this gets juicier. Not only did I find out that my little slut of a Sicilian mother got knocked up by some pig of an Irish gangster – the infamous Mick from Five Points. But that also means I'm a cousin to those scumbag Kelly brothers and their whore sister, Maureen. So that, of course, also makes me a cousin to Whitey – for fuck's sake! But then, check out this shit, Gina: My *dago* mom, the psycho drunk that she is, is also a sister to Pazzo's wife. So now that's makes Rocco, you and me all cousins! This is so damn confusing . . . it's almost interesting," she said, laughing doubled over. Then Danni sat up straight and slapped her Levied thighs. "Hoo-wee! I feel like I just took a swat off a stem full of crack!"

Rocco looked at me with a solemn expression as he stroked his bushy beard with the nailed hand: "The funniest part is we didn't become related till years *after* all that sex happened. It's not like we're like those fucking Mormons or goddamn inbred Amish assholes that deliberately have family orgies."

Danni, still in somewhat of a daze asked, "Hey, wait a minute… Now I'm not so sure if this is all that good or not... Does this make me and Rocco blood relatives?"

"No, not at all." I assured them. "Pazzo is a blood relative, not his wife or her sister."

"Whatever," Gina sighed. "Sounds like a bunch of sluts."

"I hear you loud and clear, sister. . . or cousin," agreed Danni with half a laugh, her short black hair all tousled.

"Guess what? Far as I'm concerned, fuck-it. And fuck all the sluts!" declared Rocco, as he tried to fold and refold his arms the best he could across his chest. "I salute the united sluts of America. The only thing better is bisexual sluts and threesomes."

"Okay, that's enough! This is where I step in," Tessa said, with a raised finger of her petite hand with perfectly manicured nails. "First of all, I told you a million times to watch that filthy mouth of yours, Rocco! And as far as you two *prima donna's* are concerned: you sit there calling everyone sluts like you're both still virgins – for Christ's sake. Let's get real. What you both are is goddamn lucky. Let's keep in mind that I got knocked up by a *guinea* gangster, too. Okay?" Tessa said, with emphasis, as she gave me a sideways glance. "And that was the first time I ever had sex in my life. So am I a slut, too? What's done is done."

"I'm good," said Rocco, trying to stretch on his recliner.

"But the best part of all this is that we're together. Besides the fact that we're all related, we're also best friends. We love and trust each other, right? And we can share anything. So now we're on the bonus plan. This is great! I love it! We're just one big happy family. I can't speak for the rest of you. But as for me, this right here is all I've ever wanted. And it was worth the wait."

"I'm really sorry, Ma," Gina said, as she ran to give her stepmother a hug. "You're so right. I'm pretty far from being a virgin and damn lucky not to have gotten knocked up by that piece of shit I was with for all those years."

"Me too, I guess," Danni said, hugging Gina and Tessa at the same time. I *was* pregnant by some Italian gangster." She looked at Rocco: "But timing is still on our side. Right, buddy?"

"Well, we're back," I added, clearing my throat again, "and stronger than ever." Then attempting to lighten the mood I said, "And after all this good news, there's another bright spot – especially for me. Because out of all of us, I'm the only one who's not related to Fingers. HA! Take that, you poor bastards."

"Hey, I'm the only bastard here," Rocco said. "These other three are bitches."

Tessa ignored him to focus on me. "Real funny, asshole. But let's recap. You weren't related to Fingers till we got married. But you are now, buddy," Tessa smirked.

"Then I guess we'll all be triple related after Rocco and I get married," Danni giggled while Rocco stared at her, stroking his beard the best he could with his temporary disability.

"How about it, Gina? Now that we're spilling our guts. You have anything to confess?" Rocco gave his evilest grin.

"HA! How about all that shit, Daddy-O?" Gina smiled as she twirled an auburn ringlet around an index finger. "Looks like we all have something in common now, eh little bro? Except for one little item. Even though I'm the only one here who's not married or about to get hitched anytime soon," she laughed. "But all of us either have been or currently are pregnant."

No longer smiling, Tessa and I quickly twisted around to face Gina and Danni with startled looks.

Gina continued, "And since we're all being so honest here, and even talking about sex and all, I think it's time. But you go ahead, Rocco. You should tell them."

Rocco said, "On second thought, maybe this isn't the best time, sister-girl. Okay? We've all been though a lot."

"Hey man, you brought it up! But if you won't tell them, I will," Gina said, with a stern expression. "I'm not ashamed!"

Tessa and I sat frozen. She held Gina's hand. Danni asked, breaking a full minute's silence, "Tell them what, sweetie?"

Gina smiled at Danni and then looked at her father. "Well, Dad. You remember when that pig of a boyfriend cheated on me? Well, the thing is, I briefly dated some biker. He was a guy I barely knew. He was this sexy Italian guy about my age who I'd seen a few times at a bar I used to go to. Sometimes I'd see him fly past on his chopper. But it was innocent enough, just a rebound thing with a stranger. Truthfully, just a one night stand. What can I say? It is what it is."

I sat mute. Tessa asked, "Is this your way of apologizing for indirectly insinuating that your mother and grandmother and I were sluts? Because there's no need for that. I know it wasn't deliberate. If you dated one of Rocco's friends, that's in the past. There's no reason to make amends – or even to discuss it. Mistakes happen, and we do what we feel we have to do. But thank you anyway for trying, sweetie. You're very kind."

"Well, actually, there's a little more to it than just humanism," Gina added, looking at her brother.

Tessa looked at me, her eyes pleading for me to speak up. I couldn't talk. We both stared at Gina till she finally spoke again.

"Well, the thing is, that biker and I got loaded and things went a little too far. You know how it is." Next, Gina next did a thing we both dreaded seeing. She looked directly at Rocco, but he avoided her gaze. "But that was way before we knew anything about all this family stuff. You gotta understand that. Please…"

Tessa and I just stared at each other in disbelief.

Gina said, "Rocco, I think it's your turn to talk."

Rocco cleared his throat and said with a stern expression, "I thought you were comfortable with *omerta*? Now I'm beginning to questions you on other levels."

"Fuck you, asshole!" Gina shouted. "You have no right to talk to me like that. And you certainly have no right to judge me, you fucking horny bastard!"

Rocco lowered his eyes. "You're right. This is family. Nothing should be secret between us. I apologize for what I—"

"What does this all mean?" Danni whispered, mouth slightly open, bottom lip trembling. She squeezed Gina's hand.

Rocco tried to scratch underneath his cast with his badly bruised hand: "All I can say is, thank Buddha she didn't have it. The timing was all wrong."

"I don't understand," Danni said. She began to weep.

"It means Rocco and I were *together* one night, a very long time ago, before we knew we were related. We barely knew each other, and we were very loaded. It just happened, and then…"

"Oh…," mumbled Danni, sniffing and dabbing at make-up smeared eyes with her forearms. "Okay…"

The problem wasn't that I couldn't form words in my mouth. It was that there were no words in my brain to use. I had completely shut down. Tessa looked paralyzed.

"Yes, Daddy. I'll say it. It was my brother who took me for a ride that night on his Harley, when I… Well, he took me into a house – actually my own mother's house, and … Well, I guess you can say: he came and he left." Gina said, looking at me.

"Hey, Pop, you taught us in rehab that honesty is a cornerstone. You said to never be sorry for what's already done. You said instead of being sorry and living with guilt and shame, to learn from it, grow from it and then it's no longer a mistake."

"Oh, baby, it sure enriched my life at the time. I still have dreams. How about you, Roc? Be honest."

Click We both noticed it at the same time. Together we silently let out silent sighs of relief and settled in for the ride.

"Yeah. Sometimes dreams even feel better than real life."

Then Rocco and Gina both cracked up, the type of laughter that releases pent-up emotion, a guttural type from deep within which sometimes follows periods of stress or trauma.

Rocco laughed, "We got you again! That's twice in a row! Man, you should have seen your faces. Ah shit! That was choice!"

"So then nothing happened, right?" asked Danni, still in shock, with the look of a timid fawn mesmerized by headlights. "Or you really were together, but just for one night? But it meant nothing. That's it, isn't it? That's what you learned, right?" she smiled valiantly with welled-up tears in her tragically dark eyes.

That made Rocco and his sister laugh even harder, and Danni cry even more. Even Tessa and I had to laugh at that one. Then Danni held both of her hands up by her mouth and began to weep and giggle at the same time, like juggling a hysterical set of emotions prior to a meltdown, a prelude to a psychotic break. Danni's eyes vacillated between joy, despair and panic. Watching her fold up like a Yahtzee board prompted us to lose it even more. Our laughter wasn't from lack of concern, because we loved and accepted her as part of the family. Nevertheless, we were falling over ourselves watching Danni curled up in a fit of silly hysterics while hiding her eyes.

Gina grabbed Danni's hands: "I'm sorry, sweetie. The whole story's pure bullshit. We were just playing *Gotcha* with Ma and Daddy-O over there. It was just jokes."

"By the way, Rocco, where did you get that nasty looking vest?" Tessa asked. "Why is it all faded and worn out already? I don't remember you ever having a Levi vest like that."

Gina giggled, "Oh, you didn't notice the back? Because Rocco the coward walked in and sat down right away. He's probably ready to piss himself but won't walk to the bathroom."

Tessa sat with her mouth slightly open. Danni scratched her head and rubbed her face. Gina beamed a huge smile.

Then I asked, "Speaking of truths, Rocco; is there anything you'd like to share with us, son?"

He said, "Yeah, I guess so. But Gina's right. I'm about to burst a bladder. Go ahead and chat among yourselves. I'll be right back. Anybody need anything while I'm up?" he stood, groaning, and made his way to the bathroom.

There was a good reason why Tessa hadn't ever seen our son wear that worn out Levi vest. And that reason was because to him it was new, even though it was old and used. It was sleeveless, all tattered, and the back of it held a read, white and blue patch down by the waist shaped like a rocker that read, "Cleveland, OH." The rest of the vest's back was blank. I'd seen cut-off vests just like that too many times not to understand its ramifications. So had Tessa, from living in Collinwood for all those years. Evidently, Gina and Danni already knew.

When Rocco returned we talked about why he would, at his age, agree to be a prospect for the Wong Gongs – till the phone rang. We all pretended to ignore it but laughed a little quieter, the reckless spontaneity of the moment gone. The smile vanished from Gina's face and was replaced with fear. Tessa dropped a book she had been reading on the floor. Danni curled up in a ball next to our dog, hugging him. Rocco, wearing an expression of hatred, folded his good arm across his chest to embrace his cast.

I said, "Okay, fuck-it." I walked to the phone, staring as if it were a foreign object, hoping it would answer itself. I breathed deeply as I said, "It's just the phone. Damn, we're acting like a bunch of great-grammas."

I picked up on the fourth ring before voicemail captured its message of silence, because I finally put on my glasses from the top of my head and recognized the caller ID. It was the same phone number from another memorial day, that same caller ID from an early evening when I had walked outside to find a car bomb waiting for me. I clenched my teeth and held my breath in dread. I picked up and said, "My *nigga*! How's it, brother Hank?"

He whispered, "Who's with you right now, Jackie?"

Before I said the words, "Just family, Hank. Why?" I turned to my family to track their emotions. They didn't seem relieved. And I felt a knot growing in my stomach.

Then after listening to him talk for a few minutes I said, "Hmm, okay. Yeah, I hear what you're saying, but I wouldn't think the worst. Of course. See you in 20. We're ready now."

Horrible Hank was at our front door in 15 minutes. He walked in without knocking. That big and intimidating black man stood in our front-room, terrified. Tessa ran to give him a hug, which was accepted with one huge hand gently patting her slight back. Gina and Danni huddled together on our big couch. My son and I approached one of my oldest friends without hesitation.

Rocco was the first to speak: "Well, it don't look like good news – that's for sure. But considering what a wild ride it's been so far, nothing surprises me anymore."

Hank blurted out, "My boy, Little Hankie is gone. We haven't heard from him for days."

Rocco said, in not too convincing of a tone, "You know Hankie. He's probably chasing tail. How long's he been gone?"

"Three days. Normally I wouldn't sweat it, Roc. But Carly phoned me today. The thing is, Curtis Junior's gone, too. I don't know… This just doesn't feel right."

"Hankie and Junior are *both* missing?" asked Gina. "Why didn't Auntie phone us?"

Hank answered, staring blankly, "Carly said after what everyone's been through she didn't want to cause a panic and then have Junior's lazy ass come stumbling through the door all hung-over. But in light of all that's happened with Curtis…"

"What do you need, Hank?" asked Tessa. "Just name it and it's done. That's what family's for."

"I'm all messed up, *cumare*. I didn't know what to do and still don't. That's why I'm here," said a weary-looking Hank, whose normal rigid stance of strength and confidence had turned into the slouched over posture of a broken old man.

Danni said, "Maybe those players just wanted to disappear for a minute," a sweet smile betrayed by concerned eyes.

"Yeah, maybe so, honey. But my ol' lady's freaking. She thought Little Hankie's been killed. Now she thinks our boy and Junior might have been kidnapped," Hank said, through the glaring eyes of a trapped animal. His black skin shone with sweat, a single droplet trickling from a corner of one of his slanted eyes.

I stood there trying to piece together a scenario that hopefully would make sense. Finally I had a rational thought: "That's it! Fuck-it! I'll get my gun. I'll be right back. I know right where to begin looking. We'll put in a call in to—"

That first ring of the phone hit us like a shower of ice. We sat or stood, frozen in time. Rocco walked to the phone. "What the fuck? It's your number, Uncle Hank. But you're right here!"

Hank's voice trembled, "Get it for me, son. I just can't."

Rocco picked up to hear the familiar voice of Hank's wife. She was crying. "Okay, Auntie. Please calm down a second, okay? I'm gonna put you on speakerphone, alright? Yeah, Uncle Hank's right here. Go ahead. We're all right here and we can hear you."

Rocco hit speakerphone and turned up the volume. Hank braced himself, a large black hand against a lightly papered wall.

What everyone heard was a hollow sound of a woman crying. The sad voice of Hank's wife, "Those son's of bitches!"

Hank silently wept. He had never heard his wife curse till that moment. He braced himself for some crazy news

She screamed. "I'll fucking kill them myself!"

Hank slid to the floor. Tessa ran to him, sat next to him, holding an arm. Then there was an echoed sound of laughter in the background. Hank's expression changed from helpless to curious as he rose. Rigid posture returned. He marched over to the phone and switched off speakerphone. "Is that who I think it is? And is it *what* I think it is?" He paused for about a minute, intently listening. "Tell your son I'm on my way, for him to stay put. And you tell Junior not to step out of that house till I get there. And let them know I'm steaming hot!"

"So then you mean nothing happened, right?" asked Danni. "That means they really were together, but just out for a few nights, right? That's all of it, isn't it? They're okay, right?" she forced a smile, her tragic eyes filled with tears. "I knew it!"

Hank filled his lungs with warm air and said, as he wiped the last tear from a smiling face, "Yeah, honey, Hankie's back. Junior's back. Even my man Jack is back." He put one arm around Tessa, the other around me and squeezed: "Family is everything. We're back!"

"Tell Junior I'm super pissed about this and I'll speak with him tomorrow," Gina said. "Tell him not to even think about leaving Auntie Carly's till I get there."

I had to cough before I spoke, to choke away emotion: "I've been telling you since we were kids, brother. It's all about timing . . . and family and gameness . . . and loyalty and truth . . . and integrity and timing . . . and a bunch of other things I can't think of right now," I laughed, as I walked Hank to the door. "Now go home, *coom*, and enjoy your family."

I opened the door. He and I surveyed my extended family in that familiar room: "I saw this picture right here a thousand times. While I thought I was dying, or being held prisoner, I had a recurring dream of a snake eating its own tail, an inch at a time, devouring itself to get enough nourishment from itself in order to fend off the thing killing it. Being without my family was one of the things killing me. Yet is was the motivation I needed to do whatever it took to save my life – even if that meant losing it. Just having *this* right here, right now, is all I thought about while I was dying and all I've ever really wanted."

Then the phone rang again. Everyone froze again. Rocco smiled and said, "Let's not get like a bunch of old great-grammas every time the goddamn phone rings. No worries, I got this."

With all of us getting a good look at his Wong Gong's prospect patch, he said, "The caller ID says *Unknown*. It's probably a salesman or some other bullshitter." Instead of answering, Rocco pressed speakerphone and pretended to be an answering machine. He smiled and said, "We can't come to the phone now, so please leave a detailed message and we'll get back with you as soon as we can. BEEP!"

Click Then Rocco's face changed. We noticed his eyes weren't smiling. A loud voice said, "We be watchin' yo slim ass real good. We da big dawgs up in dis mah fucka now. And we ain't neva gonna foget dis shit. You cracka-ass best be shittin' bones from now on, baby. 'Cause dis muh fucka ain't *even* over."

Rocco's features hardened; face flushed; eyes morphed from cool slate to pools of boiling black tar. I raised an index finger to keep my son calm and mouthed the words, "Be cool!"

Another voice said, "There's a new sheriff in town. See you soon." Click. A loud dial tone broke the connection.

Horrible Hank and I locked eyes. My old friend said, "Damn! This isn't good, my brother. This is gonna get uglier."

"Yep, it ain't over," I said, wearing a disgusted look.

Just then a loud motor with its radio blasting roared into up our driveway. Two doors slammed. Two large men charged into our open front door and ran past a stunned Horrible Hank.

"You kill 'em, we chill 'em, baby. It's your neighborhood movers." Whitey laughed. "And we're Collinwood ready."

Filo yelled, "Who do we have to kill to get a hot cup of coffee around here?" He handed a fat rednose pup to Rocco. "This is the pick from Bull and Bella, and the only bitch. She's a venomous thing. I call her Queen Kong, because if she had balls she'd be King. You might wanna take better care of her than you did her pops. She's the last bitch from this family, inbred on Ch. Biddy top to bottom. It's all yours if you want it, bro."

Rocco narrowed his cold gray eyes while holding that fat, squirming red pup growling at him: "Like I said, Pop, I got this."

Glossary (Collinwood Definitions):

Agida: Italian term for an upset stomach.

Addiction: Tissue hunger; mind disease; temporary biological need manifested as self-abuse, obsession and compulsion.

Bounce: Movement from despair to growth; the arc of life's upswing; an act of gameness.

Brother: Biological fact; emotional connection; psychotic episode.

Bust-out: Man not to be taken serious. Jokingly, it means someone behaving silly. While serious it describes a low-life.

Capiche: posed as a question: "Do you understand my meaning?" A statement implies, "You'd better understand, or else."

Cin don: Toast wishing someone a hundred years of bliss.

Click: Reptilian brain telepathy; primal extrasensory perception.

Codependence: Psychological *need* versus a *want*. To define oneself by opinions of another; dysfunction to fulfill a void. Can also be friendship or love.

Coglioni: Literally: testicles; figuratively: bravery.

Collinwood aka "The Neighborhood:" Ethnic area on Cleveland's Eastside of Italian, Irish, Slovenian, Hungarian, Polish and African derivation.

Consigliere: Counselor but not a lawyer. Man trusted to counsel to a Mafioso chief.

Coomba or Coom: Best man at a wedding, best friend or godfather of a child. A bro closer than a friend and more trusted more than blood family. A *coomba* or *coom* is not necessarily Italian but is always *paesano*.

Cumare: Woman's best friend; matron of honor or godmother.

Cravings: Classical Conditioning; triggers external and intrinsic; euphoric recall. An obsession with a feeling, regardless of negative experiences.

Cur: Opposite of a game-dog. In humans: coward & liar..

Dialectic: Merging old truths with new facts to construct a newer reality to once again be merged.

Drop-shot: A want-to-be gangster, a sucker, a cowardly fool.

Euphoric recall: Recall only the honeymoon; selective memory.

Existentialism:; Existence before essence. Choices pertaining to freewill and life. Randomness concerning birth and death.

Finocchio: (Fin-oyc) Anise flavored celery; sweet fennel. An Italian-American slang used to represent a male homosexual.

Freedom: Balance; state of mind and/or physical condition.

Fuck-it: It is what it is. Whatever happens, happens.

Game-bred: Dogs, fowl or people bred from game heritage. Most game-bred dogs are too friendly to be used for protection, yet too prey-driven with other 4-legged animals.

Gameness: Bravery or courage, the opposite of a cur; the *Bounce*.

Guinea (WOP, dago): Derogatory slurs to Italian-Americans.

Happiness: Enjoying what one has, not what one used to have or what one thinks is owed.

Heaven: Clear conscience to savor positive memories in old age. Can be a sangwitch. Commonly, an empty promise taught to children for control.

Hell: Recurrent negative recall; personal ghosts; remorse. Threat of a non-existent place used by "holy men" to scare children.

Hillbilly: In Collinwood, everyone not Italian, black, Asian, Latino or American Indian. Hills have nothing to do with this term.

Loss: A void, which like pain does, creates a place for newness.

Malocchio: Italian evil-eye removed by passing a Bible over a cursed head 14 times, reciting the Lord's Prayer over a bowl of water containing oil droplets.

Match: gameness contest pitting two game-dogs, gamecocks or humans till one quits.

Mick: Derogatory ethnic slur meant to degrade Irish-Americans.

Mind-meld: Psychic connection; non-verbal communication; *Click*.

Mind-movies (Head-flicks): Realistic memories and/or lucid dreams as real as life.

Minchia: Pronounced "mink-yah;" Italian word for a man's crotch. When used in Italian-American dialect it is meant as an exclamation of surprise.

MMA (Mixed Martial Arts): combination of jiu-jitsu; wrestling; boxing; judo; karate; savate; muay thai, etc...

Nigga: term of endearment used by African Americans.

Nigger: Slang to insult African Americans; can define any race considered to be below a morally, culturally accepted standard.

Ol' lady (wife/ girlfriend): monogamous relationship with a man who has or will have children; a marriage; divorce, child support, alimony and misery.

Omerta: Code of silence; honor achieved by either sex at any age.

Padine: Godfather, in the religious or spiritual, or in the sense of chosen family.

<u>*Paesano*</u>: In America, friends sharing area and mindset – not necessarily Italian or a *coomba*.

<u>Pain</u>: Survival mechanism. Physical or emotional injury; the driving force for healing.

<u>Pazzo</u>: [Pot-so] Italian word meaning crazy.

<u>Pit-bull (Bulldog)</u>: Generic term for any breed used in gameness contests and money matches.

<u>Punk</u>: A male person easily taken advantage of; coward of an extreme degree; a he-she willingly used for sex in prison.

<u>Powerlessness</u>: Unmanageability; may be forms of choice-driven slavery. Although it can be a very real response to a chemical.

<u>Religion</u>: Political mysticism; excuse to judge others; abstract addiction; herd mentality; philosophically the downfall of true freedom; possibly the cause for a WW III.

<u>Rush</u>: Feeling from injected or inhaled drugs; a chemically-induced mind-fuck from synaptic implosions which can be as intense as a sexual climax.

<u>*Sangwitch*</u>: A man with two nude women, all willing and uninhibited in a sexual state of affairs.

<u>*Schifoso*</u> or *schivi*. [ski-voso or ski-vee]" Something or someone disgusting.

<u>Scratch</u>: In martial arts, "jamming." In boxing or MMA, answering the bell. In the pit: advancing back to the source of pain to extinguish any further threat.

<u>*Sfacim*</u>: [Sfa-cheem] A person with no pride; having no *face*; a low-life jizz-bag.

<u>Spirituality</u>: God; love; creativity; integrity; sobriety; humanity; dignity; compassion; freedom; energy; dialectic; the *Click*; connection with nature.

<u>Swear to Buddha:</u> In Collinwood, a term holding more meaning than "Swear to God."

<u>Sweetie</u>: Female friend to share wild-times. Defines why a man pays child support, is divorced and separated from his children.

<u>Timing</u>: Everything:

<u>Weakness</u>: Unwillingness to do the next *right* thing.

<u>Yankee Terrier</u>: hybrid of a Staffordshire Terrier or American Bull Terrier crossed to an Airedale for the large type, or to a Fell Terrier for pocket-pits.

<u>Youse</u>: Plural form of "you;" mid-western version of "ya'll."

About the Author

Author of the sequel, *I'm Jack & I'm Back: The Basement Pit*, and of critically acclaimed, *I'm Jack & I Want More,* and of *Fighting for Life,* a book that changed the Pit-bull world, turned 19 in 1969, as a gang member in the murder capitol of America. Non-traditional morality imprinted in the Collinwood neighborhood, an Italian-American community made famous by documentaries and Hollywood films, as well as novels and non-fiction books. A 10th grade education and then a GED at age 33 became a BGS from Kent State University in 2003 – Magna Cum Laude. A student of the martial arts and freethinker since age 12 provided discipline throughout a chaotic and reckless path to becoming an ex-abuser turned conformation dog show judge in six countries for over 35 years. Working for a decade as an Internationally Certified Chemical Dependency Counselor, crisis interventionist, lecturer and primary counselor, provided an intense yet darkly humorous writing style from dealing with the murkier and more vulnerable sides of human nature. The author is enjoying early retirement while living in rural N.E. Ohio. His hobbies include writing and raising dogs, bocce ball and FreeCell, baking and horticulture, MMA and researching for his sixth book.

Made in the USA
San Bernardino, CA
18 November 2013